Redskins and Lobsterbacks

A Remembrance of the American Revolution

A Novel

By

Shawn C. Roberts

Published by Longhunter Press
Copyright 2018

ISBN number 978-1717521842

Prologue
A Life Remembered

It was a beautiful day in Montgomery County, Kentucky in the fall of 1832. William Tipton had just finished the eggs, grits, and ham that he had eaten for breakfast and was going outside to sit on his front porch. He looked down the dirt road and saw a buckboard coming up the hill in front of the house. His daughter, Sarah, was sitting beside her husband Alexis and their seven-year-old son Alexis Jr. was with them. Little Alexis was in the back of the buckboard, standing up waving to his grandfather. William rose from his rocking chair and waving back at his grandson started for the gate. The little boy jumped off the buckboard before it could come to a full stop and came running up to his grandfather.

"Granddaddy, father said he is coming to take you to the courthouse and lock you up".

Sarah looked at her husband, the county sheriff and gave him a half smile and a playful punch on the shoulder, "I told you to stop telling him your crazy tales".

William began to chuckle at his little grandson who had a concerned sad look on his face. The old man looked up at his son-in-law and grinned.

"Well, your father was just elected sheriff and he is going to take me to the courthouse, but he is not going to lock me up in the jail. Today is a lucky day son. You know good luck comes in threes. First, my nephew, the honorable John Shields Tipton, was elected to our United States Congress from Indiana, and second your daddy was elected sheriff, and today is my turn, I'm sure to get my pension. Come on, let's get on the wagon and go to town."

Little Alexis, in a much better mood, looked over at his father and began to smile. Sarah helped her father step into the buckboard, and then jumped on herself and together, they all started to Mt Sterling, the county seat.

"Why are you going to the courthouse granddaddy?" the child asked.

"Well, that's where I'm going to give my deposition. I am going to tell a man there about me being in the war when I was young."

"I'd say it's about time," Sarah said, "It's been 50 years since the war was over and the money, you'd get from a war pension would be nice Daddy, you are 78 years old and our government can finally do something for you men who won our independence from the British. I believe you qualify for a pension, you did so much in the revolution, and they will be able to give it to you now."

"Well if they don't, me and Junior here will lock them all up for a long time, won't we Sonny?"

"That's right, we will, won't we father?" Little Alexis ask his father as he waved his toy gun high in the air.

"Have you been thinking about what you are going to say to them, Daddy?" William looked at his daughter and said, "What you say is true Sarah, I may be 78 years old, but I know exactly what happened and I remember it like it was yesterday. Days like some of those, a man will never forget."

William looked out over the countryside and saw the fields that had been cleared and planted. Looking at the houses and barns that had gone up on all the farms between here and town in his lifetime he thought how much this very view had changed along with the times, since he had first come to Kentucky so very long ago. As he thought about the past he could not help remembering his brothers, Thomas, Sylvester, and Joshua, and those days when he and they were still young, and of course his dear wife Elizabeth and it made him happy and a little sad at the same time.

Sarah broke in on his train of thought. "Daddy,' she said, "I can't stop thinking   about this. I don't want you to be like old William Bell. He was in the revolution and died before he got his pension. There are a lot of you old soldiers that never got any acknowledgment from the government that you men helped to establish. There is Joseph Clark and Henry Wilson and old Mr. Thomas Hall."

Alexis broke in and said, "You've got a point, there are plenty of men around like that, men who served our country well. Remember how James McCulloch started out as a private and ended up as a Lieutenant."

"That's right," Sarah continued, "and then there's Uncle Thomas and Sylvester up in Ohio. I believe our country wants to recognize the men like them who fought for it."

"Yeah, you two are right, and that's why I believe we'll all receive our pensions. I don't believe our young country will forget its first and oldest soldiers. If a man put in more time than a month or two, he'll receive his pension just like I will. Either way, we have already gotten something out of the war, things like our pride in this country and seeing the faces of the redcoats when Lord Cornwallis didn't come out onto the   surrender field at Yorktown."

As he thought of those bygone days, William pulled his old felt hat down over his eyes and said, "I am going to take a little nap now so I will be rested up for the court, so just leave me be for a while".

Sarah said, "That's a good idea Daddy, but I don't think you will get much sleep on this bumpy road, but we will leave you alone for a while to try."

William was not really so tired, nor did he need that much rest anymore, he just wanted to think about his youth, and so he did.

Chapter 1
Another Reason for Church

Mordacai Tipton looked up at his son, Joshua who was standing at the top of the stairs and said, "What are you boys doing up there? Get yours and your brother's butts down here." Joshua didn't say a word; he just turned and walked back from the stairs to his and his brothers' room.

"Come on Thomas, let's go. Dad's having a fit. aren't you ready yet?"

"I'm always ready to go see Mary", replied Thomas. The two young men came down the steps together, combing their hair on the way. Mordacai looked at his two sons and shook his head saying, "You two sure do like church a lot better than you used to, but I'm thinking it's got more to do with the two young ladies you see there instead of the Holy Spirit these days. Vester, Billy, what do you two think about your brothers here being all dandied up?"

"I don't care father I just want you to stop calling me Vester! I'm big enough to be called Sylvester now and William here don't like being called Billy much either. Do you William?"

"Yeah, that right," replied William, "come on, let's go." The four boys and their father left the house. The boys all walked to their horses and mounted up. Mordacai walked to the buggy, where his wife, Sue, was sitting already waiting to go.

"I see you got the boys out from in front of the looking glass," she said.

"And a hard job it was too, but I got them here by telling them we are going to be late and they'd not be able to talk to their sweethearts before church. Isn't that right boys?" The boys didn't hear their father because they had all ridden off and left their parents behind. All but William who rode along beside them, not in such a rush to get to church as his three older brothers were.

"What are you doing still back here with us William? Why aren't you up there ahead with the other boys?" asked his mother.

"It's because I don't have a giggling girl to see when I get to church.".

Mordacai smiled and looked at his son and said, "All of that will change someday."

"Well come on Mordacai, I don't want to be late either," urged Sue. "There is a new family here in the county and I want to have time to talk with them and make them welcome in our church." Mordacai nodded his head. "Yes, I've heard about them. Porters they are, from Baltimore County, I believe, seems like there is a lot of folks coming to Hartford County from Baltimore these days."

"Pop, why do you think they keep coming out to this part of Maryland?" asked William.

"Probably to get away from the British and the Tories son, there are a lot of redcoats in Baltimore and Ole King George is getting a little antsy. He is sending a big
herd of soldiers over here and the people are starting to be afraid of what is going to happen in the cities up and down the seaboard."

"Well, that's enough talk about when, or if we are going to have a war or not, on a Sunday. I can see the church up ahead, so let's stop talking about redcoats and think a little about what God wants us to do." said Sue.

"Your mother is right William, that is enough talk about revolution, and you noticed that I said 'William' this time." William sat a few inches taller on his horse when his father used his given name instead of his childhood nickname of Billy.

After reaching the church, William got down from his horse and tied the reins to the hitching post outside the church and walked over to where his mother sat and helped her down from the buggy. Then he took the team of horses from his father and led them over beside his own horse. Mordacai walked over to a group of men who were gathered under a big oak tree beside the road next to the church graveyard.

"May I join in on your conversation?" Mordacai asked. "Oh, wait a minute," he said as he turned and looked behind his back. "I better look and see if ole King George is spying on us first. He doesn't like it too much when men like us start talking about him under big trees like this one here."

One of the men said, "He's making a joke but the sad thing is there is some truth in what he's saying."

Sue had already gone inside the church to talk to the other women so William began to look for Thomas. He spotted him leaning up against the church wall talking to his girlfriend, Mary. Joshua was standing next to his horse gazing up the road, looking for his girl Polly who was just coming down the road with her family. Sylvester must have already gone inside the church, because he was nowhere to be seen. William began to walk to the front door to go inside and find his brother, when out of the blue, and out of that very same door walked the most beautiful girl he had ever seen.

She had bright green eyes that met his from under the white ruffled cap that she wore under her hat. He stepped over the threshold, nodded his head and let her go by with a smile. She smiled back with her small bow shaped mouth. Her face was perfect as far as he was concerned. She had high cheek bones and a well-formed nose with an ever so slightly dimpled chin. As she walked by and made her way to the group of men under the oak tree he was able to see that the brim of her straw hat was turned up just enough to reveal her pale blond hair. William watched her walk up to the group and began to speak to one of them. He did not recognize this older fellow, but guessed he was her father. Then it popped into his mind, 'The Porters'. This must be the Porter family that his mother and father had been talking about earlier this morning. He could not take his eyes off this lovely girl. It was the first time in his young life that the opposite sex had made him feel the way he was feeling now. She was so beautiful he could hardly stand it. She began to walk back to the church with the man William hoped was her father by her side. Her light green dress reminded him of spring. The sleeves had two stripes of white with little pink flowers that ended in a fall of white lace at her small wrist.

William did not want to be caught staring at her, so he turned and walked into the Church. He looked over to where Sylvester was sitting and saw that Thomas and Joshua had come inside and sat down without him ever seeing them. They had walked right past him as he was watching this new girl, and he had no idea how they had gotten by without him noticing.

'She sure is pretty. I guess I wouldn't have heard a gun go off when I was watching her,' he thought to himself.

All of his brothers were looking at him with smirks on their faces. William's face flushed as he walked over to the family pew and sat down beside his older brothers.

Thomas looked at Joshua and said, "Next week William will be the first Tipton at church, I'll bet."

At this point their mother Sue gave everybody *the* look. Leaning over and looking directly at them all, she said in a low, but strong voice, "Act like you've got some sense now and I did say act!" And that was the end of all talk in that pew.

The Porters made their entrance through the door and down the aisle past the Tipton's pew and sat down in the row in front of them. William was as happy as he'd ever been in his life. This was no ordinary Sunday; he finally understood how his brothers felt about rushing to church, thanks to this lovely young girl who sat in front of him. Her hat was held by a long wooden hatpin that pierced the matching green ribbon that hung down her back and drew the eye. He especially liked that, because he could look at her as much as he wanted without giving the appearance that he was really staring at the back of her beautiful neck.

The Reverend Smith began his sermon by welcoming the Porter family to the congregation. He introduced Thomas Porter, his wife Sarah and their daughter Elizabeth. William thought to himself that Miss Elizabeth Porter was a lovely name, but Mrs. Elizabeth Tipton, the wife of William Tipton had a much better ring to it.

Chapter 2
Holes in Homespun

Joshua and Thomas were out in back of the house, shooting their long rifles at a small piece of homespun that they had spirited away from their mother. They had painted a red dot in its center and pinned it up on a shock of corn in the field about 100 yards away. William would get a turn every now and then, when his brothers would let him have one, but not as often as he would have liked. Mordacai stepped out the back door of the house and walked over to his sons and said, "Joshua, let William have a shot."

William took the gun and put some powder in the pan. He raised the rifle to his shoulder, hit the set trigger, aimed at the red dot, and pulled the main trigger all in one quick motion. A puff of blue smoke came rolling out of the rifle and floated into the air as a neat round hole appeared in the target. Thomas looked at Joshua, whistled, and said "dead center. That was some shot." They all ran to the target and sure enough the ball had cut into the red dot.

Mordacai looked at his son and said, "William, last year our tobacco crop was as good a crop as I've had, and you had a big hand in its outcome. You worked just as hard in the fields as Joshua and Thomas, so you will receive the same reward as they did when they became men. It's in the house on the table". William ran back to the house without saying a word, he couldn't talk around the big smile on his face. Mordacai turned to Joshua and Thomas and laughingly said, "You boys are in for it now. William will be able to shoot as much as you do and I suspect he'll give you a run for your money".

William hit the back door in a full run. His mother was in the kitchen cleaning up the dishes. "William, slow down, don't tear up the house!" William didn't hear her for he was looking down in the center of the table at his own rifle. It had a stock made of maple with a mellow gleam from a hand-rubbed shine. The patch-box was brass and hand cut into the stock. William picked up the gleaming new rifle and ran his hand down the length of the barrel and turned it over in his hands taking in every detail.

"Mommy it's just beautiful." William breathed.

"Yes son, it is. Your father and I are happy to give it to you. You deserve it."

"You are not as happy to give it as I am to get it!' William told her.

"Oh, I don't know about that son, your father and I have been smiling for weeks every time we would think about giving it to you."

Giving his mother a hug, William snatched up the gun and ran back out the door. He called out, "Come on Thomas, let's load it." Thomas gave William his shot bag and William began the process of loading the gun.

"Thank you, father, this makes me so happy."

"You are welcome, son, you worked hard for it."

By the time Mordacai could reply, William had the rifle loaded and ready to fire. He took aim and let go. The red dot on the homespun had a new hole.

"Who's the gunsmith that made it Pop?" asked William.

"The same one that made your brothers' for them, Samuel Boone." replied Mordacai.

"I thought so," replied William. "It sure has the look of Samuel's work. There are not many gunsmiths who can turn out a gun like he can. He has a touch like no one else."

"Now you will have to spend some of that money that you have been hording on powder and lead," Thomas said with a smile at his younger brother.

Chapter 3
A Barn Raising

Thomas Porter shouted to his daughter Elizabeth to fetch some water as she came walking out of the house. Elizabeth turned around and went back inside the door and out of sight. When she re-emerged from the house, she had a wooden piggin in her hand. As she was heading for the well she heard her father say, "Mordacai, I sure am thankful for the help you and your sons are giving me building this tobacco barn. I couldn't have put it up without your family's help. It's nice to have good neighbors around."

"Well, it's the right thing to do," replied Mordacai. "You'll need it this fall when you harvest your crop. Look, here comes Elizabeth with that water you called for."

"Here Pa, it's good and cold, straight out of the well."

Thomas took a drink from the wooden noggin that hung from the piggin but not before giving some to Mordacai first.

"That's real good water to be from a new well that's just been dug Thomas," said Mordacai.

"Yes, it is, the water is not so brown these days, and it's had time to settle, just like we have as a family. Here Elizabeth, go give some to the other men, it's been a hot day and I know they need a good shot of cool water."

"Joshua and Thomas have already gone home I believe, but William is still here," Elizabeth told her father.

"Well, I am sure he could use some water, so go and give him some, dear."

Elizabeth smiled and headed around the corner of the new barn to see William.

Thomas Porter looked at Mordacai and said, "Well, I believe we may be building something more than a barn here. Elizabeth and William are becoming good friends."

"I know, William is the first one here and the last to go home," his father said. "He does enjoy your family's company but Elizabeth is the real calling card for him"

Thomas nodded his head. "She enjoys having him around too. She's always talking about him at night after you have all gone home. She can't stop talking about what he has done, what he said to her that day, and what he is going to do next. But I must say that I like having the young man around myself. Almost as much as she does, well maybe not that much," he chuckled. "Who knows, maybe someday we'll be in-laws."

"Maybe so," Mordacai said with a chuckle of his own.

Elizabeth walked around the new barn to where William was working. He was climbing down from the rafter just inside the barn door.

"I heard your father yell for some water, so I thought I would come down from up there under to the roof and get some too." William smiled at Elizabeth.

"Well, here it is help yourself to a drink," she said. He took the wooden noggin from Elizabeth's hand and drank the cool water.

"Will you be back tomorrow?" she asked.

"I don't think so, we are almost done with the barn and I believe your father is going to finish things up tomorrow by himself."

"Oh, well in that case I will miss seeing you," she said. "I enjoy having you around. It's been pleasant having you here."

"I was hoping you would say something like that," William replied, a feeling of relief coming over that little tight spot in his chest that he got whenever he was around her.

Elizabeth's face turned a bright red, but she had a smile on her face. She put one hand over her mouth to hide her embarrassment. When William saw her blushing cheeks, he continued "I will see you at church on Sunday. It's only two days from now."

"Well, I think I will be able to live without seeing you for two days," Elizabeth said, "I am going back into the house and you need to start for home." Elizabeth turned to walk away, but William took her arm in his hand. He turned her back around so he could look into her eyes. He pulled her close to his chest and said, "But I don't think that I can, at least not without a kiss."

Elizabeth looked up at William and even though she was not sure exactly what she wanted him to do, she knew she wanted him to do something. She had never been kissed, and she was nervous, but she trusted William.

She told him, "I have never been kissed before, not once."

"Well then, I would be honored to be the first and perhaps the only man that will ever kiss you," William said. She smiled as she thought of what he had just said to her. She liked the idea of being kissed by William, and she liked what he said about him being the only man she would ever kiss.

William slid his arms around her waist and drew Elizabeth to him for her first   kiss. Afterward, he raised his hand and touched her long silky hair before walking away. Then he turned back to her and said, "I'll see you Sunday, my love". After giving her one of the slow smiles that always made her heart melt, he turned and walked away. She stepped back and leaned up against the barn. She was happily excited about her first kiss, but what she didn't know, was that it had been William's first kiss as well.

Chapter 4
Turkey Tonight

The next morning as the family was sitting down to the breakfast table, Joshua told his mother, "Boy Ma, your pancakes arc thc bcst I cver ate. Here, give me some more of that sorghum to put on my cakes."

"Thank you, son," his mother laughingly replied, "I do spend a lot of my time cooking every day for you boys and your father, so I appreciate you're noticing. Now that brings me to a chore for you boys today. Sylvester is on his way home from school and I think it would be nice to have a turkey for supper tonight to welcome him home. I believe that the three of you should go out and get us a nice big fat bird."

"Sounds good to me," said William, "let's gather up our rifles and go hunting fellows."

"As soon as I eat that last pancake." said Thomas.

"How do you think Sylvester is doing up at that school?" asked Mordacai.

"Well, his letters say that he is doing really well," replied Sue as she was picking up the dirty dishes from the table. "He always wanted to be a teacher so I believe he has worked as hard at this as he always does when he sets his mind to a task. He seems to be really smart and he always does well in whatever he puts his mind to."

Mordacai got up from the table and said, "I am going to work that ground up some more today so I can start planting in a few days' time, so you three can get that turkey for your mother but hey, you boys be careful."

Thomas looked at his father with an odd look as he said, "All the times we've spent out in the woods hunting with each other and you still think that we are going to shoot or kill each other?"

"Son, I don't think you'll wound or kill each other, I simply said 'be careful'."

"Careful of what?" asked William.

"The British or maybe a group of loyalists. We are not at war with our mother country yet, but I do think it is going to happen someday and likely someday soon. So, do like I said, and be careful while you are out there."

"Come to think of it maybe you should go with them Mordacai," Sue said with an anxious tone in her voice.

"No, they're not boys anymore, Sue. They'll be all right. Just be careful like I said, and don't shoot each other," Mordacai said with the fatherly smirk on his face that they had all come to recognize.

Sue waved goodbye to her sons from just outside the kitchen door as they disappeared into the woods.

Joshua looked at his two brothers as they entered the trees and said, "You know, father is right about the redcoats. Sylvester said in his last letter that they are getting mighty arrogant in Baltimore."

"What are we going to do if the war does start?" asked William.

"Well, I am going to join the army", said Thomas, "and you two are going to as well."

"The army likely won't take you, because they need good shots and if I remember rightly, I got the last two turkeys that were on our supper table," William said boldly.

"I don't think so." replied Joshua.

"No, it wasn't you" said Thomas, "I know who shot the last one and it was me".

"Maybe so," said William, "maybe then, but not today!"

The three brothers split up, each taking a different direction into the woods, all confident in their own ability to come home with a big tom turkey.

Thomas returned first with a turkey slung over his back. He walked up to the house and opened the door and said "Turkey tonight mother."

"Are you already back son? You haven't been gone but an hour or so."

"I didn't want to waste too much time on a hunt this morning. I want to go see Mary today. Will it be alright if I go and see if she could come over and eat with us tonight?"

"That would be nice Thomas, its fine with me, go and see if she might."

"I will be back as soon as I can Mother." Thomas called as he went out the door at a full trot. He met Joshua walking up the dirt road to the house.

"I heard that shot come from over on the hill where you were, so I came on back. Did you get one?"

"Did I get one!" said Thomas sarcastically.

"Hey, slow down, where you going in such a big rush anyhow?" Joshua asked. "To Mary's to see if she can come over tonight," replied Thomas.

"You think the same way I do. Let me put my gun up and we'll go together and then we'll go see if Polly can come over too", Joshua said as he ran into the house. He was inside just a few seconds before he shot back out the door, jumped on his horse and galloped up to the edge of the road, where Thomas was impatiently waiting for him. At that moment William came out of the woods and saw his two brothers atop their horses.

"You two don't have to run away from home just because I got the biggest, fattest turkey anybody ever saw come out of those woods."

Thomas looked down at William and asked, "Didn't you hear my shot?"

"Yeah, I did," said William, "but I thought you would most likely miss, so I shot this ole tom here," William grinned as he held up a huge turkey.

"Well, that's good, you can just go and clean that old slow flying bird of yours, and while you are at it you can gut and clean mine too," Thomas shouted over his shoulder as he and Joshua rode off on their mounts, leaving William standing in the middle of the road.

"That's all right, you two go on, I'll clean them, but I bet mine is the biggest!" William called to his brothers through the cloud of dust the horses left behind.

Chapter 5
Respected Young Men

Sylvester pushed his chair away from the table and raised his arms over his head. He took a long stretch and placed his hands onto the armrest of his chair and said what most young men say when they have been away from home for the first time.

"Boy it's good to be back home and with a full stomach to boot. Mother, I do believe that I missed your cooking more than anything else here at home."

That put a smile on Sue's face as she said, "Well, it is wonderful to have you back home again son. It's good to have us all under the same roof again."

"That's true enough", Mordacai replied, "We better enjoy this time together while we have it. Our children are not so childlike these days. You are all becoming well respected young men."

"That's kind of hard to believe, isn't it?" Joshua said as he took one last bite from his supper plate. The rest of the family smiled at what he had just said, yet they all realized that it was true. They still liked to poke fun at each other when the chance arose, but the prospect of what the future would bring made them all realize that they would soon be going out into the world as men in their own right. It would mean getting married and starting families of their own, and it would be happening soon. What they all needed was land, which meant that most likely some of them would end up west of the mountains, a long way from this childhood home.

"Now that you are full of mother's home cooking, Sylvester, can you tell us what is going on back in Baltimore?" asked William.

"A lot is going on these days. People are beginning to get more than a little mad about all of the taxes that King George has come up with, and they are not just standing around talking about it anymore. They are becoming more organized. A group of men are going around at night making it hard on the loyalist and the tax collectors. A great number of newspapers are being printed and passed out all over the seaboard after what happened in Boston that night the redcoats fired into all those people.

"And what happened to them redcoats? Not a damned thing!" said Thomas.

"That's enough of that kind of language." Mordacai interrupted.

"I'm sorry father, but I just get hot when I hear all of this talk about how the English are treating us. After all, we're still Englishmen too, even though we live across the ocean from the old country."

"You're right son. We are indeed still English and I don't know why they will not allow us to migrate west. They say there is a whole world of great land over those mountains, with soil so rich that a man could eat the dirt and live off of it! I would love to have land like that, but I'll be way too old to move out there by the time they decide to let us have a crack at it."

"Oh Pop, Mother is too good a cook to have to eat dirt, even dirt like that," said Joshua as he leaned over and gave his mother a kiss on the cheek. "And besides, the Indians might not like it too much if we moved out West."

"She is a mighty fine cook son, but I'd still like to get my hands on some of that Kentucky lands. But you are right about the Indians. It will take some work to get them out of our way, but we could do it if the crown would just open the western lands up to us. I don't know," Mordacai continued, "maybe the fur trade is just too good for King George to pass up."

Joshua looked at his father and nodded his head in agreement. "Your right father, just imagine what we could do with land like that!"

William got up from the table, walked to the door and pushed it open, but he stopped before stepping out into the cool night air. Looking at Thomas and Joshua, he said, "I thought you were going to have some female company over here tonight!"

Thomas shook his head and said, "Their fathers wouldn't let them come without a chaperone."

"Well, that's most likely a good thing," William replied, "All they would have heard is how bad the redcoats are, and what a sorry shot you two are, because it was me who put that bird on the table tonight!" Grinning broadly, he bolted out the door before his two brothers could say a word in their defense. William walked out into the yard and looked north, the direction where Elizabeth's home was and even though he couldn't see it, he knew she was there. He had begun to envision what it would be like to have Elizabeth by his side every night on his own piece of land somewhere west of the mountains. It was a vision that he liked very much indeed.

Chapter 6
Relax Brother

Thomas had a nervous air about him as he looked into the back door of the church and saw the biggest part of the county's population sitting inside.

"Whew, there sure are a lot of folks in there," he said.

Joshua took a turn looking inside and said, "Yeah, there sure are. There's a whole heap of them in there and they are all going to have their eyes on you brother."

"Nope, the smart ones will be watching Mary." Thomas said. "Man alive, it sure is hot out here. I wish we could have got this thing rolling earlier in the day."

William looked Thomas up and down. It was no trouble to see just how nervous his brother was.

"Relax brother, folks always love going to weddings. All the food and festivities that go along with them lead to a real good time for everybody, besides this is the day you have waited for ever since you first laid eyes on Mary." William told Thomas.

"I know," Thomas said sharply, "but there is a whole herd of them in there!"

"You just think of how pretty Mary is going to look. All you have to do is just say whatever Reverend Smith says and you will be all right," William said in an effort to settle Thomas down a bit. Joshua on the other hand would have none of that.

"That's right," Joshua piped in, "just don't trip and fall down, or stutter your vows. Oh, you'll be alright, I guess. Besides it will all be over soon enough and nobody will remember how badly you messed things up 20 years from now." Joshua's outlandish statements gave all three brothers a good laugh and allowed Thomas to settle down a bit and think about what lay ahead.

"Boy, I sure do love Mary" Thomas said, "she is a grand young girl and I'm lucky to get her for my own."

"Yeah, you're right there. You are lucky to be marrying her, but I don't know how smart she is, because she did say yes when you proposed." Joshua grinned as he got in one last dig at his brother's expense.

Before Thomas could think of a comeback, Sylvester stuck his head out of the door and said, "Come on, Reverend Smith says it's time to start this wedding."

With Thomas leading the way, the three of them stepped through the doorway out of the heat, into the cooler shade of the church. The pews were filled with friends and neighbors gathered for Thomas and Mary's happy day. As Reverend Smith began, William looked out over the congregation and spotted his Elizabeth sitting with her family. She was looking directly at him with a small smile on her face. William gave her the same smile right back. He thought of how his love for her had grown over the years, ever since that first time he had seen her in this very church. Reverend Smith had begun reading from the Bible at this point, but William was still lost in his thoughts and not paying too much attention to what was being said. He was too busy thinking about what his own wedding with Elizabeth would be like and how different it was going to be with Thomas being married and not around as much. Realizing how important this was to Thomas, William began to pay more attention to the proceedings. Thomas had settled down and was standing tall beside Mary, repeating his vows in a strong and steady voice as he looked into his bride's eyes. Then, just as Joshua had said, the wedding was over and Thomas was a married man, but the thing the Tipton family would remember most about this occasion was not Thomas' performance, but how much the day had changed their family.

Chapter 7
Farewell Thomas

It was the day after Thomas' wedding and all the family was helping him load what little belongings, he and Mary had onto two pack horses and in a small two wheeled cart. Watching, William realized that all the feelings he had feared for the last couple of weeks had come to life. His brother was actually moving away; moving not just out of the house and off the farm, but out of the county and even the colony of Maryland. Thomas was going to take his new bride and settle in Virginia.

William was holding one end of a large black trunk while walking backwards down the steps he and his brothers had raced up and down throughout their childhood. Thomas was holding the other end of the massive old trunk. The weight of it was beginning to poke into William's side, making it difficult for him to maneuver his way down the stairs.

"Stop pushing!" William exclaimed.

"Why, is it too heavy for you brother?" Thomas answered back.

"It won't be, when I drop it," William shot back. "I hope there's nothing inside that will break when I let go. But come to think of it, it won't matter much anyhow. It's not my belongings inside now is it?" Hearing his threat, Thomas lowered the trunk to its proper position and the two went on down the stairs and out the door with sheepish grins on both their faces. They set the trunk on the back of the cart and gave it one last push to settle it into its place for the long journey ahead.

"Well, that's the last of it I believe," Thomas said, slapping William on the back. "I sure do wish that you'd be at my new home to help me unpack all of this."

"I wish it wasn't so far away, so I could help you with it too," William replied.

"Fairfax county may be in Virginia, but it's not all that far from here," stated Mordacai. "But I sure am going to miss having you around here son."

"I know father, but it is the best opportunity that Mary and I have at this time. It's a good piece of land, in a river bottom, and we can't pass it up."

"Yes, I know that's true, but we, and I mean all of us, are sure going to miss you. Your mother is already upset about your leaving and you haven't even gone yet. I don't know how she will be when you do finally go. I don't believe she has been able to eat a bite for two days now."

"I know. Where is she?" asked Thomas.

"Out in the back yard," said Joshua who had been watching and listening to his father and brother.

"Let's all go around back and see what she is doing back there."

Sue was sitting under a cherry tree when her men came around the corner of the house. She was weaving a basket and placing the last strip of wood in its place when she looked up and saw them walking toward her. She turned her head and looked down as she wiped a tear from her eye.

"We're all packed Mother, it's about time for me to start." said Thomas.

"Here son, take this with you." she said as she handed the basket to him. "It's
not much but you will need little things like this when you set up your new home."

"It's a nice one mother. I'm sure Mary will like it as much as I do."

"So, when are you leaving?" asked William.

"As soon as I give mother a kiss goodbye," answered Thomas. "I have to go over and pick up Mary from her mother and father's. She lit out early this morning. She wanted to see her parents and spend some time with them before we go."

"Well son, you better be off then, daylight waits for no man."

"I know father," Thomas said as he gave his mother the kiss he had promised her. The whole family walked back around to the front of the house where the horses were tied.

"Wait before you go son, I believe we need to say a prayer." Mordacai said as he removed his hat and began to pray. "Dear kind heavenly Father, we ask that you protect Thomas and Mary on their journey to their new home. Be with them on their way, day and night. Give them the blessings of a safe trip. Bless this union and give them the strength not to stray from your path. In the name of your Son Jesus Christ we pray. Amen."

Thomas took his brother's hands one by one in a farewell handshake and kissed his parents one last time. As he jumped in the cart he said "Don't worry the Lord will watch over us all. You'll be getting letters from us soon. Good by all." The family stood and waved calling out goodbyes as they watched him go over the hill out of sight. Mordacai and Sue shared a look between them, and just like that, Thomas was gone.

Chapter 8
News from Baltimore

Late April 1775 found William a mature man, inside his father's barn grooming Mordacai's favorite horse Star. His shoulders had grown thick and broad. He stood a couple inches over six feet tall, taller than any of his brothers. His strong jaw line could have been completely covered by a beard, if he had wished, but he always took the time to shave, hating the way the short stiff whiskers felt when he touched his face with his hands. His complexion was dark and deeply tanned from spending so much time in the sun. His slightly hooked roman nose sat proportionately between his dark brown eyes. He patted Star's back, running his fingers through his slightly wavy black hair as he walked toward his father's workbench to store away the grooming brush. He was putting on his black felt hat when he heard a voice calling from outside. He could not make out what was being said, but he could tell that it was something important. The cool spring air rushed in as he pushed open the door and saw Joshua running at full speed straight for the barn. Before he came to a complete stop Joshua began to speak, but William was not able to understand anything he was trying to say.

"Slow down for a minute Joshua and catch your wind."

William was afraid he had a fairly good idea what his brother was about to say, and he was not looking forward to hearing it.

"It has begun, it truly has started!"

"What has?" William asked.

"War." Joshua cried "outside Boston."

 "How did you come to hear this?"

"Sylvester sent a letter and a copy of the Baltimore newspaper to father. Come on let's go back to the house."

The two of them ran back to the house, jumped up on the front porch and bolted through the front door. Mordacai was sitting at the table with his back to them. Sylvester's letter was on the table and Mordacai was reading it.

"What does it say?" William asked.

Mordacai licked his dry lips reached down and picked up the letter and began to read it again for a second time but this time aloud. He wanted to get a full understanding of his son's letter.

It happened on April 19th. The redcoats marched out of Boston. They were going to a small village called Concord. It seems they were after the militia's stores. But before they got to Concord, they stopped at a place called Lexington Green. For some reason the redcoats fired on a small group of militias, killing eight or ten men before moving on. When they arrived at Concord, they set part of the town on fire. But while they were setting the fires the militia began to fire on a group of redcoats that were left on the bridge north of the town. At this point the redcoats began a retreat back to Boston, but it was a hard march back, because the militia had placed themselves all up and down the road behind the stone walls and trees taking whatever shots they could get and killing over a hundred of the regulars before dark.

Mordacai paused and looked to his sons "That's pretty much what the papers say, but Sylvester's letter goes on to say that the army is sealed up tight in Boston and that 15 to 20 thousand rebels are outside the city and have them bottled up pretty good for now. The word is that more troops are on the way to Boston from England and will arrive at any time. Now, that seems to have settled the whole question doesn't it boys?"

Sue was looking out the window and had not said a word the entire time her husband had been reading the information Sylvester has sent them. She finally broke her silence as she said, "My dear Lord, what are we going to do? You know Thomas will enlist as soon as he discovers the war has begun, if he hasn't already. He's made it perfectly clear that he would bear arms against the King if it would win independence for America."

Mordacai turned to Sue and said "Well, Sylvester says in this letter that he's sent the same newspaper to Thomas that we have here. So, he'll have the same information we do, provided he hasn't already gotten word some other way. But you need to know that Thomas is only half of the situation. Sylvester goes on to say that he plans to enlist as well." Sue turned and sat down on the window seat and said, "This war is not yet a month old and I will have two sons in it."

William began to think of what he was going to do. Thomas had always said that if the war ever came, he expected all of his brothers to fight for the American cause. And his father had made it very clear that he had no love for 'ole King George. William felt he was a patriot and was not afraid to go to war. In fact, he liked the idea. However, that being said, it was arriving too soon for his liking. He had big plans for himself and Elizabeth. It was time for him to marry and go out into the world and start his own family with the woman he loved. But now, this damned war had jumped up and changed everything in a heartbeat. Questions were running around in Williams mind. Should I go on and marry her now? Should I wait until after the war is over? Would Elizabeth wait that long? How long will the war take? A year, two, maybe more?

William consoled himself in the knowledge that Elizabeth loved him and that she would surely respect his wishes and do whatever he asks of her. But, then again, maybe she wouldn't and that thought put more fear into his heart than the most seasoned redcoat could ever do.

Mordacai got up from his chair and walked across the room to his wife and put his arm around her and said, "Don't worry. Twenty thousand rebels around Boston may be enough men to end this war quickly. Maybe our sons will not have to go off to war. Don't jump to conclusions so fast, my dear."

Joshua picked this time to let his thoughts be known to the family.

"I sure don't want this war to be over too fast, at least not until I can enlist anyway. I always wanted to take a shot at a redcoat and this will be my best chance at it. Now, is not that right William?"

William nodded his head yes, but did not speak his thoughts to his brother.

"If I have to go into battle, I will gladly do so." William finally said. "If we are going to have a piece of that western land, I feel that this is our only course to obtain it.

Besides, it's our duty to protect the people we love. If the king's solders are attacking and killing his subjects in and around Boston, then they will do the same here. I will not stand by and let that happen, not by a long shot."

"Then you are willing to wait and see what happens before you let your passions get the best of you?" Sue asked her son.

"Yes mother, I will." replied William.

"I am not so sure I can say the same," said Joshua. "If the battle in Boston goes badly and the American Army or whatever they decide to call themselves need men, then I will go at once to their aid. No ifs, ands, or buts about it."

William looked at his brother and weighed what Joshua had said, then began to nod his head in agreement. He may not be able to choose his path in this war. The lines may already be drawn for him. William remembered what he was thinking about when he first saw Joshua running through the field toward the barn only a few minutes ago. It was what he had expected and dreaded. The war had begun and he knew deep down in his heart and very soul that he, William Tipton would have a role of some kind in its outcome and now, he realized that he relished the opportunity.

Chapter 9
The Patriot's Letter

Thomas sat down beside the night campfire as it began to cool down. Its embers were beginning to turn white and the coals had dimmed from the red blaze it had been at its peak just a short while ago when it had provided the heat to cook the small meal he had just eaten. Now that he had had a few hours rest and a little bit of food in his stomach, he pulled out a small wrinkled piece of paper and a quill from the pocket of his shot bag and began to write a much-delayed letter home to let the family know how he was getting along. He began:

My Dear Parents,

I have just decided to take my quill in hand to write down a few lines to let you know how life is treating one of your sons. I am well, as I hope all of you are back home. Times are awfully intense here in General Schuyler's army. They march us all day and drill us most of the night by camp fire. I have just finished my supper and we will most likely start to drill again in a short time. I still have not seen hide nor hair of a redcoat but we did see some Indians the other day, but they were at a great distance from us. I am not even sure whose side they were on. I hope they were friend, but most likely they were foe. Now you know your son Thomas is still upon this earth and well. You must forgive me for the poor condition of this paper, but it is hard to get paper out here in the field. I do have one good piece, but I aim to save it for Mary back home. She does seem to get the most of my letter writing time. But you both know that I still love you both as much as ever.

Your loving son, Thomas

Thomas stuck his finished letter back into the shot bag as Captain Galloway walked by.

"On your feet, Tipton time to get back in the ranks." Thomas got up off the log he was sitting on, stretched his cramped muscles, picked up his musket and ran off into the night at a quick step.

Chapter 10
Something New to Ponder

William and Elizabeth had stepped out of the front door of the church as soon as the Sunday services had ended and made their way down the road as quickly as they could. They did not stop to make small talk with fellow church members today. William had big plans in his head and he wanted to talk them over with Elizabeth. He took her small hand into his bigger, calloused one and led her to the old oak tree beside the road where they had so often talked before, but not on such an important subject as this one.

"Alright William," she said, "What is so important this fine Sunday noontide?"

He reached out and took her other hand and pulled her up close to him, so he could see into her eyes and said, "I am going to Virginia, and it is not for the reason you think it is."

"Yes, it is! I know perfectly well why you are going. It's the war isn't it? Two of your brothers have gone off and you believe that it is your responsibility to go as well." she said as she pulled away from him and leaned up against the tree trunk.

"No, that's not it. You're not letting me tell you what I have on my mind. You're telling me what you think I am going to say. Just let me finish what I started to say. I am going to Virginia. But on a land hunt. There is land right over the border that is for sale. I plan to see that land. It's good land they tell me land that I need to look into now. It's not the war. It's for us. We got a letter from Thomas just the other day. According to him he's not doing much but marching around in the dark. He hasn't even shot off his new musket yet. It sounds like a lot of work to me for a new blue coat. I want to make this trip before I decide what to do about the war. I'll be back in a week or so."

William began to smile as he realized that Elizabeth had gotten upset at the thought of his being gone for a long time. "I'll be back soon, just you wait and see. But you should know that someday I may go into the ranks but that's not now, not yet. However, that day most likely will come. What will you do if I do go off to the war?"

"I don't know for sure," she replied as she turned and began to walk back toward the church. Then she turned back around to face William and said, "You know I have already waited a long time for you. I might not wait forever."

William looked down at the ground and started to ponder on what he had just heard. He looked back at her and saw the same smile on her face that he'd had on his a few moments ago, when he'd realized she was sad at the thought of him being gone. Now the shoe was on the other foot. He could see the happiness in her eyes when she realized how he'd feel at the thought of losing her. All of a sudden everything had changed, just as fast as that shot heard around the world had changed things in Lexington, Massachusetts. He knew now that he had something new to ponder.

Chapter 11
The Ferry

William rode his bay horse Fly onto the ferry. As he dismounted, he soothed the big animal, "Steady, Fly. That's a good boy. We'll be off this boat and back on dry land soon enough." he told the horse as he rubbed its soft black nose. William turned and took a good long look at the land along the bank on the Virginia side of the river. This could be it...my new home, he thought to himself. He was excited about this new opportunity for land. It had been working out all right for Thomas in Fairfax County before the war started so why not for him in Frederick County now?

An older man was standing beside the edge of the ferry looking at William and his horse. William saw the man from the corner of his eye as he focused his attention back away from the shore to the nervous horse by his side.

"I had a horse named Fly when I was about your age," the old man said. "And he could fly too. Just like the wind. What about this one here? Is he fast or is the name just a lie?"

"No, it's not a lie, he's fast. Maybe not as fast as he was five years ago, but fast enough to keep the name I would say." replied William.

"Well, I believe you young man. He looks like a fine horse; maybe we will have a race someday. My Fly is dead and gone but I have other horses that are just as fast as ole Fly was. Hell, my King back home is even faster. Aquilla Price," the old man said as he presented his hand to William.

"Tipton is my name sir, William Tipton." William replied as he took the old man's hand into his own "Pleased to meet you sir."

"What's a fine young Maryland gentleman, like you doing going over to Virginia?"

"Land, I'm out looking for a good tract of land along a river bottom that is for sell and not too expensive."

"Well, you're not going to find much bottom land that is going to be cheap here along this river. Son, you better have deep purse strings is all I got to say to you. And you better have coin too, not that Continental paper money either."

"Well, I don't have all my money with me now, just enough to get by on. The rest is still at home; I hope it is enough to make a respectable bid at this time." William told the man.

"Well, I see you have a good head on your shoulders. It's not wise to keep all of your money on your person. It's a fine idea indeed with all that is going on in these times. What with all the highwaymen and the British solders running up and down the river a man could lose his money real fast if he's not careful."

"That's why I am armed," William said as he pulled open his coat to reveal the pistol that he had tucked into his belt. "Are you from around here, Mr. Price?" William asked.

"Yes, I have been here in Frederick county most of my life. That's how I knew you were out of Maryland. I would have seen you somewhere before now if you were from these parts."

"Oh, I see," said William, "do you know of a tract that is for sale around here?"

"Maybe I do at that, replied the old man, maybe so."

The bottom of the ferry hit solid ground and William and his new-found friend both mounted their horses and took to the shore.

"Mr. Tipton why don't you come along with me lets ride along together, a company of two is much better than a lone man by himself, wouldn't you say? And I have an idea of a few men I could introduce you to that might be interested in the sale of some real estate. But keep in mind that this is not any 'over the mountain land', but some of the best land in all of Virginia. As I said, it will take deep purse strings, my boy, very deep indeed."

As they rode along the riverbank together William began having second thoughts about the so-called low land prices he had heard about across the river in Virginia. Maybe the land was not so cheap over here after all. He hoped that he was not wasting old Aquilla's time. The old man seemed to be very likeable and William did not want to put him out and loose the friendship of his first Virginia acquaintance.

Chapter 12
Dragoons on the Road

William and Mr. Price had been off the ferry for a couple of hours and had ridden about 10 to 15 miles together. William was having a good time scoping out the countryside and talking to his new companion. Aquilla knew the land well and all of the landlords fairly well too. As the two men road along he would say, "This land here is nice but about ten miles further south its much better," or he would talk about how good a certain plantation's owner was in his farming practices, or how many slaves were on each plantation.

As they rode along, William noticed a dust cloud rising in the road ahead, and his heart began to race when he saw what it was coming from. It was ten or so redcoats.

"Damn," William said, "what was it you said about being robbed by redcoats on the ferry?'

"Not to worry", replied the old man as he pulled the reins of his horse to a stop. "You are safe with me."

The Dragoons slowed their pace and came to a stop facing William and Mr. Price. Their horses were all lathered and steaming hot. The horse's nostrils were working hard to take in air and catch their breath. An officer was riding out in front of his men. He was not very tall but well built, about 35 to 40 years old. He had a large cut on the side of his face that looked like it was only a few days old, and he did not appear to be in much of a good mood.

"Good afternoon Captain Price, I see you are still out gathering your men together."

"Yes, I am," replied Aquilla. "This young man here will fit right in with the rest of my loyalist. The good King's Men Brigade. Isn't that so Mr. Tipton?"

William just looked on in shock, not knowing quite what to say, so he nodded his head up and down in slow motion.

The British officer glanced at William with what could have passed for a smile on his face and said, "I saw your men starting to gather at the crossroad a few miles up the road, Captain Price. Would you like for two of my men to escort you the rest of the way? They will be able to catch up to me after they get you to the crossroads. It would be no trouble."

"I was hoping you would volunteer a few men, I might need them."

"Well, two are all I can let you have this time." replied the dragoon.

Then the officer motioned to his remaining men and they rode off, leaving two to stay with William and Captain Price. One rode next to William, the other on the far side of Captain Price with all of them riding down the road four abreast.

"So, are you really the Captain of a Loyalist Brigade?" William asked.

"Yes, I am, and from now on, you are to address me as Captain Price." said the old man in not quite as jolly a tone as the one he had been using earlier in the day.

"Well, where do you stand, boy? With the King or with those damn so-called Sons of Liberty?"

Now William understood how this Mr. Price was so well acquainted with all the people and land in this part of the county. He was a well to do man indeed, but not on William's side of the war.

"My family members are loyal subjects of the King Sir, as am I." replied William, trying not to give himself away.

"That's good to know," replied the old man.

"Now that you see that you have no way to buy land in this country you will come along with us, don't you think?"

"I am not ready to give up on that idea yet. After we get to this crossroad where your men are waiting, I will keep on looking. We'll just part ways and I will go on my own alone."

"No, I don't believe so," the old man said as he reached into his saddlebag and drew forth a fine red coat. "You are one of the King's men now boy, one way or the other. I have the need of young men with good horses in my Brigade."

William knew for sure now that there was no way out of this but to make a run for it. "You know Captain Price, you said that someday we many have to have a race between Fly and one of your animals so why not now?" Reaching into his coat and pulling out a knife, William made a quick slash into the arm of the British dragoon riding by his side, causing him to drop his reins and grab his wounded arm, while giving forth a good yell. Captain Price was in the process of putting on his red coat. William leaned over to the opposite side of Fly and pulled his leg up and gave Aquilla a good kick on his shoulder, pushing the old man off his mount and against the dragoon on the far side. The startled dragoon's horse reared up on its hind legs as Captain Price fell to the ground, landing hard onto his back. William gave Fly a kick in the side and off they went down the road fast enough to give truth to the horse's name. The wounded dragoon pulled his pistol and fired, but his arm was bleeding so badly his aim was unsteady and his shot veered off to the left of William who was speeding down the road, putting as much distance between himself and his new enemies as possible.

The other dragoon pulled his saber, turned his mount and began the chase. William looked back over his shoulder and saw the dragoons were in full charge after him and that Captain Price was remounting his horse. William knew that he had been on Fly's back a good part of the day, but not in full gallop like the British had been. He felt he and Fly should be able to out ride his pursuers in no time. But the crossroads had to be close by this time and he wanted no part of that. Up ahead and around a sharp bend was a large brick house and a woman was standing next to its gate. She took one look at William and seemed to come to a decision; she waved her arm in a motion for William to turn in at the gate. He hoped she had heard the shot and was going to help him, but he had no way of knowing if she was waving at him or the men, he could hear coming up behind him. Was she friend or foe? With no time to think about it he had little choice. As he made a sharp turn into the gate off the road, she shouted for him to ride into the house itself. He looked up toward the house and on the stoop stood a boy, standing with both of the double doors open, waving William inside the house. William ducked his head and inside he went on the back of Fly as the boy pulled the doors shut behind him. In one quick heartbeat he and Fly were out of sight from the road.

A tall male slave opened the back door of the house and said, "Don't stop, and keep on going." William rode out the back door of the house without a word. Down a hill he went into an apple orchard. He turned Fly around under the trees and looked back out at the road to see what he could without being seen himself. The woman at the road was lying on her back on the ground as the two dragoons rode up. She got up from the ground and dusted herself off and said something to them. She pointed across the road to the opposite side where a barn stood. By this time old Captain Price had ridden up and she began talking to him and pointing again at the barn. The wounded dragoon got off his horse and sat down on the ground under a tree as the captain and the other dragoon rode to the barn, dismounted, and ran inside with their weapons in hand.

The wounded dragoon had his back to William but the woman was facing him, so he rode out of the orchard into her line of vision. She saw him come out from under the trees and gave him a quick look. She then laid a hand on the wounded man at her feet as she bent over and made him lay down on the ground on his back so that all he could see was the blue sky above. She looked back at William before giving a quick glance at the barn. Looking once again at William she nodded back up the road the same way William had come. William took her gesture as the best way for him to complete his escape. He gave her a nod of his head and rode off, but not on the road. He stayed under cover, just keeping the road in sight. The last thing he needed was to meet Captain Price again on this day.

That night William was back on the ferry where he had met up with his 'good friend' Captain Aquilla Price a few hours before. This time he was looking at the Maryland side of the river. He gave Fly a good pat on his rump,
"You were indeed fast today old boy. You helped save my hide that's for sure."

He also thought about his true savior standing in the road at that gate. William did not know who she was or what her name might be, but he hoped that someday he could find out who she was to give her his heartfelt thanks.

The War had now truly come to his door and it had an ugly face to it. When a man could not ride thru his own countryside without being pressed into service for an army, he wanted no part of, it was indeed time to fight.

Chapter 13
A Dark Figure

William rode into the small village of Frederick Town that night. It was very dark and late, near to 10:00 or 10:30 he thought. It was late enough that all the British would be asleep soon and there would be less chance anyone would pay much attention to one man riding into town by himself. The last thing William wanted or needed was to run into that British Dragoon with the cut on his face. Up ahead, under a tree, stood a man nailing a poster to the tree trunk. William slowed his pace by pulling on Fly's reins. At this distance William could tell the man was not a British soldier, but Captain Price had given him a valuable lesson, not to believe everyone was on the patriot side of the war. So, William let the man finish his task and walk away from the tree and down the street before he approached to look at the poster.

It was a notice for the men of the country to join up with the Continental Army. It stated that all men who would join up for one year would be given pay in gold coin and a bounty of 500 acres of land. This was the first William had heard of free land to be given to solders on the patriot side of the war. This could be the end of his land problems, just one year of service and he and Elizabeth would have their farm.

William walked across the street to what looked like a tavern and peered into its window. Sitting at the candlelit table was the officer with the cut on his face holding a pewter cup in his hand and talking to none other than Captain Price. Aquilla stood up and slowly limped across the Hessian filled room to the bar, obviously feeling the   effects of his fall earlier in the day. William stepped back away from the window, turned and strolled as easily as could be back across the street, remounted Fly and made his way out of town. He was happy he had stayed off the road on his way back to the ferry; the old Captain was indeed looking for him, but to no avail.

Now William knew why that dark figure was putting his poster up so late at night. The town was full of Hessian soldiers who had arrived today to guard the crossroads.

This was war. Real war and a man could be hanging from a tree pretty easily if he wasn't careful. William was getting a real education on his first trip off the family farm. He was beginning to understand what his father had been talking about when he told his sons to be careful on that hunt long ago.

William leaned down and rubbed Fly's neck and said, "I'm sorry boy, but we've got to go on before we stop for the night. But at least you can eat some grass when we stop and that's more than I can do," William said as his stomach rumbled. "There's not a tavern around here that I can go into and eat tonight without the chance one of those damned redcoats, who might recognize me from the road, walking into it." He also knew he was closer to home now and that if they pressed on, he could see Elizabeth soon and tell her about his trip and the poster on the tree with the offer of free land.

Chapter 14
Staying the Night

William and Fly sure could have made a better appearance when they finally made their way up the lane to the Porter home in the next morning. Fly had his head hanging low and was acting like he wanted to stop and eat at a patch of clover by the barn, but William pulled at the reins to bring his head up. William gave the horse one more tap on each side of his belly.

"Come on ole boy, a few more feet and we will be safe. I'll take your saddle off and you can go eat all you want."

William was not sitting quite as high in Fly's saddle as he had been when he had set out this morning after seeing Captain Price last night. His neck and arms were covered with road dust. He had not shaved in the three days he had been gone and he had a white ring around his mouth where he had been licking his lips to keep the dirt off and they were starting to crack a little. Suddenly Thomas Porter opened his front door and stepped out onto the porch with a gun in his hand.

"Who's out there at this time of night?"

"All clear and good Mr. Porter, It's just me, William. No redcoats or highway men here."

"You are back!" said a small voice from just inside the door. Elizabeth stepped onto the wooden boards of the porch. She placed a small hand on her father's shoulder as he lowered his weapon and turned to go back inside. William slid off his saddle onto the ground.

"Yes, I Am." he answered. He bent over and gave her a light kiss and then put one arm around her waist as the other hand was still holding Fly's reins. Mr. Porter came back outside this time without the gun.

"I guess you want to stay the night, don't you? It looks like you're pert near wore out."

"I was hoping you would say that, but I was not so sure, the way you came busting out of that door a while ago."

"That wasn't busting out, if it was, you would have been dead my friend." Thomas said with a grin. "Now give me the horse and we will take him over to the lot." The three of them walked across the darkened lawn, Mr. Porter holding Fly's reins while William and Elizabeth followed, hand in hand. They stopped at the gate and William unfastened the belt on the bottom of Fly's belly, then reached up and grabbed the saddle, pulled it off and took it thru the barn door and dropped it on the ground.

Thomas had let Fly go and sure enough Fly went straight to the clump of clover he had been eying just a few moments before. Thomas went inside the barn and laid down the bridle beside William's saddle.

"I appreciate you letting me stay over tonight Mr. Porter. I know it's not that much farther on to my father's place, but I am dog tired tonight. I also want to tell your lovely daughter what happened out there.

Elizabeth broke in and asked, "Did you find us some land over the river?"

"Well, yes and no," said William.

Elizabeth took his hand into hers and said, "Come on, let's go inside and you can tell us all about it."

Chapter 15
A Proposal

The next morning William and Elizabeth were back outside by the barn. William was re-saddling Fly for the short ride home to his parent's house. It was just the two of them. The sun was beginning to come up and there was a light fog lying in the bottoms around the Porter farm. The sun was starting to break through the fog to begin another day.

"So, what are you going to do William, about getting yourself a piece of land? It looks like you have more than one option. What will it be?"

"I'm not sure what I am going to do, but it's going to happen fairly soon. I'm ready to do something. It's time for me to get out of my parent's home and under my own roof."

Elizabeth pulled an apple from under her apron. She had cut it in half and she pitched one half to William and then turned and fed the other half to Fly, letting him eat it out of her hand.

"I always love to feel the soft part of a horse's nose against the palm of my hand," she said as she patted the side of the horse's head. William watched her do this as the sun's rays lit her face. He loved the way the sunlight made her long blonde hair shine. And when she looked at him with her big bright green eyes he knew this was it and that it was time. He walked over to Fly and gave him the other half of the apple.

"Don't you want it? I brought it out for you," she said.

"No," he said, "I want something a little sweeter. He pulled her close and gave her a soft kiss on the lips. You know Elizabeth that I love you with all my heart and I can't stand not having you with me all the time." He took both of her hands into his and said, "Will you marry me? I will make the best husband that I possibly can and I will work as hard as I can to make us a good life together. You will never find a man who will love you more than I will. Please, would you be my wife and I will love you to my dying day."

Tears slid down her cheeks as she nodded her head up and down.

"Of course, I will. You know that you are all that I want in this world. I've loved you from the first day we met. I knew this day was going to come and I am very happy that it is today." she said as she began hopping up and down a little with excitement before jumping up into his arms. William was holding her off the ground and he began to twirl her around in circles. Then he sat her back down on the ground and gave her one more kiss.

"Let's go back inside and tell the folks," she said.

The young couple turned and ran back into the house, hand in hand to break the happy news.

Chapter 16
Promised Land

Joshua and Mordacai were working over a split rail fence when William came down the road. It was about noon and the fog had burned off the countryside but not from William's head yet. He was still fairly excited about Elizabeth's acceptance of his proposal. Mordacai looked up at his son and said, "Well you surely had some good luck on your outing, because you've got a big smile on your face. Did you find that tract of land you were looking for?"

"No, I didn't," William said, but he still had that lingering smile.

"Well then, what's the big grin all about?" asked Joshua.

William let out a chuckle and said. "It was late when I got back last night so I stopped over at the Porter' place and spent the night before I came on home this morning. Just before I came home, Elizabeth and I were talking and I couldn't help myself! I asked her if she would marry me. And she said yes."

"Well, that's not much of a surprise. We all knew that she would say yes if you ever got around to asking her to marry you. But what does surprise me, is that you asked the girl to marry you without a home to take her to afterward." his father said.

"I've got that all worked out." William said.

"Then let's hear It." said Joshua cutting in.

"Just let me finish what I was saying," William replied. "When I got over to

Virginia, I found that the price of land has gone up a whole lot since the beginning of the war. It's gotten way too high for my blood. But on my way back I saw an enlistment poster that said they were giving land away as payment for one year in the Continental Army."

"Whoa son, what if you get killed on some battlefield somewhere? That's not going to help feed a wife now is it? General Washington has lost New York after the battle of Long Island and he might have lost the whole damn war if it were not for his victory at Trenton. A losing army is not going to be able to pay its solders any promised land if it's on the losing side now is it son?"

"Father that's not all that happened on my trip. Some damned loyalist captain tried to press me into his unit by force. That was the last straw. It made me realize that it's time for me to join in on the fighting like Thomas and Sylvester has."

"Price! That son of a bitch" Mordacai yelled.

"You Know Him Father?" Joshua asked.

"Of course, I do. He is the biggest ass in all of Virginia, as well as a lying, no good for nothing piece of filth." Mordacai said through gritted teeth. "Son, how on God's green earth did you not know or hear of Aquilla Price? Was he the one who told you land was so high?"

"Yes." William replied.

"Did you speak to anybody else over there?"

"No."

"Well why not?"

"Because, I was running for my life, that's why. He and two other redcoats were after me. One even took a shot at me as I was getting away. I didn't have time to discuss land prices with anyone else!"

"Why did they shoot at you?" Joshua asked.

"Because I laid one of their arms open with my knife." William answered.

"Alright brother" Joshua said with a chuckle on hearing William's explanation.

"If you want Virginia land son, then we're going to have to go back over there and make some inquiries of better people than Price." Mordacai said. "But that's for a different day. Let's go tell your mother the good news about you and Elizabeth getting hitched, but leave out all this business about Price and getting shot at. That's one thing she can hear ten years from now!"

Chapter 17
A Letter from Mary Ann

Mordacai went to the door and shouted out to William, "Come in the house son, I got that letter we've been watching out for." William came inside and sat down at the table and looked across at his father who had also pulled up a chair and sat down. Mordacai broke the wax seal on the back of the folded paper. Sue walked up to look over Mordacai's shoulder so she could watch him unfold the letter and begin to read it aloud.

To Mr. John Taylor
I believe it is the best time for you and your son to come on over to our side of the country and see all of the opportunities that are available to you here at this time. There are a lot of more available prospects than what your son was told the last time he was over here. The bad weather has blown up north and you will have a much better time than before when you arrive this time. Hope to see you soon.
Mary Ann

"Who is Mary Ann?" Sue Asked.

"Captain Buxton Babb of Frederick County Virginia" Mordacai answered. "His letter is in code; the bad weather is a reference to Price. That no good for nothing loyalist group of vagabonds who are under his command have gone north. So, it is safe for William and me to go back to Virginia to see about buying that tract of land." Mordacai continued, "This Captain Babb is a sharp one I can tell you. This code is easy for us to see thru, but if it fell into the wrong hands it wouldn't look like much to the enemy. Just some unknown woman named Mary Ann corresponding with a man named John Taylor who of course, is not a real man at all. They can't find a man who doesn't exist. Sharp indeed."

"That's very good news!" William proclaimed. "We'll start out at first light in the morning. I'll get our supplies in order for the trip right now. This Captain Babb sounds like a right smart man to me too. He wouldn't be wasting his time and ours if there were no opportunities for Elizabeth and me in Virginia."

Chapter 18
A Home

Captain Babb looked William straight in the eye and said, "That's it, Mr. Tipton. For 180 pounds of current Virginia money, paid into my hands now and 250 pounds of tobacco to be paid next year, you and your new bride to be will own 103 acres of prime Virginia bottom land, with some of the richest soil in all of the colony. So what do you say to that fine sir?"

William extended his hand and said, "It's just perfect Captain Babb. It's all I wanted and more."

"Now William, I have one more small condition, but it will be a deal breaker if you do not agree to it. I want you to be one of my minutemen once you have moved here and taken over this land. I know you are not a Tory because of that run in you had with Price, but are you a true patriot?"

"Yes, I am," answered William. "That sits well with me. This way I can still be with my wife and we can begin our family together and still serve my fellow man in my new country by being in the militia when I am needed most. When the British finally make a threat at our backdoor which we all know they will, I'll be able to fight and defend what belongs to me and who belong to me as well."

"That is exactly what I wanted to hear from you, Mr. Tipton. Then we can count on you when that time comes." The two men shook hands to seal the deal.

"Until we meet to record the deed, I bid you farewell and God speed." With a tip of his hat, Captain Babb mounted his black horse and rode off leaving William and Mordacai standing in a flat piece of bottom land that was soon to be William's new home.

William turned to his father and said, "Can you believe that just happened? Look at it. It is beautiful, absolutely breath taking and it already has a house on the property. A very small one, but we don't need a big home, at least not yet, not until we have two or three children. I will make the land over by the creek a pasture for my cattle so they can have plenty of water and the land over by the house I can plant in crops. And then there are the woods, with all of that timber just ready to be cut for whatever I need to build. And all of the game that I could possibly need to feed my family with is running all over the place. We will have plenty to eat until I can build up a beef herd. I can't believe it is going to be mine in just a few days. Wow! I can't wait for Elizabeth to see it. She is going to be happy here, I just know it."

Mordacai looked at his son and said, "Well done William, you have handled yourself really well here today, but remember it's still going to be hard work and the job is just beginning. Do your work on time and pray to the good Lord to keep dropping his blessing on you because he surely gave you one today."

William jumped on Fly's back and said, "Come on let's ride over the farm again before it gets dark. I want to take it all in one more time before we go."

"We don't have to go now, not until after you record the deed on Monday, so why not stay here? Tomorrow we'll go hunting on your land and tonight we'll sleep in that little house of yours. How does that sound to you Mr. Land owner?"

"Good," William answered, "very good indeed".

Chapter 19
Saratoga

Thomas had been in the northern army under the command of General Gates for some time now and he held a great deal of disgust for the way Gates ran the daily operations. Maybe it was on account of the fact that Gates had been a British officer before the war and felt like he was far superior to all the other American officers, or maybe it was because Thomas felt General Schuyler did not deserve to be the scapegoat for General St. Clair's decisions that led to the fall of Ticonderoga and now General Gates was about to reap the rewards for his predecessor's work. But as much as he disliked Gates, he loved Captain Daniel Morgan, who was now Thomas' commanding officer. Thomas also held Benedict Arnold in high respect but he too had an arrogant air about himself, but Arnold got the job done and he butted heads with General Gates regularly. Anything that got under old granny Gates' skin put delight in the hearts of all the common solders in the field and Thomas was just that, a common soldier on this October morning in 1777.

The northern Continental army was here in this tree covered wilderness to stop the British forces of General John Burgoyne whose attitude toward the American troops was not very good either; his being even lower then Gates'.

"They are just a group of fools, running around playing solder." Gentleman Johnny had said before he had marched his army out of Lower Canada into the wilds of New York. But now these rebellious American fools were beating up on his well-trained British troops and Burgoyne was in trouble and everyone knew it.

Just a few weeks before, 'the fools' had Burgoyne beat at Freeman's farm, but General Gates would not finish the task after a hard day's fight. Morgan and Arnold had tried to persuade him to make one more attack the next morning on the British lines but Gates refused and let Burgoyne slip thru his fingers. But now here near Saratoga at Bemis Heights with Freeman's farm still in view, the Continental

Army had its second shot at Burgoyne's wilderness weary army. Neither camp had moved much since that first battle at the small clearing named after the Tory, John Freeman. The opposing armies' pickets were very close to each other, and every night saw the Americans mount some kind of attack to keep the invaders from getting any sleep inside their newly constructed earthworks.

As Thomas sat in the dark waiting for the sun to rise, he began to ponder what this day would bring. He had heard that Gates had fallen out with Arnold the night before and had relieved him of his command, sending Arnold to the back of the lines. But surely this was not the case. It had to be another one of the wild rumors that were always running up and down the lines. Surely to God Gates was not that stupid. If it was true, Thomas was glad he was with Dan Morgan today. Being one of Morgan's sharpshooters meant that he could stay behind trees and rocks and not lined up in a straight column exposed to British fire, because he knew that's how Gates always deployed his men. Morgan's Indian tactics had worked well at Freeman's farm when Thomas had shot down more redcoats than he wanted to remember. He felt that whenever the decisive battle came, Morgan's battle tactics would be just as effective here.

As the sun came up over the tree line Thomas heard the beat to arms coming from the drummer boys. Wasting no time, he picked up his rifle, the one Peter Renfro, the gunsmith whose name the gun bore, had made for him just last summer.

Thomas then walked over to where Captain Morgan was standing, hearing the old teamster say, "Take a tree boy, we're in the front again." And off they went, but the morning passed uneventfully, and by noon they were back in camp, but by two o'clock all had changed. Burgoyne was on the move. Gates had responded by redeploying Morgan's men on the redcoat's western flank.

Thomas stood next to an old oak and looked out over a newly cultivated field. It must be a winter wheat crop he thought to himself. Then into the field marched a line of German Hessians. Thomas picked out his man, a tall lean mustached soldier who had no idea this was the last steps he would ever take. Thomas waited for the order to fire, putting his aim at the spot where the German's heart would be. The German battalion covered over three quarters of the distance of the field when the order finally came down...FIRE. Thomas pulled the trigger and hit his mark, the brass gorget the German wore around his neck. The Hessian fell back into the dirt like so many others of his fellow countrymen who fell at the same instant. Morgan's sharpshooters were at it again.

Thomas watched as a new British battalion began to march over the bodies of the Hessians down on the field. Then out of the tree cover charged Benedict Arnold on his horse. He rode up to Captain Morgan and pointed to a British officer. Nodding his head, Captain Morgan turned to his men and shouted, "There, that officer. Put him down in hell boys!" Thomas had reloaded by now and he took his aim on the officer in question as he sat upon his gray horse. Black powder rolled out of the end of Thomas's Renfro's muzzle as the man leaned back in his saddle grabbing at his arm.

General Simon Fraser was the British officer that Arnold had pointed out and like the Hessian before this would be the last battle of his military career as well, for more bullets passed through him knocking him from his horse. The fatal shot came from an easy going, tobacco chewing Irishman named Tim Murphy who was perched high above the field in the forks of a yellow leafed sugar maple. True to his reputation as a crack marksman among his fellow sharpshooters, Murphy had again hit a valuable target. Fraser's men risk life and limb to carry him away from the battle to a house nearby where he would die later that night. At this point of the battle, the British began to retreat and the Continental Army gave chase. During the Continental advance Arnold was shot in the leg and fell with his horse which pinned him under its weight. Realizing that Arnold was out of the fight, Captain Morgan pushed the men onward, once again showing his superb military skills as he gave out commands for the rest of the day. Morgan's actions made the retreat even more dangerous for Burgoyne's defeated army leaving no sanctuary for the fleeing men.

Late that night American cannons were placed to fire on the reformed British position. They were deployed at the captured German lines where Thomas's Hessian had fallen at the beginning of the battle. They would fire all the next day and night.

By then Burgoyne was desperately running out of provisions. Supplies of all kinds were about gone and he knew the continentals would be upon him within hours. With no hope of being rescued he ordered a night time retreat to Saratoga. Once there the British again found themselves under fire from Thomas and the rest of Morgan's sharpshooters. This was Burgoyne's last gasp. He surrendered his army to General Gates, who took little part in the battle, but who would take all of the credit for the victory.

Thomas was thunderstruck to learn that Gates had indeed stripped Arnold of his command the day of the battle, but Arnold had nevertheless gone into battle on his own accord, without men under his official command. He just rode up to the hottest part of the battle and did what he could to defeat Burgoyne while Gates sat in his tent over two miles away.

At the beginning of this campaign when Burgoyne had marched out of Canada, he had under his command three thousand British regulars, three thousand Hessian mercenaries, six hundred loyalist and over five hundred Indians. Now having lost at least a thousand men, those who had survived the battle were prisoners of war. This was the biggest American victory of the war so far, and Thomas was proud to have played a part in the battle's outcome.

Chapter 20
Sarah Lee

William had been sitting outside under what little shade was left from the walnut trees that stood around his home. He had finished this day's work, but the hardest part of his day was yet to come. Mrs. Babb was inside the house with Elizabeth and she was hard at work at what had to be done.

Marriage had been good to him so far. He and Elizabeth had had a wonderful first year together. His first tobacco crop had been perfect. They'd had a dry spring when he plowed his fields and planted this year's crop. The summer had been hot, but he'd gotten all the rain he needed to produce a great crop. Enough to make the last payment to Captain Babb for the land and a little left over for some extra cash and maybe a cow or two. The corn and wheat crops had come through too, and they had plenty of grain for Elizabeth's good bread this winter. And today William had seeded his fall wheat. All it needed now was a light rain to make it sprout though the soil but William's present thoughts were far from the daily operations of his farm.

"I can't sit out here anymore," he said. I've got to go inside." He got up from the ground and dusted himself off and went inside their front door.

"Go on back out William, nothing has happened yet and there is nothing for you to do here," said Charity Babb, Captain Babb's wife.

"Well I'm staying," answered William. "I have done everything outside that I could possibly do, there's nothing left to do out there. So, I can do that sitting inside   right here."

"Well I guess you can be of some help. I usually don't have the husband inside when his wife is in labor but I don't believe that I could persuade you to leave anyway."

William walked around the bed to where Elizabeth was lying and sat down beside her after giving her a kiss on her forehead, he reached down to take her hand in his.

"How are you feeling honey?" he asked.

"Not too well." was Elizabeth's reply. Then she had a strange expression come over her face. "Oh, I think I just wet the bed."

Mrs. Babb raised the blankets covering Elizabeth.

"No dear," she said "your water just broke."

"Thank God." Elizabeth said.

"Help her William, while I put some dry bed sheets down. It still will be a while before that baby decides to come, no need for her to lay in that mess."

Elizabeth took William's hand and stood to her feet as he helped her up from the wet bed.

"Can you stand up? Is it all right for her to stand like this?" William asked.

"I'm fine," Elizabeth said looking him in the eye. "I feel better standing up."

"Let her walk around a little William, it helps if she moves around some," Mrs. Babb said as she dropped the wet bed clothes on the flood in the corner of the room.

She came back to the bed and laid dry sheets down and covered the bed with them and placed the pillow back at the head of the bed and said, "Come on little girl, get back in here"

Elizabeth sat back down and William lifted up her legs and laid them gently on the bed as she turned her body and lay back down on the cool clean sheets of the freshly dried bed.

"What now?" asked William?

"We just wait, that's about all we can do for her now. Just make her as comfortable as we can. It's up to her and the Good Lord now."

Elizabeth took William's hand and gave out a small grunt as she closed her eyes.

"That's her first big pain," Mrs. Babb said. "That child is coming down and it will be here soon if we are lucky. This might be a good time for you to go outside now William."

"No, I'll stay here," he said as he looked down at his wife, thinking to himself, what if this was the last time, he was going to be with her, Mrs. Babb had delivered lots of children over the years but women did die in childbirth. He was not about to get up and walk out now.

"I'm happy you are staying." Elizabeth said as she sat up and placed her hand on her stomach as she was having another contraction.

Mrs. Babb raised the sheets and said, "I can see the top of its little head, Elizabeth. You are doing a great job sweetie. You are a strong healthy young girl. You're going to be fine, so give me a good push baby, and bear down."

William watched as Elizabeth pushed and pushed and Mrs. Babb went on telling her what to do next. He had always loved his wife, but now it had risen to an even greater plain. His heart was filled with emotions as he looked into the face of his wife and he knew that his love for her would never die.

"William, hand me that knife," Miss Babb told him as she looked up from the tiny child she was holding in her hands. "We've got to cut the cord. You two have a beautiful little girl here."

She made the cut and handed the child into the arms of her mother. William could not believe the love that was in his heart for what his wife had just done for him. He was now a father as well as a husband and he loved them both dearly.

Elizabeth touched her newborn child's face and took her tiny hand into her own and said, "She is truly beautiful. Look at her William, she is absolutely perfect."

"They are going to be fine William." Mrs. Babb said, "Both of them are in good condition and are very strong. So, what's the little one's name?"
"Sarah Lee Tipton." the proud father replied.

Chapter 21
Late Night Fires

William was a happy man in January of 1778. His new family life was going to plan, just as he and Elizabeth had hoped it would. They'd had a good crop that first year together on the new farm and best of all; Elizabeth had given birth to their first child, Sarah. Elizabeth's confinement had gone well and Sarah was a fine healthy little girl. She was small, but she amazed her parents with the strength she had in her small hands and how hard her little grip was on their fingers. She would kick and fling her little arms and legs about all the while giving out her little giggles. She would cry out two or maybe three times a night but that was to be expected from a newborn babe.

William's arms were full of wood as he came inside the house, pushing the front door open with his shoulder. He stopped inside and raised his foot to close the door behind him with the tip of his shoe. He walked over to the wood box and dropped the wood inside it. He carefully placed the split pieces of wood on the fire, placing them just right amid the coals so the draft would draw just the right amount of air to keep the fire going, but not to burn up too fast.

Elizabeth picked up her broom and began to sweep up all the wood chips and dirt that had fallen off the wood and William's shirt onto her clean floor. "That sure is some messy wood you've got there" she would always say as she did her work.

"It gives you something to do, my dear. The good Lord knows you have nothing to do with yourself around here. It's not like you have a little girl to take care of." William said with an endearing smile on his face.

Elizabeth just smiled back and made no reply as she pitched the chips into the fire and turned back around from the warm hearth to put her well used broom in its corner.

"Yes, I have nothing at all to do these days and nights," she said as she picked Sarah up from the cradle William had made for her this fall. Holding the child in her arms she sat down by the fire.

"That's a little hot," she said as she stood back up. "Pull that chair back away from the fire for me a little, would you please William."

William did as she asked. He pulled the chair back toward the middle of the room away from the heat. Elizabeth sat back down in the chair and pulled the drawstring on her blouse to open its front. She withdrew her breast and placed Sarah at the perfect position to latch onto the nipple so the child could begin to nurse.

William had pulled his chair up close to his wife's side and sat down placing his elbow on the armrest and putting his hand under his chin to rest his head as he watched what he was sure was one of the most beautiful sights he would ever see.

"I tell you Elizabeth you are gorgeous. I love to watch you do that. It is a beautiful thing to see."

Elizabeth smiled at her husband as she looked into his eyes. "I know you do. I can see it in your face every time we do this."

She looked back down at her daughter and placed a loving hand on the back of the child's head and pulled her ever closer to her breast and began to hum a tune in a soft voice.

William got up from his chair and walked around in back of his wife and bent over and gave her a kiss on top of her head as he slipped his hand down inside her blouse and cupped her other breast in his hand. He held her there for a moment, holding her firmly against the palm of his hand. Then he released her and walked over to the fire where he pulled his shirt off over his head and began to get ready for bed.

"Did you hear that?" Elizabeth asked.

William pulled his shirt back on and walked over and picked up his rifle and looked out the window to see who was outside his house at this time of night.

"It's two riders," William said as he looked back over at Elizabeth, who had put Sarah down in the crib and was retying the drawstring of her blouse.

William did not know one of the men, but he had no trouble recognizing his neighbor James Tate. James sat atop his horse Trace's back in the same strong and easy manner that marked all his movements. Like William himself, James was a tall lean man, but there the similarities ended. Where William was dark, James was fair. He wore his blond hair long and drawn back and tied with a rawhide string. He looked at the world through a pair of light blue eyes that seldom showed his emotions, but left no doubt that he was ready to meet whatever situation that arose.

"Everything's alright," he said, "Its James Tate and he has someone with him, but I can't make out who it is."

"William opened the door and stepped outside to greet his neighbor.

"What are you doing out tonight James?" William asked, "Is everything in order over at your place?"

"All is well William, you can put that gun back down," said James "At least, for the rest of the night that is."

"What do you mean James?"

Captain Babb has called out the militia, my friend. We are to assemble in the morning at the ford. We've been called up."

"Up where?" William asked.

"Fort Pitt," replied Tate. "I was out and about this afternoon and I came across the Captain. He gave me the news and asked me and Dave here to spread the word on this side of the creek. So here we are, doing just that."

"Do you two want to come inside for a while?" William asked.

"No. You're the last soul up this bottom, so I'm heading on back home. Every Tom, Dick, and Harry up and down this bottom has asked us in and we've stopped for a drink too many times as it is. I have no real news to tell anyway. I just know what I've been told by the Captain. He'll let us know more tomorrow. So, we'll see you in the morning. Don't forget to bring Ole Betsy there. I hear you're a good shot" James shouted back over his shoulder as her rode off into the night.

William smiled as he went back inside the house and closed the door.

"Did you hear what he said Elizabeth?" William asked. But he already knew she had heard their conversation. He could tell by the expression on her face.

"Fort Pitt," she said. "I had hoped it would not be Ft. Pitt! That's way out in the wilderness, William."

"I know sweetheart," William said, "but we both knew this day was coming. I'm just surprised it took this long to find us."

William went back across the room and took his clothes off and lay down in his bed. He patted the mattress for Elizabeth to join him under the covers.

She undressed across the room in the firelight as he watched. She walked naked over to the bed and slid in beside him. He laid his arm over her shoulder and pulled her up close to him. She was on her side so he could feel the soft skin of her bottom against him. He put his hand back in its normal resting place on her breast as she began to cry.

"Don't cry now my love. You can do that in the morning when I have gone; right now, we have better ways to spend our last night together before I go."

Chapter 22
An Uncertain Future

The Tipton homestead was abuzz early this morning. William and Elizabeth had been up most of the night. Neither one could sleep much, but for different reasons. William was nervous to be on his first military tour of the war. In his heart he had wanted to be involved from the beginning: as soon as he had first heard of it way back in his father's barn when Joshua ran in with the news. But it could not have come with a worse sense of timing for him. But now, it was a different matter altogether. He was married to the woman he loved, so he did not have the worry of whether she would wait for him. He had been able to purchase the farm and it was now theirs, free and clear. Knowing these things made him feel he had done the right thing for his family. But on the other hand, Elizabeth would be left alone with Sarah, here on the homestead by themselves with no one close enough by to help her out if something came up. Most of all what he really dreaded was the thought of an Indian attack. She would be all alone with little defense if they should come. Not to mention the Tories, and the British regulars. The Indians would most likely kill a little girl and take a woman up north into the Ohio country. The British and Tories were little better. They would not hurt a small child, but the rape of a rebel's wife and the act of killing her afterward had been done in this war. All this put William in a difficult position as he prepared to leave.

Likewise, Elizabeth had her own reservations about their parting. But her thoughts were of William and the thought of his scalp hanging on some redskin's belt on the Ohio River haunted her. She would be left a widow without the man she loved, with a small child and possibly with a second child on the way, a real possibility after the night they had just spent together.

The sun was up now and William had his things ready to go. His rifle was in good order. His powder horn was full and his shot bag was equally full of lead balls. He had two extra flints plus all his gunsmith's tools were packed.

Despite her anguish at his leaving, Elizabeth had been busy as well. She had filled a second bag with some jerked beef and two loaves of bread. Along with a small amount of coffee to keep him warm at night.

William came into the kitchen where Elizabeth was preparing his packs and said, "I'm going out to get the horses ready for the ride, be ready to go when I get back. You are going with me; I'm not letting you two stay here by yourselves. They must have some place set up for the women folk to stay while we are gone. If we are headed for Ft. Pitt, we will be gone for a couple of months and that is way too long for you to be at the end of this bottom all alone."

Elizabeth assured William that when he came back from the barn she and Sarah would be ready to travel. True to her word, when William came back a few moments later, she had them both ready to go.

Now, the three of them were on horseback leaving their much-loved home behind as they rode up the creek and out of their bottom land farm into an uncertain future.

When they arrived at the ford William was happy to see that Elizabeth was not the only female at the gathering point. There were at least thirty women in and around the makeshift camp. William had learned from James Tate that maybe 40 more had already left their husbands here and had gone back to their homes, not willing to abandon their homesteads. However, they had large families with older men and young teenage boys to help out while their men were gone. This was a luxury Elizabeth did not have. As William started to take notice of these women as they moved about. He saw right off that not all of them were wives to his fellow militiamen.

"Who are all of those gals running around here James?" William asked.

"Some are the wives of the men here but most are going to be camp followers. Single women, looking for work at night after we stop the march. Washing clothes, cooking food. They maybe even try to catch a husband before we get to Ft. Pitt. And I also see a couple of outright plain bad women that sell themselves to lonely men."

"You arc not planning on taking your family with you on this march are you William?" James asked, looking at Elizabeth holding Sarah in her arms.

"No, I don't want that, but I can't leave them at home either. Just the two of them all alone, no way will I do that," replied William.

"Well that's good, because you don't have to. They can stay at my place!' said a voice from between two horses. It was Captain Babb. You have a couple horses with you don't you William?"

"Yes, I do sir," William answered.

"Well, they can't go with us. They have no room for more horses at Ft. Pitt. We are going to march up there, not ride. Is Elizabeth good with a horse? Can she handle two at one time with that little one the of yours there?" asked the Captain.

"Yes, I can Captain Babb. I grew up on a farm, been on one all my life. My father put me on a horse's back when I was very young. They will be no problem for me to handle." answered Elizabeth.

"Well, that settles the matter then; you can take them to my plantation and turn them out in my pasture with the rest of the ladies' horses who will be staying with my wife. Elizabeth, I believe you will be the sixth lady to stay with my family. That is, if we have Williams' permission here. How about it my boy" Captain Babb asked?

"Thank you, Captain. Once again, you have been the perfect gentleman to me and mine. Sir, we gladly take you up on your generous offer."
"She can either stay until we return or until someone comes to get her. The two of you can work that part out without my help. Good day Mrs. Tipton, I have other matters to settle before we leave here today," the good captain said as he tipped his hat and walked off into the mob. But then he turned back and started walking backward as he called, "By the way Mrs. Tipton your traveling companions should be meeting up at that grove of trees by the ford."

Elizabeth nodded her head in response and waved back to the Captain to let him know that she understood him as he disappeared into the mass of militiamen.

"Now don't worry about us, William. We will be just fine at the captains. If there is a group of us wives at his place, we will be perfectly safe. And we will have plenty to talk about while you men are gone."

William took little Sarah into his arms and gave her a kiss on her soft cheek and said "goodbye my little angel." Then he placed the child back into her mother's arms and said. "Take good care of her. I know you will. You had better go on to the grove with the other women so you will be there when they start the trip to the captain's place. It will be late by the time you arrive." William said as her brushed his hand down Elizabeth's face. He gave her one last kiss then turned and walked away; leaving her behind before she could cry. Crying was not the way he wanted to remember her before he took his leave. He wanted to remember her the way she was last night in the firelight, lying in his arms.

Still, there was something more he needed to hear. Turning back to her, he asked, "Do you love me Elizabeth?"

"Of course, I do," she answered.

He smiled at her and said, "Then that's all I needed to hear, my love." And he walked away.

Chapter 23
The Deer Hunt

It was very cold this February night in 1778, but at least it was dry. That was what all the men were most grateful for. Dry wood always burns better than wet wood. The fire was nice to have because of the warmth, but even better, it meant they could cook a hot meal. It was a whole lot easier to keep warm when a man had a piece of roasted meat in his stomach.

William had gotten a lot of pats on his back tonight, for he had bagged two deer this afternoon. James Tate had killed a couple as well. James and William had been given two of the ten horses that were allowed to make the northwest trek with the militia to Ft. Pitt. Captain Babb had called the two of them up at midday and said.

"Fellows, when I ride by your homes, I always see deer hanging up in a tree or hides being dried out in the sun, so I know you can both hunt. What I want you to do is, take these horses and ride on up ahead and do some hunting for tonight's meal. This will probably be the last night we can afford to cook out in the open without Indian trouble, so I want two good men out there."

William was surprised to have been hand-picked for this task out of all these men, but he had confidence in his ability to deliver on the job. He had just met

James Tate back in the spring, but they were already becoming good friends. They were about the same age, but James was not married so he had more of social life than William. He was maybe a little wilder than William, but that was one of the things William liked most about him, all of his big tales and all.

They were about what they thought was ten miles or so in front of the militia when James spotted a well-used deer path coming out of a wood and into a wheat field. He stopped his horse and motioned to William saying, "There's our killing field, don't you think?"

"Looks good to me," was Williams reply, "but I'm going in the woods not the field, it's just a little after two o'clock. I bet the deer have already eaten in the wheat field and have bedded down inside those woods for an hour or so."

"We'll most likely do better by splitting up anyway," James said. "You take the woods and I will stay here in the field, keeping the horses in view."

William jumped off his horse and circled around behind the woods and entered into the trees. Both he and James had two rifles each, for the captain had supplied them one apiece on the horses so they both would have two quick shots without having to reload. William took his time, knowing that if there were deer inside the wood, they would be very alert as usual. If he walked in too fast, they would see him first, jump up and run out before he could get off a good shot.

A smile crept across his face as he saw six deer lying in a gulley in the lowest part of the small woods. They were facing the other way and down wind from him. He sat his rifle against a tree and took his first shot with the Captain's rifle at the second deer from the back of the herd. He hit the deer on its jaw. It fell dead without ever knowing what happened. Grabbing his own rifle which he was more at ease with, he made his   second shot. This deer had jumped to its feet and looked back at him as William fired. This shot was also true. By this time the other four deer had raced out of the woods and into the waiting sites of James' gun. William heard James' first shot as he ran to the edge of the woods. William saw James' last shot. The deer was in a full run when the ball entered its back snapping its spinal cord. Its forward momentum caused the deer to slide across the short wheat, pulling the roots out of the ground as it came sliding to a stop. It was one great shot. It had been a fun afternoon for William, almost like being back home hunting with Thomas and Joshua again.

Now, back at the fire with his stomach full, William could tell his own tales tonight about his former hunts and the difficult shots he had made in the past years without raising the eyebrows of his fellow soldiers because today he had proved his skills with a gun.

Chapter 24
The House Boys

Captain Babb's' route to Ft. Pitt had taken his men on a march down the Potomac River, almost to its end. At this point he turned on a northwesterly course going past Great Meadows then on to Redstone Fort where he made camp. The weather had been fair most of the way, but now the men were getting what they hoped would be the last cold spell of winter. They had been here two days and William was happy to get some rest. Redstone Fort was not really a true fort, just a few cabins put up close by each other. It took its name from a long-deserted fort built during the French and Indian War. What was left of those walls was now useless, having been neglected over the years, but however meager it was, it still gave the men some protection.

They could again cook hot meals and it was here William got the news of the frontier from two brothers named Andrew and Adam House. These two were cut from a frontiersman's mold. They had the appearance of experienced long hunters. Their dress was that of true frontiersmen. Buckskin shirts and pants, beaver hats, tomahawks, and Indian scalps hanging from their belts. William had seen them as soon as he came in with the militia a couple of days ago as they were trading pelts in the small store for more gunpowder and lead.

James Tate was out of chewing tobacco and had asked William if he would like to come along inside the store with him. William sent James on ahead because he saw the two-House brothers were standing outside the tavern. William knew these two would know the situation in the wilderness and making friends with these men could not hurt, so he approached them and introduced himself.

"Hello, I'm William Tipton; looks like you two have been having fairly good luck trapping around these parts."

"Not really," said the older of the two. "The beaver is about trapped out and it's too dangerous to go down to Kentucky right now. This is my brother; Adam House and I am Andrew. You're with the militia that came in a few days, ago aren't you?"

"Yes," replied William.

"Where are you all heading for Kentucky, maybe?"

"No just Ft. Pitt," James said right before he bit into his new cake of tobacco.

"Ft, Pitt. Well they can use you boys up there, that's for sure. Come on, let's go and find a fire, maybe even get us some rum," said Adam, the younger of the two brothers.

"Sounds good to me," James said as he spit out some tobacco juice onto the ground.

The four men went inside one of the cabins. It had a bar with nine or ten men inside sitting around the tables with mugs in their hands. The room was full of smoke from the poorly drawing fireplace and the tobacco being smoked. William and his companions sat down at one of the last available tables and began their conversation.

"This is the first time I have been out this way, so what is going on up here?" William asked.

"It's bad. It's getting more dangerous every day, that's what's going on" Andrew said. "The Shawnee are on the warpath in Kentucky. The Iroquois are about to go over to the British. Alexander McKee and Simon Girty are talking with the Iroquois, but I don't believe they will get much done.

"I don't trust either one of those two." said Adam.

"Why?" asked James.

"Girty was raised by the Indians, captured as a boy, lived with them for years. And McKee was one of John Connolly's ole boys."

"Whose John Connolly" asked William?

"Boy, you two are new. Ft Pitt was under his command until he ran over to the British. He is as big a Tory as they come." Andrew explained. "But I like Simon. He's alright. The war's been going on for a while now and he's still working with us at Ft. Pitt."

"I didn't say I didn't like him. I said, I don't trust him," Adam replied. "He's just stuck in the middle of two worlds, white and Indian. I think when it's all said and done, he's going red."

"When are you going to head out for the fort? "Andrew asked William.

"I'm in the militia," William said, "whenever our Captain says so probably when this bad weather breaks."

"Well Adam what do you say we go along with these boys here on up to Ft. Pitt?

There's safety in numbers and all," Andrew said to his brother.

"Makes good sense to me the red devils can't kill us all, now can they?" Adam asked as he got up from the table and started back to the bar with an empty mug in his hand.

"Hey, where is that little redheaded gal that usually fills our mugs?" Andrew yelled across the room to the barkeeper.

"I would like to know that myself," said the man behind the bar. "She should be here by now. Maybe some old trapper beat you to her Andrew."

"Not that redhead! She's had her eye on me for a while now." Andrew answered back to the barkeeper. "She knows the big wood from the little brush, old man. I got her right where I want her."

Adam had refilled his mug and taken one more drink when he sat his mug down on the bar. He reached down and pulled out his tomahawk and threw it across the room, sticking it into a huge piece of elm log that had been cut just to be a target for the men inside the tavern. It gave them something to do that would help keep them out of trouble. He walked over and pulled it out of the wood and placed it back on his belt and returned to the table with his mug in his hand.

"Alexander, what do you mean she's not here?" Andrew asked.

"Just that, she's late she should have been here an hour ago. That's not like her either; she's usually here by now."

"Maybe she ran out on you Alexander." Adam said as he sat back down at the table.

"Not that one, she's too hard a worker for that." replied the barkeeper.

"Have you checked on her to see why she's not here?" Andrew asked.

"No, but maybe we should." said the old barkeep.

"Is she still down in that cabin on the creek the one out by itself?" Andrew asked as he got up and grabbed his buffalo coat.

"That's the one."

Out the door went the two House brothers without another word. William thought of Elizabeth back home and how if she had disappeared, he hoped someone would go looking for her if she was missing. He tapped James on the shoulder and said, "Come on, let's go with them." They went outside and followed the Houses down a small hill to a one room cabin sitting huddled next to a creek bank. As they came to the cabin the door appeared to be shut, but on closer inspection, they could see it was open a few inches. To the side of the cabin lay a dead dog, it had two arrows in its side, telling the story of what had happened here this morning.

Andrew said, "Damn Indians. They sure are getting awful brave, hitting a cabin here so close to all of us. Even with your militia in town. Go get the horses Adam."

"You boys want to come along with us?" Andrew asked.

"We're on foot," replied James. "We'd need horses."

"The captain will most likely let us have two," William said. "I'll go see."

William turned and ran back up the hill to find Captain Babb. When he reached the top of the hill Adam had already given the alarm. Redstone was abuzz, with men milling around cussing the Indians for this morning's raid, while others were trying to take a head count to see if everyone else was accounted for. William saw Captain Babb and told him the situation.

"The door was open at her cabin but she was not inside. A dead dog was outside, killed by arrows. Not much doubt of what happened to the poor girl. James and I would like to go along with the rescue party, if you will give us leave to go Captain."

"Well the militia can't go along, we have to get to Ft. Pitt, but I will let you two go if you promise to come back in when all this mess is over with." Captain Babb said as he walked to the pen where the horses were kept. "You boys can have two horses. Take any you want, but mind you, don't take mine."

That was all William needed to hear. Within moments the five men were across the Monongahela River in pursuit of a party of Indians holding captive a girl that William didn't even know.

Chapter 25
Hot Pursuit

The rescue party had been tracking the Indians due West. Andrew House was reading the signs left behind by the Indians, but then it began to snow. Big flakes the size of coins, the ground was cold and the snow was beginning to stick and the rapid accumulation covered the tracks of the fleeing war party. Andrew slowed down the pace of the chase, stopping ever now and then, getting off his horse looking for some indication of which way to go.

"Damn it to hell, they are on foot. I wish they were on horseback instead. We could track them a lot better. I don't see any moccasin tracks."

"Then what are we going to do, we can't see anything in this snow which way should we go?" William asked.

Andrew got back on his horse. "We keep going west."

"Yes," said Adam. "They're Shawnee. The Iroquois would most likely not be raiding this far south of Ft. Pitt. They wouldn't want to pass the fort with a white woman with them on their way back."

"I thought that too," Andrew said, "You're right. They're heading for Cresap's Bottom. They've probably got some sunken canoes hidden under the water. All they would have to do is pull the rocks out of it and pull it up out of the water and go across the Ohio to Captina Creek. They most likely have left one of their warriors behind on the other side to have some horses ready for a fast way back to whatever village they   came from. If they get across the river, we'll lose her. How fast do you think we should go after them Adam?" Andrew asked. "If we run up on them in the daylight and they see us first, you know they'll kill her right then."

Adam looked at his brother and said, "If we knew when they took her, it would be a great help. If it was last night, we've got to keep on going fast because they will get to the river fairly soon, if they are not there already. But on the other hand, if it was this morning, we've got to be close to them by now, and if that's the case, we need to go slow so as not to give ourselves away.

William spoke up and said, "It was this morning, but before the sun had come up."

"Now how would you know that?" Andrew asked.

"The fire," William answered, "I looked at the fireplace and there were still hot coals in it where she had banked the fire last night. If she had gotten up this morning as usual, she would have replenished it, but she didn't. The door was open, but just a little. If they had broken in last night, the room would have been much colder. I think they got her just a few hours before sunup."

"If you're right they'll reach the river about dark." Andrew said. "We'll ride hard for a while. When we get close, then we'll head on to the river on foot. Maybe we'll catch them camping on this side if they get there after it's too dark for them to cross tonight."

"If we are really lucky, maybe we will catch them asleep and we can cut their throats while they sleep."

Having decided on a plan the men were back in pursuit of their quarry. They   were working the horses hard, but it gave William time to think of what lay ahead of him. He was not going to be shooting at deer this time, it was going to be at a man and men could shoot back. William rode up beside Andrew and asked "How many do you think there are in this war party?"

"Six, including the girl, but who knows, they may have met up with a larger party by now." Andrew said, "But that makes it more fun for us."

Chapter 26
We Got 'Em Boys

William got down from his horse and tied his reins to the trunk of a small walnut tree. The snow had continued to fall, but not at such a rate as it had been earlier. Now the snow was a help because it had covered the ground enough to make the Indian's tracks visible, but not too much, so as to cover them back up. The House brothers had made the right decision about what direction to take and here, looking down at the tracks in the snow, Andrew had a smile on his face as he proclaimed, "We got 'em now boys!"

"We're on foot the rest of the way."

"The river bottom is close by," Andrew continued, "so everyone be careful and keeps your eyes peeled. If the Indians believe that they are safe and have made a clean escape they may camp on this side tonight. But most likely they will have left a rear guard here to watch their backs and to keep an eye out for us."

"Let's go."

They had followed the trail for about half an hour when William saw the glow of a fire up in the distance. The Indians had stopped for the night on the east side of the river. It was dusk now and would be completely dark soon.   William's eyes were scanning the countryside looking for any motion that might be the Indian lookout. The wind was starting to lie down and he cocked his head trying to pick up the sound of anyone moving about. That's when he saw someone's breath floating in the cold air. William raised his hand motioning everyone to stop. He pointed toward the tree where the Indian was hiding.

Both House boys nodded their heads. Andrew moved to the right of the tree and Adam to its left. Each one moved at a slow careful pace and even though William was only a few feet away he couldn't hear the two frontiersmen move.

William then made his own move toward the unsuspecting Indian. All three men were just a few feet away when out from around the tree stepped the Indian. He was looking down at the ground but then to his surprise he looked up and his gaze fell on William. As he raised his musket Andrew threw his tomahawk, hitting the Indian in the shoulder. William leaped forward with his knife and plunged it deep into the warrior's chest, pushing him back onto the snow-covered ground. Adam fell upon the Indian, putting his hand over his mouth to muffle his scream and slit the red man's throat.

William pulled his knife from the body and stepped back as he watched Adam remove the scalp from the top of the warrior's head with one quick slash of his knife. As Adam stuck the still dripping scalp into a buckskin pouch, Andrew handed William the dead man's tomahawk.

"You may need this a little later on tonight. Take it." Andrew said in a low whisper. "Now when we get up to their camp, we'll all take a tree. Then we will each pick out our best target. After we shoot, we all rush in with our tomahawks. But not you Alexander, you reload, so you can be ready to fire, in case another one comes in out of the dark."

Once again, they were moving through the dark, but this time towards the light of the fire. As they approached, William saw the silhouettes of the Indians moving around the fire, but the girl was nowhere to be seen. William stepped behind his tree and waited for the others to do the same. Then thru the darkness, William heard the faint sound of a woman crying. She was sitting down and her hands were tied to her feet. There were four Indians in the camp, one was standing by the fire and he was not armed. Two others had their guns sitting on their laps across their legs as they sat on the ground, talking to each other. This was the first time William had heard the Indian language and it had an odd sound to it he thought. The last Indian was standing next to the captive. He was looking down at her with his back turned away from William and the rest of the party.

William picked out his man, the one standing by the fire and pulled back the hammer of his rifle until it clicked. Then he pulled the set trigger and placed his finger on the main trigger and waited for Andrew's order to fire.

Then shots rang out and William fired, hitting the Indian in his back causing him to fall into the fire, head first. William dropped his gun and ran into the camp with his new tomahawk in his hand, giving out a loud yell as he ran. All four Indians had been hit and two of them were dead. James had just finished off the third with his knife as the fourth man ran off into the dark with Adam running on the warrior's heels. Andrew ran to his little redheaded girl and cut the cords of rawhide that had bound her feet and hands as Alexander stood by with his newly reloaded rifle in his hands.

"It's alright now," Andrew told the woman as she got up and grabbed him around the neck. "You are safe now," he said.

William walked over to the fire and grabbed the feet of the dead Indian and pulled the body out of the flames. Hearing the sound of someone approaching in a fast gate he looked up to see Adam running back into camp and began to take the scalps off the dead.

"Did you get that one that ran out?" James asked.

"He didn't get very far." Adam answered, "I got his hair."

Then Andrew did something that William could not believe. He turned to the red headed girl and asked her, what's your name Red?"

"Hannah Snapp." she answered back.

"What!" William said, "You don't even know her name? I thought you knew this girl, met her back at Redstone."

Andrew walked over to William and put a hand on his shoulder and said, "I told you that she had her eye on me, never said that I knew who she was but what a way to meet her, 'eh? And besides you came along just like I did. Why don't you tell me her name?"

William just shook his head and said, "You got a point there Andrew. I couldn't tell you her name either."

Andrew walked back to Hannah and led her out of the camp as he said." Let's go Miss Snapp. If there are more Indians around, I don't want to meet them tonight. We better get on back to our horses."

James, Adam and Alexander picked up the Indian's weapons and whatever else they could carry and left William in the camp alone. William turned the body of the Indian that he had shot over and looked in his face. One side was burned away, but the other side was still in good shape. His face was painted red with a little yellow war paint on his cheek. His hair was shaved on each side of his head, but the middle was three inches tall with a bit of white paste holding up the hair and making it stand on its ends. This Indian was a fierce looking man. William was glad he was dead. He would not raid any more cabins and maybe the frontier was a little bit safer now that he was dead.

When William left the camp, he put his hand on his new tomahawk and realized that within the last hour he had just killed two men and he wouldn't lose any sleep over it tonight, or any other night for that matter. At least that was what he hoped.

Chapter 27
Hannah's Story

Now that Hannah was safely back in the hands of her own people, she could hardly believe what had happened to her and how lucky she was to be heading back to her own home. Riding along behind Andrew and holding tightly to his big warm body, she felt safer than she had in a long time.

Andrew had wanted to go up the river to Ft. Henry at Wheeling, but she wanted no part of that. She wanted to get back to Ft. Redstone and to her own home. She also wanted to return to her job at Alexander's tavern. It was not easy for a good woman to get work that did not compromise her virtue and morals. Alexander was running a clean establishment and she had no plans to lose a good job. Alexander was also ready to get back as well, so Andrew gave in to their wishes.

The sun was beginning to pop up over the trees and its warm rays along with the safety she felt with Andrew were beginning to loosen her tongue, so she began to tell Andrew her story. William rode up beside them so he could take in what she was about to tell.

"I was asleep in my bed, just as warm as a bug," Hannah began, "Then I heard Buck, my dog begin to bark outside and then he let out a little whimper. Before I could get out of the bed, the door was knocked open and they were in the cabin. One of the Indians grabbed me by my hair and pulled me up against his chest. He raised his tomahawk above my head, making a threat to lay it open if I was not quiet.

Two others ransacked the room, but I don't have much of anything for them to take. The one that was holding me gave me a hard push into the corner of the room and picked up my dress and pitched it at me so as I could get dressed. I turned my back to them and pulled it on over my nightgown as they laughed at me. Before I could turn back around, he placed a cord around my neck and tied my hands behind my back. Then they stuck a rag in my mouth and tied a rawhide thong around my head. And then they led me out of the cabin and across the creek. I was barefoot and I cut the bottom of one of my feet on a rock or something in the water and boy, that water was cold. When we got on the other side they stopped for just as long as it took to dry their feet and put on dry moccasins. That devil, which had pulled me out of bed, pushed me down to the ground and grabbed my leg and pulled it up into the air and put a pair of moccasins on my feet. He jerked me back up off the ground and grabbed that rope around my neck. Then he put this old blanket around my shoulders and off we went along the creek to the river. When we got there, I could see that they had captured someone else. It was one of the Wetzels. They had him along with his canoe. It was Casper I think, but I am not sure, he was up front and I could not see his face. They forced me into the back of the canoe and we paddled out into the middle of the river. That's when the one sitting behind Wetzel tomahawked him and threw his body into the water. When we reached the other side, they pulled me ashore and off into the trees we went. At first, I was not moving very fast, but then he gave a hard tug on that rope and it cut into the back of my neck as it pulled me down to the ground. And they all thought that it was funny and they began to laugh at me.

Then he pulled me back up and said in broken English, 'I kill you. You go fast or be dead'. So, I stayed up as best as I could from that time on, keeping poor Wetzel in mind, but sometimes I would still fall behind, and he would give another jerk on the rope. They did not give me any food, but they ate some kind of raw meat that they had in their bags. We did not stop for nothing. Once their leader while holding my rope did stop to relieve himself, so I stepped in back of a tree and did the same. But before I could get back to my feet, he gave another hard pull on that darn rope and pulled me down into the snow.

I thought I was lost for good when we got to the river. They began to talk to each other a little more. I guess they thought they were safe and had gotten away clean. They sat me down on a log and tied the loose end of my rope to a tree so as they could start a fire. One of them pulled a raw piece of meat out of that bag and began to cook it. I believe it was the same meat they had been eating on all day. Then the one who had been leading me came over and said, 'you good squaw. We not kill you if you good. Take you to Frenchman and sell. Or maybe I keep.' At that he finally cut the rawhide from around my mouth. Then he said 'no talk or back on', so I did as I was told, but every now and then my emotions would get the best of me and I would cry, but he never did put that rag back in my mouth. Then you came in a shooting and a shouting and it was all over. I am grateful to you Andrew for coming after me. I didn't know if anyone would, me being all by myself and all."

Andrew reached around over his shoulder and placed his big hand on the back of Hannah's head and pulled her down so her chin rested on his shoulder and said "Well Hannah, I hope you don't mind if I call you by your given name. You don't have to be alone anymore. You're with me now."

Chapter 28
Dividing Loot

The next day William, James and the House brothers met back at Alexander's tavern to divide up what loot they had taken off the Indians. Most of it was small weapons, knives and hatchets, but there were three poor Indian trade smooth bore muskets and one shotgun. Adam House passed on the weapons saying that the scalps he took were more than enough for his share. Alexander took the shotgun to place behind his bar. James took one of the trade guns; the one with a blue panted stock. Andrew gave his to Hannah to keep in her new cabin that he had rented for her, one that was not as isolated as her old one had been out on the creek. William planned to sell or maybe trade off his, once he got to Ft. Pitt.

Andrew had changed his plans about going on to Ft. Pitt with Captain Babb and the militia, now that he and Hannah had truly caught each other's eye, so to speak. He had decided to stay at Ft. Redstone to be with her.

True to his word Captain Babb and his men had moved out for Ft. Pitt the day before, but Adam assured William and James that they could easily catch up with the militia, since they would be on horseback and the militia was still on foot.

William said his goodbyes to his new friends before riding out. Andrew had said that if William would stay in the area for anytime at all, most likely they would cross paths again. William hoped that it was true, but wondered, the way these two lived, with such reckless abandon they could be killed at any moment. But then again, they were such good woodsmen they most likely could fight their way out of any scrape they might get into.

As William and James rode out of the village, they began to talk over the last twenty-four hours and how it had been some kind of wild introduction to what frontier life could be like. But the real frontier was further down the river, in Kentucky. Where no forts would be built like the one at Pittsburgh, just a few small stations thrown up by men who were more concerned about making tomahawk claims, than building a safe fort that could withstand a siege like the ones Ft. Pitt could hold off.

It was late in the afternoon when the two men caught up with Captain Babb and the rest of the men. William told and retold the story of Hannah's rescue, as did James. He noticed he could tell a difference in the way he and James were being received by the rest of the men. The fact that the two of them could bring in food for the men had been greatly appreciated, but now that he and James had been in combat with wild Indians and been victorious as well had really vaulted their status among the men. William began to enjoy his new-found reputation in the ranks and was looking forward to seeing Fort Pitt.

Chapter 29
Fort Pitt

William was astonished by what he saw at Pittsburgh when he arrived. It was nothing like what he thought it would be like. Not the crude rough wild frontier outpost that he had envisioned. All the descriptions that he had ever heard about Ft. Pitt were out of date. Yes, it was true that the country could still be wild and dangerous, but not quite as bad as when Braddock's army was defeated back in the French and Indian War.

The streets were full of people going about their business and they were occupied with the same purposes as the people of any town on the seaboard. The streets were lined with shops, inns, and lots of trading posts. There were a few stables and even some talk of a couple of Churches going up and the taverns, all kinds of taverns. Some were of a family nature, but most had a rough clientele. But what really made William's day was the thought of a post office! Now he could get word back to Elizabeth and maybe even get a letter from her.

Yes, Ft. Pitt was definitely a surprise. However, most of the people on the streets did have the look that William had expected to see. Most of them had the appearance of frontier types. Nine out of ten men had a rifle on their person. Some even had the same look and general appearance as Andrew and Adam House. The same experienced look in their eyes. Farmers were here too, William knew the look of a farmer all too well.

And the Indians, not a whole lot but quite a few more than William had thought to see here. Not all of the tribes had lined up with the British. Some were still friendly to the Americans, but it was odd to see them on the streets. These Indians were not quite as fearsome looking as when their faces were covered in war paint. Some of them had a hate filled look in their eye when William looked deep into their faces and it was easy to see that unrest and mistrust ran deep between the two sides.

Now Ft. Pitt was impressive indeed. It was located between the two rivers, the Allegheny and Monongahela at the mouth of the great Ohio. It was star shaped, with five points sticking out from the fort's walls. Each wall was about six hundred to seven hundred feet long. It was built so high there was no way to see what was inside the stone walls. Earthworks outside its walls would make any attack that much more difficult. William could see how it had withstood all of the attacks over the years from the Indians, and how the redcoats had little chance of taking it out of the American's hands now. It would take a massive amount of large artillery to damage this fortress. The gates were huge and stronger that any William had ever seen before.

The barracks looked like they each could accommodate five hundred men. The powder magazine was located in one of the star points of the fort. It had the look of a magazine that could hold all the powder it would take to win this war all by itself within its walls. But now that William was inside the fort, he could see why he was here. There were nowhere near enough men inside to garrison a fort of this size. There were maybe fifty or so Continentals and a few more local militiamen and that was about it.

The fort was under the command of the newly promoted General Edward Hand. Before the war had started, he had been in the British army having enlisted as a surgeon's mate back in 1767. In time he acquired an ensign's commission and was stationed here at Ft Pitt. However, by 1774 he had become disgruntled with the crown and resigned from the military. Once the war of Independence began the Continental Army quickly approached Hand for his services. Once back in the military he had made a name for himself at the battles of Long Island and Princeton as well as the siege of Boston. For his reward his new countrymen had again posted him here at his old stomping grounds: Ft. Pitt. Most of his time had been spent trying to keep the Indians out of the war. He had sent his Indian interpreters and agents out to treaty with the Wyandot and Seneca, but it was of no use. The Indians were already in too deep with the British and everyone knew it was a losing battle to try and win them back over to the patriot side now. What little hope there was of keeping the Shawnee Indians out of the war was lost when Cornstalk had been killed at Ft. Randolph and no one dared to talk to them now.

So now, General Hand was ready to stop talking with these Indians. He was determined to show them the error of their ways. He wanted to crush them as quickly as possible. In doing so, he would win the West for the Patriot cause. In addition, the General knew that a swift victory in the Ohio country would get him back East once more to where the large battles would be taking place, and that's where General Hand wanted to be.

Once again William found himself at the right place at the wrong time.

Chapter 30
The Barracks

The next day after Williams' arrival at Ft. Pitt, all of the militiamen were still inside their barracks when Captain Babb came inside and told the men that General Hand was planning to address them that morning. The captain went on to say that General Hand had not given him any indication of what he was going to tell them. But Captain Babb did tell them what to expect from their new commander.

"He was polite to me in every way boys, but he was very professional. No horse playing around him now boys. He is a real solder and a true officer of the Continental Army. He will not put up with any kidding around like I allow you boys to get away with. It's true we are militia and we can come and go on our own leave, but while we are here, we are under his command, so be on your best behavior If not for me, then for your own good." After completing his little speech, the captain turned and left the room.

William did not have much to do except wait for the general. He had kept his clothes on last night as did most of the men since the barracks was not warm. It had just one fireplace inside to heat a very large room.

"Cold last night, 'eh James" William asked?

"Hell yes," James shot back, "and that damned rope laced bed didn't help me sleep none too well either."

"I know," William replied, "I believe I could have been more comfortable on the floor. I sure do miss that old feather bed back home."

"That bed's not all you're a missing from back home I dare say," James said as he sat back down on his cot. "Look at this, my ass is almost hitting the floor. These damn ropes are so loose in the frame of this sorry cot. I got to tighten them up before tonight."

William smiled at James as he said, "You better be careful, if you get a splinter in your ass, no one here will pluck it out for you."

Williams' statement had lightened up the mood in the room a bit. Most of the men got a good chuckle at James' expense and now they began to fall out of the barracks and into the center of the fort. William said, "I'm happy to catch the smell of frying bacon in the air, they may not have a whole lot of men around here, but by the smell of things this morning, we won't starve to death.

"That's fine with me," James replied, "and we didn't have to kill it before we ate it either. That's good for a change."

All of the men got some bacon and a piece of cornbread and a mug of milk with a little splash of rum mixed in to wash their food down with. As William was finishing up his meal, he saw a man enter the fort's gates. He was a fairly young-looking man, about William's own age. He was dressed in Indian drab and about five foot eight inches tall with a strongly body build. The man was riding a fine bay horse without a saddle. He jumped off the bay before the animal could come to a stop. He left the horse unattended as he went inside one of the blockhouses.

"Who was that?" William asked one of the sentries who was standing by the blockhouse door that the rider had gone into.
"Girty." was the reply.

About that time Captain Babb came out the same door that Simon Girty had just entered.

"Change of plans, my boys," Captain Babb said in a loud voice. "That was one of the General's spies and he has the General's ear for now. So, if you boys want to see what the town has to offer then now's your chance. But, be back inside the fort by noon that's when General Hand plans to speak to us, so off with you now."

William knew the first place that he was going to see in Pittsburgh, and it was the post office. A much-needed letter could be sent back to Elizabeth. He was not going to miss this opportunity. This could be his last chance to write to his wife for a long while and he was not going to let it pass.

Chapter 31
A Slave and Samuel

William went out of the gates of Fort Pitt and down into the streets of the town. It was beginning to warm up and a few more people were out in the streets. William had taken along the trade gun that he had picked up in his little skirmish at Cresap's Bottom.

He was looking for the tavern of David Duncan. Andrew House had told William about it. He had said that it was one of the most popular taverns in Pittsburgh. William was hoping he could possibly sell his gun there.

As he walked along, William saw what he thought was a trader standing up ahead. The man had a full beard and a toboggan on his head. He had the look of a man who had just come in out of the frontier.

"Sir, would you be willing to buy this gun?" William asked as he held the weapon out towards the man.

The man looked at the gun and began to speak in French, but William had no idea of what the man was saying. Then up stepped a black man. "He's my new master," said the slave. He does not know English very well. When he needs to talk, I do the translation for him. He just bought me in New Orleans. We came up the rivers together. How much do you want for the gun?"

"I don't know, how much do you say its worth," asked William?

"Four dollars," assured the slave, "but he will just offer you two, he's a tight old ass."

The Frenchmen hit the slave on the back with the palm of his hand, while speaking in French and raising two fingers into the air. The slave nodded his head as he spoke a few words back in French to his master while pulling his thin worn coat together trying to keep out the cold. Then he turned back to William saying, "See, I told you he would just give you two."

"Did you take that off of some savages? If you don't want that gun back in the hands of the Indians, I would not sell it to this fellow here," continued the slave.

William shook his head, "No, I don't believe I will sell it to him. I would hate for this gun to kill anybody going up river just because I sold it to someone who would give it back to the Indians." When the Frenchman saw that William was not willing to let the gun go at such a cheap price, he gave out a small grunt in disgust and in a fast motion raised his arms into the air and flung them back down to his side and walked away.

As the slave followed his master, he looked back at William and said with a grin, "He's not having much luck on this buying trip. And I sure don't know why."

As William watched the two men walk on down the street he laughed under his breath, thinking that that poor slave would never get a decent coat if his master didn't make any money, but then, winter was almost over now.

As the two turned the corner and was out of sight William's eye picked up a sign hanging out over a doorway that read Duncan's Tavern in old English. So, he made his way down to the door and stepped inside. It was just as Andrew had said it would be, full of men and a few women as well. William got one of the last tables and sat down when one of the two girls that worked there came up to him and asked what he wanted. "Coffee would be good," was the answer he gave her and off she went to the kitchen. William sat looking out over the room seeing if he could spot someone that he could sell his gun to, but almost everyone had a much better rifle at their side than the musket William was trying to sell, so he gave up the idea of selling it here.

When the barmaid came back with his coffee he asked if he could get a quill and paper. She said, "At a cost." William just nodded his head 'yes' as he took the first drink from his cup. It tasted really good and he was surprised that coffee was still available here. It was hard to find back home, ever since the war had begun and especially since most of the ports were under British control. The girl returned to his table and set down an inkwell and handed William the paper and quill and walked away. He began to write his thoughts to Elizabeth.

Hello my love, I have made a safe arrival here at Ft. Pitt and all is well with me here. I hope for the same blessing for you and our little one back home. I have already had one good adventure with the Indians that I will tell you about when I come home. I have met a couple of brothers named House out here and they have become my newest friends, but we have parted ways. Hope to run into them again. Tell Mrs. Babb that the captain is well at present as all of the men are out here. I hope you ladies are getting along well back home. I have enjoyed seeing the fort here and Pittsburgh as well, but I do miss having you by my side and seeing little Sarah grow, but I will be back soon, God willing, so that's all for now.

William drank down the last of his coffee, paid the bill and asked the barmaid where the post office was. She smiled as she looked down at him sitting in his chair.

"Just arrived didn't you, I can always tell when a new fellow arrives. You all walk down here and ask about the post office, its back at the fort." William smiled and nodded his head. He left the tavern and began his walk back. He had not gotten far when up stepped a young boy about 15 or 16 years old who asked William,

"You want to sell that there gun? I'll give you three paper continental dollars for it."

"Sold," William told the boy, "as long as you don't plan to sell it to an Indian."

"No," said the boy, "I am going to shoot one with it."

As he watched the boy handle the gun, William saw what he thought must have been the same glow in this young man's eyes as he himself had in his, when his parents gave him his rifle back home in Maryland all those years ago.

"So, you're going to bring down an Indian with that musket, are you my boy?"

"Yes sir, I'm Samuel Farra," the young man said as he grasped the musket in his hands and gave the weapon a good going over. The boy was looking down the barrel and then he turned it back around and started pulling on the hammer. "I sure am glad to finally get my hands on a rifle," Samuel said. "It is a good one now, ain't it? I don't know much about guns, I just know I need one."

"I hate to tell you this, but that's not a rifle, it's a musket you've got there." William proclaimed to the puzzled youth.

"Rifle, musket, what's the difference they both shoot the same, don't they? I mean a ball comes shooting' out the end of the barrel now don't it?" Samuel asked.

"Well, yes they do," William said, "but there is a difference. Your musket has a smooth bore where; a rifle has a ribbed barrel. Yours will load faster but it will not shoot as far or as straight but, it has a larger caliber than say, my rifle. And too, you can also fire buckshot in yours where I can't, so you see there is a difference between the two."

"Where did you get this here rifle?" Samuel asked.

"It's a musket, Samuel not a rifle," William corrected this new confused friend. "I got it a while back off some Indians that had gotten a little wild one night."

"You mean they just let you have it?"

"No, we had to kill them first but they did not mind too much after that."

"You've really killed Indians?" Samuel asked. "Did you put these feathers on the end of the barrel?"

"I am not lying to you, that was the musket of a Shawnee warrior and he was the one who put the feathers on it, not me." William told Samuel.

"Well, I'll be the son of a suck egg mule! I never would've thought that I'd own something an injin had once had. You don't think it'll be bad luck for me to own the gun of a dead man do you now?"

"No, it was just bad luck for that Shawnee," William answered. "Where's your family Samuel? If there are any more out there like you, I've got to meet them."

"Dead," Samuel replied. "I don't even remember them too good now. They died on a ship on the way over from Cows, England. I was only eight at the time. I was an indentured servant for seven long years after that and I just finished my contract with Christopher Robinson."

"What did this Mr. Robinson have you doing those seven long years?" William inquired of the young man.

"Cleaning out his stables, most of the time he never did teach me a trade. I just scooped out a lot of shit and straw over the years."

William was laughing at Samuel's story when he said, "I know what that's like. I've done my share of cleaning out stalls in my time too."

"Well, I've got to get back to the fort." William told his new friend. "We believe we will be getting our orders this afternoon, so I've got to get on back."

"Who's we?" asked Samuel.

"The militia, I'm in Captain Babb's company. We just got here a few days ago."

"Do you think that Captain Bob will let me join up with you and be part of the militia?"

"Well, I don't see any reason why he wouldn't," William said, "but his name is Captain Babb, not Bob. Boy, you ask a lot of questions. Come on, let's go and see."

Captain 32
Chattering Teeth

Samuel Farra was not in as good a mood as he had been back in Ft. Pitt when William escorted him into the fort and introduced the young man to Captain Babb. Samuel had been ecstatic when the captain allowed him to join the militia but this was not what he had in mind. He had been hoping that they would set out the rest of the winter in a nice warm barracks. But now, he was learning life in the ranks was not always easy.

William was right about getting their orders that afternoon. When Simon Girty told General Hand that the Indians were lost to the British and in a few weeks would be sweeping up and down the frontier in war parties the aggressive Hand thought, 'Why sit back and wait to be attacked?' So now, earlier this morning five hundred men had marched out of Fort Pitt and crossed the Allegheny River to take the fight to the Indians in their home country. This small army was traveling on a northwestern course following the Ohio River from its mouth up towards the Beaver River where its waters would roll out into the Ohio.

They had only been on the move about two hours when it began to snow.

"Winter sure is hanging around this year." James said to William.

"Yes sir, it sure is," William replied. "This would be a good day to still be back at home feeding a nice hot fireplace with a good smelling pot of stew hanging over it. Then we could sit back down in our favorite chair and watching our pretty wives do the cooking for us."

"When do you think we will stop to eat?" asked Samuel.

"I don't know," William said, "we just follow the fellow in front of us and we'll stop when he does. You know as much as we do. The general doesn't come back here and let us know what his plans are."

"Well, at least we have horses this time around." stated James. "It's good to have our feet off of the ground."

William, unlike his new fellow militiaman Samuel, was truly enjoying his initial trip down the Ohio River. Now he could understand how it was becoming the buffer between the Indians and the settlers. It is a natural barrier.

The wind began to pick up and it was blowing directly into the faces of the men. William reached up and pulled the brim of his hat down a little tighter around his head. As he looked back up, he spotted Captain David Scott riding down the line going in the opposite direction from the rest of the column.

"No talking in the lines boys. We don't want to give ourselves away now do we" he said as he rode by. "We're about to make our turn up the Beaver."

William turned around in the saddle and watched the captain go on down to the back of the line where he turned his horse around and fell in line beside Simon Girty.

William wondered to himself why Simon Girty, the man that knew this country better than most of the men here, was in the rear of the line and not up front with the officers leading the way to the Indian villages.

About then a drop of rain hit the top of William's felt hat with a loud plop. Then it started to pour. Within a few minutes every man was dripping wet. As they rode along the rain began to freeze. The ice was sticking to the trees and the limbs began to hang low and then they began to break under the weight of the ice. The woods all around were full of the sound of falling branches. The rain was covering the snow with a thick layer of ice and the ground was turning into soup from the mixture of snow and mud under the horses' hooves as they broke thru the ice making a crunching sound.

William knew it was going to be a long miserable night ahead. A little before darkness fell, General Hand ordered a halt to the line; they had finally reached the forks of the Mahoning and Beaver Rivers.

William dismounted from his worn-out horse and bent over to take off the animal's saddle, but ice had formed on the buckle of the girth. He pulled out his tomahawk and gently tapped the buckle to break the ice free. Then he slid the saddle off the horse's back and dropped it on the ground under a cedar tree. He led the tired animal to a walnut tree and tied the reins to the tree trunk. Giving the horse a pat on the nose he softly said, "I'm glad that it's you here, and not ole Fly. At least he is back home in a dry stall and not out here freezing with us". He walked back over to the cedar tree and sat down on top of the saddle beside James and said, "No dry firewood tonight boys, we're going to freeze our asses off when it gets dark."

"My teeth are chattering," Samuel announced just as Captain Babb walked up.

"Well son, take some of that jerked meat out of your waste bag and sticks it between 'em that will keep them from chattering."

Then Captain Babb came to the point of their situation. "Men, this expedition is going poorly. We have just gone about thirty or forty miles and our food supply is already running low. One of the pack horses has disappeared along with the fellow who was in charge of it. Damn thieving bastard and Captain Scott has just reported that he is missing another man. He thinks the poor soul fell off his horse and got swept down the river. So, I want a head count made right now to see if all of my boys are present and accounted for." The captain ordered William to take the roll call after the men had gathered around under the cedars, trying to keep themselves out of the rain as best they could. As William was taking the count, he began to see how bad off the men were becoming. Many had the fevered look of sick men in their eyes and some were beginning to cough, but the good news was that everyone was accounted for.

General Hand did not want to waste any time now, because he too saw how bad the condition of his army was, so he called for Girty. The general told his best Indian spy to proceed on out into the darkness and find out where the Indians were. After receiving this order Girty approached Captain Babb and asked for a volunteer to come along on the spying expedition. The Captain told Girty that of all his men, he had two who had crossed paths with the Indians before.

"Well, call them up. I want to look them over," the scout replied.

Captain Babb called out, "William, James, Front and center lads."

The two men approached their commander, but as they lined up James coughed. He tried to hide it by covering his mouth with his hand, but it was too late. Girty's sharp ears had picked up the sound.

"I can't use him," said Girty "One cough like that and we'd be dead. What about you?" he asked William, "are you sick too? Now don't lie to me. I don't want to find out once we are out there that you are."

"I'm fine," answered William.

"Say you've been out against the Indians before?" Girty asked.

"Yes," William answered back, "but just once, with the House brothers."

"Andrew and Adam House" Girty asked?

William nodded his head, "Yes."

"Well then, that good enough for me get your horse." Simon Girty seemed well satisfied with William's credentials as the two rode through the night up along the side of the Mahoning River. Once again, William found himself going out into the night with a great woodsman, on the lookout for Indians. William thought to himself that this was a good opportunity to learn from one of the best men on the frontier, but he also remembered what Adam had said about Girty back at Ft. Redstone, that he may turn red at any moment.

Chapter 33
Out spying with Girty

William was exhausted but now he had a fresh mount, one of the horses that had been held back as a reserve. This horse was one of the fifteen animals that were led along in the rear without a rider, each one being tied behind the other. Although he was tired, he knew that the men left behind would get little rest in these horrible conditions either, so he felt like he was not missing much in the rest department. William wished that Girty had allowed James to come along. He was going to miss his friend. They had become close in the last few weeks. Besides, James was good with his gun.

At last the rain slowed down, now it was just a light drizzle and it gave William hope that the storm was about to blow over.

Girty was up in front of William, weaving in and out around low-lying limbs and fallen logs, avoiding all the hazards, and even though it was dark, he never took a misstep. Then the two came out of the woods and onto a well-traveled path. Girty pulled on the reins to stop his horse and dismounted. He motioned for William to do the same.

"This is the way we should have been coming all along," Girty said in a low voice, pointing down the path. "That stupid guide took us the wrong way at least four times. I don't know why a blacksmith was hand-picked to be our guide. We would have been dry sleeping in a captured longhouse tonight and if I had been up in front leading the way. Out of this damned for sure. We're going on foot the rest of the way. There is a village just up ahead. Follow me and step where I do."

"I'll do just as you say Sir," William replied.

"Just call me Simon. I'm no dandy."

At that Simon Girty turned and led the way to the edge of the woods about two hundred feet from where they had left the horses. There, under a large hickory tree the two squatted down low and looked out into a meadow where a village lay.

"Look, there in the center," Simon said as he pointed to a large building. "That's their longhouse," he continued, "All of the villages decisions are made there."

"Is that a blockhouse over there?" William asked pointing across a clearing.

"Yes, they put it up back in the spring. I believe that was the first indication that we were losing the negotiations battle to the British," Simon said sorrowfully.

Scanning the village, Simon pointed out to William the fact that not too many men were out of their lodges. "They are inside, staying out of the God-awful weather. Let's head on back and tell the general."

The two quickly remounted, with Simon once more in front, leading the way back to the camp.

William was wondering why so many people did not trust this Simon Girty. After all, like Andrew had said he was still with the Patriot Army. It was very clear to William that Simon should have been the guide on this expedition, but General Hand had picked a man who had little knowledge of the country, unlike Simon, who knew it like the back of his own hand. In any event, William was glad that he had met Simon and he hoped that maybe someday the two would become friends.

Chapter 34
What the Hell Am I Doing Here?

It was very late when the two rode back into camp at the forks of the two rivers. It was just as William had thought it would be. The men were standing around talking to each other and not getting much rest. But now, at least, it had finally stopped raining.

Simon got off his horse and handed the reins to William. "Here, have someone take care of him for me. I am going to tell the general what we saw tonight." Simon was walking away when he turned and said, "you handled yourself well tonight, you can ride with me any time William."

As Simon went to find General Hand, James approached William and asked what they had seen.

"Indians, that's what we saw," William answered. "Tomorrow we'll do what we came here for, fight the Indians. He took me straight as an arrow to a village, and it was a big one too. We'll need every man that we've got tomorrow."

James asked, "What's he like?" as he nodded his head in the direction that Simon had taken to find the general.

"I have no problem with him, in fact I liked him."

Having said that, William looked down at Samuel who was sitting on the ground leaning back against a log and said, "Boy, you sure are a hard-looking tater, sitting down in the mud. Do me a favor and tend to these horses."

Samuel slowly got up and took the reins from William and led the two animals down to where the rest were tied. As the young man walked along he began to mutter to himself, "Called me a hard-looking tater. What's he talking about, a hard-looking tater?"

William flopped down under the trees in the driest place he could find, in an attempt to get some rest. He was going to need it tomorrow. Within a moment he was in a sound sleep but, just a few minutes later he was awakened by the sounds coming from a very angry man.

It was Simon, coming back from his meeting with General Hand. He was cussing loudly as he walked by and William heard him say in discuss, "What the hell am I doing here?"

As William rolled to his side he looked up and saw Captain Babb approaching. "What is the matter with Girty" he asked?

"Difference of opinion," the captain said, "General Hand sent out another scouting part after you all left and they came back with news of a closer village than the one you boys saw. The general decided that the other village would be the best one to attack, and Girty didn't take the news too well. He will be alright when the sun comes up, you'll see."

Chapter 35
The Squaw Campaign

The sun had come up, just as Captain Babb had said it would, but Simon was far from being alright with the news of the new target. Sometime during the night, a horse, belonging to James Brenton, had somehow gotten loose and run off into the surrounding countryside. Brenton was one of the few friends that Simon had with him on this trip, so Simon agreed to go along with his friend and help find the horse. William watched the two as they rode out of camp heading south back towards the Ohio River and out of sight.

Captain Babb told the men to saddle up, that they were heading out for the Indian village. As William rode out of the muddy camp he look around, to see if Simon had made his way back, but he was nowhere to be seen. Several of the men grumbled that Simon had most likely gone off to warn the Indians of the coming attack, but William was not of the same opinion. After the time he had spent with Simon, he realized he had come to trust the man. The simple fact that he had been raised with the Indians did not mean that he was not trustworthy.

Within two hours Hand's army was strung out and had become separated from each other. The fields were very muddy and the creeks had risen out of their banks. It was easy to get left behind if one had any trouble at all. However, William was able to keep pace and stay to the front of the long drawn out line.

When they reached the Indian village, William knew why Simon was so upset. This village was small, not half the size of the one he had scoped out with Simon. It was midday and the militia had surrounded the cabins with ease. The small town was now completely encircled.

James had suggested that he and William keep a sharp eye on Samuel and keep him between the two of them, because this was his first taste of battle. If he needed help they might be able to provide him with some protection.

The plan was for the men to all rush in at the same time and overwhelm the Indians before they could put up much of a fight. As William looked into the village, all he could see were children and women walking about. He was looking for a warrior as his target but his eyes could not pick one out. Then someone discharged his weapon into the village and the rush was on.

William ran into the middle of the chaotic scene, but again all he saw was crying children or frightened women who ran in to scoop up screaming children in their arms before darting inside one of the cabins or into the surrounding woods and out of sight.

But the off to his right, William saw an old man who raised his gun and had just gotten off a shot at one of the running militiamen. The old man's ball struck Captain Scott in his arm spinning him back around, where he fell to the ground breaking the bone.

The old warrior shouted out a victorious war cry as he saw that he had hit his mark. He began the process of reloading his musket when he was tomahawked by none other than Samuel Farra, who came running past William and gave a killing blow to the old Indian's head. Then, quick as a whistle and the blow from

Samuel's tomahawk the battle was over and William had never even pulled his trigger, because there were no male Indians here to fight.

As it turned out, the only Indian killed was the old Delaware war chief named Bull that Samuel had struck. But now that the heat of battle had passed Samuel was not so happy about his first kill. He watched as a very old woman came running up to her dead husband and fell at his feet and began to cry. She had not even noticed that the small finger on her own left hand had been shot off in her run to get to her husband.

Samuel stood with a wild look in his eyes. He was very upset with himself now that he could see what he had done. In his mad dash all he had seen was a flash of a pan and the smoke from the report of a rifle, not the aging husband of this grief-stricken old woman.

James saw the boy's face and led him away, telling him that he had no choice but to kill the old man. "You saved someone else's life. You know that don't you Samuel? That old man had already shot Captain Scott. If he had gotten off a second shot someone else would be dead now. Don't let it gnaw at you. Come on; let's go tell the Captain you got the Indian that shot him. I'll bet he'll give you some mighty high praise."

In the aftermath of the skirmish, the men ransacked the cabins and set them all ablaze. Several of the squaws had gotten away by running into the woods. Only five had been captured. Their hands had been tied and they were waiting to go with the first group of men leaving the now burning village.

As William walked out of the smoke, he met Simon Girty, who had just arrived. He was talking to the squaws in their own tongue, trying to console them and put their fears to rest as best he could. He looked over at William and said, "All this turned out to be was a damned squaw campaign."

Chapter 36
A Ham from Home

Now that William was back at Ft Pitt his thoughts were beginning to wonder how his two girls back home were getting along. He was enjoying life in the militia, but he was missing his wife and child badly, now that he was staying inside the stone walls of the fort most of the time. On occasion, he would go out and down to Duncan Tavern, but that too was losing its appeal. He could only listen to James and Samuel for so long now and they were starting to run out of thing to say, so they were not much help.

The fact that they were both single men was also a hindrance to William. He longed for female companionship, but only Elizabeth's. James was with a different woman almost every day. And Samuel, he was just young and dumb when it came to women. He was like a lost ship at sea, slamming into the rocks night after night.

The sun was going down and William really had nothing much to do but stand on top of the stone walls and watch the movement of the people outside the fort. As he sat there, he saw the figure of a man coming up a path by the river with what looked like a large saddlebag on each side of his horse.

"That has to be the post rider arriving with all of the mail." William said as he jumped down from the wall, ran to the ladder and slid down to the ground before trotting over to the lone rider. The man had his back to William and he was standing in the shadow of the walls of the fort as he removed a bag from his horse.

"Do you have letters from Virginia?" William asked.

"No," the rider said, as he walked around his horse and stepped even farther into the darkness and began to take off the remaining bag from the opposite side of the animal.

"Why? Are you expecting a letter?" he asked from out of the darkness. "Well, I got something better than a letter for you right here. Come and take a look, it's one of mother's hams, but I must confess, I've already been eating on it some. It's a long trip from Maryland you know."

"Joshua! Is that you?" William cried.

"None other." was the reply as Joshua stepped out into the moonlight and grabbed William by the shoulders. Although he was older, Joshua was not as tall as William. They didn't look alike in many aspects. Joshua had dark brown hair that showed auburn in the sunlight and had a natural curl that William's darker hair didn't have. Joshua's eyes were hazel and usually filled with the merriment that marked his disposition.

"Hot damn, it is good to see you again brother," William said. "What are you doing way out here?"

"Kentucky. I'm heading down river to Kentucky. I plan to get my hands on some of that good dirt before it's all gone," Joshua answered.

"Do you really have one of mother's hams?" asked William as he looked into the bag and pulled out the wrapped ham. Aw man, let's go down into town, I know a good tavern where we can go and eat this while we get caught up on what's going on with the family."

As the two brothers walked out of the fort William saw Simon Girty with a man William did not know saddling up two horses just inside the gates of the fort. "Come on Joshua, I want you to meet someone."

"Simon, this is my brother Joshua."

"Joshua, this is Simon Girty, the best spy in this fort," William stated.

Simon took Joshua's hand and said, "Hello Joshua."

"Looks like you've got your horse loaded down pretty good there Simon, where you off to?" William asked.

"Over to Alexander McKee's place. Me and Matthew here are going over for a visit tonight, "Simon said as he mounted his horse, but before riding off into the night Simon said, "Watch your hair William, I'd hate to see you get caught by the Indians now, my friend." Hearing this all the other rider began to chuckle as he rode off with Simon.

"Who is that other fellow there?" Joshua asked.

"I don't know too much about him," William said, "Elliott's his name, Matthew Elliott."

Chapter 37
An Old Longhunter

William led Joshua down into Pittsburgh. The streets were crowded with the town's usual people but with one difference, the absence of Indians. He did not see a single one in the stores. It seems that most of the tribes had gone for the British now and the ones who were still friendly to the rebels were staying out of the town. All the tribes most likely were doing their trading in Detroit now.

"What do you think of Pittsburgh?" William asked his brother.

"It's bigger than what I thought it would be. It's not just a Fort," Joshua said as he switched the ham to his other hand and tucked it in next to his hip.

"That's what I thought too when I got here," said William. He looked at the ham his mother had sent him and his mouth began to water.

"How much longer will you be here?" asked Joshua, as he looked down at William's old worn out boots.

"This tour is about up, spring is finally here. As you know we are all mostly farmers and we need to go home to start our new crops. I believe we will be out of here in a few days."

"Well, I hope you are not walking home in those old boots you got there. I don't believe you will get back to the fort before they fall off your feet."

"Yeah, they're about shot. They were in fairly good shape until we went up the river two weeks ago. It rained and snowed all the time we were up there.

Having them wet all the time nearly wore them out. I was hoping to get home with them, but I don't know now. Here's the place I was talking about, let's go in and cut into mother's ham. I haven't had anything nearly as good as her sugar-cured ham in a good while."

William opened the door and Joshua walked in first with William right behind. The room was full like most nights and all the tables were filled but, over in the corner sat an old man by himself. Two empty chairs sat by his side. The old man's legs were stretched out in front of him with his arms folded across his lap and he appeared to be asleep. Sitting on the floor under the table was a bundle of pelts tied by a tug. A pewter pitcher was knocked over on the table and the point of a knife was stuck in the wooden tabletop.

"Joshua strolled over to the table and was staring down at the sleeping man when he said, "Do you know him William?"

William shook his head, "No."

Joshua raised the ham a couple of feet above the table and dropped it so it fell hard, hitting the tabletop causing the pewter pitcher to roll off onto the floor and making the table bounce.

The old man opened his eyes with a wild look on his face. He reached for his knife, but Joshua beat him to it. Holding the knife himself, Joshua asked the old man,

"When was the last time that you had a good piece of sugar-cured Maryland ham to eat?" as he was cutting into the meat.

The old man rubbed the whiskers on his jaw and pushed the hair out of his face with his hand and said, "Too long for me to remember."

"We'll remedy that for you right now," William said after he had picked up the fallen pitcher and sat it back down on the table. The old man called out to the barmaid, "Mary! Another pitcher over here and bring us some bread while you are at it girl." She came over to the table with a new pitcher and sat it down and said, "Me and David are trying to make a living here serving meals and here you are coming in with your own food. What's that all about James Knox?" she said with a smile.

"Girl you go on and leave us alone. I've already spent enough money in here tonight."

"Yeah, yeah," she said as she reached over and pulled the old longhunters' beard before walking back to the bar. By this time the two brothers were seated at the table and watching Mary and her friend have a little fun with each other. As she came back and dropped a loaf of bread on the table and then stormed away. Knox chuckled at her and said, "Boy, she's a good one. I like that gal."

William looked over at Joshua and said, "How are our parents doing back home?"

"Good," Joshua said, "They are fine. Pop's feet hurt him sometime but that's about it. Mother's just getting along like always," he added.

"What about our brothers?" William said as he cut into the bread and handed two pieces of it to Knox.

"Sylvester has gone up north with General Lee, but Thomas is back at home. His tour is up and he went home for a while to be with Mary. But he is not going to stay for long. He said he was going back soon. You know how he is."

"And what about you?" William asked, "Going to Kentucky 'eh?"

"That's right and I was hoping you would come with me. You always said you wanted to see what you could do with virgin dirt. Well, here's our chance. But we got to go now, before it's all gobbled up.

"You are right about that," the old long hunter said, "I just got back from Harrodstown and a whole lot more folks are coming down the river and up from the Carolinas through the Cumberland Gap as well. All of the good land is going to be gone soon."

William was staring into the fire as he listened to this old Kentucky hunter continue. "All a man has to do is mark a tree with his tomahawk to stake the claim. Then plant a small plot of corn. After that he has to build some kind of shelter. It doesn't even have to be a cabin. Some are just putting up a lean-to. And just like that, a man has four hundred acres of Kentucky land. What you need to do is make damn sure that you have not claimed someone else's land. Cross claiming is going to be a big problem, you can mark my words. Take the time to look around and make sure you don't cross lines with someone else. Then all a man's got to do is record the claim."

"That's why I want you to go with me brother," Joshua said. "We can't let this slip by; it's too good of a deal. Man, this is free land, ours for the taking."

"I do love my place back home, but it's not four hundred acres." William said as he stood up and opened the door of a brass lantern hanging on the side of the wall. He reached inside and removed the lit candle which provided much of the light in the room. Reaching inside his pocket he took out a pipe and put it in his mouth and lit it from the candle, taking a few draws through the stem of the pipe. He put the candle back in its resting place and shut the little glass door of the lantern and sat back down.

"When did you pick up smoking?" Joshua asked.

"Oh, a while back," William said as he blew out a puff of smoke. James, one of my neighbors got me into it. He first tried to get me to chew, but I couldn't stand that."

"Well, if I was you two boys, I sure would be going down river. Hell, I'm an old man, not young like you fellers and I've already made four claims. You boys are going to miss out if you don't go soon. Now boys, let me change the subject here," the old man said. "That's an awful good ham you got there. How about a trade? Do you need anything, powder or flints maybe?"

Joshua spoke up, "Naw, nothing like that. But how about a pair of boots?"

"Afraid I can't help you there," Knox shook his head as he bent over and pulled out his bundle from under the table. "But I do have a couple of shoepacks," he said, while pulling the tugs of rope made of buffalo hide and hair. He unfolded the outer hide of his bundle and it fell open to reveal its content. Inside was a small treasure trove of supplies that included a pair of scissors, some buttons, gun flints, assorted beads, and a belt of wampum, a few pipes, handkerchiefs, leggins, and finally the pair of shoepacks that he handed to Joshua.

"Not me, him," Joshua said as he pointed over to William. Knox turned and pitched one of the moccasins over the table to William.

"They're plain," the old man said, "but comfortable and better than the ones the yellow boys use. They got a good sole inside that I took out of an old pair of boots. They are sewn in real good made 'em myself."

William took off his boot and slid his foot down inside the moccasin. "That's not half bad," he said as he got up from the table and walked over to the door and back.

"You've got yourself a deal Mr. Knox, but can I have a few of those buttons, maybe just two?" William asked.

"Sure, why not?" the old man said. "I got a whole heap of 'em, help yourself boy." Having concluded the trade to the satisfaction of both, the old hunter picked up the half-eaten ham from the table, dropped it down inside his bundle, and folded the buffalo hide back around it and finally retied the tugs. He bent down and picked up the rest of his belongings from the floor and said, "Well, that's it for me tonight boys. I better see you two in ole Ken tuck. You'll wish you had, if you don't come." Retrieving his rifle from beside his chair he walked off, but not before saying goodbye to his favorite barmaid, Mary, on his way out the door.

Joshua looked over at his brother and said, "See, I've only been here a little while, and you're already a pair of moccasins richer, so why not go with me to Kentucky and we will both become rich men."

"You forget I've got a wife back in Virginia," William said.

"No, you don't, she's back in Maryland with her folks. She gave me a note to give you when I was still back home. It's back at the fort in my other saddlebag."

"A letter from Elizabeth why in heavens name didn't you give it to me when I asked you if you had a letter for me when you first got here." William asked.

"Because I wanted to talk you into going on this trip first. If I gave you that note first you would have had your nose stuck in it all night. You can read it when I have gone to sleep later tonight."

William jumped up from the table and started for the door. He tossed a terse, "Pay the tab. I am going to get that letter," over his shoulder to Joshua as he shot out the door.

Joshua dropped a few coins on the table and ran out the door after William, who by now was far down the street.

Chapter 38
Elizabeth's Letter

William broke the wax seal on the back of the folded letter and opened it, but he had too little light to see what his wife had written him. He turned and ran to the barracks and sat down on the wooden floor where he lit two candles and stretched out on his stomach carefully placing a candle on each side of the letter and began to read.

My Dear Husband,

Let me begin by telling you that all is well with our daughter. She is growing fast and she is starting to eat solid foods now. She misses you very much, as do I. I have sent you this letter to let you know that we are safe here, back in Maryland living once more under the roof and protection of my father's home. The living conditions at the home of Captain Babb were quite tolerable and pleasant. However, it was not my home and even though Mrs. Babb was most helpful and hospitable, I felt it would be best for me to return to my family. I am happy to tell you that your parents have seen our little Sarah, and were overjoyed with her, just as much as we are. Your father said that I did some mighty fine cooking with his granddaughter. Now, let me come to the most important part of my letter, Joshua has told me that he wants you to go to Kentucky with him. Know that if this is your wish, you have my blessings. Do not have any reservations about going now and leaving us behind. We will be fine here until your return. However, if you do decide to go, please be careful, for I love you so. I will always keep you in my dreams and most importantly, in my prayers.

Your Most Loving Wife,
Elizabeth

William carefully refolded Elizabeth's letter and put it in his pocket, over his heart. The letter was a welcome thing to have at this time, but it made him want to go home all the more, now that he had heard Elizabeth's voice come from the page he had just read. It made him want her more than ever. All he could think of was being in her arms back in their home on that creek bottom. But if she was safe at her father's home, it would be the perfect time to go to Kentucky. He was here, at the mouth of the river that led into Kentucky. His brother was willing to go with him and he knew that what Knox had told him was true, because he could see it himself almost every day now, when one party or another of men would head down that river. He knew what they were going after land. Land like he had wanted for himself and Elizabeth for years.

His farm in Virginia was paid for now so he did not have to come up with a payment for Captain Babb. He could get by one year without putting out crops, so why not go and claim some of that land waiting for him? He made up his mind to then and there to follow his dream. He was going to Kentucky.

He got up to tell Joshua that his decision was made. He opened the door and walked over to where Joshua was standing outside by the well-used by the fort. He was shaking water off his head where he had just poured a bucket onto himself to wash off the day's dirt.

"Well brother, Kentucky it is." William said as he picked up a second bucket and poured the contents over his own head. "We'll have to find some way to get down the river though. Maybe we can hook up with another party going down."

"Do you know anybody?" Joshua asked as he shook the water out of his dark hair and pushed it back over his head.

"Maybe," said William, "Maybe I do."

Chapter 39
Turncoats

The next morning William was awakened by the sound of men's voices raised in excitement outside the barracks. There was a lot of movement out in the fort and William could tell that something was wrong. It sounded as if someone had picked up a hornet's nest and tossed it over the walls of the fort. He got dressed as fast as he could and darted out the door to see what all the commotion was about. He spotted Captain Babb standing over by the fort's powder magazine, with several other officers. They seemed to be having a highly heated discussion when Captain Babb saw William standing there and motioned for him to come over.

As William was making his way over to the captain he had to stop and let the ten or so riders go by who were being led by Captain David Ritchie. They were in full gallop as they rode past William. The hoofs of the horses were throwing dirt high into the air as they rode out the gates of the fort. In all the time William had been at Fort Pitt he had never seen such a furious exit. By this time William was joined by several of his fellow militiamen, who were also curious about what was about to happen. Among the group was James who asked William, "What in the devil is going on out here?"

"I don't know," William answered, but I believe we're about to find out."

"What's all the commotion about Captain?" James asked as the men made their way over to where the Babb was standing.

"Well, it's not good news boys," the old Captain shook his head as he addressed his men. "We have good reason to believe that Simon Girty, Matthew Elliot, and Alexander McKee deserted us for the British last night. General Hand got wind of it late in the night. He ordered a patrol to go over to the McKee estate, but no one was there, not even his slaves. Girty and Elliot are missing without leave. It looks like they have all gone Tory on us boys."

Now William knew what Simon had been talking about last night when he had said not to fall into the hands of the Indians. At the time, William just thought that Simon wanted him to be careful, but now, he knew that if he was ever captured by the Indians, it meant that Simon would be his enemy and not his friend. William felt Simon's warning was sincere and he hoped that he would never find himself in a situation where he needed to heed his friend's warning.

Captain Babb was pacing back and forth with his hands clasp behind his back as he continued, "The general has informed me that in one week's time from today, he expects the arrival of more militia from Westmoreland. I know you boys are itching to get back home so that's when we will be pulling out of here, unless some unforeseen event should pop up. So that's about it except we now have the honor to be the garrison of the fort today. You all know what to do, so get at it boys."

As the men were dispersing, William approached Captain Babb and said, "Might I have a word captain?"

"Of course, William I've always got time for you, my boy. What's on your mind?"

William waited a few seconds, giving the rest of the men time to walk off before he continued his conversation with Babb.

"Kentucky, Captain. My brother Joshua came in last night and we plan to go down the river together and see what the country is like. But I don't plan to go until we are mustered out by you first. What I was hoping for was that maybe you could help us get a way down river."

"Sakes alive, I sure hate to lose you as a neighbor William. Are you sure you want to go West? That bottom land I sold you is a fine piece of property. Are you sure you want to leave it behind?"

"No, I don't," William explained. "We are just looking for now, but who knows, maybe someday I may settle out West."

"Well, it's pretty much a wild country from what I've heard from the boys who have been down that way. But if your heart is set on going, I heard that a boat is heading down to the Falls of the Ohio fairly soon. Maybe they could use a few extra men. I'll let you know something before the day is over. I'll say one thing for you boy," the old captain continued shaking his head, "You sure are going to put a few gray hairs in the head of that pretty young wife of yours. But I can't say as I blame you for going. If I was your age, I'd probably go myself."

Chapter 40
Captain Rogers

Late last night Captain Babb had called for William and Joshua to come to the East Blockhouse of the fort where the captain's quarters were located. He told the two brothers that a riverboat captain named David Rogers was going down the river to the Falls of the Ohio and that he needed a few more men to come along with him. However, Rogers would not take any men that he had not met in person.

He had told Captain Babb that there was nothing like a face to face meeting to tell what a man was made of. Rogers was planning to pick his crew today from the men who would be at the docks on the waterfront early this morning. Rogers would make no promises that he would pick the two brothers, but he did say that at least he would talk to them before he made his final decision.

William had little trouble talking James and Samuel into coming along on this proposed trip down river, because they too had wanted to see Kentucky. William had also hoped that Rogers would take men that knew each other and had gotten along well together in the past. He knew they would be cooped up together on this boat for a good while and thought this would be the best method to sell themselves as a group to the riverboat captain.

Now the four men made their way to the docks to see if they could secure a way to Kentucky. They had taken along their weapons and gear in an effort to make the best possible impression. The riverfront was busy with men who were engaged in boat building, now that the weather had improved. They were making all types of crafts, flat-bottomed boats, keel boats, and even crude rafts and small canoes.

Captain David Rogers was not hard to spot. He was standing on the deck of a long flat boat. He was a tall man, over six feet tall and he was wearing the blue coat of a Continental officer, with a gold sash wrapped around his waist. He had two pistols stuck down in the sash and a sword on his left hip. His boots made a loud thump on the deck as he walked from one end of his boat to the other looking out over the riverbank at the men who stood by his boat.

"Now I'm sorry to say that I know most of you here, so at least half of you can just head on back up to the taverns and get yourselves a drink, because I am not hiring on any drunks this time around." The Captain went on to say, "Go on! Cull yourself out now. You know who you are."

At that, most of the men turned and walked off, but not before some turned back and hurled a few choice words to the Captain. "You can sail that boat to hell for all I care," shouted one of the men. But the Captain just acted like he had not heard, as he continued to peer out over the remaining men.

"Where are the men that Captain Babb was telling me about yesterday?" he asked.

"We're here, Captain Rogers," William shouted as he raised his rifle high in the air over his head.

"How many is in your party?" Rogers asked, "Captain Babb said it was just two of you."

William answered back, "Well sir, there are four of us. I am William

Tipton, this is my brother Joshua and these two fellows here are James Tate and Samuel Farra. We are all in the militia together except Joshua here. So, we are used to taking orders and we will do whatever you ask of us. We all get along really well together and will not give you any problems, Sir."

"Come aboard, all four of you and we will talk matters over," Captain Rogers said as he waved them onto the boat.

William and the others came aboard, walking up a plank that was extended from the boat out to the docks. The captain looked them over, each in turn as they boarded.

At the front of the boat, which was about fifty feet long, was one of the two cabins built onto the deck. Captain Rogers walked over to a table that stood by the door of one of the cabins and sat down. He took off his hat and set it on the corner of the table and pulling a handkerchief from his pocket wiped his slightly balding head.

"Alright, this is the deal. I am going to meet up with Major Linn at The Falls of the Ohio. Therefore, at that time we are going to help him make a portage around the water falls. Then we'll come back up river here to Ft. Pitt. The Major is navigating up river from Spanish held New Orleans. We will be in Kentucky for at least two weeks before he arrives. You can have ten days to comb the countryside. I know that is why you boys want to go. Captain Babb told me as much, but if you do not come back on time, I will leave you behind and you will receive no pay for your work. I will not pay anyone until our return back   here. Your pay is to be a dollar a day. You will still be considered a part of the militia while you are under my command. Is all that understood? There will be ten of us going down, I have already hired on six other men, and you boys will fill out my crew. So, what do you say, do we have an agreement?"

"Yes sir, we sure do Captain Rogers," William said, "that sounds real good to us, don't you think fellows?"

Joshua, James and Samuel all agreed to Captain Rogers's terms and each in turn shook his hand to bind the agreement.

"Alright, we will embark at first light in the morning, so don't be late. I want this trip to be as slick as a cat's ass. I don't want it to get off on the wrong foot," said the captain as he got up from the table and entered the cabin.

Chapter 41
River Rat

The men got up well before dawn this morning, the first day of June. The last thing they wanted was to be late on their first day as one of Captain Rogers' crew.

It had been a wet night so when the men started out of the gates of the fort, they were met by a dense fog coming up from the river.

Samuel was walking down the hill to the river's edge when he tripped on a rock, and lost his balance. As he stumbled, he grabbed onto James' arm to keep from falling.

"Damn, I can't see a thing out here. How is Captain Rogers going to see where in the hell he is going?" he asked no one in particular.

After James helped Samuel regained his balance he reached over and lightly punched Samuel's shoulder and said. "Damn boy, you're about as graceful as a hog on ice".

Joshua pondered Samuel a question for a moment then answered, "He's a riverboat captain. I'd say he has seen this before."

"William," Samuel asked, "How long do you think it will take us to get to the falls?"

"I've been told that it usually takes seven or eight days to go down river. They say it's about six hundred miles to Corn Island.

"Where's Corn Island?" asked Samuel.

"That's where George Rogers Clark has started some kind of settlement at The Falls of the Ohio" James answered, "You'll see when we get there."

"Tipton, is that you I hear?" a voice said coming out of the fog from the river.

"Yes sir, we're all here." replied William to Captain Rogers.

"Then stow away your gear and weapons in that back cabin and get back out on deck. We got some work to do before we push off this morning."

Joshua was the first to board the boat and went down to the cabin and opened its door to let the other men go inside bending over and making a waving motion with his arm for them to enter. The room was very small, a space about eight by ten feet. There were bunk beds on three sides of the room with one table in the middle with four chairs. Each bunk had a couple of boxes underneath so each man had a place for his belongings. William dropped his bags into one of the boxes and laid his rifle down onto one of the bunks. After looking around the small room for a second all four of the men stepped back out on deck.

"Are we the first ones here?" William asked Captain Rogers. "I didn't see the other six men you told us about yesterday."

"They will be along soon enough," the captain said, "Now you boys go down to the dock and load those poles laying there onto the boat. There are twelve in number. We may need them on our way back up river if they don't take our boat apart."

The four men did just as they were told. They went down to the dock and picked up the poles as the captain had asked. By now the sun was up and they could see a lot better. The poles were all about the same length, around ten feet. As they came back aboard the captain said, "Now take them over to the middle of the boat and slide them through those post holes."

There in the middle of the boat were four upright posts, each with three holes cut through its center. As the men slid the poles into the holes, they began to form a small corral. This enclosure formed a cattle pen in no time at all. When the poles were in place the Captain came over and set down a bucket of nails and a couple of hammers and said, "Nail them down, boys."

"What did you mean captain, a while ago when you said they may take our boat apart?" asked James before he stuck four or five nails in his mouth.

"This is a flat boat we're on here. It's good for going down river, but it's very slow heading back up," the captain explained. 'Most of these types of boats will be torn apart and the lumber reused downriver. Most likely she will be torn down and we will come back in a keelboat. But that's not my decision to make. Major Linn will make that call."

"We're here captain," called out a voice from the bank.

"It's about time," said Captain Rogers, "I was about to come ashore and skin you alive, Ross Gibson."

"Naw, there ain't no need for that now Captain. I got all the boys right here. They just had too much to drink last night," the man answered back as he pushed the last member in his group onto the boat.

"The hell you do. I only see five men"

Aw well, Watson was too drunk. We left him in the road up by the fort.

Do you want us to go back and get him?"

"Hell no, leave his drunken ass up there, I've had enough of drunks. I should leave all of you here too, but I probably couldn't get anybody any better. Oh, hell yes I could," Rogers went on to say, arguing with himself, "I got these boys here and they are sober, most likely better men too."

William was setting on the top pole of the just finished pen, looking on, wondering if Captain Rogers was about to kick this late arriving crew off the boat. Then he caught the steel eyed gaze of Ross Gibson. If looks could kill, William would be a dead man right now, no doubt about it. The comparison Captain Rogers had just made between the two groups had been a mistake. Ross Gibson, a man of fifty years or so had just picked out his newest enemy and his name was William Tipton.

Gibson's dark eyes were staring a hole thru William. His anger was seething and growing deep down inside his soul. He began to grit his rotten teeth together as he turned away from William.

"I know this river Captain. See how far this one here can steer a boat down river without running onto some damn sandbar someplace," he said, pointing his finger at William.

"Don't you be telling me how to run my own boat Ross Gibson," shouted Captain Rogers. "If I had more time I would replace your ass, and I may just do that when we reach Wheeling, if you haven't sobered up by then. Cast off those lines and push us out into the current."

Gibson picked up a pole and stuck it down into the water to the riverbed and gave a hard push, letting out a loud grunt as he pushed the boat out into the river. Turning, he let his eyes linger on his new adversary and stormed off to the back of the boat.

Joshua walked up to his brother and said, "We're going to have to keep an eye on that river rat."

Chapter 42
Gibson's Bounty

It had been two hours since the boat had made its much-heated departure from the docks of Fort Pitt. William was sitting in the front of the boat with his rifle lying on his lap. He had just finished loading the weapon about an hour and forty-five minutes ago. After Ross Gibson had made his feelings known to the rest of the crew about how poorly he thought William's river boating abilities were going to be, William wanted to make his own feelings known as well. He went into the cabin and pulled out his rifle and shot bag and had proceeded back out on deck. William did not know this man, Gibson, but he sure did know a threat when he heard it, and Gibson had just made one. In full view of the entire crew, William had carried out his own well cared for gun and proceeded to demonstrate his ability to quickly load his rifle. The entire process took less than 30 seconds. William accomplished this while looking the crazed Gibson straight in the eyes, sending his own threatening message to the other half of Captain Roger's crew. Within a few moments, Joshua and James and even young Samuel had emerged from the cabin with their own guns in hand as well.

Gibson looked the young men over, as he wiped his forehead with the back of his arm, showing his black teeth in a smile that never reached his eyes. He turned and walked over to the men that had boarded with him and said something in a low voice. Two of the men laughed at what he had said. Turning back around to face William, Gibson said, "That's not the first time I ever saw a gun, boy."

"Well, let's hope it's not your last time either old man," William answered.

Fire leapt into Gibson's eyes as he jumped forward, but two of the other men pulled him back into their circle, trying to calm him down.

"Not now Ross, let it go," one of the men said onto Gibson's ear.

"Rogers will get rid of us at Wheeling if you start something now."

The door of Captain Rogers's cabin swung open and the Captain walked out into the sunlight. "All right Ross, you take the tiller from Basil. William, you take your boys there and go on up to the front of the boat. Keep an eye on the water. Be on the lookout for any driftwood that might be floating down our way. Give out a good yell if you see any. I don't have much for you boys to do going down river. Just keep your other eye on the bank".

Now that William had had some time to settle down, he was enjoying the view of the river as they made their way downstream. He had hopes that the same was true of Gibson, back at the tiller. Gibson obviously enjoyed steering the boat and there did not seem to be any reason he would think William was a threat to him. The alcohol had to be working its way out of his system by now, so maybe the two of them would get along. William could only hope so.

As the flatboat drifted down the river, William realized that this was the point where the Ohio made its first sharp turn, as it past the mouth of the Beaver River where, just a few weeks ago he and the rest of General Hand's army had made the march on its way to the Indian towns in what had become known as the Squaw Campaign. The course of the river had to make just one more southward turn before they would arrive at Fort Henry in Wheeling.

"New country for us James, this is as far as we have been on this river," William said as he looked on down the river with the sun in his eyes.

"New land up ahead too, fellows," James answered holding the barrel of his flintlock under his chin, resting his head. "I'm looking forward to seeing Kentucky. I've been hearing about it ever since I was a boy."

"Well, we're not there yet," a strange voice said. "We are fairly safe for now, but the further South we go, the more dangerous it will become. The Indians can always take a shot at us from the banks around here, but once we pass Wheeling, it's really their country on the North bank. On the south side, we have a few folks to help us out in Kentucky but not much, and in all reality, they will be looking at us for protection."

"What's your name Mister?" asked Joshua as he was looking the man up and down with a slightly suspicious look.

"Basil Brown," the man said.

"Yeah, you were the first one on the tiller after we pulled out of the dock." Samuel said.

"That's right," the man answered.

"If you came in with that Ross fellow what are you doing up here talking to us?" Samuel asked, "That won't make your friends too happy. We all saw how fast he gets mad back there."

"He's not my friend," Basil said as he sat down on the boat's deck beside William and swung his legs over the side of the boat. "Ross Gibson doesn't like anyone who takes the tiller. I mean, he's crazy when it comes to that. He thinks that anyone who does the same job that he does is out to get him. It's insane. Hell, He's insane. Anybody that would kill his own family has to be crazy. I may have come aboard with him, but we're sure not friends. I would dare say that none of those other boys are either. They're just too afraid to let him know it. He's a dangerous man and everyone knows it too. Just a word to the wise, you all need to watch him close. Don't go out on deck at night by yourself and sure as hell don't go ashore alone with him. He will come back with some wild story about how you got killed by some damn bear or got shot by the Indians". Then Basil Brown tapped William on the back and said, "You definitely need to keep your guard up at all times. I saw the way he looked at you. He hates your guts. He'd as soon cut your throat as look at you. He is back there right now, just thinking of a way to kill you, so if I was you, I'd sleep with one eye open and one hand on that pistol of yours."

"Why would Captain Rogers hire on a man like that?" William asked.

"First of all, Gibson is good at what he does. He knows every inch of this river. He speaks Spanish and some of the Indian languages as well. And the captain doesn't know about what happened to his family. Now I've come this far, I might as well spill the rest of my guts." Basil said as he got up off the deck an looked back down to the far end of the boat, and around the captain's cabin to check and see if anyone was nearby to see or hear what he was about to tell.

"He sure would spill mine if he knew I was telling you this."

Basil walked over and looked down the other side of the boat just to be safe, then the continued with his story.

"When I first met him a few years ago, he would speak of his wife and his two little girls on occasion, but he talked about his boy all the time. I thought they were still alive the way he spoke of them. It seems that he was some kind of trapper and in order to keep the Indians happy he married a squaw to stay in good with them. Now, I don't know if an evil man can love his family or not, but the way he talked about that boy, I know he loved him. Well, one night we were at Fort Pitt and he got real drunk, even more that he usually does. We were sitting at a table and he began talking about how much he missed going out hunting with that boy of his. And I said, "Well, the next time you go home, you can go out with him then." He just sat back and stared down into the fire that we were sitting by and said, "I can't he's dead now. Back in Pontiac's war, the British was paying real good money for Indian scalps, so I killed all five of 'em one night took the scalps to Detroit for the bounty." And all the time he was telling me this he never once looked away from that fire and the son of a bitch's face never once changed expression. He's not spoken of that boy since, at least not to me anyhow. Like I said, he's evil. I don't know if the devil himself would want Ross Gibson's soul."

"William we are going to have to watch him all the time," Joshua said, "even when we're asleep, one of us has to stay awake and keep watch."

"We'll have to take turns," Samuel said, as he was sharpening his knife on a small whet rock against his knee.

Basil Brown looked out over the water and said, "I've been on this earth for 36 years and I've never been afraid of anything or anyone until I met Ross Gibson."

Chapter 43
Wheeling

The sun was beginning to set and there was less than an hour's sunlight left in the day as Captain Rogers' flatboat ran aground at Wheeling. William recalled that Andrew House had wanted to come back this way after they had rescued Hannah Snapp back in February, but they had decided to return to Redstone instead.

William looked up beyond the bank and saw a few cabins lying close to the river, just above the floodplain he supposed. On up from the cabins, about 500 feet stood Fort Henry. It was small compared to Fort Pitt. No earthworks outside its walls, and the walls themselves were much shorter than those at Fort Pitt. They were about ten to twelve feet tall and you could see between the cracks of the pickets, which were made of white oak logs. It had the usual blockhouses on its corners with port holes cut into the wood, which would allow the men to fire their flintlocks rifles from the safety of the blockhouses. To the east of the fort was a field that had recently been plowed. Beside this field stood the home of Col. Ebenezer Zane, the founder of this settlement. The river bank had a few canoes that had been pulled out of the water and one was sitting on the grass with a man lying down inside asleep. A poor lookout, William thought. On down the riverbank was a second flatboat. It had also been beached. There was a long rope tied to a chestnut tree to keep it from floating downriver. It was the boat of a family by the look of it. There were all kinds of trunks on its deck as well as farming tools and even household furniture. A clothesline had been strung across the boat and clean clothes were flapping in the wind. William knew this was the work of a woman. Not too many men were concerned about how clean their shirts were on the frontier. At least, not the men on this boat anyway. The family had also dug a fire pit to cook in on the bank away from the boat and by the look of things they had camped out here for a while. William's gazing of the countryside was interrupted by Captain Rogers who said, "Tie her down for the night boys."

William jumped off the boat and caught the line that Samuel had just pitched to him. He tied the rope to the roots of a large sycamore tree that had been unearthed by the waters of the river during some recent flooding. As he gave the rope a hard pull to make sure it was secure, and that his knot would not slip in the night, he watched Gibson disembark from the craft.

What little hope that William had had of Gibson becoming mellower, now that they had been on opposite sides of the boat the better part of the day were quickly crushed. Gibson never took his eyes off William as he walked by on his way up to one of the cabins. The look was just a vicious as the first one William had received earlier in the day. The three men who had boarded with Gibson followed him up the bank and into one of the cabins above. Basil Brown joined Captain Rogers and the rest of William's friends on the riverbank. Already mindful of the threat Gibson had become, they all had their weapons in hand. Joshua had picked up William's and handed it over to his brother as soon as he had finished tying down the boat.

"Somebody has to stay here with the boat; we can't leave it unattended, do I have a volunteer?"

"I'll stay captain, there is nothing up there that I haven't already seen before," Basil replied. "You fellows go on, I know you never been here before." Basil jumped back on the flatboat and sat down on a bench in the center of the boat. He reached into his pocket and pulled out a piece of jerked meat and proceeded to eat his dry supper.

The rest of the crew began the walk up the bank with Captain Rogers in front. "Boys," he said, "I'm going up to see Colonel Zane at his home, to talk over some things. You have the run of the town, if you can call this place a town. Stay out of trouble now, I'm already one man short and I can't afford to lose another." He walked on leaving the group of men standing there looking at each other.

"Well, let's head over to those cabins," James said as he nodded his head in the direction that Gibson party had just taken. "I've been in a fort long enough as it is, I don't care to see the inside of another."

James and Samuel took off towards the cabins, packing their flintlocks in the folds of their arms with the barrel's sticking up in the air.
"William you know Gibson is down there in one of those cabins," Joshua said to his brother, "we need to keep our rifles handy. Maybe we should go back to the boat."

"Nah" William said, "I'm not letting him stop me from doing what I want to do. Besides, he can't be in all of them at the same time."

"Alright, we can kill him tonight just as well as any other, I guess." Joshua said as he laughed, "Let's go."

The two strolled on towards the cabins. The first cabin they came to had a locked door, but the second one was open. Inside stood James and an openmouthed Samuel who was staring at a fairly rough looking woman. She was sitting on top of a bar with her blouse open. She was leaving nothing to the imagination of the men around her. Her breast was completely exposed for all to see, making her the center of attention in the small room.

"Well, that's not for us!" Joshua said, "Let's head on over to the next one."

As the two turned to leave, Samuel called out, "Hey, where you two going? Come on back here." William just shook his head and turned the corner and was out of sight.

Samuel followed but stopped at the door and called to the men one more time, "Come on back here. You don't want to miss this."

"Oh yes we do!" William said as he walked on, not even looking back over his shoulder. Samuel stood scratching his head at William's and Joshua's departing backs.

"I'll tell you one thing brother," Joshua said as the two headed for the last cabin, "If that's the best-looking woman that they've got here, then I sure am glad that I'm from Maryland!"

"Speaking of Maryland women, I haven't heard you say a word about Polly. Are you two still an item?" William asked.

"You know what father always says, 'you can't marry a wife without having some place to take her to first'" Joshua said. "That's why."

"Kentucky!" both brothers said at the same time with a laugh.

"If this trip works out like I hope it will, I'll ask the question when I get home, and she will surely see that I am worth waiting for." Joshua explained to his grinning brother.

"You think so?" William asked in jest.

"Well, it worked out good for you didn't it William?"

"Yes, it did, Joshua, it most certainly did. You want a good home to take her to after you get hitched, that's for sure."

The last cabin was more to William and Joshua's taste. It was a small store run by an old lady who looked to be a hundred years old. She had the usual stock for a frontier outpost, beads, blankets, tobacco, traps and an assortment of tools and tin cups. She had a pile of shirts sitting on a table that she was working on. She was stitching one of them together with her needle and thread. Her work was so smooth and speedy she made it look easy. Her fingers were pulling and pushing the needle through the cloth with the ease of long practice. She made small stitches with her old gnarled and wrinkled hands, but they were strong and tight stitches that would withstand the test of time, just as she herself had. She put the thread in her mouth and bit it in two with what had to be her last two good teeth. As she tied off the threads she asked, "What can I do you boys for?"

"I could use some smoking tobacco," William said.

"I got some hanging above the door there," she said as she picked up a different shirt and looked it over. Then she laid it back down and said, "All the light is about gone for the day, these will have to wait for tomorrow. I got a few jugs of whiskey under the table here," she said trying to drum up some more business.

Nah, the tobacco will do just fine." William said. "What about you Joshua, you want anything?"

"Nah, just looking," Joshua answered as he reached into a bag sitting on the floor in a corner of the room and pulled out a handful of seed corn and poured it back down into the bag.

"On second thought, we'll have some of this seed corn you have there." he told the old woman. "Ten pounds should do it."

The old woman got up from her chair and hobbled over to the bag and scooped out the yellow grain with her hands then turned and dropped it into a smaller bag and said "You got to plant two acres to make your claim legal." William nodded his head yes as he paid his bill and the two brothers left the store. As they stepped out of the door they noticed that the sun had set and the day was all but gone. The only light showing was coming out of the cabin doors on up ahead. As they got closer to the number two cabin they could hear the sounds of shouting men and above it all was the sweet sound of a fiddle floating out to them on the night air. When the brothers got to the door they looked inside and saw the same woman as before doing some kind if dance and it surely wasn't the Virginia reel. But Samuel and James didn't seem to mind.

Once again, William and Joshua passed on going inside. Instead, they headed on back down the path towards the river, but they still had to pass that first cabin, the one whose door was locked on their first pass. This time the door was open with a young woman standing just outside. She was holding her arm in a manner that made William think she was hurt. As the two brothers approached, she tucked both her arms behind her back and stood up as straight as she could. And like the woman in the cabin they had just passed, she too had her blouse open, but unlike the other one, she was pretty.

The brothers slowed their pace as they looked at her, but they did not stop. She stepped up to them and reaching out, took William's arm and said. "Come on inside and stay with me for a little while."

"No, we have to get back to our boat," William said, "but, thanks all the same."

Releasing William's arm, she started walking backward and turned her attentions to Joshua. She reached down to her blouse and pulled it open further, revealing a great deal of her smooth white skin.

"Are you sure you want to back go to that boat? There is no one like me down there, I can tell you that much."

Reluctantly, Joshua told her that he could not stay either, but as he passed her by, he walked away a few steps then stopped and turned back around and said, "I'll say one thing for you girl, you sure know how to make it hard on a fellow. It was hard to say no to a girl who looks like you." As he turned away from his would-be temptress, there just as he had warned William earlier, sitting at a table in the far corner of the room watching the door and paying less attention to the women inside than to the scene unfolding outside, sat Ross Gibson. Both brothers saw him as they passed the door and both realized at the same time that the girl most likely had been the bait Ross Gibson intended to use to spring his trap on William.

William stopped on the way back down to the river and turned to his brother and said, "We may well have foiled this plan of Gibson's, but the night is still young.

We sleep in shifts tonight."

"That's fine with me" said Joshua, "I won't be able to sleep much tonight anyway I'll see that pretty girl's bosom every time I close my eyes"

Clasping him on the back William teased his brother, "Well, Joshua you just learned one thing back there, not all the women here are ugly, now are they? She may have just come from Maryland."

Joshua laughed at his brother and said, "Maybe you're right. Maybe she is from Maryland. Maybe she is at that."

Chapter 44
God is Watching

As the two brothers arrived at the boat, they met Captain Rogers standing on the riverbank. He was watching a man and his wife kindling a fire. This was the family that had beached the boat with the clothesline. They had two children playing on the bank. One was a boy of six or seven years. He was standing on the edge of the bank holding onto a tree branch trying to splash water on this smaller sister who was running up and down the bank laughing at her brother's antics. The husband finally got his fire burning and left his wife and teenage daughter to begin preparing the family's nightly meal. As his wife was tending the flames, he headed over to say a few words to captain Rogers, arriving about the same time as William and Joshua.

"I have been told that you are Captain Rogers," the man said.

"Your information is correct sir, I am indeed Captain Rogers, what may I do for you?"

"Well Captain, I was hoping you would escort me and my family down the river. We've been waiting here for five days now, looking out for another boat going down river. It will be a whole lot safer for us if you would let us tag along. We had decided to stay just a few more days and if no one had come along we were going to pull out and go on down by ourselves. We were up inside the fort this afternoon, and I didn't see you land. We sure were happy to see that boat of yours on the bank when we came down the hill. Like I said we've been here for a while and the wife is ready to move on.

This is not the best place for a family to be. The Zanes are good people, but there are some godless folks up in those cabins. I would be much indebted to you Captain."

"I see no reason why we can't go down together," the Captain said, "as a matter of fact I prefer to have a second boat with me on my voyages downriver. The more of us that travel together the safer we will all be. But you're going to have to keep up with us, I'm not going to drop anchor just to let you catch up."

"That will not be a problem, Captain; I have rigged up a sail for my boat. If the Indians take after us, we may outrun you."

"That's fine," Captain Rogers said with a chuckle, "we are going to push off as soon as we load up a few things in the morning."

"We'll be ready Captain," the man said, "by the way, my name is Richard Chenoweth."

Last night William fell asleep on the riverbank next to the Chenoweth fire along with Joshua, James, and Samuel. It didn't make much sense for them to sleep in that cabin aboard the boat while they were still so close to Fort Henry. No Indians had been spotted on this side of the river so they felt like it was not too much of a risk to be sleeping outside. However, they did take turns keeping an eye out for Gibson. Joshua took the first watch, and later in the night James and Samuel had also taken a turn. That left William with the last watch of the night. The early morning hours seem to be the ones that were hardest to stay awake, but William kept his eyes open by feeding the fire and walking around his sleeping friends, and playing with a stray dog that had come to the fire to warm up in the damp predawn hours. As the sun began to rise with its pink glow climbing over the horizon, William began to feel a little silly, having stayed up waiting for Gibson to come down and cut everyone's throat. Now that nothing had happened William wished that he had gone to bed. Gibson was most likely passed out up in one of those cabins with a prostitute by his side. As William sat there poking a stick into the fire and looking at his sleeping brother, he began to think about the night before. William was proud of his brother. Joshua had showed his good character by turning that young woman down. She was attractive and except for William, no one would have ever known that he had taken her up on her offer. Joshua had to have known that William would not have held it against him. After all, Joshua was a single man. No vows would have been broken. Then William remembered what their mother Sue always said when it came to matters like this. "God is always watching". Joshua must have remembered too.

"Is that fire hot enough to make coffee?" Captain Rogers asked as he emerged from his cabin, pulling on his blue coat before he jumped off the boat onto the riverbank.

"We have a lot of hot coals Captain." William answered back as he tapped Joshua on his foot with the stick, he had been using to poke the fire.

"Good, we're going to have a big day ahead of us," the Captain said, "and coffee will be just the thing to get us moving this morning." Rogers turned and yelled back in the direction of the boat, "Basil, bring a pot with you when you come."

Joshua was still sitting on the ground when he leaned over and shook James' elbow to wake him up.

"Damn, I wish that I'd been smart enough to leave that cabin last night when you boys did." James said as he held his head and rubbed his eyelids with his fingers. I had way too much whiskey last night."

Basil placed a pot of coffee over the fire and stood up and said, "Looks like he did as well," pointing a finger at Samuel.

William reached down and pulled off the blanket covering Samuel and said, "Rise and shine boy, time to get up."

"Where are Ross and the rest of the crew?" Captain Rogers asked Basil, as he watched Samuel scramble to his feet.

"They didn't come in last night Captain. I really don't know where they are, but they can't be far. Probably up there with those gals I'd say."

"Well, they better be here by the time I am done with this cup of coffee," the captain said. "We have to load two barrels of salt onto the boat and drive down those two head of oxen and get them in the pen before we shove off this morning,"

Captain Rogers said as he let Basil pour more coffee into his cup. Just then the gates of the fort swung open on top of the hill and out came Gibson, leading the two red oxen with a rope. The two animals followed him down the hill to the boat without giving him any trouble at all. But they came to a dead stop when they arrived at the ramp that led up to the deck of the boat. Gibson handed the rope to one of his companions and walked around the beast and said, "Come on boys, let's go." He gave one of them a slap on its flank. "Get on up there," he said while giving the animal a push in the rump and up they went onto the boat and into the pen.

Basil leaned over to William and said, "See, he always knows when he's got to do something to save his ass. He may be mean, but he's not stupid."

Chapter 45
Once More at Cresep's Bottom

The day's travel downriver had been fairly uneventful so far. True to his word Richard Chenoweth had kept his boat within a few hundred feet behind Captain Rogers, always staying within eye contact.

Captain Rogers had recruited one more man from Fort Henry to fill out his crew. His name was Andy Forbes and he needed a way to Corn Island. He wanted to catch up with his brother who had joined George Rogers Clark's army earlier that year. It was a perfect fit for both parties. It didn't take long for this new crew member to realize that the boat was divided into two separate factions. Forbes was staying to himself, trying not to get stuck in the feud. He talked to no one and did as he was told.

"That's Captina Creek." Basil pointed out to William and James, as they passed the small stream. "So, that makes the south bank Cresap's Bottom then," William said as he turned and pointed for the benefit of Joshua. "It sure does look different in the daylight now, don't it James?

"Yes, it sure does, I wouldn't have known that was it if he hadn't pointed it out to us," James replied. It had been very dark the night that William and James had been here with the Houses, chasing after the Shawnee who had captured Hannah. The little battle had taken place up in the trees just above the river. William did not get the chance to see the Ohio that night even though he was so close to its banks. Looking out over the waters, William wondered if the bodies of the dead warriors were still lying up in those trees.

Captain Rogers called out to Gibson, "Put her ashore Ross, let's take a look and see if we can find some game for our evening meal." Gibson pulled the tiller with all his might and the big clumsy boat began to make its slow turn to the bank. As the men walked up to the front of the boat Samuel spotted a flock of twenty or so turkeys run into the trees. "There goes our supper running off up that hill," he shouted. As the men jumped off the boat, William had an eerie feeling come over him. It felt odd being back here. He never thought that he'd be back, but here he was. James looked over at William with a grin and said, "Let's go see if we can find them."

"Ross, you and your boys stay here and be ready if the Indians are afoot" Captain Rogers instructed, "We may have to leave here fast."

William looked at the sand and mud along the bank. He didn't see any fresh tracks. There was a well-worn path through the dead weeds that led up in to the woods. William felt like this was the spot where the Indians had decided to cross. As he and the other men entered the trees, William cocked his rifle and nodded at Joshua to do the same.

Seeing that Captain Rogers had pulled ashore, Chenoweth pulled his boat close to the bank but he did not let his boat hit bottom. He just came in far enough to be out of the fast current and to slow his boat down. His family was out on top of the deck, watching the men on shore. Richard Chenoweth was going to be very careful on this stop. He was not willing to put his family in danger.

Samuel fired his musket at one of the turkeys that was bringing up the rear of the flock. The bird rolled over a few times as the blast hit its backside. The wings of all the other turkeys made a thumping sound as they took to the air, putting distance between themselves and the hunters. Samuel let out a cry, "I got him!" as he saw his target lying on the ground. William was scanning the trees for any movement that might present a threat to them, but he saw nothing but the tree trunks. James, too, was not taking anything for granted and was also keeping his rifle up in firing position, just to be safe. Joshua stepped in between the two and said, "I believe it is safe fellows."

William spotted the old campsite and in the middle were the remains of the Indian's fire. It contained a few blackened logs that had not been completely consumed by the flames lying in the pile of ashes.

"This is the spot James," William said, "but there are no bodies here. There must have been another party across the river just like Andrew said. They probably came over the next day and took them away."
"Look William! Look at what I found!" James said as he held up the rope that Andrew had cut from around Hannah's neck.

William walked over to where he had left the dead Indian that had fallen into the fire. Then he turned and looked further down into the trees. "What about the first one we killed? Do you think they found him too?"

"I don't believe they did, I smell something bad coming up from that way,"

James said, "if he's down there his body has got to be rotted pretty badly by now."

Joshua said, "Let's go and see. All we have to do is follow that stench."

As William and Joshua followed James down into the woods they knew the body was there when they came upon a detached arm. It had been ripped off by wolves or maybe a bear. Just a few feet ahead was the body. One leg was missing and the body cavity was open, all of the organs were gone, replaced by a mass of crawling maggots.

"Boy he is ripe," James said, as he covered his nose. "Let's get back to the boat.

As William was walking back through the trees, he saw Samuel standing by the burned-out fire and he called out to him. "Samuel, if you want to meet the fellow who used to own your musket, he's laying down here."

"Hell no," Samuel answered, "That may be bad luck." He reached down and picked up his turkey and headed back to the boat, ignoring the calls of his friends.

"After seeing that redskin back there I can't say I blame him too much," Joshua said to his brother.

Chapter 46
The Chenoweth Family

Now that the second day of the voyage was almost completed, the two boats floated past the spot where the Little Kanawha River fed its waters into the Ohio. Captain Rogers would never stop at a junction where two rivers came together. He would always say that it would be a bad place to spend the night, reasoning that it would be the very same place that the Indians would pick for their stopovers. He would always go down far enough to be just out of sight of the last river junction and land on the southern side of the river. He said it just wasn't smart to land on the northern bank and expose oneself to the Indian shore. One of his other standing orders was that for no reason were there to be any fires built at night. The Indians would be able to see or smell the smoke making the boat a sitting duck for an Indian attack. This policy meant that all of the evening meals would have to be cooked aboard the boats as they were still traveling downriver, and ready to eat before the boats stopped for the night.

The flat boat had a stone hearth on deck made for just this purpose, but one still had to be careful not to set the boat on fire, just as William and Samuel had been this afternoon while they were cooking up Samuel's turkey for supper. A little before dark Captain Rogers ordered Gibson to put the boat over next to a giant white oak tree that had fallen into the water. This gave the two boats some camouflage behind its' massive branches.

Captain Rogers' boat pulled in first then the Chenoweth boat followed, pulling up besides, so the two boats could be tied down together. They were so close to one another that a man could step from one boat to the other in one stride. As Gibson and his men tended anchoring down the boat, William's side of the crew jumped ashore and made a quick reconnaissance of the area. This was a dangerous task, but for some strange reason William truly enjoyed doing the work. Having his rifle in hand, moving slowly through the woods, looking for any possible dangers gave William a thrill.

Joshua and William had grown up hunting in the woods of their father's farm. This gave them some knowledge of how to watch out for the Indians, and being out with the House brothers had given him and James even more experience. Not to mention what he had picked up from watching Simon Girty back at Beaver River that night in the ice storm. Another thing William enjoyed was watching Samuel. He was getting a kick out of seeing how fast Samuel was picking up on things himself. The boy was growing up right in front of William's eyes. Samuel had first given William the impression that he was not the sharpest knife in the drawer, but William could now see great potential in Samuel. All he needed was someone to just take the time to show the young man the things he would need to know, if he was to survive this untamed country. The trees had already budded out by this time and the woods along the river were completely leafed out. This would make it even harder to spot an Indian moving through the woods. But for now, at this spot, William and his friends could still see a good distance. The river bank seemed to be safe as the men finished up their patrol around the boat, but James and Samuel had volunteered to stay on the bank and act as a two-man picket. They had picked out a fallen giant chestnut tree to hide in, setting between its still leafed out branches. This would make it difficult for them to be seen and would also give them some cover if they were shot at by any Indians lurking nearby.

William and Joshua returned to the boat as the sun was setting and the day ended. Richard Chenoweth came over the edge of his boat and invited the two brothers aboard by waving his hand for them to come and talk awhile.

"Well fellows," he said as he pitched a fish trap into the water. "If we are going to travel together, we should know something of each other. This is my wife Peggy and my oldest child, Amelia. Those two over there on the floor asleep are John and Eunice."

"Pleased to meet you and yours, Mr. Chenoweth I am Joshua Tipton and this is my brother William."

"Where are you from Mr. Chenoweth?" William asked, as he watched the trap sink in to the dark river water.

"We have a farm near Fort Redstone, but I keep hearing about how good the land in Kentucky is, so here we are."

"Do you ever catch anything in that trap?" Joshua asked as he looked over the side of the boat and into the water where Chenoweth had just dropped his wire trap.

"Yep, almost every night we'll catch something and Peggy will cook it up for our midday meal." Chenoweth answered. After hearing the splash of the trap hitting the water, Peggy Chenoweth, with the help of her oldest daughter Amelia woke up her two other sleeping children and said, "Come on you two, time for bed." Amelia took her little brother by the hand and pulled him to his feet. She began what looked to William to be a nightly ritual, to lead the little boy down the deck. She was holding his hand in hers and together they both went inside the cabin of their parent's boat. Amelia was a very pretty young girl William thought to himself. She had the same pleasant air about her that Elizabeth had had when William first met her. As soon as she had disappeared into the cabin, her mother, still carrying her other sleeping child walked over to her husband and said, "Go ahead and ask them Richard." Then she turned and made her way down the long deck of the boat and also disappeared into the cabin. Joshua sat down on the rail of the boat beside William as he placed the butt of his rifle on the wooden deck letting the weapon rest against his shoulder as he sat and said, "Do you have a question Mr. Chenoweth?"

"I didn't pay too much attention to it at first but Peggy did. And once I started to look for it I saw it too," the concerned father said as he led William and Joshua to the other side of the boat.

"It's that man you all have got on the tiller," Chenoweth whispered.

"His name is Ross Gibson," William said, "Why, what has he done?"

"Nothing yet," replied Chenoweth, "but what's got us spooked is the fact that he keeps staring at Amelia. He is always looking over in her direction. It's just strange the way he does it. But there may be nothing to it. What me and the wife would like to know is, do you think he is harmless, or not?"

"We don't know the man personally." William said, "But from what I have seen and heard about him makes me believe that your wife is well within her rights to have concerns about him.

"We sure don't trust him and your family shouldn't either." Joshua said as he looked over to the other boat.

"Have you said anything to Captain Rogers?" William asked.

"No." replied Chenoweth. "I don't know the captain that well. I don't want him to think I was trying to make trouble for him."

"Then why ask us?" Joshua inquired.

"Like I said, we're from Fort Redstone. I knew that you two boys went after that Snapp girl and brought her back home safe. It was all the talk there for a few weeks. I feel like I can trust you. By the way, did you hear that Andrew House married that girl?"

"Did he really?" William asked.

"He sure did, right before we left home." Chenoweth assured William.

"Well that's good to know, looks like something good came out of that night after all." William said.

Joshua pointed over at William and said, "For the record, he was the one who got the girl back not me. The other fellow was James Tate, even if I would like to take the credit for it. James is the one on the bank tonight. But William is my brother," Joshua said.

"Well all the same, I would like to thank you boys for telling us what you know about Gibson. I am going to tell Peggy what you all said. I know she is anxious to hear what you told me, so I will see you later tonight." Mr. Chenoweth walked William and Joshua off the boat and turned and headed down to his cabin.

The two brothers stepped over to their boat and as Joshua said, "Well brother, looks like your name is becoming known on this river. Seems like I am going to have to kill me a few redskins before anyone knows who I am.

Chapter 47
A Shadowed Figure

A few hours after dark James and Samuel made their way back to the boat. They had been setting in the woods for some time now and all was quiet. Their stomachs were starting to talk to each of them and they knew that Samuel's turkey was on the boat waiting for their return. Samuel had wanted to come back sooner, he was afraid that Gibson's half of the crew would devour the bird before him and James could get a chance to eat their share. James had assured his young companion that Captain Rogers would make sure that their portion of the meal would be saved and if he didn't William and Joshua surely would.

But now James finally gave in to Samuel's wishes, believing that the Indians were not close by and if they had known of the boat's presence, most likely they would have made an attack by now. He felt like it was safe enough to go back, at least long enough to eat their supper. As the two approached the boat they saw William and Joshua standing alongside Basil on the back of the boat. All three were looking downriver while Captain Rogers was standing on top of the men's cabin by Gibson and his half of the crew, looking through his brass telescope trying to get a better view downstream.

"What are you all looking at?" Samuel asked as he boarded the boat. William turned around to the two and said, "A campfire on the northern bank."

"Can you see anything Captain?" asked Basil.

"No, not really it just makes the glow a little bigger," he answered. "But I can see that they are across from the Little Kanawah".

"Damn, they're close." Gibson said. "We should cross over the river and sneak down to where they are Captain. Maybe it's just a few of them. We could take them all out before they knew what was happening to them."

"No," the Captain replied, "that would be foolhardy. Why take the chance, they may just as well out number us two to one, who knows? No, we will just have to keep an eye open tonight and slip away in the morning. Hopefully, they have not spotted us yet."

Richard Chenoweth stepped over to Rogers' boat and said in a very low voice, "Keep it down boys you know how sound carries at night on this river. They are over a mile down but they still may be able to hear us even that far away."

"You are absolutely right," Captain Rogers said whispering, "This is what we're going to do. William you take Joshua, James and Samuel down the river a little way. The moon's out tonight so you should be able to see them if they are paddling up to us. One of you needs to keep an eye on the bank. They could come up by land, but I doubt it. Ross, you have your men ready on the boat. Keep those poles at your sides; we may have to push off fast tonight if they do attack."

Chenoweth glanced over to his boat and said, "I will need some help getting my boat out into the water if we have to leave in a hurry. I can't do it as fast as you all can. If I go out with William's party can someone board my boat and help me push off, if we are attacked?" he asked Rogers.

"That's fine with me," replied the captain. "We have more men than poles anyway so William and his boys can help, but hopefully it will not come to that."

William and the other men disembarked from the boat and made their way down the riverbank to take their positions. James took to the woods by climbing on top of the root ball of a fallen tree. This put him about five feet above ground level, giving him a good view of the land down river. Samuel stayed by William's side, each on opposite sides of a walnut tree on the river's edge with Joshua taking a tree just a few yards further up river. Here they could see the distant Indian fire very well. If the Shawnee decided to come up the river their shadows riding up over the moon lit water would be easily seen.

Richard Chenoweth had stayed a little closer to his boat, always keeping it in his sight. He did not go quite as far up the river as the other men.

As William stood there in the dark, he thought to himself that this was the first time he was the hunted and not the hunter when it came to Indian scuffles. The two other times that he had been engaged in battle with the Indians he was the one on the offensive. He had always had the advantage in the past, but not this time. This was a whole different situation sitting here waiting to be attacked. It made the hairs on the back of his neck stand up every time he heard a sound in the night air. All the noises that he had heard hundreds of other nights without a second thought were now heightened to a new level of awareness. The rustling sound of several raccoons playing up in the woods had first gotten his attention, but he soon recognized what they were, by the sound of their chatter. The sudden sound of a splashing frog jumping into the water made his heart jump with anticipation of an Indian attack. The sound of a beaver hitting his tail on the top of the water's surface across the river made a sound similar to the discharge of a rifle. All of this made him a bit nervous, but yet he was somehow not truly afraid, just on edge. But as the hours passed by and the light from the Shawnee campfire grew dimmer in the distance, it became clear that tonight the threat was just that, only a threat. Their fire was about out and most likely they had eaten their last meal of the day and had fallen asleep.

"Samuel," William whispered, "I believe that we are safe for now, or at least until the sun comes up in the morning. I am going to check up on Mr. Chenoweth. You stay here with Joshua." Samuel just nodded his head, as he leaned his back against the tree and slid down the trunk to the ground into a sitting position, giving his feet a much-needed rest.

William turned and started back toward the boat. There, he saw Mr. Chenoweth with his back to William. He was watching his boat very intently, in a squatting position as William took a knee by his side.

"Do you see something?" William asked.

"I don't know maybe." was the reply Richard Chenoweth made. "Look, there on the bank next to where the rope is tied down."

As William peered into the moonlight, he saw a shadowed figure moving toward the Chenoweth boat. It was a man, and he had his rifle hung over his shoulder, but in his hand was a tomahawk. William could hardly believe one of the Indians had managed to slip past all of the men on the bank, but there he was, about to step foot on the boat. Chenoweth raised his weapon to take a shot. As he was setting his sights on the man's head William pulled down the stock of Chenoweth's rifle and whispered, "Don't shoot. Let's rush him. The report of your gun will give us away." William pulled out his own tomahawk, and Chenoweth agreed by nodding his head. As they made their way to the boat, the Indian had already boarded and was peeping into the cabin window where the Chenoweth family lay sleeping. He heard the sound of Richard's boots on the wooden deck, but it was too late, the two were upon him before he could defend himself.

William made a diving leap, grabbing him around the neck and knocking him to the floor. Richard ran up and hit the man with the butt of his gun, causing the assailant to drop his tomahawk. As William and the man began to roll around on the deck, William realized that he was not fighting an Indian, but was in the grips of a white man. The foul breath and rotting teeth of Ross Gibson had given him away. As the two men were fighting and grabbing at one another William got a hand free and delivered a strong blow to Gibson's head, causing his nose to bleed. Quickly, William and Richard had Gibson pinned down to the deck floor between the cabin wall and the rail of the boat.

"I knew you were no good," Richard proclaimed as he pulled Gibson up from the floor and slammed his body against the cabin wall. Hearing the sounds of the struggle coming from the Chenoweth boat, Captain Rogers led the rest of his crew quickly aboard. Everyone had their weapons drawn; believing the boat was under attack from the Indians, but there was no warrior to be found. All they saw was William, sitting on the side of the boat's railing trying to catch his breath while Richard held Gibson at gun point.

"What the devil is going on here?" Captain Rogers asked.

"We found him trying to get inside at my family," Richard explained. 'He had his tomahawk drawn. He thought I was too far up the riverbank to see him."

"That's a damn lie." Gibson said, as he spat blood into the water. "I heard something over here. I was trying to protect them. This sure is a fine way for you to show some thanks for me sticking my neck out to save your family"

"You lying bastard" Richard replied through gritted teeth "I was watching from the bank and William saw you too. There was no one on this boat but you Gibson. You came over here after my daughter. You can lie all you want but I know what you were up to." By now Peggy Chenoweth was outside on the deck, listening to her husband and Gibson arguing when she said, "Richard is telling the truth, Captain. I saw him looking in our window. He was looking at Amelia sleeping in her bed. He was coming after her. I know he was."

Captain Rogers let out a groan in deep disgust and turned to Basil and said, "Clap the irons on him Mr. Brown. Take him over to our boat." Suddenly, Gibson dived off the boat into the water. He had made two or three strokes under the water's surface before he raised his head up out of the water to suck fresh air into his lung. Then, he submerged himself back under the water and was quickly out of sight. The men on board the boat spread out, looking out into the dark water for Gibson. William and Richard jumped onto the bank, William going up river and Richard down, but they too, saw nothing of Ross Gibson.

Captain Rogers was still standing on the boat looking out into the water when he said, "Ross, you stupid bastard. You've got to be guilty as hell if you would rather face those wild savages than stay here and face us."

It had taken Gibson almost an hour to get across the Ohio. He had swum out into the center of the river, where he grabbed onto a piece of driftwood. He was able to rest as he floated farther down on the current before he began the last leg of his swim. Now, as he crawled out of the water onto the shore, he rolled over onto his back and looked up at the stars, and then he managed to smile. His head was hurting from the blows he had received in the fight with William and the butt of Richard's rifle had not done his ribs any good either. As he started walking east back up the river, he realized he had lost most of his gear, but he had managed to keep his rifle slung over his back. Although he could not tell if it was still in working order in the dark, he felt sure his Shawnee friends would let him borrow one if he needed it.

Chapter 48
Shooting Fish in a Barrel

When dawn broke, the two flat-boats made their way out onto the river as fast as possible. No one had gone to sleep after Gibson's escape. Even though the boat was in more dangerous waters now, William still felt that he and the rest of the party was far safer now that Ross Gibson was gone. As far as William was concerned it was good riddance.

Basil had taken over on the tiller, steering the boat downriver. Joshua and Samuel had helped the Chenoweth family get their boat off the bank and into the water. True to his word to Captain Rogers, Richard had no problem keeping up with the other boat. He had put up his sail and was making good speed. With the help of a strong wind on this spring day, he was able to sail far ahead of Captain Rogers's boat. The Captain had elected to stay in the rear position which put him in a much better situation to fight off any Indians that might try to overtake them and capture the boats. William and James, along with Andy Forbes were stationed on the back of the boat. They were watching back down river to see if any of the Indians were paddling upriver after them. They had continued down river about twenty minutes when Joshua and Samuel both jumped into the water. They swam away from the Chenoweth boat a few yards before stopping. They just kicked their feet and floated on their backs, waiting for Captain Rogers to catch up and fish them out of the water so they could rejoin the crew.

As William extended his hand over the rail to give his brother a pull out of the water he asked Basil, "What did you say a river rat looked like? Maybe something like this?"

"Pretty much," Basil answered.

Samuel had grabbed onto the boat with one arm without any assistance from the crew. He raised his leg up on the deck and pulled himself out of the cold water.

"Damn, it's too early for this," Samuel said as he shook the water out of his hair and body, much like a big friendly dog.

"Yeah, but you boys sure do smell a lot better." William teased. "I should have pitched you two a bar of soap before we let you back on deck."

Joshua pulled his wet shirt over his head and dropped it onto the deck. Then glancing down river said, "We got company fellows."

William looked and saw four Indian canoes paddling fast after their boat. The canoes were long enough to hold eight to ten men each. The warriors were making long strong strokes with each pull on the paddles.

"Captain," William yelled up to the front of the boat, "Here they come!" As the Captain made his way down the boat carrying his ever-present rifle, both Joshua and Samuel passed him on their way to the men's cabin to get their weapons. Captain Rogers drew out his brass telescope and looked at the pursuing canoes saying, "They're catching up to us boys. We need to slow them down some." Running back to the rear of the boat with his musket in his hand, Samuel asked, "Well, how are we going to do that Captain?"

"There's not much you can do with that musket, but William and Joshua sure can do some damage with those long rifles," the Captain replied.

"At last" Joshua said with a good deal of enthusiasm!

"You boys wait until I come back," the Captain told the men. "Samuel you come with me. Lay down your musket, I have something for you." As the Captain and Samuel took off for the Captain's cabin, Joshua looked over to William and said, "It's going to be just like shooting fish in a barrel, 'eh brother?"

"I hope so," William replied as he primed the pan of his flintlock.

"How many grains of powder do you have loaded up there?" Andy asked Joshua.

"About a hundred and ten, maybe a hundred and twenty it's loaded for bear." Joshua told his new, shy friend.

"That's just dandy," Andy replied as he cocked the hammer back on his own rifle. We'll put the fear of God in those damn yellow boys."

Samuel and Captain Rogers both ran out the door of the Captain's cabin, each with a rifle in his hand. They made it back to the rear of the boat in just a few seconds. As the Captain propped his extra rifle against the back wall of the cabin he asked, "Are they in range yet?"

"Yes sir." replied William as he looked at the approaching Indians down the barrel of his rifle.

"William, you take the canoe on the right and Joshua you take the left." Captain Rogers told the two brothers. "Then Andy and will take our shots while you two are reloading. Samuel, you and James fire last."

Taking off his hat William pushed the hair back from his face with a swipe of his hand and replaced his hat, pulling it down low over his eyes, to help cut down on any glare that might reflect off the surface of the water.

"All right boys, at your leisure," the Captain said.

"Are you ready, Joshua?" William asked.

"Aw yeah, I've got mine in my sights," Joshua answered, as he placed his finger on the trigger.

"On the count of three then," William said. "One... two...three."

Both rifles fired at the same instant, and both Shawnees paddling in the front position of their respective canoes were knocked back by the impact of the lead balls. One fell over the side of the canoe into the water, and the other slumped back onto the man directly behind him. Before the smoke had a chance to clear the air form the initial reports, Andy and Captain Rogers each fired their weapons, also hitting their marks.

Samuel stepped up to take his shot, but before he could get it off, Captain Rogers ordered him to wait. "Look at how they are ducking down in the canoes, Samuel. They will be hard to hit like that. So you just put a hole through the bottom of that canoe. Aim just under the water level." Samuel raised his rifle to his shoulder, drew aim and let go. A splash of water rose up in front of the canoe putting a hole in the Indian's craft.

One of the Indians raised his head up from behind the wall of the canoe and James made him pay with his life for his curiosity. By this time, the front two canoes were falling back, but they were quickly being overtaken by the two canoes that had been bringing up the rear. As William and Joshua stepped up to take their second shots, William saw an Indian fire his rifle from one of the new canoes. At almost the same instant, before he even had time to take cover, William heard Andy cry out to his left. The Indian's aim was also true, hitting Andy in his leg just above the knee.

William fired his gun one more time. He was aiming at the warrior who had just hit Andy. The ball cut through the Shawnee's neck, killing him instantly. Joshua had also taken his shot at the same Indian and he too hit the warrior in the chest.

Seeing that too many of their fellow warriors were being picked off by the white eyes the Indian's slowed their pace and started to turn their canoes toward the northern bank of the river. Realizing that the chase was over, Captain Rogers bent down to pick Andy up under his arms and helped him down to his cabin to tend to his wound.

Samuel shook his fist in the air and screamed out to the Indians as their canoes began to run upon the shoreline, "What's the matter boys come on back we got some more for you, you damn cur dogs."

William placed his mouth over the end of his muzzle and blew down the barrel of the rifle to make sure the weapon's touchhole was clear and ready for its next use when he heard Joshua say, "Just like fish in a barrel."

Chapter 49
At the Point

That afternoon Captain Rogers docked his boat at Fort Randolph at the mouth of the Kanawah River. This was the last settlement on the river until they would reach the falls. With Andy's wounded leg, it was the best place for him to receive medical attention. Captain Rogers had dressed Andy's leg as best he could, but everyone felt it would be best for him to stay here at the Fort. As it turned out there was no doctor there, but there were a few women who were willing to do the best they could for the wounded man.

As they carried Andy from the boat up to the Fort, Captain Rogers told them what he knew about the area.

"The land here between the two rivers is shaped in a V formation. It was because of this feature that they called it Point Pleasant. It was here in October of 1774 that the Battle of Point Pleasant had been fought. As it turned out, it was the last joint military effort we had with the British. Lord Dunmore, the Governor of Virginia who was just an arrogant bastard, had called for the militia to come out with him under the command of General Andrew Lewis. Dunmore, not acting like the best military mind in the world, had decided to divide his troops into two separate armies one under himself and the other under Lewis. General Lewis had camped here at the point for the night and was attacked the next morning by Chief Cornstalk, of those scalp-taking Shawnees, along with a few Delaware. I've even heard there were some Wyandot, Miami, Ottawa and Mingos along. During the night Cornstalk had led his Indian forces across the river by canoe and was able to attack the Militia from the east, penning their backs in the Point against these two rivers. The battle had been hard fought and had lasted until right before dark, but eventually Andy's militia won the day and drove the Indian army back across the river. But for one reason or another, Lord Dunmore never reached the battlefield while the fighting was going on. He only arrived on the scene after the battle was won. Personally, I always thought, and I wasn't the only one to think it, that the Governor had hoped the Militia would be massacred by the Indians and allow that pompous ass to march himself in and defeat an Indian force already battle weary from their encounter with the Militia. By doing so, it would give the impression that only the British could win a battle, and make the Militia look incompetent. He thought it would also cool any thoughts the Americans had of going to war against Great Britain. But by winning the battle, our boys had done the exact opposite, and spoiled Dunmore's treachery.

Soon afterwards, Fort Randolph was established and in that odd way that things sometime work out, it was here where Cornstalk met his own end. He had come into the Fort for peace negotiations, along with his son Elinipsico. Old Cornstalk was a sly leader and no one knows for sure, because he denied knowing anything about it, but right before he arrived here for these negotiations, two white men were fired upon while on the river and killed. This did not make Cornstalk and his men very popular when they got here. So, to try to keep the peace they were taken into custody by Captain Arbuckle and put in the fort's stockade. A night or two later, hell, maybe it was even that same night, I don't know for sure, but a mob of men broke into their cell and murdered the chief and his son. Revenge was the main motivation for those killings. Cornstalk had a long history of warring on the white settlers hereabouts. He had led war parties into the white settlements as early as '63, killing men and taking women and children prisoners. By doing this, he had made many an enemy on the frontier and it led to him losing his own life here at the Fort. One of the things that made it such a firestorm was the fact that Cornstalk was so highly thought of by all the Indian tribes. Of course, that made the cost still higher for our American cause, for the Shawnee will never forget how their beloved chief met his death. Fort Randolph has become one of their favorite outposts to attack and the dangers are still very present here."

As they reached the gates to the fort, William realized from what he had just heard the captain tell them that he was once more in a place where every step that a man took could well be his last.

Chapter 50
Cowbells

Captain Rogers was still inside Fort Randolph the next morning, looking for anyone who would be willing to sell him a canoe. This would allow the crews of the two flatboats a way to travel back and forth to each other without getting wet as Joshua and Samuel had yesterday.

The Captain had sent William and Joshua out into the woods to find the two red oxen that had been turned off the boat to graze the night before. This would be the last opportunity for the animals to go ashore until they reach the falls.

"Do you see them anywhere?" William asked his brother when the two stopped at the edge of the clearing.

"No," replied Joshua as he was looking into the woods, "But I hear their bells tinkling down that way."

"Well then, let's see if we can call them up. I'm not real crazy about running off into those trees." William said. "Let's see if we can call them up like a cow. They may think we've got some salt for them." William raised his free hand to the side of his mouth and called out in a loud voice, just like his father had always done back home when he called his cattle. "Whoo, Whoo, here boys come on. Sook, sook, come on boys, Whoo."

"Here they come," Joshua said as he watched the two animals emerge out from under the tree limbs at a fast trot. As the front one ran along the cowbell that was hanging from a rope around his neck was ringing as it bounced back and forth across his massive chest.

"Looks like we need to give them a bit of salt today," William said as he began driving the two oxen down to the river.

"Do you hear a bell ringing down in those trees?" Joshua asked as he stopped and looked back to the tree line.

William noticed that the second ox was missing its bell. "Come on Joshua, there is no good reason for a lost cowbell to be ringing down there by itself. Let's get out of here; we're not fools. That's some damn Shawnee down there ringing that bell. He's trying to lure us into some kind of trap."

Just then James and Samuel came out of the fort's gates to help with the cattle. Unlike William and Joshua, they were unarmed, having left their guns inside the fort.

"Take them on down to the boat Samuel," William told his friend as he stopped and looked back down into the tree line, still hearing the ringing bell.

"Come on Samuel; let's get them on the boat and in their pen." James said, as he fell in behind the two oxen and led them around the corner of the fort and out of sight.

William and Joshua raised their weapons and began to walk backwards, all the while watching the woods behind them. Then suddenly, the bell stopped ringing and a shot rang out. The lead ball flew over the heads of the two brothers, slamming harmlessly into the wooden wall of Fort Randolph. As the two turned and ran around the corner of the fort, they heard the war cry of an Indian who had just missed his best opportunity for a kill today.

Chapter 51
Like Old Times

William was disappointed that Captain Rogers had not let him and the other men go back out after the Indian who was ringing the bell and had taken that shot at him and Joshua from the woods this morning. "It would be too dangerous" the captain had said, "That would be just playing into the Indians hands. Besides there will be plenty of opportunity to fight other Indians form here on out. Why waste time on one redskin when there is more down river in Kentucky."

The men stationed in the fort had said this was not the first time a bell had been used to ambush someone who had been out gathering his animals. Usually when the Indians took a pot shot at someone, they always ran off soon afterward, not leaving much of a trail behind to follow. So now that they were back on the water heading down to their next stop, the Big Sandy River, William had time for his blood to settle back down and he knew that he and Joshua had been lucky this morning. If that Indian had had a better aim, one of them would be in the ground by now, but as things had turned out, William was sitting on the boat reading his Bible to Samuel and all was well.

Another good thing that happened was that the Captain was able to get his hands on a canoe. It was made from buffalo hide. The hides were stretched over a wooden frame made from a willow tree. The hairy side of the hide was placed so it was inside the little craft. The smooth back side of the skin was placed in the water. The seams of the hides were chinked with a homemade paste made from hair and bone marrow that made the canoe waterproof. It was light and easily handled by two men so no more cold early morning swims had to be made. As William was finishing up his lesson to Samuel, James came walking up and said, "It's your turn to clean up after the oxen, Samuel."

Samuel just nodded his head as he got up off the deck and picked up the scoop and climbed over the rail fence into the pen that held the oxen. He put one of his hands on the rump of one of the animals as he walked around behind it, while watching William and James, who had followed him over to the pen. William laid one of his hands on the top rail of the pen and James put one of his feet on the lower rail. Both men were standing there with smug looks on their faces. As Samuel scooped up a fresh pile of manure and pitched it over the side of the boat into the river, William said, "Just like old times back at Mr. Robinson's, 'Eh Samuel?"

Chapter 52
Kentucky

Last night had been the first time William had laid eyes on Kentucky. Captain Rogers had, as usual, docked just below the Big Sandy River. The men had stayed up, taking turns keeping the all-night watch on the bank. But the night had been calm and at first light the two boats were back on the river heading down into Kentucky. William and the rest of the crew were becoming more excited the further down into Kentucky they traveled.

Basil was at the tiller when he waved to William to come over and talk awhile. William was on top of Captain Rogers's cabin, looking out over the Kentucky landscape. The trees were in full bloom now and spring had finally sprung. The wildlife was unbelievable. Perched on top of the cabin William had already seen his first black bear, and countless deer and elk that had been grazing along the riverbank. If the interior was like the land along the river, William knew this was going to be his home someday. Jumping down from the roof of the cabin, he made his way to Basil.

"Well, William what do you think of Kentucky?" Basil asked as he steered the boat down the river.

"I know what all the fuss is about now." William said as he waved his hand up and down the Kentucky shoreline. "It's unbelievable. All of the game and the land looks good on both sides of the river."

"Yeah, it's worth all the trouble," Basil proclaimed, "If we can get a good foothold here and keep the Indians on the north side of the river, this can become a great place to live. But don't get so overjoyed that you lose sight of what's going on over on the northern bank. Just up ahead is the mouth of the Licking River and that's where the Ohio is at its smallest distance across. It's probably the most dangerous part of the river, so don't be daydreaming up there during the day."

William nodded his head and walked up to the front of the boat to talk to the rest of the crew. Now that Gibson was gone, the other half of the crew had become more tolerable. These men would never be his friends, but at least they were not so hostile now.

"Tell me Samuel, are you planning on making a claim now that we have seen the land?" James asked as William joined the men.

"Sure, I am," Samuel said laughing, "I plan on following you inland to claim the same tracts you do. We can fight it out in court I guess."

"That sounds like something you would do." James said as he hit Samuel on the back with the palm of his hand in a friendly joking manner.

"Look over there," Joshua said as he pointed to the Indian Shore.

Up on a huge bluff sat four Indians next to a roaring fire, cooking what appeared to be a bear. Two of them got up and watched the two boats float on by, but they made no threatening motion. However, one of the warriors sent his own message. He stood silhouetted against the sun facing the boat, and extended his arm over his head, holding aloft his weapon and slowly turned his body to following their progress, never relaxing his stance until they were out of his sight.

Basil and Richard had kept the two boats close to the southern shore. They were way out of gunshot range, so neither party took the trouble to fire their weapons at the other. Everyone ran to the back of the boat to see if there were any canoes coming after them but it soon was apparent that no one was coming after them this time.

The boats had traveled about ten miles further downstream when Captain Rogers announced that it was time to go ashore on the Kentucky side of the river. He wanted to cut some cane for the oxen to feed upon at the canebrake that lay just ahead. This was the first time that the boats were to spend the night without some kind of protection from a fort. They had gotten feed for the livestock at each stop, but there was no fort to stop at now and the oxen were about out of hay. The last thing he wanted was a hungry ox bellowing on the boat at night, giving away their position to the Indians.

As the boat ran aground the same four men who had gone on gathering expeditions at all the other stops upriver stepped onto the shore with rifles in hand. Captain Rogers had warned the party that canebrakes were a favorite spot of the Indians to lay in ambush. This one was not real big, less than an acre, William thought plenty big enough for a war party to hide in. So James and Samuel had volunteered to walk through the middle of the break while Joshua and William circled the cane, looking for any Indians. This plan soon fell apart, because the cane was so thick that James and Samuel couldn't walk through it. They began to cut the cane as William and Joshua kept an eye out for any hostiles that might be lurking about. Within a few minutes they had cut enough cane to feed the oxen for the day. As William stood watching James and Samuel cut the cane he thought about one of the many qualities that he admired in James Tate. He was just as good a shot as William and Joshua, maybe even better, but he never complained about not being the one with a gun in his hand. No one had told him to do the hard work of cutting cane, he just did it on his own accord and this made him a good man in William's eyes.

As soon as they finished William handed James his gun and helped Samuel carry the fresh cut cane to the boat and everyone climbed safely aboard. They were quickly back out into the river going downstream once again.

Captain Rogers had one more order for the men to carry out. He wanted fresh meat tonight, so William, Joshua and James stood in the front of the boat, looking for a deer to shoot on the bank. It didn't take long for them to find one.

"There's a doe James," William said as he tapped Joshua on the shoulder and said, "Watch this. Go ahead James, knock her down." James fired his rifle at the unsuspecting deer. The ball hit the doe's side causing her to jump high into the air. The animal tried to run away, but it managed only a few steps before it fell over dead.

"I have seen James shoot all spring," William told Joshua, "and I have not seen him miss his mark yet. Not once."

This gave the men their first opportunity to use the new buffalo hide canoe. They dropped it into the water and James and Samuel paddled over to the bank, grabbed the deer by its legs and tossed it into the canoe. Within a few moments they and the deer were safely back aboard the boat. Turning to face them, William told the men,

"Now, it's only fair that we all do some of the work on this deer. James shot it, Samuel retrieved it, so Joshua can clean it and Basil can cook it." With a puzzled look on his face Samuel asked, "What are you going to do to it William?"

"Why, eat it of course!"

Chapter 53
A Burned-Out Flatboat

In all of William's travels he had never seen anything that could compare to what he was seeing now. Here, opposite the Licking River on the Indian shore were the remains of a burned-out flatboat. Captain Rogers never liked going ashore on the northern bank of the Ohio, but this time he had little choice. The Chenoweth family had once again decided not to beach their boat, just as they had back at Cresap's Bottom. William believed that Richard could handle this gruesome sight but the children had no business seeing it. Joshua was the first to spot the doomed boat. He was watching the river banks for tonight's meal when the smoldering boat had come into view. He called everyone's attention to the sad scene. It was obvious what had happened. The unfortunate family's belongings were scattered along the riverbank, having been ransacked by their attackers. The bodies of two men had been left lying on the shore in clear view. Captain Rogers might have passed on by if not for the woman that Samuel pointed out. She was crawling on her hands and knees under the trees up above where the boat rested. She had seen the two boats floating downriver and she began to scream for help when she saw them. She came crawling down to the waterline calling out for them to stop. The effort proved too much for her and her strength gave way as she collapsed, falling into the water.

William and Joshua dropped the buffalo canoe into the water and quickly paddled over to the wounded woman as fast as they could. While the rest of the men on the boat shouldered their rifles to give the two brothers covering fire if needed, William stepped out of the boat and pulled the poor woman out of the water while Joshua stood guard over the two of them. She was old. What little hair she had left on the side of her head, not having been taken by the scalping knife was graying to almost white. The blood had run down her face and had had enough time to dry there, but the top of her head was still bleeding. On the back of her dress was another bloody spot, left by a gunshot wound.

"We will help you as best we can," William told the crying woman as he held her in his arms. "What's your name?" he asked, but all she would say was "Tom, Tom, go and see about little Tom. He is up there next to the trees". William laid her head down as gently as he could, and picking up his rifle, headed for the tree line that the old woman had just crawled away from. There, under the trees, was the small body of a baby boy, less than a year old, even younger than Sarah back home. His head had been smashed in. Some heartless savage had obviously ripped the child from its mothers' arms and taking it by the heels had flung him against the trunk of one of the trees, smashing out little Tom's brains. William dropped his head looking at the ground, not wanting to see the remains still on the tree. He shut his eyes and shook his head in disbelief. How could anyone do such a thing he thought as he placed his free hand out on a tree to steady himself? He turned away and started back down to the burned-out boat to meet the rest of the crew who by now had also reached the shore. Like the old woman, the two men had also been scalped. The older of the two had been disemboweled. He must have put up a good fight to save his family, but sadly, to no avail. William thought that was probably why the Indians had mutilated his body so badly. Captain Rogers was now down by the old woman, trying to comfort her as best he could. He asked her, "How many people were in your party my dear?" but she was losing her battle. She was trying to say something but all that came out were a few jumbled words that made little sense to Captain Rogers or the other men of the party. Then, breathing her last few breaths she died on the banks of the Ohio in Captain Rogers' arms.

James came down out of the trees and said, "Well, fellows there are at least twenty or thirty tracks left behind up there. Looks to me like there were some survivors taken captive. There are women's shoe prints left in the mud up there must be this poor woman's daughter or daughter-in-law."

"Well, we can't go after them," Captain Rogers said as he stood up from the ground where the old lady lay.

William turned and stepped into the water and waded over to Captain Rogers's boat and jumped aboard. He walked across the deck and opened the boat's toolbox. He reached inside and pulled out two shovels. The river water splashed around his legs as he jumped back into the Ohio and said to no one in particular, "Well, we can give her and the rest of them a Christian burial. That's the least we can do."

Three graves were quickly dug between two redbud trees and William placed little Tom in the arms of the woman who was most likely his grandmother in one of the graves. When all three were taken care of, Captain Rogers read words from his Bible over the unfortunate family. William had never seen this side of Captain Rogers before. It was the first time the Captain had shown much emotion on the trip. He was visibly upset by the killings. Even in the heat of battle with the Indians in the canoes or during Gibson's desertion, he'd not been this angry, and the last thing he said before he boarded his boat was, "someday they will pay for this day's work. At least they will if I have any say in the matter."

Now as William and the rest of the crew were back out in the river, heading west, he knew that this country was just as deadly as it was beautiful, for he had seen it with his own eyes.

Chapter 54
Rain On His Face

Today was to be the last day of the voyage and if all went well, the two boats should land at the falls by mid-afternoon, according to Captain Rogers. William and his friends were looking forward to finally getting off this boat and having their free week to explore in the central part of Kentucky.

It was here at the mouth of the Kentucky River where James Harrod had turned off the Ohio with his team of Pennsylvania surveyors back in 1775. They had come to establish his settlement at Fort Harrod after traveling a few days down the Kentucky River into the central part of Kentucky. In doing so, he and his men had found the first white settlement in Kentucky. Although they were not the first white men to enter Kentucky, they had beaten out Richard Henderson's party led by Daniel Boone by a few months when they arrived to settle Boonesborough. No one knew for sure who the first white, English speaking man was that first stepped foot into Kentucky. Some credited Archibald Wood, but Dr. Thomas Walker of the Loyal Land Company was the first to lead an official expedition to Kentucky back in 1750 by going through the Cumberland Gap. However, several longhunters had beaten even the doctor here. Men like John Findley and Casper Mansker and even William's ham eating friend James Knox. The first white woman was Mary Draper Ingles of Virginia, who had been kidnapped by Shawnee Indians back in 1755, twenty years before Harrod's party ever entered Kentucky. But no one had ever dared to stay here until Harrod had, just three short years ago.

The land had now flattened out some, just a few rolling hills here and there. William knew that this part of Kentucky was the best suited for farming. It had the look of the land that his father Mordacai had always dreamed of and now he and Joshua had an opportunity to claim some of this land for themselves. As the boats pushed off this morning the weather turned bad and it began to rain. William could see the rain falling up ahead on the horizon before it reached the boats and heard the sound of the falling drops hitting the water as the storm rushed in on them. All of the other men had ducked inside the cabins to get out of the rain, leaving only William setting up front and Basil, at his usual spot at the tiller. As the raindrops ran around the rim of his felt hat they fell onto his lips. William stuck out his tongue and the fresh water drops that landed there tasted good to him. He looked up into the sky, shut his eyes, and let the rain fall on his face as he thought of the family that had been ripped apart back at the burned flatboat. They would never realize their dream of settling here as a whole family. Maybe someday the women could manage to somehow get back to the white world, but they would have to start anew without their husbands, and somewhere out there little Tom's mother would always be haunted by his memory. Seeing what had become of this family made William proud of his part in being able to save Hannah from the Shawnee. His train of thought was broken by a bolt of lightning that shot across the sky over the

Kentucky shore, followed by the loud crack of thunder that gave the oxen a good scare. William was sure that the men were not the only ones that would be glad to get off this boat. The oxen would surely be happy too. Theirs' had been a long hard trip as well, being penned up all this time. He was beginning to have a new-found appreciation for these two good-natured beasts. William got up from the deck and walked over to their pen and said, "Just a few more hours boys and we will be there."

Chapter 55
At the Falls

It was late in the day when the boats finally arrived at Corn Island. The rainstorm had slowed their pace somewhat, but they did make it before nightfall. A lot had happened in the past seven days. The trip downriver had seemed to take longer than just a week, but today's date was June, 7th 1778.

The island itself contained about seven acres of land and was about a mile long. It was positioned closer to the Kentucky side of the river putting most of the distance of the river between the island and the northern bank, the Indian shore. Any attack that the Indians might make on the island could be seen very easy by just a few men placed on the corners. The odd thing about the island was that a channel cut through its southern side and divided it in two. This would give the Indians an even more difficult approach if they were to attack. The island had first been surveyed by Thomas Bullitt back in '73 which turned out to be one of the reasons that led to Lord Dunmore's war the following year of 1774 at Point Pleasant. The Indians realized that settlers would surely follow survey teams to the Island and Kentucky. Cornstalk knew that this would cut the Indians off from their sacred hunting grounds. Nothing had happened on the island until back in May of this year when George Rogers Clark had made it the military post for his western campaign, or so everyone thought. Clark too, had come down the Ohio with his army of over one hundred fifty men along with ten or so families that wanted to settle in Kentucky.

As the boat ran ashore on the sandbar of the little island, William could hear the roar of the rapids off to the right of the Island.

"Can you hear that?" William asked Joshua with a grin on his face.

"Yeah, I do. They sound huge," Joshua replied. "Let's go and see how big they are."

The two brothers jumped off the boat and headed towards the sound of the rapids. The Island was partly wooded, but not completely and true to its name there was even a crop of corn planted in a small meadow. As Joshua and William were walking through the knee-high crop, Joshua bent oven and picked up a handful of soil and said, "By the way, brother, I don't know what the Captain has planned for our supper tonight but I am not eating this dirt!"

William just laughed as he too scooped up a handful of the dirt and he began to look it over while rubbing it between his thumb and fingers. "It is indeed rich," William said, "just like everyone said it would be. Joshua, I sure am glad you talked me into coming down here," William told his brother as he dropped the soil back to the ground. As the two of them walked out of the corn patch and entered a small grove of beech trees that lay next to the waterline there they stopped. They set the butts of their rifles on the ground and gazed out over the wide expanse of river and at the white caps of the rapids. Joshua said, "I am happy you came along too. It wouldn't be the same if you weren't here with me William."

"Yeah, I know," William answered as he rested his chin on the tip of his rifle   barrel. "So, these are the Falls of the Ohio. They are not nearly as big as they sound, but it has been a wet spring this year, so the water level may be higher than normal making them smaller."

Joshua nodded his head in agreement as he looked further down the river and said, "I reckon so. Looks like to me that a canoe could easily shoot down the rapids and maybe even a keel boat, but there's no way for any craft to come up them from the west. This Captain Lynn will most certainly have to make a portage around the falls and this island as well."

The two brothers were joined by Samuel and James as William bent over and picked up what he thought was a rock, but after further examination, he realized that it was a small, light blue fossil. He skipped it out over the water with a strong side arm throw. Seeing this, Samuel picked up a piece of driftwood that was about five feet long and flung it out into the water. The men watched as it picked up speed as it floated down over a series of rapids and went quickly out of sight.

"Boy, that water sure is moving ain't it?" Samuel said to the others as he picked up a second piece of driftwood and dropped it into the river.

"Yeah, it sure is. Well, I am going to head on back up to our boat," James announced in a loud voice so the men could hear him over the sound of the rushing water. "I want to meet some of the soldiers around here. See what they've got to say. Maybe we can find Andy's brothers and tell them what happened to him. I'm sure they would want to know how he is."

Hearing this, all four men headed back towards the corn patch. The light of the sun was starting to dim as it was setting and it soon would be dark. The oxen still had to be tended to, but tonight the men could wander around the many campfires that would be burning and relax by talking to the men here in Clark's army. Not having to worry about the Indians sneaking up on them as they slept in their beds would be a nice change for a least one night and be the biggest boon of the day.

Chapter 56
Night on Corn Island

As William walked around that night with the rest of the crew, moving from one campfire to another, he realized that he had definitely made the right decision about not waiting any longer to see Kentucky. All the men here wanted to claim land for themselves and drive the Indians out of the area so they could bring in their families. But not all of the talk was of land. William had also heard his share of tall tales, and jokes, even some down and out lies around the fires, but they were amusing to hear and added to general all around good time. But some of the men were getting upset at how long they had been stationed here on the river. They wanted to go inland to Fort Harrod or maybe Boonesborough to get a better look at the land, but Clark would not grant them leave to go. The big tall redhead had instead instructed his men to build a few rough cabins. This they had done, and now they were ready to go fight off the Indians who were making life so hard on the settlers. William was standing at his latest campfire stop, again listening to some buck skinner tell how he could kill all the Indians in the world, all by himself if Clark would just let him go. This was a tale he had already heard more than once tonight, so he stepped over to the next fire where he saw a tall young man talking to a group of men, but he was not as long winded as the others had been in telling their tales. He was not a braggart, what he was saying had the ring of truth to it. As he listened to him speak William formed the same opinion of this man that he had about the House brothers. As he leaned against a tree, William thought this was someone to take notice of, and he was not the only one who thought so. There was a group of men taking in every word the man was saying. One of the men in that group asked, "How are things going at Boonesborough. Simon?"

"Not great." was the reply Simon Butler gave. "Ever since Daniel got captured at the Blue Licks with all his salt boilers things have been bleak. Richard Calloway has been stirring up trouble as usual. Captain Smith has taken over the fort but he has a very small number of men at his command. The Indians are running all over the countryside. It's not very safe out there right now. Some of the settlers are losing heart and heading back over the mountains. Blackfish seems to have taken over from Cornstalk and he has the Shawnee in high spirits right now. Hamilton, up in Detroit is providing all the powder and weapons the Indians need." Hearing the name of the British commander, Henry Hamilton mentioned, one of the men kicked a log into the fire with such force it knocked apart the fire base and caused sparks to fly up into the dark night air. "I would love to get my hands on that hair buying son of a bitch!" the enraged man said.

"I know, Hezekiah," replied the sandy haired Butler, and then he sighed and said, "I believe it's going to be an awful hard summer coming up boys. And the fact that Simon Girty has gone over won't help much either. But we can still hold on."

Another voice came out of the darkness saying, "Come on Simon, you have Clark's confidence, why has he not taken us to the forts like we all expected him to do when we enlisted?"

"Lt. Clark is a good man," Butler answered as he ran his ramrod down the barrel of his rifle, giving the weapon a good cleaning as he addressed the question. "I have a good idea what he is up to, but I don't know for sure. He'll let us know when the time is right. He didn't have you fellows come all the way down here to just sit on your asses."

Another Simon, William thought to himself as he watched Simon Butler slide his ramrod back into its proper place under the barrel of his gun just before he walked off into the night. There must be something to that name that made William like the men who carried it so much, first Girty and now Butler.

"Here Hezekiah, eat some of these buffalo ribs," a man said to the fellow who had kicked the fire.

"Naw," replied the man who was still obviously very upset.

"Aw, come on brother, get yourself some," the man tried one more time as he extended his hand out, holding a slab containing several pieces of the ribs.

"I don't want any John, just leave me alone. Go on now."

Hearing this William realized the two men were brothers. Maybe they were Andy Forbes' brothers. After all, how many sets of brothers could there be on this island? William walked over to the two and said, "Hey fellows, I came downriver with an Andy Forbes, is he by any chance your all's brother?"

"No, he's not, our last name is Foree, John answered, "but there are two men here someplace by the name of Forbes. I meet them the other day. They are usually over at that cabin." he said as he pointed the blade of his knife at a cabin across the line of campfires.

"Why do you need to talk to them?" Hezekiah Foree asked.

"Their brother Andy got shot in the leg up river, and we had to leave him at Point Pleasant. I just wanted to find his family and let them know where he is and what happened to him." William replied.

"Too bad, there has been a lot of that sort of thing going on around here," John said as he bit into one of the ribs but by God if we ever get off this damn island, we could put a stop to some of that stuff."

Chapter 57
The Warning

The next morning James grabbed the toe of Samuel's foot as he lay sleeping in the boat's cabin and gave it a hard pull and said, "Come on boy, shake a leg. Let's go!" The rest of them will leave us behind if you don't get moving." Looking over at Basil, James asked, "Are you coming along with us?"

Basil shook his head no and said, "Nah, I like my hair right where it is. Besides it's a lot safer here with Clark than out there with those damn Indians. I'll see you boys when you get back." Then he rolled over pulling his blanket back up over his head. By now Samuel was up and as he slipped his shot bag over his head and shoulder and was positioning it on his hip, he asked Basil one last time, "Are you sure you don't want to come along with us? It should be a grand time." Basil looked out from under his covers and said, "No, I am staying right here. Like I said, I'll see you when you get back. That is if you get back." He extended his hand and gave Samuel a hand shake and said, "Good luck fellows, I hope you won't need it but you most likely will." Then he flopped back down onto his bunk and rolled over facing the wall of the cabin.

James and Samuel stepped out the cabin door and walked down the boat to the ramp that led to the bank where William and Joshua were waiting.

"Basil's not coming." Samuel said as he shifted his rifle to his other hand and jumped onto the ground.

William looked at Samuel's weapon and asked, "Isn't that one of Captain Rogers' rifles?"

"Yeah, it is," Samuel replied with a smile. "He said I could take it along with me as long as I brought it back."

"Looks to me like he has taken a liking to you Samuel, if he'll lend you a rifle like that one there," Joshua told the still grinning young man.

William was standing by the remnants of last night's fire that was still smoldering. He took the side of his foot and kicked aside the ashes, putting out what little fire was left, and then turning to face his companions he said, "We all agreed to come down here to see Kentucky together. We all know it is going to be dangerous and that some of us might not come back from this little adventure, so now might be a good time for a prayer. After all, if I'm right about the date, this is a Sunday and if it's not, a prayer won't hurt us anyhow." Removing his hat, William bowed his head, closed his eyes and said, "Lord, protect us under your watchful eyes and keep us safe as we go out into the wilderness as Moses did all those years ago. If any hardship should fall upon us we pray that you will give us the needed strength to survive any ordeal that we may encounter. We also ask that you watch over our loved ones back home until our safe return. In the name of your Son, Jesus Christ, we pray. Amen."

The men then made one last check of their weapons to make sure they were in good working order before they headed out. The flint on William's hammer was a little loose, but just a few turns of the screw and the flint was once again tightly secured in its place.

Joshua patted William on the back and said, "Well, let's go."

The four men headed towards the southern side of the island and in just a few moments they were looking out over the water at the mouth of Beargrass Creek that would lead them into the heart of the bluegrass region of Kentucky. There were twenty or so canoes tied to the bank and in no time, they had paddled one the short distance to the Kentucky shore and stepped foot onto the bank and disappeared into the tree line. William and James walked side by side in the front while Joshua and Samuel brought up the rear. Now that they were off the island, they could no longer speak in a normal tone of voice. Everything that was said from this point on was whispered in a low voice and hand gestures were used whenever possible. Every step that was taken had to be made lightly and carefully. All eyes were focused on the lay of the land. Every tree, bush, rock and hillside were a potential ambush spot that had to be carefully checked out before passing it by. The land was flat and covered in waist high green grass that was beginning to seed out. There were also a few canebrakes scattered here and there and the woods were full of grand old oak trees along with hundreds of other strong tall varieties of trees and plants. Deer and buffalo paths were going in every direction, and the air was full of the sound of a thousand different kinds of birds chirping. Within two hours they had crossed four creeks with some of the clearest water running in them that William had ever seen. It was as if they were in the Garden of Eden, with no one but themselves, as if this land had been untouched by man. But soon this illusion was broken by the sight of a sycamore tree that had its bark peeled off and on the smooth trunk was painted in red and black, a warning, left no doubt by an Indian who wanted no white man in this Eden. The painting was crude, but the warning was simple enough. All it had was a sketch of a man tied to a stake with his body painted black and the flames of a fire licking at him, while the Indians were dancing around the condemned victim. Joshua looked at the tree trunk and then to his brother, while shaking his head and said, "This is without a doubt the most beautiful land we will ever see, but what price will we pay for it?"

Elizabeth walked across the kitchen floor of her parent's home and sat down at the cherry table that her father had just brought into the house this very morning. Thomas Porter had promised his wife that he would make her a new table and even a set of sturdy matching chairs to replace the old ones they had been using. Now that he had fulfilled half of his promise, he was back outside in his barn, working on the chairs.

As Elizabeth sat at the table, she ran her hand over the newly finished tabletop, admiring the workmanship of her father's efforts to please his wife. The table was beautifully done; maybe she could talk him into making one for her and William someday. She reached over and picked up a bowl of onions and began to peel off the outer skin and cut away the roots. They would cook up well with the roast that she and her mother was about to prepare.

Little Sarah was sitting on the floor by her mother and grabbing the hem of Elizabeth's dress with her small hand. She stuck the fabric in her mouth and began to chew away on it in an effort to relieve her aching gums. She already had her first tooth come in and now she was working on some more. Sarah had the same dark complexion as her father and she also had his black hair to match, but her eyes were the green of her mothers, as well as her high cheek bones.

Elizabeth finished cutting up her onions and got up from her chair and walked over to the bucket of water that she had drawn out of the well this morning. She washed and dried her hands off on a towel as her gaze fell upon William's latest letter to her, sitting on the window sill. She had read it more than once since it had arrived but one more time wouldn't hurt, she thought as she picked it up and walked back over to the table and sat down. She carefully unfolded the paper, laid it on the table and smoothing out the wrinkles she began to read.

Hello My Love,

Your letter could not have arrived at a better time for me. I was feeling kind of lonely here all by myself. And now that I have received word from you, I am in much better spirits. I was overjoyed to hear that all is well with my two girls back home. I also believe that you made a wise decision in going back home to your folks. It also made me happy that my parents got to see our daughter too. I know that it pleased them very much. Having Joshua here has also been a blessing and yes we are indeed going to Kentucky together. I know this will keep us apart for some time longer, but I believe it will pay off in the long run. But my dear Elizabeth please know that you are here with me in my thoughts and in my dreams. This will most likely be my last letter that I will be able to send to you, because there is no way to send one from Kentucky. I don't know when this letter will find you as it may take a while to arrive, but don't despair for the next time you hear from me, you will be in my arms and I'll be back home with you. So, keep an eye upon the road.

Until then,
William.

Elizabeth refolded the letter and placed it back on the window sill so she could read it again in the morning or maybe later tonight. She turned around and saw Sarah crawling towards the open front door of the house. She rushed over to the doorway and scooped up the little girl as she was going out onto the porch and stood looking out over her father's farm. She pointed down the road that one day would bring her husband home to her and said, "Do you see your daddy out there somewhere?"

Chapter 59
Splashing Buffalo

The explorers had traveled in a southeasterly direction after they pulled out from the falls this morning and now, they had reached what they all hoped was the Salt River. Simon Butler had told them to follow its water course until it turned due south. At that point they should keep on going east until they arrived at Harrodsburg, which was situated just east of the Kentucky River. Since this was their first time in the region, William and James were not completely convinced that this was the Salt River. Butler had said that it was not a real wide river and at spots it was no more that 80 to 100 foot wide. The water course that they were looking at now was not all that wide.

"This has got to be it," Joshua said, "all the other streams that we have passed have been small. This has to be a river; it's just too big to be a creek."

"Well, Butler did say we should reach it a little before sundown," William said, trying to convince himself that this was indeed the right way. "We have maybe an hour or so of daylight left, so this is most likely it."

James nodded his head in agreement and said, "I think we should stop here for the night. That will give us time to look around some before it gets dark. I really don't want to sleep right next to a party of Indians and not know it until they shoot a hole in one of us. Besides, look how long Samuel's hair is getting. We sure would hate to see him running around here tomorrow morning with it all scalped off now wouldn't we?"

All of the men had smiles on their faces except Samuel, who had taken off his hat and was running his fingers through his long dark hair and said, "That's not funny boys. He's telling a joke, but I remember those poor dead scalped fellows back at the river. It could happen you know."

"I know," replied James, "that's why we should look around some before we bed down for the night."

"Makes good senses to me," William said, "let's circle around some, but I don't think we should split up. We will be safer together, I would say. I also think we should all check the powder in our weapons before we continue."

Samuel held his rifle in the fold of his arm and rose up his frizzen from the top of the gun's pan and said, "Damn, all my powder is gone."

"You have to be careful Samuel," William scolder his young friend. "Look, you have to try to keep your gun level so your powder will stay in the pan. If you don't it will all fall out on the ground. Look, I am not mad at you Samuel; I just don't want to see you get killed because of something as simple as not having powder in your pan."

Samuel said, "I know that," as he poured black powder into his pan while William watched.

"Not too much either," William said, "watch here, push your frizzen back down into its place. See that crack between the frizzen and the pan? That's where you are losing your powder. Be careful not to use too much powder either, the more powder you have in your pan, the longer it takes to burn down through the touchhole. When you pull that trigger, it takes a second or two longer for your rifle to go off. That can cause your aim to be off, because it's hard to hold still that long holding a gun that's as heavy as these are. And if you could by the grace of God hold aim, the other fellow has shot his rifle at you while you're sitting there waiting for yours to go off."

William touched Samuel on the back and said, "Now, don't forget that. It could save your life someday and maybe mine too."

Hearing all of William's instructions Joshua looked at his brother and said, "You sound just like father back home when he was telling us the same thing."

William didn't answer that, he just said "Come on, lets go."

The four of them spread out about one hundred feet apart from each other and down through the woods they went, moving as quietly as they could trying not to disturb the ground under their feet. They all knew that if just one of them stepped on a fallen branch, the snapping sound could be heard hundreds of yards down through the trees giving them away to anyone who happened to be listening. All seemed to be clear until William saw some movement up ahead in the underbrush of the tree line. He could not quite make out what it was, so he stepped behind a tree and motioned for the others to do the same. As he peered out around the trunk a large herd of buffalo came running down towards the river and jumped in causing the water to splash high into the air as they entered the river and started the swim to the other side. As they climbed up onto the other bank all four men ran to the water's edge and watched in awe as the large beast disappeared into the trees. James looked at William and said, "Did we spook them or did someone else down that way spook them up to us?"

William shook his head back and forth and said, "I don't know." They all four fell down behind an old moss covered fallen tree trunk and stared down into the woods watching for any possible threat that might present itself. But, after a tense fifteen-minute wait, the sun fell below the treetops and their nerves began to calm. Then they heard the sound of leaves rattling and the pop of a small twig. All four men cocked their hammers back and propped their weapons on top of the log and waited to fire when they saw a lone opossum come wandering down towards them in a very non-threatening manner. James chuckled out loud as he took his hand and swatted away a buzzing mosquito from his right ear and said, "Boy, I thought for sure that was Blackfish himself coming here to kill us all!"

"Yeah, me too" William confessed as he spun away from the log taking the pressure off his cramped knees and sat back down on the ground putting his back against the log once more. Then in the distance, they all heard the report of gunfire and the howls of Indians as the startled opossum jumped over their log and ran out of sight.

Once again, they shouldered their weapons and peered out over the log into the darkness. William reached down to his belt and pulled out his pistol and put it on top of the log beside his rifle. He also pulled out his tomahawk and handed it to Joshua and said, "Here, take this. You may need it before this night is over.

Chapter 60
Horse Thieves

A few hours had passed since the Indians had shot off their weapons and screamed out their war cry for all to hear. The moon was almost full tonight and William could still see far down into the trees, but that was all he could see, just the trees, and nothing else except for the hundreds of lightening bugs that sparkled in the night. Every now and again, he could hear the sound of a nickering horse somewhere in the darkness.

William looked over to James and said in a low voice, "Do you know what we would be doing if Andrew and Adam House were here with us?"

James nodded his head yes, and said, "I sure do. We would be talking over some plan to sneak off down that way and take a few scalps of our own."

"That's right," William answered, "and here we sit like four rabbits in our holes waiting for the sun to come up. I don't know about you boys, but I am getting kind of sick and tired of sitting around and not doing anything. Boys there are horses down there. I don't know how many, but a few, and riding would be a lot faster than walking."

"But there is one big difference this time around," James whispered. "We don't know how many of them are down there. Andrew could tell by the tracks in the snow. That's an advantage we don't have tonight."

Joshua stood up and said, "That's a chance I'm willing to take. You all stay here I'm going down there to see what's afoot."

"Wait, I'll go with you," William said as he tucked his pistol into his belt and raised his leg up over the top of the log and slid off the other side.

"What about us?" Samuel asked. "We should go too."

"No," James said, "We'll stay here. You boys go on and see what's down there. If they realize that you are watching them, they will rush you. If that happens you all high tail it back here and we will give you covering fire."

William nodded to James and turned to Joshua and said, "Look Joshua, let's take it easy going down. We have all night to get there. Let's take our time."

"I know you've been out spying on the Indians before with Girty and those House brothers you keep talking about, but you're not the only Tipton that's good in the woods," Joshua said sharply.

William nodded his head yes and said; "Don't you think I know that? If I thought you were going to get me killed, I wouldn't go down there with you."

James and Samuel watched as the two brothers worked their way down towards the unsuspecting Indian camp. Each one took his time and in a little while they were both out of sight. The wind began to blow, not really hard, but strong enough to make the sound of rustling leaves help cover any sound made by the two men moving towards the horses. Unlike the last time, this Indian camp had no firelight to guide William to its exact location. The two had crept about two hundred yards when they stopped and peered out into the night looking for the camp. Joshua spotted one of the horses swishing its tail over its back, swatting at some irritating insect. Joshua waved over to William and pointed to the bedded down horses. William counted ten tethered animals as he and Joshua made their way over to take a closer look. But only four of them had the look of an Indian's horse, with all the painted symbols on their necks and hind quarters. The others surely had belonged to white men. They still had saddles on their backs. These horses were either stolen from some isolated cabin or had had their riders shot off in an ambush. Off to their far right, stood a Shawnee warrior, holding his rifle and standing guard over his sleeping companions.

The two brothers backed up slowly and turned away from the Indian and towards James and Samuel behind the log. As they walked along, they dared not speak but they had confident smiles as they glanced at each other. Soon they were back at the log, telling James and Samuel what they had seen. All four agreed the horses were worth the risk and the four of them began to stalk their prey. When they got back to where the horses were tied, William noticed that two of the horses were now standing, and the lone Shawnee guard was talking to his horse, rubbing its mane and patting its neck. William could tell that this man truly loved his horse and somehow it made him feel bad knowing he was here to kill him, but then he thought of the saddled horses and remembered that they too had owners who cared for them until this Shawnee had most likely killed them yesterday or the day before. However, this was not the time for a forgiving heart so William began to stalk his pray. Maybe he could take him out without killing him he thought to himself.

William jumped from behind one of the horses directly in front of the warrior and delivered a knockout blow to the man's head with the butt of his rifle. The unconscious Indian fell to the ground with his head split open. William's companions fired on the rest of the sleeping Indians, but this time someone missed his mark allowing one of the warriors to make a running attempt to grab a horse and escape. Having heard the shots all of the horses had jumped to their feet causing William some difficulty in getting off his shot at the fast approaching Indian. As William fired one of the animals bumped into his side causing his shot to veer left of his mark. The Indian jumped into the air as he kicked his foot into William's chest knocking him to the ground. The maneuver caused the attacker to lose his balance and like William, he too fell to the ground. Both men rolled away, trying to avoid the stomping feet of the newly frightened horses. Then, they both reached out for the other at the same instant, in what would become a fight to the death for one or the other. William reached down and pulled out his pistol and somehow managed to fire off a shot into the warrior's stomach. Joshua bent over and grabbed the Indian by the throat and jerked him off his brother, throwing him to the ground. He fell upon the Indian's back sinking the tomahawk that William had given him just a few hours ago into the back of the warrior's head. William jumped to his feet and quickly picked up his rifle and began to reload it, but something was not quite right. His arm had a sharp pain and the palm of his hand was dripping wet with his own blood. James reached over and took William's arm and pulled out the Indian's knife that was still sticking in his arm, between his hand and elbow.

"Samuel, reload my rifle," William asked as he fell back against a tree, taking the weight off his wobbly legs.

"Are you alright William?" Joshua asked.

"Yeah, I'll live," William answered as he watched Samuel finish reloading his rifle.

"Let me have it," William said as he reached out and took the weapon form Samuel's hand. He stepped over the dead Indian who had just stabbed him and walked over to the unconscious Indian who He had hit first with the butt of his gun at the beginning of this little skirmish. William lowered the barrel of his rifle to the warrior's chest and pulled the trigger.

Chapter 61
Powder Horns

William was relieved when he saw the wooden walls of Fort Harrod from the top of his new mount. His forearm was hurting badly, but he could still move his fingers. That was what bothered him most about his wound. He was afraid of losing the use of his hand. At first the wound was not so bad, but as the hours went by, the stiffer and sorer it had become. He had not looked at the wound since early this morning when Joshua had washed the blood away and wrapped it in a couple of handkerchiefs. He hoped he would not find any red streaks running up his arm when he got the chance to examine the wound.

The ambush had been a success, despite his wound. They had recaptured the horses with the saddles, and they had also taken the Indians horses as well. Horses were a mighty valuable asset to have on the frontier. In addition to the horses, they had also gathered up the Shawnee weapons, and unlike the poor-quality trade gun the Indians had at Cresap's Bottom, these were of high quality. Two Brown Bess muskets, supplied by the British in Detroit no doubt, and two long rifles that were most likely taken from some settlers who lost more than their weapons to the Indians. Along with the rifles were several powder horns full of powder and an equal number of shot bags full of lead balls. Each of the Indians had worn silver armbands and earrings, and a couple even had silver gorgets around their necks. William had heard of the Brown Bess muskets the Redcoats used, but this was the first time he had seen one up this close. The size of the lead balls was so much bigger than the ones the long rifles used, maybe three times its size. One of them had a bayonet on its end. That in itself was a prize any Continental soldier would love to have.

Joshua had given William's tomahawk back to him, having taken a tomahawk from one of the dead Shawnees as a trophy of the battle, along with his share of the weaponry and silver that they had all divided evenly.

Samuel took one of the long rifles to be his own. Now when he returned the weapon Captain Rogers had so garishly loaned him back at the falls, he would have a fine long rifle of his own, one that was a far cry from his first trade musket.

William's share of the loot was to be one of the long rifles, two of the horses and one fourth of the powder and lead, plus the deer horn handled knife that James had pulled out of his arm. "Something to remember your dead Indian friend by" was how he put it as he presented it to William.

As the party rode up the small hill that the fort was situated on, their eyes fell upon its walls. It was built in a rectangle, being about seventy by ninety feet in diameter. Its four corners had the normal two-story blockhouses and six or seven cabins were built between in a straight line with the blockhouses and their back walls forming the outer wall of the fort itself. They were all connected by ten-foot-high pickets made of oak trees standing upright and buried in the ground. The fort gates were swung open as the horses approached. Two long haired, full bearded men stepped out with weapons in hand. They were wearing tattered clothing and they wore the look of exhausted men, but they were happy to see some new faces entering their fort. James and Samuel were the first to enter the gates, leading the Indian horses behind them as they rode along. As soon as they were inside they were quickly surrounded by the forty or fifty inhabitants of the outpost. Joshua rode alongside William, keeping a concerned eye on his brother.

"Damn William," he said, "I wish we had kept our asses behind that log and left those redskins alone last night. A few horses are not worth losing your arm over."
"Oh, I'll be alright in a few days," William said as he slid off the horses back onto the dusty ground inside the fort. He turned back around to the horse and pulled off the new powder horn that he had won in the skirmish and hung its leather strap over his head. With his good hand he grasped his rifle and stepped back from the horse as Joshua took its reins and led it along with his own mount to the fort's watering trough in the center of the yard.

A middle-aged woman, who was standing in the doorway of a cabin stepped out and walked over to William and said, "I see you've been shot in the arm. Let me take a look at it. Come on inside with me, I'll fix you right up."

"Thank you very much," William said, "but it's not a gunshot, it's a stab wound,"

"All the better," she replied as she stepped back into her cabin, "stab wounds heal up a heap better than gunshots do. Don't tear things up as bad and all. Let's take a look," she said as William removed the powder horn from around his head and hung it on one of her chairs. She removed Joshua's handkerchiefs from around William's arm and said, "I'm Ann Poague, my husband was one of the fellows that opened the gate for you. The clean one now, not that dirty Thomas Denton. Why, he's not so much as taken a bath since he's been here, and that's been over two years!"

"Yes Ma'am," William replied as he looked around the well-stocked cabin.

"Well, you're in luck son, it's not too bad," she said as she looked over his arm it's a clean puncture. Did it go clear through?" she asked as she turned his arm over to examine the back of the wound. "Yeah, it surely did now, didn't it?"

"Do you think I will lose the use of my hand?" William asked.

"Naw," she replied, "can you move your fingers now?"

"Yeah," William said as he wiggled them to show her how much movement he had but I don't have much of a grip in that hand."

"Well, if you can move them now, you can when it's all healed up. Let me put some of my salve on that before I bandage it back up." She walked over to a cupboard and opened its pokeberry stained door and removed a small jar of some sort containing her homemade remedy. She liberally applied it to William's wounded arm and finally, she wrapped the wound in a clean piece of linen and said, "Now, don't you be upset about it none. I've fixed up a whole lot worse than that since we've been here."

After again thanking her William rose and looked around the room. Something in the far corner of the room caught his eye and he said, "Mrs. Poague, however, did you get that spinning wheel to this wild country?"

"Well, I can tell you it wasn't easy. My husband tried a hundred different times to throw it away on our trip over the mountains, but I wouldn't let him. That's why he's got those ratty clothes on out there now. I won't let him have any of my homespun!" she said laughing. Then her eyes fell on the powder horn that William had taken off the Indian and looking him full in the face, she asked, "Where did you get that horn?"

"Off the Indian who stabbed me" William answered.

"Did you kill him?" she asked, as she picked it up off her chair and began to rub the scrimshaw work on the horn with her fingers.

"Deader than a doornail, why do you ask?"

"It belonged to a friend of ours," she answered in a sad voice, "see his name is carved right here."

William took the horn form her hand and read the name out loud. "Barney Stagncr. Say he was your friend?"

"Yes, he was. Those savages beheaded him outside the walls of the fort last year down by the spring. They took his horse that was grazing by his side. Did you take that Indian's horse too?" she asked "Because if you did I would like very much to see it."

"Yes, we took him and of course you can see it," William told the teary eyed woman, "I'll take you to him right now."

As William and his new doctor were walking across the fort's enclosed yard to where the captured horses were tied she pulled her apron up and wiped her eyes on its corner and looked at the animals from a distance and said, "I can't tell if that's him or not." After reaching the spot where the horses stood, Mrs. Poague finally reached up and rubbed the back of the horse's ear and said, "That's him. My husband sold Barney this black gelding. Well, I guess he belongs to you now." She said as she turned to William. "You know, he's saddle broke, but you couldn't tell it by the way he looks now, what with all of this paint all over him. You wouldn't mind if I washed these Indian markings off, would you?"

"No Ma'am, you go right ahead," William said as he placed his hand on his shoulder above his wound and said,

"I'd sure appreciate it. I'm in no shape to do it." She just nodded her head yes, and led the horse toward the gates of the fort. As she was passing through to the outside she was stopped by a tall man with a black beard. William could not hear what the two were talking about, but he assumed that it had to be the horse. After they had finished their conversation the man started to approach William, and Mrs. Poague picked up the rope that the Indians had used as a bridle and she led the horse down to the spring where the animals' former master had been killed.

William watched as the man approached him from the gate. As he drew nearer, William began to realize how big this fellow really was. Down by the gate he looked tall, but not this tall. He was well over six feet, maybe as tall as six foot three. The rifle that he was packing in his hand was much longer than a normal Kentucky long rifle, maybe a foot longer. He was dressed in a blue hunting shirt that went below his waist, halfway to his knees. He had a set of leggings around his legs and on his feet was a pair of moccasins. He was leading his horse, which had the hind quarters of a buffalo lying across its back, no doubt just shot and dressed this very morning by this impressive looking man. He reached up and pulled off the yellow and black checkered bandana that he had tried around his head and stuck it inside his belt. He ran his fingers through his wet black hair and said to William, "So, you killed the Shawnee that had that horse, did ye".

William nodded his head and said, "Yeah, but not before he stuck me in my arm."

"Well, let me shake your hand then," the big fellow said. "That's one redskin I am happy to see dead. My name is James Harrod," he said as he presented his hand to
William.

"Take no offense, but my handshaking hand is out of order right now," William said, feeling a little cautious about having this big frontiersman take hold of his wounded arm. A handshake from a man of this size might be a little more than his arm could take at the moment.

"None taken, I understand," the leader of the fort said, "I've had my share of Indian battles myself, they can put up a hard and fearsome fight when they have to, can't they? We all liked old Barney, the fellow who owned that horse. I guess he was the oldest man here among us. That's what made us all so mad last summer. The fact that they would kill someone that old," Harrod said as he cut one of the ropes that tied down the buffalo meat. "No honor in that. Where did you boys come from Logan's Station maybe?"

"No, we came from the falls," William answered.

"Your one of George's men then" Harrod asked as he bent over and grabbed the buffalo and slung it over his shoulder as though it were a small child.

"No, we came down river to help a Captain Linn at the falls with his cargo, but he's not due for a few more days, so we're out looking the country over. Simon Butler told us how to get here. We'll just be here a few days."

James Harrod faced William, still holding his kill on his shoulder as if were of no consequence and asked, "Have you ever eaten Buffalo before?"

"No, not yet," William replied.

"Well you will tonight. Come on with me. My wife will fix you a nice plateful."

William walked along behind the strong captain of this young settlement and followed him into one of the corner blockhouses to try a new dish.

Chapter 62
McCray's Offer

William's arm was still giving him some trouble after two days at Ft Harrod; however, it was healing to his satisfaction. Mrs. Poague had continued her treatments of his wound. She changed the bandage twice a day, always applying her salve. Aftcrwards, she re-wrapped the bandage tightly, making sure to pull his skin together, so it would not gape open. When she had finished, she would always say to William as he was stepping out her door, "You take care of that arm William, don't try to lift anything yet, take things easy, and don't push it." Knowing that she was probably right, he also knew that he had let all the time that he could afford to lose slip by.

Joshua was willing to wait a little longer, but James and Samuel were anxious to go out and stake their claims. Although they had not said anything about pulling out to William just yet, he could tell they were as ready to go as he was.

Captain Harrod had already taken William's three companions south of the fort to see his land. Most of the land in that direction had already been claimed by the men in Harrod's 1773 party. John Clark, Azariah Reese, William Fields, Silas Harlan and even later arrivals like Hugh McGray and Thomas Denton had taken up land in that area. That being the case, the four of them felt like their best chance was to head over to the north, past where the MacAfee brothers had made their claims.

William had saddled Barney Stagner's horse and was waiting at the fort's gate with Samuel for James and Joshua to join them when Hugh McGray came walking up and said, "I understand you boys are looking for land to claim."

"That's right," William answered as he shifted his weight in the saddle looking down at McGray and his stepson, James Ray.

"Well then, hear me out." McGray said as Joshua and James rode up to the gate on their new mounts. "North of Boonesborough, there is unclaimed land. I have already made one claim up there for four hundred acres. As of now, as far as I know, no one else has been up that way. My boy James here will show you the way if you agree. It's too far away for me to keep. I always planned to sell, or trade it off someday anyway. You boys came down on a flat boat, right?"

"Yeah," Samuel answered.

"And you're going back up river on a keelboat?" McGray asked as he looked over at the horses that William and the others had brought in, that were penned up inside the fort's corral.

"You want to trade your claim for our horses?" William asked.

"That's right," McGray replied as he continued on, "I need more horses and you boys can't take them back on a keelboat. We will draw up the papers before you go and if you like what you see, all you have to do is sign them. Young James can go to the falls with you and he can bring them back here after you all are safe on Corn Island. If not, he can come on back and you boys can go on your way. But you don't know the country really well and it will take more time for you to find a good track of land. It will be faster for you and good for me. You've already had one run in with those damn savages. The less time you're out in those woods the better off you will be. What do you say to that, do we have a deal?"

"But you just have one claim to trade," Joshua said, "There are three more of us that wants land. What about us?"

"You can claim what you want." McGray replied in an aggravated tone, "no one else has made any claims up that way. Like I said you can go off by yourselves, but you won't know where to go, not without my boys help."

"Give us a moment to talk thing over Hugh," William said as he and the others rode out the fort's gate and down to the spring.

"Well, what do you say fellows?" William asked, sitting on top of his gelding. I kind of like the idea."

"Yeah, it's fine with me," James said right after he spit a stream of tobacco juice over the top of his horse's head onto the ground below. "You trade the horses for his claim and we'll all blaze tomahawk claims. Having young Ray guide, us to good land where we can all be together is worth the price of horses that we may not even be able to sell once we get back to the falls. It's like he said, if we don't like the looks of it, we can go on our way, but the way he acted up there that would most likely piss him off."

William smiled as he turned his mount around and said, "Yeah, but that will be young James Ray's problem, not ours. He will be the one that will have to tell Hugh that we refused." They all laughed as William headed back up to the fort to tell McGray to draw up the papers.

Chapter 63
Fort Boonesborough

Yesterday's ride had been hard on William's arm. Early on it had not been that bad, but by late in the afternoon it had become very painful. Every bounce made in the saddle had taken its toll. However, thankfully, the party had not run upon any trouble during the days ride. James Ray might be young, but he knew this country very well, just as Hugh McGray had said he would. This afternoon, a few hours out of Boonesborough they had had the good luck of running across a hunting party of five men from Boonesborough. They were led by a fellow named John Holder. This eased William's mind a good deal. The additional men would greatly increase their chances of reaching the fort safely. William had learned from his past encounters with the Indians that it took all of a man's strength to fight just one of them off, and with his wounded arm he would have little chance of surviving a fight today. If a small party of Indians did spot them now, most likely they would let them pass on by, and if it was a large war party, then they would all be doomed anyway. The one thing that had kept his mind off his arm during this journey was the countryside and all the good water courses that flowed through the fields. This land was worth fighting for he thought to himself.

As they rode down the hill away from Otter Creek, William looked out over the bottom that lay next to the Kentucky River. There were about fifty acres lying in the bottom and about a hundred feet from the river stood the fort. William remembered what Simon Butler had said about Daniel Boone having been captured during the winter and he had no trouble believing it when he saw what poor condition the fort was in at this time. One of the fort's walls was not yet complete. The whole place had the look of a fort without a leader. Upon seeing the riders enter the fort a man he later learned was named Richard Calloway called out to John Holder, asking if either of his nephews, Cage or James Calloway were among them. Holder just shook his head no as he rode on by. William learned the two Callaway's had also been captured along with Boone at the salt lick known as the Blue Licks.

As William dismounted from his horse, for some unknown reason one of the dogs from the fort began to bark at him and Joshua. It was beginning to unnerve the two when Joshua made a fake lunge at the dog, causing it to run off and leave the two exhausted men alone. Samuel had taken William's horse form him and was tending to the animal's needs when a pretty young woman approached the two brothers and motioned them to one of the fort's empty cabins. She told them that the cabin had been her mother's, who had just recently returned to North Carolina and that it would be alright for them to use it until they left in the morning. She did not say what her name was, and William was too tired to ask her. Looking around the dim cabin he saw a straw filled mattress on the cabin floor, and he simply fell upon it and was soon asleep. He woke up a few hours after dark, and found some stew that the young woman had left. He gratefully ate the savory meal and once again fell into a deep sleep. He had obviously not even rolled over in his sleep until just a few minutes ago when he awoke to a new morning. His arm felt much better after the good night's rest and he was hoping that the wound had made the turn now for the good and was on the road to being healed. But he also knew today's ride was yet to come and that would tell the story if he was truly healing or not. As he stepped out of the cabin into the common yard of the fort, a few drops of rain began to fall. It was not a hard rain, just a light steady one. Reaching into his shot bag, he pulled out a piece of a deer's hide that he had killed a few years back. He had tanned the back side of the animal's skin while leaving the hair on its front side. He had formed it into a small hood that would lay over the pan and flint of his rifle. This would keep his power dry in wet weather conditions like todays.

James Tate and James Ray were talking as William walked up to the two and said, "We need to get moving fellows. We can't let this rain stop us from going out today. Time is a luxury we don't have; besides the rain might keep the Indians off our backs for a while."

"That's fine with me," the young James Ray answered as he walked off, "I'll get my horse."

"Where are Samuel and Joshua?" William asked as he shouldered his rifle and pointed it out towards one of the open gaps in the picketed walls of the fort.

"They're saddling up our horses," James answered as he watched William handle his gun. "How does the arm feel? Can you hold your arm steady enough to get off a decent shot?"

William lowered his rifle and said, "I'm not a hundred percent but, I can manage, hopefully I won't have to." He sat the butt of his rifle down on the ground and propped the barrel against the wall of one of the cabins. Cupping his hands together, he dipped them into the rain barrel that caught the water running off the cabin's roof and took a drink. He wiped his mouth off with his shirt sleeve just as Joshua walked up, giving him the reins of his horse. William put his foot into the stirrup and pulled himself up onto the horse's back. Then Joshua handed him his rifle and mounted up himself. As the men were making their way out of the fort the same young woman who had let them sleep in her mother's empty cabin stepped out into the rain holding her apron over her head, trying to keep dry and walked up to James Ray and looked up at him through the rain and said, "I'm sorry to hear about your brother James. I know how hard it is."

"Thank you, Jemima," he answered, "I guess you do at that. We both know what it is like to lose a loved one to the Indians now that your father is gone. She nodded her head yes, and said, "You boys be careful out there now." James Ray tipped his hat to her and rode on out of the fort, leading William and the others through the sycamore trees down at the river's edge when Samuel rode up beside him and said, "Hey, James, who was that little gal back there? Is she single?"

Ray stopped at the riverbank and said, "Who her, don't you know who she is? Why, she's Daniel Boone's daughter Jemima. She got married to Flanders Callaway a while back. Don't go casting your eye at her, Flanders is a big ole boy! Well, this is where we cross the river fellows, let's go." Ray walked his horse out into the water first and within a few seconds his horse was swimming across. Samuel's horse likewise   took to the water fairly easily, but Joshua's mount was balking, not wanting to enter the water. The horse reared up on its hind legs, refusing to enter the current. It spun around wildly, trying to break away. Joshua jerked at the reins, turning him back toward the river to make another attempt to get the horse into the water. Just then James rode up behind the frightened horse and smacked it on the rump yelling, "Get across there." The horse jumped out into the water, wild-eyed, making a huge splash. At first, the animal tried to climb back out of the river onto the bank but Joshua finally got control of the horse and the two of them began their long swim across. William patted the neck of his horse and said, "Come on boy, let's go." The horse stepped out easily into the water, as though he was walking into his favorite pasture back home. William could feel the horse's powerful legs working under the water. The level of the water rose over the top of the animal's back and was around William's waist. As they made their way out to the middle of the river, William looked back over his shoulder and saw that James, too, had little trouble with his horse and they were also swimming across. As they reached the opposite shore, Samuel's horse floated downriver a little too far, missing the best spot to climb out onto the bank. Samuel slid off the horse's back and climbed out of the water as his mount floated down to a spot where the bank was not as steep and it was able to climb out of the water to safety. Everyone else had gotten to the bank with no trouble. Samuel's rifle had gotten wet, as did Joshua's when his horse first jumped into the river, but other than that the crossing went well and they were soon out of sight.

Chapter 64
Spider Web

Hugh McGray's property was just what William wanted his Kentucky farm to be and more. It had a creek running through the front of the track with bottom land on each side. The larger of the two bottoms had canebrakes growing in its center. The smaller one lay next to a hill that rose up so as you could see the entire bottom from its summit. This would be a perfect spot to build a house William thought. The land on top of the hill ran all the way to the back-property line and was mostly flat, with just a few rolling fields. There were already several open fields with tall grass blowing in the wind. With a few years work, other fields could also be cleared and made ready for cultivation. As far as William was concerned, this was it for him four Hundred acres of heaven. He and Joshua agreed this was what they both wanted and if Joshua could find a nearby tract to his liking, they both would settle here.

Joshua had ridden off with James Ray to see if any of the adjoining land had any new tomahawk markings that some other settler might have made in McGray's absence. James and Samuel took off in the other direction to do the same, taking old James Knox's advice about not cross claiming. William would have gone along with them, but once again his bad arm was beginning to bother him after the long days ride, so he decided to sit here on top of his would be hill and take in the view that he hoped would become his and Elizabeth's someday. He sat down under a large oak tree and leaning his back up against its trunk, he looked out over the

Kentucky landscape when his eye fell upon a spider web by his side that was the home of a large black spider. The web was about two feet around in the shape of a circle. William took his finger and gently tapped one of the main threads of the web, causing it to vibrate. This action made the spider run to the center of its web. For safety, William supposed. Then, shifting his attention back to the view in front of him, he began to visualize what his home would look like with several out buildings sitting around his yard, with Elizabeth and Sarah darting in and out of the buildings carrying out their daily chores. Then once again William's attention was drawn to the spider web at his side but this time a small butterfly had unfortunately flown into the spider's trap. The spider quickly ran down to his pray and soon had the butterfly completely wrapped into a neat ball of webs, no doubt the spiders next meal. William once again looked out over the bottom below him and there, coming out of a grove of wild cherry trees, in the far bottom he saw two Indians walking up the opposite side of the creek. Reaching for his rifle, he quickly crawled down the grass covered hill and waited for his prey to come into his shooting range. The Indians seemed to be alone, just the two of them walking along. They were taking their time, not in any rush. One was much taller than the other. Soon they had made their way directly across from where William was laying in ambush. William cocked his weapon and placed his aim on the smaller of the two when he realized the Indian was a young boy, about twelve or thirteen years old, obviously out on a hunting trip with his father. Their faces were not painted with war paint like any of other Indians that William had fought in the past. William didn't know what to do; it just didn't feel right to fire upon this father and son. He took his sight off his target as the two stopped and looked over to William's side of the stream. William once again placed his sight on the father as he stepped into the water and began to wade over to Williams's side. The Indian stopped in midstream and said something to his young son, over his shoulder and began to laugh as the young boy stepped into the water. William knew that he had two choices. He could simply dill the father and go after the son or he could let them go on by and hope that they would not see him in the grass. By now the father was stepping up on the bank and he was way too close not to spot William.

Without thinking William raised to his feet in front of the father, no more than twenty feet away and pointed his rifle at the Cherokee's chest, but still holding his fire. The father stopped but did not raise his musket. He just raised an outstretched hand to his son, telling him to stop in a very calm manner. He was a middle-aged man with tattoos running down his arms and around his neck. He had a silver ring in his nose and brass armbands around his upper arms. And William had not frightened him one bit. The two men just stood there for a moment not knowing what to do, and then William lowered his rifle. The Indian slightly cocked his head and stared into William's eyes and stepped back into the water, walking backward very slowly across the creek to his son, but never breaking eye contact with his adversary. He placed a hand on the boys back and spoke to him in a low voice. Then, the boy ran back across the bottom into the safety of the grove of trees as his father turned back to William and nodded his head. He arced his hand out away from his chest with his palm turned outward to William as though he were saying 'so long', and walked away leaving William in the bottom all alone wondering to himself if this farm would be his web and the Indians the unfortunate prey of William in the guise of spider or was it to be the other way around, with him stuck in their web with no way out someday'?

Chapter 65
New Brothers

"I can't believe that you didn't fire on that Indian yesterday." Joshua said as he dug a small hole in the ground with his tomahawk.

William just shook his head as he dropped one of the grains of seed corn into Joshua's hole and covered it back up with the side of his foot. "I don't know, maybe I should have, they know where we are now, but it just didn't feel right."

"Well I hope it doesn't come back to haunt us." Joshua said as he dug another hole. "How much seed do we have left?"

William looked into the small bag of seed corn that he had bought from the old woman back at Wheeling and said, "Just a handful. We'll be done in a few minutes. I think we have already planted enough to say we got your acre out."

"It's awful late to be planting a corn crop." Joshua said through a sly grin, "but I don't know who is going to come out here and see if we harvested this corn or not. I do believe that ole Patrick Henry's got more pressing matters to attend to than this here crop."

William laughed at his brother and said, "as far as I know, all the law says is that we have to plant a corn crop, it didn't say anything about us tending to it afterwards. Once we have moved out here, we'll have to take better care of our crops than we have this one here. You know Joshua, it's a shame that Thomas and Sylvester didn't come out here with us. Why they could have gotten the same claims that James and Samuel have claimed for themselves. We could have all been out there together."

Joshua nodded his head yes and said. "I thought that myself last night." But then he looked over to the end of this would be cornfield and saw James and Samuel standing guard with their weapons in hand and said, "We could have gotten worse neighbors than those two over there I suppose. James is a good man and Samuel is well on his way to being one."

William nodded his head in agreement and said, "You know in a strange way somehow, they do feel like brothers. Don't they? James even resembles

Thomas in some ways and they do act a lot alike too."

"Yeah, and Samuel is just like everyone's little brother," Joshua said as he dug one more hole

.

"That's the last one you'll have to dig. I've just got one seed left." William said as he planted the last one from his bag. "You know the folks are not too old to come out here with us. Dad may get to see Kentucky after all.

The two of them picked up their rifles and walked back over to where James and Samuel were standing. "Boy, its awful hot for June." Samuel said as he wiped the sweat from his brow, "look, my head is soaking wet and all I've done is stand here. I wonder how hot July and August is going to be."

James pushed his hat back a little with the end of his gun barrel and said, "I guess it's going to be just as hot on this side of the mountains as on the other. Then he looked out over the field and said, "Well, all we have to do now is throw up some kind of shelter and we're done. Within a few minutes, two forked branches were driven into the ground by James and Joshua laid a third branch into the forks connecting the two together while William tied them down with a rawhide thong. Samuel placed some smaller limbs on top of the cross branch and laid the other ends on the ground making a quick lean-to. Now they could say they had fulfilled the last requirement to acquire Joshua's claim, just as they had done earlier in the day at Samuel's and James's new farms.

William laid a hand on Joshua's shoulder and said, "Boy that's a real nice home you got their brother."

"Yeah, yeah, come on," Joshua answered, "let's go find that Ray fellow and get out of here."

As the four men walked along through the trees they heard a loud crackling noise. Taking cover, they silently moved toward the noise and were surprised to see a large black bear tearing apart a fallen tree. The bear was biting into the wood and smashing it apart with its powerful paws looking for any insects that might be inside. Joshua raised his rifle and pointed it at the bear as she raised her big head up from her work and looked at the men only a few yards away.

"Don't shoot," James said as he pointed to two small cubs standing behind a redbud tree just a few feet away from their mother. "She's got cubs with her."

Joshua lowered his weapon as he watched her pound her paws on the ground and pop her jaws several times warning the men to stay away before she turned and walked away with her cubs by her side. Within a few moments the bears had blended into the shadows of the trees and were out of sight, leaving the men behind, looking at each other.

"You know, we probably should have gone on and shot all three of them," Samuel said, "If we are going to settle out here, we'll need to get rid of all these bears so our cattle will be safe out in the fields."

"Yeah, but that's a few years away from now," Joshua said. "We'll just let them go for now."

"Just like those two Indians I saw yesterday," William said as he looked at his brother, "see, it's not always easy to shoot."

"Yeah, I reckon not." Joshua answered.

Chapter 66
Back to the Falls

It had taken a day and a half to get back to the falls safely. Yesterday's ride had been much easier on William's wounded arm, as the party had decided to take a slower pace in the days travel after they re-crossed the Kentucky River. The weather had cooled down some and everyone enjoyed being able to ride their new horses even though they were about to give them over to James Ray. They had decided to stop for the night at the foot of a high knob about fifty miles from the falls. The knob was in the shape of a horseshoe and its summit was densely covered with all types of hardwoods. William had seen it from a good distance away, and thought to himself that it would be difficult to get lost in this area because the knob could be seen from miles around. Ray had informed William and the others that Squire Boone, the brother of Daniel, had built a small station about eight miles northwest of this knob on the waters of a creek he called Clear Creek. Unfortunately, like so many other settlers, he too had trouble with the Indians and had to flee his Painted Stone station back to Boonesborough for safety. This brought a smile to William and Joshua's faces, because they both knew that Samuel Boone, the gunsmith who had made their rifles was the uncle of none other than this Squire Boone, Jr.

While out hunting for supper, Samuel had killed a doe and even though it was probably a stupid thing to do, the men decided to build a fire and cook it. After eating they agreed it would be best to move on to a cold camp where no more fires would be made, so they traveled about five more miles and stopped for the night. There was a little daylight left, so William brought out his Bible and read the story of Jephthah from the Old Testament to the others.

Finally, late this morning they arrived back on Corn Island. James Ray did not stay very long, he wanted to put some miles behind him before dark so he soon had the horses tied together, one behind the other for his return trip home. William bid him goodbye, shook his hand, and wished him well as he watched the young man head back towards Ft. Harrod all alone. It was hard to believe that Hugh McGray would allow his stepson to travel by himself after James' brother William had been killed just last summer, but every family is different in their ways.

William had overheard what Jemima Calloway had said to James as they left Boonesborough. And last night after dark, Ray had told the men his story of how he and his brother were ambushed while working in the fields tapping maple trees. William Ray was killed outright but James. Being fleet of foot had outrun the Indians back to the fort. Once James told what had happened, James Harrod and Hugh McGray had gotten into an argument over what to do next. Harrod felt that McGray was letting his emotions take control of his better judgment by wanting to rush off in pursuit of the Indians, but he cautioned that they needed to take time to form a plan of attack and proceed with a bit more caution. The situation had become so heated and the two became so angry at each other that they actually pointed their rifles at one another. They may have even pulled their triggers if not for Mrs. McGray, who boldly stepped between the two and stayed between them until cooler heads prevailed.

Later on, that fall, McGray had killed an Indian who was wearing the shirt of his dead step-son and had completely mutilated the Indian's body. William feared that if young James was captured. he would most likely fall to the same fate as that Indian. The Indians and the McGray and Ray families most definitely had it out for each other.

Beside his concern for James' safety William had another reason to hope his young friend made it back alive. If not, his and his friend's deeds would never be recorded and their dreams of land in Kentucky would die with young Ray. As William lost sight of his brave new friend he marveled at the resolve and character bred in the men who daily faced and conquered the hardships of living on the frontier. It would be men like James Ray who would keep the western migration moving.

William turned and noticed that while he and the others had been only gone a few days things had changed here in their absence. The settlers had moved off Corn Island and were in the process of building a stockade on the Kentucky side of the river. Richard Chenoweth had already torn apart his flatboat and was using the lumber to build a cabin for his family. William also heard from Basil that Captain Rogers had given his flatboat to the Chenoweth Family as well. That meant they were definitely not going back upriver on it, but they could still sleep on it at night for the captain had retained use of it until their stay on the island was over. So, tonight William and Joshua once again walked Corn Island. They were surprised to see sitting among the many fires burning non-other than their old friend from Duncan's Tavern, James Knox.

"You don't have any Maryland hams to trade, do you?" asked William as he sat down next to the old hunter.

"No sonny, I'm afraid that ham is long gone, but I see you still have my shoepacks," Knox answered as he laid a buffalo bone on the fire in front of him.

"Well, it looks like you boys made it down here after all. So, what do you think of Kentucky?" he asked as he picked up another bone from the fire.

"Well enough to claim one tract and buy another," Joshua answered.

"Really" Knox said as he smashed open the end of the bone with his tomahawk against a flat rock. He put the opened end of the bone into his mouth and sucked out the hot marrow, all the while looking over to William. "So, you've already been out into the woods then and made it back alive." he continued as he turned his bone around and placed the other end into the fire, so he could finish off both ends of his delicacy.

"Are you going to stay here with Clark?" William asked.

"Nah, I'm heading further on down to the Green River. Going to try my luck at hunting this beast here." he said as he cracked open another bone. "You boys want to come along?"

"Nope, can't. We're waiting for Major Linn to come up from New Orleans." Joshua answered.

"Well hell boys, I think he is already here. A keelboat is tied up down there on the other side of the falls. You all better go and see if it's him."

William and Joshua made their way down to the westernmost end of the island and there they saw a keelboat beached on the Kentucky shore. It had to be Major Linn's boat for there were several men on the well-lit deck armed with rifles and mounted on the boats front bow was a small swiveling cannon. Cannon would be needed to protect a boat such as Major Linns which would be carrying a large load of gunpowder. Having seen this well armed boat, William could not help but feel that his return trip back upriver would be much safer.

Chapter 67
The Portage

William grabbed the reins that ran from the yoke and down the backs of the two oxen that he had come to love on his trip downriver. He gave them the usual flip of the wrist and said, "Come on boys, give her a good pull. Walk forward." At his command, the two oxen began their first hard hauls of the day, pulling Major Linn's keelboat out of the Ohio River and onto the Kentucky bank. On each side of the oxen was another tow line connected to the boat with 25 men on each line helping to pull. After a small amount of digging away of the riverbank, slowly but surely, the keelboat began to rise up out of the water and onto dry land. As soon as the backside of the craft ran upon the grass, ten more men fell in behind the boat and began to push. The portage around Corn Island and the Ohio Falls had begun. Joshua and Samuel were on the right line while James and Basil were on the left one. Major Linn was directing the men on the lines while Captain Rogers was in command of a crew of axmen cutting a path for the boat to pass thru the woods and around the island and back down to the river. The men had already unloaded the cargo making the craft as light as possible. The boat was moving at a fairly good rate William thought. Its hull was cutting just a few inches into the topsoil as it ran along on top of the ground. The valuable kegs of gunpowder were waiting for the boat on the other side of the island. George Rogers Clark was making sure it was kept safe by putting several men on guard around the desperately needed powder. William and the other men in Major Linn's crew were thankful to Clark for the assistance of all the extra men on the lines. If his small army had not been here, this would have been a much more difficult portage that it was now. Their presence also gave Major Linn another greatly appreciated asset, an army to guard the boat while it was on dry land. What Indian wouldn't give his right arm to find a boat and a supply of gunpowder on dry land with only a small crew to watch over it?

As the boat was being dragged along, a group of spectators walked beside it, watching this odd sight of a boat with no water under it going over dry land. Occasionally, they would stop and cheer the men along who were manning the lines.

The lay of the land was also a big help for there were no big hills to climb, but there were a few small ones here and there. The boat only stopped on two occasions. Once to remove a large rock blocking the way and the second time for the men to get a good foothold as they went up a small hill. As the day heated up, Major Linn called for a stop to change the fatigue detail, allowing fresh men to take up the lines to pull the last half of the portage. Now they were pulling while their predecessors laughed and cheered them on for a change.

William stayed with the red oxen, not wanting to leave them in the hands of someone who might push them too hard. After all they were a part of his crew. As he walked behind the cattle, he could hear the water running over the rapids to his left even though he could not see them for the trees that were blocking his view. It was a welcome sound for it let him know that the end of this portage was almost at hand. He knew that soon he would be heading back upriver. He had been looking forward to seeing Kentucky on his trip downstream but now he was looking forward to getting back home to the loving arms of Elizabeth and his small daughter, who had to have grown quite a bit while he was gone.

After a lot of blood and sweat, the keelboat finally reached the waters of the Ohio one more time. The boat was pulled up alongside the river as close as they could get it with the two oxen, then a group of men walked up to the front of the boat and pushed its nose into the water, where it stuck in the mud. Then the rear of the craft was likewise pushed down causing the water to splash as the boat re-entered the river. Soon a few well-placed poles had pushed the keelboat out into the deeper waters of the river and the portage was over.

Chapter 68
So Long Captain Rogers

Late that afternoon Captain Rogers and Basil were unloading their belongings off the flatboat, but unlike William and the rest of the Captain's old crew they were not storing their gear away on Major Linn's keelboat. They were packing a canoe instead. As William watched the two finished their work, he approached the Captain and said, "It looks as though you two are not going back to Fort Pitt with us".

"That's right." the Captain said as he stepped away from the fully loaded canoe. "I guess the cats out of the bag now, so I may as well tell you. We are going on down to New Orleans. My orders were if Major Linn's buying trip went well, then I was to do the same. Strike while the iron is still hot so to speak. You never know when the Spanish will stop selling to us, so we're going to get it while the getting is good. Basil here is going along to steer our new keelboat back upriver. He's not in such a hurry to get back home as you are. Major Linn will pay you boys when you get back, so don't worry about that."

"Oh, I wasn't thinking about our pay Captain," William answered, "I just wanted to know what's going on."

"Is that why you stayed here instead of going inland with us?" William asked Basil.

"Yeah, we had already talked it over," Basil said as he nodded his head towards Captain Rogers. "After Ross pulled his stunt the Captain thought it would be best to keep it as quiet as possible."

"I can understand that," William said as he took Basil's hand into his and said, "I want to thank you for all the help and information you gave us on Gibson. We'll miss you going back upriver."

Basil just laughed, not knowing quite what to do then he put his hand on William's shoulder and said, "All you boys will get back just fine, the major's crew know what to do. I'll see you back at Pittsburgh."

"When are you pushing off?" William asked as he turned back to Captain Rogers.

"As soon as you push us out into the water," Rogers replied as he stepped into the canoe and sat down in its front picking up an oar. William gave the back of the canoe a good hard push out into the water and gave the two men one last wave goodbye as the Captain yelled back over his shoulder. "We'll miss having your gun William, take care."

As he watched the two shoot over the white caps of the falls and go out sight, William wondered how much money Captain Rogers must have hidden away on that canoe. It had to be a large sum to buy a boat load of black powder. If Ross Gibson had known about this, he probably would have stayed away from the Chenoweth girl and kept a closer eye on the Captain.

William walked away from the riverbank wanting to find Joshua and tell him the news. As he was walking through the new Kentucky settlement, he could hear the pounding of hammers and see the swinging of axes. This was not going to set really well with the Indians he thought to himself as he walked along. Then at the edge of the still unnamed town he saw Simon Butler who must have been out on a spying mission, talking to George Rogers Clark under a chestnut tree. Clark was sitting on a stump, listening intently, while Butler was giving his report. Clark jumped to his feet and gave Simon a slap on the back, seemingly very happy with whatever it was Simon had just told him. Then the two of them walked away down into the trees and out of sight. William thought that the two must have some kind of plan worked out from the way they were acting, but whatever it was he would not find out what it was unless they told it tonight because, tomorrow morning Major Linn's keelboat was going to take him home.

Chapter 69
Shoulder Poles

Going back upriver was a whole lot more work than it had been going down. This new method of using shoulder poles was hard on the back as well as the hands. It took ten men at a time, five on each side of the boat. They would stick their poles into the water and let it sink all the way to the bottom, and then they would push off the riverbed, walking along the side of the boat for the entire fifty-five-foot length of the craft from bow to stern. The only good thing about this whole process was that Major Linn's crew was big enough that they could take shifts. If the wind would cooperate, the sails could also help with the constant fight against the hard, swift head current of the Ohio. If all went well, the boat could go upstream about twenty to twenty-two miles a day, so it would take a month of long hard days to pole back to Pittsburgh.

The first ten days had been routine and uneventful, but on occasion William would have a good day, when he and the boys could get off the boat and do some hunting for the crew's nightly meals. Last night a canoe had come downriver with two hunters who had stopped and was staying with the keelboat at least until the sun came up this morning. Like old James Knox, they too were out for buffalo, but they had some news that would greatly change the course of the war. The French had finally entered the war. Their army would be much appreciated, but their navy was the most important asset they would bring to the American's cause. The British could move their troops much easier and faster with their navy and they had blockaded most of the harbors along the seaboard. The French navy should be able to help neutralize the English fleet. At any rate this should help speed up the outcome of the war one way or the other, if these two men knew what they were talking about. William hoped it was not just another wild rumor, but Major Linn had also heard while he was still in New Orleans that a French alliance was very much in the works, so maybe there was truth in what the two men had told them.

Once again, William found himself under the command of a man he liked. Captain Babb had become much more than just William's militia commander, he was a good friend. His time under General Hand had been short but not too bad. Simon Girty had treated William with respect while out spying on the Indians, and Captain Rogers was a good and fair man while coming downriver. So far, Major Linn had been more than tolerable on this trip. He didn't say much, but that was a good thing as far as William was concerned. The last thing the crew needed was an overbearing commander on this long return trip upriver. William had felt tuckered out from the day's work and had gone inside the boat's cabin and had quickly fallen asleep. Not long afterwards Samuel, who was just coming off guard duty had entered the cabin and woke him up with a shake of his arm and said, "Come on William, get up, you'll want to see this." William got up from his bunk and walked out onto the deck and there he and the rest of the crew watched the beginnings of an eclipse of the moon. The light began to fade little by little and soon the men standing on deck were leaving no shadow at all on its wooden floor. Within minutes the moon was in full eclipse. William looked over to Samuel and said, "Maybe like the moon, ole King George will soon be losing his power over the landscape of this continent and we will be able to provide it with our own light instead.

Joshua looked over to James and said, "We need to get him off this boat, he's thinking way too much."

Chapter 70
A Cry for Help

James was entertaining the crew up at the front of the boat with one of his wild tales of love and conquest. The young woman in question was not far away, but just up ahead at Fort Randolph. It seemed that while Captain Rogers was out rounding up his canoe that night and the rest of the men were sleeping away in the fort. James had indulged himself with the company of one of the few females at the fort on their way down river just over a month ago. She had a beau who was out of the fort that night and James had managed to steal away a few kisses from her while he was gone. Now that Major Linn's boat was inching closer to civilization, James was hoping that this fellow would be out hunting again. "Yeah, she is a pretty little thing," he said as he stretched out his arms up into the air and cinched his fingers together before placing them back down on top of his head.

"Why didn't you let me see her?" Samuel asked, "Where was I at?"

"Hell, I don't know," James replied. "I sure wasn't going to look you up while I had her in my sights," he said laughing. Then he looked Samuel in the eye and said, "I mean you're a fine looking fellow and all, Samuel, but she had you beat!"
"Well I sure hope she does," Samuel shot back, "If I look better than she does, I sure wouldn't be bragging to everyone or even telling anybody at all that she was that ugly, and that I was kissing on her as well. Nah, I would keep my mouth shut if I was you." The entire group began to laugh and chuckle at Samuel's quick response when over the water everyone heard the sound of a man's voice.

"James, I hope that's not her man looking you up," Joshua said as he looked over to the northern bank with a grin on his face. "What's he saying anyway? Can anyone tell?"

"Stop, please stop. I need help." the lone man shouted from the shore.

Major Linn looked out over the water to where the man was and then ordered his helmsman to keep the boat in the center of the river. Then he raised one of his hands to his face and cupped it around his mouth and yelled, "Who are you?"

"Paul Johnston, my boat was attacked by the Indians last night, I out ran them but now I don't have a gun. Please come over and pick me up. If you don't they will catch me for sure."

"Swim out to us." Linn called to the stranded man.

"I can't swim," replied Johnston, "come on, stop for God's sake. I am no threat to you. Look at me!" he yelled as he held out his arms in a non-threatening manner.

"If you can't swim out at least part of the way, then I can't help you," Linn called back. "This is your last chance to come aboard. Now swim out now or we'll leave you behind."

"I can't. I'll drown for sure." the man yelled as he was walking along the river bank parallel to the boat.

Major Linn turned his back to the man and walked up to the front of the boat and sat down in his cane bottomed rocking chair and said, "Don't pick him up."

William looked to the canoe at the back of the boat and thought 'why not pick him up in it instead?' He approached the Major and volunteered to paddle over to the shore and help the man.

"No, you stay where you are Tipton; let's see how he reacts for a while."

William didn't answer, he just walked over to the rail of the boat and primed the pan of his rifle and watched the man run along beside the river begging for them to stop.

"What do you think William?" Joshua asked.

"I don't know," William answered. "It could be some kind of trick. He is on the Indian shore and there are a lot of trees up on that bank. They could be hiding up there in an ambush.

"But you wanted to go and get him," Samuel said as he watched the man still walking along the bank.

"Yeah, but that was my heart talking, not my head. The major could very well be right. He may have just saved my life."

James looked over at the Major and said, "He's right, and what kind of name is Johnson anyway? Maybe a made up one, don't you think. We better watch the shoreline for canoes.

Soon all the men had their weapons in good firing order and ready for any attack that may fall upon them, if this man was not telling the truth.

An hour soon went by, then two, but Johnson did not change his story. He kept pace with the boat all the while pleading for help. But the more he talked the more suspicious the crew got. He was far enough away that you could not make out his facial features but something about this Johnson seemed to be familiar to William. Something about his walk reminded William of someone, but he couldn't quite put his finger on who it was. Finally, the Major stood up out of his chair and walked over to where William and the others were and said, "This is where we find out if he's telling the truth or not. Look ahead, no more trees to hide in on the bank." Johnson fell to his knees at the end of the tree line and screamed out one more time, "For the love of God, please stop. I can't go on anymore."

As the river made a little turn in its course Ross Gibson stood up off the ground as a war party walked out of the trees and came down to the water's edge and stood beside him. As they watched the boat go on upriver one of the parties handed Gibson his gun. He took it and laid its barrel up on his shoulder and said to Blackhoof, "We'll get 'em next time my friend."

William looked over to Joshua with an astonished look on his face and said, "Another kind of cowbell."

Chapter 71
What Times We Live In

The crew of the keelboat could see that Fort Randolph had a hard summer while they had been gone to Kentucky. The corn that had been planted outside the walls of the fort had been completely destroyed by the Indians. They had simply pulled the stalks out of the ground and left them lying there in the hot summer sun to die. The corn had tasseled out but the ears had not been fully developed. All the work of the settlers inside the fort had gone for nothing. The remains of several rotten cows still lay outside the fort walls giving off the foul smell of death. They too had fallen victim to the Indians, they were shot as they grazed on the grass outside the fort. The Indians had lurked around outside the walls of the fort long enough to prevent the settlers from even butchering the meat of their dead cattle. This shooting of cattle had become a common practice of the Indians, because they thought if the white eyes killed their buffalo, it was only fair for the Indians to do the same to their cattle. It looked as though these people were going to have to endure a hard winter with the loss of their grain and cattle.

Major Linn had ordered two kegs of powder be left here for the fort's defense and that four men were to accompany him and the powder to the fort's gates while the rest of the crew were to stay aboard and watch over the remaining of the cargo.
William wanted to see how Andy Forbes was getting along, as did Joshua so the Major let them help escort the powder in. James was hoping to meet up with his sweet kissing gal while Samuel wanted to see what she looked like. So, as the boat ran   aground, Samuel and Joshua quickly jumped off the boat and began to steer the wheelbarrow carrying the gunpowder up the hill to the fort's gates. William and James walked alongside with their rifles at the ready while the major brought up the rear of the landing party. "Come on boys, let's get that powder up that hill as fast as possible," he said. Hearing this, Samuel and Joshua each holding one handle of the

wheelbarrow picked up their pace as they pushed towards the fort. William had been holding his rifle in just one hand next to his hip, but then he saw a freshly dug grave about fifty feet from the fort. Seeing this last resting place of some unfortunate soul, he quickly raised his rifle to a firing position as he peered into the surrounding tree line.

The gates swung out as they reached the fort and out stepped Captain Arbuckle with several other men. "Good Lord is that powder?" he asked as he looked into the wheelbarrow. Samuel sat down the wheelbarrow and said, "Yes sir it is and it's never been fired either. Not once."

Smiles crept over William and James's faces, but they quickly disappeared when they saw how little the Captain thought of Samuel's joke. One of the men took the handle away from Samuel and wheeled it inside the gate. The Major and Captain Arbuckle entered the fort behind the powder leaving the others still outside.

Joseph Casey one of the fort's defenders looked to the others and said, "They're not here anymore. If they were, they would have killed these boys by now." He reached into his belt and pulled out his knife and turned to the wall of the fort. He stuck his knife into the wood wall and carved out a spent lead ball. He looked over to Joshua and said, "Did you bring lead too? We're running low on that as well."

Joshua answered "No" as he too began to pick out the remains of some Indians' missed shots. Soon most of the men who were inside the fort had come out and were also retrieving lead from the fort's riddled walls.

Samuel and James went on into the forts to find the young lady in question, while William helped carve out the lead balls. He dropped one into the pail that all the balls were being placed in, soon to be melted down and remolded into new ones. He asked, "How is Andy?" to the buck skinner standing beside him.

"Who's Andy?" Casey asked, still intent on the task at hand.

"You know, the fellow who was shot in the leg that we left here when we came down river back in the spring."

Casey began to nod his head at him and said, "You just passed his grave. He died about a week ago. His leg finally went bad and they cut it off, but he died a few days later." William, Joshua, and their new talkative friend walked back down to the grave and looked at it. They had not known Andy very well, just a few days really, but they were nevertheless upset to find him dead.

"Hell, nobody will ever know where his body was laid to rest in a few years' time without some kind of marker or stone." William said as he looked down at the grave. "Why hasn't there been one put up?"

"We don't put up stones anymore. The last time we did them damn varmints packed them off so we don't bother anymore" answered Casey.

Major Linn re-emerged from the fort and said "Come on boys, we're not staying here tonight, too many Indians running around here for my taste. I believe we will be safer to keep on moving upriver. Is that your friend you were talking about?"

"Yeah," William said.

"Sorry to hear it," the major said as he continued onto the boat. "What times we live in."

As the boat was being untied James and Samuel came running down the hill to the river pushing the empty wheelbarrow in front of them. With one toss they pitched it onto the boat and jumped aboard.

"Well now, did you get that kiss?" Joshua asked as he looked at James.

"Not this time around." James answered laughing. "Her man was the one who helped us unload that powder. He was even loading up his rifle as we were leaving, so I thought it best to just go while we were ahead."

"Did he know who you were," William asked?

"No but I was not going to stand around and let him find out either," James replied as he looked back over his shoulder to the fort's gates.

Chapter 72
Gibson's Lie

Gibson lay under the low-lying branches of a cedar tree next to his ex-Brother-In-Law, Blackhoof, the Shawnee sub war chief.

"That's them for sure," he said as he was spying on the keelboat across the river at Point Pleasant. I was not quite sure that it was him when I was walking along the riverbank calling to them, but now I am."

"Which one is he brother, point him out to me, so I may know who to kill for the death of my sister and her children," spoke the Shawnee.

"The one up in front, that's him! The killer of women and children! I'd know that son of a bitch anywhere," yelled the lying Gibson.

"This is good. We have been waiting a long time for his blood. Now is our time to sell his scalp to the British."

"What is that they are unloading from the boat?" Gibson asked as he peered across the river to the other shore with squinted eyes.

"Fire powder," answered Blackhoof. "They are taking it to the fort. We will not only kill the white eyes we will take his power to make war as well" Blackhoof relished.

"How much do you say is in the boat? She looks low in the water to me," replied Gibson." I'd say enough for one whole summer and maybe one winter as well my brother.

"So that is him in the front." Blackhoof said, as he reached down and pulled out his knife. He looked back across the river to the man he hated most of all in this world, but this was the first time he had ever seen the man who had killed his beloved sister. He made a long cut along his forehead with the blade. "We bleed for my sister tonight, but soon he will bleed much more for her."

"Soon he will be ours," Gibson said as he took the knife from Blackhoof's hand and made a small cut on his own brow. Blackhoof crawled backward out from under the tree as the blood ran down the side of his face. He walked around to the other side of his horse where he reached into a buckskin bag and pulled out some black and red paint and began to rub it on his face. Half an hour later Gibson came out from the trees and said, "They are not staying here tonight. They are going on up to Wheeling."

"Good." Blackhoof said as he jumped on his horse's back with one side of his face painted black and mixed with his own dried blood and the other side painted red. He looked down at Gibson with wild looking eyes and said, "We'll ride ahead and pick our killing field for the killer of mothers.

Gibson mounted his horse with a solemn look on his face, but inside he was smiling, because his plan was coming together. Major Linn's appearance matched the fictitious description he had given Blackhoof of his sister's supposed killer all those years ago. Linn was of the right age and height while all the other men on the boat were way too young to have taken part in Pontiac's war. If everything went according to plan, both men would be happy. Blackhoof would have his revenge, and take Gibson back into his good graces and as a bonus Gibson would get another shot at William.

Chapter 73
Ambushed

"Fort Henry," William said as he looked out over the small village of Wheeling from the deck of the keelboat. You know what's after that, don't you Joshua?" he asked as he primed the pan of his rifle.

"Yeah, I do. Fort Pitt," Joshua answered, "and after that, sweet Polly's arms. We're almost home brother."

"That's right," James added, "so you boys better look up those girls in those cabins this time around. It's going to be your last chance to see them before you get home."

"Haven't you been paying any attention to that Bible reading I've been doing all summer?" William asked.

"Yes, I have and I've enjoyed it too," James answered as he jumped off the boat and tied down the anchor line to a tree on the bank. "But we don't have to worry about Gibson tonight like we did the last time we were here, so you can see them tonight."

"That's true enough," William answered, "but this time around I plan on getting some sleep. Pushing those poles all day can take it out of a man. Here's your rifle."

Upriver from Wheeling, pulled from the water onto the bank and hidden under some brush were ten canoes belonging to Blackhoof and Gibson's war party. They had been in place since morning and now the long wait was going to pay off, for Major Linn's boat had finally run aground. The Indians could see his crew out on deck. The crewmen had their weapons in hand but were not paying any attention to the tree line above because they were engaged in talking to one another. Blackhoof's plan was to let them get halfway up the hill to the fort before his warriors were to open fire. This would make it difficult for the white eyes to run for cover, no matter in which direction they would decide to run. Halfway to the fort or back to the boat either way they would be exposed to the Indian's fire. But the most important order Blackhoof had given was that no one was to fire until the major was off the boat.

Blackhoof pulled back the hammer of his rifle as he watched a man jump off the boat and tie down the keelboat to the shore line. Then one of the other men handed him his rifle and he too jumped onto the bank with his rifle in his hand. Soon the entire crew was off the boat, standing around the bank, talking to each other, about fifteen in number, but the Major was nowhere to be seen. This made Blackhoof a little anxious; for he had been waiting a long time to kill the murderer of his sister. This may be his only shot at this man and he wanted to make it count.

Gibson also had his man picked out among the crew. He had graciously given Blackhoof the honor of killing the killer of his sister, but there was a man on this boat who had challenged his own manhood and Gibson wanted him to pay for that mistake with his life. So as the ambush party sat in the tree line, Gibson leveled his aim on that young man as he walked up the hill talking to his brother.

Blackhoof looked down his ambush line and motioned for all his warriors to hold their fire until the white eyed Major stepped off his boat, but one of the Indians at the end of the line took this signal to be the order to fire and he did. The shot rang out and his aim was true, the ball slammed into a crewman's chest killing him instantly after it had ricocheted off the rifle he was carrying. He would never know what just happened to him.

Fire raged in Blackhoof's eye as he saw the white eye Major duck behind the cover of the keelboat rail. Gibson, seeing that the surprise of the ambush was over also fired his musket at his mark. His target fell to the ground and rolled over behind the protection of a nearby stump, but Gibson felt he had delivered a killing shot to the man. By now all of the Indians had shot their weapons but their fire was ineffective, hitting only a few of the crew members. The Indians rushed forward screaming at the top of their lungs as they ran into the clearing of the fort's outer yard. The boat's surviving crew returned fire on the rushing Indians, knocking many of the Shawnee to the ground but now they too had empty guns in their hands. The white eye major seeing what was happening, fired his small cannon from the front of his keelboat into the rushing Indians tearing a hole in their line. The cannon's percussion knocked Blackhoof and Gibson off their feet and they both rolled over behind the same stump where Gibson's victim had fallen.

William had already fired his rifle as soon as the Indians rushed out of the trees and now, he had only his pistol left to fire at the two men who were on him at close range, but they both seemed a bit dazed by the fire of the cannon. William reached over for the closest man and put the muzzle of his gun to his head and held it there not wanting to fire it, leaving him with no shot to kill the other Indian with. For the second time in William's life he realized he was not fighting an Indian, but just like on the boat it was Ross Gibson that he was holding his pistol on. Blackhoof began to regain his wits and rolled over onto his knees and looked into Williams' eyes. He pulled his tomahawk from his belt as he watched William pull back the hammer of his pistol leveled at the head of Blackhoof's brother-In-law. There they all three sat for a few seconds, each thinking over his options.

William finally broke the silence and said to Gibson, "If I can only kill one of you, you can bet your ass it's going to be you, you son of a bitch. Any man who can kill his own wife and children for scalp money deserves to die like the devil you are."

Blackhoof screamed out as he jumped forward from his kneeling position and sunk his tomahawk into Gibson's skull. William dropped Gibson's body and scrambled backward away from the two men while Blackhoof delivered a second blow into the chest of his sister's killer. William heard the Shawnee say a few words to Gibson in the Indian language as he pulled his tomahawk free from Gibson's chest. Gibson opened his mouth to say something but all that came from between his rotten teeth was air. He died looking up into heaven, a place that he would never go.

William pointed his pistol at the Shawnee chief, not knowing what has just happened as the Indian ignored him and lifted Gibson's greasy scalp. Why would this Indian kill Gibson like that? Then William's eye picked up the retreating Indians running past the two of them and Blackhoof ran off with them leaving William behind with Gibson's dead body.

William jumped to his feet and called out, "Joshua! Are you alright? Are you hit?"

"No, I'm alright," Joshua answered.

"Samuel, what about you" William asked?

"Still alive, but James has been hit." Samuel cried as he stood over his wounded friend as the two Tipton brothers ran to Samuel's side.

James sat up and put his hand on the side of his neck where a ball had just passed cutting through his flesh. "Damn," James said as he looked up at his comrades, "four inches to the center and my head would have come plum off. William where is your Bible? My wild days are over!"

William closed his eyes and shook his head saying, "That was a pretty sharp battle."

Chapter 74
Take Him For A Swim

The ambush was bloody for both sides. Besides Ross Gibson the Indians had lost thirteen warriors, nine of which had been killed by Major Linn's cannon fire. Several others had also been wounded, but they were either carried off by their comrades or had limped away on their own power. Some of them would very likely die from their wounds later on. The Major had lost two of his crew for sure and maybe a third. The first was a German immigrant who spoke little English. He had been the first to fall probably never knowing what had happened. The other, ironically was one of the men who had come aboard with Gibson back at Ft. Pitt as part of Captain Roger's flat-boat crew. The Captain had always called him by his last name, simply Hardin and since he was with Gibson no one had ever asked what his given name was. He had been on the friendliest of terms with Gibson, but after Gibson escaped, he stayed to himself, hardly talking to anyone. Five others including James, had been wounded. All were gunshot wounds from the initial volley made by the Indians. No doubt many others would have died if not for Major Linn's timely cannon fire. The Indians were running in with tomahawks and scalping knives, ready to finish them off when the cannon shot turned the tide of battle. James had the least serious wound; the ball had only grazed his neck. He was bleeding heavily, making it look much worse that it really was. He was able to walk with little trouble, so it seemed he would do alright. The worst of the wounded was a man from Westmoreland County, Pennsylvania by the name of John Richardson. He had been gut shot and had little hope of survival. The other wounds consisted of a fellow with a broken arm below the elbow, one with a leg wound and the last man had a hip wound. All three should heal up fairly well, but you never knew about things like that, Andy's wounded leg did not look that bad at first either, so who knows what condition they will be in five or six days from now.

Ebenezer Zane had led a group of men from the fort after the retreating Indians upriver. A few gun shots had been heard in the distance, but no one had come back yet with news of what had happened or which side had fired their weapons.

The Major had moved the wounded Richardson into Fort Henry and told William and the others to stay at the boat and stand guard over it while he was inside. Soon after, a detachment of men walked out of the gates toward the river.

"What are they doing?" Samuel asked as he ran his ramrod down into his rifle to clean its barrel. No one answered as they watched the men split up into groups of two. Then each pair bent over and grabbed a foot of a dead warrior.

"They must be going to bury them," William answered as he watched them drag the Indians toward the river.

"I don't know about that," James said as he stood up from the chair he was sitting in while holding a blood-soaked rag to his wounded neck. He began to smile as he watched the men dragging the Indians' bodies over to the water's edge. One man walked around and bent over and grabbed the hands of the corpse while his partner held on to both feet. Together they hefted up the body and after a few swings they let go and watched as the Indians' body splashed into the Ohio. The warrior's body turned over onto his stomach, leaving only his shoulders and the back of his head out of the water as it floated down past the keelboat.

"That's some kind of sendoff, ain't it?" Joshua said as he raised one foot up on the boat's rail and leaned over resting his elbow on his knee. "Hell, I believe I shot that one."

"I don't know if I would even do that." announced James. "If they wouldn't stink up the place, I'd just let the buzzards have at 'em."

"Well, you know we need to tend to our dead too." William said. "It's going to be dark soon, so we better get at it."

Within thirty minutes two more graves were dug. Hardin was placed in one while the German was laid to rest in the other. As William and Samuel were covering the bodies with the topsoil they had just dug from of the grave sites, two soldiers from the fort walked up packing Gibson's body and said, "You boys missed one of your men."

"No, we didn't!" answered James, "that son of a bitch was with the Indians. You can throw his ass in the river too as far as we're concerned!"

"He's not with you then?" the other soldier asked.

"No," replied William as he wiped the sweat from his forehead. "He was probably the mastermind of the whole ambush. He's a damn turncoat. You can take him for a swim too."

Hearing this news, instead of carrying Gibson's body as a show of respect as they had been when they approached William and James, the two soldiers dropped his body and drug him to the river like they had the Indians. But before they could let the fish have at him Ebenezer Zane returned with his men.

"Stop that! What on God's green Earth are you doing?" he bellowed. "Give that man a proper burial!"

"He was with the Indians according to them," the soldier explained as he pointed up to William and the others.

"Oh, is that so? Well we need to make an example of him then." Zane said as he drew out his sword. He walked over to where Gibson lay and with one quick downward slice of his sword, he decapitated Gibson's body. "Put it on a pole high in the air down by the waterfront as a warning not to go over the Indians." Zane ordered as he picked up the head by its ear. "Maybe then the next fellow will think twice before he jumps sides."

Chapter 75
Weary

August had been a hot month and the mosquitoes had been extremely active on the river, but they were much less fearsome than the Indians who seemed to have disappeared since the attack at Wheeling. Only a few fires had been seen on the northern side of the river and they were always at night, far up in the woods. The river traffic had slowed down as well. Few boats or canoes had passed by going downriver as Major Linns party made this last leg of the keelboat's return trip home.

William and the other crew members were beginning to fall prey to riverboat fever. They had been on this damn boat for a good while now with little news of what was going on with the war back east. The last news they had received was of the French entering the war and that had been a good while back. But that was nothing compared to what William was feeling about the lack of news about his young family back home. He missed the feel of Elizabeth's soft skin and the sound of her voice. The good-natured smile she always had on her face when he was teasing her, the smell of her long hair and the feel of her gentle touch. And then there was little Sarah. How much had she changed since his departure? Could she be walking now, or maybe even saying a few words? William was not even sure what he was missing, since she was his first child. He had never paid much attention to how other children had grown in the past, but he knew he was missing out and he wanted to be home. He was weary of being stabbed and shot at, as well as seeing families destroyed by Indian attacks like the one with the burned-out boat. He was tired of digging graves for men who had gone to Kentucky, men very much like himself. But now that he could once again see the tall walls of Fort Pitt from the deck of this boat, he knew he would be back in Elizabeth's loving arms soon. His first venture into Kentucky had been hard but profitable. He was coming home with a new tract of land for his family, but he knew it would be a good while before he would settle there. He loved his family way too much to risk their lives in a move there now. The war would have to be won and the Indians dealt with somehow before he would return with Elizabeth and Sarah to build his home on top of that hill.

"Well, we made it back alive boys!" proclaimed Major Linn as he stepped up onto the deck. "I still believe that it was worth the trouble," he continued. "We have a lot of powder here to throw into the war. You boys can be proud of what we've done. It's going to be a great help to the cause."

Reaching into his pocket he handed each crew member a slip of paper as they made their way off the boat. "Take that to the paymaster inside the fort. He'll settle all accounts. There will be another flat-boat heading back to the falls in a few days to meet Captain Rogers on his way back up from New Orleans if you're interested."

"I'll go." said a voice from the bank.

"Watson, is that you?" Major Linn asked.

"Yeah, I was drunk and missed him on his way down, but I would like to meet him at the falls and head back upriver with him."

"Well, I don't know who's going to lead that party downriver, it's not going to be me, but I'll put in a word for you Watson." the Major said. "I know you're a good river man. Just be sure to keep the cork in the bottle this time, eh?"

William looked over to Joshua and said, "Watson may be on that boat, but I sure as hell won't be!"

Chapter 76
Mustering Out

Captain Babb had once again come through for William and his friends. As soon as they had all gotten off the boat they headed straight to the paymaster's office inside Ft. Pitt. They wanted to get their pay as soon as possible and head for home. Joshua had come here on horseback. He had left the animal at the fort's stable while he was gone downriver, so he needed no mount for the return trip home. However, William and James had marched to Ft. Pitt, only riding when they were out hunting for the militia. Their plan was to buy a couple of horses so they could ride back home as well.

Samuel was the first to present his voucher to the paymaster who was sitting behind a rough oak desk. After he received his pay, he stepped to the side and waited for the others to do the same. William was next in line and handed over the paper to the paymaster who read William's name on the document. As he began to hand over William's pay, he looked up and said, "We weren't sure if you boys were coming back for those horses or not. We were beginning to think the fort would have two more mounts for our men this fall, but I guess not."

"What horses?" William asked.

"The horses that Captain Babb left here for you, what's the other man's name?" the paymaster asked as he pulled open the desk drawer and reached inside picking up a piece of paper and looked down over the top of his glasses and said, "James Tate, yeah, that him, James Tate."

"That's me." James said as he handed over his voucher.

"Damn Tate." the officer said as he pushed his eye glasses back up to the top of the bridge of his nose while taking the paper out of James' hand "Looks like we almost got to keep your horse by the looks of your neck."

"Well, I'm glad you didn't." James replied as he placed his hand on the side of his neck where his wound was. The paymaster just smiled as he handed over the money to James. Then Joshua took his turn. Once more the paymaster read the name on the paper, but this time he read it out loud. "Joshua Tipton, we don't have a horse here for you. That means you're walking I guess."

"Already got one," Joshua answered as he saluted the paymaster before stepping out the door where the other three were waiting for him. Joshua was recounting his money when he announced, "This is the most money I have ever held in my hands before. Hell, it's the most I've ever seen in my whole life. I sure am going to live high on the hog for a while."

William watched as Samuel stowed away his pay into the rawhide change purse hanging around his neck. William suddenly realized that his young friend had nowhere to go now that their tour was up. Samuel had never said what his plans were after they had all mustered out. William liked him and was not looking forward to leaving another new friend behind.

"Come on, let's go down to Duncan Tavern and celebrate." James said. "Let's have one last drink in Pittsburgh before we all go home."

"Sounds good" Joshua said as he patted James on the back. "Let's go."

William was watching Samuel's face as James made his request and he could see that Samuel's spirits had dropped like a ton of bricks. He had suddenly realized that he had no place to go now that their adventure was over. He didn't say anything but he didn't have to, William could see the hurt in his eyes.

As the four of them headed out of the fort, James and Joshua had put some distance between themselves and William and Samuel. William said, "Better hurry Samuel; we don't want to get left behind now do we?" William picked up his speed and ran on up to the others while Samuel lagged behind, not in such a rush to get to the tavern as the others were, knowing full well that once their drink was over he would be parting ways with them.

"Hey fellows," William said as he caught up with the other two, "what are we going to do about Samuel? We can't leave him behind."

"I have been thinking about that for a while now," James said as he walked down the street. "I like the boy, and if he agrees I am going to ask him to come and winter with me back home. I don't know if he'll want to, but I'm going to make the offer anyway. He would be better off with us than here all by himself. Who knows what kind of crowd he could get mixed up with here?"

"Good." William said, "if you didn't ask him, I was going to ask him the same thing, but it will work out better for you than for me since you are single and all."

The three of them all stopped at the same time and waited for their companion to catch up with them. He was moving at a slow pace with his head down.

"Samuel if you walk that slow, you'll never stay up with us on our way back to Virginia." James said, "We better get you a fast horse."

"Virginia, me in Virginia where would I stay," Samuel asked, "I have no one there."

"You're staying with me." James said, "That is if you want to. My door is open to you anytime. We can't bust up a crew like the one we've got here."

A smile spread across Samuel's face as he picked up his pace and said, "How long will it take for us to get there?"

Chapter 77
Together Again

The stay at Duncan's Tavern wasn't long. Once inside Samuel made a few inquiries and found a horse trader and made a deal for a six-year-old red horse. His back was bowed a little but other than that, the animal looked fairly good. There was not a whole lot to pick from anyway, so Samuel paid the man, feeling lucky he had gotten a horse at all. They stayed one last night at the fort and as soon as the sun was up, they began their journey home, going back the same way they had come with Captain Babb.

William was hoping to run into one or perhaps both of the House brothers at Fort Redstone for a quick visit, but they were nowhere around. The homeward bound party did stay over that night at Alexander's Tavern. Alexander told William that Hannah had stopped working for him ever since she had married Andrew and shortly afterwards the two had left town for Pittsburgh and maybe even Kentucky after that. As William went to sleep that night, he hoped that the Houses would stay at Fort Pitt for a while and let things cool a little in Kentucky before they settled there for good. He was sure Andrew would not risk losing Hannah to the Indians a second time, but then again, he did love fighting the Indians. They would most certainly fit in with the other settlers in Kentucky if they did decide to go there. He knew too there was no reason to lose any sleep over Andrew and Adam House. Those two could take care of themselves better than most men could and William soon fell asleep.

It was hot the next morning as William's party pulled out of the settlement, but unlike last time, all was calm and clear with no Indian's about Old Redstone fort. They reached the Great Meadows that afternoon and the Potomac River safely by nightfall. It had been a good day's ride and they felt they would soon be out of reach of the Indians. After another day's ride along the river together James and Samuel wished William and Joshua well and crossed on over the river into Virginia. Unlike the Tipton's they had no reason to stay in Maryland not having any family to see or pick up before heading on home. The two brothers continued on alone and were soon in very familiar country. William pulled on the reins of his horse as he and Joshua stopped under the old oak tree in the Churchyard where they had both grown to manhood.

"Well, which way will it be brother?" William asked as he looked at the fork in the road, "Do you take the road to Father's or do you go the other way to Polly's?"

"I'm going to see my girl," Joshua answered, "I'll see the folks later on tonight. Who knows, now that I got that land in Kentucky, I may just ask her to marry me today. It worked for you."

William offered Joshua his hand from atop his mount and said, "Well, good luck. If she's the one I hope it works for you."

"Oh, she's the one alright," Joshua answered as he shook William's hand. "If it wasn't for her, we wouldn't have gone to Kentucky together. She's the reason why I went. It's time for me to start a family you know."

"Well I am glad I've got an older brother that was smart enough to take me along." William said. "It's going to work out perfect for us. Just think our farms will be side by side. Our Children will grow up together just like we did."

"Yeah, it's going to be good." Joshua said as he leaned back in his saddle "Where are you staying tonight, the Porters or over at the folks?"

"I don't know," William answered. "I would like to stay at home but we may have to stay at her parents place. I guess it depends on what Elizabeth is doing and how much time we will have to get over to father's place. But I will definitely be there tomorrow. I haven't seen the folks in over a year and I want to hear how Thomas and Sylvester are getting along as well."

"All right, see you then," Joshua said, as he gently kicked his horse's side and rode off at a fast gallop, heading down the other road leaving William alone under the oak where he and Elizabeth had shared so many Sunday talks together. He reached up and pulled his hat down tightly on his head and took off after his two girls. Four more miles and I'll be there he thought to himself as he rode along. With each stride of his horse his heart began to beat a little faster, knowing that he was that much closer to Elizabeth. It had been a long time since he had kissed her goodbye back at that ford near Captain Babb's home. As the road made its last turn before it reached the Porter homestead, through the trees his eye caught sight of the rooftop of the barn that he had helped build just a few years ago.

'Oh God, I hope she is home and not away,' he thought as he entered the gate of Thomas Porter's farm. He slowed his horse as it galloped to the front yard, but no one was anywhere to be seen. He quickly looked out over the yard but again he saw no one, not at the well, or in the lots around the barn. He did see Fly grazing in the late afternoon shade of the barn. He jumped off his horse and ran onto the porch and opened the door and stepped inside the house. There he saw his wife and daughter sitting at a cherry table eating their supper. Elizabeth jumped from her chair and quickly flew across the room where she buried her head in his chest and wrapped her arms around his waist as she began to cry tears of joy. He placed his hand under her chin and raised her head up and looked into her green eyes and gave her a tender kiss.

"It's been a long time, my love." he finally said. "It's good to be back in your arms. Now where is my little girl?"

Chapter 78
A Soft Bed

It was late at night at the Porter homestead but William and Elizabeth were still up talking to one another in her old bedroom. William was lying on his back looking up at the ceiling, while she laid on her stomach resting her head on the top of his bare chest. He had one arm free to gently scratch her back, and she in turn was taking her fingertips and running them up and down the scar on his forearm.

"Downstairs, you told us all about the farm on top of the hill and of the rescue of that Hannah girl, as well as the Indians on the river and the ambush at the fort but you haven't told me about how you got this scar. It wasn't there when you left. William, how did it happen?"

"It was after most of all that. It happened between the Falls and Harrodsburg. We had come across a party of Indians who had stolen some horses from some settlers. We fired on them as they slept, but one charged into me with his knife. He stabbed me before I gut shot him with my pistol."

"So, you had to kill him?" she asked as she let out a deep sigh.

"Yeah, I did and one more after him." William answered as he ran his hand down her lower back.

"How did it make you feel?" she whispered.

"Mad at first," he replied, "it happened so fast I didn't have time to think about it. I mean he had knocked me to the ground and it was him or me. I didn't even know he had stuck me until James pulled the knife out of my arm."

"My God," she said, "you could have been killed William."

"Looking back on it now, it's the second one that haunts me. I had already knocked him out. He was unconscious. I didn't have to kill him but I did it anyway. We could have just left him there."

"Some say they are not human William. I don't know if it's a sin to kill them or not," Elizabeth said as she looked deep into his eyes. "Some say they may not even have a soul."

"Yes, they do." he replied, "I saw a father and son together. They didn't know I was there for a good while. It was just like watching me and father out hunting together. They were talking and laughing, just having a good time. That's how I know they have a soul. I had them both dead in their tracks before I let them go. The father looked me in the eye as he was walking away. I still believe that he was wishing me well as he walked off. That Gibson fellow I told you about on the river. He was a white man but his soul was dark and evil, much worse than that Indian's soul ever was."

"So, you didn't kill them." Elizabeth said as she rolled over and propped her head on her open palm, resting her elbow in William's stomach.

"No, I didn't" he answered.

Looking deep into his eyes she said, "See William you always make the right choice. You have good judgment. She rose up and kissed him on the lips and said, "You're a good man William Tipton, that why I love you so."

"I hope I'm a good man."

"God thinks so too," she answered. "He has brought you back to me alive and well. That Gibson man sure didn't have His protection."

"That's another thing that's been baffling me." William said "The Indian that killed Gibson. I don't know why he did it. Maybe he put two and two together when he heard me talk to Gibson. For some strange reason he let me go. No, they have a soul all right. He could tell good from evil somehow. They're just so different from us in the way they live. They believe that the land in Kentucky is just for hunting and we want to farm it. As long as the King keeps on giving those weapons and supplies, they will fight us for it; I can't say I wouldn't do the same"

Elizabeth frowned while she was brushing away a stray strain of hair out of the corner of her mouth and said "I am still afraid to go out there William. It sounds so dangerous I hope you won't think the worst of me for it."

"No, that thought would not ever enter my mind my love, but the land is ours." William said as he pulled her close to his side. "I have the papers in my saddlebags but we still have our farm back home, so we don't have to go out there until it is safe. It may be as long as ten years before we settle in Kentucky. I'm not going to risk losing my family just to move out there. I may have to go back by myself from time to time, but that is in the future. Let's just concentrate on tonight for now. It's good to be back in a soft bed and have you back by my side."

Chapter 79
Bad News All Around

As William and his family rode into the yard of his childhood home at his parent's place, he saw Joshua's horse walking around the pasture along with several others of his father's horses. He had no doubt that Joshua would have told the folks that he would be arriving sometime this morning. The front door of the house stood open to help let out some of the heat from his mother's hot fireplace. He could see her inside thru the open doorway. She had her back turned to him, and was busy preparing the midday meal. He glanced over to Elizabeth who had by now ridden her own horse up beside him. He pressed his finger to his lips, motioning her to be quiet. He looked back inside the house where he saw his mother shoot back across in front of the open door with her arms full of ears of corn, freshly picked from the field. She still had not seen William outside. She had her head down, not paying much attention to what was going on outside as she began snapping and stringing green beans, she had picked from her garden earlier that morning. Grinning, William looked back at Elizabeth and shook his head. Then not being able to contain himself any longer, he yelled at the top of his lungs,

"Hello, in the house. You have visitors outside, show yourself."

Sue Tipton raised her gaze from her bowl of beans and her eyes fell upon her son for the first time since he had moved away. Her face broke into a smile and she seemed frozen behind her table looking out the door at her son, sitting atop his mount holding his daughter in his arms.

"Hello Mommy," he said thru his own smile, "I sure have missed you!"
He handed Sarah over to Elizabeth and jumped off Fly's back and leaped onto the porch to meet his mother who was laughing and crying at the same time as she came thru the doorway. She gave him a tight hug and said, "It's so good to have you home once more, son." Stepping back a few steps she looked him up and down with a glow on her face and a tear in her eye. "Oh, come here," she said, "and give me another hug." The two came together in a fierce embrace and this time William picked her up off floor, spun her around and gave her a kiss.

"Where's Father?" he asked as he carefully sat his mother back down.

"Right here, behind you." proclaimed Mordacai while holding a chopping hoe in one hand and holding little Sarah in the other. Turning around he pitched his gardening tool into the yard and turned back to William and shook his son's hand.

"You sure have an awful sweet little girl here; son looks like your young family is well on its way son."

"Yes, it is." William said with a smile.

"Well, come on let's go inside and sit down." Sue said as she placed and arm around Elizabeth's waist. "Oh, look at the muss I made," she said as she looked at her table where she had knocked over her bowl of green beans, scattering them everywhere in her haste to get to her son. William and his father sat down at the table where they had eaten so many meals together in the past and watched as their wives began to gather up the split beans and start snapping the last of them.

"Well William, are you as happy with you land in Kentucky as your brother is?"

Mordacai asked his son across the table.

"Yes, father, I am very much so indeed." William answered. I suppose Joshua has told you all about it by now."

"Yeah, pretty much." Mordacai replied.

"Good," William said as he looked to his mother. "Now tell me how everyone is getting along. What's the news of the family seems as though you two are getting along fine."

"Oh, our health is good enough." Mordacai said, "The crops are in fair condition, I guess. Tobacco worms are about to eat the tobacco up. I pick them off every other day it seems. Got a few weeds coming back in, that's what I was doing when I heard you call out."

"Are any redcoats around giving you any trouble?" William asked.

"Nah, not yet anyway I guess I am too old for them to mess with." Mordacai answered angrily as he smacked the tabletop with the palm of his hand.

"I am glad your home, William." his mother said as she reached out and took his hand from across the table. "The family could use some good news right about now." she continued. "We've got a newspaper over there that you need to see," she said as she nodded her head towards the mantel over the fireplace.

"Thomas sent it to us," Mordacai said as he got up and walked over to the mantel and picked up the paper and brought it back and handed it over to William.

"It's about Sylvester," he said as he sat back down.

"He's not dead, is he?" Elizabeth asked.

"We don't know," Sue answered as she began to cry.

William looked down at the Philadelphia paper and read the small headline, *'Men missing from the battle of Monmouth fought June 28, 1778.'*

The list was in alphabetical order and William quickly scanned down to the T's where he saw the name, Sylvester Tipton, recorded among the missing.

"Could it be another Sylvester Tipton?" Elizabeth asked.

"We don't believe so." Mordacai answered. "Sylvester was with General Lee and Lee was at that battle. From what we have been able to put together from the few paper's we have seen and what Thomas has heard, Lee ordered a retreat from the field and some of his men were captured by the British as they tried to do so. General Washington reformed the lines and eventually won the battle, but he never did get Lee's lost men back. We haven't heard a word from Sylvester since. We just pray that he is alive somewhere." Mordacai said as he shook his head, "At least his name is not on the list of known dead from that damned battle."

"Maybe he is wounded in a hospital somewhere and has not been able to write us yet." William said as he laid down the paper. His face had completely changed now.

What had been a great homecoming just a short time ago had suddenly become the biggest disaster of his life. He dropped his head onto the tabletop and covered it up with his hands.

"No, I've been up there to see for myself," Mordacai said. "I couldn't sit here and not know. I just got back home two days ago myself. I looked everywhere for him. I wasn't alone; I was with several other families who were missing relatives of their own. We didn't find Sylvester or any of the others anywhere. Maybe the British will release a list of prisoners soon. Crazy as it sounds; we're praying he is with them, because if he's not, then he's dead in some unmarked grave somewhere that we will never find."

"Where is Thomas?" William asked with his head still bowed.

"Back with Washington's Army" Mordacai answered. "He was home when the battle was going on so he missed it. I think that's bothered him some, that he wasn't there to save Sylvester, but there is no way of knowing if he could have even if he had been there.

"How is Joshua taking the news?" William asked again.

"Bad." Sue answered. "At first I didn't want to tell him, but we knew he had to know."

"Why would you not tell him?" William asked his parents.

"He got some bad news himself yesterday." said Mordacai, "when he got in last night, he told us he had gone to Polly's to ask if she would marry him. But when he got there her father told him she got hitched to one of those Miller boys while he was gone to Kentucky and has moved away. Her father wouldn't say why she didn't wait for him to come back. This morning he took off on one of my horses and rode off without saying where he was going. We haven't seen him since."

"Damn," William said as he jumped up from his chair. "What's going to happen next? It's bad news all around. Joshua can get through this. Hard as it seems to him now, he can find a good woman somewhere who will love him the way he deserves to be, but poor Sylvester, that's another story altogether. You mean to tell me the best thing we have to hope for is that he is in some damn prison somewhere?"

Mordacai got up from the table and walked over and put both his hands-on Williams two shoulders and said, "I'm afraid so son, where else could he be?"

"I'm going to find him." William said as he pulled away from his father. "I'll leave in the morning."

"Son, I have already been there. Both armies have moved on. I looked for a whole week. You've got your own family to think of now. You have to wait and see like the rest of us. That's all we can do now. Wait and Pray." William had always been for the war, but up until now it had been just politics. The high taxes and not being allowed to settle over the mountains had made it seem that the war could procure good things for them all, but now it was personal. He may have lost a brother.

William turned back to his father and said "If Joshua's gone off after Sylvester without me, I'm gonna kill him."

Chapter 80
His Hell on Earth

William had spent the whole afternoon yesterday reading over all the letters that both his brothers had sent home to his parents. Sylvester had written more than Thomas. Reading them helped William catch up with what they had both been doing during the last year. Mordacai had also saved several newspapers with news of the war but not much had happened while William was away when it came to major battles. The biggest engagement of the summer had been at Monmouth and the fact that Sylvester was lost there had taken away all the sweetness of an American victory for the Tipton family. William had gone out to the field this morning to help his father with the weeds in his tobacco crop. Now that he saw all the hog-weeds in the normally clean rows, William could tell that his father had been away a good while looking for Sylvester. A weed would never dare to grow in his fields if Mordacai was home. As the two men were working their way down the rows, they saw Joshua returning to the house. He jumped up on the porch and wave with his hat for them to come in. He yelled, "Come on, I've got news."

As they entered the house Joshua handed his father a New York paper. "I was over at Robert Shields place talking to his son John. I was there asking him if he knew why Polly got married while I was away. That's when Robert came up and handed me this, and said he was sorry to hear about Sylvester. It is a list of prisoners being held in New York. He's on it."

"Well, at least we know now, he's alive and we know where he is." Sue said as she grabbed onto her husband's arm. Now, how do we get him back?"

"I don't know," Mordacai answered, "If you're not an officer, it's hard to get exchanged. The British have New York bottled up tight. We can't just walk in and get him."

"What I have been told is that they are being held in prison ships in the harbor." Joshua said as he sat down next to his mother and put his arm around her shoulder. "The most important thing is that at the time this here paper was printed Sylvester was still alive. He's not dead." Joshua said trying to console his mother.

"The next thing we need to do is find out who is in charge of prisoner exchange." William said. "There's got to be somebody in charge somewhere."

"A prison ship, well, that's got to be better than a dungeon in the bottom of a prison somewhere, doesn't it?" Sue asked as she wiped a tear from her eye. "They've probably got him working on its decks so he can at least get some fresh air. Who knows, they may even let them do some fishing so they can eat the fish, don't you think?"

Mordacai, William, and Joshua's eyes met over the top of Sue's head, for they all knew this was the wishful thinking of a mother who was trying to find some good in a bad situation.

Sylvester knew there would be no good come from this situation as soon as he stepped foot on the HMS frigate Bristol Packet. The ship was very old and she had been stripped of her sail rigging along with anything else that might make this old, dry rotted hull seaworthy. It would certainly be a floating death trap to anyone who was foolish enough to try to sail her into open waters and that was what Sylvester thought it would be to him when the British soldier in charge of his group of prisoners opened the steel doors that lead down into the ships interior. An ungodly stench rose up from inside the ship's bowels to meet him as they were led down the steep dark stairs that he knew would be his hell on this earth. His hands were bound with iron shackles, but at least his legs were free. The first four prisoners he saw were dead piled up on each other at the bottom of the steps.

"Bend your back laddie," the guard said as he hit Sylvester with the butt of his musket. "Use your strength while you still have it. Drag their dead arses back up those steps so as they can receive their parole." Sylvester grabbed the dead man under his armpits and drug him up to the ships deck. "Halt right there," the soldier commanded as he leaned down and ran his bayonet in the corpse's side. Just making sure," the soldier said as he gave Sylvester the benefit of what passed for a smile. "Drop 'em over into the boat you came over on, ye ungrateful rebel." Sylvester made three more trips up and down the stairs all the while listening to all the reasons why his guard hated the American colonist. "If it wasn't for ye trouble making bastards, I would be back home in Edinburgh, but nay, here I am stuck on this damned ship with a bunch of dead men, just because ye won't pay your taxes." Well you're sure in hell going to pay them now", he said as he followed Sylvester back down into the ships damp hull. Those prisoners who were still alive inside looked to be at death's door, and they were filthy as well.

They were wearing rags and looked as if they had not been fed in months. The guard pushed Sylvester down one last time beside a man who was surely living his last day on this earth. Taking out a key, the guard unlocked the ankle iron from around the soon to be dead man's foot. "Here," he said, "put these on, I don't believe your friend here is going to be around too much longer. If he could talk I know he would want you to have these, so put them on." Sylvester did as he was told and locked the irons around his ankle watching the guard climb back up topside, but not before firing one last salvo at Sylvester. "I'll be sure and bring your evening meal in about a week or so." he said just before he slammed the door shut. Sylvester knew the only way he would ever get off this ship was to die so he began to hold his breath.

Chapter 81
Answered Prayers

As much as William hated to go, he knew he had to leave for his own home. He had been gone for the whole growing season and his small farm would be overgrown with weeds and young sapling trees if he did not go back soon to clear them off. It wouldn't take long for his fields to simply turn back into wild country. There was even the chance of squatters moving in on his homestead. If his wheat seed was still safe and in good shape, he still had enough time to put out a winter wheat crop. He had little choice but to go.

With Sylvester being held prisoner on a ship out in the middle of New York harbor, the family knew there was little hope of rescue. Mordacai felt the only hope of getting his son back was if there was a mass exchange of prisoners, but that was one of the things that General Washington wanted no part of. The head of the Continental Army was not willing to trade seasoned British regulars held prisoner for unreliable militia or ill trained Continentals. Washington hated letting his former soldiers be held, but he was hoping the British would simply let them go instead of having the burden of feeding them. He knew it wasn't easy for his soldiers, but it was best for the cause. Now that Joshua had returned home, Mordacai was planning a trip to Philadelphia to see if he could help drum up support for an exchange. The elder Tipton also understood that he was not a rich or a powerful man, but maybe there were such men in the young nation's capital who could help and just maybe he could persuade them to get something done.

The Porters and Elizabeth had planted more corn and potatoes as soon as she had arrived back in the spring realizing her and their daughter would not have a whole lot of food to winter on with her husband away if nothing was done to provide for them. Their foresight and hard work would make the coming winter months a whole lot easier for William and his young family. Now, with William's pay he could buy extra supplies once they got back home, providing there was anything to buy.

So, after only a short four day stay at his parents' home, he and Elizabeth, along with little Sarah, said their goodbyes. The family gathered to say a prayer for Sylvester's return and a safe trip home for William's family as they started the trip to Virginia.

Before leaving, William told Joshua to keep his head up and not be too upset over Polly not waiting for him, it was better to learn now that she was not the one for him than it would be after they had married. Joshua assured his brother that he would indeed be fine and he even went on to confide that he already had his eye on a girl named Jeanette who was the younger sister of his friend John Shields. She had grown up quite a lot in the last year and if it was alright with her family he intended to start a courtship with her soon.

William had missed seeing Thomas this time but he felt like they would cross paths sooner or later, but he did leave a letter for him in their mother's care, for when Thomas came back this way. Knowing that a difficult trip lay ahead, William had taken one of his father's wagons to pull his family and food supplies to their farm. Captain Babb's horse pulled the wagon while Fly walked along behind on the trip home. William had second thoughts about not keeping Samuel with him. It was going to be a hard ride back home and Samuel's gun would have been nice to have along if something should happen on the road. He was afraid that if he ran into either army, they would most likely take his food from him to feed their soldiers, and there was always the chance of running upon Captain Price and his Tories again, so it was going to be a worrisome journey back home.

Luck was on their side this time however, and by the time William had gotten his family back over the river away from the ferry a few miles, he felt like all would be well the rest of the way home. He didn't know why, bad luck could find him now just as easily as anywhere else, but his mind was at ease for some strange reason, and sure enough their good luck held all the way home. As they made their way up the creek bottom that led to their farm, both he and Elizabeth were happy to see their home still standing. With the militia being gone most of the spring anything could have happened to the house while they were away. The Tories would love nothing more than to burn down the home of a rebel while he was out fighting and away from home, but it had not happened here. All that met William at the farm was a few new weeds in the field, just as he had thought they would be. He could see a small herd of deer grazing in his yard, but they jumped over the split rail fence and ran off into the nearby woods. He was thankful to God that all of his prayers had been answered this past year that had been so full of dangers, and that he and his family were once more safely back in their home.

Chapter 82
A Christmas Dance

It had been as good a Christmas as William could possibly have enjoyed this December 25, 1778, but not a great one. The food was delicious and the company was good, but every time he began to enjoy himself, his thought would drift to a cold ship frozen in the harbor of New York City.

Samuel was eying the last piece of Elizabeth's apple pie that was sitting on the table. It was the last batch of apples she had stored way back in the fall and would also be the last they would have until next year. She had been saving them for this glorious day, the best of all holidays. Being away from his extended family, William had decided to invite James and Samuel over for the day. They quickly accepted his invitation, not having any families of their own nearby.

"Go ahead and take it Samuel. You have been watching it like a hawk for over an hour now," William teased his young guest. Everyone laughed as Samuel's face began to turn red with embarrassment. Elizabeth got up from her chair and picked up the pie and placed it on a wooden plate and handed it over to Samuel with a smile. William had always been proud of his wife and now she had given him another reason to be. Samuel sat the plate down on the floor by his side and grabbed Sarah as she tried to run by his chair. He scooped her up and sat her down on his knee as he said, "Hummm, apple pie." He picked up the plate and fed the little girl a bite of the pie and said, "If this is all of the apples on this farm, then she will be the one to eat them, not me."

"Well, aren't you a gentleman," Elizabeth said as she sat back down next to the fireplace very pleased that William had brought this young man back from the frontier.

"Maybe in a couple of years from now, we'll all be eating apple pie on one of our farms in Kentucky on Christmas Day." James predicted as he patted his full stomach.

"Thank you for the meal, Elizabeth. I surely enjoyed it. Now I have a gift for you and William outside, so I guess I better go and fetch it for you two." He stood up and walked over to the oak door and opening it, stepped outside and closed it behind him to keep the cold wind out of the small, warm house.

William looked over at Samuel and asked, "Do you know what it is?"

"No, I don't." Samuel replied as he gave Sarah another bite of pie, "and if I did, I wouldn't tell you anyhow."

Within a few minutes James reopened the door and stepped back inside the house. In his hands was a blue blanket that had something wrapped inside.

"I sure am thankful it didn't snow last night. If it had, as cold as it is out there, we may not have been able to get over here today. Now be patient with me, it's been a while," he said as he sat the blanket down on the table. As he was unfolding the blanket he looked over to Elizabeth and said, "When we were in Kentucky, if William was not shooting at some Indian, he was usually talking about you, and one of the things he said was that you loved a good dance, so here we go!" He raised a fiddle from the blanket and placed it under his chin and ran the bow over its strings, and to everyone's surprise James soon had the little room full of music. He looked at William and nodded his head toward Elizabeth. With a smile on his face William got up from his chair and walked across the room to where Elizabeth was sitting and bowed to his wife as he took her hand in his and said. "May I have the pleasure of a dance, my love?" She nodded her head without saying a word and soon they were moving across the wooden floor of their home to the sounds of James' fiddle and for the first time today William truly forgot about his brother.

Chapter 83
A Fearsome Ghost

The wind outside was blowing hard this afternoon, causing the death ship to rock a little more than it normally would, but by now Sylvester was well over his sea sickness and was used to the ship's constant movement. However, he was in no way used to the cold and it was just the last of December with the cold months of January and February yet to come. He was beginning to lose heart.

From the very first day of his imprisonment his strategy was to escape somehow. He had come up with several plans. The first and simplest was to conserve his strength and pray to God for an exchange of foot soldiers and just wait it out. But now, he was growing weaker every day, and if he was to pull off his second plan, he would need all of his remaining strength to get away. Like his first option, the second seemed to have little chance of coming true. The plan was for him to stab the loud-mouthed guard with the large piece of dry rotted wood he had managed to pull up out of the ships deck. He had managed to keep it out of sight of the guards by sitting on top of it. It was about six inches long and sharp at one end. Plenty sharp to deliver a killing blow to any man who got close enough. But herein lay the plan's problem; the guard never got that close. The son of a bitch always threw what little food the prisoners got at them, always keeping out of arm's length. If by some miracle he did come close enough for Sylvester to kill him and if he staggered back a few steps after being stabbed and fell to the deck he would be out of reach, with the keys to the shackles hanging around his neck, leaving Sylvester sitting on the floor still chained to the metal ring mounted in the ships deck, waiting for the next guard to come down to take his revenge out on whoever had killed his fellow guard. He had lost weight while he sat inside this God forsaken ship and his feet and wrist were bloody from the shackles he wore, but that was part of his third and last plan. He felt today would be the best time to pull it off. The guard that Sylvester hated the most was not here today, at least if he was, the Scotsman had not walked down into the hull. Sylvester had been keeping up with the red coated guard's rotation and felt like the Scotsman who hated the prisoners the most, the one who liked to stab the dead before they were thrown overboard, was not here today, and if the pattern held true, he would not be here tomorrow either.

As Sylvester sat there with the rest of his fellow prisoners, he picked at one of the larger scabs that had formed on the back of his left hand, causing it to bleed. But it wasn't bleeding enough to his liking, so he raised his hip and took the splintered piece of wood he had hidden and jabbed it into the wound making it bleed more. He stuck his would be weapon back into his ragged trousers out of sight. He carefully smeared his own blood from just under his nostrils down to his mouth and on to his chin. Then he applied a little more to one of his ears and slumped over onto his side and waited for the guard. He had not told his fellow prisoners of his plan, he was afraid that one of them might turn him in to get a favor form the guards. He had seen men turn on each other while he was here and that was a chance he was not going to take. He had told the man chained next to him that he felt like he was dying earlier in the day, hoping it would help with the deception it would take to fool the guard. As he lay on his side he prayed to God for help and that if he was discovered to still be alive by his captors and was killed, he asked Jesus to forgive him his many sins and that his soul would be accepted into the Kingdom of God. After what seemed a long time, he heard the sound of the steel door being opened at the top of the stairs. He had been practicing holding his breath ever since the first day he had been led into this sour smelling place. Each week he had been able to increase his time and now he would see if it would pay off. As the guard walked down the line to his spot, Sylvester stopped breathing.

"Another dead one," the guard said as he stopped and looked down at the dead rebel. He glanced at the dead man's ribs to see if his lungs were moving for a few seconds and saw no movement or sign of life in the man's body. As Sylvester played dead he heard the sound of the guard's boots walk back towards the front of the line of prisoners and he heard the key turn to unlock the shackles of the newest and strongest prisoner. Who would be used to drag Sylvester to the foot of the stairs? Sylvester did not dare to move or make a sound as he was being drug down the ship's length by his feet, even though the rough wooden planks were cutting into his back. Then he heard the prisoner turn and walk away back down to where the guard was waiting.

"'Ere's another one for ye, come and get 'em too," he heard the cockney accent say.

At last Sylvester was able to breathe in some air, now that he knew the guard was not close enough to see him. He had been able to hold his breath for over four minutes now. As he lay there, a sick feeling began to come over him as he realized that he would have to spend the long night ahead next to a dead body. He had hoped that no more men had died today, knowing if they had they would be stacked upon each other like cord wood and he would be at the bottom of that gruesome pile.

"Jest two for the reaper today," the guard said as he followed behind the other dead man who was being dragged to the foot of the stairs where Sylvester already lay. The dead man's chest fell across Sylvester's legs as he was dropped, confirming Sylvester's worst fears. Within a few minutes the prisoner who had been forced to drag out the dead was locked back down into his place and the guard walked back past Sylvester and headed up the stairs and shut the door. Once again Sylvester prayed, thanking God for allowing the first part of his escape plan to work. Soon the sun fell from the sky, and with it disappeared, what little light that had filtered into the bottom of the ship. As soon as it was completely dark, he pulled his tingling, aching legs from under the dead man's body. All he had to do now was to wait for the row boat to come and pick up the dead in the morning. As one of the other prisoners began to cough at the back of the ship he reached down to the bottom of his trouser leg to the hole in the hem where he had hidden his Masonic ring, to see if it was still there. He had hidden it there when he was first captured. He was hoping that it had not fallen out while he was being dragged down the ships flooring. He managed a rare smile when he felt the ring, safely tucked away. Having done all he could, Sylvester shut his eyes and tried to get some sleep for it was going to be a long night. Early the next day, before the sun came up, Sylvester stuck his legs back under his companion, the two of them now lying just as they had when he fell atop Sylvester the night before, and waited two more anxious hours for the guard to come down and remove the dead. He prayed once more that it would not be the Scotsman and his prayer was once again answered. As he lay on his back gazing up, he kept his eyes open, trying to make them have that glazed look that dead men have come over them. This would allow him to see some of what was going on around him. Now he began to worry if the ship's temperature had been cold enough to lower his own temperature, and was his skin cold enough to pass as a dead corpse? He could only wait and see. A few seconds past before another newly arrived prisoner came down the steps just as Sylvester had on his first day, and he too was ordered to pull the dead from the bottom of the ship. He bent over and picked up Sylvester's body and slung it over his shoulder and carried him up and out of the ship's belly. The sun blinded Sylvester's eyes but he did not squint them even as hard as it was to keep them open, but soon they adjusted to the light and he was able to see as he was being carried over to the edge of the boat. Bracing himself for the long fall from the ship down to the rowboat waiting a good ten feet below, he wondered how he would end up. A fall like this could easily break a bone, or even kill him, but he had little time to think of what might happen in the fall, as the big prisoner swung him up and over the side of the ship and into the rowboat below. Luckily his fall was broken by the bodies of other dead prisoners who had no doubt been dropped from some of the other prison ships that were nearby in Wallabout bay.

"Ahoy there, wait we got another for ye", the guard yelled down to the two men in the rowboat. At the oars was an old man and the other was an armed British guard wearing his red coat. Even so, he looked cold and had laid down his musket and stuck his blue hands under his armpits to try and warm them up. He was more concerned with keeping warm than with the dead men lying inside the boat with him. The waves pushed the boat out away from the ship and the oarsman had to paddle the boat back alongside the ship for the second prisoner to be dropped inside. As the old man maneuvered the small row boat he said to the cold guard, "Thank goodness this is the last ship. I am ready to get to my home and the fire the old lady will have waiting for me."

Sylvester felt the boat rock as the other body fell into the waiting craft. It fell next to him and he could see that the corpse had a new wound, where the guard on the ship had bayoneted the body. Why he had decided to just stab the second body and not the first was a mystery to Sylvester but he was thankful to God that he had.

The boat had rowed about half the distance to shore before Sylvester made his move. He had planned to use the sharpened sliver of wood but now that the soldier had put his Brown Bess down, Sylvester quickly picked it up and ran the bayonet into the soldiers back and pushed him over into the water. The old oarsman stopped rowing as his mouth fell open. The sight of a half-starved man rising up from the dead was more than he could take and he dove over the side of the boat leaving it to this fearsome ghost.

Sylvester began to cry as he rowed the boat to the other side of the harbor on the Brooklyn shoreline because he did not have the strength to row against the current of the incoming tide. His strength finally gave out after fifteen to twenty minutes of rowing and he was no longer able to carry on any further under his own power. The mudflat along the shore was just too difficult for him to manage in this weaken state. He simply let the waves take him where they would. The boat soon ran aground on one of the open pastures of the Brooklyn farmland across from the city of New York. He knew freedom was not yet his; he could still be easily recaptured if he couldn't muster up enough energy to get out of the boat. With nothing but pure determination, he grabbed onto the rail of the boat and pulled himself up and over into the frigid water. He reached back inside and retrieved the Brown Bess and struggled to dry land. Looking up and down the shoreline, he saw just one house, but most importantly, he saw no British soldiers around. Relief poured thru him, and placing his free hand atop his head, he said to himself, "Get you wits together man and think!" Turning back to the boat, he stepped once more into the cold water and gave it a hard push out into the current and watched as it floated down the coast line. He began walking toward the lone house he could see in the distance and thought to himself, 'I hope there are no Tories there, for if there are, I'll have to kill them and that is something I definitely don't want to do, but I am not going back to that damned ship'.

Chapter 84
Business to Attend

As Sylvester stumbled along through the waist high brown grass that was between him and the house, he saw its back door open. He fell to the ground and waited to see who would emerge from the small one room house. The door was still open, but whoever had opened it had not yet come out. They had just left it open, and Sylvester could still see them moving around inside. When they finally stepped out into the sunlight, he could see that the first was a black boy about thirteen years old, followed by a man who looked to be in his forties. Sylvester thought they were father and son. The two of them were walking over to a wood pile about one hundred feet from their door. The fact that they were most likely slaves eased Sylvester's mind some. They probably didn't care who won the war, and if they were pro-British, they definitely wouldn't have any weapons in their house. Sylvester knew that he would need some food at some point soon and he also needed to get out of the open. The oarsman had by now surely reported his escape. Sylvester had hoped the British wouldn't spend too much time looking for one lone escapee, but he had killed a soldier. That fact alone would almost surely make him a high priority on the British list of things to do and with little else for the redcoats to do here in their winter quarters he knew he couldn't stay out in open view much longer. As the two slaves made their way back to their home with their arms full of firewood, Sylvester's eyes fell upon the dwelling's chimney. Black smoke was swirling out of its top which meant they were most likely cooking something inside. As quickly and quietly as he could, he made his way to the door. He put his ear to the wooden boards and listened to what was going on inside. They sounded as though they were alone in the house. He could hear a baby crying and the voice of a woman trying to console the upset child.

Sylvester knocked on the door and stepped back a few paces and lowered his musket, pointing it at the closed door. The door was opened by the father, ever so slightly, only the few inches needed to stick out a smiling face to see who was outside, but his smile melted away as soon as he saw the weapon pointed towards him. The man stepped out of the house and shut the door behind him.

"All I want is some food and a place to sleep tonight. I'm not here to hurt anybody." Sylvester said to the slave as he lowered his musket down toward the ground.

"Will you help me?"

"If anybody need help, boss, it sure would be you." the man said. "Come on inside. We don't have much, but what we do have is yours if you want it."
"Who's inside with you?" Sylvester asked.

"Just my woman and two children," answered the slave as he stepped back inside, "No one for you to fear anyway. Come on in and see for yourself. You can sit by the fire".

Sylvester followed his reluctant host inside the house where he found the slave's wife holding a crying child in her arms with her older son standing by her side. Both mother and son were startled by his presence in their home.
"Don't worry," Sylvester assured them. "Everything is going to be fine. I just need some help for today and tonight. I'll be gone in the morning."

"Lizzy, give him a bowl." the man said to his wife as he pulled out a chair from a dark corner in the room and sat it next to the fireplace, "Here mister, warm yourself up some."

Sylvester gladly accepted the offer, but kept his musket across his lap, not willing to risk laying it down just yet. He looked up into Lizzy's eyes and nodded his head in thanks as he took the bowl from her hand. His arms shook from fatigue as he drank down the potato soup inside the bowl.

"When was the last time you ate mister?" the man asked.

"I don't know." Sylvester answered.

"You come off one of them ships, didn't you?"

"Yeah," Sylvester replied before taking another drink of the hot thin soup.

"I know what it's like to be on one of them ships." the slave said quietly. "Don't worry; you won't get any trouble from us Mister."

Sylvester handed the now empty bowl back to the woman and laying his musket down by his side, he stretched his cold feet out to the fire. "What's your name?" he asked as he looked over to the male slave.

"Moses is my English name," he answered as he stared at this sorry dirt covered man by his fire, but he wasn't sure if he heard him because his head had fallen down onto his chest. The man had the look of someone who had just fallen asleep in his chair, but Moses waited a little longer to be sure before saying, "Boy, go and tell master what   happen here this morning. Go on now", Moses said as he walked ever so slowly over to Sylvester's chair, where he picked up the musket off the floor. "We shore don't want master mad at us over this." The boy ran out the door and down the hill away from the harbor towards the center of Brooklyn. His master's house was just a short run away. If Sylvester had gone on a few hundred feet more, he would have seen the plantation's main house. The boy knocked on the back door of the house and was met by the head house slave. The boy told his story to the older white haired, well-dressed man who said. "You wait here. I'll go and get the Major." He walked down the hall, past a dining room, and past the parlor which held two British officers who had come to call upon the major's daughter. He walked around behind his master who was sitting in his favorite chair drinking a glass of wine, and touching something on his hand. The man's servant leaned over to him and said something in a low voice into his ear. The Major stood up and announced, "Well now, it seems I have some business to attend to. Remind me to put this away when I return, he said as he gestured to a velvet lined box resting on his desk. Having issued this order, he arose and strode from the room.

Chapter 85
A Fellow Mason

Sylvester's eyes flew open as he felt his chair being kicked out from under him. After he had fallen to the floor, he reached for his musket, but it was nowhere to be found.

"Wake up, you good for nothing rebel," an older well-dressed man was ordering, while standing over him with the tip of his sword pointed at Sylvester's throat. "Be still or I'll run you through."

Sylvester looked over at Moses in disbelief, very disappointed in himself for falling asleep in the slave's quarters. 'Why would I trust this man just because he was a slave?' he thought to himself. He knew he had just made the biggest mistake of his life and he just might pay for it with his very life and he had no one to blame but himself.

"Sorry mister," Moses said as he stood in the corner of the dark room.

"Don't be Moses," the slave's master announced. "If you hadn't told me about this, I would have beaten you like the devil himself when I found out, and I would have learned of this you may be sure. You made the right decision today."

"So, you escaped from one of those ships, did you? The Jersey or the Bristol Packet? Well you're going back now." The Major stepped back a few steps and said, "Tie him up Moses. Put your hands behind your back and don't try anything." Sylvester stood up very slowly, looking at his adversary, who was still pointing his sword at Sylvester's chest. As the major watched him come to his feet, he stepped away from Sylvester and into a beam of light from the one window in the dark cabin and Sylvester saw a flash of gold coming off the Major's hand. There on one of his fingers was a Masonic signet ring just like the one tucked down in Sylvester's trouser seam.

"May I show you something?" Sylvester asked.

"I said don't try anything." the major said as he stepped forward, thrusting his sword in the direction of his prisoner, placing the point of his blade under Sylvester's chin.
"Just let me sit down and show you something before you tie me up Sir. Please, I am begging you."

"Very well, go on, but you can't buy your way out of this." the Major said as he stepped back another pace, still pointing his weapon at Sylvester. "No amount of money can buy your freedom. I am a loyal subject of his majesty, the King."

"I am not trying to bribe you, but I believe you will reconsider my fate after you see this." Sylvester replied as he picked up his chair and sat back down in front of the now low burning fire. He raised his leg onto his other knee and reached into the seam of his trousers and pulled out his ring. He slid it onto his thin finger and presented it to the major.

The Major looked down at the ring and lowered his sword. He turned and walked over to the corner of the room and sat down, glancing back across the room at Sylvester and said, "Brother, you are a free man. Moses, go up to the house and tell Edward to come down here as soon as my guest depart. In the meantime, have him prepare a bath and get some clothes for our guest here. He stood up and strolled back across the room and extended his hand and said, "You are a lucky man indeed. I wore my ring to a lodge meeting last night and was just preparing to put it away when Edward interrupted me with the news of a prisoner on my property. A few moments more and my ring would have been safely put away. I am Kasper

DeVrees, a loyalist Major in the Kings Militia and your newest friend. Sylvester told Major DeVrees who he was and the story of his capture and of his escape that afternoon. Later that night just before he fell into a deep sleep in the finest guest bedroom of the Major's mansion, he realized that becoming a Freemason before the war began had just saved his life.

Chapter 86
A Familiar Voice

It was the first warm day of March, this Saturday afternoon on the Tipton farm and Mordacai Tipton was out in his field plowing the ground for this year's new crops. He was anxious to finish his work because as soon as he was done, he was going to New York. The previous fall he had been in Philadelphia trying to persuade anyone who would listen to him about a prisoner exchange but nothing had come of his efforts. So now he was going to travel to British held New York to see if five thousand pounds of tobacco would buy his son's freedom. He had only sold enough of last year's crop to buy a slave to help with this year's growing season. If he was going to produce one thousand pounds an acre, he was going to need some help to get the job done, and a slave would be the best way to keep his fields in good order while he was gone trying to ransom Sylvester's release. As Mordacai guided his draft horse into the last row of the field behind the horse being worked by Ben, the only slave he had ever owned, he was looking forward to this new opportunity to get his son back. As much as it went against his grain, if it took buying a slave to get his son back, he was willing to do it. Indentured servants were much harder to come by now that the war was dragging on another year, and with most of the men in the area being away fighting there was little help to be had for hire, so he had settled on Ben who appeared to be happy to get away from his former master who had died this spring. Mordacai had already treated him much better than his old owner had in the few days he had been here on the Tipton farm. It was quite different from the years he had spent with his previous master; however, he greatly missed what was left of his family and friends from his former plantation home. He was depressed being here alone, although he tried to keep it well hidden from his new owners, always hoping to be reunited with his sons someday. Sue watched from the porch as the two men led their horses into the barn after they had left the newly plowed field behind. She had their supper ready and went back inside to set the table. She sat down the last plate as her tired husband walked into the room. He picked up Ben's plate of food and took it back outside and handed it over into the slave's hands and said, "See you in the morning, Ben, that's all for today." The slave took his plate and headed off to his new cabin that had just been built this winter on the back of the farm.

"Odd having him here, isn't it?" Sue said to her husband as she watched Ben head toward his quarters.

"Indeed, it is," Mordacai answered, "a necessary evil."

As Sue turned around, she asked, "How do you think he is adjusting to his new surroundings Mordacai?"

"Well enough I suppose," Mordacai replied as he followed his wife to their table. "He did say his wife had passed a few years ago, so he probably left no family behind to speak of."

The couple sat down to eat their own meal when they heard the sound of boots walking across the front porch.

"Ben, is that you?" Mordacai asked, "Is there something the matter with your supper?"

"No, it's not Ben, whoever he may be," a familiar voice said from just outside the door, "but I sure would like to have some of mother's cooking again."

All that Sue could manage to say as Sylvester stepped inside the door of the house, he had grown up in was, "Thank you Lord," over and over again. She jumped to her feet and ran around the table to her son and gave him the hardest hug he had ever received in his life. She finally pulled away after holding him in her arms for a few moments longer and led him to the table and sat him down at his old spot beside Mordacai, and for the first time in his life, Sylvester saw his father cry.

Mordacai rubbed the brow of his forehead as he looked into his son's eyes. "However, on God's green earth did you get here son?"

"I escaped." Sylvester announced proudly, "but not without a little help from a Tory afterwards, believe it or not. It's a long story so I'll start at the beginning.

Chapter 87
Where To

Capt. Babb sat under a grove of oak trees at the head of a long table out in the south lawn of his plantation home. As he looked down at the families who had gathered at his home for the local meeting, he saw familiar smiling faces of the militiamen he had led to Ft. Pitt the year before. About halfway down the table sat William with Elizabeth by his side holding Sarah in her lap. James and Samuel were on his other side, eating away.

"Do you think he is going to call up again today?" James asked right before he bit into a fried chicken leg.

"I would say so," answered William looking up and down the table. "We're all here, by the looks of it."

"I wonder where to this time," Samuel remarked, "Fort Pitt again, maybe?"

"Could be," William replied, "with George Rogers Clark having taken control of the Northwest the way he has, I don't believe it will be Kentucky. With that hair buying Hamilton being shipped off to Virginia in irons, I would say that would have to slow down the Indians out there some, at least until this fall."

"Yeah, I would have loved to have seen him being dragged through Kentucky by some of the very same people that he was sending the Indians out to scalp." James added. "I bet they were hard on him that trip! But it still could be Kentucky. Just because Hamilton is gone doesn't mean that Blackfish and the rest of the Shawnee will give up on their hunting grounds that easy. You know Girty is still out there, as well as McKee. And I even heard that Chief Joseph Bryant may be heading out that way as well."

"James have you gotten any word on Captain Rodgers?" William asked reaching into his pocket and pulling out his pipe.

"Not a word," James answered as he stood up from the table.

"Me neither," Samuel added as he wiped the edge of his mouth with his shirt sleeve. "But I'm sure he's alright though."

After William had lit his pipe and blew out a few puffs of smoke, he got up from the table and walked over to Captain Babb's well where James and Samuel had already joined a gathering of some of the men. Most of the women, including Elizabeth were busy cleaning up from the meal that everyone had just enjoyed. As the men were watching the women talking to each other as they went about their work, William saw the Captain making his way down the table stopping every few feet to say something to one of the ladies still seated before moving on. Each time after he left, those seated would smile and chuckle at something he had said.

"Look at that." William said. "He gets along with the women folk as well as he does with us men. I have to say the Captain is a real good man. It'd hard not to like a man like him, ain't it?"

"Yeah, he is indeed. Oh, look here he comes. I guess we'll find out what's afoot now." James said as he spit out a long brown stream of tobacco juice.

"Man, alive James! How can you ruin the taste of a good meal like the one we just ate with that nasty stuff?" William asked with a grimace on his face.

"Well boys, I got to say that meal sure did hit the spot." Captain Babb said as he approached the well. "I tell you, there are some really fine cooks in these parts. They can make a man fat if he's not careful, 'eh." he chuckled as he looked up into the sky and said, "Looks like its going to be a great evening for a dance. You got that fiddle James?"

"Yes sir, I sure do!"

Samuel looked over at James and said, "I sure am hoping that you spit that tobacco out before you start playing your fiddle. I surely would hate to see you spittin' out over the top of that bow of yours and hit some little gal that was dancing' by."

"Don't you worry about that Samuel, I'm gonna use your hat for a spittoon. You just make sure you leave it on the ground so I can reach it."

"I'll let you boys work that part out later on by yourselves," the captain laughed as he clapped each of them on the back herding them along with him, "but for now, let's head on over to the front of the house. I've got an announcement to make and that will be the best place to make it I suppose."

The men followed Captain Babb over to the front steps of his white frame house and watched as he climbed to the top step to address the men below. He cleared his throat and straightened his cloak and placing his hands behind his back said, "Boys, I'd like to have everyone's attention for a moment if I may. First of all, I would like to thank you all for coming out this evening. I know you already have a fairly good idea of what I am going to say, so I'll just go on and say it. The militia has been called up once again fellows. General Smith needs us to guard one of the lead mines on the border between us and Maryland. I don't have to tell you how important lead is to the cause right now. The Tories have been causing some trouble over that way, trying to stop the shipments going out. I know it's not the most exciting tour we could have, but that's what needs to be done. The good thing is, it's not real far away and our enlistment time is just for forty days this time around. We'll be back soon enough. So, go on and have a good time tonight with your wives and sweethearts. We'll be pulling out in two days' time and we'll meet at the ford like the last time. So, that being said you boys go cut a rug."

"Lead mines," William said as he turned back to his friends, "sounds like a lot of sitting around and doing nothing. But hey, you never know, we may get to shoot at ole Aquilla Price. He did say something about Tories, didn't he?"

"At least we won't have the redskins trying to take our hair this time." James said as he walked over to retrieve his fiddle. William like the rest of the men, made his way back through the crowd until he came upon Elizabeth talking to Mrs. Babb at the back of the house where they had been doing the dishes.

"Well, I guess you have heard by now, haven't you?" William asked his wife.

Elizabeth nodded her head yes. "I am happy enough with it. I won't have to go back to my parents this time either. The Babbs are letting me stay with them again. I can even go back over to the farm and check on it from time to time, if it is alright with you." she said bravely.

"As long as someone goes along with you, I guess." William answered taking her hand in his.

"I'll make sure someone's with her," Mrs. Babb said as she was holding little Sarah's hand. "My, haven't you grown since the last time I saw you child."

"Excuse us would you Mrs. Babb, I hear James warming up his bow. Come on Elizabeth, let's take a turn."

"By all means, go ahead. I'll watch after this one here. Don't worry about her; I'll keep an eye on her for you."

As the two of them made their way to the courtyard where the dance was to take place, Elizabeth pointed across the yard to Samuel who was leading a young lady of his own into the dance. "Do you know who she is?" she asked.

"No, I don't, but I'm sure he will tell me all about her while we're gone."

Chapter 88
Not Just Lead

William was riding along on Fly in front of the column as the militia reached the peak of a large hill that was just a few miles over the Virginia and Maryland border in the western part of the colony of Maryland, somewhere between the two towns of Hagerstown and Fredrick. Down in the valley below laid a field that did not have a single blade of grass growing on it anywhere. It was covered with just rock and dust and a few weeds could be seen here and there. To the right of this dusty expanse was an open furnace about ten feet around with a large fire burning under its center, melting down the raw lead inside? As William and the rest of the militia rode down the hill, they could see the mouth of the mine. It was not too big, just large enough for a draft horse to squeeze out of, like the one that was coming out of the mine now, pulling a sled full of lead ore behind.

"Joshua's not missing anything on this tour." James said as the column reached the bottom of the hill.

"Is this it?" Samuel asked, stepping down from his horse. "Damn, there's nothing here but that hole in the side of this hill."

"No taverns like in Pittsburgh to amuse ourselves in this time around." James said as he looked around the mine. Hell, Wheeling has this place beat. I don't even see a store anywhere nearby. Forty days in this place! Damn!"

"Well boys, I believe this is our mine." Captain Babb announced as he dismounted from his horse. Turn our houses loose over there in that lot while I go inside that office to see what we're here for. William, come along with me would you?"

William handed Fly's reins over to Samuel and walked along beside the captain to the small wooden building that stood next to the mines entrance. William opened the door and stepped aside allowing the Captain to enter ahead of him. The room was as dark as the mine itself would be William thought to himself as he looked around at its dark corners. It had just one window to light the room and it didn't even have a pane of glass in it. At a desk in the center of the room sat a young man in his twenties. He was reading over a few pages of paper in his hands.

"How do you do, Sir," he said as he stood up from his work and extended a hand to the captain. "I am George Kelly, the owner of this mine. I assume your Captain Babb."

"You assume correctly, sir, I am indeed. What can we do for you?"

"Keep the Tories off our backs. They have been running all over this part of the countryside doing all kinds of mischief. That damn Aquilla Price and his men killed my father back in the spring when they burned down our home. They've been doing everything they could possibly think of to stop our production. Lately, they have been hiding out up on top of that hill outside and taking shots at my men working down here. They cause some kind of trouble almost every day. Last week they shot out my window and hit a poor fellow in the back of his head killing him right where you're standing.

Continentals come and take the lead out of here once a week but they can't stay here all of the time, that's why I asked General Smith to send us some help. I was hoping that you and your men could put up some kind of picket line up there and keep them away for a while.

"We'll get right on it." Captain Babb assured the young mine owner. He and William turned and walked out the door into the mine's yard. "Aquilla Price," the Captain said as he walked over to the horse pen. "Well, William you bested that old rascal once before, maybe we can do it again."

"James, pick you out a man and come along with us. We're going up to scout out the best place to put up a picket line on top of that hill," the Captain continued. To no one's surprise, James picked Samuel, and the four men mounted up and rode back up the hill above the mine. As they combed over the landscape, William began to think of his first adversary of the war. He had not seen Price since that night he had looked through that tavern window over two years ago. But he had kept up with his movements during that time and had heard of the captain's exploits in the war. Burning down this poor man's home and killing his father in the process sounded much like all of Prices' other deeds in this war. Putting an end to his military career would be very satisfying to William. But, if their paths were to cross here once more, William wanted to have the upper hand on the situation. Aquilla Price was a vengeful man. If he ever found out who William was, he most certainly would attack Mordacai's homestead and maybe even go after Elizabeth as well. He would not dare attack Captain Babb's home because that would open the door for retaliation on his own plantation by the patriots, but a plain ordinary soldier's home would look just innocent enough that he might try to pull it off. Sylvester's capture had made the war more personal for William, but if Price ever were to try something like that, the war would be secondary to William then.

"That's our spot boys, right there behind that stone fence," Captain Babb announced, "we can see forever from here across that open field. They will have to come that way don't you think? This way we won't have to dig a trench line and it won't look one bit out of the ordinary. They may just ride up on us without even seeing us behind it then you sure can put those long rifles to good use then. You boys stay here while I go back and bring the rest of the men up here. Kelley said they've been here almost every day so keep a sharp eye out. You never know when they may show up. Tie your horses up one behind the other and I'll take them back with me as I go."

Within a few minutes Captain Babb was heading back down to the mine with the horses walking along behind him. But William and the others were not watching him, they were sitting low behind the stone fence with their weapons lying atop the fence, ready if need be, looking the other way.

"This may not be that bad of a place to be after all," William told James and Samuel, "If we can welcome ole Aquilla in a day or two, there could be more here than just lead here."

Chapter 89
Fallen Horses

Captain Babb's entire command had been lying in ambush behind the stone fence for over four hours now. He had ordered them to sit on the ground and not look over its top, across the open field to the other side. His plan was to completely take Price's mounted loyalist by surprise. If just one of Babb's forty-six men stuck his head up at the wrong time, he would give the whole element of surprise away. The men were not completely blind, for behind the fence every fifth man had loosened a few small stones knocking them out so they could see through it, providing the company with a perfect view of the landscape below.

"Do you see anything out there?" Samuel asked William who was peering through a hole.

"Aw yeah, I see a lot of things, but nothing to get excited about," William answered, "here, take a look for yourself." William scooted down the row a little, giving Samuel enough room to be the lookout for a while.

"So, you met this Captain Price once, did you?" James asked.

William didn't answer; he simply nodded his head 'yes' a few times.

"Well, tell us, what's he like then?" James inquired of him.

"To tell you the truth, at first, I liked the man, but he was playing a part, trying to draw me into his well-used trap, and I fell for it. He's an older fellow; pretty well educated I would say so he knew just how to lure me in. His reputation isn't the best, as you well know now, but I didn't know it at the time."

"Well, I sure wish he would hurry and come on, my butt is getting sore just sitting down here." James said as he shifted his weight from one hip to the other.

"Here, you want to look out for a while?" Samuel asked as he pulled away from the peephole.

"No, I'd rather have my hindquarters sore than my knees, I don't need to see. Let William have it back."

Once more William found himself looking through the fence, out over the field below to the road that led down to the mine. His eye fell upon a dying elm tree that already had three or four dead branches sticking out of its top. Sitting on the dead branches was a flock of buzzards, about ten in number. One of the birds had extended its wings completely out from its body, letting the wind dry its feathers. On the other side of the road was a crop of corn about waist high, moving with the wind. William wondered to himself, would Price ride down the road in full view, or would his men sneak through the cornfield and take positions to fire down on the mine. If they had been Indians, William believed they would have done the latter, but since they were used to attacking the mine with little danger to themselves, he thought they would probably take the easier path and ride down the road, not wanting the blades of corn to cut their arms and faces as they made their way to thru the green stalks to the other side of the field. He turned his attention back to the tree and saw the buzzards take to the sky and fly away to the north. He looked down to the road and saw the black hats of the King's Loyalist brigade rising up over the small incline of the hill. A few more paces of their horses and their red coats were also in view as they made their way down the road. William was disappointed to see that there were only six of them and ole Aquilla was not among them.

"They're here fellows," William whispered as he turned away from the fence and picked up his rifle. Along with the other men behind the fence, he pulled back the hammer of his rifle, cocking it, and waited for the Captain's order to fire. As the unsuspecting men rode toward the stone fence, Captain Babb stood up and gave the order by raising his drawn sword high into the air.

William raised his rifle to his shoulder and placed a well-aimed shot through the chest of the man riding in the rear of the red line. The entire Loyalist force was knocked to the ground from the well-aimed volley, along with two of their mounts. One of the riders had managed to stay in the saddle, but he soon fell back over the horse's rump onto the ground as it tore off in the other direction.

"Boys, reload!" Captain Babb yelled as he slid his sword back into its scabbard, "there may be more yet to come. William did you see Price out there anywhere? I didn't."

"No, I didn't either," answered William as he pushed his ramrod back down under his rifle barrel, in its proper resting place, having reloaded his gun.

"Stay behind this wall boys. Time is on our side here. Let's wait and see if that's all of them." the Captain ordered as he looked out over the field. One of the downed horsed was struggling to get to its feet, but kept falling back on its side, letting out a terrible high-pitched scream. One of the wounded men lying next to the wounded horse pulled a pistol from his blood-soaked holster and raised a shaking arm and shot the animal in the head, stopping its suffering. Then, much like the horse he had just shot, he too fell back to the ground in agony.

"Captain, that man's still alive out there." James said looking to Captain Babb. "Can I go out to him?"

"I don't advise it, but it's your neck. Go at your own risk. We will give you covering fire if needed. Be quick about it my boy, but I suggest you stay here with us."

Without hesitating James jumped over the fence and ran the fifty yards distance to the wounded man, as the rest of the militia watched from behind the safety of the stone fence. As he reached the man, James fell to his knees and looked into his eyes before feeling for any sign of life. He was too late; the man had died just as James reached him. He had maybe as many as ten gunshot wounds in him. James looked back into the dead mans face and whispered, "Sorry mister," before he ran back to the safety of the stone fence and leaped back over to the other side and his waiting comrades.

"Why did you do that?" Samuel asked. "He could have just as easily shot you as he did that horse."

James was still breathing hard from his long run, looking straight ahead, at no one in particular and said, "Any dying man that would think of his horse at a time like that is a good man in my book. I felt like I had to go and see if I could help. He was my mark when we shot off that volley. This one is going to haunt me some."

Chapter 90
A Tooth Pulling

It had been ten days since Captain Babb had won his small victory over Aquilla Price's detachment. Babb's militiamen were truly enjoying their victory, even though Price himself wasn't present at the little skirmish. The Squaw Campaign the year before had been somewhat lacking in satisfaction for them, but this was a victory they could take some pride in, even though the number of men involved on the other side was relatively small, it had a bearing on the war. The mine was running much smoother now that it was not being fired upon every day. Since Price had not sent any more men to harass the mine, Babb's men felt as though they had put some fear into his heart. Believing he was too fearful of another ambush, they hoped he had moved on to greener pastures elsewhere. But having dispatched the enemy, boredom was starting to kick in and some of the men were counting the days until they could return home.

"I'm telling you, we've been here ten days now and we marched for another three getting here, so that's thirteen days in. So, we have twenty-seven more to go until we can get back home" one of the men said to his companion.

"But the three days on the road don't count." the second man argued back. "We still have thirty days left in this enlistment." he yelled.

"Which one do you think is right?" Samuel asked as he and William were standing on opposite sides of James, who was sitting on the ground holding his jaw, watching the two men about to have at it with each other.

"I don't know for sure," William answered, "but if they don't calm down soon we may get to see a good old-fashioned throw down before midnight gets here."

"That's not all you're going to see tonight!" James proclaimed, "This bastard is coming out. I can't stand this any longer. Five days is enough. We'll need some whiskey" he continued. "Maybe Captain Babb has some stowed away somewhere." he said as he got up still holding his throbbing jaw.

"Well, he won't let you have it just to get drunk on." Samuel said as he watched the two men who were still arguing raise their clenched fist and begin walking in a circular motion around each other.

"Well, I can't pull this tooth sober either!" James vowed. "I got to have something to dull my senses down some."

"Hot damn, there they go!" William shouted as the two men began their fight.

"I guess we'll find out which one is right now, Samuel. I'll take the little one for a buck. How about it? You do want that big fellow, don't you?"

"You're on", Samuel answered. "I'll take that wager for a dollar. Damn, get up, you big clumsy ox! Now why did I take that bet, one good punch and he's on his ass. Come on, get up!"

"You can pay me when we get back home." William told him as he slapped Samuel on the back. "Come on, let's go see if we can find some licker somewhere for James."

"Aw, he might get up yet." Samuel said hopefully, "let's give him a second or two. Ah hell, your right. He's out. Maybe that little fellow can knock that bad tooth out for you James."

"By God, I just might let him do it," James answered back sharply.

At first Captain Babb wasn't too convinced about James' request for the whiskey, but after a look into James mouth at the condition of the tooth in question, he soon gave in and let James have two jugs. The first one had gone down with little effect, but the last jug was putting a contented smile on James' face.

"Well, that's enough time spent standing and waiting around." James announced as he reached into his shot bag and pulled out a small pair of pliers that he carried for making repairs to his gun. He took one more long pull from the jug and reached inside his mouth with his new dental tool and began to pull.

"Hell no," he said spitting out some blood, "not yet, that hurt like hell."

"Make sure you got the right one now James." William laughed as he watched in disbelief, "You sure you don't want me or someone else to pull it for you?"

"No," James answered, "give me another ten minutes or so, I'll get 'em out."

"Alright then," William said as he sat down by the fire next to Samuel, "have it your way then."

"If I pass out you can go ahead and do it for me, but I don't think there is enough whiskey left in this little jug here to get the job done." James said as he lifted it to his lips one last time. Five or six big swallows later the jug was empty. James shook his head back and forth like a mad bull, blinked his eyes a couple of times and said, "She's coming out this time boys." Using both hands, one on each handle, he placed the pliers in his mouth and gave the offending tooth a might tug as he bent over moaning.

"He he, he, I got the little bastard." he said as he turned back around to face his friends, holding the bloody tooth in the palm of his hand. "Anybody got a big rock? This damn thing has been hurting me for a good week. Now I'm going to smash it all to hell."

"Here, take this mister," a big black eyed man said as he handed a horse shoeing hammer over to James. Taking the hammer, James laid his tooth down on a rock and delivered a smashing blow that sent the tooth flying into a hundred pieces.

Chapter 91
Old Acquaintance

The next day was William and Samuel's turn to be posted on the picket line at the stone fence. They had been there a few hours when James came walking up from the Militia's campsite to help pass the time of day.

"How's that jaw of yours?" William asked as he was biting into a rabbit's leg he had cooked earlier in the day. "You want a bite?"

"Naw," replied James as Samuel began to laugh at William's joke. "All that whiskey is out of my system now, but the pain sure as hell is hanging around." James answered as he put a hand to his swollen jaw. "It's gonna be awhile before I chew anything. It still hurts every time I drink something, hot or cold. Maybe I'll be able to handle a bowl of soup soon."

"Then why did you come up here?" Samuel asked. "The captain said you could take the day if you needed it to recoup."

"It doesn't hurt any less up here than it does down there." James answered, turning away to spit out some bloody saliva.

William wrinkled his face and said, "You're not chewing any tobacco, now are you?"

"No," James answered as he sat on top of the fence. "It's hard enough to just talk right now. Besides, I tried it right after you boys left this morning, I thought it might do it some good, but it didn't take me long to spit it back out I can tell you."

"Well, you haven't missed a thing up here." William said as he looked out over the countryside. Neither a hide nor hair of a redcoat to be seen this afternoon, I suspect we might have run them all off, or so it seems.

"Listen!" Samuel said. "I hear something coming this way."

"Sounds like wagon wheels to me." William declared as he threw down his rabbit bone and took a knee behind the fence raising his rifle. "Now let's don't get too trigger happy," William said. "It may be some of the Continentals returning for more lead. Let's make sure who it is before we fire on them."

The sound of rolling wagon wheels became louder and louder as a string of wagons made their way toward the stone fence. William lowered his weapon and stepped out into the road to greet the four wagons being escorted by ten Continental Dragoons at the front of the wagon train.

"What can we do for you fine Gentlemen?" asked William as they came to a stop in front of him.

"You can point us to the lead mine." the dusty commanding officer said from atop his horse. "We're out of Ft. Pitt and this is our first time down this way."

"Well, you're here." William told the officer as he pointed down the road. "The mine is just down this hill. You're just a quarter of a mile away."

The dragoon nodded his head as he tapped the sides of his horse's belly with his brown boots and rode off with the rest of the wagon train following behind. Each wagon had two worn out horses pulling them along. There were two teamsters on each wagon, one holding the reins while the other acted as armed guard beside the driver. At the rear of the wagons rode a group of militiamen on horseback. One looked down at William as he was riding by and slowed his pace a little.

"Well, I'll be Adam!" the buck skinner said to the man riding to his left. "That's William Tipton."

"Yeah, and that's James on top of that stone wall." Adam House replied to his brother Andrew. The two men veered off the road and jumped off their horses and clasps hands with William and James as the four of them made their way over to a large chestnut tree.

"Sorry I didn't recognize you there at first." William said as he shook Andrew's big hand, "but with you not having those beaver hats on, it does make you boys look a little different this summer."

Yeah, I guess it does." Andrew agreed, "It's not every day you meet a man that can look this good in either a beaver hat or his bandana. Its way too hot for beaver this time of year, that's why I'm wearing this bandana instead." he said with a grin. Andrew looked down the road and waved to the Captain of the dragoons to go on. "I swear that man thinks I am one of his men. That's why I like being in the militia. Those officers can be awful stuffy."

"Damn James, have you been rolling' around with the Indians again?" Adam asked, looking at James swollen jaw.

"No, he pulled a tooth late last night. William answered.

"What about you Adam? You still have all your hair under that rag of yours?"

"Look for yourself," Adam laughed as he reached up and pulled off his blue bandana revealing a full head of black hair. "Yeah, I still have mine, but there are a few Indians out there without theirs, I'll tell you."

"How's Hannah doing?" James asked through locked teeth.

"Still got her eye on me" Andrew answered. "Hell, she better. We're hitched now you know."

"Yeah, we heard that from a fellow named Chenoweth who came from Ft. Redstone, and Alexander told us about it too as we came back through last fall." William replied. "I was disappointed that we missed you then, but it sure is good to see you boys now."

"What are you doing down this way?" James Asked.

"Aw well, General Hand is gone from Ft. Pitt these days and the fort's new commander, Colonel Brodhead sent us after some lead with these boys here. But the main reason was to recruit some men for a militia that's going up the Allegheny River as soon as we get back." Andrew explained. "How about you all want to come along? It'll be like old times. There will be a whole lot of plunder to be divided up amongst whoever goes along easy money to be made. It will only take us a few days to do it, besides it will be fun!"

"I'll go," Samuel said. "It sure will beat sitting around here doing nothing. Maybe we can get some of those redskins that got away at Wheeling last fall."

"Who's this cub here?" Andrew asked just before he took a drink from his bull horn canteen.

"Samuel Farra," William said. "We picked him up at Ft. Pitt. He's a good man to have along if you're in a scrape."

"That's one," Adam said, "how about you two?"

"Well, we'll all have to see if Captain Babb will let us run off with you two again first." James said, "but I'm chomping at the bit to fight some more. What say you William?"

"It won't make Elizabeth too happy," William said with that crooked smile of his, "but she won't find out until it's all over, and a cut of that loot would be nice to have when we get back home. I'll go ask if the Captain will let us have leave."

Andrew clapped his big hands together and said, "That's what I wanted to hear. We wiped their red asses once before and we can do it again. Let's go and find that Captain of yours, 'eh."

"We can't abandon our post just yet," William answered, "but we'll find out something tonight before you all go back. So, what have you two been doing this year?"

"Well, I'll tell you, it's like this," Andrew said as he stuck the end back into his horn canteen.

Chapter 92
New Love

Joshua walked up to Jeanette Shields' horse and laid a loving hand upon hers and said, "Good night sweetheart, have a safe trip home."

"We will be just fine," she answered, "Don't worry. John will get me home in one piece. He always has." She reached down and brushed her fingertips along Joshua's jaw line and said, "See you soon, I hope."

"Tomorrow?" he asked, "Is that soon enough?"

"Come on you two, break it up won't you? The things I do for my sister!" John Shields said to himself under his breath as he tugged on the reins of his horse, turning the black mount towards the road leading away from the Tipton house. Joshua slapped the rump of her horse with the palm of his hand as she turned away and laughing all the while, called out to her brother, "How much longer are you going to chaperone us John?"

"Until she has a ring on her finger" John replied as he rode off into the darkness, escorting his sister back home.

Joshua turned back to his parent's porch and walked back up its steps and pulled up a chair and sat down next to his brother Thomas and said, "Well what's your impression of her Thomas?"

"She's lovely young woman, I like her."

"Good," Joshua answered as he leaned back in his chair raising its front legs off the porch floor. "I love her."

"I believe the feeling is mutual." Thomas said looking over at Joshua. "I never saw Polly look at you quite the way that one does. I would say she is yours if you want her to be."

"Well, I want her to be, but I don't like all that talk of Tennessee that John and her father are always talking about. I want no part of Tennessee, its Kentucky for me and mine. It sure is good seeing you brother. It's a shame William's not here. I believe this would have been the first time we all would have been back here under this roof at the same time since you got married, but he's not here."

"Yeah, we keep missing each other somehow," Thomas said getting up from his chair and walking over to the porch rail. "I haven't even got to see his child, or him mine for that matter maybe next time. Tell me, Joshua, how do you think Sylvester is these days? He didn't say much at supper tonight."

"Aw, he's just fine," Joshua answered as he sat the front legs of his chair back down on the floor. The main thing is that he has filled back out some. You should have seen him when he first got back home. He would have had to run around in a rain storm just to get wet he was so thin, but mother's cooking is bringing him back slowly but surely.

How about you Thomas, how has the army been treating you?"

"Well enough, I guess, but I haven't done much fighting since Saratoga. Oh, I might get to fire off a shot every now and then, but General Washington's more concerned about keeping his army together than fighting in another major battle and loosing manpower, but I wish he would sometimes. Maybe that would shut Gate's big mouth some. I still hate that I missed Monmouth, but I had to go home at some point. From the way Pop was talking inside tonight, it sounds as though you and William have had your fair share of scrapes."

"Yes we have indeed; you should see him moving through the woods, Thomas, He is something to behold!" Joshua said proudly.

"I'll bet he is, you know he always was the best among us, but don't tell him I said so! Now tell me some more about Kentucky." Thomas said as he sat back down in his chair. "I may have to go out there myself after this damn war is over."

Chapter 93
Up the Allegheny

The appearance of Fort Pitt had not changed much since William and the others had been there the year before, but the situation inside its walls had. General Hand was no longer in command of the fort. He had gotten his wish and was reassigned back to the war in the East. The fort's new commanding officer was Colonel Daniel Brodhead. Also new to the fort was part of the eighth Pennsylvania Continental Line. Captain Babb had once again agreed to let William and James have leave to go with the House brothers, as well as Samuel this time, but before they left, he had warned them that no other Virginia Militiamen would be at the garrison this time. He wanted them to know that the rift between the two colonies of Virginia and Pennsylvania over which one would control Ft. Pitt could possible pose a problem for them. In anticipation of this, he had written them orders to carry on their person to return back to the lead mine as soon as Brodhead's campaign was over. He was not about to let the Pennsylvanians keep three of his best men. That was all William and his companions needed to hear. They were more than willing to get away from the dull post at the mine, sitting and waiting for something to happen had become disagreeable to them, and even though this would be much more dangerous, it would put them back into the war.

"Damn William, do they ever ride horses out of this fort?" James asked as they marched out of the gates of Ft. Pitt with the rest of the six hundred and five men who were going on this campaign.

"Doesn't look like it does it?" William answered as he looked back over his shoulder to the fort's corral where Fly was being stabled while this small army was gone.
"Don't worry about him; they'll feed him just fine while we're gone." Samuel said.
"I know that," William replied, "I just hope we have no problem getting them back on our return."

"Well, it looks like they are going to take better care of us on this march than they did on that squaw Campaign," James stated as he looked down on the Allegheny River at the skiffs and boats loaded down with provisions for this tour. "No food shortages on this trip. They are even going to drive a small herd of cattle behind us this time."

"Hey, does anybody know what date this is?" William asked.

"August the 11, 1779." said a man as he ran by on his way to the front of the line.
"Who was that?" William asked.

"Samuel Brady." answered Adam.

"Heard of him" James stated as he walked along. "By the way Adam, where is Andrew this morning?"

"He's out looking for Jonathan Zane. We heard he was going to be the guide on this here march. If that's the case, we want to be with him. Andrew has drunk down several kegs with Jonathan over the years. So, don't be surprised if we're running up ahead to the front in a while. That is, if you want to."

"Of course, that's where we want to be." William said. "We were in the back of the line when we were out on that squaw campaign last year and we didn't learn anything until Simon took me out spying with him."

Adam walked up beside William and said in a low voice, "I'd keep that to myself if I was you. Girty's name is not too well liked around these parts now days. Hell, I like the man too." Adam said, "but I'm sure in hell not going to tell everybody about it either."

William nodded his head yes and said, "That's the last time I'll say his name. So, tell me about these Indians. Are they like the Shawnee?"

"Injins are Injins," Adam said. "The Senecas fight as hard as any of the rest of them, that's for certain." Then he looked at Samuel with an evil grin and said, "But I do think their scalps come off much easier than do the Shawnees."

"Well, I just hope we stay on the East side of the river." James announced. "I want to keep my feet dry this time, if I can."

"We will," Adam answered. "There's no reason to go over unless we're ambushed someplace."

As William marched along beside the rolling Allegheny River, he began to think of what Elizabeth had said back at Captain Babb's plantation about the mine tour not being as dangerous as, say one of the major battles someplace else. 'She would skin me alive if she knew I volunteered for one of those battles, of course come to think of it, this one is likely to be just as bad.' Then a slow smile came across his face as he thought, 'she may just kill me herself when I get home after this is all over.'

"There you boys are," Andrew yelled as he came walking down the column. "Come on with me. Jonathan is leading the way and he wants us up there with him and Brady. Colonel Brodhead is going to stay with the main army while we are up front spying out ahead of him. Tom Nicholson, that half breed is with us up there too. They say that General Sullivan is going to hit the savages on a second front. Hell, we're going to wipe some redskin ass up this river. If I had known it was going to be this damn easy, I would have brought Hannah along. Western Pennsylvania is going to be a whole lot safer after we're through with them, 'eh boys?"

William's walk turned into a dead run as he and the rest of the spying party ran to the front of the procession and passed the eighth Pennsylvania line. He could not keep from smiling as he heard a young private ask an older soldier, "Who are those men running by?"

"Why, they're the spies," answered the older man. "They're tougher than old pine knots, scalp takers they are, my boy."

Chapter 94
No Small Matter

That night Jonathan Zane took one look at Samuel as he stood by William and James under a locust tree and shook his head as he spoke to Andrew. "That one there really is young, are you sure he is ready for this Andrew?"

"I haven't been out with him myself, but I have the other two." Andrew answered trying to reassure his concerned friend. "William and James helped me get my Hannah back from the Shawnees. All three of them have been down to the Falls and they've even been through Kentucky by themselves and got back with their hair. I wouldn't go out with them if they were greenhorns. They've had their share of battles. They'll do whatever they're told. They're good men to have along in a scrap. Hell, come to think of it, young Samuel there was the one who killed the red devil that shot Captain Scott back on Hands campaign up the Beaver River last year. Their militia captain sure did hate to let them go, but he told me they were plumb too good of a man to be guarding a lead mine. They'll be fine."

"Alright," replied Zane, "I'll take your word for it. They sound as though they have already proved themselves to you. I just wanted to make sure. You know how good Brady and his rangers are. I just don't want any of my men to look bad out there, that's all. In the morning we will be going on ahead of the main army. I don't have to tell you to be ready."

Andrew nodded his head and turned back and walked over to the locust tree.
"I was under the impression that he already wanted us, Andrew," William said. "It looked to me as if you had to talk him into it again."

"Aw, he just wants to look good," answered Andrew. "I can't say I wouldn't do the same. He knows this country as good as the Indians. That's why Colonel Brodhead hand picked him. He just wants everything to go smooth tomorrow, as do we. Remember, we will be the eyes of this army. That's no small matter."

"This army is no small matter either," James said, reaching into his pocket for some of his chewing tobacco. "They are going to make some noise as they march along through these hills."

"That's why we have to be on our toes out there in front of them tomorrow." Andrew said as he watched James begin to chew away on his plug of tobacco. "We can't let any redskins see what is coming or slip past us to spy on our army."

James just nodded his head as he cut another piece of tobacco from his cake and handed it over to Andrew. Then he turned his gaze to William with a gesture asking if William wanted some.

"No, you can keep that nasty stuff for yourself," William said. "I would as soon chew on a dead horse as that stuff. I'm going to get some sleep now boys, so leave me be." William continued as he lay down on the damp ground next to the fast-moving waters of the river. He looked up into the night sky and wondered if Elizabeth might be doing the same thing at this very moment back home. Then he shut his eyes and surprised himself as to how easily he could fall asleep, knowing that he may be going into battle in the morning, but that was becoming an ordinary event.

Chapter 95
Delaware

As William was moving through the woods east of the river, he stopped every fifty or so feet to scan the countryside for any sign that hostile Seneca might be in the area.

His sharp eyes were picking up almost every movement that was in front of him. A gray squirrel's tail was twirling around as he cut into a hickory nut in the low-lying fork of a tree. A young fox ran behind a fallen log with a rabbit in its mouth.

Samuel was moving just as cautiously as William was himself, down in the bottom of the hollow below, and although William could not see him, he knew that Andrew was just over the ridge out of sight doing what he did best, being a woodsman. To William's left was James, going up the riverbank watching over the water to the tree line on the opposite bank. Adam had been taken by Brady out even further into the woods with the rest of Brady's rangers. Then even further in front of them was Jonathon Zane, leading the way, being the first who would make any contact with the enemy, all by himself.

The general idea was that Zane would be able to avoid any Indians while Brady and his feared rangers would turn back any Indians that may present themselves. This last line of defense that William was in would act as a buffer between any Indians that may have slipped past Brady or that might have outflanked the rangers, or any that might be attacking form due east, and the main body of the army bringing up the rear. But William also knew that this was all a precautionary way of moving into the Indian country. The Seneca had no way of knowing that this force was marching up to their back door, so to speak, but it was better to be deliberate than lying dead on the banks of this river, having been taken by surprise.

The ground was still wet this morning from the heavy dew that had fallen the night before. The moccasins that William had on his feet were doing little to keep the moisture out, and off his feet. It made him miss the stockings and boots he had left back at Ft. Pitt, but Andrew had advised against them, leaning more toward the moccasins because they would leave much less of a trail behind and be much harder to track by anyone who might be looking. They also made little noise on the forest floor if a man was careful where he stepped much less than William's hard soled boots.

The sweat had begun to pop out on his forehead as the sun and temperature rose together. It was going to be a long hot day. William took a drink of rum form his wooden canteen and stuck its cork back into the hole as he began to once again move forward up the river. He avoided a thicket of briars by stepping up on the log that the fox had gone behind. As he was making his way down the long tree trunk, he heard the high-pitched sound of a deer snorting up ahead. Then he saw the buck's white flag rise as the animal made its way down toward Samuel. William thought to himself that it was a shame that he could not fire upon this fast-moving deer. It would be quite a good shot if he could hit his mark, but there was no need to shoot this time. The army had all the meat it needed in the rear and the report of his weapon would only give them away and alert the Seneca up ahead. Before he stepped back down from the top of the log, he stared into the surrounding trees and like every other stop this morning; he saw nothing to fear in them. He glanced over towards the river and saw James looking at him from the top of a large rock next to the water's edge. James gave the all clear sign and jumped off the rock and continued to head northward.

A smile came over William's face as he took a step forward. Andrew was starting to rub off on him. He was having a good time being out against the Indians in their own land. It was dangerous work but he still enjoyed it for some reason. It got his blood up and it made him feel more alive in a strange way. He looked back down toward Samuel's direction, but he was nowhere to be seen. William sprinted to the peak of the hill he had been walking up and looking ahead, he saw that Samuel had outdistanced himself from the rest of the line. William shook his head and reminded himself to have a talk with Samuel tonight about getting too far in front by himself. He needed to keep close so the other men could watch his flanks. He motioned for Samuel to slow down, but the young spy was enjoying himself too much, and did not see William's signal. William became upset with his young friend, knowing if they were fired upon, he would be out in front too far to be helped if things turned bad. William turned his gaze back down the line to where Samuel should have been and his heart stopped as he saw a tall Indian, hunched down and making his way toward Samuel from his rear. William was amazed at how well this

Indian was stalking Samuel, moving from tree to tree silently and deliberately, only stepping where Samuel did. The warrior had his musket hanging over his shoulder, but in his hand was a bow with an arrow notched in its proper place, ready to be shot. He was closing the gap between the two of them gaining ground with every step. William leveled his rifle toward the Indian and pulled back the hammer. He did not want to be the man who gave away the army's position, but he wasn't going to let Samuel die at the hand of this savage either. All the Indian had on was his breech cloth and black war point from the belt line up. Suddenly, to William's complete surprise a bronze arm reached up and pulled down William's rifle, then he heard a low voice speak into his ear, "be still and watch." William lowered his weapon and watched as the tall, painted Delaware closed in on Samuel.

'Turn around,' William thought to himself. 'Don't let them catch you like they have me.' But Samuel never heard the Delaware until he reached up and pulled Samuel back against his shoulder. There the two stood until the rest of the advancing line reached them. William uncocked his rifle as he watched the party of friendly Delaware disappear over the hill going towards Andrews' direction. They had been invited by Colonel Brodhead to accompany his army and help lead the way.

Once again, William had learned a valuable lesson from someone who knew Indian tactics far better than he did. Keep your eyes on your back as well as your front, for these woods were full of deadly men. William was upset with himself on two accounts. One, for not watching his back well enough. And second, for not recognizing the evergreen sprig in the Delaware's hair that distinguished the friendly Delaware from the hostile Seneca. This would be the last time he would make that mistake he promised himself.

Chapter 96
Tobacco Pipes

The day had ended with little else happening that afternoon. Zane had piloted the army through another day's safe march and all was well in camp tonight. Brady and his rangers were sitting together telling each other lies and some half-truths as well, passing the long night hours away. Although Brady himself was somewhat guilty of telling too many jokes, he reminded his men from time to time to keep the sound down.

Colonel Brodhead was inside his white canvas tent, listening to the reports of his officers and giving out the next day's marching orders. So far, everything had gone according to plan and he was pleased with his army's efforts, He had already told Zane that he wanted more men to be with him out in front tomorrow, as they traveled deeper into Indian Territory each day.

William was outside the tent holding his pipe by its stem, tapping it against the palm of his hand. He had knocked out all of the burned-out tobacco ash from it and then refilled it with new leaf. He stuck it in his mouth and drew a few puffs as he lit the pipe. He leaned back against a tree and gazed over to the Delaware camp just across the meadow. They were part of this army in the daylight in every way, but by night they kept a separate camp and William enjoyed watching them interact with each other from this distance. He had seen Indian camps before, but this time he could really watch them as a group, not having to pick one out as a target. They were all dressed pretty much the same, the difference being in their war paint. They were all bare chested, their entire upper body being covered in the paint. Their only clothing was dark blue or black breech cloths hang around their waist with tanned brown deer legging that came up a little over their knees. They wore no copper or brass armbands or earrings. Their belts were heavily laden with tomahawks and scalping knives. A few beads hung around their necks, but they were dull colored ones, pale reds and blues, nothing shinny that would reflect light. Powder horns hung around dark necks and shoulders very much the same way as William wore his. A few had smaller knives hanging around their necks, safely tucked into leather sleeves. Heads were shaved almost completely except for a round knot on the top back portion of the head. These had been decorated with black and red feathers entwined with their hair, the red feathers indicating life, the black for death. One man was very much the center of attention. He was carving a ball headed war club from what looked to William to be a piece of maple.

"First time you seen Indians in camp?" asked a voice from the darkness behind William.

William turned and shook his head no as he answered the stranger's question, "but it is the first time I didn't fire on them within a few moments afterward."

"So, you're a scalp taker, are you? Shoot in amongst them and ask questions later, 'eh? Just like Hand did up the Alleghany a while back," the short broad-shouldered man said in a somewhat unfriendly tone.

"No," William replied as he cocked his head and frowned at what he hoped was not his next Ross Gibson. "I've never lifted one yet, but I promise you the ones I did kill had it coming to them, my friend, and I have let others go on their way as well. Can you say the same?"

"I surely can." the man said as he walked on by.

William didn't say any more as he watched this odd man walk into the Delaware camp. James stepped in behind William and peered over his friend's shoulder and said, "What's got his tail all tied in a knot? Ain't we supposed to be out here to kill Indians?"

"Aw, don't pay him any mind boys," Andrew said as he joined the other two. "He knows everyone here but you all. I guess that's his way of feeling you out. He has seen you all here with me and Adam. Everyone knows how we feel about the redskins and he asked Adam once something along the same lines. He didn't like what Adam had to say, but I do believe your reaction was more to his liking."

"Who is he?" William asked as he and the others watched this man sit down between two of the Delaware Indians and take a pipe from one of them.

"Tom Nicholson is his English name," answered Andrew. "He has an Indian one too, but I don't know what it is. His mother was a squaw, I don't know out of what tribe though. He has had family killed on each side, red and white alike. He just can't stand a man who hates every Indian he sees, that's all.

"That's all well and good, but do we have to keep an eye on him from now on?" asked William.

"Nah, he's all right." Andrew answered, "He never gave Adam any grief."

"What did Adam say?" asked James.

"Something like the best Indian is a dead one. Far worse that what you said here tonight I'll tell you. Hell, go on over and talk to him, it will be alright."

"You sure about that" Samuel asked. "What about the Indians?"

"They're with us ain't they? Unlike the Seneca, not all the Delaware are hostile. These men could just as easy be fighting on the other side. General Hand did attack an unmanned Delaware village last year, didn't he?" Andrew said with a smile "Go on over."

"Alright," William answered, "I'll go over if you say it's permitted."

Before he walked over to the Indians William made his way to the side of beef that they had all just enjoyed and cut a few hunks of meat off and then headed for the Delaware camp. As he was approaching the camp, he looked back to his friends and saw they were watching his every step, but gave no indication that they would soon follow.

Then he thought, 'what am I getting myself into here?' He considered turning around, but then reconsidered and continued on. He walked across from Nicholson and sat down on the ground and looked into his eyes before offering each of the Indians a steak. Each one in turn shook his head no, as William made his offering. Nicholson leaned forward and smiled as he placed a hand under his chin and said, "Don't be offended by their refusal. Most Indians will not eat before they go into battle. Our hunger makes our fight that much more fearsome, but come back in a night or two if we don't have any luck tomorrow."

"I see." William said as he stuck the meat into his shot bag. As he looked around into the faces of the warriors who were engaged in rubbing bear fat on their upper bodies to keep off the deer flies and mosquitoes, he saw some familiar ones. "You are the ones who came up on me and my friends this morning from behind which one of you spoke to me in English?"

"I am he," answered the Indian who was carving on his war club, but he never raised his head from his work to look at William.

"Well, I have to tell you that your war paint surely is intimidating. You scared the hell out of me."

"It is meant to do so, but we also wear it for another reason. When we go into battle, we know that sometime we must do horrible things. Things we do not want the Great Spirit above to see, so we wear our fearsome paint so he will not know who we are. When we go to the river and wash it off, we wash our bad deeds off with the paint and he once again knows his children."
"Well, I have to hand it to you as much as I hate to. We never heard you boys until you were upon us. I am happy you're on our side this time around."

"That's nothing to be ashamed of," Nicholson said, "if you're in the woods long enough, I don't care who you are, and it's going to happen sometime or another.

On hearing what Nicholson had said, the Indian finally raised his head from his work and said, "It is true what our friend just said. You can never be too careful on the warpath. But what I saw in your face was not fear when I pulled down your rifle. It was worry for your fellow warrior. That is good; just don't forget your own back next time." Then the older Indian again lowered his head to continue work on his club and said, "We have had words over you tonight. You say you only kill bad Indians and let good ones go. How you know who is good, who is bad?"

"I can't tell just by their looks," William answered. "It's more of what their doing at the time than anything else. What a man does or doesn't do tells what is in the heart more than words I would say, Indian or white."

"You like tobacco?" the Delaware asked as he looked at William's pipe sticking out of his shirt pocket.

"Yes, I enjoy a smoke with my pipe from time to time," William answered as he pulled it out for the Indians to see.

"Never had a white man's pipe," the Indian announced as he handed over his Indian pipe to William with his tattooed arm. A smile came over Nicholson's face as he heard William say to his Delaware friend, "Well you can tonight my friend. Try mine."
As William watched the Indian try his pipe, he knew that he would never forget this night when he had his first real conversation with a Red man on the banks

of the Allegheny River.

Chapter 97
Maybe A Girty

Colonel Brodhead was listening very intently to the courier who had just come running into camp. Samuel Brady had sent this fleet footed young man back with word of a party of Indians heading this way. However, Colonel Broadhead was getting frustrated at the small amount of information he was hearing. "So, you don't have any idea as to how many are coming this way?" the colonel addressed his courier in a strong voice.

"No Sir, I do not. We just spotted a single file column of injins walking up the riverbank pretty far down in front of us. The Captain told me to run back as fast as a wildcat and let you know. He said if they were in small numbers, he would fire on them from ambush, but if they were too many, he would let them pass on by, so as they   would be penned in between the two of us."

"Well, I didn't hear any shots, did you?" asked Brodhead as he stepped from his tent and motioned for Andrew House to come over.

"No Sir, I didn't." replied the runner.

"You're dismissed then, but wait outside my tent for now. House get in here, I have orders for you." Brodhead said as he led Andrew back inside his tent.

When William saw the flap of the colonel's tent fall down, he turned to pick up his rifle and said to Samuel, "Get your gear ready. I believe we'll be moving out of here real quick. Something's afoot."

"Damn it to hell," Adam swore, scrambling to his feet. "Your right, I just knew the one day that Zane left us behind something good was going to happen and we would miss out. They will get all the good plunder before we can get there!"

James laughed at Adam's antics as he sat under his maple tree, holding his rifle over his lap and watching the rest of the men hurry about the camp. "You boys are a whole lot faster when the Indians are about," he said as he stood up from his seat. "Do you think you'll need your powder horn today Samuel?" he asked, "Because it's over here if you do."

William took the horn from James' hand and hung it around Samuel's neck as he sat on the ground pulling on his moccasins. Then he turned his attention back to the colonel's tent just as Andrew stepped out and came running over.

"Come on, a war party is on its way here," Andrew yelled as he ran by William. "That runner said they're about two miles out."

"That's good," Adam proclaimed. "I haven't taken any scalps in a few weeks now. I don't want to get out of the habit just yet."

As William fell in behind Andrew on the run through the camp and into the heavily wooded forest, taking the same route the runner had just come in from only a few minutes ago, he began to clear his mind of all thoughts that did not pertain to the upcoming skirmish. All jokes and frolicking were to be laid aside now. As they made their way down the newly beaten path along the river's edge, they began to spread out on Andrew's command. "Here, up on that rise. Don't you think Adam?"

No one took the time to answer as they made their way up the small hill. William and the rest of the men all knew that whoever held the high ground held the advantage when it came to combat. No other orders were given because they were not needed. Every man took his tree, high above the path and stood quietly waiting for whoever was to come walking down the trail into their trap.

William brushed away a small spider and its cobweb with the side of his hand. It had gotten stuck on the brim of his felt hat as he was running through the forest. He suddenly realized his breathing was heavy from the long run he had just completed, so he began to gradually slow his breathing and calm down. Using the side of his foot, he began to rake away any debris that might make any sound under the weight of his feet as he waited, just as if he were deer hunting back home. He looked to his right and saw Samuel and a little farther down, behind an elm tree was James. William smiled as he thought back to the Squaw Campaign, when he and James had decided to keep Samuel between the two of them for his protection. Samuel had come a long way since that day, but it seemed that they still kept the practice up anyway. William turned to his left and saw Andrew about fifty feet down with Adam between the two of them. He made one more quick check of the powder in the pan of his rifle before he glanced back at Adam. That was when he knew the Indians had arrived for Adam was wearing that devilish grin of his.

The war party was walking along just as the runner had said they would, down below in single file, one behind the other. There was no doubt what they were planning to do on this march, for they all had their war paint on, looking ready for battle. They planned to make some white settlement pay dearly, either today or tomorrow.

Once again, William picked out his man with the sight of his gun and calmly waited for someone else to fire and starting the melee and Adam did. On hearing Adam's shot, William likewise pulled his trigger and felled his mark. The Seneca and Wyandots were completely taken by surprise. The first four warriors in line were all hit. Two were already dead. The others began to retreat back up the path they had just come down, unknowingly heading into the sights of Brady's riflemen. However, their numbers were still much greater than the men firing on them. William and his companions were not going to make any tomahawk charges on foot after forty or fifty Indians, so they all reloaded their weapons as the Indians ran away, knowing that Brodhead was on his way with the rest of the army. William looked back to the path and saw his Indian lying dead on his side with a bullet hole in his head. The two wounded warriors were backing their way back up the path, very slowly, scanning the trees as they went, but no one fired on them, believing they were not much of a threat any more. Besides, no one wanted to get overrun with an empty gun if the war party decided to regroup and charge back at their attackers.

Then up in the distance, more shots were fired, no doubt by Brady's men. Adam shouldered his weapon and looked once more to the path below, William did the same, waiting for the soon be retreating Indians one more time. But after only a short wait they lowered their rifles, as from the opposite direction they watched, as Colonel Brodhead came down the path, with his army behind him.

"William are you still passing on taking your scalps?" Adam asked as he started down the hill at a fast pace.

"Yeah, go ahead; you can take mine if you want." William answered. After reaching the bottom of the hill and making two quick slicing motions with his scalping knife Adam had two bloody trophies in hand, ready to be hung on his belt. As Adam was wiping the blood from his knife, another runner appeared, coming from Brady's direction.

"Colonel Brodhead, most of them got past us but we killed a lot of 'em." he reported. "And sir, one of those friendly Delaware's is saying that one of the dead is James Girty, the brother of Simon."

As William and the rest of the army made their way up to the second ambush site, he was hoping the Delaware was mistaken about one of the dead being James Girty. Even though Simon had gone over to the other side, William still liked him for some reason and he didn't want to see the dead corpse of Simon's brother lying on this path.

"That is him." said a young Delaware. "I see him many times in my old village. It is James Girty."

William watched Tom Nicholson shake his head no as he walked up to Colonel Brodhead who was surveying the dead man and say, "that could be one of the Girty's, but it's not James or Simon either for that matter. I have talked to them both many times and that is not either of them. But he could be some other Girty I have not met."

William looked at Andrew and asked, "Have you ever met his brothers?"

"Yeah, once," Andrew answered as the two of them made their way through the mob of men standing around the body. Andrew bent down and looked the dead man in the face and said, "Well he's definitely a white man. I have only seen James Girty one time, so I am not going to say that Tom is wrong, but I think he's a Girty." As Andrew stepped away from the corpse the Delaware leaned in and took the scalp from the questionable Girty.

William walked out of the mob and made a quick body count of the dead. Twelve Indians lay scalped and dead on the ground at this spot, and there were the two killed by Adam and himself at the first ambush site, and some of the wounded that had managed to escape would probably die later tonight. It was a victory Colonel Brodhead could be proud of, he had lost only one man in this fight and that was from an accidental   shooting by one of the Pennsylvanians who shot himself. The only other drawback to the battle was that the Indians who had escaped would most definitely alarm the villages upriver that the white eyes were on their heels.

Chapter 98
Blackened Skies

A fast-moving rabbit shot out of the edge of the burning cornfield that lay next to this small village of Custaloga at the headwaters of the stream called French Creek. The small animal had waited as long as it could, but the heat from the fire was growing too great for the small creature. Whatever waited for it outside this field could not possible be as bad as this heat. It ran as fast as it possible could, under the wooden platform that the Indians had put up to be their watchtower over this, their most precious of crops. William stopped as he was climbing the ladder to the top of the platform and watched as the rabbit made it safely into a hole left behind by a groundhog a year or so earlier. He made three more steps up and reaching the top. There he stood looking out over the burning field. The rabbit was not the only animal fleeing the flames. He could see a flock of turkeys running out the other side of the field, followed by a deer and her two yearling fawns. The smoke from the flames shifted as the wind blew in a more westerly direction, into William's face. He turned his back to the wind to avoid the smell and to keep the smoke out of his eyes. As he looked in that direction, he saw the evacuated village had turned to ash, with only two wooden cabins remaining standing, but they too would soon fall. Flames were running up the sides onto the roofs, dooming them to the same fate as the rest of the village. Like the cornfield, Colonel Brodhead had ordered that the Indian's bean, squash and gourd fields on the other side of the village be destroyed by fire too. William could see the Continentals torching them and fleeing the flames at a hard run, just as he had fled this cornfield just a few moments ago.

"Come down from there." James called out to William, "you've got to see this." William wasted little time climbing back down the ladder. The black smoke was growing denser by the minute and soon the platform itself would be ablaze.

"What do you fellows have there?" he asked as he walked away from the burning fields and toward the river.

"It's a copper kettle," announced Samuel.

"Nothing odd about that," William said as he approached his friends. "I've already seen ten or more just like that one back at the village."

"At first glance, maybe so, but I don't think you have seen one like this one here," James said as he rolled it over on its side so William could see its flat bottom. Take a close look at that stamp."

William reached down and rubbed the bottom side of the kettle and read the words stamped into the metal by a hammer "Tipton Copper Company, Baltimore, Md 1722."

"Well, I'll be!" William said as he looked at the old beat up kettle. "That's got to be made by some of my kin. My great granddaddy Jonathon Tipton came from Jamaica to Maryland sometime around 1700 according to father. This kettle was surely made by him or one of his sons, I'd bet on it.

"Jamaica?" James asked with an odd look on his face.

"Yeah, that's right," William answered. "He even named his plantation, "Poor Jamaica Man's Plague'. That's what I always remembered about his story. I wonder how the Indians got it way out here. I'm going to take this home to father." William picked the kettle up by its handle and took it down to the river to stow it away in one of the skiff boats that Colonel Brodhead had brought along to supply the army and to help take back whatever plunder the army might capture on the campaign. At the water's edge laid a virtual treasure of confiscated household goods. Kettles like the one William had cast iron pots and pans, bolts of cloth, sewing needles and even mirrors and salt. The fleeing Indians had taken all of the military supplies and weapons with them. There wasn't so much as a single arrowhead left behind, however there was a great quantity of abandoned pelts, beaver, otter, deer and black bear. As William walked away from the river to join the rest of the spies, he spotted one of the men from the Pennsylvania Eighth walking toward him with a powder keg in his arms.

"So, we did find some powder here after all. Was it in one of those last two cabins up there?" William asked, pointing to the village.

"Yeah it was up there," answered the soldier as he sat the keg on the ground next to a large pile of pelts. "But it's not powder. But it sure as hell is going to go off like black powder when everyone sees what's inside." The soldier took his foot and kicked the keg over knocking its top off. He reached down and picked it up and dumped its contents onto one of the pelts.

"Damn, how many would you say are there?" William let out a low whistle as he reached down and picked up one of the scalps that had fallen out of the keg.

"I don't know," answered the soldier "At least fifty, maybe as many as a hundred. I'll have to count to see. It looks as though they had them all ready to be shipped off to Detroit though."

Soon the pile of scalps was completely surrounded by angry men who had lost loved ones to the Indians.

"This could very well be my father's, he had long gray locks like this one here," one man said.

"Oh, God, That's Mary's!" another began to cry. He was holding the scalp of a woman that still bore the blue ribbon that she had tied into her auburn hair the day she had been killed.

William dropped the small child's scalp that he had been holding in his trembling hand back into the pile. It had given him a sick feeling deep in his stomach. This poor child was no older than Sarah, back home he thought. He looked up into the blackened sky overhead and said to himself, 'the souls of the men who could fill this keg had to be as dark as this sky.'

Adam raised an eyebrow as he looked at William and said, "I don't think I will get any disapproving looks the next time I take one of those bastard's hair."

The whole mood of the campaign had taken a drastic turn now. No one really had any reservations about burning the Indian's food supplies before the keg had been found, but now the men were even more inspired to make this one hellish upcoming winter on the scalp taking savages. The hatred of the British as also heightened as well, because everyone could see that this keg was not made to hold gunpowder. It was a whiskey keg supplied by the British Indian agents to keep the Iroquois nation on the King's side by a sick form of bribery. The burning of the village was a good start, but it was not enough. The militia wanted blood and not the blood of women and children, but the blood of the warriors who had lifted these scalps. But time was working against Colonel Brodhead now. He had planned this campaign very well, but six hundred mouths was a lot to feed. The cattle that he had driven along with them were thinning out every day, and the supply boats were not sitting so low in the water anymore. In a few more days he would have to turn back for Ft. Pitt and he, like the rest of his men wanted more revenge than this.

Chapter 99
Brokenstraw Creek

Every mile that passed under William's feet was making him more and more anxious to go into battle. Colonel Brodhead's army was still slowly marching north, up the Allegheny River, but the Seneca warriors that everyone wanted were being as elusive as they usually were. The colonel was beginning to think that most of the male Indians of fighting age were off to the East engaging General Sullivan's force. However, he still had hopes of finding a war party now that his spies were coming up on the mouth of Brokenstraw Creek, but he was running out of time.

Early this morning when the spies walked out of camp no one said a word when Andrew House's small lot of men joined the ranks of the spying party leading the way. William and James, and even Samuel Farra were now part of the elite woodsmen. The Delaware were also completely accepted as a unit of the spies now. It was the largest group yet to front the army. Jonathon Zane was again piloting the way, a little in front of Samuel Brady and his rangers.

William put out a hand onto an ash tree's trunk as he stopped his smooth, quiet movement through the forest. He had outpaced himself from the man to his left and he was waiting for James to catch up. James was having trouble making his way up and around a sink hole that had fallen in next to the river sometime this spring. As William stood there, he could feel the hairs on his right arm tingle a little. He removed his hand from the tree and turned his arm over so he could see what was crawling up his forearm. He sat his rifle barrel up against the tree and took his free hand and flicked off the tick that was running its small legs over William's sensitive hairs. The tick landed on the tree trunk form which he had just removed his hand. William reached for his knife as he thought, 'here, suck on this for a while,' right before he took the point of the knife and stabbed the little blood sucking parasite.

He picked his weapon back up and returned his attentions back to the more dangerous foes that might be close at hand. As he looked up ahead, he could see the river waters converging back together as it flowed around an island that had formed in the river. The trees on this side of the bank were thinning now and he could see the smooth round stones lying on the riverbank just like they had for several miles.
He looked back down to James who had made his way around the hole and was back in position, but as William was watching, James pointed up ahead to the river. William turned his attention back to the riverbank where he saw Jonathan Zane running at full speed back to the rest of the line where he was met by Brady. William didn't have to hear what the two were talking about to know what lay up ahead. Like all the other men who could see what was happening, William checked his rifle and was preparing himself for battle.

Brady stepped away from Zane and made a waving motion for Tom

Nicholson to join the two-man parlay. William watched as Nicholson nodded his head yes and walked over to the water's edge after listening to what Brady had to say. Zane and Brady each took a tree, but not before Zane had a few words with Andrew. After hearing what Zane had to say, Andrew ran to his brother, Adam and told him to send word down the line for everyone to form around Nicholson for an ambush. Several canoes loaded down with Indians were traveling downriver and would arrive within minutes.

William hunkered down inside a small ditch that ran into the river along with the rest of his fellow militiamen and watched Nicholson sit down next to the bank in full view of the river in a cross-legged position with his rifle resting on his lap. Within a few minutes the rest of Brady's rangers were also in place on the opposite side of Nicholson, taking their stance behind whatever tree they could find, completing the trap that was soon to fall on the unsuspecting Indians if Nicholson could lure them ashore.

From his own position, William watched as the first canoe made its way around the island. Nicholson stood up, holding his rifle over his head by one arm and gave out a long, loud war cry to get the warrior's attention. He spoke a few words in the Indian's own tongue as the canoe turned in towards the bank. One of the Indians stood up in the middle of the canoe and spoke back to Nicholson in a welcoming manner as the canoe ran aground. The war chief that stepped from the canoe was no doubt about to hit the white settlements again this fall. He and his warriors were dressed to kill, carrying nothing but their weapons. They would be a fast moving and hard-hitting war party if they got to the settlements. By now the second and third canoes had come ashore beside the first one.

As William gazed upon the powwow he was amazed by how at ease Nicholson appeared and at how well he was playing his role. He had managed to get three of the four canoes to fall into his trap and he had not given up on the fourth just yet either. He stepped away from the chief and tried to lure in the last canoe. Two of the Indians from the second canoe stepped onto dry land and began to walk towards the ditch that William and some of the other men were hiding in, with their rifles at the ready. The first of the two Indians approached a poke weed and raised his breech cloth to relieve himself while his companion, who carried a flintlock, scanned the tree line behind the ditch. Seeing nothing to give him any cause for concern, he turned away and walked back across the clearing. He stopped and watched as several of his fellow warriors also stepped away from the water's edge, but then he gave out a yell as he spotted one of the half-concealed bushwhackers in the trees. He quickly ducked down to one knee as a shot flew over his head, having been fired from the ditch. He fired off a shot at one of the spies across from him, but it would be his last shot for William put a ball through his lower back, killing him instantly. The battle was on. The first volley from the woods was very well aimed, all of the Indians on the bank were down, either dead or wounded, including the chief who had fallen back into the river on his back. He would lead no more raids on the settlements; his body was badly torn apart by a series of bullet holes. Nicholson, being completely exposed to the Indian fire with little cover to protect him was also hit by a shot from one of the canoes. Seeing him go down, William and James jumped from the ditch and ran to Nicholson as the rest of the men were engaged in reloading their weapons as the surviving Indians tried to push the canoes back into the water. Each grabbed an outstretched hand and pulled Nicholson back the twenty feet to the safety of the ditch. As William picked his rifle back up he heard the second volley being fired by his comrades. Several more Indians fell from their respective canoes, leaving just a few unharmed warriors inside. They quickly dove under the surface of the water abandoning the canoes and trying to avoid the third, upcoming volley. By now, the fourth canoe, the one Nicholson had not managed to lure ashore was heading downriver, leaving the other three beached canoes behind. Two of the Indians who had jumped into the river water were hit as they crawled out of the river on the island, but a few more had made it to safety in the trees, making their escape. Only a few of them had managed to keep their guns as they swam across the river, not that they would be of any use, since they were useless when wet. With the Indians being unable to fire back across the river, the whole battle had lasted only about ten minutes and was now over.

As one of the Delaware was attending to Nicholson's leg wound, William saw that Jonathan Zane had been hit as well. Brady was standing over him, looking at his shoulder. The wounded Indians that had survived the volleys were soon put down by the tomahawk and were being scalped by the spies who came rushing in with Adam leading the way. And for the first time in his young life Samuel Farra took one himself. As William walked down into the carnage of the battle he was met by Andrew.

"Are they all Seneca?" William asked.

"No, I see what looks to me to be a few Munceys in the group as well." Andrew answered.

Suddenly, the report of a distant rifle was heard and one of Brady's rangers standing beside the water's edge was hit. A fifth canoe had paddled down the river from the back side of the island undetected. It had picked up several of the surviving Indians who had made it to the other side. One of them had pulled off a great shot from the fast-moving canoe. The warrior cried out a triumphant yell as he saw that he had hit his mark from a standing position. As William rose from the position he had instinctively ducked into at the sound of the gunshot, he saw Andrew pull the trigger of his Kentucky long rifle and when he turned his head back toward the river, he saw the Indian tumble into the water to the cheers of Brady's Rangers.

"Damn Andrew, you sure do know how to shut them up," William said as he looked to the river. Andrew just grinned as he pulled the wooden stopper from his powder horn and poured black powder into his barrel.

"I just hope Brodhead heard the shots and is waiting for them downriver,"

Andrew replied, as he placed a lead ball on a patch and pushed it down to the bottom of his barrel with his ramrod.

Chapter 100
Couldn't Pull the Trigger

As Tom Nicholson hobbled over to one of the captured canoes, he motioned for Colonel Brodhead who by now had reached the battlefield. Seeing that the colonel was heading his way, Nicholson leaned his backside up against the rear end of the canoe and slid over its top as gently as he could, and dropped into its bottom, while holding his wounded leg on top of the craft's sidewall. Reaching up, he picked his bad leg up with his hands and swung it into the center of the canoe, letting out a small groan.

"Is he coming?" asked Jonathon Zane as he lay on his back in the front of the canoe resting his head on a pile of pelts.

"Yeah, he's on his way," Tom answered, "looks like they got the bleeding stopped. How does it feel?"

"Hurts like a son of a bitch," Zane answered. "What about you?"

"About the same as you," Tom replied, "but I'm afraid it will hurt something fearsome in the morning."

"Damn fellows," Colonel Brodhead said as he looked down into the canoe, "how in hell could I lose two of my best spies on the same day? Jonathon, they tell me you are a lucky man. That ball just passed under your collar bone. I have seen enough shoulder wounds to know that if that bone is hit, it'll shatter like a piece of ice with fragments of it flying everywhere into the flesh. It may be hard to believe, but God was with you today. What about you Tom? Bleeding much?"

Nah, one of the Delaware put this rag on my leg and twisted it tight with a stick from a tree and it's doing the job for now."

"Well boys, let's have it, what's on your mind? I know you called me over here for some reason and it sure in hell is not for a dance," Colonel Brodhead remarked as he raised a booted foot up to the side of the canoe and leaned forward, resting his elbow on his knee.

"Brady most likely already knows this, but a Muncey village is only a few hours march away," Zane said. "I know supplies are running low, but don't stop on our account. You can lay it to waste by nightfall."

"He's right," Nicholson joined in, "they have a trail cut through the woods just a little way off the river. I'm sure that any of the Delaware could lead you to it with little trouble."

"We'll take care of it for you," the Colonel replied. "Thanks for the information boys, your efforts and knowledge has been so crucial to this campaign. See you back at Ft. Pitt in a week or so. He shook each man's hand before tapping the side of the canoe with his palm and said, "All right then, off you go." Then he turned and walked away. The canoe began to rock slightly as it was being pushed out into the water by some of Brady's rangers so the wounded men inside could have a more comfortable trip back to Ft. Pitt. With the protection of an armed escort traveling along with them in other Indian canoes they should be guaranteed a fairly safe trip home at least as good of a guarantee as a man could have on this wild frontier.

By now the Colonel had made his way over to Brady who was looking over the spoils of war that had been won today. Brodhead eyed all the captured rifles, muskets, power horns and even a keg of rum and said, "Well, that's a fairly good day's work, but according to Zane and Nicholson we could easily add to these riches. They say there's another Indian village close by. We're going to attack while the iron is still hot. We can still do some damage to these British loving Indians today."

"Brady, I have let Zane pilot most of the way, but I know you are just as capable of leading us, so let's pull out of here and set some fires."

"Yes sir, I know exactly what village they are speaking of," Brady replied, "but with our two losses today, I would like to have Andrew and Adam House along with those other boys of theirs tag along with my rangers. I would like to put them on my flanks, two on a side. That is, if you will allow it."

"Deploy them as you wish Samuel, you're guiding the way now," the colonel answered. "Take whoever you need." As Colonel Brodhead made his way back to his mount, he stepped between Andrew and William who had taken in all that had been discussed.

"If we are on the far flanks Andrew, we'll be the first to run up on the Indians this afternoon if they attack from the east, or from the west for that matter." William said wearing a concerned expression.

"See," Andrew said with that cunning smile of his, "If you're good at what you do like we are, sometimes you're the one with your ass hanging out. Brady saw you and James pull Tom into that ditch. That's the type of men he wants with him."

"That's right," Brady said as he approached the two. "Andrew, you and Adam take the East flank, Tipton, you and Tate head along upriver while me and my rangers take the middle, but we're going to veer off the river some. So, Andrew, you will be a little further out in the woods now."

"What about Samuel, William asked.

"He can stay with us", Brady said as he nodded to his men. I don't want too many men out there. Two on a side is all I need. Keep in mind now, all that you are is just something of a moving picket. Don't try to take a large force on by yourself. If you see any danger come a running and let me know. Let's go."

"William and James did as they were ordered and started up along the side of the river as Andrew and Adam made their way through the rangers to cover the other flank, leaving a very disappointed Samuel Farra behind."

After walking along for about a hundred feet or so, William turned and waved to Samuel as he and the rest of the rangers disappeared into the trees.

"I would rather be on our side than Andrew's." James said as he turned away from William. "At least we've got the river for some protection, if the Seneca cross it will have to slow them down some." William nodded his head in agreement and continued on his way. He was proud of his new-found status of securing the point, but as he looked around and all that he could see was James, moving in and out of sight, depending on the landscape he realized how serious it was. This was the most vulnerable he had been since that night he was rolling around on the ground with that Indian back on the Salt River in Kentucky. The old adage of *be careful what you wish for, you might get it,* came to mind. Thoughts of Elizabeth to his mind as well. She was still under the impression that he was guarding that mine. This mission most certainly wouldn't make her too happy with him. A smile crept over his face when he remembered another of his father's old sayings; *this is one of those things she can hear about in ten years or so.* Realizing that he had his mind on other things than what was at hand, William cleared his head and began to concentrate more on the countryside.

The trees were thickening up ahead and the distance of his vision was shortening with every step he took. Then suddenly, a covey of quails taking the air down next to the river grabbed his attention, and he came to a stop. He cocked his rifle and raised it to his shoulder, placing the weapon in its firing position. He held his ground, waiting to see who or what had spooked the birds into flight. Then, from under the cover of the trees, out stepped a lone armed man with his back to William. He was peering down into the water, walking upriver very slowly. Keeping his sights on his target, William followed the man at a slow, careful pace. After looking up the river for about twenty feet the man stopped and laid his rifle on the bank and waded out into the water to his waist. He reached down under the water's surface and pulled up a stone, and then another, and finely another after that. With the weight of the stones gone up popped a small, one-man canoe that he quickly pulled onto the bank. As he reached for his rifle, out stepped William, pointing his gun at the man's bent back and said, "Let it lie where it is Mister. Now, rise up slowly or I'll put a hole clean through your back."

"The man pulled his hand away from the rifle and straightened up taking both of his hands and pushing back his long, wet black hair, away from his face.

William narrowed his eyes as he said, "Simon? Simon Girty is that you?"

"None other," replied Girty. "You're not going to shoot your old guide now are you William?" he asked as he looked up to his captor.

"I sure don't want to, but I will if you try something foolish, Simon. You were good to me back at Ft. Pitt, but we're on different sides now. What are you doing out here?"
"Getting away from that army of yours William I saw them heading for Muncie town, but they won't find anyone there of any importance. All of the warriors are off on the war path. It's just mainly women and children along with the old ones."

"Are you going after the warriors to bring them back?" William asked.

"No, I'm going west," Girty said as he turned back to his canoe and dumped out the water that was still inside. I'll be taking my rifle with me now William, it's a long way to Detroit and I'll need it." As William kept his rifle at the ready, he watched Girty pick up his rifle by its stock with one hand in a non-threatening manner and lay it in the bottom of the canoe. As he stepped over into it he said, 'Well, if someone was going to catch me out here, I sure am glad it was you. So long William, maybe next time we will have a little longer to talk."

As William watched Girty row across the river to the western bank, he remembered his last conversation with Simon that night at the gates of Ft. Pitt, when he told William to watch his hair and not to fall into the hands of the Indians. William knew that Girty couldn't pull a trigger on him if he were ever to be in Simon's sights, just as William couldn't now.

As soon as the canoe ran aground on the far bank, Simon picked up his rifle and laid it on the ground. He submerged his canoe back under the water and disappeared into the tree line without a backward glance across the river.

Chapter 101
Side Saddle

Elizabeth scratched her nose just before she dropped one of the last remaining red apples from the top of the tree that stood in the side yard of her and William's home. The apple fell into the basket that she had set on the ground below, but it rolled off the overfilled basket onto the grass along with several others that had made the same drop. She smiled as she stepped down from the ladder, she was using to reach the higher ones on the top of the tree. Six bushels was quite a good amount for a tree this size she thought to herself as she reached the ground. Hessian soldiers had been combing the ridges in and around Winchester, purchasing and eating apple pies from the noncombatant Quakers who lived in the vicinity, so last thing she wanted was for these apples to draw some unruly German mercenaries to her door while William was away. As she picked up her basket and began to make her way to the barn to store away the fruits of her labor, she noticed how low the sun was hanging in the sky. Realizing that she had stayed here way too late, she had a decision to make. Should she stay the night here all alone, or should she head on back to the Babb plantation? It would most certainly be dark by the time she reached Mrs. Babb's house. She had been riding over here every Saturday afternoon since William had been away but this was the first, she had come alone.

Everything had been so quiet here in the bottom that she felt she would be safe here by herself this afternoon. It made her feel closer to William and not quite so lonely for him when she was here at their home, even though William himself was away. However, time had gotten away from her while she was doing her work and she realized there really was no decision to be made. She had to get back to Sarah. And poor Mrs. Babb would be so worried, wondering what had become of her beloved house guest if she did not return. Even though she knew she was going to be very late, she felt the proud feeling of accomplishment come over her as she sat down her basket inside the barn. She had way too many apples for the amount of crock jars she had to store them in for the upcoming winter. She still had time to dry some of them and maybe if William returned in time, they could even make some into cider. They would most definitely last deep into February and maybe even into the first of March she found herself musing as she stepped outside and latched the barn door.

She made her way across the barn lot to her mare, Lilly and bent down and picked up the reins, patted Lilly's soft nose, fed her one of the small apples and said, "Sorry old girl about not taking off that side saddle while we were here, but I just didn't want to have to handle it again today." She led the horse over to a stump that had not been cleared away from the barnyard and using it as a step, mounted up on Lilly's back. She pulled on the reins and the two of them made their way down past the barn and house onto the lane that cut through the cornfield William had planted this spring. The stalks were no so green now, they were beginning to turn brown and dry out. The ears would harden up fast now that fall was coming. They were already far too tough to eat off the cob now. William would have his hands full when he returned home, picking the corn and putting up the shocks. She was happy that he had passed on raising any tobacco this year. He felt like there would be a good chance that the militia would be called back up in the late summer or early fall, making it too difficult to harvest the crop while the war was still on. And as it had turned out, that is exactly what had happened.

Her shadow was growing taller on the ground now that the sun was setting and soon it would be dark. She tapped Lilly's side to make her pick up some speed and cut down on the dark time she would have to travel on the road. Suddenly she remembered the last promise she had made to William before he left with the militia, *not to go to the farm alone,* and here she had done exactly that, and to top it off, it would be dark when she finally arrived back at the Babb plantation. William would certainly be upset with her, as she was herself for not paying more attention to the time. *But why tell him about it?* If nothing happened on the way back, no one would know but her and Mrs. Babb. The two women had become fast friends over the last two years. She would surely keep a small secret from William if Elizabeth asked her to. At any rate she was just under a half-hour away from her destination now that she had made her way past James's dark homestead and she knew the road well enough to get back, even in the dark. Just up ahead was the lone fork in the road that she would have to pass, but the Battle Town crossroad appeared to be clear. It seemed that way back in the Fifties, a rowdy tavern was established here at this crossroad, leading to its notorious name. Even old Colonel Dan Morgan of Saratoga fame had taken a fancy to the place back in his youth. At least that was how Captain Babb had told the story to her anyway.

As she rode past the intersection, she noticed how at night all the fall crickets sounded so loud when they were singing to one another. She began to hum along with them, trying to keep herself calm now that it had grown dark. She was on about her fourth song when she reached where the road turned away from the creek and made its last turn until it wound past the Babb plantation. Just a couple more miles and she would be safely home, but then she heard a sound coming from behind her. She looked back down the road and saw two horsemen riding fast up the road and one called out for her to "Halt in the name of the King." Hearing this she flattened herself low on Lilly's back and tore off down the road as fast as she could go, hoping that Lilly could see where they were going. As Elizabeth looked back over her shoulder, she could see that she was not pulling away from here pursuers, but they were not gaining on her either. She reached down into her saddlebag and pulled out William's pistol, praying that she would not have to use it. One more backward glance showed her the riders were beginning to gain on her. As Lilly ran down the dirt road, Elizabeth noticed the road had been cut down by all the carriage and wagon traffic that had passed over it during the past hundred years, leaving a high bank on each side. Hoping she could lose them in the dark in the underbrush she gathered herself and leaped from Lilly's back onto the high bank. She hit the ground hard, rolling over several times until she came to a stop under some bushes as
Lilly ran on followed by the dragoons. Fortunately, poor Lilly was just as afraid as Elizabeth was and never stopped running and soon outdistanced the British soldiers who could not see that their quarry had disappeared from the horse's back. Elizabeth quickly ran down the field until she came upon one of the rock fences that Captain Babb had surrounding his property. All she had to do now was follow the fence to the Babb home. Other than a few cuts and bruises she had escaped unharmed. But

how in the world was she ever going to explain this to her husband; especially if Lilly was lost?

Chapter 102
Where the Devil Sleeps

The Muncey towns had been just as Simon Girty had said they would be. No big force of warriors to engage. Just like the village on French Creek, it too had been set ablaze and quickly consumed by the flames. Several more hundred acres of cropland had been destroyed in the wake of Brodhead's fast-moving army yesterday. The highlight of the day had been the discovery of Simon's deserted cabin. Inside they found a stack of documents addressed to Girty from the British command back in Detroit, along with a few of his own reports that he had not managed to send off North to his superiors, having left them behind on his crude bed in his haste to escape. The discovery had energized the army, giving them something to look for in the woods in and around the sacked village. It also made the Delaware even more convinced that the white man killed back on the river was indeed James Girty and now they wanted his brother Simon as well.

William had known that Simon was a hated man, but he did not fully understand how badly his turncoat friend was hated until that moment. Men were running around the village as though their lives depended on finding this white savage. William, knowing more about the situation than any one of them, elected to stay in the village and not take part in the wild goose chase. He knew Simon was long gone by now and he certainly was not going to tell anyone of his encounter with Simon on the river. He had worked too hard to build his reputation and he wasn't going to put it in jeopardy now that it was made. Besides, he could lose more than his good name if it ever got out.

A firing squad was not out of the question. Brodhead was a good commander, but he could be a hot head at times and he just might not understand why William had let Simon go. He wouldn't be as forgiving as Captain Babb in a situation like this. At the time, William had not had enough time to think of it as letting an enemy go, to him it was just not being able to kill a man he considered his friend. So, as the army combed the countryside looking for their villain in the woods, William went into Simon's lodge. There wasn't much left of it after it had been ransacked by the mob. There were a few broken bowls and cups lying about on the dirt floor along with a few articles of clothing. Simon had no furniture inside or any personal belongings to speak of for that matter. Simon may have stayed here some, but it certainly was not his home. As William stepped back out the door a torch was thrown inside by one of the Continentals.

"The devil may have laid his head there last night, but not tonight." the

Pennsylvanian said as he ran to the next dwelling.

Today had been little different from the one before. Except for the fact that this doomed Seneca village of Yoghroonwago was the home of Cornplanter instead of Girty. It had fallen to the same fate as all the others on this river. Cornplanter was also away and not able to defend his own home. This would be the last of the Seneca towns to be attacked on this campaign for Colonel Brodhead had turned around and was leading his army home and out of eastern New York.

As the army marched South, Adam's hip was almost completely covered by all the scalps he had hanging from his belt. He was walking in front of William, beside Andrew and William was listening to the two of them as they walked along the river's edge.

"This is the hardest we've been able to hit the Injins so far Andrew. How bad is this going to hurt them do you think?" Adam asked as he lifted his rum filled canteen.

"Greatly," Andrew answered, "we haven't killed many this fall, but our actions will come winter when all their food supplies are gone by February. And maybe next year not so many of them will raid south or to the East. I would dare to say a great number of them will stay behind next spring, remembering what we have done these last fifteen days."

Adam nodded his head in agreement and said, "I believe so too, but before we start patting each other on the back and handing out commendations to one another, we still have to get back to Ft. Pitt in one piece. I sure would sleep a lot better if I knew where and what Girty was up to. He is out there someplace and he needs a victory to give the Indians something to feel good about this winter. With Clark taking the Illinois country and us kicking their red ass here, he is going to make someone pay and I don't want it to be us."

"Don't worry about him." William said, "I have a feeling he is heading west."
"Well, I hope your right about that," Andrew said as he looked back at William. If you aren't, I sure in hell wouldn't want to be in Kentucky right now."

William just nodded his head, hoping that the House brothers were wrong this time about Simon, even though they had always been correct about him in the past. William had let Simon go and he prayed that someday he would not regret the decision he had made on the river that fateful day, but somehow deep down in the pit of his stomach he knew it had been a mistake to let him go. It had all happened so fast, he hadn't had a whole lot of time to think about it then, if he had it to do over, he might have held him prisoner, but then he remembered Cornstalk's fate back at Fort Randolph. Simon's death would have been very similar to that of the chief's if he had turned him over. It was a hard position to be put in, but he had made his decision and it was over and out of his control now. Second guessing himself couldn't change the past so it did no good to dwell on it now.

Chapter 103
A Blue Dress

William hung his copper kettle over Fly's backside, just above the horse's rump. He had tied a string to the handle and ran it under his saddlebags and tied the other end to the saddle itself. This was his entire portion of the plunder that he would be taking back home with him. The rest he had elected to sell off in an auction that had been held inside Ft. Pitt yesterday. He had planned on giving the kettle to his father, Mordacai from the first moment he realized where it came from, so it had to make the trip back home. Other than it, nothing else had grabbed his fancy, so parting with the rest was easily done. Hard currency would be much easier to carry home, besides he wanted to bring something back for his girls and having money to buy it with would be better than anything he could trade for.

"Fellows, I'm going to look around some down in the town before I leave today." William told James and Samuel as he swung up into his saddle. "Would you all like to tag along?"

"Sure," James replied, "I could stand to buy a few items myself, but nothing too big. Samuel here can watch our rigs while we're looking."

"Now why would you think that I wouldn't want to look around some too, maybe pick something up for myself?" Samuel asked as the three of them rode out of the gates of the fort.

"Calm down, you can go in if you want to," James answered laughingly, "all I'm saying is someone will have to watch our horses while the other two are inside, you can have a turn."

"What are you looking for anyway Samuel" asked William. "I have a family to buy for and James has his home to maintain. Maybe that little girl you were twirling around at Captain Babb's dance? I've been waiting for you to tell us something about her, but you have been as silent as the grave about that pretty little one. I thought you would talk our heads off about her on this tour, but you haven't. Going to take your sweetie back a red ribbon?"

"Well, maybe I will at that," Samuel replied. "She's one of the Riley girls, they just moved into the bottom this spring. Lydia is her name. I only spoke to her once before that night, but we had a good time at the dance. She's a good girl, not like those women back at Wheeling. Maybe something will come of it."

"This is the place I had in mind," William said as he pulled his horse to a stop.

"Nothing in there for me," James said as he leaned back on his horse with a grin.

"I had a clock more in mind, you go on in with William if you want Samuel, and I'll stay with the horses this time."

William tied the reins of his horse to the black hitching post that stood in front of the store and walked through the door of the only dress shop in Pittsburgh. He had never shopped for a woman before and he had no idea of how to go about buying for one now. Elizabeth surely could use one store bought dress. Blue was his favorite color on her, but she was more partial to green. But he was going to be the one looking at her, so blue it was going to be. As William walked around the shop, waiting for some assistance, he saw Samuel pay for his red ribbon and quickly make his way back out the door with a sly grin.

"What can I do for you?" the man asked from behind the counter.

"I need a dress for my daughter and one for my wife as well." William answered.

"How old is the girl?" asked the man, "and what color do you want."

"Two, she's two and make it green if you have it."

"Sure, I have green," the man said as he walked over to the other side of the shop. "At that age one size fits all. How about this one"? He said as he presented a dark green dress of a child's to William.

"Looks good to me," William replied.

"Now, on to the difficult one." the storekeeper said. "How tall is your wife, Sir?"

"She comes to right under my chin," William answered with a grin.

"Is she thin or round in the middle,"

"Thin," William replied.

"And the top," the storekeeper asked again, "small, middle sized, or big?"

"She is somewhere in the middle," William said. "I sure am glad you're a man. I don't know if I could have spoken to a woman about such matters as this."

"We thought as much," the storekeeper said as he nodded his head towards his wife who had just come out of a back room. "Most of the men coming from the fort prefer me instead of her. She sells to the women folk while I tend to the men's needs. What color do you want sir?"

"Blue this time," William answered, feeling more comfortable with the situation.

"We have one with a little amount of white lace on the neckline and down along the end of the sleeves over here. Right this way sir and I'll let you have a look." William followed him over to the front of the store and watched as the man pulled a dress from a shelf and unfolded it onto a table so that William could see it in the sunlight that was coming thru the window.

"That's the one!" William said.

"She will need white stocking to go with it," the storekeeper prompted, "and maybe a pair of shoes?"

"I'll take the two dresses and a pair of stocking to go with them," William answered, "but I'll pass on the shoes."

"Very good sir, I'll have the missus wrap them up for you."

"William looked down at the dress and felt the fabric between his fingers and said, "You know, I believe you're correct. Show me the shoes as well. She deserves them."

Chapter 104
The Love of His Life

It was late Sunday afternoon as the Tipton family was making their way back from church services. The congregation had held an after services meal in the churchyard to celebrate the safe return of the militia. All of Captain Babb's men had made it back safely, unharmed once again, and most of them were in attendance at the meal. Samuel had even managed to drag James along to the delight of William and Elizabeth. It had been a most pleasurable afternoon for all who attended. Samuel had truly enjoyed himself in the company of young Miss Lydia Riley. She had stayed by his side most of the day and soon after the end of the morning sermon, a neatly tied red ribbon had appeared in her long black hair. But what had turned everyone's head was the fact that James had stayed by the side of Lydia's sister-in-law, Prudence. She was not wearing her black mourning clothes, because for the first time she had left them at home. Her husband, Drew Riley had been killed at the Battle of Long Island and she had elected to stay with her in-laws even after their move from Maryland to Virginia. If this match between her and James took, they would make a very handsome couple.

"That was nice wasn't it?" William asked as he turned his newly purchased carriage in to the lane that led up to their home.

"Yes, it was," Elizabeth answered, "It was divine. It almost makes things feel normal around here again. I am happy for James and Samuel. Maybe we'll have a couple of wedding to attend before long."

"Could be," William said with a smile, "and this carriage sure does make it more convenient to travel with Sarah."

"Captain Babb had certainly taken a liking to you, William. You are deep in his good graces. He sold it to you for a most reasonable price," Elizabeth continued on, "It seems his generosity has no end when it comes to you."

"I think you are right about that." William answered, "But don't sell yourself short, a lot of it is on your account too. The Babb's have you in their good favor as well."

Elizabeth just nodded her head a little and said, "Maybe they see a little of their younger selves in us."

William pulled the carriage to a stop and looked over at his wife and said, "I think so too. Here, let me help you down." He stepped from the carriage and walked around to the other side and reached up and took Elizabeth's hand and helped her down. "You sure are something to behold in that blue dress, my love. You're still the belle of the ball." Then he pulled her up close and gave her a kiss on her cherry red lips, "Sweet as ever." he said as he released her from his embrace.

"Elizabeth chuckled as she straightened her dress and gave William a loving look as she turned back to the carriage and said, "Sarah sure did have a time today. She is out like a candle in the wind. She was so cute in that green dress of hers running around the churchyard." Then she picked up the sleeping child and said, "I'm going to put her down to bed for a while" and started to take the little girl into the house. As William was leading Fly and the new carriage to the barn, she turned back and said, "I sure do like those yellow wheels. They really make the whole carriage shine."

As William was taking Fly's gear off, he glanced outside to the cornfield and said, "Fly, old boy, tomorrow we harvest that corn and not with a torch mind you, but with a corn knife and a wagon. Today may be for black carriages with yellow wheels, but tomorrow it's a farm wagon for us." He reached down into one of the six apple filled baskets that sat beside the barn door and picked up two and fed one to Fly. As he turned the horse out into the pasture, Lily saw the apple and ran up to the gate for hers. William obliged by giving her the other apple, before making his way back to the house.

Elizabeth had left the front door to the house open, not being able to shut it with Sarah in her arms. The fall breeze had felt so good blowing thru the room; she had let it stay open for the fresh air. William entered the open door and took off his hat and hung it on the wooden peg that he had driven into the wall for just that purpose. As he turned away from the wall, he kicked off his boots and asked his wife "is she still asleep?"

"Yes," Elizabeth answered as she walked away from the child's bed. "I like to watch her sleep when I can."

William watched her walk over to their bed and sit down on it. She raised her dress a few inches so she could look at her new shoes.

"Do you like them?" William asked.

"Oh yes, I do" she answered as she looked down at the black satin shoes.

"Good," William replied, "I almost didn't get them for you, but I'm glad now that I did. Why don't you pull that dress up a little higher so I can see the tops of your white stockings?"

"Alright," she said as she stood up from the bed. William leaned his back against the wall and watched as she bent over and pulled up the hem of her dress ever so slowly, until the garment was above her knees. Then at his encouragement, a little higher, to the top of her stockings, then, just high enough to reveal the white flesh at the top of her thighs "Would you like to take them off for me?" she asked in a soft girlish voice as she sat back down on the bed and extended one crossed leg.

William walked across the room and took a knee at Elizabeth's feet and unfastened the buttons of her shoe and slid it off, dropping it to the floor. He kissed her toe through her stocking and laid her foot down and picked up the other with his strong hand behind her calf and took off the remaining shoe. He placed his tanned hand on her knee and spread her legs ever so slightly apart. Gently sliding both hands up her soft legs until they reached the top of her stocking, he slowly began to unroll them down her leg. Her eyes never left his as she reached around behind her back to pull the draw string to her dress. As he pulled the stocking from her foot he returned her gaze and said, "Don't take it off, I want you in it." She ran her fingers through his black hair as he rolled down the remaining stocking. He stood up and walked around behind her and loosened the string that bound her dress and pulled the neckline down around her shoulders all the while kissing the back of her neck. William lay back upon the soft mattress of their bed and reaching up to her, took her hand in his as she straddled his body in a sitting position, still in the dress. She bent down to give him a kiss, but before she reached his lips he stopped her so he could gaze down into the top of her dress at the round deep cleavage before him. He put his hand on the back of her head and pulled her down for the kiss that she delivered so well. She rose back up and placed both of her small hands atop his chest and leaned forward as William thanked God for the love of his life.

Chapter 105
Unattainable Revenge

Two years was a long time to be on the Ohio and Mississippi Rivers, but that's how long Captain David Rogers had been sailing up and down the two extremely important waterways. If this new nation was to be won, it would need a way to ship in and out all kinds of cargo from its interior. Captain Rogers, along with a handful of other riverboat men were proving that the navigation of these rivers would be the future of commerce in an independent America. He and Basil Brown had been very busy since they shot the rapids at the Falls of the Ohio last summer and paddled on down to the Mississippi bound for the port of New Orleans. Major Linn had made a successful run the year before with a single keelboat but now Captain Rogers was leading back a small flotilla of four keel boats bound for Ft. Pitt, loaded down with military supplies.

The Kings Navy could blockade the eastern seaboard, but as long as the Spanish controlled the mouth of the Mississippi, the American's could still bring in supplies through this back door. The Captain had been in New Orleans for only a few months, building his fleet and making purchases with everyone from Spanish officials to outlawed pirates to fulfill his young nation's needs. Progress had been slow coming back up against the constant downriver current of the river, but under his leadership the fleet had made it to the Ohio and back up to the falls. Last week he had made a very difficult portage around the falls and dropped off some desperately needed supplies at Corn Island, and picked up some additional men as well. Richard Chenoweth had assured his old friend that the next time Captain Rogers found his way to the falls a newly constructed fort would be waiting for him, but that would be a year or two away. Now the little flotilla was making its way towards the Licking River. Captain Rogers was beginning to relax some, believing the hardest part of his journey was now over.

A young teenaged Shawnee warrior sat on a high hilltop that lay next to the Ohio River. He had his horse hidden away and tied to a hackberry tree right behind him just as he had been told to do. The long hours of the day had been dragging by slowly and he was wishing he had not been selected for this uneventful task. Although he would much rather have been back with the rest of the war party on the Licking, he was determined not to take his task lightly. He had kept his eyes intently on the bend in the river that lay just down from his lookout post. He was lying on his stomach holding his musket in his hands when he spotted a large piece of driftwood floating down river in the fast-moving current. Pretending that it was a heavily laden flatboat, the young warrior pointed the muzzle of his weapon at the target and followed its course downriver, shooting off many "big knives" from its deck. As the driftwood floated on out of sight, his mind once again drifted back to camp. Simon Girty, the much talked about white Indian was there in charge of the war party and the young Shawnee just knew he was missing out on seeing this great man. He had hoped to watch and listen to this man that could walk in both worlds Indian and white alike. He knew it would be a great learning opportunity for him, but instead, here he sat shooting at imaginary boats. He reached out to wipe away a drop of moisture that had formed on the barrel of his musket with his thumb, when he saw four keelboats make the turn around the river's bend going upstream. Wasting little time, he crawled back away from the bluff's edge and untied his mount, leaped upon its back and raced off to give the alarm.

Simon Girty had given another of his inspiring speeches this morning to the two hundred Shawnee and Wyandot warriors that had come along with him to the river bank. Although it had been a shorter version of the one he had given at Chillicothe, he still had managed to inflame the war party tempers by reminding them of George Rogers Clark's victory over Hamilton in the Illinois country and his settlement of Corn Island in Kentucky. He had also pointed out that now the white men were showing less fear of traveling down the Ohio River and only a complete rout of the upcoming flotilla would slow down their settlement of Kentucky and put fear back into their land hungry hearts. Now that he had received word that the keelboats were close by, he had put his plan into motion.

John Watson dropped his shoulder pole down into the water in the rear of the boat and began to push into the muddy riverbed, propelling the boat upstream. As he walked toward the front of Captain Rogers's boat, still pushing away, he saw a small two man canoe up ahead, crossing the Ohio from the Indian side of the river.
"Basil, look at that!" he said as he pulled his pole out of the water, "Do you see them?"

"I surely do," Basil answered making his way to the Captain at the rear of the boat. "Captain, we have caught some Indians in midstream up ahead and I don't think they have seen us yet." he reported to Rogers.

"How many of them are there?" the Captain asked.

"Just two, in a single canoe, they seem to be heading for the Licking."

"Abraham Chaplin," the captain yelled, "you and Robert fire on those redskins.
"Which Robert" asked Chaplin?

"Bentham, Robert Bentham," replied Captain Rogers.

"That's an awful long shot to pull off Captain," Chaplin said as he pointed his rifle at the canoe.

"I know," Rogers said, "but they will be in the Licking and out of sight fairly soon. If we are going to get them it's got to be now. I am not going to turn into the Licking just for two Indians. Both men fired their rifles but both shots came up short, missing their marks. The two Indians, now seeing the keel boats began to paddle frantically for the mouth of the Licking River.

"You didn't hit em, but you boys sure did scare the shit out of them," laughed Basil, "look at 'em go. Hell, Captain the way they're acting I would say they are all alone. Why don't we pull in and kill them and do some hunting while we're on the Kentucky shore afterward?

Captain Rogers looked across the river to the northern bank where just last year he, along with the rest of his crew had dug the graves of the passengers of that doomed, burned out flatboat. What had been left of the charred craft had been washed away by the heavy spring rains, but not from his memory. How could he ever forget that old woman and her dead grandchild? Two lone Shawnee would not put his four keelboats at much risk, he thought. "Alright Basil, let's go get them. Who knows they may very well be the same bastards that captured that flatboat last year."

"Let's hope so," replied Basil, "I just wish William and his boys were here to see this. I know they were just as bent on getting revenge for that deed as we are."

"A deadly wicked smile came over Simon Girty's face as he saw the first keel boat turn up the Licking, about to fall into his trap. He, along with the rest of his men stayed out of sight as the two-man canoe ran aground and the two decoys ran up into the trees. A few shots rang out from the keel boats, but again they missed their mark.

Captain Rogers jumped ashore with both his pistols in hand followed by Watson and Bentham. Basil even came ashore this time, packing his long rifle with several other members of the crew. They soon took to the trees after their prey, still feeling confident that it was only a matter of time until they would have their revenge, but it was not to happen today.

Girty let out a war cry as he stepped from behind an oak tree, leveling his rifle at Captain Rogers's chest. The black smoke rolled from the barrel as the ball hit the Captain in the stomach. The ambush was on and one hundred screaming Indians charged into Captain Rogers's small crew in the woods, while the rest climbed up on the keel boats in the river. The Indians also launched ten canoes from the far bank paddling for the other keelboats that had not landed on shore.

Captain Rogers fell to his knees, knowing that his life was about to come to an end. He could not believe that he had foolishly led his men into this killing field. All his past experiences had told him to stay off the shore, but his emotions had gotten the best of him this time. He had made a deadly mistake and he knew it.

Watson and Bentham were also wounded in the devastating volley, Bentham in the legs, Watson in both arms. To his amazement, Basil had somehow not been hit. He simply dropped his gun and took off in a run as fast as he could possibly muster. As he was running away, he could hear the screams of his fellow crew members coming from the water. If he was lucky he may be able to reach Ft. Harrod in a few days or maybe Ft. Boonesborough and bring back some help if any of the wounded could hold out that long.

Only one of the four keelboats had managed to escape, it having been last in line and never turning off the Ohio. As they watched in disbelief from their deck they could see that it was a complete massacre. Their Captain was gone.

As Girty picked up Captain Rogers pistols and stuck them into his belt he looked out over the battlefield. His plan had worked to perfection. Only one boat had gotten away and it was the smallest of the group. It was his finest hour so far in the war and he had just captured tons of valuable supplies for his Indian allies. As he was making his way to the river, walking around the scalped bodies of the dead and dying he spotted the young Shawnee spy who had brought word of the approaching boats. He placed a hand on the young man's shoulder and asked, "What's your name, my friend?"

"Tecumseh," the proud youth answered, "Tecumseh."

Chapter 106
Closing Doors

William was having a hard time trying to get the barn door shut; it was hard to push closed with all the snow on the ground. He had to stop and rake away the small pile of snow that had formed just to be able to finish the task. He turned around and picked up the two rabbits he had shot while out hunting this afternoon and headed back down to the house thru the path he had cleared so many times this winter just to be able to get to the barn. This had been a long, snowy winter and he couldn't very well climb thru knee high snow every time he had to see to his livestock. As he stepped up onto the wooden porch, he stomped his feet hard, trying to knock off as much of the snow and ice that had frozen to the bottom and sides of his boots as he could, before stepping inside.

"I see you had some luck," Elizabeth said as she smiled up at him from her chair in front of the fire where she sat sewing on a new night gown for Sarah.

"Yeah," William answered as he closed the door. "It sure does make your chickens feel a little safer, at least for another day. I could see it in their eyes while I was cleaning the rabbits inside the barn."

"You can tease me all you want about my chickens," She laughed up at William, but I don't care how cold it gets out there, we are not going to eat all the chickens before spring comes. I have something for you though. The postman finally came by today while you were out. You got a letter from your father and one from Joshua too. They are on the table, inside your Bible. Not a word all winter and then two in one day."

William kicked off his boots and walked over to the table and opened his Bible and took out the two letters. He moved to his chair in front of the fire and sat down, stretching his cold feet out in front of the hearth. As he broke the wax seal from the paper, he let out a small sigh. As he was unfolding his father's letter, Elizabeth could see the concern in her husband's eyes and said, "Don't worry honey, I'm sure they are all in good health. It will be good news, they will be pleasant letters." William didn't look up from the unfolded letter in his hand; he just began to read it aloud, so she could hear its contents too.

Dear Son,
It is another cold day here and not much is going on at present. So, I have taken up my paper and quill to write you a few lines. All is well here as I hope it is at your home. I am feeling fine as is your mother and as far as I know all of your brothers are as well. Sylvester and Joshua have awayed to Baltimore together, but have promised to return the first week of March. I have already written Thomas asking him to do the same. I am sure that you are just as aware as your mother and I are that our family has been blown to the winds over the last few years. It is our hope that you and your family could also return on that week so we could all be under the same roof once more, God willing. Today is the Twenty eighth of December. I am hoping this letter will come to your hand before March arrives. If time allows, please send us a response.

Until then, I remain your father,
Mordacai.

"See, I told you they are all alright. Joshua's letter will be the same," Elizabeth assured him. "What about going back in March? Are we going? It sounds delightful.

I could even see my family as well."

"Of course, we're going," William replied. "It has been ages since I've seen Thomas and Sylvester. Come hail or high-water, we'll be there."

"Good," Elizabeth said as she put her sewing down to give William a kiss. "I am going to start supper now." William handed her the letter and ask her to place it back in the pages of his Bible for safekeeping and began to open the last letter which was dated January 4, 1780.

Dear brother,

Joshua here, I along with Sylvester am in Baltimore at the present time. Sylvester had some business to attend to here in the city and being in such a weak state from his captivity, I have consented to accompany him on his travels. Not wanting to lose another sweetheart while I was away, I have proposed to Jeanette Shields. I now relate to you the good news of her answer. Yes. I was going to tell you this in person, but as I am penning this letter, I felt obliged to give you some good news to go along with the bad. I now come to the point of this missive. I am not sure if you have already received the bad news elsewhere, but I regret to tell you that our old Captain and friend was killed in ambush on his way back from the Falls near the mouth of the Licking River along with most of his crew. I do not know the fate of Basil Brown but, God willing he made it out alive. It has been said that Simon Girty led the war party that did the deed. I just can't fathom how Captain Rogers fell into a trap like that. He was always so cautious while out with us. May God have mercy on his soul?

> *Until better times your brother,*
> *Joshua*

William bit into his upper lip as he sat there in the firelight, hardly able to believe what he had just read. He had let one friend go, only to lose another to the hand he had shown mercy to. Captain Rogers had been a good commander and he had become a true friend to William and now he was gone. Placing a shaking hand under his chin William closed his eyes and wished that he had never left that damn lead mine or even met Simon Girty for that matter. Deep down he knew that he was not responsible for Roger's death but it didn't make him feel any better. He knew that like the barn door outside, he had to close this door as well but it was going to be a hard one to shut.

Elizabeth dropped pieces of flour-coated rabbit into her skillet and swung it in over the hot coals of her fireplace as she asked her husband "What did Joshua have to say?"

"Well, you were partially right," William answered, "there is some good news; Joshua is engaged to a girl names Jeanette Shields."

"You don't seem too enthused about it" Elizabeth said as she turned away from the hot hearth "You don't believe it's a suitable match?"

"Oh, I'm sure they will be fine for each other," William answered "I'm happy for Joshua, but that wasn't the reason for the letter. Capt. Rogers is dead."

Chapter 107
Brothers Once More

Mordacai opened his front door and stepped outside as Nancy, one of Thomas's little girls ran inside the house followed by Sarah who bumped into his legs as she too ran by, leaving their grandmother Sue sitting outside alone on the front porch.

"Whoa there, slow down youngins. You'll get a knot on your head if you're not careful," he called after his rapidly disappearing granddaughters. "You look a little ragged around the edges," he commented to Sue as she leaned back against one of the porch posts, obviously happy and contented. "They sure have livened things up around, here haven't they?

"Shhh listen, you hear that racket inside? That's our children in there."
Mordacai just smiled at her and nodded, "You're enjoying having a house full of children, again aren't you?"

"Yes, I am," she answered. "It's a God sent blessing to have all my boys' home again. He has answered my prayers. First Thomas runs off to war, and then Joshua and William went west together, out there with all those Indians. I was worried sick. But when Sylvester was captured, I thought I would lose my mind. I had many long nights that I thought we had lost them forever. I never thought I would get them all back alive, much less all here at the same time again, with their families."

"Well, they're back home for now, so why are we out here all alone while they are inside?" Mordacai asked. "Come on, let's go back in." The two of them got up and went inside the house to rejoin the family reunion. Both Sue and Mordacai could see how the faces of their young boys had turned into the faces of mature men. Men they were very proud of.

William and all his brothers were sitting around the table enjoying each other's company for the first time in years. Days gone by were revisited; tales were told and retold over again to the sound of laughter. "Remember when..." had begun several conversations today and everyone has a least two stories to tell. But now, by the evening meal the subjects were becoming more serious. Thomas wanted to hear about Kentucky from William and Joshua. But Joshua was more interested in talking about his intended instead, so it fell to William to tell his older brother what he wanted to know about their land in Kentucky. Sylvester announced that he had been hired as a schoolmaster in a small school in Baltimore. He had had enough of the war and was afraid that if he were captured again, they could put him to death because of his escape. His record would show that he had not been paroled or exchanged for. He had no way of knowing if the British had his name listed on a document that would bode trouble for him and finding out was not a risk, he was willing to take. Not that anyone could blame him; the war had been hardest on him. He had been in one major battle and several small skirmishes before he was captured. He had done more that his part of fighting even before his time sitting in the hull of that death ship.

Sylvester leaned forward at the table and resting on his elbows said, "You know, when I was in that harbor I sometimes felt all alone. It was like I never had a family. All of your faces had somehow disappeared from my memory. And for a while there, I completely lost you. It's good to have brothers again. So, tell me, what's in all your futures now." All four men glanced around at each other even though they remained silent a moment as they each felt that connection that only brothers can have.

"Not many changes for me," William spoke first. "I plan to return home and go about my life."

"And the war" Thomas asked?

"When the militia calls, I'll go," William replied, "but not until. What about you?"
"Captain Galloway said I was to be a sergeant upon my return, so that should answer that question. I am in until the end. You all know General Lincoln's army is bottled up and may soon fall at Charles Town in South Carolina. My guess is the war is going to shift more to the South if that city is captured. I'll most likely be sent down there soon."
"And what of you Joshua" Mordacai asked as he sat looking down at his sons from the head of his table.

"Tennessee maybe," Joshua answered as he looked directly at William. "The Shields want to go and see what it's like down there. I may go with them, but don't worry Brother I sill plan on settling in Kentucky. But that may all change if Thomas is right. We might all be heading south."

William nodded his head and said, "There's no big hurry to get out there. I have seen enough of Kentucky to know that it's not safe for women and children just yet, maybe in a few years, but not now. I definitely plan on settling out there, but not before the war is won. It may sound foolish, but I would still like to engage the British army somewhere before I go west. What about you father, do you ever see yourself moving out west with us?"

"Don't tell your mother, but I just may tag along with you boys one of these days," Mordacai replied. "I'm not dead yet. This old farm has about worked itself to death, and I don't see why I have to die with it. It would be nice for all of us to stay close together out there someplace. You know, Sylvester, they are going to need schools out there someday too. No reason you can't come along as well."

"Oh, he may have one reason." Joshua put in with a grin, "and it wears a skirt! He seemed to be fairly well acquainted with General Starks' niece Mary back in Baltimore. Aren't you brother? He spent most of the time we were away with her. I may not be the only Tipton with a wedding on the horizon."

William stood up from the table, drawing the attention away from his smiling brother Sylvester and said, "Well, while we're making announcements, Elizabeth and I have one to make too. Come over here, my love and stand by me. Elizabeth walked to her husband's side and took her place beside him as he took her hand in his and said, "I am overjoyed to let you all know that my beautiful wife here is once more with child.

We will have a new addition to the family come this fall. I am hoping for a son this time so pray for us. This is the start of a new decade, so let's all pray that the Eighties bring an end to this war and our sons and daughters will inherit a peaceful America."

Chapter 108
War in the Bottom

The topsoil was turning over well as William ran his plow down through his cornfield. It was soft and loose under his feet as he walked along behind Fly. A good crop always started with a timely plowing like this one. The ground was not too wet or too hard. He was happy with the condition of his field. As he reached the end of his row, he noticed that his beloved horse was not as fast as he had once been. The years were piling up on Fly now. "This is your last time to be hitched behind a plow ole boy," William promised. "Green pastures are all you'll see next year. One lazy day after another, but not today, come on. Turn around and fall back in line." William bore down on the plow handles as its sharp blade bit into the soil. He glanced down to the south end of the field to make sure his rows were straight when he saw black smoke rising in the afternoon sky. He stopped Fly and wiped his forehead with his shirt sleeve. *'Someone must be burning off one of their fields somewhere. It's an easy way to get rid of last year's weed seed'*, he thought as he went back to work. But his eyes were once again drawn to the smoke as he was making his way back down the field. *'That looks to be coming from James' farm'*, but that didn't make much sense. James had burned off his field last week. Maybe he was misjudging the location of the fire. It could even be coming from Captain Babb's plantation instead. It was hard to judge distance by smoke. As he completed another round in the field, William knew something was wrong

Grass fires burned up quickly, and disappeared much quicker that this one was. He pulled the pin that held the plow to Fly's singletree and jumped on his back and rode back to the house. As he ran inside he called to Elizabeth who was out in the barn gathering her chicken eggs to come inside. Quickly grabbing his rifle and powder horn, he stepped back outside the door and met Elizabeth with a full basket of eggs in one hand.

"William, what's the matter?" she asked.

"I don't know for sure," he replied, "but something's afoot. I'm going to see you stay here and watch the road from the woods around back. If you see anyone coming up our lane that you don't know, you and Sarah take to the trees on Fly.

Elizabeth watched as William disappeared inside the barn, returning with her mare Lilly. They set off at a fast gallop down the lane and up the road that led out of their bottom. She stepped back inside the house and picked up Sarah's doll from off the kitchen table, and trying to stay calm for Sarah's sake said, "Come on little one. Let's you and me go out in the woods with Fly and play a game until your daddy comes home."

As William made his way toward the smoke, he knew it was not coming from James's farm; it was still too far away to be his place. He took the end of his reins and slapped Lilly on each side, urging her to keep up her pace. As he made his way up the bottom, he could see James standing outside his barn looking at the smoke while he saddled his horse. William never slowed down as he past James' gate, just yelled from his saddle, "It's at the Captain's!" as he rode by, knowing that James would soon catch up on his faster and fresher mount. And by the time William had reached the   crossroads James had indeed made up the ground and was racing to the fire beside William. As the two of them rode up beside the stone fences that bound the Babb plantation, they could see the Captain's home and outbuilding were ablaze. When they made the turn up the plantation lane they could see that the roof had already collapsed, leaving only the blackened outer walls of the mansion standing. They quickly dismounted from their winded horses in the circular drive that ran in front of the house, both armed with their rifles and neither knowing what or who had started the fires.

"My God," James said as he ran as close to the flames as he could, holding his hands and arms up to block the searing heat form the fire, trying to see inside. "I don't see anybody William. You don't' think they are still in there do you?"

"I don't know," William answered, "but if they are, those flames have surely consumed them by now. Let's circle around back and see if anyone is back there." They quickly made their way around to find the detached kitchen still standing, but no one was inside, or anywhere else in sight for that matter. William was losing hope of finding anyone alive when he and James stepped out of the kitchen and walked around the last remaining side of the Babb home. There under an oak tree sat Charity Babb on the ground with her husband's head lying in her lap. William ran to her and fell to his knees while looking down at his friend. The Captain's eyes were swollen shut and his face had several cuts. He was bleeding badly from the beating he had taken and he was coughing up blood."

"Who did this Charity?" William asked as he took her hand.

"Aquilla Price and his damned Tories," she sobbed, looking up at him with anger in her eyes.

"How many" James asked. "Which way did they go Mrs. Babb, can you tell us?"

"I don't know where they went, but he had maybe two hundred men with him. You lads can't go after them. There are too many for you, but you can help me with Buxton. We've got to get him away from here and into a bed. They took the best horses with them, but you can catch a few loose ones that they ran out of the barn before they set the fires".

William and James picked up their old Captain, as the flames from the main house began to spread to the roof of the kitchen, setting it ablaze too. As they carried him away from the heat of the flames, Mrs. Babb told them to be careful of his ribs when they set him back down on the ground. "I fear some of his ribs are broken. They gave him such a devilish beating. They thought they had killed him, and I did too at first, but after they fired the house and rode off, he regained his wits for a minute or two before passing out again."

"Try not to worry, Mrs. Babb, we'll run down a couple of your horses and take you two back to my house," William said. "I know it's further away that James' but, its more isolated, being at the far end of the bottom. If Price is still out there somewhere looking for you, we'll make you harder to find, besides Elizabeth can help you nurse the captain back to health. Now it's our turn to help you."

They left Mrs. Babb with her husband and began to scan the grounds for some sort of transportation to move him on. The Tories had burned the carriage along with the barn it had been stored in which left the two desperately looking for another option.

William had managed to run down one of the draft horses with little trouble. The big footed animal was of a quiet nature and easily cornered. Meanwhile, James had run down to one of the outlying sheds that Price and his men had left still standing, and there, between it and a corn crib was an old wagon. It was still useable, so he quickly motioned for William to bring down the draft horse to hitch to the wagon.

William drove the wagon up beside Captain Babb and pulled the horse to a stop. James tied Lilly to the back of the wagon while William leaped down from the seat. Then gently as possible the two of them lifted their bloody captain into the back of the wagon. As William drove the wagon with the Babb's riding in the back, down the lane leading away from what had only this morning been their home; James rode up beside him and said, "I'm not going with you to your place William. If we come up on Price my single gun will be of no consequence. Instead, I'll go and gather up the militia and have them assemble at my house, if it's still standing." William nodded his head as he turned onto the main road and James' mount road off in the opposite direction in a full gallop.

"How would you have me go, Mrs. Babb? Fast with haste, or slower, not jarring the captain as much?" William asked.

"Let's try a normal pace," she replied, "I want to get him in bed, but not at the risk of doing him more damage."

"How about you" William inquired, "You have a goose egg sized bump on your head. Did they hurt you other than that?"

"No, I was out for my afternoon walk in my garden when I saw their long red line riding up our entrance. By the time I got back to the house, it was already in flames and they had Buxton tied up to the lattice of the grape arbor. Price was standing by as one of his men was having at it on poor Bux. I ran up to stop them, but one of those dogs knocked me to the ground. I guess that's how I got the bump. Price never addressed me personally; he just turned his back and continued to watch Buxton's beating. When they finally stopped, his only words were, 'That will teach you to fire on my men from behind stone walls.' Then, without another word, he mounted up with his men and rode off. It might have been twenty to thirty minutes before you all got there."

"Don't you worry," William said. "If they had turned our way when they left you, me and James would have run up on them. I don't think even Aquilla Price would take his men down a dead-end road, so they must have gone the other way. We'll soon have the Captain in my home under your and Elizabeth's good care.

Chapter 109
Twenty Men

William had taken Lilly into the barn and quickly saddled her up and was off to James's homestead, but not before saying a prayer for his friend. Having left Captain Babb in the capable hand of Elizabeth and Charity he had headed out with a heavy heart. Although he had continually told Mrs. Babb that her husband was a strong man with a good fighting spirit that would help him overcome his injuries and help him recover, he knew he was lying to her as well as himself. The type of beating that Buxton Babb had taken could kill a man in his twenties. Captain Babb was a man of advanced years and William knew his life was very much in danger. If, by the grace of God he did survive, it was going to take quite some time for him to recover. And what kind of recovery would it be and for what not the war. The Babb plantation had no bearing on the outcome of the war. There was little military value there of any kind. No, Aquilla Price had done this evil deed for his own satisfaction and little else. William sincerely hoped that enough men from the militia could gather together in time to make Price regret this day's work.

As he rode up to James' yard he was met by Samuel who had no idea of what had happened today or even where James was for that matter. He had been at the Riley farm courting Lydia. After hearing the bad news Samuel had bolted into the house and was quickly back out the door, armed and ready to go. The two of them walked out into the road and looked down its tree lined sides and saw nothing but dirt and rocks.

"I don't know how long I can stand here and do nothing." William said gripping his rifle. "But I don't know what else to do. James took off toward Winchester to call out the militia, but Price could have gone the same way, maybe only an hour or so ahead. Who knows what lies down that way? He said he was going to have the men rendezvous here, but no one is here. Some of them should have gotten here by now."

"Why don't we ride off down that way and see what's afoot?" Samuel suggested. "No one will be coming from your way. We could stop at that Battle Town crossroad and wait there instead." William agreed and took little time making his way to the horses. Both men quickly mounted up and were off down the road at a hard gallop only to once again see no on at the crossroads. The smoke from the fire could no longer be seen in the distant sky over the Babb Plantation, but the smell still hung in the air, making William all the more frustrated. As he sat on Lilly's back he began to ponder which direction that son of a bitch Price had taken. William already knew he definitely hadn't gone north towards his and James' end of the bottom or they would have run into them. James had ridden west toward Winchester, but William felt that Price would want little part of that Patriot filled town, but on the other hand maybe that was the reason James wasn't back yet. The Babb Plantation was on the eastern fork, so if all his musings were correct, that only left the southern fork. William pulled Lilly's reins to the South, hoping he would see some evidence that this was the route Price had taken, and soon he found it. Several piles of fresh manure dropped onto the dirt and numerous divots that had been kicked up by a large body of horsemen left little doubt that this is the way Price had fled. Now that he knew where to go, his frustration only grew, because he knew two men could do little damage to such a large force. Then, to his vast relief, he saw James riding up from Winchester ahead of twenty men on lathered mounts armed to the hilt.

"How's the Captain?" James asked as soon as his horse came to a stop.

"At death's door, I'm afraid," William answered. "They have taken the southern fork my friend, but from Mrs. Babb's description and the looks of their trail our small party will be greatly outnumbered, but I still want to go."

"That never stopped us when we were in Kentucky." James answered.

William narrowed his eyes and nodded as he turned his horse's head toward the rest of the militia and said, "I don't know for certain what awaits us down this road, but Captain Babb is one of the best men I ever had the privilege to meet and I don't believe he is going to live to see the dawn. We've bested Price's men once before at the mine, and I don't see any reason why we can't again if we all go now. How about it? Do we make that bastard atone for his bad deeds?"

No one objected and no one cheered after William had said his piece, they simply fell in behind him at a fast pace, soon to be biting at the heels of Aquilla Price and his Tories.

Chapter 110
One Clear Shot

Night had fallen upon the road as the militia chased after Price and his red coated Tories. The chase had been going on now for some time and it was apparent that their chance to overtake him in the daylight was over. Realizing their situation, William slowed the pace of the pursuit, allowing the horses some rest as he rode along between what he discovered had become his two best friends in the entire world. He was bone weary, but nevertheless, he continued to go over their options in his head.

"Damn, I wanted to find them before now," James spoke from his left. "We'll lose their trail in the dark."

"I don't think Price will keep going due south," William said, "that would put him in the mountains someplace. What reason would he have to go there, but to hide? And we all know his pride is too big to allow him to do that. If Mrs. Babb's count is reasonable, his numbers are far too big to cause him concern. No, I think he is going to follow along beside the Rappahonnock. Then they will cross over to the other side sometime tomorrow and put its waters between him and us."

"Do you think he knows we're coming after him?" Samuel asked as they continued down the road at a steady pace.

"I would bet that he does," William answered, "but who knows what's in his mind?'

"But I know what's in yours," James said as he pulled his horse Trace to a stop "Cresap's Bottom."

William nodded his head as the rest of the men circled around the three. Realizing that he, James and Samuel had become the unofficial leaders of this band of militia, he spoke in a clear loud voice. "The element of surprise is our best tactic since they greatly outnumber us. If we had come up on them this afternoon, we couldn't have done much but shoot at his rearguard. But, if we can catch them tonight, we can fire off maybe four or five rounds before they know what's hit them, or more importantly, how many of us there are. That's assuming they don't bed down in a town tonight. If we can catch them out in the open, we can do some real damage. All we have to do is find their campfires. Samuel, you're not going to like this, but I want you to stay here and keep the boys on the move and together, while James and I scout out ahead for those fires. You'll be in charge here until our return."

"Good Lord, me in command?" Samuel said with a nervous laugh.

"You've got more experience that anyone else here." James told Samuel. "But remember, you can still ride into an ambush yourself. So, keep those big ears and squinty eyes of yours open. When we spot them, we'll come back and get you all. But stay on the move until then."

William and James turned their mounts and continued down the moonlit road. With the help of its grayish glow the road could be see well enough to maintain a fairly fast pace. When a large cloud moved over the moon, blocking its light for a long moment, William looked to the heavens and wondered if this was some kind of sign from God, letting him know that Captain Babb had left this world and its earthly problems behind. Any other night he would not have given a dark cloud a second thought, but tonight was not just any other night and he was afraid it could be a bad omen. Not able to see as well as they could only a moment ago, they had little choice but to slow their mounts to a walk. Then up ahead, a large owl took flight, across the night sky giving out a high pitch screech warning anything or anyone of their presence.

"Did you see that," James whispered. "Someone's under that pine tree."

William nodded his head yes, as he reached for the pistol he had tucked in his belt. They both left the road and approached the tree, William on the left and James on the right.

"Who goes there?" William asked pointing his pistol at whoever was hiding in the low hanging branches.

"Don't shoot!" a young voice said.

"I won't," William replied, "not if you come out of there right now."

William lowered his weapon as he watched a young Quaker boy of about twelve or thirteen emerge from the cover of the pine tree onto the once more moonlit road.

"What are you doing out here all alone, boy?" James asked the frightened youth. "'Why aren't you home with your folks eating your supper?"

"I've been cut off by a bunch of redcoats," the boy answered. "Father always said if the British were to ever come this way to our home, I was to take to the fields until they left."

"You mean to tell me that Aquilla Price is at your farm right now, as we speak?" William asked.

"I don't know what his name is," answered the boy, "but there are men staying in my father's yard and the officers are staying inside the house. I saw that much from the creek around back."

"How far away" James asked, "Why don't you show us the way, but we'll have to stay out of sight now."

"It's not far, they are on my father's farm now."

"One more question," William said, "Do they have a picket line set up away from the house?"

"What is a picket line?"

"A group of soldiers staying out away from your house, on guard" William said.

"No, I don't believe they do," the boy answered, "come this way, I will show thee; it's just up around the bend and down that hill."

"Can you see the house from the top of the hill?" James asked.

"Yes," the boy replied as he pointed a hundred feet up to the top of a small hill. Hearing this, William and James dismounted and handed the horse's reins to the young Quaker and told him to stay put as they proceeded up the road until they reached its summit. Lying on their stomachs they could see the Quaker homestead down below, just as the boy had said it would be. The farm's cattle lot was full of horses with several others tied to the fence. There were men walking around the house and grounds. A few fires were burning in the front yard, but most of the

Tories were across the road camped out in a pasture. They were very lively and loud and the two spies could easily hear their conversations. They seemed to be very much at their ease, casually moving around with each other, not paying much attention to their surroundings.

William turned to James and whispered, "If we could get our men in those small woods by the big camp across the road, we could have a turkey shoot."

"But we'd have no shot at Price," James said as he pointed to the house.

"You know he's sitting on his fat ass in that house with his feet under a dinner table feeling awful proud of himself."

"Your right," William answered, "and that don't sit too well with me. If you're willing to take command in the woods I'll go over behind the cattle lot and wait for Price to step out of the house. He'll come a running when we fire off our volleys. Maybe I can get a clear shot off at him before he gets out of the yard."

"If they charge you, William, you'll be all alone out there by yourself. We may not be able to save you. Hell, it's going to be hard for us to get away ourselves," James pointed out. "Are you sure you want to do this?"

"Oh yeah," William answered as the two crawled back down the hill. "But we'll wait until they're bedded down for the night before we attack."

"Alright," James answered, "We have a plan."

During the past three hours William had been busy. First, he and James had made their way back to Samuel and the rest of the militia. There they explained the new plan of attack. William's thoughts then turned to Lily. She was not going to be a fast-enough of a mount for him to complete his upcoming escape. Not wanting to leave Elizabeth's mare behind for the enemy, he had decided to take her back down the road a few miles and hide her away in a hollow, out of sight. Now, here behind the cattle pen, he had selected one of the Tories better horses, a solid black Friesian who was tied to one of the wooden split rails of the fence. He had also picked out one of the better saddles and bridles and had silently saddled the animal. Now all he had to do was stay out of sight and wait until James made his surprise attack across the road.

One by one, the loyalist was falling asleep in their respective camps. Only a few targets were walking around the dimming fires. William and James had already predetermined that this would be the best time to make their attack. So, William knew that all hell was about to break loose on these brave men who would beat a single older man to a pulp while his wife stood by helplessly watching. William had placed himself at the corner of the fence facing the house, giving him an excellent view of the front porch and providing him with the shot that would send his old adversary to hell. He felt that and James had put together a solid plan. His only reservations to it was that it was going to unfold in front of the peace-loving Quakers who would never take part in any war, but he had little control over that now. From his hunkered down position, every now and then he could see someone inside the house cross in front of the side window, but he could not make out who they were. He had hoped to see Price before the attack took place. He could not even be sure Price was in the house. This being the home of a modest Quaker family, old Aquilla might not have taken a liking to their simple ways and traveled on down the road to find more luxurious lodgings instead.

Growing anxious for something to happen, William peered across the road into the woods where James should have deployed his men by now, but he couldn't see any of them moving about. This was a good thing, he supposed, because if he couldn't see them, the sleepy enemy most likely couldn't either. Without warning, the front door of the house opened, drawing his attention back to the house. As William watched concealed behind his fence he saw Aquilla Price walk onto the porch. He was holding his favorite tobacco pipe, confirming his presence here tonight. William carefully set his gun barrel atop the fence and calmly waited for James' volley. Across the road, hidden in the woods, James too had seen who it was that stepped out of the house and sat down in a chair to take his ease in the fresh night air while he enjoyed a good smoke from his pipe. William did not see the flash that lit up the woods as James' men fired off their first round into the Tories camp, for he had his eyes on Price. He did hear the thundering of the reports from the militia's rifles. The first volley had been very effective, knocking down most of the men standing around the fires. The rest leaped to their feet in complete confusion, not knowing where or who was firing on their position. Price rose up from his chair, calling out in a loud voice, "To arms men, to arms!" as William pulled the trigger of his rifle. The ball flew across the yard striking Price's arm and tearing deep into his shoulder, causing him to tumble off the porch into the dark. The men who had camped on the western side of the road beside the house, rose to their feet and were making their way to the horses that were penned up in front of William when another round of shots came from the woods and into the camp on the other side of the road, hitting another ten to fifteen men. But this second volley gave away James and Samuel's position to the Tories in the yard. As William mounted his new horse, he saw an officer organizing his men into a two by two firing formation in the road, preparing to fire into the woods that were filled with William's militiamen. From atop his horse, William pointed his pistol at the officer and delivered a killing shot to the officer's body before he could give the order to fire.

Having been fired upon by two well aimed volleys, the King's Loyalist Brigade took to their heels across the other side of the pasture abandoning their commander, their horses and their fellow men in the house and yard. This gave James the chance to deliver a third round into the remaining forces that came pouring from the yard onto the road and giving William time to bolt into the cover of the woods. This last volley had little effect, hitting only two men, but it gave away their position, allowing the Tories to fire off their first volley into the woods, but doing little damage to James' concealed men.

As Samuel was reloading his rifle from behind a black gum tree he saw that the retreating men in the pasture had reformed and were running back across the field in a bayonet charge and closing fast. Realizing that even though their battle plan had worked to perfection thus far they still were vulnerable to a counter attack, Samuel fired his rifle at the charging line killing another of Price's men. Seeing that they were still greatly outnumbered and not being able to slow down the determined rally, he called for a retreat. Hearing Samuel's call, James gave the same order. Quickly the militiamen mounted their horses and dashed out of the woods onto the road as the bayonet charge entered the now empty woods on the other side of the trees. A few shots were exchanged between the fleeing militiamen and the Tories that were still formed on the road, but like a swift moving wind, the militia was back over the hill and out of range of the Tories Brown Bess muskets. William who was closest to the road and out in front of his men when the militia made their well-executed retreat stopped his horse and made a quick head count of his men as they rode by. Of the twenty-three men that had made this successful attack, twenty-one rode by including James and Samuel. Not wanting to leave anyone behind, William rode back to the top of the hill and saw no one approaching, Patriot or Loyalist. What was left of Price's so-called Brigade was content to retake the field and tend to their wounded. As William turned his Frisian around and galloped back down the hill he knew the Tories would likely claim a victory here tonight since they had retaken the battlefield. He also knew that with four or five more victories like this one they would soon lose this war, but what made him most proud was the fact that good Captain Babb had been avenged tonight and by William's very own hand.

Chapter 111
Sampson

James was sitting on his horse just off the side of the road, with one leg bent over the saddle horn resting it on Trace's neck. He was still holding his rifle across his lap, as he had all morning watching for any of Price's men who might be forming a counter attack. It had been several hours since he had gotten any sleep and it was beginning to take its toll. He looked down at his rifle through bloodshot eyes and took his free hand and rubbed his tired heavy eyelids with his thumb and forefinger in an effort to stay alert. As he raised his head he heard the snap of a twig down in the hollow below him, across the dirt road. He slid his leg back down his horse's side and put his foot back into the stirrup as William led Lilly by her reins out of the tree covered hollow from the back of his new Frisian mount.

"I declare William that is the best piece of horseflesh I have ever seen. If I was one of those Tories and that was my horse, I sure would be coming after him sometime soon," James declared.

"Well, if that's the case," William answered, "let's hope his former owner is one of the slain this morning. Your right though, he looked good in the dark last night, but good heavens, when the sun hit his black coat this morning, I knew I'd picked the right one."

"You know, he very well could have been Price's horse," James said as he raised his eyebrows and smiled at William.

"That thought crossed my mind as well. Wouldn't it be some kind of justice if he was?" William replied as he glanced back down the southern end of the road. It looks like we gave them all they wanted last night. If they were going to come after us, they would have done it by now. Come on let's get out of here while the getting is still good."

The two of them turned their horses around and began their ride back toward home at a slow walk.

"So, you believe you got him" James asked?

"Who Price?" William replied as he looked over at his friend. "Oh, yeah, I hit him alright. It was a side shot. I either got him in the ribs or the shoulder. It knocked him plum off that porch. When I fired he was calling out some orders and I never heard his voice again afterwards."

James looked back over his shoulder and said, "Well and good. That bastard had it coming. I hope they bury him in a mulberry coffin, so he can go through hell a popping'. If their captain is dead then maybe the rest of 'em will give up this war. They were all so scattered I don't think they're coming after us, but I hate having my back to them. What are we doing walking along here anyway, let's pick up our pace?" At that they kicked their heels into the horse's sides and galloped off, leaving only a trail of dust to show of their passing.

Samuel, along with most of the militia was waiting for them when they reached Battle Town crossroads again. Not wanting to chance being taken by surprise like the Tories had been the night before, Samuel had spread out his men, up and down the road in a defensive position, Indian style, behind trees and anything else that could conceal them from view. Only Samuel had stepped out to meet the two riders as they pulled the horses to a stop. Samuel laid his rifle in the fold of his elbow, it's barrel sticking in the air as he walked out of the tree line and onto the road "Are they gone, or do we have more work to do today?" he asked.

"As far as we can tell," William answered, "they're still at that Quaker farm, licking their wounds. My guess is they'll soon be heading on down the Rappahannock River and out of our country."

James dismounted from his horse and turned to William and said, "It probably would be a wise idea to set up a couple of pickets, one to the South as well as one on the road to Winchester. They could come back tonight or tomorrow. Price sure took his time coming after the Captain he may do the same with us."

"William nodded his head in agreement from the top of his horse and said, "It looks like word has spread across country that we're back."

"Yeah," Samuel answered, "the crossroads is becoming a gathering place for the families to welcome us home. There are a lot of womenfolk down in those trees. I keep telling them to stay out of sight and away, but everyone wants to hear the news of what happened last night. More are arriving all the time. Things are breaking down around here. It will only get worse when the Pennington and Hite families get here and find out that Peter and Ezekiel didn't make it back".

"Any word yet of Captain Babb" William asked.

"Not a peep," Samuel answered, "I hope that's good though."

"James, set up your pickets," William said as he handed Lilly's reins over to Samuel. I am going home to see how he is. I only pray he's still alive. Here, tie her up. I really don't want to mess with her now; I'll get her when I come back this afternoon."

"Do what you have to William, but come back as soon as you have news, we all want to know how he is too." James requested.

William nodded his head yes, as he turned his new mount around and galloped off down the road toward home. With every stride the Friesian took, William was amazed by the animal's speed and strength. This was his first opportunity to turn this magnificent mount loose without having to drag Lilly along behind. As he was riding down the bottom, William realized he would need to name this powerful horse. It had to be a name that would match the quality of its owner, something noble. Maybe he should name him after King David from the Bible, for there was no doubt this horse was young and powerful, like David had been in his youth, but naming him after a king just didn't quite feel right. This war was being fought to rid America of a King. Then, William looked down and saw the horse's long black mane flying in the wind, reminding him of someone else of unusual strength from the Bible, someone who got that strength from his long flowing hair. Sampson. The name fit perfectly William thought as he turned into his gate. His homestead looked to be still untouched and everything seemed to be in good order outside as he prayed it would be inside. He rode Sampson straight to the front porch, not bothering to take the time to put his new prize in one of the stalls in the barn. He dismounted and tied the reins to the Babb's wagon that still stood where he had left it the day before. With four long strides he was on the porch knocking on the locked door.

"Open up Elizabeth, it's me, William," he called as he kept anxiously knocking. He stopped when he heard the door's heavy deadbolt slide out of its place, allowing Elizabeth to pull the sturdy oak door open. She stepped forward into his arms and buried her head in his chest, very relieved that her husband was once more safely home. William pulled away from her embrace and looked into the room over her head where he saw Mrs. Babb sitting beside William and Elizabeth's bed holding the hand of her husband.

"How is the Captain?" William asked as he stepped into the house.

"Not good," Mrs. Babb answered, "but he's still with us. He's asleep for now, but he was awake a few hours ago."

William walked over to the bed and looked down on the badly beaten man. His eyes were both bruised and swollen shut. His nose appeared to be broken. The two women had removed his shirt and had tightly wrapped his chest with strips of ripped sheets, binding his ribs.

"Well, praise the Almighty," William said as he put a hand on Mrs. Babb's shoulder, "I told you he would pull through."

"What happened last night William?" Elizabeth asked as she looked out the door at the black horse standing in the yard.

"We caught them late last night around the midnight hour and this morning we put the fear of God into their souls. I believe old Aquilla Price met his maker today   along with several of his men. I got off a good shot at him and I hit my mark."

"That's my boy," a weak voice sounded from the bed. "Tell me all about it, spare no details."

Chapter 112
Run for the Bottle

Life in the bottom had returned to somewhat normal in the few weeks since the return of the militia. The Babbs had stayed at William and Elizabeth's home for ten days, but had since traveled to their daughter's home in Norfolk, the port of Hampton Roads. His recovery was coming along slowly, but he finally felt his ribs could withstand the long trip to the coast where he would complete his recovery. The Virginia Gazette had reported on the burning of the Babb plantation and the injuries the captain had sustained. The same issue reported on the skirmish that had unfolded at the Quaker homestead. According to the report the Loyalist had lost eighteen men with numerous others wounded, including their captain, Aquilla Price, who had lost his arm in the battle along with his prized Frisian mount. William was surprised to learn that Price had survived his marksmanship, but was overjoyed to read that Sampson had indeed been Price's horse.

But these events were far form William and Samuel's minds today. Once more the two were about to go into action in what they both hoped would be another successful attack, this time just outside of James' home. Both were mounted atop their respective horses and took off at the firing of James' rifle. Sampson quickly out distanced Samuel's older, slower horse and was soon well ahead. William ducked and shifted his body from side to side, displaying his own abilities on horseback, avoiding the low hanging branches on the two-mile course of the Run for the Bottle. Having jumped over a few fallen logs and a five-foot-wide ditch, William glanced over his shoulder and saw that Samuel had fallen too far behind to be much of a threat. All he had to do now was emerge from the forest and gallop to the big elm tree and grab the brown bottle hanging from one of its branches to assure his victory. As he and Sampson bolted from the trees into the clearing back at James's home, the wedding party gave out a loud cheer as he rode under the elm and snatched the bottle with a victorious yell. Samuel just made his way out of the trees in time to see that the race was over. William turned Sampson toward the house and trotted over to the bride and presented it to the newly wed Mrs. James Tate.

"Here Prudence, you may need this on the long nights to come when you discover that James is not the man you thought he was before you two got hitched today," William teased. She took the bottle from William's hand but assured him she would not use it for the reason he had just suggested.

"You keep taking like that William and I won't let you have your supper here tonight," James threatened his good friend.

The newlyweds escorted their guest around to the back of the house were a feast was laid out for this happy occasion. Pork and beef were to be the main course, along with an abundance of vegetables that included potatoes, cabbage, squash and green beans all laid about the table with different types of fruits and breads to be enjoyed with butter and molasses or honey.

James and Prudence's courtship had been swift but they seemed to be very much in love with each other. William was glad to see his friend settled down with a good woman. Elizabeth was beginning to show signs of her pregnancy and was enjoying a rare chance to have a good meal without having to prepare it over a hot fire. All that was missing from the celebration was the good cheer of Captain Babb, but he had assured everyone that he would be back before fall to rebuild his home and start anew
.

After everyone had finished the meal, Samuel pulled James' fiddle from its case and showed everyone that he had learned more than just woodsman ship while staying with James, by running the bow over the strings and allowing James and his bride to have their first dance as a married couple. The merrymaking and dancing continued for several more hours before Elizabeth and several of the other ladies stole Prudence away and escorted her to her bridal chamber. James was still at the table with William and the other men who pressed him with a well-deserved drink.

"Well, my friend," William said as he clapped James on his back, "I sure am happy for you. She is a fine lady. You're a lucky man today. Maybe this time next year you'll have a little one in the house as well as a wife."

"I hope so," James replied taking a drink from his mug. "A son would be nice. Anyway, I appreciate all that you and Elizabeth have done for us tonight. It's been a good wedding hasn't it? By the way, where have all the women gone off to? I haven't seen a one since Samuel stopped playing."

"I haven't the foggiest idea," William answered as James set down his mug. All of a sudden James' eyes rounded as he realized what was in store for him.

As he looked back at the house and saw all the womenfolk filing out the door, he yelled, "Oh no, I'm way too old for that!" but he was too late. William held one arm while Samuel grabbed the other and with the help of several other men, they picked up his entire body. James found himself lifted into the air and carried across his yard to his house.

Elizabeth was laughing as she opened the door and said, "All is clear. She's tucked safely away under the covers in the back room."

"You too, Elizabeth" James asked smiling as he ducked his head under the door frame.

"I wouldn't have it any other way, James." she said as she stepped outside and shut the door behind her.

James' wedding escort gave out a cheer, as they set him down on the floor. Samuel quickly opened the door to the bedroom as William gave James a shove in the back, pushing him into the bedroom and quickly slamming the door. "We'll let you two out in the morning," William announced as he slid the kitchen table in front of the door, securing the newlyweds inside.

"If you want any food or drink, look to your nightstand. God bless you two. See you tomorrow. We have a dance to get back to."

Chapter 113
Down South

General Horatio Gates, having won over the favor of the Continental Congress   had been appointed High Commander of the Southern Army. The victory at Saratoga had vaulted Gates over General Washington's choice, General Nathaniel Greene to replace General Lincoln, who along with better part of the southern army had been captured at Charles Town. The Surrender of over five thousand troops was a hard pill to swallow. The war in the South had been one setback after another, first the loss of Savannah in 1779 and now Charles Town. However, the confident Gates was sure that he could turn this trend around. William, himself, had doubts about this new southern commander, remembering Thomas's remarks about Gate's conduct at Saratoga. However, a call of the militia had been made by Patrick Henry, the Governor of Virginia to help rebuild the decimated southern army, so it appeared William would get the chance to decide for himself about Gate's qualifications.

"I really don't want to go this time around," James said as he looked out over his field. I have one of my best crops out this year and I don't want to leave it behind. Besides, Prudence is a little gun shy of my going off to war anyway. She's already lost one husband in this war. It just wouldn't be fair for me to go off and leave her alone so soon after our wedding."

"I can understand that," William said as he pulled himself into Sampson's saddle.
"I'll miss having you along though."

"Then you're going anyway," Samuel asked as he walked up and patted Sampson on the neck.

"Yeah, as soon as Joshua arrives, William answered. "What about you Samuel, are you staying behind as well?"

"Hell no," Samuel answered back sharply. "I've been itching to get out of here and off this farm. James may be newlywed, but I'm not besides, it's time for me to get out of their way for a while. When is Joshua due?"

"Any day now," William answered. "He sent me a letter a few weeks ago, so I expect him anytime. James, I have a favor to ask of you if you are staying here."
"You don't have to ask," James interrupted, "Elizabeth and Sarah is more than welcome to stay here with us while you're gone. We have plenty of room for them. They'll be as safe as they can be here with us until you return."

"Thank you, James, I'll sleep a little better at night knowing they are here with you instead of being all alone at home. As soon as Joshua gets here Samuel, I'll let you know. See you fellows later."

William turned Sampson and began his ride back home. He had only made it a few yards when Samuel called for him to stop. "Hey, are we riding or marching this time?"

"If I'm not riding, I'm not going," William answered. I had enough of that back at Ft. Pitt."

"Good!" Samuel replied, "You're going to ride Sampson down, right?"
"That's the plan," William answered. "Why?"

"Then will you let me take Fly?" Samuel asked. "Buck's getting in bad shape and I need a better mount to take on such a long ride. I'd hate to catch a bullet in the back just because I have the slowest horse in all of Virginia."

"Sure, you can take him," William answered, "but are you sure you don't want Elizabeth's side saddle and Lily instead? But no, on second thought I guess you better take Fly, it would be awful to see your reputation compromised. You know how we southerners are when it comes to our horseflesh."

"Are you crazy?" Samuel shot back, "I'd rather ride a hog than take that mare."
"All right," William laughed, "Fly it is, see you in a few days."

William turned Sampson around once more and took off for home, not quite sure if Samuel had taken him seriously or not. He knew his way of teasing Samuel sometimes left the young man scratching his head in wonder if William was serious or just pulling his leg. He was glad that Samuel was coming along, but he was a little disappointed that James was staying behind this time. He could understand very well how James had reached that decision. William had very nearly decided to stay here himself, with Elizabeth being with child, but she had assured him that the child would not arrive until October and if anything, unforeseen did come up he could be back home in no time at all. That was one advantage of staying in the militia and not joining the Continentals. Besides, it would most likely be a year before Gates could get his new southern army in fighting order. The militia would only be needed for a short time until the army was reorganized William felt sure.

There was another reason William wanted to go. Thomas was indeed going south just as he had predicted back at father's get together and this would give the three brothers even more tome together if the militia was close to Thomas' company. William was proud of the fact that Thomas had become a sergeant and just maybe Thomas could pull a few strings and get William and Joshua assigned to Captain Galloway's unit, but if not surely they would cross paths somewhere in camp.

As William made the turn into his gate, he felt Sampson begin to pull up. He quickly dismounted and bent over and raised Sampson's front right foot and saw that he had thrown a shoe. "It's alright boy," William said, as he led the horse into the barn. "This will give me something to do until Joshua gets here. Besides, I hear Banastre Tarleton is in the Carolinas now. I sure don't want you to lose a shoe with him on our heels. I'll give ole Fly a good going over too."

Chapter 114
Making Fur Fly

It was late at night and Elizabeth had already fallen asleep snuggled up in her and William's bed, but for some reason he couldn't get to sleep like she and Sarah had done. He had already been in bed once tonight, but all he had done was just lie there in the dark, staring up at the ceiling. No matter how hard he tried to drift off, he couldn't manage to do it. Feeling like lying there was just a waste of time, he had gotten up.

He lit one of the candles that Elizabeth had make just this week and put it in the center of the table giving him enough light to work by, but not enough to disturb his sleeping wife and child.

He wanted to finish his new powder horn. He had already fitted and pinned in place the wooden top to the horn and he had also cut off the tip and replaced it with a wooden plug that would keep his powder inside. All he had to do tonight was file down a groove deep enough onto the two ends to tie a rawhide strap onto it so he could hang it over his shoulder. This was the biggest powder horn he had ever made. When finished it would hold twice as much powder as his old one had. He had never tried to do any of the work they called scrimshaw on his horns before. Andrew House's horn was the first to grab his attention back at old Fort Redstone. It had elaborate carvings of deer and bear running over rocks and streams. When he was at the falls, he noticed that ninety percent of the men there had some kind of scrimshaw work on their horns. Even old Barney Stagner had carved his name into the horn that William had taken off of the Indians on the Salt River back in Kentucky. Now sitting here rubbing his smallest file over the new horn, he began to think of what he could carve on it. Some he had seen had poetry on them, but he knew he wasn't much of a poet so he quickly dismissed that possibility. He had seen one with a very detailed map and some others with rougher maps, but that didn't grab his fancy either. Still others had had scenes of their owner's adventures with the Indians and British. These were more to Williams liking, but would be the hardest to make. He could put the Salt River ambush on one side and the Quaker homestead skirmish on the other, but that would take more time and light than he had tonight. At least he had an idea of what he wanted so he snuffed the candle's flame and stepped out the front door and sat down on the top step to and gazed out into the darkness

As William looked up into the star filled sky, he thought to himself how fast time had passed since he and Elizabeth had first taken in this view. The two of them had been on this farm for four years now and it had been two years since he had been in Kentucky. He knew that sooner or later he would have to head back to the wilds of Kentucky if he wanted to hang onto the land, he had gotten from McGray. Someone else would most definitely try to claim and settle that tract of land if he didn't keep an eye on it, but he felt that was at least another year away. William surprised himself when he let out a small yawn, and his eyes had begun to feel heavy. Maybe now he could get some sleep. He stood up off the step, raised his arms high into the air over his head stretching his long-tired body. To his left he saw a fox run out from under one of the split rails that formed his fence, moving toward Elizabeth's new hen house. She had mentioned that two of his chickens were missing this morning and now he knew why. He turned back to the door and as quietly as possible went back into the house and snatched his rifle from the wall and stepped back outside. He had not bothered to put on his boots and the night dew was cold on the bottom of his bare feet. He was making his way toward the hen house, thinking, *'I'll make your fur fly this time'*. As the fox got closer to the coop the chickens trapped inside were becoming very agitated. William spotted the fox scratching at the wooden door of the hen house and shouted; "get out of there!" as he fired off a shot at the fast-moving predator. It let out a yell as the ball tore into its side, ending its night raids forever. As William was making his way back to the house, Elizabeth came running out the door, still half asleep, with William's pistol in her hand.

"Where are they?" she cried wanting to help fight off whoever her husband was shooting at, be it Indians or British soldiers.

"No one is out here but us," William assured her, "it was just a fox after one of your chickens. I've already put him down."

"Good heavens, William the next time you go shooting off your rifle in the middle of the night, outside my window, I sure wish you would let me know first," Elizabeth said as she lowered her pistol. "There is a war going on, you know."

"I'm sorry honey," William said wrapping his arm around her shoulder, laughing at his brave little wife. "Your right, there is a war going on, but Lord Cornwallis himself, along with a thousand of his men would have turned heels and run away if they saw you come busting out of that house with that pistol of yours. Come on let's go back to bed and get some sleep.

"Sleep," Elizabeth said, "I couldn't go back to sleep now if I wanted to. My blood is up now. I just knew you were out here fighting someone off. I sure am happy it was only a fox instead of those Tories. So, that's what happened to my chickens last night."

Chapter 115
The Dan

One week later, Joshua finally arrived at William's home, a married man. He and Jeanette had gone ahead and pulled the trigger. At least that was how he had put it when he made his announcement to William and Elizabeth. William was disappointed that he had not known about the wedding sooner, but as Joshua had explained it was a fast wedding out of necessity. Jeanette, like most other women, had wanted to have a grand wedding, but with Joshua going south the couple had decided they would rather go on and have a quick ceremony so they could have a week together as man and wife before he went out on another tour. None of Joshua's family was able to attend except for his parents. Thomas had already marched off with Captain Galloway's company to the Carolinas and Sylvester was away in Baltimore getting ready to start his teaching career.

The next day, William made another of his painful departures from his wife and daughter before leaving them with James and Prudence. He had been away at least once every year since they had been married, but it was not getting any easier. It was also the first time that James wouldn't be by his side on one of these outings and it felt strange not having him around. James was always so steady and level headed under fire, not to mention his superb marksmanship, but what William was really going to miss most was his easy mannerisms, wit, and all-around good fellowship. Somehow, James always knew just what to say at the right moment, serious or making a good joke at someone else's expense, and he never minded when the shoe was on the other foot. His camaraderie would be missed by all, William realized as the three riders were about to lead their mounts up to the wooden deck of Boyd's Ferry on the Dan River.

The leather of Sampson's saddle creaked as William dismounted from atop the horse to pay the toll. "Damn, my back is killing me," he remarked as he placed both hands behind his back just above his kidneys while he stretched forward, arching his back. "It's been a long ride today. Maybe we'll spend the night here before going over in the morning."

"That suits me fine," Samuel agreed as he too rubbed his backside. "My pain is a little lower than yours, but it sure does hurt. That God forsaken rain storm we rode through back there didn't help much either. My ass is galled for sure."

Joshua began to laugh as he walked around his horse and reached inside one of his damp saddlebags and began to dig around inside it. "You should have said something sooner." he said pulling out a small tin container. "This will have you fixed up by sunrise, but you'll have to put it on yourself."

"Where did you get it?" Samuel asked.

"Let's just say it's good to have a smart wife back home," Joshua answered still wearing the smile on his face. He pitched the tin over the horse's backs into Samuel's waiting hands. Samuel turned and in a slow, stiff legged gait moved off into the trees next to the river.

William handed Sampson's reins to Joshua and said, "Here hold him while I find the ferryman."

"No need in that," answered a voice from a barn at the water's edge. "I'll be right with you." A man appeared carrying four boxes stacked one atop the other, from inside the barn. He walked past the brothers and continued up the bank and sat the boxes down on the ground next to a pile of just about everything a man could possibly store in a barn.

"That's it," the ferryman announced. "If the water gets up any higher, all it's going to get is that old barn now. Are you boys going across tonight?"

"Can you get us across?" Joshua asked as he looked across the swollen river.

"Sure I can," the old man replied, "that is if you got two halfpennies apiece. I usually just charge one, but when she's up like today I have to double my rate. I guess you're trying to catch up with General Gates ain't you? He came thru here with about fifteen hundred men last week. Took all day and half the night to ferry them across, but I got it done. Best day I ever had in the ferrying business."

"You don't know where he was heading do you?" William asked.

"Hillsborough," the ferryman answered. "Just keep on going due south after you cross over. It's about ten miles to the North Carolina line, then about forty more on to Hillsborough."

"If you'll let us stay the night, we would rather go over in the morning." William told him.

"You can stay if you want to, but I wouldn't if I was you. Both armies use my ferry and you never can tell when one of Cornwallis' men will ride up. That green coated   Tarleton is one mean son of a bitch. If I was you boys, I'd go on over and camp out in the countryside somewhere."

"Pay the man," Joshua said. "That sounds reasonable to me. It's just one more night out."

"All right then," the ferryman answered, "but you boys are going to have to help pull on the lines, she's rolling fast this evening and I'll need your help to get over to the other side."

Within thirty minutes the ferry, with the help of William and Joshua had made its way over the darkened river. Samuel held the horses as the others pulled it across by its tow lines.

"You boys got some well-trained animals there. I knew King would handle the crossing, but I wasn't sure about the other two." the ferryman observed.

"What do you mean, King?" William asked.

"King's been over this river more than once," the ferryman laughed. "Like I said Captain Price uses this ferry all the time. I know his mount when I see him."

"King may have crossed this river before, but this is the first time Sampson here ever has. Isn't that so Mister?" William asked with a harsh gaze.

"Oh, sure it is. It's his first time over." the ferryman remarked as he drew his fingers thru his long hair before replacing his hat. As the ferry struck the shoreline and his three passengers remounted the old man called out, "I understand. I ain't seen King all summer."

William pulled Sampson around as a bolt of lightning shot across the night sky.
Leaning forward he tipped his hat to the ferryman and said, "I thought as much. You better get on back over before that water gets any higher mister. It'd be a long night out here all by yourself.
"Don't your worry none sonny, I'll get back over and it'll be my last crossing on this pitiful night," the ferryman yelled as William rode away. "I don't care if King George himself is on the other side waiting for me to come back over."

Chapter 116
Gates Comes Marching In

July 25th was a hot, humid day on the Deep River in North Carolina at the Hollingsworth farm, but Sergeant Thomas Tipton was letting his men cool off some by allowing them to take a swim in the cool waters of the river. Here was where the Baron DeKalb was waiting for the arrival of General Gates with his vanguard. DeKalb had come over to America as a soldier of fortune back in '77 with another famous Frenchman, the Marquis de Lafayette, but he soon fell in love with his newly adopted country and had become one of the most hardened patriots that could be found. He had been sent with his Maryland and Delaware Continentals to help take off some of the pressure that Lord Cornwallis was pressing on General Lincoln in

Charles Town. But now that the port city had fallen it had made Dekalb's army Cornwallis' latest target. DeKalb's troops were the only ones left in the south for the British to engage other than the militia and Cornwallis was not unmindful of that fact.

Thomas was sitting next to the river on a large brown boulder, watching his men try to catch some of the trout that were swimming around them in the water just under the surface. A couple of the men had come close to hanging onto the slippery fish with their bare hands, but once out of the water the fish had always managed to wriggle out of the soldiers' grasp.

"By God, I'll just shoot one of them damn fish with my rifle," one of the frustrated men announced as he waded out of the water and collapsed on the bank

.

"No, you won't, Patterson." Thomas ordered, "We don't have the ammunition for that nonsense. That's what Cornwallis wants us to do. Go over there to that barn and look inside and see if you can find a gig or maybe even a net. There's more than one way to skin a cat or in this case, a fish. Hell, they live next to the water; they have to have something to catch fish with around here someplace."

"What about one of the officer's spontoons asked the soldier?

"Now that's a fine idea," Thomas answered sarcastically. "You just go right on up there to the house and knock on the door and ask one of them for his spontoon. I'm sure they'll hand one right over and let you bring it on down here and jab it into a rock filled river bottom. Just look in the barn like I said."

Having already taken a dip himself, Thomas reached down and picked up his black boots from the bolder he was sitting on. With a hard shove of each leg, both boots were quickly back on. As he rose to his feet, away down in the distance he could hear a familiar sound that he had come to recognize over the long course of the war, the unmistakable sound of an approaching army on the move. It was easily recognizable, tins tinkling on the backs of marching men, the sound of their feet all moving together, and the hooves of the horses stamping on the road. Disregarding the heat, he put on his blue sergeant's coat and hat and began the walk up and away from the river's edge to the road, to see the size of Granny Gates' Army. Morale was low and all sorts of rumors had been circulating through the camp as to the numbers that Gates would bring with him and now Thomas was able see the size of this grand procession for himself. As the blue coated veterans filed pasts, Thomas was pleased with their appearance. They wore the hardened look of men who had been standing toe to toe with the British in New York and New Jersey and had lived to tell about it. But their numbers weren't exactly what he had anticipated, less than two hundred men. More men than this would definitely be needed to take on Cornwallis and Tarleton.

"Damn, is that all Washington can spare?" he said aloud. "They may push our numbers over a thousand, but that's about it." *'The men from the Maryland and*

Delaware lines who were already here are good fighting men, but if all we have are these boys and the local militias, it will be next year before Gates could take on the enemy', he thought to himself.

As Thomas stood at attention, his eye fell on the line of officers who were riding in the middle of the presentation. First, there was Gates himself, sitting on the most beautiful horse Thomas had ever seen, followed by several other officers that he had not seen before. As Gates dismounted form his horse and was making his way to the house, DeKalb had a grand thirteen-gun salute fired off to ceremonially welcome the new commanding Officer of the Southern Army. DeKalb was followed out by the young General Mordacai Gist of Maryland flanked by General William Smallwood, also of Maryland, to welcome the hero of Saratoga. Smallwood had been well tested in many battles right from the beginning of the war. He had been wounded at White Plains, and although Gist was young, he too had been very active as far back as the Battle of Long Island where three fifths of his command had been killed or wounded while taking the brunt of the fighting while the rest of the army escaped. He had come from a family with a long line of fighting men in its history and was of very good stock. As Thomas stood and watched the ceremonial gestures taking place between the high command, he wondered if Gates was up to the task. The other generals gave him no pause, but Thomas still remembered how poorly Gates had treated Arnold and Morgan back at Saratoga, but that had been a victory. Thomas knew that Lord Cornwallis was no Gentleman Johnny Burgoyne either.

"Right, then," Thomas said as he turned back to the river. "I know Gates is going to eat well tonight, but damn it, I would like to as well. Where is that net Patterson? Did you find one?"

"Yes Sir, I surely did."

"Well, what are you waiting for, throw it out over into those white caps next to that blue rock and pull us in some supper, would you? That short allowance of bread just isn't enough

Chapter 117
Left on the Side of the Road

As William and the others rode out of the village of Hillsborough, North Carolina he was beginning to wonder just what kind of army he was trying to enlist in. As far as he knew, none of the other men from Captain Babb's Militia had taken up this call to arms. William felt it had more to do with the raid on the Babb plantation by Price's Tories than with anything else and the men were just reluctant to leave home and families unprotected. He had his own reservations about leaving home now that the war had raised its ugly head so close to his own door, but being able to leave Elizabeth and Sarah in James' able care had made his decision to answer the call easier. As the three of them rode south he had expected to join up with men from other parts of the colony heading in the same direction, also looking to join Gates' forces, but so far it hadn't happened. Last night while taking his only meal of the day, at a tavern in Hillsborough he had learned from the long-winded barkeep that the North Carolina Militia was already in the field under Major General Richard Caswell. Word was that Caswell was not real excited about handing his command over to Gates. If that in itself wasn't enough reason to give William concern, the present situation certainly did. He was trotting up on five deserted cannons obviously left behind by DeKalb, probably due to the lack of horses to pull them. He was beginning to realize just how bad the situation was down here.

"It makes a man wonder if they would have taken our mounts to pull their artillery with, doesn't it?" Joshua said as he pulled his horse to a stop.

"I don't think they would take these animals," William replied patting Sampson's neck, "they're way too fine of horseflesh to do that type of work, but they just might try putting them in the cavalry. It sure seems odd seeing good field pieces like these, just sitting here out in the open like this, unprotected."

"Well, they must be planning on coming back for them, because they didn't spike them, "Joshua observed from still atop his mount.

"I sure do hope they will, I would hate for the British to get their hands on them," Samuel remarked. "Think of the damage those things could do in the wrong hands. Maybe we should go on and spike them ourselves."

"No, let's head on down the road," William answered, "If they had wanted them spiked, they would have done it themselves. Besides, we don't have anything to do it with anyway. Come on, let's move on we aren't going to catch up with anyone standing around here talking to each other."

"Maybe he was going to spike them," Samuel remarked, "but just didn't get the chance."

"Who" William asked as Samuel walked Fly across the road and looked down into a ditch where the body of a dead man was lying face down in the weeds.

"I don't know who he is," Samuel answered, "but he sure looks dead to me." All three of them pulled their weapons and quickly dismounted. William and Joshua both shouldered their rifles, scanning the tree lines that shaded this dusty dirt road, while Samuel turned over the body of a young man. "Yeah, he's dead for sure," Samuel said as he looked up at his friends. "Hell, I'm not even sure what side he was on. He doesn't seem to be in either side's uniform. Could be militia thought, I guess.

"Yeah, but who's side?" William asked, knowing full well that his companions couldn't answer his question. "That barkeep said the Tories have been acting up really bad all year long, ever since Charles Town fell. My guess is this fellow was of one of their ranks. If he was a patriot, whoever killed him would most likely have taken the cannons with them when they left."

"Or gone after some horses to pull them away with," Samuel said as he remounted Fly's saddle. "Whoever they were they've been gone awhile, because his body is already stiffening up."

"How was he killed?" William asked.

"Shot in the back," Samuel answered, "by the looks of the hole in him it was a shotgun that did the deed."

"Our talkative barkeep last night said that Salisbury was almost completely patriot," William said as he and Joshua climbed back up on their horses. "He said Gates would most likely be heading this way, southwest, because most of the people due south of here are still fairly loyal to the king. I say we keep going this way and as much as I hate to say it, we better leave this poor soul here as he lies. I think he was on the other side fellows, and I for one, don't want to get shot digging a grave for some Tory I don't even know."

"Me neither," Samuel replied as he slapped Fly's side with his reins. "Come on; let's get out of here while we still can."

As the three of them made their way down the road, William looked back over his shoulder to where the dead man lay by the side of the road and hoped that he would not leave this earth the way that poor fellow just had, but he knew full well that he could do just that if he didn't use his head. Even if he did his part, he knew there was more than one way to die in this war. He also knew the army here didn't fight the same way he always had in the past, on the frontier. No Indian style of fighting in Gates' army. He would line up his men across from the enemy in the European formation as each side fired off volley after volley at one another until one side turned and ran. It was just a matter of dumb luck as to who lived and who died, according to what Thomas had told him about his time with Gates' army up north. It was going to be very different here, especially if Cornwallis attacked before Gates could rebuild the Southern Army.

Chapter 118
Hell Bent

As Thomas walked back down the wooded hill to where his men were breaking camp, he shook his head in bewilderment. He had stood back just far enough to hear what was being said at the officer's meeting that had just broken up a few moments ago. *Gates has got to be off his rocker. How in the hell could a man who just arrived in this country tell men who had been here their entire lives what was the best route to march through? In their own countryside now, mind you. And why was Gates so hell bent on Camden being his next objective anyway? It's far too close to the British lines for my taste.* All these thoughts were running around in Thomas's mind as he stepped around a clump of rhododendron bushes.

DeKalb had suggested marching the army southwest to Salisbury thru Rowan County. Although he had never been there himself, DeKalb had engaged in more than one discussion with the locals about the surrounding countryside and everyone had agreed that it would be the safest and best way to go. It may be a little further out of the way than the direct route that Gates had settled on, but the road was more traveled and in better condition. In addition, the inhabitants would be a lot more hospitable than the Tory laden route to the south that dumb ass Gates wanted to take. It seemed that Gates had still not learned to take advice from his own staff and was as arrogant as ever. But what really had Thomas worried, was Gates' aggressive attitude. From what conversations he had heard, it was obvious Gates was well satisfied with the condition of what he called the Grand Army of the South. By marching to Camden, he was putting the last remaining army in the south within striking distance of Cornwallis. Not pulling back to buy more time and to rebuild what General Lincoln had lost, a foolhardy decision in Thomas' eyes. And he was not alone in his opinion. In comparison, General Washington had won a few battles, but he had never put his troops in a bad position for very long. He knew when to fight and when to retreat. If he had marched in and fought every army that presented itself the war would have been lost way back at Long Island. Gates may have guts but, did he have enough brains to go with them? Thomas wondered as he walked in among his men. "Put out that fire Patterson. We're off to Camden," Thomas ordered as he walked past.

"Camden!" Patterson said as he started to kick out what little flames that were left in the fire, "not Salisbury?"

"No, we are going due south, straight to Camden." Thomas answered. "General Gates says there is a supply train coming down from Virginia and will overtake us in a few days, so we should have plenty of food to keep us moving when it arrives, so get cracking boy." As Thomas reached down and picked up his black leather waist bag, strapped it around himself and fastened its brass buckle, he hoped that Patterson and the rest of his men had bought into Gates' story about the supply train, because he had his own doubts about its arrival. One thing was sure about it, if it didn't show fairly soon, it was going to make a long and hot march more difficult.

Chapter 119
German Hospitality

It was about seven o'clock in the evening when the three tired riders came upon a very impressive two-story stone house that was made from tan colored granite blocks. It's well shaded lawn was covered with tall Short-leaf Pines mixed in with a few redbuds. This handsome home was by far the best plantation that William had seen in the western part of the North Carolina Piedmont.

"Where ever on this green earth could Gates' army be" Joshua asked his two dust covered companions as they pulled their horses to a stop next to the open wooden gate that lead to the front of the house.

"I don't have the foggiest idea" Samuel answered while shaking his head. "You would think that we would have run into some of their outer pickets by now if they were camping around here. Hell, this may not even be Salisbury."

"Well let's find out where we are" William replied as he dismounted from Sampson's back. "Here Joshua take my rifle, I don't want to knock on that door and have someone fire a shot out of that top floor just because I'm armed. They have portholes cut into the walls up there. That barkeep said most of the folks around here are against the king and these folks most likely are too but, they could very easily not be either, so I'll keep my pistol handy just in case." After tying Sampson's reins to the split rail fence that enclosed the dooryard, William made his way down the short lane that led to the house. As he approached, he could see movement inside the house through its many tall windows. Before he could step onto the flagstone walkway that led to the darkly stained front door, it was swung open by someone inside. Out stepped a short stocky gray-haired gentleman who looked to be in his late fifties. He was holding a musket, but he was not pointing it at William, but held it at the ready and would be able to quickly bring it to bear on William if he thought it need be.

"You have no need for that, Sir," William told the man as he stopped ten feet from the gentleman's door.

"You never know these days," replied the homeowner in a thick German accent. "What is on your mind?"

"We are trying to find Salisbury," William answered, pointing back to Joshua and Samuel, who had now dismounted their horses, and were holding their weapons in clear view. "Are we near the town?"

"Nearby, yes, it is only four more miles on down the road, "was the reply William received. "This is Granite Ridge. I do not see any evergreen twig pinned to your hat."
"No and you won't," William answered, "We're not Tories. That's my brother, and over there by the bay is one of my neighbors from back home. We have come down from Virginia to join up with Gates' army. We were told that he was in Salisbury."

"You have been badly misinformed then," the German replied as he handed his weapon to a young woman standing just inside the door.

"No disrespect, Sir, but are you sure? Is there a chance the army could be in Salisbury without your knowing about it? Perhaps they arrived just a short time ago maybe they came since your last trip into town?"

"I have a printing shop and the wheelwright business in town; I tell you there is no army in Salisbury. The whole southern army seems to be spread from here to kingdom come. I have a son who is ensign in the North Carolina line. I have no idea where he is now either. My name is Michael Braun" the older man said as he looked up at the sky. "It is near to dark, you will not find your army tonight. You can pass the night here if you want. My daughter Margaret will have our supper ready soon. You are more than welcome to partake if you wish. We have food to spare. I will have Carl show you where you can stable your horses." Mr. Braun stepped out into the yard and called out. At the sound of his voice, a young slave came toward the house from the stable across the road. "Carl, show our guest where they can feed and bed down their horses for the night." William and the others gladly accepted this gracious man's offer and introduced themselves before walking over to the stables to tend the horses.

Twenty minutes later, the three men were back from the stable and knocking on the door to the stone house once more. Margaret, the daughter of their host opened the door and invited them inside by motioning them with her hand. She led them into the kitchen, just to the left of the main room of the house. The room was dominated by the biggest fireplace William had ever seen. It was large enough to accommodate a whole side of beef if need be, but tonight the table was well covered with a variety of dishes, all contributing to a pleasing aroma that made him realize how hungry he was. The main dish was a spicy sausage served in shredded cabbage. There were green beans and fresh corn and sweet potatoes in steaming bowls place along the length of the table. Hot rolls and plenty of fresh churned butter sat at each end of the table beside jars containing honey still in the comb.

Mr. Braun was already seated at the head of the table when they entered the room. He politely rose to his feet and gestured to the many empty chairs sitting around the long table that had accommodated his once large family. William, Joshua, and Samuel wasted little time settling themselves for the evening meal. Their host proceeded to say grace over the food in his native tongue, while Samuel peeped out over his crossed hands and looked down to William with that odd smile of his, not quite knowing how to take this odd sounding prayer.

"If I wanted to find the army," Braun said, as his daughter served him from a large platter, "I would turn back for Camden. One of my business partners just came from Charlotte a few days ago and he said nothing of Gates being there. He must be heading east instead. You can be there in two day's rides if you push yourselves. Now do not be shy gentlemen, help yourselves to the food. I can see that you are hungry."

"Thank you very much," Joshua answered as he began to fill his pewter plate. "So, you have a son away in the army now?"

"And a son-in-law as well," Braun answered. "Margaret's husband, Fredrick is out with the militia as we speak. He is under his father, Captain Wendell Miller's command. They are off fighting the Tories someplace down is the swamps. She is staying here until he gets back. How do you like her German cooking?"

"Mighty fine," Samuel answered, "Sure beats raw apples!"

"In that case, you do not have to waste time talking to me," laughed Braun. "Help yourself, but save room for Margaret's apples. She bakes them is the best strudel you'll ever eat. After you finish, I will take you upstairs to where I have a large loft. My wife has a loom that she uses up there. There are some beds there too, from when my children were all still at home. I dare to say it will be nice to have a roof over your head tonight."

"Yes sir," William answered, "It surely will. We appreciate all you have done for us tonight, but if I may ask, why would you do this for us? You could just as easily let us sleep outside."

"It is like I told you; my boys are out there somewhere. Just maybe there is someone helping them tonight like I am you. At least that is my hope; beside it is the Christian thing to do."

"This is a real nice home you have here, Mr. Braun. How long have you lived here?" Joshua asked.

"Let me see, I bought the land back in 1760 from Mr. John Dunn, but it took me until '66 to complete the house. It was a virtual wilderness here in those days. It was a lot of work but we are proud of it," Braun replied as he pushed back his plate. "We will have some of that strudel now dear."

"How long have you been in the colonies?" William asked.

"Long time, I came over from Germany as a boy with my father back in 1737. Father first settled in Pennsylvania before he brought us down here. I told you she was one good cook, didn't I?" asked Mr. Braun as he watched his guest eyes roll as they bit into his daughter's dessert.

"Yes, you surely did," Samuel mumbled thru a mouthful of strudel, while cutting his fork into another bite. "So, you built the house yourself then," he asked, remembering his manners and trying to carry on polite conversation while eying another piece of the delicious strudel.

"Every timber and stone of it, my wife told me what she wanted and I did it. It was her idea to have all these double-sided fireplaces in the corners of the rooms. Heats two rooms with the same amount of wood it would for one. She sure was proud of those fireplaces. She passed back in June of '71. God rest her good soul. She is buried across the road."

"Sorry to hear it," William replied. "That was one fine meal. You didn't lie about your daughter's cooking abilities, not one bit."

"Ya, it is maybe a good thing Fredrick is away in the war," the proud father said as he stood up from his table. "If he were here, he would be getting fat like me," he chuckled. "Come, I will show you your quarters for the night."

He took the three of them back into the great room with its white plastered walls and a light green painted chair rail running around the room that matched the deep window sills, and led them up an enclosed stairway to a massive loft where they were to spend the night under the huge open trusses that held up the roof.

"We never did get around to plastering the walls up here, I always liked the rock showing anyway," Braun explained, "but there is a finished room around the corner that you can use, but it is too early for that. Let us go back downstairs and have a good pipe and a good talk. You can tell me the news of how the war is going up in Virginia. My son-in-law has it in his mind to find out about Kentucky. Do you boys know anything about it out there?"

"Not as much as some, but more than others," Joshua replied as his and Samuel's eyes met over the old man's head.

Chapter 120
Skin and Bones

As Patterson marched down the little traveled path through some of the harshest and most isolated parts of North Caroline he stopped and took off his tri-cornered hat and wiped his sweat soaked brow and turned to look back over his shoulder, down the trail he had just traveled.

"Keep moving Patterson," Thomas ordered, as he dusted off his red epaulettes that distinguished his rank of sergeant from the other exhausted men moving down the line. "Looking back over your shoulder won't make that supply train arrive any faster. I know you boys are getting hungry, but maybe they will catch up before sunset and we'll eat better tonight." Patterson put his hat back on his head and muttered something under his breath before marching on down the road as he was told. Thomas knew he had made some highly inappropriate remark but he also knew that Patterson was a good soldier and even good men needed to blow off steam every now and then, so he let it pass without comment. Patterson was well within his right to complain about this barren countryside that was providing so little to sustain a growing army. Now that most of the food being carried in the few wagons that Gates had on hand was almost gone, this swampy area would have to bear fruit of some kind, and do it soon. Few friendly faces had been seen in the wilderness on this trek and they had little to give Gates' Army. The men were already on half rations and Thomas knew those might be cut even more if that supply train didn't arrive soon.

The concerns of desertion and mutiny running thru Thomas' mind seemed not to have affected Gates' thoughts at all, as of yet. Even the fact that what little artillery they had left was being bogged down in this sandy swamp land had not given Gates any pause in his plan of attack. If they were lucky, they might run across a cornfield like the one they found yesterday before they crossed the Pee Dee River or find a peach orchard like the one the day before. But Thomas and the men all knew that raw corn and peaches would not sustain a soldier's dietary needs for long. Even worse a fellow could suffer the back-door trots, as his mother used to caution him and his brothers when they ate too much corn as children. His thoughts turned serious again as he realized that if they did come upon a part of the British Army their poor condition would put them at a great disadvantage in a fight. Hell, even that small band of Tories who had been taking crack shots at Gates' rear guard every now and then could probably overrun them now, Thomas scoffed.

Thomas had never been the type of soldier to pat his men on the back, but he knew now was the time to encourage the men and not the time for harshness if he didn't want them to mutiny. He had never seen this play out himself, but it had happened more than once during this war when food was scarce like it was now. As he walked along beside his men, he struck up a conversation with Patterson, trying to keep the man's mind off his stomach.

"Why are you in this war anyway, Patterson," he asked the aggravated soldier.

"Well, at first it was glory," Patterson answered. "My brother and I joined up at the same time. We thought how exciting it would be to go into battle. He got cut up pretty bad at White Plains and died soon afterwards," Patterson answered. "I guess it was revenge after that, but now it's got more to do with land. A grant after this war is over would be nice,"

"What about the revenge?" Thomas asked.

"Oh, I can't deny that I don't smile every time I shoot one of those damn Lobsterbacks, but I also know no matter how many I kill, I'll never see Lewis again. Have you lost anyone close yet sergeant?"

"Not yet, thank God," Thomas answered as he moved along with the men. "I had one brother captured at Monmouth but he escaped, and another stabbed in the arm, but they're all still alive."

"Well, let's hope they don't have a brother starve to death down in North Carolina," Patterson said with a sarcastic smile.

Thomas laughed at Patterson's joke as they continued down the trail. He could tell that their talk had raised Patterson's spirits some, at least for a little while. Then off to the right of the road Thomas and his men heard a sound that made their mouth's water. Thomas looked over at a smiling Patterson and said, "Did you just hear a cowbell ringing over there is those pines, or am I hearing things?"

"Yes Sir, I surely did, and still do for that matter," Patterson assured him.

"Well, don't just stand there, Patterson. Take four men and go get us some meat for supper, if not for yourself, then for my brothers' sakes."

Needing no other encouragement, Patterson and three other men ran off into the tree line followed by Thomas. There, lying under the pines was one of the poorest Jersey cows Thomas had ever seen. She was taking advantage of the shade from the trees and was contentedly chewing her cud.

"Hell, she's nothing but skin and bones. I don't know if she's worth the trouble of skinning." one of the men said as he stared at the unsuspecting animal.

"She may not be fat, but she's got some meat on her." Patterson assured them as he raised his rifle and pulled the trigger. She was quickly gutted and to everyone's surprise, the poor cow had supplied enough meat for Thomas's men and a few others as well. Each of the men had cut off a good size hunk of meat, more than enough for a beefsteak to be cooked later on for supper. They were all still hungry but the rest of the afternoon's march would go easier now that they had something to look forward to tonight. Just maybe those slow-moving supply wagons would get here tomorrow. At least that's what everyone was hoping for.

Chapter 121
A Lost Horse

When William and the others arrived at the Pee Dee this morning, they knew they were finally on the right trail. Gates' army had been here and camped on this site within the last few days, prior to ferrying across the river. They could tell by the empty barrels that the army had left abandoned by the burned-out campfires.

At the beginning of this march the barrels had been filled with pork, that was heavily salted to keep it from spoiling, but now that the army had consumed the contents, they had simply discarded the empty barrels for anyone to see. Joshua dismounted his horse and was kicking the ashes of a couple of the fires, hoping to find some hot coals under the gray ashes, but all he found was dead coals. "They're long gone from here fellows," he said, but Samuel and William had not heard what he'd had to say. They had ridden down to the water's edge and were gazing across to the other bank in disbelief.

"Why would Gates burn the ferry like that?" Samuel asked, "He might need to use it again sometime."

"He didn't burn it." William answered, "The Tories did."

"Just to slow down Gates' supply lines" Joshua added as he joined the other two.

William nodded his head in agreement as he remounted Sampson's back. "And to keep any reinforcements from joining him as well, I'd say."

"That's a real long swim for the horses to make," Samuel said, looking at his two friends. "Further than any we crossed back in Kentucky. I don't think they can make a swim like that."

"I'm not sure either," William again agreed. "Let's head down river, maybe we'll find a better crossing spot on down somewhere."

By now it had been a good four hours since they had left the ferry, and they were becoming frustrated, not able to find a suitable place to cross this wide river.

"Damn, we're losing way too much time." Joshua said as he rode up between William and Samuel. "We have to cross over this river and cross it now. If we don't, it might take us another two or three days to find Gates," he said angrily.

"Well, we can't cross here," William said as he pulled Sampson to a stop.

"Why can't we?" Joshua asked, "It's just a little water."

"Just a little water" Samuel said in a sarcastic voice. "Noah and his ark would have trouble crossing that piece of water, much less us on these horses."

"He's right Joshua. We'll just have to keep going downriver until we find a better spot to cross over," William told his brother.

"I just don't know about you two sometimes." Joshua teased, "Are you two old women or two men? Sometime I really can't tell which you are. I'll tell you what, you two stay here and watch while I cross on over to the other side."

Without giving William or Samuel time for further objections, Joshua turned his horse Lightening, towards the river and plunged into the swift current.

Samuel turned to William and said, "That damn fool of a brother of yours is going to drown right before our eyes."

William yelled at the top of his lungs for Joshua to turn back, but his headstrong older brother ignored his calls and kept on going. The water was already over the horse's back and the two of them were still not halfway across the river.

Samuel turned to William and said, "Well, he may be just crazy enough to make it, they've got a good start."

William didn't answer; he was keeping his eyes on Joshua's back as he was making his way across, knowing that Samuel was trying to give him hope that Joshua would make it across in one piece. Then just as William had feared, the swift moving current began to push Joshua and his horse down river, now that the two were in the center of the current. As William and Samuel walked their mounts down the bank, keeping up with Joshua as he was being pushed along, Lightening began to struggle to keep his head out of the water. Joshua had already floated off his back and was only holding onto him by his long tail.

"Good God, they're not going to make it." William said as the horse disappeared under the water's surface. "Do you see him anywhere?" William screamed as he looked out into the water.

"No," Samuel answered, "Not so much as a hair, but he can still make it if nothing hits him while he's in the water. He's a good swimmer."

William once again took off down the river, yelling Joshua's name, hoping to get a glimpse of his brother. Then he saw Lightning's belly roll over in the water with his legs sticking above the surface for just an instant before he once again disappeared under the muddy water. William pulled Sampson to a halt, looked at Samuel and said, "He's gone under again, if he doesn't come up soon, he's a dead man for sure."

"We can't stay here!" a frantic Samuel yelled. "He's being washed down. We got to keep move and try to stay up." For the second time, the two of them rode down the bank calling Joshua's name. He had been out of sight now for over ten minutes and both men knew if he had not been washed ashore, he was most certainly dead. Then, on the far side of the river, Samuel saw Joshua struggling out of the water onto the bank. "There he is William! He made it! I don't believe it, but he made it out alive, Thank God!"

William looked over the river as he raised his hands and ran them through his long black hair, realizing he had lost his hat while riding down the river bank and was thankful that was all he had lost on this day.

"Are you hurt?" William yelled across the river.

"No," Joshua answered, coughing up river water, "just my pride, I'll live."

"Now that you got that settled, just where are we going to cross?" Samuel asked.

"Downriver somewhere, we certainly can't cross here, but first I got to go back and get my darn hat." William replied.

Chapter 122
The Battle of Camden

It was close to ten o'clock on this moonless night of August 15th when the order for a night march was sent down through the camp of General Gates' army. Their objective was only seven miles away, down the Waxhaw Road and all that stood in their way of that town's food supply was a force of about a thousand British soldiers, a branch of Lord Cornwallis' army under the command of Lord Francis Rawdon. After defeating Rawdon, Gates would sweep down upon Cornwallis' Highlanders and Welshmen, completing his grand victory. Even with Tarleton's horse, Gates had estimated that Cornwallis' forces numbered no more than twenty-five hundred men, while his own force had grown to over seven thousand men, now that the North Carolina and Virginia Militia had joined his ranks along with the Virginia State Troops, under Charles Porterfield who had come in just a few days ago. Gates was so confident that he was about to have an easy victory here tomorrow that he had detached one full company of Artillery along with one hundred of his best Continentals from the Maryland line to General Sumter who was miles away. These were some of the best battle tested men he had at his disposal, not to mention the three hundred men from the North Carolina militia who tagged along with the Continentals. This had reduced his field pieces to just six, but he was confident that they would be more than sufficient to blast Rawdon out of his way. He would then simply overrun Rawdon's lines and turn Rowdon's captured field pieces around, thus enlarging his own artillery.

DeKalb had recommended a flanking motion to the north where the army could out maneuver Rawdon and enter the town without firing a shot. Then, after the army was rested, they could march out and engage the British on their own terms under better conditions. But Gates would have none of that. The troops had already been fed tonight he explained. Caswell's North Carolinians had arrived with a full baggage train of molasses and cornmeal along with some beef. Rest and food were no longer a problem in his eyes, but Gates has not finished ignoring his officer's advice yet. Colonel Otho Williams, the deputy adjutant general, had reported that Gates' manpower was indeed at the seven thousand mark when at full force but only three thousand and fifty were in good fighting order at this time. Gates, believing this to be utter nonsense, assured the rest of his staff that these numbers were grossly inaccurate. Refusing to be dissuaded, Gates proceeded to explain how he wanted his Grand Army deployed.

General DeKalb was to take the Second Maryland, while General Gist was to command the Delaware Continentals. Both were to take positions beside each other to the right of the Waxhaw road. The North Carolina and Virginia Militia were to take the other side of the road under General Caswell and General Stevens. Both men were to command the troops from their home colonies, supported by Colonel Charles Armand's small light cavalry. General Smallwood was to stay in the rear with his First Maryland Continentals while General Gates would follow behind with the rest of his staff, in order to see the battlefield as a whole and thereby dictate whatever needed to be done. The last statement General Gates made to his staff as they were exiting his tent was, "Gentlemen, I tell you this, tomorrow Lord Cornwallis will dine at our table in irons and the south will be ours."

Thomas had been reassigned to Porterfield's Virginians who were having a hard time walking through the dark woods to the left of the road. The moon had been hidden most of the night and what little light was getting through the clouds could not penetrate the pine canopy overhead. Thomas had stumbled into some kind of thorn bush and was trying to back his way out of its sharp reach when he heard gunfire up ahead. With little regard to for his skin he pushed forward ignoring the pain caused by the thorns. Armand's Cavalry was firing back over their shoulders as they came galloping through Thomas' line. Thomas shouldered his own weapon as Porterfield yelled, "Stand at the ready". He could not make out who was charging toward him, but he could hear the distinct sound of oncoming horses. It was most likely some of Bloody Benny's dragoons. Then as the moon light finely emerged from the clouds, he saw the unmistakable bearskin crested helmet that Tarleton's green coated men always wore. Thomas, along with the rest of Porterfield's line, fired off a volley into the dark, stopping the dragoon's blind charge. They quickly spun their mounts and returned the same way they had come. Thomas' marked horse continued on its course without its rider. Not knowing if his enemy was dead or alive, Thomas stood his ground and reloaded his rifle in the dark. The smoke from all the firing was making the dark woods even more difficult to see in, but gradually it began to clear and Thomas saw the fallen dragoon limping away back toward his lines no more than fifteen feet away.

"Halt or I'll fill your backside with more hot lead," Thomas commanded. Hearing Thomas's order, the wounded man turned back around and faced his captor, "If you have a belt on drop it." Thomas said, still pointing his rifle at his prisoner. "You better not have one of those sabers in your hand either. Hold your arms up so I can see what you're doing over there."

The Englishman never said a word, he just dropped his belt and raised his hands up as he was told and limped over to where Thomas was standing. Within a few minutes, other prisoners have been brought over to join Thomas and his prisoner, under the direction of one pissed off Virginia officer that Thomas had never seen before. "Are you the wretch who killed Porterfield?" the officer yelled, shoving one of the prisoners to the ground.

"Hell, I don't know," answered the defiant Brit as he stood back up, "but I sure hope I did." Hearing this remark, the officer stepped forward and struck the prisoner with the hilt of his sword, knocking the man to the ground along with a few of his front teeth. The officer then turned angrily on Thomas and said, "You men come and go with me, we're going to take these devils to the back of the line for questioning. Fix your bayonets if you have not already done so. They took some of our men prisoner and I'm sure they will be interrogated, so turnabout is fair play."

The sun was coming up as the prisoners were led to the back of the American line. They were made to sit on the damp ground with their hands tucked under their butts as the officer began his interrogation within full view of General Gates. The unlucky man he had chosen to begin with was the toothless dragoon he had hit earlier in the night.

"How many men does Rawdon have under his command?" the tall officer asked.

"You'll find out soon enough," was the defiant reply, "when he overruns your lines this morning. Once again, the Captain of the Virginians delivered a hard punch to the stubborn prisoner's face.

"Don't trifle with me, you can see I am enjoying this can't you?" the Captain said as he rubbed the red knuckles on the back of his hand. Seeing that the beaten prisoner was not going to answer, one of his fellow dragoons spoke up and said, "three thousand men."

"That's a damn lie!" The Captain shot back.

"No, it is not and Cornwallis has three thousand as well," the prisoner continued on. "Not to mention the local militia and the New York Irish that Cornwallis had brought from Ninety-Six."

"That's enough," Gates intervened from his seat in front of his tent. "That's the same numbers the last group said. Damn, our forces are about even if they're telling the truth. Have my horse saddled, so I can take to the field."

As new guards took the prisoners away, cannon fire was heard in the distance, back toward the front lines. Thomas turned toward the sound and ran off in its direction as fast as he could manage on foot. Out on the battlefield General Grist's brigade took the first volley of the battle, no more than two hundred yards away from Rowdon's line, along with heavy cannon fire from the British six pounders. It was tearing a large hole in the American lines as the seasoned

Continentals held their ground, but on the other side of the road the North Carolina and Virginia militia were slow in advancing   from the trees, allowing Cornwallis to order a bayonet charge that drove fear into the hearts of both militias. Panic ran rampant up the Virginia line after they fired off one ineffective volley that did little damage to the advancing British. The majority of the Virginia then turned and ran away while almost at once a thousand Carolinians dropped their weapons without even firing off one volley, and ran to the rear, pushing Smallwood's force back with them in a wild disorderly retreat, just as Thomas reached the line. As the retreating men came running by, Thomas tried to stop one to find out what had happened, but none would stop. He had little choice but to join the retreat. General Smallwood tried to reform the line, but could do little to stop the flood of panic-stricken men that ran by. Seeing that it was useless, he too turned and rode away on his mount. The militia had completely collapsed and was being hacked to pieces by the victorious British troops.

All that was left of Gates' Grand Army now was its right wing. Generals DeKalb and Gist, not knowing the fate of the militia on the other side of the battlefield continued on with the fight. The two were under the impression that they were winning the day. They had already held off three different charges by the British and no call for retreat had been given from Gates, so all had to be going well. However, the few men in Smallwood's line who had not run off knew better and under the orders of Colonel Williams tried to charge up to their fellow Continentals, but the British had cut the field in half by now and charged into the Marylanders, soon routing that brave brigade before they could get word to the right wing. Not willing to sacrifice anymore of his men Williams pulled his men out, leaving DeKalb and Gist to their fate.

By now, Cornwallis could very easily see that he had won the day. All he had to do was concentrate on the isolated right wing and he would have demolished Gates' Army. DeKalb had his horse shot out from under him, but not willing to give up just yet, he ordered a full bayonet charge in which he was killed, receiving as many as eleven wounds to his body. The fighting was at point blank range, hand to hand. The killing blow to DeKalb was a bayonet wounds to his chest.

General Gist had managed to fight his way off the field with a small number of his men as Tarleton finished off whoever was left behind. The American casualties were going to be horrific and no one near the front seemed to know the whereabouts of General Gates. As Thomas was making his way back through the trees, he had marched through just the night before, he began to curse the commanding General. He had never had much confidence in Gates' leadership. He had always known Gates had more than his fair share of faults, but Thomas never dreamed that being a coward was one of them until now. And soon the rest of the world would too.

Chapter 123
Scattered to the Wind

The sound of cannon fire had been echoing over the countryside all morning, but now as Joshua dismounted from Fly's back and jumped onto Sampson behind William, the air was still and quiet. William tapped Sampson's side and the horse took off again with both men on his back.

"When was the last time you heard a shot fired?" Joshua asked William.

"It's been a while, maybe twenty minutes, but they sure did sound close," William answered. "But I never did hear any small gunfire."

"Me neither, but good heavens, there sure was a lot of cannons going off," Joshua observed. "I'm no expert on artillery, but I would say there were close to fifty cannons in that battle. It sure sounded like a major battle to me. I pray that Gates won the day. We need a victory down here pretty bad. I wonder if Thomas was there."

"I would say so," William answered. "If we could have ferried over that damn river back there we would have been there as well."

"Or if I hadn't of lost my horse we've been slowed down quite a bit since I've been doubling up on your horses. I'm glad I didn't lose my rifle too. That would have been a mighty bitter pill to swallow. Can't you just imagine a man trying to join a volunteer army without a horse or a rifle?"

Samuel pulled Fly to a halt and called for the two brothers to do the same. "There's something moving down there next to that marshy land beside that road. "See, between those two trees," he said as he pointed to the east. "That looks like the hind quarters of a horse to me. You may get to ride into Gates camp yet Joshua, but we better take it easy on our approach, we don't want to spook him." The stray horse was grazing on what little greenery it could find under the small grove of trees he had taken shelter in. As the three men approached, Joshua slipped from behind William and was walking toward the animal, very slowly, directly in front of his prize. William and Samuel, where still mounted in case the horse bolted and they had to give chase, the two horsemen drifted apart a couple of hundred feet and waited to see how the horse would react. Joshua reached up and took off his hat and held it out in front of him, upside down, giving the impression that he had feed inside, as the horse had spotted the approaching men.

"Whoa boy," Joshua spoke softly, as he stepped in front of the big chestnut who still wore his saddle. "Look what I've got for you here big fellow. Whoa now. Come on and gitcha some boy." Joshua's ploy worked just as he had hoped it would, and the tall well-bred horse walked up and gingerly stuck his inquisitive nose into the hat. Joshua took hold of the black leather reins and captured his prize.

"He's a British Dragoon's horse," Joshua announced as he looked over the horse's gear. After he had pulled the reins back over its neck, he walked down to its midsection and took the green and red trimmed saddle blanket in his hand. He rubbed its royal emblem between his fingers. "There's dried blood all over the saddle. I would say that's a good indication as to who won the battle." he said with a smile. "Hell, Thomas probable shot his rider off! That is one fine saddle," he said as he ran his free hand over the smooth leather seat. It even has a pistol in the saddle holster."

"That's why the British has the best army in the world," William said as he looked the horse over. "They're not only well trained and battle tested, their equipment is the best in the world as well."

Samuel dismounted from Fly and walked up to the other side of the horse and patted its neck. "He's got a wound here that looks like a bullet grazed his neck. It's a few inches deep, but I don't see anything inside the wound. You're going to have to keep an eye on it for a while, boy he is one fine piece of horseflesh. Wonder if there are any more around here? I could use one like him myself."

Joshua closed the bearskin holster flap back over the pistol grips and ran his fingers through its black fur with a satisfied look on his face. He put his boot into the brass stirrup and pulled himself up onto his new mount and fell in between William and Samuel as they made their way to the road just up ahead when they heard the sound of shouting men running through the pines. William's eyes narrowed as he saw four dragoons ride into the retreating men who were running on foot without weaponry to defend themselves. He pulled Sampson to a stop and was reaching for his rifle when he saw the sunlight glimmer off the blade of a dragoon's saber as he swung it down upon one of the defenseless militiamen, cutting him down with a deadly blow. The men on foot began to scatter as the pursuing dragoons picked out their next victims. Smoke rolled out of the end of William's rifle as he delivered a killing shot into the advancing dragoon who had just hacked a man to death, knocking him from his mount before he could overtake his next mark. Samuel and Joshua had likewise discharged their rifles into the unsuspecting dragoons, each not wasting their lead. The last remaining dragoon quickly whirled his horse and raced off into the tree line leaving his comrades where they fell. The nine surviving men turned towards their saviors, still in a hard run. William and the others had dismounted and were reloading as the panic-stricken men came running by.

"What's happened?" Joshua asked as he remounted his horse. "Did we win or lose that battle?"

"It's a disastrous defeat," a North Carolinian yelled as he ran by, not taking the time to stop. "Our whole army is scattered to the wind. Take to your heels. Tarleton's men are giving no quarter."

"Wait, we'll gather their mounts," Joshua yelled.

"There's no time!" the man replied, "that dragoon will be back with more men any minute, but they won't take to the swamps, it's too hard on their horses and they won't risk it on foot."

William watched as the fleeing men took to the swamps and quickly disappeared into its muddy waters as Samuel and Joshua ransacked the dead dragoons, ignoring the warnings of the fleeing men. Samuel had pulled a heavy purse from one of the dragoon's vest pockets, while Joshua had looted a fine leather covered telescope from the other dragoons' belt along with his cartridge box.

Samuel jumped on Fly and said, "Come on, let's run down those other horses before they get away. They're just on the other side of the road," as he and Joshua rode to the crest of a small hill in the road, they saw thirty or more of Tarleton's men tearing into another small group of fleeing militiamen on the far side of the clearing.

"You'll have to wait another day for that horse," Joshua said. Both men spun their mounts around and throwing sod high into the air, raced back toward William and the swamp.

William, seeing they were in full gallop realized they were most likely running from more British troops shouldered his rifle from atop Sampson's back and waited until they reached him. Then all three of them rode into the trees. Joshua's new horse had hidden in just a short time ago. There behind the low hanging limbs of a giant oak the tree watched as the dragoons rode by.

"Where do we go from here?" Samuel asked the two brothers.

"Back to Salisbury," William answered. "Or maybe Charlotte," as he continued. "Whatever is left of this army has to reform somewhere. We'll just follow the tide and try to outrun those damn bastards until we get back to North Carolina."

Chapter 124
Has He Lost the War?

Thomas propped his back up next to the wall of a silversmith shop in Charlotte and slid down the ground in slow motion, letting out a small groan as he reached the bottom. He pulled up a small stool as a substitute for a table and sat his half-filled plate of food on it. He bit into the cold chicken leg that the shop owner had generously given him. It was a little on the greasy side, but tasted good going down. It was the first morsel he had eaten since the battle. He took a mug from the owners' young granddaughter and sat it between his outstretched legs, protecting it so it would not spill the rum inside. Holding the half-eaten chicken leg in one hand

and a dried-out piece of cornbread in the other he listened as the shop owner told his story.

"Oh yeah, Gates was here all right, but not for long," the old silversmith explained. "He rode into town kicking up all kinds of dust. He ran into that tavern across the street, ate some food, paid the owner, stepped back outside, remounted on a new horse and shot out the other end of town like a bolt of lightning, leaving his old mount behind. Damn fine horse it is too."

"Did he say where he was going?" asked Thomas after he washed down a dry mouthful of cornbread with his rum.

"Don't think so, but he did ask how far away Hillsborough was. So, I would say that's your best bet as to where he was going. But who knows for sure? The way he shot out of here, he may not stop 'til he reaches Philadelphia."

"You mean he didn't leave any word at all as to where he was going, or any orders for what's left of his army? No instructions as to where to go?" Thomas asked angrily. "Leadership is needed more than ever now and no one knows what to do."

"None that I know of," the old man answered as he shooed his granddaughter inside the back door of the shop. "He acted like a damn coward, an embarrassment to the whole country. What a disgrace he is. If anyone had acted that way back in my day, during the French and Indian War, we would have tarred and feathered his pompous ass," the old man said through gritted teeth. "Do you think he has lost the war for us?"

"Hard to say," Thomas replied. "If he had stopped somewhere between here and Camden and reorganized the men maybe not, but now, I just don't know. Most of the North Carolina militia is returning to their homes. They seem to be pretty demoralized and from what I have been able to put together from the regulars who lived to tell the tail, the Continentals have been ripped to pieces and DeKalb is said to be dead. All the artillery is lost as well, not to mention all the supplies in the baggage train that was left behind, looks like the numbers of our casualties is going to be sickening. Maybe we can get ole Dan Morgan back after this. At least, that's what I am praying for. What about Generals Gist and Smallwood?" Thomas asked. Have you heard any news of them?"

"Gist is here in town somewhere," the silversmith said as he took Thomas' empty plate and mug. "Don't know about Smallwood as of yet. Sorry that's all the food I got left for you. I know you could have eaten more, but It's late at night you know, and that's all I have left."

"No, I thank you for what you could spare, I was happy to get it," Thomas replied, "I'll tell you the countryside is not too friendly to our cause between here and Camden, lots of Tories in South Carolina."

"Yeah, and they've been making out awful good too," the old man said as he handed the dirty dishes back inside the door to a dark hand. "The last group of soldiers who came in here before you said they were robbed twice by those wretches. But there are a lot of wigs down this way too. It's just that they have to lay low now that Cornwallis is down here. They give you any trouble? The Tories I mean."

"No, not after they discovered I hadn't lost my rifle and that I could still shoot," Thomas said laughingly. "That's the first time I've been able to laugh since before the battle. It's good to know I still can after that debacle."

"That's the spirit," the old man said, "Washington's still holding out up North. It's too early to talk of the war being lost just yet. We just need the right man down here to take command. What's your name anyway, Sergeant?"

"Thomas Tipton. I'm out of Virginia, but from Maryland originally."

"Now that's odd," the old man scratched his head, "I fed two brothers named Tipton a few hours ago. William and Joshua Tipton and they had a fellow by the name of Farra with them, any relation?"

"Brothers" Thomas responded loudly as he rose to his feet. "Where did they go?"

"I sent them down to the stables a few hours ago. They were looking for a place to bed down their horses. They said they were planning on sleeping with the horses, being afraid someone might steal them during the night if they didn't stay with them. It's just down the street from here."

"How much do I owe you?" Thomas asked.

"Nothing for that sorry meal it's on the house. I'm too old to fight, but I can help in other ways. Good luck to you Sergeant."

Thomas picked up his rifle, thanked his host and ran down the three-foot-wide alleyway that led out of the silversmith's back yard and onto the main street. Stopping only to shut the green gate at its end, he pulled down his tri-cornered hat and ran on down the street looking for the town's stable.

William was sitting next to the stable door working on his power horn. It was going to be a long night but he was not about to lose his two prized horses because he didn't watch over them. With all the militiamen fleeing home after the army's defeat, he was not going to take the chance of one of these desperate men riding off with one of his beloved horses while he slept in one of the town's taverns. The scrimshaw work was going as slow as ever. But he had managed to finish one side of the horn. It was his version of the Salt River ambush, but the Quaker homestead depiction was giving him trouble again. He had already filed away two other efforts from the horn's surface and was now starting his third attempt. It too would be made by firelight. He never had the time to try it in the daylight hours. Working on it now would help pass the time. Samuel had walked down into town to see the sights, most likely hoping to meet a real southern belle and Joshua, being a married man now, elected to stay behind here.

He had drifted off to sleep just inside the door on a pile of hay and was very little company, so William was free to carve away on his horn. He had decided to use a new tool tonight, discarding his knife and using his touchhole pick that he always used on his rifle. It had worked well on the house and it seemed to do a better job on the smaller detains such as the men and horses. But now the firelight was fading and he had looked up from his work and rubbed his eyes making his vision a little bleary. He glanced down the street, letting his eyes refocus, where he saw another Continental soldier approaching the stable. William couldn't make out the man's face in the darkness but he knew he was of some rank by the man's red epaulettes on his shoulder. Shaking his head as he looked back down to his work, he knew it was another officer trying to gather up some of his lost men. He wouldn't be the first to do such a thing today. William heard the man walk up, but he really didn't feel like having another conversation with an upset soldier here tonight. He just ignored the man as he stopped in front of him. "On your feet, Tipton I have fatigue work for you," the man said as he tapped the bottom of William's boot with the tip of his own.

A smile came over William's face right before he blew some of his carving dust from his horn. "You always were the bossy type Thomas, but I'm still glad to see you." William said as he rose to his feet to greet his older brother. "It's good to see that you're still alive and well brother. I was hoping to run into you somewhere down here, but with all of this disorder and confusion going on, I was having some doubts. You look well. No cuts or wounds."

"Oh, I'm fine," Thomas replied as he grabbed onto both of his brother's shoulders. I didn't know that you all were down here with the militia. Seems like we would have crossed paths somewhere in camp before now where's Joshua? He's not hurt, is he?"

"Naw, he's just inside the door there. No, the reason you never saw us in camp was because we were never there. We missed the battle by a few hours. We came down when the militia was called up, but it was such a poor turnout in our part of the country that we were slow getting here. We heard the cannon fire, but never got to the battlefield. But we did shoot some dragoons that were on the North Carolina Militia's heels."

"Well that's more than they did," Thomas replied. "At least you did some fighting. The militia's feet just couldn't hold the day. Say Joshua's inside?"

"Yeah, but he's asleep. Did you know he's gotten married?"

"No, I didn't," Thomas answered, "but it doesn't surprise me. He had that look in his eyes every time he was around that Shields girl. That is who he married isn't it?" William just nodded his head, yes.

"Just making sure," Thomas said with a grin. "Don't want to call her by the wrong name when I rib him about it." William sat back down and asked Thomas, "What's your take on the situation down here brother? It looks as though Gates has confirmed your worst fears about his abilities."

"It's too early to say yet," Thomas answered as he sat down next to William. "But this has to have ruined Gates' career. Everyone in the army knew that Washington wanted General Green put in command down here. But Gates had enough power to get congress to appoint him instead. Maybe congress will heed Washington's word now. If Gates is not replaced within a few weeks, we'll have another disaster on our hands and the cause cannot withstand that, I'm afraid."

Chapter 125
Hope

As William rode out of Salisbury acting as the rear guard of this short procession of soldiers, he was amazed by how fast his and everyone else's frame of mind had improved in the last five days. Disappointment and depression had run rampant among the surviving troops back in Charlotte. Some soldiers had come into town with their weapons, but many had not. A soldier rejoining his unit could do little good without anything in his hand to fight with if Cornwallis attacked again, and that was everyone's worst fear. Then there were the camp followers straggling in adding dejected faces to the scene. Many of these women were now widowed, having lost their husband to the point of a British bayonet. Others had lost young children in the mad dash to escape and were frantically looking for them in the streets of the town. There were also single women among them, some of whom had lost the man they hoped to marry and some who lost one who was willing to pay her way in life.

Many of the civilian families that supported the American cause out in the surrounding countryside had abandoned their homesteads in fear of reprisals from the local Tories who now had little fear of the defeated Southern Army. But gradually, the situation began to change. General Smallwood had arrived with a few men and he and General Gist had done a good job of reorganizing the pitiful fragment of an army, along with the help on one highly capable Sergeant. In addition, word had spread that more men were further on up in Salisbury, so as these ragtag remains of an army marched to Salisbury the fear of another attack from Cornwallis lessened with each step, and had disappeared altogether by the time they finally arrived at that small village. The townspeople had proved very generous, feeding as many of the troops as they could. Gates had eventually let his whereabouts be known by sending dispatches back to Salisbury, instructing Gist and Smallwood to rendezvous with him at Hillsborough, where he had secured DeKalb's abandoned artillery. He had also sent dispatches north with request for more men along with the news of his loss to congress.

Once again William and the others had spent the night at the home of Michael Braun. The old German had his own good news for the Tipton brothers and Samuel. At least it was good news if the rumor was true. He had been told that Dan Morgan, the old teamster himself, was coming out of retirement to take a bigger hand in the southern theater of this long drawn out war. Maybe the war was not lost after all, but it had certainly been one hellish week.

"Back to Hillsborough," Joshua sighed as he rode along. "This trek is becoming old hat for us, 'eh boys?"

"Too old," William replied as Sampson stopped on the side of the road to take a bite of some low-lying branches that William was not familiar with. "Let's just hope that Morgan is there waiting for us when we arrive. I pray that Mr. Braun's information is true. Come on Sampson, let's go. I'm not acquainted with that tree. I don't want you getting sick from eating something that I don't know what is."

"How long do you think it will take for word to get back to our wives?" Joshua asked. "I wrote a letter for Jeanette last night and I plan to send it off as soon as we arrive at Hillsborough."

"Yeah, I did too," William answered, "but I'm sure the news of our defeat will out run our letters. It will be a hard few days on our girls, waiting to hear from us especially Elizabeth. Let's just hope it is days and not weeks."

"Now why do you say 'especially Elizabeth'? Do you think she loves you more than Jeanette loves me?" Joshua argued.

"Well, maybe," William replied laughing, "but she is carrying a child you know. Women can get mighty upset when they're with child, but you'll find that out yourself someday if you're lucky."

Samuel just rolled his eyes as he rode along between the two of them.

"What's that look all about Samuel?" Joshua asked. "Just because you can't seem to catch yourself a wife doesn't mean we can't discuss ours. You're the only one of us that's not gotten married since we got back from Kentucky. Hell, even James has settled down. Are you going to stay a free man forever?"

"That's right," Samuel answered, "free as a bird."

"At least until Miss Riley says otherwise," William teased.

"Why don't you two go on up there with your other brother and give him a hard time?" Samuel suggested.

"Aw no," William replied. "Thomas has his hands full with his men up there. We're just fine right here. We don't want you to be lonely back here by yourself anyway, do we Joshua?"

The men had grown quiet after their little lighthearted exchange had ended. William took the time to think of his growing family back home as his eyes scanned the countryside. He hoped what he had said would not come true, but he was afraid that it would. Elizabeth was a strong hearted woman, but she had never received word that her husband might be dead before. He prayed that she would have confidence in his abilities to stay alive and make it back home safely to her waiting arms.

William tugged on Sampson's reins, pulling him to a stop. He opened the pan on his rifle and pulled out the stopper of his powder horn with his teeth and poured some black powder into the pan.

"What is it?" Samuel asked as he reached for his own rifle, "Tories?"

"No, supper," William replied. "There's a flock of turkeys running into those trees at the bottom of this hill. I'll bet you I bag the biggest bird down there!" he yelled over his shoulder as he rode off leaving the others behind.

Chapter 126
Dispatches

Night had fallen on the makeshift camp just outside of Hillsborough as William and Samuel were kindling a fire in front of their newly constructed lean to, much like the ones they had built in Kentucky on their claims. However, this time the roof was made of evergreen branches. They would do little to keep rain from dripping through, but it had kept the morning dew off them these last few days they had been camped here. This afternoon the sky had turned dark and the wind was picking up as though a storm would be blowing in sometime tonight. Samuel had placed a pile of dried grass and tow in the bottom of the fire pit they had dug and stepped back to block the wind, by standing in the direction it was blowing from, as William leaned over to light the fire. With a few strikes of his flint on a small piece of steel that he always carried with him, the fire ignited. After a few carefully placed twigs were laid on the flames the fire blazed up, burning well. With some luck the two rabbits they had shot this afternoon would be cooked within the hour providing the rain would hold off long enough to finish the job.

"Three men eating two rabbits somehow the math just doesn't work out does it?" Samuel asked as he stared down into the crackling fire.

"Yeah, lean eating again tonight," William agreed. "It would be nice to have some of Elizabeth's cherry pie to top off these rabbits with now wouldn't it?"

"Damn, William, don't talk like that. I'm hungry enough now as it is, without talk like that." Samuel laughed "Damn, Cherry Pie!"

"Look what I got boys," Joshua announced as he came walking into the firelight from out of the trees.

"I am hungry," Samuel said as he looked up from his sitting position at the cow hide that Joshua was holding, "but I'm not eating that."

"Me neither," Joshua answered as he walked past the fire, "but it will help keep the rain out tonight. Here, help me spread it over the top of our roof there."

"Where did you get it?" William asked.

"It was the last of that beef they brought in the other day. I guess no one saw any value in it. The cooks had just left it down by the creek where they had slaughtered those cows. They'll be wishing they still had them when it starts raining later on tonight."

"Well, it may keep the water out, but it sure does stink the place up some," Samuel said as he wrinkled up his nose.

"The evergreens will be in between us and it. That will keep the smell down for your delicate nose," William teased, "or you can sleep over in the other lean to with our gear instead."

"Well, if it doesn't rain, I just might," Samuel answered.

"What are you boys cooking up there, I know our beef has all been eaten up by now," Dan Morgan asked as he walked up to the fire with Thomas by his side. "A couple of rabbits I see," he continued. "Poor they are, not the best specimens I ever saw, but better than nothing I dare say."

"Yes, Sir," William answered.

"Sergeant Tipton here tells me you boys are from my home county of Frederick." Morgan stated. "I don't remember seeing you fellows when I took the county Militia up to Canada back when the war first broke out."

"We were still in Maryland at that time General," William answered. "I bought my place from Captain Babb after you were gone I guess. But we did go up to Ft. Pitt with the militia under Captain Babb."

"Yes, that's what your brother tells me," Morgan replied. "I heard that Captain Babb had some bad luck this past spring."

"Yeah, the Tories gave him a good beating and burned down his home," Samuel said, turning the half-cooked rabbit over. "But we ran them down later on." he said proudly.

"Yes, I heard that too. Buxton spoke highly of you boys before I came down here. That's why I want you men to do something for me. The Virginia Militia's tour is about up, in a few weeks in fact, and General Green has informed me that he's not going to do any fighting until spring of next year. So there is no need for you all to stay here. I am going to stay behind. If I want to turn this bunch into the army that we'll need to win this damn war and whip little Bennie's ass next year, I'm going to have to stay here and build them up. So, I would like for you to take a few dispatches back to my home in Winchester. My family will see to them from that point on, and get them to their final destinations if you can get them that far. You will need to pull out at sun up. Come on over to my headquarters in town and I will have them ready for you then."

The juices from the cooking rabbits dripped into the fire below, making a sizzling sound drawing Morgan's attention to the fire. "I would go on and eat those things before they get too dry if I was you boys. Have a safe trip back now. I'll have some extra supplies waiting for you at my headquarters in the morning. Thomas, I won't need you anymore tonight. You may stay here and chew the fat with your brothers if you want, but I wouldn't stay too long, it's going to rain soon. That's what my old bones are telling me anyway." At that, the old waggoneer turned and walked off into the night after giving William and Joshua exactly what they wanted, a good reason to go home, back to their wives and families and out of this upcoming winter tour.

Chapter 127
Teary Eyed

Elizabeth reached for the small shovel that always hung to the side of James fireplace, next to the bellows. Taking it down by the handle she scooped up some of the hot coals from the fire that was burning inside the hearth. The heat from the red coals was hot on her face and arm forcing her to hurry at her task of piling the coals on top of the cast iron lid that covered the cherry pie she had baking inside.

"Please, sit down Elizabeth before you fall down" pleaded Prudence Tate. I told you to let me do that? You're too far along to be doing all that bending over" she said pointing to Elizabeth's rounded stomach. "I declare you can't sit still for a minute."

"I know," Elizabeth sighed as she stepped away from the hearth and put her hands on her hips, "but it's hard to just sit here and do nothing. I have got to keep myself occupied somehow. You know all too well what it's like not knowing if your husband is alive or not. It's making me a little crazy."

"Yes, I do know," Prudence replied as she pulled out a chair from under the table in the center of the room. "But I wasn't with child when I lost Drew either. Sit down here, your face is as red as a beet and you're covered in perspiration from the heat of the fireplace. You must take better care of yourself dear, besides you don't know for sure that William is dead. It's only been a few weeks since that battle took place."

"I know," Elizabeth said as she sank down into the chair, but he has always written to me in the past and this time I haven't received a single word from him."

"That's true," Prudence said as she dipped clean water from the water bucket that was sitting on the table's edge onto a dish towel. "But just because you haven't received any correspondence from him still doesn't prove anything either. You know the mail has been slow since the war has been going on." Prudence walked around behind Elizabeth and pulled her head back against her by putting her hand under Elizabeth's chin. Looking down into Elizabeth's eyes, she said, "Don't worry. I feel like he and the rest of them are alive and well," as she placed the cool towel on Elizabeth's forehead. "We will just keep on praying to the good Lord. He'll come back to you. Just you wait and see."

Elizabeth smiled and shut her eyes, enjoying the soothing sensation of the cool towel on her hot forehead. "You're a good friend Prudence. James is a fortunate man indeed to have married a good woman like you."

"That's sweet of you to say, but that's not the only reason we can say that he has been fortunate this year," Prudence said as she walked back around in front of Elizabeth and took her hand in her own. "This coming spring you can come over here and fuss at me for working myself too hard while I am waddling around here with my child."

"Ohhh sweetie, that's wonderful," Elizabeth said as she stood up to give her friend a congratulatory hug. "Does James know yet?" she asked pulling away, "He will be overjoyed."

"No, not yet. I am planning on telling him later on tonight after we eat supper when we take our nightly walk down by the creek."

"That will be a perfect place and time to tell him, Prudence. I can hardly wait to see how he will react to this blessed news, I…I," Elizabeth said as she began to cry. "It's good to have some good news around here again."

"That's why I went on and told you. I thought it might raise your spirits some. And I must confess, I've wanted to tell someone about it too," Prudence said happily. "I'm just so happy that you are here to share this with us."

"Share what with us?" James asked as he walked in the front door holding his rifle.

"Supper," Prudence answered laughing as she walked over to her husband and put her hand on his shoulder, "What else?"

"I don't know for sure," James answered, "But I dare say it wasn't supper you two were talking about. However, I'm not bold enough to challenge two women all by myself either, so I'll just take you ladies' word for it at the present. When do we eat? I'm kind of hungry tonight for some reason."

"Another hour or so," Prudence answered.

"Very well then, I'll be out in the barn putting away some more wood for winter until then," James said, turning and stepping back off the porch. As he walked into the barn lot he stopped and picked up a piece of wood and carried it inside the barn, where he pitched the single stick of firewood on a large rick of wood in the corner of the barn. He put his rifle on a work table inside the door and stepped back outside to the large pile of wood that he had split earlier in the day. He picked up several split logs and laid them in his wheelbarrow until it was full. Then he picked up the wheelbarrow by the handles and began to push it inside when he heard several horses coming up the road. He pushed the load of wood toward the barn in a hard run until he was inside the door where he let the top-heavy wheelbarrow fall to the ground as he swooped up his rifle and stepped back outside to meet whoever was riding up.

Riding along beside Joshua and just a little out in front of Samuel, William looked up and saw James dart out of his barn, hunched over with his rifle in his hand. James' quick disappearance from sight behind a pile of wood gave William pause. Realizing that Joshua was now riding a strange mount, one with British gear, William called for a halt, knowing full well that if James took them for Tories, that one of them would soon be dead.

"Don't shoot James." William yelled raising a hand to the side of his mouth. "It's only us. No Tories here."

Hearing William's call, James stepped out into the open and raised his arm into the air, waving his friends on home. He walked out of the yard into the middle of the road and watched them ride up with a wide grin on his face.

"Do you always lie in wait for your friends with a gun behind a woodpile?"

Samuel asked as he rode up.

"No, just the ones I don't like too well," James answered as he followed the horses inside the gate, while eyeing Joshua's new mount. "Been stealing horses again have you boys?"

"Something like that," Joshua answered.

"How are my girls?" William asked as he dismounted from Sampson.

"They are both well," James told him as he took the reins from William's hand. "Sarah is around back of the house playing, and Elizabeth is inside. She may be the one that shoots you though; she's been mighty worried what with no news coming about you."

"She didn't get my letters?" William asked as he walked toward the house.

"Not the scratch of a quill," James answered. "Hell, I was even beginning to wonder about you all myself," he laughed.

William shook his head as he walked toward the house while the other men began to discuss how Joshua had acquired his new horse. He could see that the door to the house was open as he approached. The sound of his boots on the wooden boards gave away his presence, but the women inside were engaged in their work and, thinking it was only James paid little attention to his entrance. Elizabeth had just brushed the cooled coals from the top of the pie pan and had backed away from the hearth watching Prudence replace them with more hot coals to finish baking the pie.
"It's not been an hour yet," Prudence said as she hung the shovel back in its place, her back still turned to William.

"Well, I'll just go out back and play with Sarah then," William answered.

Elizabeth bent her head and shut her eyes as relief ran through her body. Tears began to flow down her cheeks as William placed his loving hands on her waist and said, "Hello, my Love." Leaning down gave her a tender kiss on the side of her wet   cheek. Opening her eyes, she spun around and melted into his arms. After several satisfying kisses, she took his face in her hands and said, "Where have you been?"

Chapter 128
A Place Called King's Mountain

It was one of those glorious late fall October days. The sun was shining brightly making the gold and red tree leaves shine even more this afternoon. William and little Sarah had walked down to the creek to look over his four cows that were grazing down next to the water. All of his cows had given birth to their calves this spring before he had gone down to the Carolinas, but he still liked to check on them every day or so. Sarah always looked forward to going to the creek with him; she thought there was nothing better than throwing a stone into the water while her father stood by bragging about how pretty she was. The wind began to blow a little harder than it had been earlier in the day as the two of them sat on the creek bank. With each gust of wind, a whole gaggle of maple leaves would float down from the trees to the ground and onto their heads. Sarah had jumped up and was running around trying to catch the leaves before they could reach the ground, putting on a good show for her father as she played on the natural carpet of gold.

"Look daddy, I got one, I really did get one!" she cried as she finally plucked one from the crisp air.

"That's my girl," William said as he got up. I believe you're the best leaf catcher I ever saw, and I've seen a quite few in my day, believe me. Come over here little one and give me a hug." As the little girl ran to her father who had squatted down and opened his arms, she tripped and fell to the ground.

"Busted your little butt, didn't you?" William laughed as he watched his daughter struggle to get back to her feet in the tall grass. "Look at what you found," he said as he leaned over on all fours and crawled on his hand and knees to console the little girl. "Look a here, look a here. It's a box turtle. Not only are you a leaf catcher but now you're a finder of rare turtles." William picked up the small black and yellow spotted turtle and sat it in front of Sarah. "See how he's shut up tight in his shell? He's afraid of you Sarah. See how he has pulled his head and legs inside his shell and shut it up tight?" William asked as he plucked a few leaves from her hair. "If we wait long enough, he'll pop his head back out for us. Just sit there and watch and he'll come back out in a minute or two." Standing up he glanced back up to the house, holding his ever-present rifle in his hand. To his surprise, he saw James riding his horse Trace down toward him and Sarah.

"Daddy, he's not come back out yet," Sarah informed him while tapping the turtle's hard shell with a twig.

"Well, he won't as long as you keep hitting him on his back like that sweetie," William answered.

"Have you heard the news yet William?" James asked as he rode up.

"No, I don't guess I have," William answered. "What is it? Good I hope."

"Oh, it is that," James said as he jumped off his horse. "You know how Cornwallis sent that Scotsman Colonel Patrick Ferguson out in the Carolina back country to head up a regiment of Tories?"

"Yeah," William said, "I remember hearing something about that."

"Well, it seems that Ferguson sent a dispatch over the mountains and out through the western parts of the Carolinas, telling all the militia if they didn't come in from hiding and take an oath to the King, he would ride into their own country and lay it to waste with fire and sword."

"I bet that went over big," William said as he walked over to Sarah.

"Aw, he got the militia out, alright," James continued, but the end results were not quite what he expected. Isaac Shelby and John Sevier marched over a couple hundred men from Tennessee and joined up with the McDowell brothers at Quaker Meadows. Then Ben Cleveland led a force down from Wilkes County North Carolina, while Colonel Campbell came down from western Virginia. By the time they all rendezvoused they had over a thousand men. Somehow Ferguson got wind of their plans and high tailed it out of North Carolina into South Carolina where they finally cornered him on top of a mountain."

"Damn, we missed it," William said as he sat Sarah, still holding her turtle, on top of James' horse.

"Yeah, I know," James said as he turned toward William's house, holding the reins. "And it gets better," he said as the two of them walked in front of Trace with Sarah riding on his back. "We missed out alright. It was a total rout," James continued with his story. "Ferguson was killed along with half of his men and the rest were taken prisoner."

"Where did all this take place?" William asked.

"A place called King's Mountain," James answered. "It gets better though, I'm not done yet. It seems they marched the prisoners somewhere near Gilbert Town and had a trial for some of the Tory officers and sentenced them to be hung. Ten were executed."

"Who were they?" William asked, "Do we know any of them?"

"Nine of them I never heard of," James said as he came to a stop and looked over at William, "but the other one was a one-armed fellow by the name of Price."

"Aquilla Price is dead?" William asked, "I don't believe it somehow. I always thought we would cross paths again."

"Well, not in this world," James replied." He's a piece of rotten fruit now for sure."

"Who told you this?" William asked.

"Captain Babb," James answered.

"He would know," William laughed. "Was he pleased to hear the news?"

"Yes, he was," James answered, "but I think he was a little disappointed in the fact that he's not going to get another shot at Price either, now that he's dead. But it's probably better this way. I believe Captain Babb is a getting too old for this war."

"Yeah I think you're right," William agreed, "I would say his best and last reason to go back into the war died along with Price."

"Look Daddy, he stuck his head back out," Sarah announced from atop the horse.

"Well, don't let him bite you," William answered.

"Bite!" she cried as she dropped the turtle to the ground.

Chapter 129
A Son

William walked out the front door of his house and sat down next to James after shooing Elizabeth's calico cat out from under his favorite chair. "Well my friend, it will be your turn, come spring." Williams said as he leaned back in his chair.

"Yeah, I reckon, James answered. "So, tell me, how does it feel to have a son?"

"I'm walking a little taller," William answered with a smile. "But I sure am relieved that it's over. It's not easy watching your wife in those last few weeks. You'll see. It's hard on them without question. I just pray we get the little fellow through the winter alive. He looks healthy, but you never know about winter babies."

"Yeah, that's true," James agreed as he lit his pipe. "Have you two settled on a name yet?"

"Not really," William answered. "We're still going back and forth over it.

Elizabeth is partial to Solomon, but I'm holding out for John. I told her the other day, if she let me name this one, she could name the next son Solomon. She said she would sleep on it for a while. Is that the tobacco you grew this year?"

"Yeah, and it's kind of strong, but good," James replied reaching into his back pocket for his tobacco pouch. "Here have some for yourself and see."

"Alright, I think I will," William said as he pulled out his own pipe and filled it up with James' latest crop. "It's been a good while since I had a smoke. I ran out fairly quickly when I was down in the Carolinas. Boredom sets in real fast when you're sitting around a fire at night with nothing to do. I smoked mine up in the first week down there. I haven't had any since I've been back home. Dang, you're right. That's strong."

William rested one ankle on his other knee as he blew out some smoke and watched it float across the porch and drift away into his yard. "Heard any more about what's going on down in Kentucky while I was away?"

"Come to think of it, I did," James answered. "But it's not good; you're not going to like it too well. I met a fellow down in Winchester that had just gotten back from Kentucky. By the name of Bohon...I think...Yeah... That was his name, John Bohon. Anyhow, according to him, your old friend Simon Girty is making quite a name for himself out there. He and some British officer lead a war party of about eight hundred Shawnees along with a cannon out of Detroit to a couple of smaller stations out in the central part of Kentucky. The first one was called Ruddell Station. The British blew its gates to hell with that damn cannon. Then they let those damn red demons run in with tomahawks in hand to kill almost every man, woman, and child inside. But even that wasn't enough for the bastards. Later on that day they took Martin Station without firing a shot. I guess the settlers knew they were no match for a field piece. They took every soul inside up north someplace. Hard to believe he's the same fellow that was with us back at Ft. Pitt," James finished, shaking his head. "But I did get some good news too, Basil is alive and well."

"So, he made it," William said as he jumped up from his chair. "How is he?"

"Well, I don't know for sure, but this Bohon fellow said Basil walked all the way from the Ohio River to Fort Harrod and led a party of men back to Captain Rogers ambush site. But as you know the Captain was dead when they got there, but they did find two fellows that were shot up pretty bad still alive and they managed to save them."

"Good ole Basil," William said as he stomped his foot on the floorboards of his porch. "He's probably back at the Falls trying to catch a boat right now."

"Or maybe down in New Orleans wintering with one of those French Girls he was always talking about." James chuckled. "You know that we're going to have to go back fairly soon if we want to keep our land out there," James sobered as he looked over at William.

"Yeah, next summer after your son is born, maybe," William answered as he stepped over to the doorway and took Elizabeth's hand, leading her out of the house and over to his chair.

"Good to get some fresh air, 'eh Elizabeth" James asked?

"That it is," she answered. "Now you take good care of Prudence this winter, James. Not every woman in her condition would come over to another woman's house and work as hard as she did over here before my laying in. And then to turn around and help me out yesterday like she did. Now she's in there cooking our supper. You can be sure that when her time comes, I'll be there for her, come hail or high water. You sure did well by yourself when you married her."

"I already know that," James answered, "And she knows that you'll be there for her when her time comes."

"All right then, it's settled." Elizabeth said as she shifted her weight to the other side of her chair. "William," she said turning her attention back to her husband, "John sounds like a fine name to me. How about John Solomon Tipton? It has a good ring to it, don't you think?"

"John Solomon Tipton," William said, running his hand up and down the woodwork of the doorway and looking up at the ceiling. "I like it," he answered, "but you love Solomon so much you shouldn't have to waste it on a middle name. No we'll save Solomon for the next boy," William disagreed with his wife.
"But what if it's a girl?" Elizabeth asked with a smile, "You know it could be."
"Then you can name her whatever you want my love and the next boy will still be called Solomon, even if he's the tenth child down the line."

"Ten children," Elizabeth groaned, "I don't like the name that much. Maybe we should just go on and call this one John Solomon."

Chapter 130
Thoughts of Kentucky

The redbuds and dogwoods were in full bloom this spring, reflecting the mood of the inhabitants in William's newly green bottom in Frederick County this year of 1781. The warm rays of the sun felt good on everyone's faces after the cold winter they had just endured. The newest member of William's family, John, had indeed survived the cold winter months to everyone's delight. And if that in its self wasn't enough good news, the Tate family had increased the population of the bottom by one as well. True to her word Elizabeth was at Prudence's side when her time came just a few weeks ago. Under her and Charity Babb's watchful eyes, Prudence had given birth to a strong baby boy. However, the Tates did not have the same problem the Tipton's had when it came to naming their child. For James' first son's name had long been settled on. He was to be named after his father's two best friends. William Samuel Tate.

Even the war seemed to be going better, now that General Green was in command in the South, and ole Dan Morgan's victory at the Cowpens over Tarleton had taken away some of the sting of Gates' defeat outside Camden the year before. Tarleton's dragoons were considered to be the best the British Cavalry could offer. Yet Morgan, along with the help of Lt. Colonel William Washington had sent Little Bennie home with his tail stuck between his legs. Added to these victories, General Washington had managed to keep his Northern Army together and was hoping this would be the year he would recapture New York City. The only drawback so far this year was the fact that once again William and his neighboring friends had decided to pass on going back to Kentucky. Joshua seemed to be enjoying married life too well to leave his bride behind back in Maryland and had not shown up for the trip. Remembering how hard it had been for William to go into the wilderness and leave his family behind, James had decided to wait at least until the fall to return to Kentucky. None of this had rubbed William the wrong way. He loved his family as much as the others did, besides he felt no urgency to spend another spring away from his loved ones in a dangerous land full of hostile Indians. In addition, Captain Babb had returned from the coast and was in the midst of rebuilding his home after Aquilla Price had so unmercifully destroyed it the year before. The greater part of the militia was helping their old commander in the construction of his new home. It would take a few years for the captain to complete his vision of what his new home would be, but William and the others were going to help get it under roof this spring. After that, the captain could take all the time he wanted to finish the finer details. As William sat on top of the two-story house's eave, waiting for the block and tackle to hoist up another bundle of lumber he gazed out over the bottom's green countryside. It was a bird's eye view that he rarely got to see. From his perch, he could see how Captain Babb had divided his plantation into smaller fields, all with stone fences that ran around and through his property. The crossroads were visible and he could even see the rooftops of the buildings on James' homestead, but his own was just out of sight. A view would not be a problem at his home in Kentucky he thought. He would have one like this every day as he stepped out of his front door high upon that hill in the rolling landscape where he planned to build his home once they were settled in Kentucky. He would be able to see most of his farm in one quick glance. But when would that be? The war seemed to have no end in sight. He had hoped that the Indians would be subdued before he took his young family out there. But that seemed to be a distant dream now. The more he thought about it, he wondered if it was maybe a mistake not going out there this spring after all. If he wanted to have his Kentucky home before he reached thirty he would have to take a few chances, he thought. Maybe it was time for him to go back and see how the situation out there was himself. That was always the best way to find things out, do it yourself. Maybe he could talk James and Samuel into going out there after all. If Joshua never showed up, one less rifle would make little difference. Four men could be killed by Indians just as easily as three.

Chapter 131
A Hard Friend to Have

The ramp of the flat boat fell into the waters of the Ohio River just a few feet short of the bank causing the water to splash high into the air, here at the newly founded frontier town of Limestone, at the mouth of a creek that bore the same name. William rode Sampson off the boat and turned him around and watched as James and Samuel joined him on the Kentucky shore.

"No Stockade," James said as he rode up next to William. "I don't know if that's good or not. What about you?"

"Well, let's just hope it's not needed. Maybe it's a good sign that the Indians are giving up on their old hunting grounds," William answered with a grin.

"Hell, that's a crock," Samuel said as the three turned away from the river, laughing at William's sarcastic joke.

"It's no laughing matter," a man said coming up from the river with a bucket of water in one hand and a rifle in the other. "I lost a brother last month on the river just down from Wheeling."

"We didn't mean any disrespect Mister," William answered.

"I'm sure you didn't." the man answered as he kept on walking, "There is a hell of a lot of Indian sign out there right now. I thought you should know that before you rode off into it."

"Thanks for the warning." Samuel answered, "This is not our first time out in the cane breaks."

"That doesn't matter," the man said as he stopped at a cabin door. "Lots of good men have been killed out there that had been on this frontier for years," the man said as he opened his door and disappeared inside. But before he shut the oak door, he gave one last suggestion. "If you're going out this afternoon don't camp at the Blue Licks tonight. Stop at Kenton's cabin. If you're lucky he may be there. But most of the time, he's not there. He stays out in the woods a lot spying on the redskins."

"He's right," William said as he watched the door shut. "Let's be sharp out there. They don't call it the dark and bloody ground for nothing."

A few concerned looks were passed between the three friends as they headed past the four crude cabins that made up the small town. As they rode along down an eight-foot-wide buffalo path that led out into the interior of Kentucky, Samuel asked, "Who is this Simon Kenton anyway? Our river captain spoke of him while we were coming down."

"I don't know for sure, but his cabin's a few miles inland." James answered, "Maybe that's where the stockade is." After answering Samuel's question, James turned his attention to William and said, "You were right about coming back out here William. There is a whole lot more settlers out here than there was on our first trip. We need to be here some."

"Yeah." William answered, "Word is getting out. I'm glad we already have our land out here squared away. There is going to be some wild business deals going on now. A lot of land hungry folks coming down the river. We saw more boats in one day this time than we did the entire trip with Captain Rogers. The way they talked up at Ft. Pitt one out of every four boats is being attacked, and yet they still keep on coming.

"That's why I like the idea of going back through the Cumberland Gap on horseback instead of going back up river against that current." James replied. "Besides, that's a part of Kentucky and Tennessee we haven't seen yet."

"Yeah, and I'm kind of curious to see how many people are coming up that way too," Samuel added. "If it's as many as on the river, the country will be filled in a few years. There's the cabin."

"Doesn't look like much," William said as they came to a stop in front of a small one room building. "I don't believe anyone is here. There's a lock on the door. I say we keep on riding. We have four or five hours of daylight left. Maybe we can reach Bryan's Station before dark."

"No, it's way too far," a voice spoke from the trees to the south of the house. "You would only make it as far as the licks and that's no place to spend the night with just three men. You boys stay here tonight and I'll lead you on to Bryan's in the morning."

"I remember you." William said as he watched Simon Butler prop his long rifle up against the cabin wall so he could unlock the door to Kenton's cabin. "We met at the falls two years back. You told us how to get to Harrodsburg. You're Simon Butler."

"Yes, that sounds like something I would do," Butler answered as he opened the door. "I try to help out whoever I can, but my name is Kenton now. I had to use an alias for a few years, but now I don't have to anymore. My true name is Simon Kenton. I've got some buffalo meat inside if you want some," he said turning away from the open door. "Yeah, I do remember you fellows now. You all came in on Captain Rogers' boat a few days before I led George down into the Illinois country. Damn shame about what happened to Rogers."

"That was us." William said as he dismounted his horse "And yes, it was a shame about the Captain. He was a good man."

"Hugh McGray told me all about you fellows," Kenton continued. "He still has those horses he traded that land to you for. Well, most of them anyway. I think a few have been stolen back by the Shawnee. He was starting to wonder if you all had got yourselves killed on some battlefield back east. He'll be disappointed that he won't be able to resell that land now that your back."

"Sorry to disappoint him," Samuel said, "But he hasn't resold our land, has he?"

"No," Kenton answered, "Hugh is a hot head, but he's no crook. Well, how about it boys? Are you staying or moving on?"

"We'll stay," James answered. "We came back to check up on our land and to find out firsthand what the situation is like out here. Seems to me you're the man to talk to about that. We'll stay."

"Good, then go around back and grab us a few logs and I'll make us a fire inside. Damn, I hate cooking," Simon said as he lowered his head and stepped inside the dark cabin. "After you fellows tend to your horses and come in with that wood, you can tell me what's going on back east."

It had been a few hours since William and the others had taken up Simon's offer and now, they were sitting around a crude table inside. William looked over this dirt floored cabin and a grin flashed over his face as he thought how similar the cabin was to the one Simon Girty had been using up the Allegheny. This cabin may belong to Kenton but from the look of it, he didn't spend too much time here.

"So, you have all gone back east and got yourselves hitched?" Simon asked. "That makes you fortunate men indeed."

"Not me," Samuel said quickly.

"Well, that makes you a fortunate man as well doesn't it?" Simon asked with a smile as he sat down his wooden plate. "I know it's kind of hot in here, but I don't like going back outside after I burn a fire. The Indians know I stay here some and if any are around out there and see smoke; they will take advantage of the opportunity to get a shot off at me when I step out that door. So, I don't oblige them, at least not until morning."

"Why?" James asked, "Do they hate you that much?"

"Hell yes," Simon answered. "Ever since Simon saved me from the stake back when I was captured, they've been out for me, even before really."

"Simon Girty saved you from burning at the stake?" William asked.

"He sure did. They had me stripped down and painted black, ready for the fire to be lit. At first, he didn't realize who I was, because of all the black paint. But once he did, he talked them into having some kind of vote after he made a speech to them on my behalf. It was a close vote and the ones who wanted me dead were a mite pissed off and are still after me, you can bet on that."

"When did this happen?" William asked, "After he went over to the British?"

"Yes," Kenton replied. "We met back during Dunmore's War and have been friends ever since. I disapproved of his actions," Simon said as he got up and walked over to a port hole and stared out to see if anyone was lurking around outside. "I mean, how could I not, after what he did to Captain Rogers, but I sure was happy to see his face when I was about to be burned alive. I don't see or hear anything unusual out there," he announced as he walked back to his chair and sat down. "Simon Girty is a hard friend to have most of the time, but I sure am thankful to God that he was my friend that day. I guess it's hard to understand if you don't know him very well. You know I followed his war party all the way to the Ohio after he captured all those people at Martin and Ruddell stations. Once I even had him in my sights, but I let him go. I keep on having discussions with myself as to why I let him go. Maybe it was because I was outnumbered, but I say that's not the reason I didn't fire."

"I know precisely how you feel," William said as he laid his rifle across the arms of his chair, over his lap. "I have lost a few hours of sleep over Simon Girty myself."

"Why the name changes," Samuel asked, letting his curiosity get the better of his judgment.

"That's a long story," Kenton answered after glancing around the table at his guest. He could tell the question had made William and James uncomfortable. Smiling he said "That's all right fellows, I don't mind. It was love believe it or not. At least that's what I thought at the time. A girl I was sweet on took to another. My manhood was hurt so I took it upon myself to win her back with my fist. I thought I killed him; ran away that night met up with an old long hunter and ended up in Kentucky. Turned out he was just unconscious and they put him on trial. Not being able to find me or my body, everyone thought he had killed me" Kenton laughed. "But it all worked out in the end, he got the girl and I got my name back."

"Must have been some tussle," Samuel replied with a sheepish grin.

"Yah it was." Kenton continued, "Changed my life. I've been shot at, ran after, captured, ran the gauntlet, escaped, been helped and helped others. Hell, I wouldn't have it any other way. Well, on second thought, maybe not the gauntlet and the broken bones that went with it."

Chapter 132
At the Lower Blue Licks

Simon Kenton had been in Kentucky for several years and William had little trouble seeing how he had managed to keep his hair all this time. He was a careful man, but in an extraordinarily bold way. On several occasions last night, he had gotten up and peered out the portholes of his cabin, watching the dark tree line that ran around his little used homestead. He would stand at one for a while, before moving on to the next, not stopping until had had completed scanning the entire perimeter outside.

It was still completely dark when he opened the back door of the cabin this morning. But before he led William and the others out and down into the corral where the horses were, he had shouldered his long rifle for a few seconds, holding it in firing position from the doorway, taking nothing for granted. Apparently, he felt it was safe for he gradually moved out into the open. As he turned his torso, still holding his rifle at the ready he could see from the corner of his eye that William was doing the same to his right just a few feet away and James and Samuel had taken his other flank. He had already instructed all three that for no reason were they to speak, not to their mounts or each other for that matter. But as he watched their movements, he realized he had wasted his wind for these men knew what they were doing.

He led the way off his property walking in front of his horse, leading it by the reins, taking one of the four paths that he used just to keep from being predictable. When the sun finally rose, he mounted up without a word and picked up the pace. Twice, he had dismounted to look at the ground. He would point out some partially concealed moccasin track, only to turn back and take another little traveled deer path through the woods a few miles until it came back out on the buffalo trace further down, away from what could be the ambush site of a cunning Shawnee or Cherokee. Now they were approaching the Lower Blue Licks and he had once again slowed the pace at which he guided them along. He had dismounted and handed the reins of his horse to James and whispered to the others. "Look at this," as he pointed to a nearby patch of dead foxtail grass that still stood with its stems high in the air a few feet off the ground, a part of last year's growth. He carefully walked over to the dead, tan colored grass and ran his hand over the tops, indicating that the wind had pushed the grass in an easterly direction, but in the center, the blades were pushed over in the opposite direction, giving away to the trained eye that a small party had recently passed that way. He told William and the others to stay where they were, off the trace and out of sight. "If I'm not back in twenty minutes," he said, "you all head back to my cabin." He then quickly turned and silently disappeared into the forest as William and the others checked the pans of their rifles and took to a tree.

Almost Fifteen minutes later, Kenton emerged from the trees, walking backwards, ever so slowly, watching the very woods he had just walked out of. He then quickly faced William's tree and crossed the trace and gathered them all around him.

"By God, there are eight Indians at the lick," Kenton explained. "And they've got Joseph Jackson with them. He's one of the Boonesborough salt boilers that Blackfish caught back in '79 with Daniel. I know you fellows came out here to tend to your claims, but I would consider it a great personal favor if you would help me get Joseph back. I know firsthand what it's like to be held prisoner by those savages. Two years is a long time to be in their clutches. It's not good by any means."

William looked to his friends and from their expressions, could tell they were just as eager to save the man as he was. He nodded his head, yes and asked. "What do you want us to do?"

"They're on foot," Kenton explained. "Looks to me like their waiting for someone to come along to start making salt. They're definitely setting up an ambush and we'll use that against them. If we back track a little and come up on their hind side, they will never know what hit them. Now, Joseph is wearing a blue ruffled shirt and leggings, but they have made him shave his head, so don't fire on him by mistake. He looks the part of an Indian, so remember who he is. He'll most likely fire on them after he realizes what's happening."

"Is he armed then?" James asked.

Kenton nodded his head and said, "It has taken two years for him to gain their trust. They've let him have a rifle, but he probably only has one shot. They know he can't kill them all with a single shot and they could kill him very easily if he tried to escape alone. I appreciate your help fellows, and I know Joseph will too." Kenton smiled then and said, "Damn they're going to be in one hell of a predicament pretty soon, let's go get our boy back."

One hour later William squatted behind a fallen ash tree, less than a hundred feet from his prey. He propped his rifle's barrel on top of the log and set his sights between the shoulders of another unsuspecting Indian. The Shawnee were indeed trying to take advantage of this spring. They were all hiding behind whatever cover they could find. Most were in among the trees like the one William had picked out as his target, but some were concealed in the bushes. And far to the right, hiding in a cane break was the blue shirted white man that William had come here to help save. William saw the head of one of the warriors explode to his left, splattering blood and brains all over the tree trunk that he had been hiding behind just a split second before Kenton had pulled his trigger, killing the Shawnee instantly. As William looked through the smoke of his own rifle, he saw his Indian tumble to the ground, having wasting the black war paint he had smeared on his face this morning. Two more well aimed shots rang out in the air as James and Samuel discharged their weapons, leaving two more red bodies on the ground.

As Kenton was reloading, holding his back against his tree, he yelled out, "Run to us Joseph. We will keep them off your back until you reach us."

The remaining warriors took to their heels, knowing they were at a great disadvantage having been taken by surprise from the rear. Seeing them flee, Samuel stepped out from behind his tree and raised his pistol to take one last shot at the retreating Indians as Joseph Jackson fired off a shot at his young would be rescuer, cutting Samuel's powder strap that hung around his neck and shoulder. The ball missed his chest by only a fraction of an inch, slamming into the tree trunk he had just stepped from behind. Giving out a war hoop, Jackson disappeared into the canebrake following his retreating comrades. Stunned by what had just happened, Samuel fell to the ground and fired his pistol into the cane break hoping his ball might find Jackson's blue ruffled shirt.

"Hellfire!" he cried out. "I thought you said that bastard was a prisoner, held against his will!"

"I did," Kenton answered as he pulled Samuel to his feet with one outstretched hand. "I'm sorry. I had no idea that son of a bitch had turned injen on us. The next time I see Joe Jackson, I'll put a hole through his damn traitorous head."

Chapter 133
Tories for the Night

As William rode along the North bank of Elkhorn Creek just behind Samuel, his eyes fell on the freshly taken scalps hanging off the side of Samuel's saddle. He wondered how much longer he could keep living this way and not have his own scalp or that of one of his friends' making a last ride into an Indian village across the Ohio. God's providence always seemed to be watching over them and William prayed that it would stay that way until this war ended. Simon Kenton had been up front still leading the way this afternoon, being as observant as ever, but now he pulled his mount to a stop and waved William and the others up beside him.

"Well, this is as far as I go, boys." the big frontiersman said, leaning back in his saddle. "Bryan's Station is just up ahead. You'll be there within a half hour or so. This is the best crossing spot. The creek gets a little deeper further on down."
"You're not going in with us?" James asked.

"Naw," Kenton answered. "Never did feel really comfortable there. Too many Tories inside for my taste. I'm going on down to Boonesborough instead. If you all come with me, it would take you out of your way some. If you're going to your claims that is."

"If those folks are Tories, then maybe we should stay out in the woods somewhere tonight," Samuel suggested.

"No," Kenton replied, "They're not like that. Maybe Tories is too strong a word to use. They're nothing like those fellows that were killed at King's Mountain. Let's just say they lean more to the King's way of thinking than say, Patrick Henry or Governor Jefferson. They moved out here to get away from politics altogether. No, you'll be a lot safer inside there tonight than out here. You don't want to be caught out here in the woods at night. Just don't talk the Whig cause up too much while you're inside. They're safe enough; the Bryants are even some sort of kin to Daniel Boone's wife Rebecca."

"All right then," William said as he extended a grateful hand to Kenton. "You have never steered us wrong yet. Maybe we'll see you tomorrow night at Boonesborough."

"If you don't count Joe Jackson that is." Kenton chuckled and shook his head as he withdrew his hand from William's. "Could be we'll meet up again tomorrow night, until then I bid you all adieu"

William turned Sampson around and stepped into the shallow water of the creek, bringing up the rear since James and Samuel were already midstream. He glanced back across his shoulder and saw that Kenton had dismounted his horse and was looking in his nap sack. He once again turned around and rode back up onto Kenton's side of the creek and said, "Is everything in order over here?"

"Oh, Yeah," Kenton replied. "Just getting a bite to eat, got some jerk down in here somewhere." he said as he was digging around inside the sack.

"I didn't say anything about it last night," William said as he looked across the water to James and Samuel who had already climbed out onto the bank. "I ran into Simon Girty up the Allegheny River and I had the drop on him."

"And you let him go off in that canoe, didn't you?" Kenton said still looking down inside the sack.

"How did you know that?" William asked.

"He told me all about it." Kenton answered. "He didn't say who you were, but he told me how it happened. It's not easy to catch Simon with his guard down. Here it is, I got it now." Kenton replied as he finally pulled out his jerked meat. "What happened to Captain Rogers is eating at you isn't it?"

"Yes, it is," William whispered.

Kenton's keen eyes looked directly into William's and the big frontiersmen said, "Don't let it. We can't tell what the future will bring. I can see why it's pressing on your mind. Rogers was a good man, but Simon will do some good in this war too. He saved me and he'll probably save some more before it's all over. You're in Kentucky now, he may save you someday. Hell, he may have already done it and we might not even know that he did in this wild country. It's not a bad thing to have a friend on the other side. Like I said, Simon's a hard friend to have at times, but he's still a friend, even if he is on the other side. One thing I have come to realize is that if Simon wasn't leading the Indians, the British would have someone else doing his job. Rogers would still be dead and all those settlers at Martin and Randell Stations would still be up North someplace. It would just be someone else doing it. The war is going to go on, no matter who is in charge."

Kenton pulled himself up in his saddle and looked up to the sky and said, "We better go. The sun is getting low." Then he rode off without another word leaving William alone on the bank. He let out a long breath and crossed over to the other side where his two friends were waiting.

"Everything all right" James asked?

"Yeah," William answered. "All is well, right as rain."

The rest of the trip to Bryant Station was uneventful. It passed quickly and when the three-man party arrived at the gates of the fort, they found its doors swung open with no guard outside, which seemed a little odd at the time. As William rode into the fort, he could tell it was different here from Boonesborough or Harrodsburg. No Ann Poague or Jemima Boone had come out to greet them. No James Harrod or John Holder had come over to chew the fat as they unsaddled their horses. Almost everyone inside just stared at them, wearing expressionless looks at best and the ones that did show any emotion was in the form of hard looks. The only smile William saw had come from a small boy that was shooting his toy rifle at the riders when they had dismounted their horses.

"Damn fellows," William said as he walked around Sampson. "We just got the coldest shoulder ever offered by a white man in Kentucky."

"Cold as a witch's tit" James replied.

"Well maybe it's on account of they don't know us too well," Samuel offered as he looked around the long rectangular fort. "Do you see anyone you know? Surely someone here knows one of us?"

"I don't see anyone." James answered, "Not a single soul."

"Well in that case, let's give them what they want," Samuel suggested as he began to walk to the nearest cabin door. He looked back over his shoulder and said, "Just follow my lead," to William and James. "I'll get us some good cooking tonight." James turned his back to the cabin and bit his lower lip, looking over at William with wide eyes as he heard Samuel rap on the closed door.

"Hello Ma'am," Samuel said as he took off his tri cornered hat with one hand. "We just came in from the Carolinas and we were told this is the best place for folks like us to stay here in Kentucky."

"What do you mean by folks like you?" the woman of the house asked.

"Let's just say someone who's not so dead set against the King," Samuel answered. "We don't want any trouble," he continued, "just some food for the night. We can pay."

"Oh, that won't be necessary," she said as she dried her hands on her apron. "We thought it would get fairly rough back home for folks who have leanings like we do after Ferguson was defeated. We may not have fancy fixings, but we don't mind to share with others who feel the same as us. You boys sit out there next to the block house and I'll have some supper sent out to you all after a while." She stepped back inside her doorway and disappeared as Samuel turned to his friends with a smug grin on his face and said, "Well boys, us Tories eat at six o'clock tonight."

Chapter 134
Lost

William was happy now that he was back on his Kentucky land. It was even better than he had remembered. And best of all, there was no squatters or a cross claimer on his land. The grass was just as green and high as it was that day he watched the Indian father and son wading the creek that ran in front of his future home site. The make shift lean-to that he had made on his first trip here had fallen in during his absence but that was to be expected and was of no great loss. James and Samuel's lands were also in good order. They had already been checked out earlier in the day. All they had to do now was to ride over to Joshua's claim and give the land a quick looking over before heading on to Boonesborough for the night. The visions of future homes and the thoughts of better crops had raised everyone's spirits. Seeing believed in this case and it gave the three men a renewed desire to settle out here in a few years or possibly sooner if all went well.

The three were on horseback as they rode down the hill on William's land, and like on their first trip here, the countryside was still filled with game. But this time no bears had been seen wondering around the many canebrakes that stood next to the creek.

"Is Joshua still talking about Tennessee?" James asked William as they rode off William's land and onto Joshua's.

"I think so," William answered as he pulled his horse to a stop at the bottom of the hill. "I don't see how it could be any better than this. I hope he still remembers how good this land is out here." William swept his arm wide as he gestured over the countryside. His eyes fell upon some white smoke rising up in the distance.

"Look, that's smoke coming up over there behind those trees. It looks like someone has lit a cooking fire."

"Well, let's hope it's a white someone," James said as he checked his rifle. "I had about enough Indian fighting on this trip for my taste yesterday."

"Me too," William agreed, "but we've got to see who's over there, that's why we're here in the first place. We've got to protect what's ours."

As they rode across the clearing toward the tree line that was between them and the fire, William could hear muffled voices coming through the trees. He could not tell what was being said, or even what language they were speaking, but one sounded like the voice of a woman.

"That's not an Indian," James said as he cocked his head to one side trying to make out what was being said. He dismounted from his horse, and joining the other two on the ground, pulled his tomahawk from his belt.

William like his two companions tied his horse to a tree trunk and began to work his way on foot toward the voices. With every step he took he was more and more convinced that it was a family of settlers camped on the other side. As he stopped under a huge oak tree his suspicions were confirmed. There, with their backs turned, sitting around a big campfire, and oblivious to their surroundings was a young couple, neither one more than seventeen or eighteen years of age, eating a freshly cooked rabbit. They had two poor looking horses with them, one loaded down with a small amount of household goods and it appeared to William that they had been riding double on the other. The young man had made the mistake of not keeping his weapon by his side. He had cleaned the rabbit the two of them were now enjoying and had left his shot gun sitting next to the very same oak tree that William was now under. William reached down and picked up the old blunderbuss and walked into their camp followed by James and Samuel, giving the young couple a fright, since all three were heavily armed. The young husband stood to his feet realizing the gravity of his mistake, but bravely put himself between the group of intruders and his terrified wife.

"No cause to be alarmed," William said as he handed over the gun to the anxious young man. "But always have your gun within arm's reach my friend. You were lucky this time. We could have just as easily been Indians and you would be dead now and your wife here captured and headed north into an uncertain future at best."

"What are you two doing out here all alone anyway?" James asked.

"Looking for Boonesborough," the husband answered nervously. "I have some kin there. We came up the Wilderness Road and stopped over at Logan Station a few days back. Captain Logan let us stay with him for a while. He had said there was too many Indian sightings for us to continue on alone. But when nothing more came of it, I got itchy feet and we took off again against his advice. I felt like I could handle anything that might present itself. But three days ago, I saw one of those savages on the road and we took to the trees to make our escape. Which we did, but in doing so I got turned around somehow and we have been lost ever since."

"Well you're close to the fort now," Samuel said as he stomped out the fire. "Get your things together and we'll be there before nightfall if nothing else happens to stop us."

"What's your name young man?" William asked as he presented his hand to the obviously relieved young man.

"Charles Shirley and let me present my newly wedded wife, Katie."

"Lord, have mercy, I sure am glad that you all came along," Katie Shirley said, still shaken up from their appearance.

"Pleased to meet you ma'am," William answered, "but let me give you some free advice if I may. I learned this the hard way. Don't always trust everyone you meet and see out here just because they're not Indian. There is little law out here, and although there are only a few redcoats on this side of the mountains doesn't mean the war's not being fought on the frontier.

"Anything you say mister." Shirley replied, "Just get us inside the fort safely and I'll be your man for life."

"That won't be necessary." William answered. "We're going that way anyhow, we'll be glad to show you the way."

Within twenty minutes or so William and his companions was leading the young couple out of the wilderness and safely on to Boonesborough. James and William were riding out in front while Samuel had fallen in at the rear, putting the Shirley's in between the three. As William rode along, he would glance over his shoulder every now and then to see how they were doing. And with every look he could see the anxiety disappear from their faces, replaced with relief and joy. Now he knew why Simon Kenton took so many chances helping others in this country. Not all of this world's rewards came in the form of personal gain and money.

Chapter 135
Tales of a Siege

As the party of travelers was riding along the side of the Kentucky River, William saw something moving a little further up ahead on the bank. There, to his left in what little light there was remaining of the day, he could see a recently awakened raccoon climbing out of a two-hundred-year-old dying oak tree. The fat little animal was halfway down the trunk when a second one stuck its masked face out of the hollow tree top and joined its mate for a nightly excursion. But on seeing the approaching horses the two quickly ran behind their tree and disappeared into the forest.

"We have to be close now, don't you think?" James asked as he watched the retreating raccoons scamper away.

"I would say so," William answered looking back over his shoulder at the Shirley's. "You know it's not going to be easy to get her across the river. Hell, we had a rough time of it ourselves when we did it two years ago and we don't have much time to do it in either." he said as he looked up at the setting sun.

"Less than an hour if we have that," James replied. "Maybe one of us can cross over first and bring her back a canoe if they have one over at the fort," James suggested. "I was hoping we would be there before now. We're prime targets out here now. If there are any Indians around, this would be the perfect time to fire on us. They could easily get away by just slipping into the night after ambushing us. At least that's how I would do it if I was them. We're sitting ducks right now."

"Well great day," William proclaimed as he looked up the river bank. "That's a ferryboat sitting on the far bank. No wet river crossing tonight my friends looks as though the people of Boonesborough have been making some progress in our absence. If the Indians are going to get us tonight, they're about out of time. I just hope someone's on the ferry to bring us over. I wonder how we can hail them if no one's watching."

A smile spread over William's face as he watched some men walk up out of the trees and onto the ferry. They each picked up a shoulder pole and started to push the boat out into the water, coming over to William's side of the river. As the boat crossed over William saw the now familiar face of Simon Kenton standing out in front of the ferry holding his rifle in the folds of his arm. As the ferry ran aground Kenton said, "I was beginning to wonder about you boys, but I see that you've picked up someone on the way. I suppose that slowed you all down some."

"Not too much," Samuel said as he walked his horse up onto the ferry. "Have you been waiting for us long?"

"Nah," Kenton answered as he watched the tree line along the shore.

"We didn't know about the ferry." William said as he shook Kenton's hand. "But it sure was a pleasant surprise. These are the Shirley's," William said as he nodded his head at Charles and Katie. "They've got some kin around here someplace."

"There's a Michael Shirley up at the fort." Kenton said, still watching the tree covered bank even though the ferry was already a hundred feet back out in the river, returning to the safety of the other side.

"That's him," Charles answered.

"Well in that case," Kenton remarked, "You'll be eating at his table a little later on tonight. The fort's just a mile up river from here."

"This sure does beat swimming our horses over," William said as he stomped his foot on the ferry's floor.

"Yes, it does," Kenton answered, "but it came at a high price. Richard

Callaway and Pemberton Rawlings were killed here last spring while they were building this raft. Callaway had been scalped and most of his clothing was stripped off when they were found. Rawlings lost his hair too, but he was still alive when John Holder's rescue party got here. But the poor fellow died the next day. Callaway had a few slaves with him and only one of them got away, the others having been taken prisoners. Yeah, old Callaway was planning on getting rich with this ferry. He was going to charge three shillings for every man and horse that crossed over, but he never saw any of that money. I never did care that much for him, but that was no way for a brave man to die, and he was brave. He was hard on Daniel after the siege and was always stirring something up but he fought hard here at the fort and his presence will be missed."

"Is Boone back at the fort?" William asked. "I would like to meet the man. I have heard a lot about him."

"No," Kenton answered. "After the siege was over, and that stupid court-marshal, Daniel moved out and is settling another station of his own a little to the south. But you never know when he'll show up. You may run into him somewhere while you're out here."

"Were you at the siege?" James asked as the boat bumped into the bank.

"No," Kenton answered, "but I can tell you what I've been told about it while we're riding up to the fort. Daniel got wind of the Shawnee's plans somehow and made his escape. He got back here a few days before Blackfish's war party arrived and gave the warning of the impending attack. Blackfish led a few night attacks after his arrival, but they were all beaten back. They even tried to dig an underground tunnel from the river bank under the fort's walls. So, the boys inside dug a counter tunnel out from under our walls to cut them off. They got so close to each other they could hear the other side digging. I believe even a few choice cuss words were passed back and forth. But then it began to rain and that damn tunnel collapsed in on them. Hell, they may even have a few buried out under the fort's yard for all we know." Kenton laughed. "That was the last straw. They simply drifted away after that. Squire Boone was shot in the shoulder and a German fellow was hit in the forehead and died soon after. London, Richard Henderson's slave was killed outside the fort's wall one night when his pan flashed. But other than that, everyone made out fairly well, but only God knows what this year will bring. All of the settlements were attacked at some point last year. I don't see why this year will be any different." Kenton concluded as the sun set behind the trees lining the river.

William could hear a late working blacksmith's hammer ringing through the night air as they rode out into the clearing where the fort was built. He could smell the smoke of several fires burning inside and he could even see their flickering glow through the cracks of the newly completed walls. Another day had come to an end here on the Kentucky frontier and William was grateful that he had made it through to the fort with no incident and was still alive to tell the tale. It had been a good day.

Chapter 136
The Old Warrior's Path

William, James, and Samuel stayed at Boonesborough for two nights and had gone out hunting during the day to stock up on enough meat to get back home. They decided to return as planned by way of the Wilderness Road. Simon Kenton had gone off into the woods the day after they reached the fort on one of his long hunts. After his departure they stayed in the home of John Holder. Holder had been very hospitable to them and his jovial personality, along with his colorful language had been very entertaining, particularly to Samuel. He was happy to have someone new to tell his stories to and urged them to stay a little longer, but the lure of seeing the southern parts of Kentucky was too great and the three men developed "itchy feet" as young Charles Shirley put it. So early yesterday morning, the three had struck out for the Cumberland Gap, knowing it would take a good three day's hard ride to reach the mountain pass and at least a fortnight more to reach their Frederick County homes up the Blue Ridge.

Last night they had taken a page out of their old river boat captain, David Rogers' book. They spent the night a little past the junction where Boone's Trace ran into the Wilderness Road at Hazel Patch. Their strategy was the same as the captain's. He had always advocated that a junction would be the normal stopping place for travelers, and by going on a few miles to the south they would likely be a little safer. As an extra measure, they had struck off the road, putting it completely out of view before making a campsite. This area was originally known as the Indian's old Warrior's Path.

The Shawnee and Cherokee had been using this path for many years to fight one another long before any white men had discovered its existence. The Indians knew every inch of it like the back of their hands and all three men felt it was a necessary precaution to stay as much out of sight as they could. Once off the path they had chosen to sleep under the branches of a hackberry tree that had fallen to the ground during a storm earlier in the spring. Although the tree had been uprooted, it was still fully leaved out tree, giving them a good amount of cover to hide in, but being fairly well concealed had not made them feel secure enough not to post a watch. They had taken turns during the night but none of them slept well; remembering how the horses of the Indian party on the Salt River had given away the location of that camp to William two years ago. William and his party, having learned a valuable lesson from those Indians who had thought they were being just as careful he was tonight, did not fire their weapons or burn any fires after dark. The horses had stayed quiet for the most part, only once had they nickered during the night and that was Sampson. After midnight a pack of far off wolves had howled giving the horse a fright. William had quickly calmed the big black horse and quieted him down.

When the dawn's first rays of sunlight rose this morning, they quickly broke camp. The horses were well rested as they made their way back to the path and turned south toward the gap. It was now around midday and the landscape was becoming more mountainous and their pace was beginning to slow considerably. James was riding alongside William as he reached into his shirt pocket and pulled out the sweet-smelling cake of tobacco that he loved to chew. Dropping his reins into his lap as his horse continued waking; he proceeded to cut off a morsel of the tobacco with his knife. Looking over to William, knowing full well what the answer would be, he asked William only with his eyes if he was willing to finally give it a try. William answered just as silently as James had asked by simply shaking his head, no with a crooked smile and wearing a look that plainly ask if James had lost his mind. James just shook his head and shrugged his shoulders and put his tobacco away, acting as if William was missing one of life's greatest pleasures. At that moment the silence of the day was broken as gun shots rang out a good distance to the South.

Samuel pulled his horse to the side of the road and dismounted. He flipped the reins over his horse's head and led the animal off the path and into the forest. William and James quickly followed suit, falling in behind their young companion who by now was thinking and acting as sharply as his teachers. After tying the horses, the three took to the nearest trees and waited and listened for someone to come up the path.

"I heard at least nine shots," William whispered as his eyes focused on the bend in the path four hundred feet down the road.

"How long do we wait?" Samuel asked as he pulled out his pistol and primed its pan.

"Depends on what and who comes up that road," James answered. "It had the sound of an ambush to me. Too many shots for a lone hunter or even a hunting party for that matter. Let's just hope that it was some of our people doing the ambushing and not the Indians."

William nodded his head in agreement and settled in for however long a wait it would take to find out what had happened. The wait was short. Within ten minutes a rider less horse emerged around the bend followed by four fast riding men. One was slumping over his horse's neck. As they approached, William stepped out into the open and waved them down. Three of them never stopped, just rode on by, but the last one slowed down after seeing that William was not a threat.
"How many would you say?" William asked.

"Don't know for sure," the rider answered, "but enough to shoot us up something awful. We had to leave three men behind. They're dead for sure. God rest their souls. You all better ride along with us on to Logan's Station."

"Which way were you heading?" James asked, still behind his tree.

"We're out of the Holston settlements, heading north into Kentucky," the man replied as he rode off.

William hurried back to the safety of the woods and as he stepped behind his tree he said, "I for one, don't want to go back to the Kentucky settlements. What about you boys?"

"Me neither," James answered. "Home is that away." He pointed the barrel of his rifle in the direction the men had just ridden from "Besides there could just as easily be Indians behind us as in front. What about you Samuel you have a dog in this fight just as much as we do. What do you say?"

"Home is fine with me," Samuel answered. "I don't see any reason to travel the same ground twice. If we head back to the forts, we'll have to turn around and come back this way sometime. But I do think we should stay off the path for a while. That's what Kenton would do, don't you think? Let's keep to the trees."

After waiting another twenty minutes without incident, the three of them began to make their way toward the gap, walking in front of their mount as quietly as they could, while still in the cover of the tree line that followed the Wilderness Road. No war whoops had been heard since the shots had rung out, and none of the three knew if that was a good thing or not, but still they continued on. When they reached the ambush site, there in the center of the road laid the remains of several mutilated bodies. Not wanting to fall into the same trap, the three moved on without stopping to tend to the dead. If they were lucky, the Indians had taken to the trees on the far side of the road which would allow William and his two friends the opportunity to slip by them undetected. And if they were really lucky the Indians may have already started the return trip to their homes in Tennessee, loaded down with enough loot to keep them happy and not too concerned with whoever was still on the road. Either way, it was going to be a long and worrisome afternoon.

Chapter 137
The Cave

William stopped next to a huge boulder that had rolled down from the top of the mountain overhead no telling how many centuries ago. He leaned his shoulder against the moss-covered blue stone as he peered out into the rain-soaked meadow that lay before him. It had been raining all afternoon, ever since they had passed the ambush site earlier in the day. Now, as he ran his eyes along the base of this rock cliff looking for any opening that could get them out of this downpour, he saw the pyramid shaped opening to a cave. The opening was about fifteen feet high at its peak, plenty high enough to lead the horses into. Trying to see if anyone was inside the cave, he turned and looked back toward the direction he had just come, noticing the path that he had just made through the wet, green, fern covered landscape. No matter how carefully the three had tried to be, they had still pushed the vegetation to one side while moving thru the valley. He looked back to the cave and saw that the green carpet before the opening was undisturbed. No stomped down, mud covered ferns lay between him and the cave convincing him that the cave was free of Indians, at least for now.

"There's no one in there," James said looking over William's shoulder. "I say we go on inside for the night. We can dry off our rifles and just maybe we can continue on in the morning if this weather breaks. The only drawback I see is getting trapped inside by a war party from out here. But with this rain, they will be the ones with wet powder, not us. We could hold them off for some time inside there. Hell, they couldn't even burn us out of there if they tried."

"Plus, we have an abundance of food," Samuel added. "We could withstand a fairly long siege from in there."

"I agree," William said as the rainwater dripped off the brim of his felt hat that was now nearly worn out. "I truly believe this is a Godsend for us. James, let's go inside. Samuel, you stay here with the horses while we take a closer look. No need in all of us getting killed if there are any Indian's lurking inside."

As William and James sprinted across the span of ground to the cave's mouth, Samuel squatted down to one knee, hoping that if his two companions were to have the misfortune of being fired upon; his powder would be dry enough to give them some covering fire. But he knew that one lone shot would do little damage to anyone who might be inside that dark opening that his friends were running for. A sigh of relief came from deep down inside his chest as he saw William and James split apart as they reached the cave's opening, each placing their back up against the rock wall of the cliff on opposite sides of the entrance.

William took one quick glance inside, sticking his head around the stone corner. He could see there was nothing on James' side of the cave before pulling his head back out of the breach but couldn't see what was on his own side. He glanced over at James and saw that he had seen nothing on William's side either, giving the all clear sign. Both men stepped inside the cave at the same time, pointing the barrels of their rifles at nothing but the dark walls of the empty shallow cave.

"I've been in worse taverns," James proclaimed, as he looked around inside the cave. "This will serve well for tonight," he laughed.

"It will do," William agreed as he stepped back outside into the gray light and waved Samuel in with the horses as a gust of strong wind blew his hat off his head, onto the cave's dirt floor. He stepped inside and walked to the back of the blackened cave and picked up his hat with one hand and smacked it against his leg in an effort to dust off the dirt that had stuck to the wet felt as it rolled across the floor.

James took the reins of his horse from Samuel's hand and the two of them led the horses to the back of the cave and began the task of unsaddling them. William stepped over to the opening and looked out into the storm which had grown in its fury. "We got here just in time," he said as he watched the treetops sway back in forth, bending low in the high winds. "I sure do hope this thing blows over soon," he said as he sat down to take the first watch on what would be another long night.

"A fire would be nice," Samuel said as he dropped a saddle to the ground. "It sure would help dry these damp clothes off. But as hard as that rain is coming down, we couldn't get anything to burn in here anyway."

"You're not the first to think that," James told him as he looked down at the remains of an old burned out fire. "We're definitely not the first to stay in here," he said looking up at the blackened ceiling of the cave. "It took more than one fire to do that." He walked over to his saddlebag and pulled out an old dirty rag and began to clean   the pan of his rifle, wiping away damp powder and making sure the touch hole was clear. "Let's just hope no one comes along tonight to start another fire while we're still in here," he continued as he wiped the rag down the length of his barrel. Pitching the rag to Samuel, he walked over to the opening and sat down across from William on the dirt floor, crossing his legs Indian style. He laid his dry rifle across his lap and looked outside, watching the storm blow by. He crossed his arms, grasping each shoulder with one hand in a futile attempt to keep the cold from seeping into his tired bones.

Chapter 138
Cumberland Gap

"Well, the gap is not real hard to find now is it?" William asked as he stared down the Wilderness Road. "All one has to do is look up to the mountain tops to see the great break within the range, looks as if God himself took the bottom of his mighty hand and just pushed the stone and rock aside for us."

"Well I guess in a way he did." James said as he pulled himself up into his saddle "Looks as though our approach is going to get a lot steeper today. Wonder what the other side's going to look like?"

William looked back to the cave before answering James question and seeing that Samuel had finally strolled out into the morning sunlight and was within ear shot he said, "I don't know for sure, but we may never find out if we keep waiting for Samuel to drag his sorry hide out here this morning."

"I'm coming," Samuel replied, "besides you two haven't been out here too long yourselves you know. Let's make some tracks. Daylight's burning."

At that, Samuel mounted his horse and stepped out in front of the other two and began the uphill ride. Following behind his young friend, William began to take in the beauty of this cloud filled mountain pass. It was much wider than what he had envisioned before seeing it. He had not expected the wide valley he was now riding into. The mountainside on each side of the gap was tree covered for the most part, with a few late blooming dark pink azaleas scattered here and there, spreading spots of color throughout the hillsides, with a few exceptions where the topsoil had eroded away on the steeper areas leaving only a rock face behind and no soil for them to take root. The woods contained the same familiar trees that he had come to know while in Kentucky. He now fully understood why no wagons could be driven through this pass. Knowing the river route as well as he did, he knew that he would never put such difficulties as this mountainous crossing would be on his own family. Besides they could bring almost all of their possessions with them by river. They would have to leave most of it at home in Virginia if they came this way as there was no way to lug large pieces of furniture over these mountaintops. It was true that Indian attacks on the river were a strong possibility, but as the ambush they had come upon proved, it was no safer along this route. At least you could see them on the water in their dugout canoes, not like here on this isolated road where they could be lurking behind any tree or bush.

As they were making their way up the trail with only the sound of the rolling rock under their horse's hooves, Samuel pulled his horse to a stop. He quickly dismounted and signaled William and James to do the same. With little choice, all three stepped behind a rock ledge leaving the horses out on the path exposed, having no place to hide them.

"What's up there?" William asked in a low voice, pulling the hammer back on his rifle.

"More voices." Samuel whispered. "Damn I hope we don't lose the horses."

"We won't." William said as he cocked his head to one side in an effort to hear what was being said by the party up above. Then, he too could hear in the distance the distinct sound of men speaking to each other in English, on the higher ground just up ahead. A red hound walked past the three of them and began to growl at the unattended horses. William shooed the barking dog away as he reached for Sampson's reins, putting the horse between himself and whoever was coming in from the other side of the gap. He called out in a voice loud enough to reach up the mountain trail, "Who goes there?"

"Virginians," a voice replied.

"Then all is well, for we are too," William answered. But he still wasn't letting his guard down; knowing all too well that whoever was up there could just as easily be lying through their teeth with their faces all covered in war paint. He waited to see what the approaching men looked like before exposing himself in the open. However, it didn't take long to see that they were telling the truth, for four men came walking down the trail far more trusting than William was, holding their weapons in a non-threatening manner, being followed by some dirty faced women and children.

"I'm John Cobourn, out of Hampshire County." the leader of the party announced as he looked William and the others over with his gray eyes. "Say you all are from Virginia as well?"

"Yes, we are," James answered. "We're heading back home to Frederick County ourselves. Had any trouble on the way?"

"No." Cobourn answered, "At least not of the Indian variety. We stopped at Anderson's blockhouse for a few days and while we were there, the fort's spies were saying that there was very little Indian sign in the area. So we thought it best to head on while the coast was clear so to speak. But we did lose a horse two days ago in a fall. What about you all?"

"No trouble ourselves, but we came upon an ambushed party yesterday," William replied. "So, the Indians are definitely out and about on this side of the gap. We were just lucky enough to learn of it at someone else's expense."

"You need to be prepared for what you'll see when you get there. It's something little eyes should never see my friend, if you get my meaning." James said nodding his head at the children.

"That bad" Cobourn asked while squinting his eyes. James' only answer was a nod of his head.

"Very well then," Cobourn answered as he placed a hand atop a small boy's head. "I'll attend to it. I'll have the little ones placed near the rear so we can clear the way. As for what lays behind us, I would say that you all will be fairly safe while going through Powell Valley. At least as safe as one can be out here in the wilds. Once you get on the back side of Big Moccasin Gap, most of the danger will be behind you," Cobourn predicted. Then taking William's hand in his own, he said, "Thanks for the information and God's speed to you good sirs."

William stepped aside and watched as the small group of settlers walked by. They were fourteen in number counting the two slaves that were leading a couple of loaded pack horses and a lone cow. Bringing up the rear was a young boy no older than Samuel had been when William first met him back at Ft. Pitt.

As the two parties separated and they walked out of sight, James asked William, "Do you see them making it through?"

"I don't know," William answered, "but I said a little prayer for them as they passed us by.

"I did as well," James said as he remounted his horse.

"Did either one of you two put in a good word for us?" Samuel asked as he rode up beside his two companions.

"No, I didn't." William replied, "Maybe you can do that for us while we're riding along today. I do hope that Cobourn fellow knows what he's talking about when he said there was little Indian sign in Powell Valley. But then, we all know how fast that can change."

"Too well," James replied, "all too well."

Chapter 139
An Unexpected Reunion

William dipped the point of his knife into the wooden bowl of water that was sitting between his legs. The water inside had washed away the soap and whiskers that were clinging to the end of his blade. He turned his head to one side and ran the blade once more down his jaw line in an effort to remove the last of his remaining stubble from his newly smooth face. Satisfied that was the best he could do without the benefit of his looking glass back home, he gave up on his task. He stood up off the ground under the overhang of Andersen's blockhouse and wiped the remaining soap and water from his face with a towel and tossed out the dirty water from inside the bowl. The mountain wind cutting under the overhang felt cool to his damp skin as he rubbed his fingertips around his lower jaw. Now that he, along with his two friends, had made it back to civilization, he wanted to clean himself up some. Even if this was just the very edge of the settlements, there was no reason to keep looking like a barbarian he thought. Two nights ago, he had sat inside the abandoned walls of Martin Station where he noticed how bad the appearances of James and Samuel had become on this return trip home. The three of them had even gone so far as to enter into a good-hearted conversation about how ruthless they all looked. Just maybe that was why the Indians had let them pass by unmolested on the eastern side of the Cumberland Gap they had all laughed.

He walked out into the sunlight and cast his eyes on the surrounding mountain tops in the distance as he stretched his back muscles and wondered how James and Samuel were doing. He looked back at the two-story blockhouse that John Anderson had built back in '77. It was well constructed and although it had no outer wall around its perimeter, it could withstand almost any size attack the Indians could muster against it, barring any artillery the British might supply them with. But that was an unlikely possibility. It would be quite a task to drag those heavy guns through these mountains, even if they could be spared from the war. The blockhouse was well built, even its chimney had been built in the center of the building if in the event of an attack, the enemy could not use it as a ladder to climb onto the roof. The only weakness was its outer door, but it had some well-placed portholes around it to keep away any attackers. The only real cause of concern that he could see was the fact that the corral gave the horses little protection, on account of its being so far away from the blockhouse. But William knew he would not be here long, so he felt Sampson and the other horses would be safe enough tonight, for tomorrow they would start the last leg of the journey home up the Blue Ridge.

Samuel and James had taken to the woods earlier in the day to bring down a deer or perhaps an elk. The three planned to jerk the meat tonight and hopefully, it would hold out until they reached home, so now that he had done away with his beard, William once more picked up his ever-present rifle and began to watch for their return. As he was standing there, a small gray squirrel came running across the round hilltop on the eastern side of the blockhouse. Seeing William standing there holding his rifle, the little gray turned sharply and leaped on the trunk of a walnut tree and scampered up to the safety of its top branches. Feeling that this may be a telling sign that Samuel and James had bagged a deer and were returning, he began to walk forward to see who was starting up the incline below. At first all he saw was the tops of the felt hats the approaching men had on their heads. But with a few more steps of their horses, William could see the dirty faces of the riders. One in particular had a familiar way of leaning forward on his mount with his head down as though he was asleep. Just behind that rider were Robert Shields and his two sons, John and Thomas, Joshua's newly acquired in-laws along with another man that William did not know.

"Wake up there, brother!" William said as he smacked Joshua's boot dangling off the side of his horse. All that he could see was the smile that came across Joshua's lips, since his hat was pulled down low, over his eyes. But then pushing back the brim of his hat to give his brother a better look at his face he raised his leg over his horse, slipped to the ground and gave William a fierce hug.

"William," Joshua said, still holding onto his brother's shoulders, "I'm going to be a father in a few weeks, how about them apples?"

"You don't say," William laughed, "well congratulations. You'll be a great father. It's going to give you a whole new outlook on life, I can tell you that much."

"That's what they keep telling me," Joshua said, "and I must confess that I'm looking forward to it. I was hoping I would run across you out here somewhere, but I never thought I would."

"Well, I'm sure glad you did. How are you doing Mr. Shields?" William asked as he turned his attention to the gray-haired head of the Shields family.

"Well enough," the old man answered, dismounting from his horse, "But I'll be doing better when we reach Tennessee."

"So, that's what brought you this way," William said as the men began to walk up the hill to the blockhouse.

"Yeah, maybe you'll go along with us to see what it's like down that way yourself," Joshua answered as he pulled his rifle off the top of his mount.

"I doubt it," William replied, "after seeing our Kentucky land once again; I know it's the place for me. My future is set as far as I'm concerned. Any doubts I had about settling out there I laid to rest on this last visit."

"That's fine then," Joshua teased, "all that I'd be doing if you did come along would be saving your hair from some wild Cherokee. Come on; let's go have a talk William. We've got some catching up to do. Here John, tend to my horse if you would be so kind," Joshua requested of his brother-in-law as he handed over his reins.

"Sure," replied John, taking the horses and following behind his father and brother who were already heading toward the corral. The two Tipton brothers watched as the Shields walked away with the other man William had not recognized.

"Who's that short fellow with you all?"

"Brice Matthews," Joshua answered. "He's a good fellow."

"How serious are you about settling in Tennessee, Joshua? I hope you haven't forgotten what we have in Kentucky. It is some grand country down here in these mountains, but it won't feed you like that bottom land in Kentucky will."

"Oh, I know that. I'm just going along for the ride." Joshua assured his brother. "They want me to keep Jeanette close by, but I plan on taking my family to Kentucky, just as you are. I'll let them down easy after we see the land out there. Don't worry; we're still going to be neighbors. It was just too hard to tell them 'no' without going out to see it first. Besides, this most likely will be my last adventure. Once this war is over and we're settled on that hilltop, we'll spend the rest of our lives farming. So why not live it up some now?"

"That's what I wanted to hear," William said, patting his brother on the back. "James and Samuel are out hunting. When they come in we'll have a good meal for supper tonight and you can tell us some of those wild tales of yours to pass the night hours. But as much as I hate to do it, we're heading on home at first light tomorrow morning."

"That's fine," Joshua answered, "We'll have many a day together once we have settled in Kentucky."

"So, tell me, what do you want a son or daughter?" William asked.

"Oh, I don't really care one way or the other," Joshua answered, "but if it's a boy I'm going to name him John Shields Tipton."

Chapter 140
Meeting a Heroine

The rest of the homeward journey up the Blue Ridge had gone well after leaving Joshua behind at Anderson's Blockhouse. Their route had taken a northern turn after passing thru Moccasin Gap, and as they came up on the New River, they crossed over at Ingles Ferry where they had the honor of meeting the famous Mary Draper Ingles. The ageing beauty was thought to be the first white woman to set foot in Kentucky, but it had not been of her own choosing.

Her saga had begun back in 1755, when she was twenty-three years old and living with her husband on their farm at Draper's Meadow. It was in July of that year when a party of Shawnee fell upon her homestead and a few others. Most of the men had been killed in the attacks. Colonel James Patton had died with his claymore in his hand. Mary's life had been spared, but she was captured with her two sons, Thomas and George, and her sister-in-law, Bettie, who had been shot in the arm during the attack. After setting her home ablaze, the Shawnee forced the captives to march all the way to Kentucky, as far as the Big Bone Lick. The most astonishing aspect of this trek was that that Mary was in the last stages of pregnancy when captured. She safely delivered her child, a girl on the way north and by the next day she was once again forced to continue the march on to Ohio. When the war party broke up at Scioto, she was cruelly separated from both her sons. With little hope of reuniting with her children she came to the gut-wrenching decision of leaving her newborn daughter behind and trying to make her escape back home with an older Dutch woman by following the course of the Ohio and New Rivers after being taken to Kentucky. William was amazed to think of how horrible this long walk had been without the benefit of food or weapons, but somehow, she had managed to pull through the ordeal. A few years later, she and her husband, William Ingles, who was away at the time of the attack, did manage to ransom back one of their sons, Thomas. The youngest, George, had died soon after being separated from his mother. The fate of the newborn was never discovered, but as she explained to William and everyone else who was brave enough to ask, that she had not given up on the possibility of finding her lost baby girl someday. She was an amazingly brave woman in William's eyes for she never left the frontier for the safety of the east after her escape. But from that day forward, she was never seen without a rifle by her side.

But other than meeting Mrs. Ingles and passing by the Natural Bridge in the lower Blue Ridge the rest of the trip home was forgettable, if exhausting. More good war news was waiting for William and his two fellow travelers on their arrival back home. General Green had made a much better showing in his abilities than his predecessor. After sending Morgan out after Tarleton at the Cowpens, he had stood toe to toe with Cornwallis at the Battle of Guilford Courthouse. The British had held the field at the end of the day, but lost their main objective, Green's Army. General Green, like Washington had done so many times in the past, had inflicted many casualties upon the British ranks and forced the Redcoats to waste valuable supplies as well as time on a campaign they had little to show for. Washington finally had a man who could win in the South.

Chapter 141
I'm Sorry Jeanette

The Little Pigeon River, in the mountains of eastern Tennessee was a beautiful sight to behold, Joshua thought as he stood beside the boulder filled stream. He watched the running water rush over the stones that lined the entire bed of the small river. The water was cold and not very deep, in most places a man could wade across from one bank to the other watching trout swimming just under the water's surface. He had already crisscrossed it three or four times this morning as he had been out scouting the riverbank for a parcel of land to claim. He had no real intentions of settling here, unlike his enthusiastic in-laws. But he figured while he was here; why not claim some of this free land? It could always be sold off at a later date. The terrain was rough here in the mountains and that made Joshua believe that it would be a slow developing region. There were a few good tracks of land scattered in the valleys here and there, but not enough to cause a large migration. If isolation was what a man craved this was the place for him, but Joshua wanted his family to prosper. There would be only a small amount of people settling here in this country and that would mean there would be little money as well. And that he was not willing to compromise on. This was not the place for him.

It had been a month since he and William had parted ways back at that blockhouse on the Wilderness Road. The Shields party had turned to the southeast at the Gap and had made the difficult journey here over an ancient mountain trail that the Cherokee had cut through their hunting grounds in this mountainous valley. They had crossed over the Holston and Clinch Rivers on their way here, then over the Pigeon River that fed this smaller stream where he now stood. Now that they had arrived here safely, Joshua's main concern was where were the Cherokee?

Spring was here and he had not seen a single warrior in the area, which was a good thing, but it left him with an eerie feeling. It was like they knew that the whites were in their valley and were keeping a watchful eye on them, just waiting for the right moment to fall on their prey.

Robert Shields had spoken of building a station to fort up in along this stream, not too far from where Joshua was now. That task could not be done fast enough in Joshua's mind. It would definitely be needed; the only question would be when. He reached down into the water and picked up one of the thousand small pebbles that lay in the riverbed. He rubbed the smooth blue stone between his fingers, looking at the small vein of fool's gold that ran through the small stone's center. Now if I could find some of the real stuff out here, he thought, just maybe I would settle out here. He chuckled aloud at himself and dropped it back into the water, checked the powder in the pan of his rifle and headed up the bank to where Brice Matthews was, believe it or not, plowing the ground he had picked out for himself, preparing to plant a crop of corn. He had been the butt of many a joke while carrying that plow point over the mountains. But now that he had found the land he wanted, he had carved out two wooden handles and pinned them inside his plow point and was plowing away behind his horse, around the river bend. That is if Joshua had his river bends correct in his mind.

Suddenly on the far bank, a doe ran from under the trees and dived into the rock filled water and scampered across the river. She climbed out, all wet and cold onto the bank just in front of Joshua and quickly darted into the trees. Remembering the spooked buffalo back in Kentucky, Joshua squatted down behind one of the many boulders that lined the bank and gazed across the river to where the terrified deer had just emerged. He sat there for a long intense moment, scanning the tree line, hoping that it was nothing more than that the deer had simply wanted to cross over and had not smelled Joshua on the other side. The sound of the whitecaps rolling in the water hindered his hearing so he had to rely on what he could see, and on his instincts. After a short wait, he thought it would be best to continue up the band to check on Brice. As he moved up he kept his eyes on the far side of the river, and although he had not seen any reason for concern, he felt like he was being watched. As he made his way around the curve of the river, he saw that Brice was doing fine beside his newly plowed field. He had unhitched his horse from the plow and led the animal down to the water's edge for a cool drink.

"Did you find what you were looking for?" Matthews asked, patting his horse's neck.

"Not yet," Joshua answered, "but I still haven't given up on the idea yet either. Have you seen anything to give you any alarm?"

"No," Mathews replied, "why, have you seen something this morning?"

"Naw, not really," Joshua continued as he shook his head, "but I have a strange feeling that I've been watched all morning. I guess there's nothing to it. Maybe I've been out here too long and am getting a little antsy. Looks as though that plow of yours has paid off" Joshua said smiling at Brice. "I'd say you got the last laugh on that account, my friend."

"It would seem so," Mathews agreed, "but I'll let you boys use it if you want. Come on; let's get on back to camp. I believe Robert is planning to start building his fort this afternoon, or at least get started on it anyway."

Brice Matthews was pulling his horse away from the river's edge when a shot rang out from across the river. The lead ball slammed into his back snapping his spinal cord, killing him instantly. Joshua did not have to look back to know what was happening, for he could hear the war cries of the Cherokee as they waded across the river. More shots rang out as Joshua attempted to make his escape across Brice's plowed field, but one of the shots was true. It found its mark striking his lower leg as he reached the tree line, knocking him to the ground. He quickly rolled over onto his stomach and shot his own rifle, putting the well-aimed ball into the chest of one of the war party that was already half way across the field. Joshua crawled to the nearest tree and leaned his back against the trunk while attempting to reload his rifle. Maybe he could get off one more shot before he was overtaken by the twenty or so warriors that were approaching him in a hard run. He looked around the tree and shot off his pistol, knocking down the lead Indian as he reached the end of the newly turned soil. Not wanting to be taken alive, only to be tortured and possibly burned at the stake while still alive, he ran his ramrod down the barrel of his rifle after the powder and ball had been placed in the muzzle. He did not take the time to remove it from the end of the barrel, for he knew this would be his last shot. He dropped his head back up against the tree's trunk and looked up into its green leafy top and said, "I'm sorry Jeanette. Take care of our son as best as you can, for you know I love you both dearly." Then he forced himself to his feet, ignoring the great pain that was running up his bleeding leg and said, "God, give me the strength to see this through."

He stepped out into the open and fired his rifle for the last time right before two warriors leaped upon him burying their tomahawks deep in his chest, ending his young life there on the banks of the Little Pigeon River. He would not feel the pain of their scalping knives, but his family would most definitely feel a great pain when word of his death reached their doors.

Chapter 142
A Star Filled Night

It was late night and Elizabeth had just cleared away the supper table and sat down behind her spinning wheel. She usually did the job of tending to the crockery as soon as her family finished their evening meal, but tonight William had pulled her away from the nightly task and taken her out in the back of the house to play with the children in the fading light of the day. William always enjoyed those times when his work was done and he could simply sit in his back yard and watch his two children and his wife interact with one another. But now the sun had gone down and the little ones were tucked away in bed fast asleep. He had sat down at the table was in the process of sharpening his knife on his whet rock, when he heard the sound of boots on the wooden boards of his front porch just outside, followed by a hard rap on the front door.

"Open up William. It is I your brother Thomas. I have some news," the voice said from the other side of the locked door.

William gave Elizabeth a surprised look as he put down his knife and quickly got up from the table and walked over to the door, happy that his older brother had finally found the time to make an appearance here at his home for the first time since he and Elizabeth had married and moved out here. He felt the loving hand of his wife slip over the top of his shoulder as he unlatched the heavy iron bar that always locked the door when it was shut. When he swung the door open, he saw that Thomas had stepped back away from the threshold and was leaning against the rail that ran around the porch.

"Good heavens Thomas, what brings you out our way tonight?" William asked as he punched his brother's arm. "It's good to finally get you under my roof."

Thomas took off his hat with one hand and looked down at his feet as he blew out a long pent up breath. He raised his hand to his forehead and ran his fingers through his hair with a grimace on his handsome face. As he looked up into his younger brother's eyes, and paused for a short moment, he finally said, "Look William, I can't think of an easy way to say this, so I'm just going to say it. Brace yourself this won't be easy. Joshua is dead."

"What?" William asked as he stepped off the porch, while placing both hands on top of his head in disbelief. "No. No he can't be. Not Joshua."

"He's dead William. He was killed by some damn redskins down in Tennessee. I wish it was a falsehood, but it's not."

William, stunned by what he had just heard, sat down on the grass in disbelief before falling back on the ground still holding the back of his head with his clasped hands. He shut his eyes for a second, just to make sure this was really happening. Realizing that it was, he opened them and stared up into the star filled night sky overhead as he listened to Thomas continue.

"Robert and John Shields came by father's place and told us what had happened. It seems that Joshua and a Matthews's fellow were overrun by a war party of Cherokee while they were out alone. They said he put up quite a fight before they killed him. They told father there were three bloody spots on the ground where he had shot at least that many before he died. You know how the Indians never leave their dead behind if they can help it. There were no bodies there other than Joshua and Matthews."

"Are you sure?" William asked, "I just saw him a few weeks ago. He was fine then."

"I'm sure," Thomas assured his brother. "Why would the Shields lie about something like that? No, he's gone. I'm sure."

"Damn, he was so happy," William said as he stood up off the damp ground and began to walk around the yard in circles. "He said that Jeanette was with child and that he was going to be a father soon. God bless his soul."

"He still will be," Elizabeth said in an attempt to console her shocked husband,

"As long as that child is alive, he will be too in a way."

"What was he doing down there anyway?" William asked as a single tear ran down his face. "He told me he had no real plans to move out there. What about his body? Did the Shields find him?"

"Yeah," Thomas answered in a low voice. "They said he was torn up pretty bad, but he got a good burial. They laid him to rest by the river where he was killed."
"How are your poor parents handling this Thomas?" Elizabeth asked.

"Not good. I don't know which one it hurt the most. Mother's taken to her bed and Father is real quiet, not saying much of anything, but I do have a letter for you William. It's from Father. He wanted me to bring it to you on my way down."

"On the way down where" William asked.

"Virginia," answered Thomas. "General Washington is shifting a lot of his troops down that way. As a matter of fact, I am calling on a number of the continentals who were on their furloughs. I've got orders for them to muster back into the ranks."

"Well, I'm going with you," William said angrily. "It's time for this bloody war to stop."

"I thought as much," answered Thomas as he put his hat back on, feeling relieved that his hardest task was now over. William walked over and put a shaking hand around his wife's waist and putting the other on Thomas' back said, "Come on inside and show me the letter. I want to see it tonight." The three turned back toward the candle light of the house and walked up the porch steps and into what just a few moments ago had been a happy household, but had now turned into one of despair. What had been a good day had quickly transformed into the very worst day of William's life. The world would be a little smaller and quieter now that Joshua was gone. And William would always have a hole in his heart.

Chapter 143
Come Back to Me

Thomas had mounted up and ridden down to the end of William's lane and was waiting for his brother to say his goodbyes to his wife and children this morning. He knew all too well how difficult a task this was. He always liked to have a little privacy when he was saying his farewells to Mary back home and he wasn't about to intrude on William and Elizabeth's last moments together today. He looked back to the house and saw his brother leading his black Friesian up to the front porch where he tied the reins to the railing and disappeared inside the doorway. Knowing it would take very little time for William to overtake him, Thomas gently tapped his horse's side with his foot and slowly rode down the road at an even pace, leaving William behind to tend to his task of saying goodbye.

William forced a smile to his face as he stepped inside his home for what would be the last time in a long while. As he came in the door, he reached down and picked up young John who was crawling out from under the table in the center of the room, cutting his speedy little son off before he could reach the open front door that William was standing in. He tickled the little boy's tender ribs under his arms causing the little fellow to giggle and laughed out loud as he said, "You're moving a little faster today, my boy. Why the big hurry?"

"He's like his father," Elizabeth answered from just on the other side of the table, as she finished packing the last few items away in his waist bag.

"I suppose so," William answered as he kissed his son on the cheek. He raised the boy high into the air a few times before he sat him back down on the floor, pointing the giggling child in a different direction to keep him from slipping out the open door. Turning back to the table, William asked, "Where is my little girl?" I know she has to be here somewhere." He pretended not to see Sarah, who was holding her favorite doll and standing ncxt to her mother's side.

"Here I am Daddy," Sarah called out as she ran toward her father, falling for his ploy.

"Sarah, where are you?" William kept calling as he looked over the top of her small head, acting as if he could not see her, even though she was standing right in front of him. "Elizabeth, where's our little daughter? I can't see her for this pretty girl running around in front of me." Unable to ignore her any longer, he looked down at her and said, "Wait a minute. You are Sarah, aren't you?" he said, laughing at the happy child who was used to playing this familiar game with her father. "Sarah", he continued, "I want you to take good care of your mother while I'm gone. Can you do that for me?" he asked as he picked her up and held her in his arms.

"Yes, I will," she answered in a small voice as she bobbed her head up and down with that big grin of hers on her face and twirled the tips of her hair with her fingers.

"Well that's good then. That's one concern off my mind for sure. I thank you for the favor young lady. Now, why don't you go on over there and play with your brother so your mother and I can step outside for a moment." He stepped over to Elizabeth and took the full bag from her hand and slung it over his shoulder. Reaching down he took her hand in his and led her out the door.

"William, are you sure you want to do this so soon after hearing of Joshua's death? Why don't you sit this out and stay home with me," she asked as he stepped off the porch, hoping that he would heed her plea but knowing full well that he wouldn't. He turned back to her and said, "I would love to stay here. There is no other place in the world that I would rather be, but I would go out of my mind with torment knowing that the war was going on and I was not doing my part."

"Not doing you part!" she raised her voice at him. "My goodness, you've been gone almost as much as you have been here William. You have gone far beyond what has been expected of you. What good is liberty going to do this family if you're dead? I'm afraid you'll take too many chances this time, trying to get revenge for your brother. You have volunteered for dangerous jobs in the past when you didn't have to and I don't want you to do it this time."

"I promise you that I won't," William answered. "I know I can't bring him back no matter what I do. But I need to go, it's my duty. You know that," he said as he pulled her into his arms. As she laid her head against his chest he heard her say in a soft, broken voice, "William, promise me that you'll come back to me."

"I will my love," he answered "Don't you worry. This is not our last day together. I promise you, I'll return. I love you all too much not to. You'll see. God has taken one of us and I don't believe he'll take another." But deep down, he knew that if his skills and talents were ever asked for, he would break his promise to he wife and do whatever was asked of him. He wasn't sure where this tour would take him, but if there were any Indians there, God help them for he would not, nor any British either for that matter.

Chapter 144
Rode Hard and Put up Wet

After hearing of Joshua's death, James and Samuel also decided to re-enter the war. Joshua had become a good and trusted friend over the past few years to both men. They too would have a hard yoke to bear under this anguishing news. Having William to break the news had made it all that much heart breaking, because they could see the pain and grief in his face as he told them what had happened to Joshua.

All of them now had a new founded fortitude that they had not experienced since Captain Babb had been attacked and his home destroyed by the Tories. Atonement was at hand.

The Frederick County Militia had also been called upon and was going to be leaving within the next few days. Once again, it was under the steady command of Captain Babb, who had ignored the wishes of his concerned family to stay out of the war. He had explained to his wife and daughter that he was not just going to sit about in the luxury of his newly constructed home while his good friend Dan Morgan was out in the field leading the other half of the county's militia. Morgan had embarked south, leaving just a few days before and Buxton Babb was not about to stand idly by and watch the rest of the war go by. However, William wasn't willing to wait for his old Captain this time, having already decided to travel along with Thomas who was still under orders to continue on south. James and Samuel had as always, fallen in with the two Tipton brothers, only this brother had a different name. It was Thomas, not Joshua who rode with them and it was going to be a lot different this time around. Not having been around Thomas very much, and seeing how serious minded he was about the outcome of the war, they had stayed in back of the four-man column, letting the two brothers ride side by side most of the time over the last few days. At first, the two were still in deep sorrow and were having a hard time dealing with their loss, but as the miles passed away under their horse's feet, they seemed to come to the realization that they had to move on mentally, now that they were about to reach Hanover Courthouse, because the enemy would now be nearby.

The British had been very active here in the Tidewater region during the summer. Cornwallis had conceded the western Carolinas to General Greene after losing the race to the Dan River. He returned to the seaboard where he had re-supplied his army in Wilmington, North Carolina. Afterwards, he marched north into Virginia in an attempt to capture the young Frenchman, the Marquis de Lafayette and his American Army. In doing so, he believed he would conquer all of Virginia. He had even gone so far as to write in one of his letters, "*The boy cannot escape me*".

Cornwallis had turned his troops up the James River and had traveled a little past Elk Island to the Point of Fork where he captured a great quantity of American stores, but not the Marquis. Remembering the futility of his Carolina campaign against Greene and not wanting to make the same mistake twice, he had now decided to turn back to the East and make for the port of Portsmouth. In addition, he had also received dispatches from General Clinton ordering that he was to send reinforcements to New York. He did as he was ordered and returned to the coast. But Cornwallis was not the only Brit making havoc in Virginia. Banastre Tarleton and his much-hated Legion of Cavalry had very nearly captured Governor Jefferson at his mountain home, Monticello. Jefferson had narrowly made his escape by riding down the heavily forested hill in front of his home as the dragoons raced uphill on the back side of his five-thousand-acre plantation, never halting until they had ridden onto the terrace that graced the back of the mansion. And to make matters worse, in the early spring, Thomas' old commanding officer, the traitor Benedict Arnold had sacked the newly formed seat of Government in Richmond. Governor Jefferson had offered the large sum of five thousand guineas to anyone who could slit Arnold's throat, but it had little effect on the hero of Saratoga. He kept burning and raiding as if the bounty was insignificant. This was the situation the four were about to ride into as they reached the small village in the pursuit to join up with the Marquis's army. They were definitely back in the war.

Thomas looked over to his brother and said," I have no idea how the people are living down here, much less the armies. There's nothing to eat."

"I thought as much myself," William agreed. "I haven't seen a single hoof in miles; Cow, hog, sheep, or even a goat for that matter."

"No deer either," James said as he rode in between the two. "I would say whatever hasn't been eaten up was smart enough to high tail it out of here, by the looks of things. Hell, I'll settle for a skinny chicken right about now."

"Well, I can't help you there," Samuel replied from the rear but I do have a few eggs packed away in one of these bags. If you boys want, we can fry them up tonight. Or we can wait until morning if you want."

William pulled Sampson to a stop and looked over at Samuel and asked, "Are you pulling our leg or what? It's hard for me to believe that you have eggs."

"A straw filled bag can be a wonderful thing." Samuel replied as he rode past his doubting friends into Hanover. As they made their way down the street William spotted a large number of horses under an elm just to the side of a tavern at the end of town. The horses were saddled with several different types of bridles and saddles. Very few of the horse blankets matched, which made William believe they were militia and most likely some of Morgan's men, if not the General himself.

"That's got to be some of our boys," Thomas said as he pulled his mount to a stop.

As William glanced over to his brother, he remembered the lesson Aquilla Price had taught him all those years ago. With Thomas wearing his continental uniform, there was little doubt where his allegiance lay. "Thomas, you stick out like a sore thumb in that uniform of yours. Why don't you wait here while we ride on down and make sure they are some of our boys just to be safe."

"I don't believe that will be necessary," Thomas said as he leaned back in his saddle. "But I guess it won't hurt to do it. Go on and I'll watch from here," he replied, pulling his pistol from his belt.

William nodded his head and hurried on down the street, giving Thomas little time to reconsider. As he rode past the tavern's open door he saw Dan Morgan sitting at a table littered with empty oyster shells and the remains of a pecan pie that he had not finished off. He had one leg propped up on an empty chair, being examined by a doctor who was stooping by his side attending to the old soldier's aches and pains. There was a sentry standing by the doorway, keeping a close eye on William as he turned back up the street and stood up in the saddle to wave the rest of his party on down to join the general's troop.

William dismounted and led Sampson over where the other horses were tied under the oak. As he walked across the dusty road, the eyes of the sentry once again fell upon him as he was making his approach to the tavern door.

"Halt where you are," the narrow-eyed militiaman ordered. "What business do you have here today?"

"I'm here with a sergeant from the Virginia line to join up with General Morgan." William answered as he pointed to his companions. "See for yourself, there they are."

"Well, you don't enlist here," the tall sentry replied as he eyed Thomas and the others making their way down the street. The General has more important matters to attend to than your enlistments. That Sergeant should know that. We're camped just out of town. You can muster in there like everyone else. Off with you now."

"Hold on there Moses, I know that man. Send him on in here. He's been a courier for me in the past. He's just the sort I need to talk with," Morgan said as he stuck his other leg out and up into the chair. "Are you here with Captain Babb? He said he would be along in a few days."

"No Sir," William answered as he stepped back a few feet to let the Doctor walk around to Morgan's other side.

"That's what I wanted to hear," Morgan replied as he began to roll up his shirt sleeves. "I'll need some good horsemen before this summer is out. Well, tell me Doctor, what's your verdict? Am I a broken man or not?"

A smile broke over the Doctor's face as he looked down at Morgan, who was putting on his hat. "No, you're not broken yet, but for the life of me, I don't know how you're doing this."

"It is true. I have been rode hard and put up wet a few times over the years." Morgan replied as he stood up. "But I'm not done yet. We got little Bennie at the Cowpens and now it's that Cornshucker fellow's turn. But first, we have to catch up with Lafayette my boys. He's stationed on Malvern Hill somewhere between here and Williamsburg. Yes sir, I tell you boys, Cornwallis is going to have one hot summer on his hands this year. When I was about your age, the British gave me 499 lashes; I still have the scars to prove it. They still owe me that last lash. I was sentenced to 500 but they miscounted. They'll never get another chance to get in that final lash. That's one mistake I'm not going to make, no sir. And I can assure you that old Cornwallis is not going to get off easy either.

Chapter 145
Blue Coats Instead of Red

Lafayette's army was made up from the New Jersey and New England Continental Lines supported by some Virginia Militia. They were in dire need of almost everything an army could use in wartime, William thought as they finally rode into the Continental camp on Malvern Hill. They were without enough tents to accommodate all the men at night. Some of their boots were worn down so badly they looked like the ones William was wearing the night Joshua rode into Ft. Pitt on William's first tour. He would never forget those old pieces of leather now. He would always remember that his brother had traded off his mother's prize ham so William could get those shoepacks from Knox.

This was the first occasion in William's military career that he had actually had the opportunity to go inside a Continental camp. Every man here was lacking in some capacity when it came to their rigging. And what little they did have was bought by Lafayette himself back in Baltimore, with his own money, before they marched down here. But William had learned from past experiences that the abilities of a soldier didn't always correspond with his uniform and equipment. He could tell that these men were fighters; they had been in the war a long time now. There were no cowards or shirkers in their ranks. Every man may not have the most eye-catching attire, but they all held well maintained muskets in their hands. Discipline was most certainly in their camp. It was being displayed from one end of the camp to the other. Men were drilling and carrying out their orders. They had been in the field for over five months here in the south, and were almost at the point of starvation. But rag tag as they were, they had made their commander in chief very proud, for the British had retreated for the most part to the coast for whatever reason they had concocted. Benedict Arnold had been ordered to return to New York so he was no longer in the area. So now this three-thousand-man army was sitting here, keeping a watchful eye on Lord Cornwallis and the point of his sword, Banastre Tarleton.

"Well Sergeant Tipton, where will you be in all of this mass of humanity? I may need to get a hold of you," William asked as they rode up to where the militias had pitched their tents in a grove of maple trees to the north of the main camp.

"I don't know for sure," Thomas answered, "but by the way Morgan was talking, he wanted me to stay with his men. It would be nice to have some of the freedom you boys in the militia have. Just look at the difference in the two camps. They're a little more laid back on this side, but I'll go wherever they send me. It's not like I have a choice in the matter."

"Tell me," William ask as he dismounted form his horse, "how does this army compare to what Washington has up North?"

"No difference," Thomas replied, looking back at the continental side of the camp. "The protocol is the same, the Continentals deployed to right, in the place of honor, Militia to the left, but I don't know how much difference that makes now. Most of these boys have been under Washington's command at some point in the war anyway. Hell, some of the militia is former continentals anyway, having their enlistments expire and taking up with their local militia instead of going back in their old lines. That's one advantage the Redcoats don't have over us as much as they used to. Our men are a hell of a lot more battle tested now than they used to be. We've had to learn the hard way at times, but it's put a fire in our bellies. We're not as intimidated as we were back at the beginning of the war."

"Well one thing is for sure," James said as he pulled his rifle from his horse. "It sure is good to see Blue coats instead of Red ones. But I feel like we're going to see some soon enough."

"Well, I hope so," Samuel replied eagerly as he looked into Thomas' eyes. "I always wanted to be in a big battle. This could very well be it."

"Maybe so it would be a good time for it, we have a good man to serve under," Thomas replied. "The Marquis may be young, but he has picked up a lot from General Washington over the last few years. And having Von Steuben's army join up with us will increase our chances of victory all the more. Yeah, Lafayette, Morgan and now Von Steuben, they're all good officers. Hell, better than good. But I'll say one thing for you boys," he said with a devilish grin, "You better pray to God that you're not put under that German. He's been hard on militia in the past. They say he can cuss a man in more than four languages. It might be better if he uses something other than English. At least, that way you won't be able to understand what he's calling you," he laughed. "Come on let's go into camp and see what's coming out of the rumor mills.

"Hey boy," Thomas yelled at a private who was walking by with a grooming brush in his hand. "Tend to these animals and see that they're fed, if we have anything in this army to give them."

"Yes Sir," the private answered, taking the reins of two of the saddled horses. William was a little apprehensive about letting Sampson walk out of his sight with this unknown private. He turned to Thomas and said, "Are you sure about this? We don't know this fellow."

"Chain of command," Thomas answered pointing to his red epaulettes. "I'll have his hide if he lets anything happen to our mounts. Won't I private?"

"Yes Sir, you most certainly will," the private answered. "Plenty of high trees around these parts to hang a man from, don't worry mister, your mount will be fine with me," he said as he took Sampson's reins from William's reluctant hand. "I value my neck too much to lose it over a horse."

Samuel stepped up behind William and whispered "He may value his neck, but not as much as we value our horses. Don't worry; I'll follow along behind him. I won't let them out of my sight until they are bedded down for the night."

"Yeah, that's a good idea. I don't want to lose Trace either." James agreed.
"I'll give you a hand there," Samuel announced as he walked by. "Mine can be a little wild at times. Four horses at one time can be trying at best. Lead the way friend."
Thomas shook his head as he tugged at the tail of his coat to pull it down tightly over his shoulders, making sure it was straight in line. Then giving his hat a quick adjustment, he turned towards the Regulars camp giving everyone the impression that he was very much at home in this army. "I'm going into camp to see what the mood is like around here. See you men in the morning." That said, he strolled off and disappeared into the mass of troops. William could see that someday if this war ever ended, that Sergeant Thomas Tipton was going to miss some aspects of army life. James turned and looked down into the militia camp as he bit into his chewing tobacco. With a bulge sticking out from his jaw he asked, "Do you see any Ft. Pitt boys down there anywhere William?"

"No, but let's go see, there could be a few down there that we know. Look, down next to that mass of tents and lean-to's" William said as he pointed into the center of the camp. "See where all those men are standing around that wagon? That's a peddler down there selling something."

"He's selling spirits," James grinned and wagged his eyebrows at William. "That should be a good place to start. Come on," he said as he shifted his rifle over into the fold of his arm and made his way toward the horse drawn bar. "I hope he's got some good bourbon down there. I'm sick of rum."

William didn't answer, he just walked on behind, knowing very well that James wasn't about to let this opportunity pass by. As the two reached the wagon, William saw that James was correct in his assumption of what was being sold. The owner of the wagon was a young man in his twenties and he was selling whiskey hand over fist to the thirsty militiamen.

"Got any bourbon?" James called out as he approached the young man standing in the back of his wagon.

"No, but I have some mighty fine brandy," the barkeep answered as he raised his leg up and put his black boot on top of the green wooden wall of the wagon's side.

"That will do," James replied, "how much?"

"It'll be two shillings."

"Damn, did it come from the King's own wine cellar?" James complained as he spat out his chew.

"If it's too rich for your blood, you don't have to buy it my friend. Hell, I may be selling it too cheap as it is. It's no skin off my nose. Besides I'll be out of stock in a few minutes anyway."

"I didn't say I didn't want any," James answered as he handed over the money. "I'll take one for me and one for my friend here".

"Give us four pieces of that sweet bread as well", William said, looking down at a bushel basket sitting in the corner of the wagon filled with the bread.

"That'll be another shilling," the young man replied as he stuck out his hand.

"Does Lafayette know about you selling all this stuff down here?" William asked as he paid the bill.

"I have a permit made out to yours truly, Daniel Trabue signed by the Marquis himself right here in my vest pocket. It's all legal and good my friend, so don't you worry. You won't be lined up in front of any firing squads tonight," he laughed.

"It may be priced high, but damn, it goes down awful smooth," James commented after taking his first drink.

"I told you it was fine stuff," Trabue replied proudly. "I'm not robbing anyone here."

"No, you're not," James answered as he wiped his mouth with his shirt sleeve. "Are you in the militia?"

That I am," replied Trabue, "As a matter of fact that's how I got this permit. I've run so many dispatches for Lafayette that he's showed his gratitude by letting me do this for a while."

"We just came into camp today," William said, placing his hand on top of the wagon wheel at his side, "what's the situation around here?"

"All I can tell you is that Cornwallis has about nine thousand men in Virginia. They're spread out from Williamsburg to Portsmouth and they outnumber us three to one. We've been sitting here ever since General Wayne was ambushed while he was attacking Cornwallis' rear guard when the British were crossing the James River two weeks ago. That little cocky ass Tarleton is burning half of the towns up and down the river, putting fear in everyone's heart that he doesn't kill first. They say Cornwallis has moved into the President's house at William and Mary Collage and is going to open up the old capital for the Loyalist after running all the Whigs out of town." Trabue jumped down from the rear of the wagon and as he was shutting the tailgate he looked at William and said, "I'd say everything's about normal."

Chapter 146
Tarleton's Quarter

Early this morning, even before the moon had surrendered to the sun, Dan Morgan had summoned Thomas to his white canvas tent. The old soldier was limping badly as he gave Thomas his orders. Lafayette had come by some intelligence on Banastre Tarleton's dragoons. They were heading to Petersburg and Morgan wanted Thomas and his men to accompany the general's mounted militia. Lafayette was of the same mind and agreed with Morgan, this advance had to be stopped, if at all possible. Lafayette could not afford to be trapped between two British armies. Hopefully Tarleton was just out scouting or foraging for supplies. This may not be another major offensive, but that could not be determined in camp. The task was to be attended to by Morgan's newly arrived troops while Lafayette continued to follow Cornwallis to the coast.

Morgan had also informed Thomas that after these past three nights of sleeping on the ground, the old General could no longer stay in the field. His old bones had simply spent too many nights in the open air over the years. He still had the desire to continue, but his body could not withstand the beating any longer. The pain was too great to bear. This was to be the last orders of his military career. He was returning home to Saratoga, his newly renamed estate in Frederick County this very day. He had relinquished his command.

William and his friends were now part of a one-hundred-man cavalry that was approaching the Appomattox River. The column was riding through the countryside having left the road to Petersburg. The commanding officer, Lieutenant Colonel Windsor Allison had spotted a distant fire and directed his men through several pastures filled with sheep. He called a halt on top of a hill where he could get a better view of the burning barn below. Allison dismounted his horse and was looking at the plantation through his brass telescope. "I count nine mounts down there. There are three dragoons with the horses and the other six are probably inside the house." He compressed his telescope and put in back inside its case as he looked at Thomas and said, "Easy enough Gentlemen. They're no match for us. I would like to capture at least one of them alive."

"And if they resist?" William asked as he pulled his pistol.

"Then we'll give them Tarleton's quarter." Allison replied with a raised eyebrow. "They never seem to have a problem with that philosophy as long as they are doing the attacking. What's good for the goose is good for the gander I always say. Twenty should be sufficient Sergeant Tipton."

Thomas nodded his head and quickly selected his men by pointing them out with the tip of his drawn sword. As he made his way to his horse, Thomas turned to William who was standing between James and Samuel and said, "We need to kill those three, outside tending to the horses. When we charge they'll call the alarm to the men inside. As soon as they do, I want you and your friends her to bust their asses. Make sure to scatter their mounts to the wind.

"Leaving the dragoons who come running out of the house with nothing to escape on," William interrupted.

"Exactly," Thomas replied. "We'll ride in and mop up the rest of them, hopefully with little trouble. I will give you and your men some time to work your way down through the grass. When you're within your killing range, stop and we'll come on down."

William tucked away his pistol and pulled his long rifle from Sampson's back as James and Samuel did the same from their respective mounts and followed William into the waist high orchard grass that was blowing in the wind. After entering the grass a few feet, they fell to their knees and began to crawl down the long summit.

Lieutenant Allison once again pulled his telescope from its case and watched as the three men made their way down the hill. As they reached the midway point, they stopped their descent and waited for the charge to begin, causing Allison to believe they had misjudged the distance to the plantation below.

As he turned to Thomas to inform him of his concerns, he heard Thomas give the order to "Charge". Allison spun back around and focused his scope on the three snipers, then to the green coated dragoons standing in the courtyard below. One raised a hand to the side of his mouth as he climbed on his horse, but then tumbled off the other side of his mount as Allison heard the report of three rifles simultaneously being fired from the hill. The other two riders were likewise knocked to the ground and their horses had bolted down the lane in a panic.

William stood up and reached down for his powder horn as Thomas and the others rode by and into the yard below. Four of Tarleton's men ran out of the house in a vain attempt to grab their horses. Two were cut to pieces by the militiamen who had delivered Tarleton's Quarter to the surrendering dragoons ignoring Allison's order to take them alive. Thomas quickly regained order over his enraged men, saving the lives of the other two so Allison could question them later and obtain the information he needed. As William removed his ramrod from his barrel, he saw an older woman being pushed out of the open door of the house. She was followed by a younger woman who had a pistol held under her chin by another of the dragoons, using her body as a shield between him and Thomas' men.

"Sergeant, dismount your horse," the desperate dragoon ordered as he pulled the young woman close to his chest.

"There's no need for all of this." Thomas coaxed, "Surrender, lay down your arms and no harm will come to you."

"I saw how you devils let my men surrender just now. No, dismount or she will pay forfeit for your foolish actions here today. Lower your weapons and step aside."

"Captain, once again I implore you, let the girl go," Thomas plead from the top of his horse. "I'll give you my word as a gentleman, no harm will come to you here today."

"Sergeant, there hasn't been any gentlemen left in this war since what happened at Waxhaw's. You have to know that and I know it as well. In all good conscious, I can't trust you."

"For God's sakes, let him have your horse," the older woman said to Thomas as she stood up, regaining her footing. "He will kill her for sure if you don't."

Never taking his eyes off the soldier and his hostage, Thomas replied,

"Very well good lady, I see little honor in my adversary here. I believe you are right. All right then Captain, you win." Thomas raised his hand and ordered his men to lower their weapons. Then he dismounted and stepped away from his horse, conceding the matter to this desperate man.

Pushing her forward with his free hand the captain ordered her to mount the horse.

"That's not what we agreed to Captain," Thomas objected.

"Well it is now. I'll let her go when I am out of sight," replied the captain. "You have my word as a British gentleman. A smile crossed his face as he said, "Jump up here lass," looking at Thomas with an extremely smug expression.

Seeing the fear in the young woman's eyes, Thomas tried to console her. "It will be fine young lady. He has given us his word, this will all be over very soon. Do as you're say. I promise it will be alright."

Still apprehensive she did as she was told and with one quick leap she jumped onto the horse's back, to everyone's surprise.

Seeing that his plan was working, the Captain placed his black boot in the stirrup and pulled himself up onto the animal's back just behind the girl. A soft thud was heard, followed by the sound of the report from William's rifle. The dragoon tumbled to the ground with a bullet hole just under his arm, tearing his ribs and punching a hole in his lungs. Thomas reached down and picked up the dying man's black bearskin helmet that had rolled over to his feet. As he ran his fingers through the soft hair of the helmet, he looked up to his brother high up on that hill and wondered just how far a shot William had just pulled off.

As he lay under the belly of Thomas' horse, the captain asked "Where did that shot come from?"

"From heaven," the old woman answered as she pulled her shocked daughter off the horses back. "Lucy, are you alright? Speak to me girl." she said, looking her daughter up and down.

"I'm fine," Lucy finally answered as her mother pulled her back into the safety of the house. Thomas reached inside and pulled the door shut behind the two. As he turned back around to face his men he said, "Bring those two prisoners up here beside my horse so we can have a few words."

He walked back to the dying Captain and stood by his body as the badly beaten prisoners were led to him. "My commanding officer is right on top of that hill there and he wants to have a talk with you two. So I am going to send one of you up there to him, but the other is going to stay here with me and he is going to be very forth coming to all my questions." He dropped the dragoon's helmet to the ground and put his foot on it as if it were his very own personal stool and placed a hand on the grips of his pistol. One of the prisoners, having already had his green coat and personal valuables taken from him began to complain, "You can't treat us this way. We are soldiers, not common thieves. We deserve better than this."

"That's exactly how I felt when I heard how your countrymen had treated my brother when he was held on one of those rotting prison ships in New York harbor." Thomas interrupted. "And by the way, to answer you're dying Captain's question that was my younger brother who shot him off my horse." Thomas told him as he glanced at the dead officer. "But I guess I answered his question a little too late but back to the   subject at hand. You are going to be very truthful in your answers to me. If you two don't tell the same story, I'll let my brother use you boys for target practice. And after I finish talking to you, I plan on talking to those two ladies inside. They may be able to shed some light on this matter as well. Some of you most likely shot your mouths off while they were standing by. Now, since you and I are already acquainted with one another, I'll address my questions to you sir." Thomas motioned for the other prisoner to be sent to Allison, but before he was out of ear shot, Thomas said, "Now don't forget what I said about target practice. My brother is quite a marksman." Turning to the remaining solder Thomas stared hard into his prisoners' eyes and said, "Now tell me soldier, what are you all doing out this way? And where is Banastre Tarleton?'

"Foraging," replied the nervous dragoon, "We were after the sheep. Our beef supply is about gone and our Captain remembered seeing several flocks here on the Appomattox River. We were going to drive them back to our lines. As far as Colonel Tarleton goes, he's most like strolling up Duke of Gloucester street between the capitol and the Governor's palace."

"Williamsburg," Thomas said.

"Yes sir, and Lord Cornwallis is residing in Portsmouth at the moment. We're establishing a sea base there on the James, or maybe further on up the coast at   Yorktown.

"He's not concerned about the French bottling him up in the river?" Thomas asked.
A smile stole over the dragoons face as he replied, "Why would we ever be afraid of the French Navy? We blow their ships out of the water all around the globe. Our Navy is far superior to the French."

"Maybe so," Thomas replied, "but your cavalry sure is taking a pounding these days. How many more of your comrades are nearby?"

"Not many most have already turned back for the coast."

"Have you been honest with me?" Thomas asked as he narrowed his eyes, "remember, that was no idle threat I promised."

"I have answered the best I could," the dragoon replied as he put a hand up to the cut over his swollen eye.

"I hope so, for your sake," Thomas said, as he turned back to the house's front door. But then he turned back to the dragoon and asked," why did you burn these people's barn? You could have left it standing."

The dragoon glanced at the smoldering pile of ash where the barn had once stood and shaking his head said, "I really have no answer for you on that. It was the captain's orders. You would have to ask him."

"Too late for that," Thomas replied as he motioned for the prisoner to be taken away.

Chapter 147
The Pox

William walked over to the fire, reached down and took another strip of the mutton he and his friends had been eating tonight. It had been several years since he'd had the opportunity to taste the meat from a sheep. As he walked back to their new tent on the edge of Lafayette's latest camp, he bit into his second slab, hoping it would taste better than the first, but like his initial sampling, this one was just as bland.

"It would be nice to have a little seasoning for our meat every now and then, wouldn't it," he asked as he sat down between James and Samuel. "There has to be some salt around this camp somewhere."

"You ain't a playing," James replied. "It's sure not like what mother used to cook up back home when I was a boy."

"How so?" William asked as he chewed away on the dry meat.

"The sauces she used. She would pour the most delicious gravy all over the top. It would have green peppers and onions chopped up in it. It would make you lick your plate when you finished. But you better not let her see you doing it, because if she did, she would slap the top of your head in a heartbeat."

"Sounds like it was worth it," Samuel responded as he stared into the fire. "I never heard you talk about your mother much before or any of your folks for that matter."

"Well, she's dead now. So is my father. They had me late in life. She was in her forty's when I was born and father was well into his fifties. She's been gone for about five years and papa about ten. I wasn't as lucky as William is, still having his family around, but I was better off than you my friend. I sure wish she was here to liven up this tasteless stuff we've been eating tonight. And you're exactly right, it was worth it. She never hit me very hard," James chuckled.

Samuel smiled as he looked away from the fire and into James' eyes and whispered, "I would have liked to know what a mother's touch feels like. Even if would be a slap to the top of my head."

"You'll know someday," William told him. "You'll see your wife with your children someday when you are married and settled. That is, if you can ever find a woman that deranged."

"I hope so," Samuel laughed as he stood up and walked into their new tent. "Well, our supper may not be the best, but our sleeping conditions are a whole lot better tonight. I suppose our shooting today may have had something to do with that. Don't you think so William?"

"Could be," William answered as he walked into the tent. "It is strange that Lieutenant Allison came up with a tent for us tonight. Maybe Thomas can shed some light on the matter when he comes in later. However, we got it, it sure is nice to have one big enough for us all to sleep in."

"Fellows, you better step out here," James called as he stood up and reached for his rifle. "Bring your guns with you; somebody's moving around out there in the dark."

William and Samuel quickly emerged from the tent with weapons in hand. "Where are they James?" Samuel asked, pulling back the hammer of his rifle. "I don't see anything,"

"Down there by the creek," James answered, "next to that big sycamore. You all come on out of there or we'll shoot."

"Don't fire boss. We're unarmed," a man answered as he came walking toward the fire with raised hands. "Do you have any food to spare? We're all might hungry down here."

William lowered his rifle as he watched the approaching slave enter the edge of the flickering firelight, at the head of a group of fifteen to twenty black men standing down by the water's edge.

"What are you doing out here walking around our camp at night?" James asked from behind his raised rifle.

"The British have run us off," answered one of those still standing in the dark. "They took us off the plantations here abouts back in the spring. But they turned us out now. They say they don't have enough food to feed us any longer."

"I don't know", James answered. "We know that they have offered slaves their freedom if they will take up arms for the King. I sure in hell am not going to feed some damn black that has taken their side over ours."

"No boss, I promise. They took us off the farm by force. We got no choice in the matter. We're begging you for something to eat. Anything you could see your way clear to give us would be a mighty big help. We ain't eating in a couple a days. Some of us are mighty weak."

"There is some mutton over at the fire." William said, "Help yourselves to it."

"God bless you sir," the slave said as he reluctantly walked into the firelight with his head down, trying to keep his face from being seen. But as he reached out for the food, William could see the pox marks on his shaking hands and arms.

"Take your food and go back the way you came," William ordered. General Lafayette has given us orders to shoot any British soldiers or slaves that have smallpox trying to enter our lines. Word's out about the British having the pox. You're doing just what the British wanted when they drove you out of their ranks. Smallpox is not getting this army. Take your food and go. And don't come back here again. You're damn lucky that we took pity on you tonight and that no one else has seen you here, because if they had, you'd be dead by now. How did you get past the pickets anyway?"

"Don't really know, boss."

"Well if you come back again, we will shoot next time."

"Thank ye boss," the slave answered as he slipped back into the darkness. "We won't we back."

William looked at James and cocked his head to one side with a concerned look on his face. Both men stepped inside the tent and picked up their gear and carried it back outside. As James walked behind the tent and bent over to untie its rope, William pulled up a peg at the front corner, He looked at Samuel and said, "Let's take this tent down and move it to the other side of camp. He didn't get too close, but I don't want to take any chances of getting the pox. Besides, if twenty men can walk past that picket line out there, how safe can it be on this side of camp anyway?"

Chapter 148
The Landing

Sampson threw damp soil high into the air as he made the sharp turn off the Richmond road onto the road leading to Yorktown and William got his first glimpse of Williamsburg. The little bit of the old capitol's streets that he could see was empty this morning. The road ran just to the edge of the hundred-year-old town before making a U turn to the southeast, down the peninsula. All that he really saw was the college of William and Mary. It gave him an odd feeling as he rode by the tall brick building to know that just a few weeks ago this town was completely occupied by the British.

A smile crossed his face as he remembered what Trabue, the whiskey peddler had told him about Lord Cornwallis staying in the very same brick house he had just passed. He was overjoyed to see the redcoats abandoning towns instead of occupying them, but he knew they were not giving up on Virginia just yet. Cornwallis was expecting reinforcements from New York and would renew his fight for the colonies as soon as Clinton sent orders to do so, and that would likely be as soon as the weather cooled. Lafayette's spies had brought in word of Cornwallis's departure form Portsmouth three nights ago. He was, reportedly, on one of the ships that had sailed out to sea, with his army aboard, headed for some unknown destination. Yorktown had long been rumored as a possible base for the Kings fleet. It had one of the deepest harbors in all of North America, but Cornwallis could just as easily be sailing north instead, so now once again, William and his two friends, found themselves on a spying mission to see if the British were indeed going to land on the shores of Yorktown, only twelve miles away.

It had become a well-known fact that Lafayette was completely taken by the abilities of the men that Dan Morgan had entrusted to the Marquise after his departure. Lafayette had even gone so far as to pen a letter to General Washington, telling his Excellency of their great shooting abilities and stamina. However, these were not their best qualities, in his eyes. What he appreciated the most about them was their scouting and spying abilities. This was something he sorely lacked and they filled that void very nicely.

Thomas had led several scouting and spying parties since the one to Portsmouth and he had come to depend on the abilities of his brother, as well as those of James and Samuel. Their days on the frontier had served them well and Thomas was smart enough to take full advantage of it. Now that his men has ridden out of Williamsburg he had sent the three out in front to make sure his troops were not riding into a trap.

William pulled Sampson to a stop as he looked down the road from the top of the hill they had just climbed. They always took to the tree lines instead of riding down the roads in plain sight when out scouting, and this time, like so many in the past, it had paid off.
"Do you think James can see them from the other side of the road?" Samuel asked as the two looked down at the two carriages coming from the seaport town.

"I'm sure he has, he always does," William answered. "They don't look too threatening anyway. Let's ride down and see who they are."

The lead carriage slowed as the driver came to a reluctant stop as the two riders approached, cutting it off on its way to Williamsburg. The driver of the heavily loaded carriage looked over his shoulder to the second carriage to see how it was fairing. To his relief, he saw it was fine and was making a turn back toward Yorktown, but then a third rider came down from a grove of trees with his pistol drawn making the carriage halt, to the drivers' obvious disappointment.

"What is this meaning of this?" the man asked, looking into Williams eyes with an angry expression, "Robbery?"

"No," answered Samuel who also had his pistol drawn, "That is unless you're carrying Cornwallis' payroll."

"Well if that's what you're looking for, you're going to be greatly disappointed." the driver answered. "I and my family are fleeing our home in Yorktown because of that bastard. The British fleet has sailed into the harbor this very morning and is landing on the docks from where I used to ship my tobacco as we speak."

"How many?" William asked as he put away his pistol.

"More than I cared to count," the driver announced, looking back to his other carriage. "I sure wasn't going to stay long enough to find out. Are you with Lafayette?"

"Yes, we are," William answered. "That's why we're here. We wanted to know if the British were in Yorktown or not."

"Well then, you have your answer. There are Lobsterbacks running up and down the streets of Yorktown today friend, Hessians too."

"Where are you heading Mr..?" asked William, leaving little doubt that he wanted to know what the drivers name was.

"Cox is my name. Charles Cox III to be exact and Richmond is our destination, after a stopover in Williamsburg tonight."

"Well in that case, Samuel here will give you and your family an escort into Williamsburg, Mr. Cox."

"Surely that will not be necessary," Cox replied.

"I'm sure that you're right, but it couldn't hurt to have a good shot along with you, now could it?"

Cox nodded his head as he slapped the horse's backs with the reins and drove off.

William turned to Samuel as the second carriage passed and said, "Ride along with them until you come up on Thomas and his men. Have Cox tell him what's going on in Yorktown. He seems to be telling the truth, but you can never tell these days. We sure don't want him going back to the port and telling the redcoats that we are going to be spying on them today." Samuel nodded and fell in behind the two carriages without a word. William and James took back to the trees on the west side of the road, continuing their ride to Yorktown. After a few miles the direction of the road turned alongside the York River. William could easily see why Cornwallis had selected this port for his naval base. The river was wide, very wide. It had the look and smell of the ocean he thought when he first saw it. The whole British fleet could drop anchor in this short, but wide river with ease.

The closer they rode to Yorktown, the more refugees they met fleeing the occupied village, convincing the two that Cox was indeed telling the truth about the landing. There was no doubt about it now; Cornwallis was staying in the South. To make matters worse, the land was becoming swampier the further they rode, giving them little choice but to travel on the road in certain stretches, making their approach more dangerous. They stayed to the edge of the road at all times, keeping a sharp eye in the distance for the enemy, as well as scouting for the best escape route if it was needed. Sporadic gunfire could be heard ahead giving the two men pause as to whether or not to go on. As William looked back toward Williamsburg, he knew the decision was no longer his. Samuel and Thomas were riding up on them from the rear.

"Where are the rest of your men?" William asked as the four rode off the road into a small grove of trees.

"Heading back to the old Capitol," Thomas answered, unbuttoning the coat of his uniform. "We met a company of local militia retreating from Yorktown. They had taken the Hampton road out of town and cut across the countryside to make their escape. So, I sent the rest of my boys back with them." He tucked his coat into his saddlebag and said, "Their captain implied that would be our best route to take as well if we decide to go on in. What do you think?"

"You're in command," William answered.

"Maybe so," Thomas replied, "but our mission is complete. We know for a fact that the British are in Yorktown. We can turn back and report what we heard and saw today. The militia will verify our report."

"Then why have you taken off your coat?" William asked as he pointed to Thomas' saddlebag.

"Because when I'm riding over to the other side of town, I'll blend in with everyone else a whole lot better if I'm not in uniform," Thomas answered. "I'm going on in to get a better look for myself, but I won't make any of you go if you don't want to."

"I always wanted to visit Yorktown," James quipped looking at William with that devilish smile of his.

"Isn't it a hanging offence to be caught without your uniform" Asked William.

"Only if they catch me, besides after all, I'm still in uniform from the waist down."

"All right then" William said. "Let's go see it."

The four raced across country taking the route the captain of the militia had suggested, leaving the Williamsburg road behind. After crossing a small creek and cutting through an unharvested wheat field they crossed the road that led to Hampton and passed through a cotton field, continuing on until they reached the high bluff that stood next to the York river less than a half mile from the tobacco port. No one spoke as they listened to the sound of bagpipes and drums coming from the seaport. They quickly made their way to the edge of town and there looking down its Main Streets they it was all but deserted. They continued on until they reached Read Street that led to the docks. The wind was blowing in William's face as he looked across the harbor. He quickly counted six British ships in the blue waterway between Yorktown and Gloucester Point. The wharf on Water Street and all along the waterfront was full of British infantry. To elude capture Thomas quickly led them into the yard of the Dudley Digges house. The British appeared to be waiting for the rest of the army to unload before they entered the town. For now, there were only a few who had made their way up the bluff and into town.

"Damn Samuel, they do look like lobsters running across the beach," William chuckled, remembering what Cox had said earlier in the day. How many do you figure are down there Thomas?"

"Two thousand or so redcoats," Thomas answered and no telling how many more are still inside those ships waiting to put ashore. I'm glad I'm not stuck in one of those rocking hulls; I'll bet half of them are sea sick and the other half are holding their noses from the stench of it all down there. You know it's hot as hell inside with this August heat beating down on those ships."

"Who is that way down the beach there?" Samuel asked, pointing further down the coastline.

"German Hessians," Thomas answered. "It's hard to be sure from here, but by the look of their shorter rifles they are Jaegers. They are supposed to be the best of all the   Hessians; elite woodsmen and marksmen. What do you think, maybe a thousand of them?"

"They are deploying troops on the other side of the river at Gloucester Point as well," James said, pointing to a ship dropping anchor on the far shoreline.

William let out a low whistle. "Damnation. They're rolling out artillery from that last ship. Lafayette sure doesn't have enough men to stop this juggernaut of an army. Will this war never end?"

"I was of the same mind," James said as he shook his head in disgust. "And what have we not seen yet horses that's what. That means that either Tarleton is riding his horses here overland or that there is a second fleet on its way that hasn't arrived yet. Either way, it's not good. Look. There goes the Union Jack up over the courthouse. It didn't take them long to get that rag up."

"No, it never does. I bet those damn Carolina Tories ran her up that pole. They're always with Cornwallis' army." Thomas said. "If not, they're close by. You can bet on it. There is everything down there but an Indian."

"Yeah, I know," William said as the group turned away. "And that's one bunch I was hoping would be here. Well at any rate, we've seen enough. Wouldn't you say brother?"

"Oh Yeah," Thomas replied. "Let's go spread the word."

Chapter 149
The Old Statesman

George Wythe was one of the leading citizens of Williamsburg, as well as the whole of Virginia. He was the epitome of a fine southern gentleman, having descended from a long line of distinguished public servants. Wythe had held a seat in the House of Burgesses as long as anyone could remember. This could have corrupted a person of lesser virtue, but not George Wythe. He had worked hard his entire life and had won the respect of most everyone he met. As a young man, he had attended William and Mary's grammar school. His mother had taught him Latin and Greek and he had read the Law under his uncle Stephen Dewey in Petersburg. Soon after he completed his education, he became a licensed attorney, living in the colonial Capitol with a very successful practice. His real passion in life was that of educator. During the war, he had been appointed to the newly created chair of law at his alma mater. He had taken several young men under his wing over the years, making some his private students. Thomas Jefferson, James Monroe and Henry Clay were among those he tutored. Any young man would give his weight in gold to be a Wythe protégé. The Law had paved his way to great heights, like those of his ancestors before him and by 1768 he was Mayor of his beloved Williamsburg. Men such as George Washington, Peyton Randolph and Patrick Henry were happy to be among his peers. Wythe had always considered himself a loyal Englishman, but when the winds of war began to blow, he found he could no longer stand with the King, and by 1776 his name could be seen upon the Declaration of Independence as one of the signers from the Virginia delegation. So, as William's spying party rode into Williamsburg on their return from Yorktown a little before dark, he was shocked to see none other than George Wythe standing at the head of Duke of Gloucester Street in front of the college, waving down their party.

"What may I have the honor of doing for you this evening, Mr. Wythe?" Thomas asked as he pulled to a halt and patted his horse's neck.

"I would very much appreciate it if you would lend me the use of some of your men for the night, Sergeant," the balding statesman requested. "If you would be so inclined as to indulge the wishes of an old man that is; you see, I have just arrived and have not yet been present at my home. Only the Almighty knows what conundrum awaits me there upon my return."

"If it were up to me Sir, I would send my whole company with you, but I am afraid that the information I carry is far too important to do so. However, you may have the use of two of my men. There are none better. William, you and Samuel see to Mr. Withy's needs tonight. James and I will ride on to the Marquise's camp and give our report. But on the morrow you two are to rejoin us in camp."

"I am in your debt, Sergeant," Wythe replied, stepping away from the horses and out of the road. "Have a safe ride gentleman."

Thomas tipped his hat and rode out of town without another word, quickly disappearing into the countryside as William and Samuel dismounted for their horses.

"How far is your home Sir?" William asked as he pulled his rifle from Sampson's saddle.
"Not far lad, it is on the Palace Green, just down from Bruton Church."

William shook his head as if he understood, but was reluctant to admit to Mr. Wythe that he had no idea where that was. He let out a long sigh as he looked to Wythe and said, "Well Sir, I'm afraid you will have to show me the way for I have never had the opportunity to visit your township until tonight."

"In that case, I'll give you the tour as we go along," Wythe answered as he turned and began his walk through the tree shadowed streets. "Duke of Gloucester Street here is one mile long with the Capital at the far end and the College behind us as you can see. It is ninety-nine feet across, which I believe is its greatest aspect. It gives room for all these maples in addition to all our commerce. We have approximately three hundred houses in our township, at last count, but that was before the British took control back in June and before my departure. I pray they did not do too much damage while they were here, although I can see they have broken some windows in a few of the shops and left refuse strewn everywhere. I hope that is the worst of their damage."

"So, you evacuated then." William asked as the two men walked side by side down the street followed by Samuel leading the horses.

"I felt I had little choice in the matter. Clinton has always said if he caught any of the signers of the Declaration, he would put us on the first ship sailing to England. Being tried for treason is something I would not relish. You know what happened to William Wallace."

"Once again, Sir I show my ignorance," William answered.

"Then you will have to read up on him someday. You can read, can't you?"

"Yes Sir, that I can," William answered proudly.

"Well then, my friend that will cure all of your problems caused by ignorance in the future. If a man is able to read, he can overcome ignorance with a few books. Stupidity on the other hand can never be conquered."

"Well put, Sir," William replied as he glanced up at the tall steeple of a church.

"Tell me Mr. Wythe, how did it make you feel to write your name on a document that basically told the King of England that he had lost all control of his thirteen colonies?"

"Terrifying," Wythe chuckled. But then he stopped and looked into William's eyes and said, "But what made cold chills run up my spine, was the fact that one of my boys had written that wonderfully elegant Declaration. Have you read it?"

"Yes sir, I have. Governor Jefferson made is all proud. His pen had as much to do with the rebellion as those shots fired in Lexington, I believe."

"You're a smart lad. What's your name?"

"William Tipton."

By now they had reached the brick wall that ran around the grounds of the churchyard. "Do you attend services here Mr. Wythe?"

"Always," was the reply. "I never miss a Sunday when I am home. I was appointed vestryman back in sixty-nine"

"It is quite impressive," William said stopping at the wrought iron gate and gazing inside the grounds.

"Governor Fauquier thought as much. He was buried inside," Wythe replied as he came to a stop beside William at the end of the church wall "not in the churchyard mind you, but in the church itself. He is interred right under the flooring.

Well gentlemen, this is the Palace Green. My home is just around the corner." Wythe pulled a small pistol from inside his vest, and as he looked down to examining his flint he explained, "I was on the Committee of Safety back in the sixties. They presented this pistol to me then. I've never had the opportunity to fire it in anger, and I really am not looking forward to doing so tonight."

"I don't believe you will tonight either," William said, as he looked down the long row of catalpa trees that lined the street that led to the Governors Palace. We have not heard of any redcoats still hanging around Williamsburg. But then, you are not the average citizen either. Any redcoat who could capture you would have quite a feather in his hat. Do you have anyone in the house?"

"Not a soul," Wythe answered. "It's locked up. At least it was on my departure, but I'm sure the British have forced open the door while they occupied the town."

"Well, let's go and see," William suggested, taking his first steps down the green. Samuel having not added one word to the conversation since Wythe had pulled them aside on the road put a hand on the old statesman shoulder and said, "Stay behind us Sir. This is what we do well. If anyone is inside, we'll find them." Within moments the three were standing in front of Wythe's impressive two-story brick home. William put his hand on the black front door of the house and with one light push; it swung open, confirming Wythe's suspicions that his home had been breached. William stepped inside and put his back against the staircase balustrade that came down from the second floor, as Samuel stepped in the empty dining room to the right. Seeing that all was clear in Samuel's room, William stepped inside the study beside the staircase where he found several overturned chairs and a drop leaf table that lay on its side, but nothing else seemed to be damaged, other than a few books thrown about the floor. Two more rooms on the lower floor were quickly searched but no one was found. Wythe stepped inside his home and stood looking at the cherry chair that was sitting in his hall. "That chair is from Thomas Everard's house across the green. Hell, I have a few chairs missing that should be here beside the door. Those arrogant British officers have been staying in our homes and have been moving furniture from one house to the other by the looks of it."

As he listened to Mr. Wythe complain about the condition of the lower floor, William and Samuel made their way up the staircase to the second floor and looked through all the upper rooms. Here too, they found no one about.

"Mr. Wythe, all is clear up here as well," William said as he looked into the most beautiful bedroom he had ever seen. "Look Samuel, red wallpaper. I have heard of it, but this is the first time I ever saw any."

Samuel just smiled, shaking his head as he went back down the stairs, "Hell, I never even heard of such a thing. I grew up on dirt floors you know."

Wythe had his back to his two guests, unlocking his back door as they reached the bottom of the stairs. "Say it's all clear up above?" he asked, turning the key in the brass lock.

"Yes Sir," Samuel replied.

As Wythe opened the door, he looked back over his shoulder and said, "Let's have a quick look at the grounds before it's completely dark. They're not real elaborate nothing like the ones over at the palace." He stepped out on a brick walkway that led through his once well-maintained lawn that had been sorely neglected in his absence. His objective was the little school house just twenty feet away. "They spared my door over here," he said as he looked down at the undisturbed lock. "No need going inside tonight," he told his escorts. Without another word he walked past the two and led them to his stables and a series of other outbuildings around the grand estate. Again, no one was found on the property. He completed his circuit and returned to the front of his home by going through a small wooden gate that led back out to the green. When he arrived at his front stoop, he reached into his vest and pulled out a purse.

"Tell me, where are you two sleeping tonight?"

"I haven't any idea," William answered. "We usually sleep in our tent, but it's pitched back at Lafayette's camp. We'll just have to rough it tonight."

"Nonsense," Wythe replied as he pulled a few coins from his purse and put them in William's hand. "Put your horses in my stable although I am afraid there may be no feed there, you may draw water from my well. After your animals have been attended to, enquire at Raleigh Tavern. I'm sure they will have accommodations for the night. I will most likely be away in the morning, so until we meet again, I wish you well." With that, Wythe stepped inside his threshold and shut his door.

William turned to Samuel with a smile and said, "Let's go get the horses."

The two of them walked out into the center of the Palace green and looked at the huge Governor's Palace as the sun was setting behind its tall cupola, making quite a backdrop for the two to gaze upon. William looked back to Wythe's home and said, "You know Samuel, there have been many English born governors that have ruled over us from that palace, like Dunmore and Botetourt, but I would dare say that none of them were of the quality of the man we just met."

"I wouldn't care to debate that with you," Samuel replied. "I doubt if they ever paid for a roof to be placed over their guard's heads. Not with their own coin anyway. Come on let's see to the horses and find this Raleigh Tavern before all the beds is taken. I don't want to sleep on the floor"

Chapter 150
Clover and Cheese

It had been over a week since Cornwallis' army had landed at Yorktown. The British occupation of the small town had been completed without firing a single shot. Lafayette was under the impression that Cornwallis would soon march North with his army into Williamsburg. He had never wasted time in the past. Wherever he had been deployed while in the south, he soon took to the field on the heels of whatever army was close to hand. General Gates had been the only American crazy enough to attack his army. Green had divided his troops in the Carolinas forcing Cornwallis to do the same, fighting only on ground he found favorable. Green had also won the race to the Dan, putting its wide waters between him and Cornwallis when retreat was needed. Lafayette had done the same earlier in the summer avoiding all major engagements. But September and October were still to come, leaving Cornwallis plenty of time to make war this fall.

With Lafayette needing to know when the British were planning to make their move, he kept his spies and scouting parties between Williamsburg and Yorktown regularly. It kept William, James and Samuel in the saddle, constantly riding back and forth between the American camps and the British held seaport. Although they were becoming saddle weary, they had grown to know the lay of the land between the two armies very well. Dirt paths used by local planters to move their crops and cattle were now familiar territory. They knew where all the water courses lay, and how to avoid the swamps. These were definitely worth noting, because on two different occasions they had seen deer struggling to escape the muck after wondering too far into the soggy land. They sunk into the boggy surface, stopping only when their bellies touched the mud below. William was sure that more than one of the animals had died in the swamps. If he was ever chased into one, Sampson would get bogged down and William would become easy pickings.

Luckily, Cornwallis' army had shown little initiative since their arrival, so pursuit was not something the spies had encountered. A small number of earthworks had been erected, but they were nothing formidable in William's eyes, nothing like the great walls around Fort Pitt. But all that could change today, for spies had sent in word that Banastre Tarleton's dragoons had crossed Hampton Roads by boat just yesterday, making the horses swim to shore beside the boats. Raiding and burning would slow down Tarleton's progress, but no more than a day or two, depending on how destructive he was feeling. On his return there would be no more unchallenged rides through the countryside. Cornwallis would soon have horses to give chase to anyone who came too close to his lines.

William pulled Sampson to a stop as he rode toward the York River. He spun around and looked back down the path to where James and Samuel had stopped following, for some reason. They had let their horses wander into a field. Everything seemed to be in order, neither one had pulled their weapon, or even dismounted. No shots had been fired; they were just sitting on the horses talking to one another when Samuel waved William to come join them.

As Sampson trotted back, William spotted the cause of the delay. The horses were grazing on a patch of red clover. William dismounted and dropped Sampson's reins, walked under an oak to get out of the sun as Sampson munched into the clover, filling his empty stomach.

"I guess we better let them graze some while we still can," James said as he stepped under the tree with William. "Once Tarleton's men arrive, they'll be out looking for places like this one too."

"Yeah," William replied pulling a half pound of cheese from his waist bag. "Thomas says Light Horse Harry is coming to call on us with all his horses as well. Their animals will need to be fed too. Their coming should get us back in camp and off horseback when they get here. A rest would be more than welcome about now."

James shook his head in agreement, as he reached out and took a slice of cheese from William's hand. He bit into his portion as he looked down at William's knife that had just cut the slice. Reaching up, he pulled a small hair from his mouth that had undoubtedly come from William's blade.

"Damn, William. Do you ever clean that knife of yours after you clean an animal?"

"I do," William smiled "Every time. I give it a quick wipe on my pants leg. Not just one, but both side mind you," he laughed.

"What about you Samuel? Want some hair on your cheese," William asked.

"Sure, I do. It gives it flavor in my humble opinion."

"You would say that," James replied as he stood up and looked down the path at a wagon that was approaching, loaded down with furniture. The slave who was driving looked at his master who was sitting beside him, holding a musket across his lap. The owner told him to stop as the three men stepped in front of the wagon holding their rifles in full view.

"Evacuating?" William asked.

"Yes, That I am," replied the slave owner. "Took my family out when they sailed passed my home last week. I decided to come back to retrieve some of my belongings when I got word that son of a bitch Tarleton was riding this way. He's only seven miles away at the mouth of the river. I've already lost most of my slaves to the British as it is can't afford to lose much more. Sam here is about the last slave I have left," he said as he glanced at the grazing horses. "You all need some horse and mule feed?"
"Yes sir, we sure do," answered Samuel. "My horse has lost weight since we been here."

"Well, in that case, mount up and keep on going toward the river about two miles. I have a barn with about a hundred bushels of grain stored away inside. I would rather let the militia have it than the British. They'll get their dirty hands on it for sure if you don't get there first."

"Then this is your land then?" James asked as he picked up the reins of his horse.
"Yes, this is my plantation alright. It goes all the way to the river. My home is about a thousand feet from the bank. Well, come on Sam, let's get moving." As Sam popped the reins across the horses backs the planter called out, "My name is Augustine Moore. Tell Major Carter Page that I was the one who gave it to you. He's Lafayette's aide-de-camp, if you don't know and a friend of mine. Maybe he can get me a payment for the grain someday. There should be a wagon in the barn if you need it."

James looked at William with a big grin and jumped on his mount and took off with the others close behind. Within a few turns in the path they quickly reached the barn is question. All three dismounted and approached the barn cautiously, taking nothing for granted. As Samuel raised the latch on the big wooden door and swung it open, William and James stepped inside as four slaves ran out the back door of the barn.

"Stop or we'll shoot," threatened James as he reached the far end of the barn. Then, shaking his head, he lowered his rifle watching as the runaways disappeared into Yorktown Creek running toward the British lines.

"There goes the last of Moore's slaves," laughed James as he turned back into the barn. "Cornwallis will have them shoveling dirt on their defenses before sundown, I'll wager."

"You're probably right," William answered as he pulled an old bolt of cloth from over the top of several bags of feed, sitting in the corner of the barn. "Maybe Samuel will take you up on that bet, but I won't."

"Me neither," Samuel said as he swung one of the bags into the wagon. "Come on, let's get this thing loaded and out of here before Tarleton gets here. I sure as hell don't want to load all of this stuff up only to have to abandon it on the road somewhere to those green coated devils."

"I hope your right about not abandoning the wagon, because your horse is going to be the one pulling it," James laughed as he picked up his first bag. "It would be a long walk back to camp."

"I'll cut his reins and ride bareback before I let that happen." Samuel answered. "I'm not losing Chance, even if I did pay for him with that dragoon's coin."

Chapter 151
Different Flags

Yesterday had been Wednesday, August 29th and it had been quite a day in General Lafayette's camp. William had spent most of it sitting outside his tent under a large coffee tree. He had cleaned his rifle soon after eating a cold biscuit for breakfast and afterwards had led Sampson to a nearby creek. He splashed several buckets of water over the horse's back. As far as William was concerned, Sampson was the finest animal in camp and William always enjoyed grooming the big Frisian. The afternoon had been spent pinning a letter to Elizabeth. Thomas had somehow managed to get his hands on some paper and had generously let his brother have a few sheets. He spoke of his rides through the countryside, his impressions of Williamsburg and the inner dealings of camp life. But the majority of his letter was about how much he missed and loved his wife and children and his future plans for their life in Kentucky.

Samuel complaining of hearing his stomach growling all the time had disappeared soon after awakening. By mid-afternoon he rode back into camp after purchasing two chickens from a nearby farmer, thus supplying the best meal the three had eaten since their arrival. They were sitting around the tent sucking on the bones, since no one wanted to waste the smallest morsel that might still cling there, when in the distance from the continental side of camp a loud cheer was heard. Another horse race, William imagined. Maybe some of Lee's men might have enough courage to race Sampson someday he thought, for none of the militia's cavalry would. Not even the officers with their fine mounts would take the chance of losing to Sampson. James had stood up from his spot under the tree and looked to the continentals who were moving about in small groups, then would breakup only to reform another parlay with new people. Each time they dispersed, cheers could be heard. William realized something big must have happened. He didn't have to wait long to find out what all the ruckus was about because he could see the smiling face of Captain Babb heading his way from the other side of camp.

"What's all the celebrating about Captain?" James had asked. "Has Washington taken New York, or maybe someone has captured that turncoat Arnold."

"No, my boy, none of those, but early this morning three ships sailed into the mouth of the York River."

"Why cheer about the British getting re-supplied when we're running out of everything," Samuel asked, casting his bone aside.

"Nothing," answered Captain Babb. "That would only make our situation here worse. You see, the flag flying atop those three masts is French, boy, not the Union Jack. Cornwallis is bottled up good now. If we can only get enough men in time, we can lay siege on the port and capture the largest army anybody has through this whole long war."

So, now that the sun had come up, William and his friends were once again riding with Thomas to Yorktown to see this miracle. If Cornwallis was in trouble, he wanted to be there and see it for himself. Rumors had been running rampant about what was going to happen next. The biggest concern was another landing by the Kings Navy somewhere on the James River with troops from New York or possibly even from England. That would crush Lafayette's army, trapping it between them and Cornwallis. This seemed to be the greatest threat in William's mind. Some of the rumors were completely absurd; one claimed all the western Indian tribes were combining to attack in the next few days. William could not remember any other time when so many rumors had been flying around camp.

This morning, however, Thomas had overheard Lafayette's aide-de-camp, Major Page talking with some fellow officers that General Washington was marching south with the majority of his northern army. While this was good news, it meant he was weeks away and Lafayette's army would have to hold fast until his arrival. They prayed they could hold the line until then, and now that William and his party had arrived on the outskirts of Yorktown, he would soon see what the situation really was.

"Tarleton's horse must be in the town. I don't see any horses out in the fields," James remarked as the group arrived at a plantation just outside of town. "Hell, he may have already left. But I can't believe it will be that easy."

"Good heavens," said Captain Babb who had decided to come along on this mission as he pointed down at the British lines, "Cornwallis is not wasting any time now, my lads. Look at those poor slaves down there."

William, who was the last of the group to make his way out of the trees to see what was happening, could hardly believe his eyes. Hundreds of runaway slaves like those of Augustine Moore who had been hoping that the British would free them after the war were toiling away on the British earthworks. But they were not alone. Hessians and British infantry were making dirt fly as well. What had been an unimpressive defensive position was becoming more formidable by the hour. A line of redoubts would soon run from the end of Yorktown Creek to the river. This would put two defensive lines between the town and Wormley Pond. Cornwallis was battening down. The small British fleet that was still docked along the wharf as if all was well made William uneasy. It was if they knew something that Lafayette didn't.

"" Where is the French fleet?" Samuel asked as he looked down river. "I don't see diddly squat. Have they already sailed away?"

Thomas stood up and spat out the blade of grass he was holding between his teeth and said as he mounted his horse, "Come on, let's ride upriver and see where they are. If they are gone, nothing good will come of this." Their ride was short lived, for upriver a few miles sat the French fleet, right in the middle of the river. Their sails were down and they rode at anchor, but no one was on deck.

"Hell, have they surrendered?" asked Samuel. "All I see is a white flag flying over the mast, other than those long red pennants waving in the wind at the rear."

"No," Captain Babb said with a grin. "That's the French navel flag. It's as white as snow lad. Don't worry." At that moment, coming from one of the ships, a bell could be heard ringing out across the water and the decks were suddenly alive with activity.

"See there boy, they're not surrendering!" They have Cornwallis bottled up for sure just like I hoped. If Washington gets here in time, we may just have the son of a bitch. Can you imagine? Cornwallis is within our grasp."

"But it won't be easy." William answered. "They still have cannon and we don't, at least not enough to hurt them. I would say that for now, Cornwallis still has the upper hand."

"True enough, but in a few days that may not be the case, my boy. Only time will tell."

Chapter 152
Nobility

William blew out a long breath as he approached Lafayette's huge tent. It would be his first time inside the young Frenchman's headquarters and he was a little edgy. This was not an ordinary officer he was about to meet. Few others had been able to win over General Washington's trust in so short a time, but this young soldier of fortune had done just that. The Marquis wanted to have a one on one conversation with one of his scouts. Lieutenant Colonel Allison had again sent William to Yorktown to spy on the redcoats today and now instead of reporting to Allison, he would be speaking with the General. A tall sentry, every inch of six foot three and wearing a stern look, stepped in William's path. Quickly realizing his mistake William stopped and handed his written orders over to this giant of a soldier who read them quickly and handed them back to William. He stepped back into position, without a word staring straight ahead. William stood at the entrance for a moment more before the sentry motioned him inside with an ever so slight nod of his head.

The tent had only three men inside. One was sitting behind a small roll top desk quill in hand, writing away, with a stack of papers by his side. He never raised his head from his work as William entered, but the second one did. He was setting a large table with the finest silver that William had ever seen. No doubt Lafayette would be hosting the rest of his officers tonight. The table was set for ten. And there, sitting behind a grand cherry desk, in a red velvet high back chair sat Lafayette, dressed in the finest uniform in the southern army. He had a white ruffled blouse under his double-breasted coat, which was trimmed in gold embroidery. His red hairline rose high on his forehead, promising that he would one day soon be bald. That is, if he lived long enough. He had long ago made his reputation as being one who would not balk when the cannons or muskets were being fired. He had been wounded at Brandywine in the heat of battle. His mettle had been well tested in the forges of this war and he had yet to melt. He was foreign by birth, but his love for this country was that of a patriot. He was holding a crystal goblet, filled with red wine in one hand while reading a dispatch that had arrived from General Washington's courier in the other. He took the last sip from his drink and sat the empty goblet on the desktop as William gave him his best salute.

"So, monsieur, you are one of General Morgan's men?" he asked as he ran his index finger down his long, pointed nose. He rested his head in the palm of his hand, bracing his elbow on the armrest of his chair, as he waited for William's reply. It had been rumored that he was ill with fever and William could certainly believe it to be true, by the dark circles under the Marquise's eyes.

"Yes sir, I came in camp under his command." William answered.

Lafayette nodded his head and stood up and slowly walked out from behind his desk and said, "Tell me. What did you see of our enemy today?"

"They have unloaded several cannons from the ships along the wharf today and have placed them inside the earthworks above the town. A few small rowboats rowed out toward the ocean, past your countrymen's ships. The gunners aboard fired at them Sir, but I am afraid the boats were just too fast for them to hit with cannon. Whoever was inside the boats were smart enough to stay out of gunshot range? So, they have gotten word out today that the French fleet is here I am afraid."

"Oui, that is of no Consequence," the young Frenchman replied, picking up his white powdered wig from its stand on a corner table that sat beside his bed. "They are not the first to slip past, but I do find it interesting that Lord Cornwallis has pulled his cannon from his ships. How many would you say?"

"Six that I saw," William answered, "but they were already fast at work when I got into position to see what they were doing. Unfortunately, a few dragoons spotted me and I had to take flight. But I would say that their earthworks are about finished."
"How many horses did you see?"

"Not many, just the ones after me."

"And how did you lose them?" Lafayette asked as he turned to walk around his bed.
"My Frisian," William answered proudly, "and a few well aimed shots."

"Ah, so you are the one who has everyone in camp talking about that mount of yours." The Marquise put his wig on his head as he stood in front of the full body size looking glass. "Maybe after this war is over, we can have a little wager. You know I have a Frisian myself."

"Yes, Sir" William replied still standing at attention. "I would enjoy that very much indeed."

"Maybe not after I have lightened your purse strings," Lafayette responded looking at William though the mirror. Being satisfied with his wig the Frenchman turned to William and asked "Before you go, tell me why Morgan's men are performing so well, how may untrained men have acquired such skills?"

"Many of us have grown up on the frontier and have had a gun in our hand from the time we could walk. Others, like me and my friends have spent time in Indian Territory. I can tell you first hand that Kentucky is a proving ground for honing survival skills. I don't know if there is a single answer to your question Sir, maybe the best answer is that each of these men have a yearning for freedom deep down inside, that's a powerful weapon."

After listening to what William had said, Lafayette turned and sat behind his desk and with a nod of his neatly groomed head said, "Very well then, you are dismissed."

As William made his way back to his side of camp, a smile crossed his face as he thought how different Lafayette's tent had been from the cabins of Simon Girty or Simon Kenton. It had better furnishings than those two men would ever have in their homes after a lifetime of work. William's own station in life was not that far from the two Simons, but he was a world apart from that of the Frenchman he had just left. But this cause had brought William and Lafayette together, working for a common goal. If they could win this war, it would certainly change the world. Just imagine the horse of a French nobleman racing a small Virginia landowner's animal. The King of England would die of shock and maybe the one in France as well.

Chapter 153
For the Lack of Feathers

James dropped a few coins on one of the many tables inside the Apollo room of the Raleigh Tavern as he stood up from his meal. He wiped the corner of his mouth with the large napkin that was provided for every customer that ate at this once famous establishment. Cornwallis's troops had been hard on this Williamsburg landmark while occupying the town this summer. Holes had been left in the walls by angry boots, chair rails had been ripped from the walls and damaged furnishings were evident here, like in most of the other places of business in town. He had asked the barmaid why the owners had not repaired the damages and had laughed at her response.

"They're not going to fix anything until they are sure that Lafayette can hold the town first."

The tavern may have been a little rougher than normal, but the beef and cabbage was still cooked to perfection. The prices were a trifle high, James thought as he stepped out into the street, but food was getting scarce. Tarleton had stripped most of the plantations of everything they had and it was driving up the prices. This could be the last meal he would be able to pay for. Hopefully, the French could provide Lafayette with some assistance in feeding his troops. A massive landing had taken place near James Island, but the men disembarking form those transports were dressed in white, not red as everyone had feared a few days ago. Maybe this would be a turning point in this war for independence after all. He let his gaze travel down to the distant capital building where someone had run up the new American colors, but William was nowhere to be seen. He turned and began to make his way toward the Palace Green, maybe William was waiting for him down that way. Now that more residents were returning to town the streets were becoming much more crowded, nothing like it was ten days ago before the French dropped anchor. Everyone knew that Lafayette was marching his army into town today and no one wanted to miss seeing the young General who had become so popular since his arrival. Having been out on another scouting mission yesterday, he and William had decided to stay here in town and were waiting along with everyone else for the General to arrive.

James stopped his walk up the street and looked over at the now emptied brick Magazine and Guardhouse where the local militia's weapons and powder had been stored before the war. Back in Seventy-Five, three young men had been wounded there by Dunmore's troops possibly being the first to shed blood for the cause in the colony and bring her one step closer to revolution, but again William was nowhere about.

"Hey James, over here," William called from the top step of the county courthouse directly across the street. He was sitting on the steps under one of the four windows along the front of the building. James made his way over and sat down beside his friend, who as usual, was reading.

"You're going to burn a hole in the pages of that Bible someday if you keep on reading it at this pace."

William frowned as he shut the book and turned it over, handing it to James with the title facing up. "This isn't the Good Book."

"A History of Scotland," James read aloud before handing it back. "How did you come by this?"

"George Wythe, I suppose." William answered. "It was down in the bottom of one of my saddlebags. I just saw it this morning. He told me about a fellow named Wallace being captured by the English back a long time ago, and if he was ever taken by the British, they would most likely do to him what they did to Wallace. Samuel and I stabled our horses at his place that night. He must have put it in that night or the next morning, because Wallace is in this book. That's the only explanation I can come up with."

"Good Heavens William. That's a large sum of money in your hand there. Books don't come cheap my friend,"

"I know," William replied, standing up and tucking the book inside his waist bag. "At first I was nervous about having it. I sure don't want my hands and head stuck in a pillory like that poor fellow over there," he said pointing to a man locked between two wooden boards, exposed to pubic scorn, just a few feet away.

"I heard about him up at Raleigh's," James said as the two walked off the steps of the courthouse and headed in the other direction. "He's a Tory. They're going to tar and feather him sometime after Lafayette rides in this afternoon."

"Well, at any rate I walked down to the Wythe house this morning after I found it, but no one answered the door."

"I wouldn't worry about it much. With everything the redcoats looted, I'm sure no one is looking for that book right now. Besides, Wythe put the book in your bag as a gift I'd say. Whoa!" James exclaimed as four fast moving horses bolted off the street and down the green.

"That was Lafayette on that lead horse." William said as they stopped at the head of the green. Looks like he's going to make the Palace his headquarters, he sure didn't waste any time getting here."

"He'll have it in good order when Washington arrives," James replied. "Where else would he stay?"

"General Washington," William said, shaking his head. "At first I thought it was a bunch of idle talk about him marching south, but I guess it's true. They say he's already in Virginia with his army accompanied by a French one as well. We are in the right place and at the right time for sure James. History is going to be made right before our eyes, and soon."

"One way or the other, friend," James replied as the two once again began moving down the street. Let's pray we are on the side that wins it. Lafayette must have the troop camped out in back of the college. There's none in town."

"Yeah," William answered, "but what has me worried is where in the hell is the rest of the British Navy. You know they're not going to let the French stay at the mouth of the river for long without a fight. All of this could be for nothing if that blockade is busted up."

"Well, we'll have to leave that to Washington and the French Navy for now because I'm not about to row out to sea in a dugout canoe to keep the redcoats in the harbor. I mean, the two of us can't do it all you know." James said as he punched William's arm.

William cocked his head to one side as a smile crossed his face. "Once again James, you are right, but I believe it would be wise not to speak of it again. If someone overhears us, Allison just might put us in that canoe."

Suddenly, loud cheering could be heard coming up the street causing the two to stop with their joking. A young boy of about fourteen ran by. He stopped just long enough to yell back over his shoulder to a group of smaller boys. "Come on or you'll miss it if you don't hurry."

William's smile disappeared as he looked at James, realizing the condemned man was about to have the gristly sentence of tarring and feathering carried out. "I've already seen enough in this war to last me a lifetime. This is something I don't want to see."

"Me neither." James answered as another cheer went up, "But it's too late for that now. Here he comes on a rail. What a sight."

William looked down the street and saw the mob moving towards the college, being led by a lone drummer. The victim was sitting on a sharpened plank, obviously in agony. He had been stripped from the waist up and steaming hot tar had been poured over his head and shoulders, scalding his skin under the black tar. Some feathers had been thrown on him but not very many. It seemed hardly anyone wanted to waste a good pillow on him. He had a few stuck to his back and shoulders and a few were stuck to the side of his face. The man was screaming as the crowd bore him through the town.

Having seen enough, William and James stepped inside the gate of the Bruton Church to let the procession pass by on the other side of the wall. William looked at James and said, "I don't know what that man did to deserve that. It had to be pretty bad, looks as if everyone's anger is being set loose on this one Tory."

"Oh, he's getting his due," said an older woman standing next to the church's open door. "He's given the names of several families to the British, knowing full well that their husbands were away with the militia. If it was up to me I would have had him hung."

Chapter 154
Two for the Price of One

Samuel took off his hat as he sat on his mount and wiped the sweat from his forehead with his free hand. The calendar might say September 4th, but the temperature felt more like August 4th this afternoon. Fall had not fallen yet. He replaced his hat and tapped Chance's side with his foot. As the horse took its first steps into the field, Samuel nodded at the militiaman standing in the picket line just outside of Williamsburg. Today was his turn to roam the countryside above Yorktown. William and James had ridden yesterday and were probably sitting back at camp, or if they were lucky, they could be in Williamsburg. He hoped this would be the last time he would have to do this without his friends. Somehow, they had gotten on different rosters this week. The men he was riding with now seemed capable of handling whatever situation that might arise, but it wasn't like having William and James riding by his side. After a few hundred feet the lead rider picked up the pace and put the horses to a swift trot. The wind felt cool on Samuel's face as they make their way toward the port. Things had been quiet the past few days. Tarleton's horse had been absent lately and Samuel hoped they would be today too. Maybe the French landing on the James River would keep Tarleton occupied for another day.

As he galloped along, he could tell his saddle was too loose, more evidence that Chance was losing weight. The girth needed to be tightened, so Samuel pulled to a stop and the two rode under the high branches of an old oak tree. Jumping off, he bent and unfastened the buckle and pulled the strap into the next hole and quickly remounted and rode after the rest of his party, loosing little ground in the process. But it was enough for the riders to have disappeared over a small hill and out of sight. It was nothing to worry about; he could catch up in a few minutes. As he reached the top of the hill, his gaze fell upon the last horse up ahead, only a few hundred feet away as shots rang out from a nearby tree line. The lead rider had been hit in the shoulder, but had managed to stay in the saddle, but the man riding next to him had been killed in the volley and lay on the ground beside his horse. The horse in the rear, being the closest to Samuel had also been killed, but its rider appeared to be unharmed, if somewhat dazed, from his fall to the ground. Samuel rode down to the fallen man and allowed him enough time to leap on behind him as a group of dragoons burst from the trees in a full charge with sabers drawn.

Samuel quickly turned his double loaded mount and headed back in the direction he had just come, but now that his horse was carrying the extra weight, he was quickly overtaken by his comrades who had only one man on their horses.

"Ride up next to that bay, and I'll jump," Samuel heard his passenger say, as he pointed to an unmounted horse that had lost its rider and was running along with the retreating scouts, determined to stay up with the rest.

Banastre Tarleton pulled one of his pistols from his horse's saddle and said under his breath, "Two for the price of one". Then bringing his weapon to bear on the two fleeing militiamen riding double on the crest of the hill, he pulled back the hammer with his thumb and watched in amazement as the rear rider leaped from one horse to another in full gallop, nearly falling off his new mount. As he regained his balance, Tarleton pulled the trigger adding another name to the growing list of men he would kill in this war.

Samuel heard the shot and saw the man he had just saved tumble from his horse, from the corner of his eye. Knowing he was next, he forced his horse to jump a split rail fence running beside the road, where he quickly disappeared into a field of tall cornstalks. Once out of sight he stopped his horse, pulled his rifle, and waited to see if he was still being pursued.

Tarleton and his men continued on their way to Williamsburg, having overrun the picket line just south of the college. The militia had little choice in the matter. They were outnumbered and had little chance of turning the charging dragoons. After a few ineffective shots, they just melted away, abandoning the southern end of town to Tarleton, who had no Idea that his adversary, Lafayette was on the Palace Green just down the street with only a small guard.

Hearing the shots outside of town, William and James ran down the rapidly emptying street to the stable owned by Charles Taliaferro, whose brewery and warehouse had been completely ransacked by Cornwallis's men back in the summer. Having lost his love for the British, he was allowing anyone in Lafayette's army access to his stable in the rear of his shop. As James and one of Taliaferro's slaves saddled the horses, William took his position by the stable's open door and watched Tarleton's now familiar green coated men. They were riding past the college and after learning from one of the few loyalists still in town that Lafayette's army was pitching camp a mile to the west, headed back for Yorktown to William's disappointment. If Tarleton had rode another twenty feet, he would had been in William's waiting sights.

Tarleton unaware of his escape was sure that with the intelligence that he had just gathered, Cornwallis would make a full-fledged attack on this town come morning. They would crush Lafayette's army before the French and Washington's troops could arrive. Lafayette's defeat would be nice, but would be secondary to the main objection of the assault, that being Lord Cornwallis's way out of Yorktown.

Chapter 155
Deserters

Late yesterday afternoon, a few hours after Tarleton had returned to Yorktown, General Anthony Wayne's army had marched into Williamsburg. Wayne's division was the first to reinforce the Marquis army since it had arrived at the old capital and had taken up a defensive position at the college. They were welcomed as saviors by the townspeople. Tarleton's small raid had put the fear of war into their hearts once again. The additional fire power had settled nerves and things were beginning calm down. A French reinforcement was expected to arrive soon, and if this new scouting mission William was on went well, maybe the proprietors of Raleigh Tavern could start the needed repairs.

At sunup this morning everyone was expecting the cadence of British drums or the sound of bagpipes to be heard announcing Cornwallis' advance, but as the sun rose higher in the sky and nothing was heard, Lafayette ordered a reconnaissance mission. The party of fifteen included both Tipton brothers, James and Samuel. They were under the command of Lieutenant Colonel Allison. Someone must have remembered how well the Petersburg mission had gone, William thought. Only two men from that day's heady work were absent here today. They had been replaced by two men from General Wayne's army who needed to learn the area. The distance from Yorktown to Williamsburg is twelve miles and the first six were quickly covered, but the party slowed at yesterday's ambush site, where Samuel had made his escape thru the cornfield. Two men had lost their lives here and needed to be attended to. They had been stripped of their weapons, boots, and all their valuables during the night, but at least no animals had disturbed them in that time. Both bodies had been laid over a horse's back and taken back to Williamsburg for burial by a lone scout while the others continued. Once again, William found himself tending to the dead. It felt almost normal. Nothing seemed to bother him anymore when it came to this grizzly work. This war was making him hard, he thought as he remounted Sampson's back.

A short ride later the party found themselves a short distance from Yorktown Creek. The British would no doubt have a formidable hold on the bridge that spanned its waters. Bearing that in mind the scouts took to the fields that surrounded the port. As they were making their way to the Hampton Road they were spotted by one of the newly finished redoubts on the far side of the creek. The British gunner raised the elevation of his mortar two degrees before firing his shell. William could hear the whistling sound of the projectile as it cut through the air after hearing the mortar's report. But the round was long as it flew over their heads, slamming into a wooded area two hundred feet away. Sampson was taken by surprise by the sound of the impact and the jarring of the ground and jumped wildly at its detonation. William managed to stay in the saddle, but just barely. Like the rest of his party, he took to the trees for cover after regaining control of his horse. Laughter could be heard coming from the redoubt but it stopped soon after Samuel yelled at the top of his lungs. "Go ahead and laugh it up, but all you did was waste a good round on a cherry tree. That's one less you'll have to fire at General Washington when he gets here, you pricks."

William pulled his long rifle from his saddle as he heard the British reply, "Soiled your britches, did you Yank?" followed by another round of English cheers. As he made his way to the edge of the tree line to join James, he checked his powder. "I'll take the one on the right," William announced as he pulled back the hammer of his rifle.

"Uh huh," James answered as he raised his rifle on the other side of the tree that William was using as a prop to steady his aim. "Let's hold off until two show themselves at the same time. They won't be dumb enough to expose themselves again after we fire."

"Hell, that's too far away," remarked one of the New York Continentals who had just arrived with Wayne the day before. "They're just wasting good powder themselves."

Allison looked at the man and shook his head with a cool expression and said, "Not these two."

"This will be the first time I ever shot at a blue coat," James said, watching the blue coated British artillerymen moving around on the redoubt. "There's two for the picking William."

Across the open field the eyes of a gunner in the 4th battalion of the Royal Artillery narrowed as he saw white smoke floating up in the woods. As he turned to duck down a ball ripped into his side, knocking him back over the butt of the mortar, covering its touch hole with his body. The rest of the mortar crew fell to the ground in an effort to get out of the line of fire. All but their commander who leaned over into the earthworks corner make of gabions, all stiff and erect. He stood there a few seconds before slumping to the ground with a small hole in his cheek. The ball never exited the back of his skull, it just rolled around inside a few times being almost spent.

"That will keep their heads down and their mouths shut the rest of the day," William said as he turned back to his horse. He walked up to Sampson and quickly reloaded his rifle and slid it back inside its carrier. There's another one for you Joshua, he thought to himself, not an Indian, but he wore a royal badge all the same.

Thomas looked at Allison with a proud grin on his face and said, "He's been making shots like that since he was a boy back home in Maryland. He's a natural born shot."

"That they both are," Allison replied, glancing at James. "Well, it looks like they're not attacking today. Sergeant, you take three men and ride back toward Williamsburg and inform them of the situation here, but don't take your brother or Tate. I may need them yet."

Thomas saluted, called out the names of the three men that would accompany him back to the American lines and mounted his horse. Before riding away, he trotted his mount over to William and looking down from his saddle said, "You always got the biggest bird back home, I guess some things never change. See you back at camp."

William slapped the horse's rump as it started off, realizing that he was going to be here for a while. Once again, he retrieved his rifle and walked back to the edge of the tree line to where James stood. Allison walked up beside him and looked at the redoubt across the way and said, "You were correct about keeping them down, Mr. Tipton. I can't see a one from here,"

"Can't say I much blame them," The New Yorker replied. "After a shot like that, I'd dig my way back to town before I exposed myself to that kind of fire."

"I don't know about that," Samuel called out, pointing to the last redoubt in the long line of earthworks. "They're making a bayonet charge. Here they come a running boy get ready."

William shouldered his rifle and put his sights on one of the charging British. This would be a more difficult shot this time, he thought. His target would be on the move, so he waited for the men to get a little closer before he fired, however something wasn't quite right with this charge William thought. Their numbers were way too small. He could only count eight men approaching. Suddenly all of them dropped their weapons as their leader raised a small white piece of cloth, revealing that they were about to surrender.

"Don't fire but keep them in your sights!" Allison shouted. A few shots rang out from the British line in an attempt to stop the deserters from reaching the woods, but they were too far out of range for the English Brown Bess to hit their mark. It really was an ingenious way for the British to make their escape. They had fooled their own countrymen into believing they were making some king of half ass attack upon the woods. As they entered the tree line, their leader called out, "Don't shoot! For God's sake! Please don't shoot us now!"

"That was either the smartest or the most stupid thing I have seen during this whole long war." Allison announced as he pointed his pistol at the man holding the white scarf. What is the meaning of this?"

"We have had our fill of Cornwallis," the leader answered. "When he decided not to attack today, we knew it was time to go over to the other side. We are not surrendering now, mind you. We can't be paroled back over. No sir we would be killed for sure. We want to be Yanks now. I'm Sergeant Ray Davies and we are at your mercy."

Allison walked over to his horse and called over one of his men. He turned his back as he spoke relating his orders. The man jumped into his saddle and rode off in a full gallop. Allison walked back to the British Sergeant and said, "I have sent him back to tell my superiors of our situation here. Now, tell me. Why have you done this here today? If I believe you are trying to lead us into some sort of trap, I'll have you shot in these very woods."

"No tricks," Davies answered. "We were in a bad spot over there Lieutenant Colonel. The pox is getting bad in Yorktown; those damn darkies brought it in with them. Our food is already in short supply. We know that General Lafayette has ten thousand men in his ranks, not counting the French that landed on the James. Lord Cornwallis has reassured us that Clinton's troops are on the way from New York and will arrive here before Washington can get here, but I for one don't believe it. I have been through a few sieges in Europe and I don't want to go through another. The only real hope we had was the British Navy, but we don't know where they are."

William's heart jumped with joy as he listened to Davies explanation. The Marquis' numbers were way short of what this artilleryman believed. It seemed the rumors were running through both armies now. If this lifelong veteran of the

British army panicked and threw in with the enemy, things must be bad indeed on the other side. If the British were this panicky, just maybe they could capture the almighty Cornwallis this fall. Things were definitely looking up for the American cause.

Chapter 156
A Damned Well

Thomas was lying in his tent in agony. He had rolled onto his side, drawing his knees up as tightly as he could in an effort to ease the pain. But it was not working. The poison in his system was hard at work, doing God only knows what. His hair was sweat soaked and chills racked his body, a horrible companion to the fever that had him in its grip. He and the other men who had ridden back to Williamsburg with him all suffered the same symptoms. Thomas had been the last of the group to fall ill, the first being the youngest of the four, a young boy from out of the Blue Ridge Mountains in his seventeenth year of life.

Thomas had dismissed his symptoms at first, putting it down to a case of nerves. Mortar fire could shake the most hardened veteran and this morning was this young soldier's first encounter with field artillery. But after reaching camp the other two soon were showing signs that all was not well with them either. Food poisoning then, Thomas expected would be the cause, but neither of the three had eaten together last night, nor had any breakfast this morning before going to Yorktown. When he started suffering the same symptoms, he realized the only thing they all had in common was their ride back from Yorktown. They had stopped at an abandoned plantation along the roadside only long enough to draw a pail of water from its well, but long enough to be poisoned it seemed. Thomas, having a taste more for something fermented, had only taken a small amount of the tainted water, but the young mountaineer had drunk two or three cups.

The other two men only had one cup apiece. Tarleton's dragoons had obviously made one stop themselves on their way back to Yorktown. There was little doubt that they were the ones who had poured the toxin in the well. Rats bane, a form of arsenic was   their favorite choice. The biggest question now, was how much they had poured into the well, and how much water was inside to dilute the poison. Dr. Amos Carter had been summoned to the men's tents, but there was little he could do, other than give each of them a small amount of charcoal and order that the well in question be sealed off. This could be something other than arsenic poisoning. It was unlikely, but possible, so Dr Carter had ordered the four to be quarantined at the makeshift hospital set up at the Governor's Palace. General Lafayette could not afford to have another epidemic sweep through his growing ranks at this crucial time. As a cart was being brought in for the sick to be transported, Captain Galloway, Thomas's commanding officer for most of the war, set out to find his best sergeant's brother.

William was standing in the midst of a circle of men who had gathered around his tent to hear what the British runaways had had to say. He was holding a small bowl of half cooked rice, still on the chewy side mixed in with some squirrel meat that wasn't half bad. If it only has a few peas or maybe a green pepper mixed in, it would have been a fairly decent army meal, he joked as Galloway stepped into the mob.

"Tell me Tipton, did you or any of your men stop at a well on your way back in this afternoon?" the Captain asked.

"No Sir," William replied.

"Well, that's good. What about Lt. Colonel Allison? I can't find him around camp," Galloway inquired.

"Not as far as I know, Sir."

"All right then," Galloway replied, sitting down on a wooden stump. He looked up at William with a concerned expression and said, "We have a situation on our hands here. The patrol that came in first with your brother unfortunately did. I'm afraid it was poisoned. All have fallen ill, but as of now they're still alive."

William handed his bowl to Samuel and picked up his rifle as Galloway continued, "No need to go to his tent. Dr. Carter has sent them to Williamsburg. They're on the road by now. You won't have any trouble catching them. Tell Thomas I'll be praying for him."

James reached into his vest and pulled out his light purse. He poured out the last of his money into his hand and said, "This might help. You don't know what you may need. Take it with you." William took the money, shook James' hand and biting down hard on his lower lip, and nodded his thanks to his good friend. Without any other words needed between them, he mounted Sampson's back and set off to find his brother.

He put Sampson to a hard run and soon was able to overtake the slow moving two wheeled carts as it passed by the college on the edge of town. Riding up beside it he looked down into the cart bed and saw that the youngest of the four was already dead. His head was thrown back in a convulsive position. His mouth was open, as were his unseeing eyes. Jumping from his saddle, he tied Sampson to the back of the moving cart and climbed inside its opened tailgate. He shook Thomas' shoulder, praying that he was still alive, unable to tell, since Thomas was lying on his stomach with his head facing the wooden sideboard of the cart.

"Thomas, are you still with us?"

"Still here," Thomas replied weakly, trying to roll over "A little worse for wear, but still here. I could use something to drink thought. But not water.

"

"Got some green tea," William replied as he pulled the plug from his canteen. He put his hand under Thomas' wet head as he gently lifted his brother's head.

"How did you come by that?"

"Just because you may feel like you're dying, doesn't mean I'm going along with it. I'm not telling you where I got it."

"It's going to take more than a little poison to get me out of this world," Thomas replied.

"I know. That's why I have no intensions of revealing my source. Once you're well, you would be buying it all for yourself and I'd be out in the cold."

A soft smile broke across Thomas's pale face as he took a small sip from the canteen. "Damn, that hurts going down," he said. "How are the others doing?"

"Lost one, the youngest." William answered.

"He drank the most," Thomas said, rubbing his eyes.

"How much did you have?"

"Just a little but I don't believe it was enough to kill me. But God, my gut is on fire and this damned bouncing cart isn't helping matters any."

Well, we're here, so your ride is about over," William observed as the cart stopped in front of the palace's white wrought iron gates. The driver slid off his horse's back. The big draft horse was pulling double duty, not only was he pulling the cart, he had his master riding in a saddle as well.

"Stay here, I'll go inside and find out where they want to put them. Front, side, back, there are so many doors in this place you never can tell which one they'll send you through."

"Get me up," Thomas requested. "I've got to get above this stench. I need some fresh air."

"What? Set you up? Are you sure?" William asked

.

"Yeah, and I want to see the other two."

William pulled Thomas into a sitting position, resting his brother's back against his own body, and swinging his legs over the edge of the vomit covered cart.

"Are any of you boys alive down there?" Thomas asked as he was looking over at his comrades?

"Me," replied the one laying in the middle. "But I'm beginning to wish I wasn't. Oh, what I wouldn't give to be able to sleep this off if I could."

"Joseph died," Thomas told him, looking at the youth while holding his own aching stomach.

"I heard," replied the other man. "Damn shame. He was a good boy by all accords."

The driver came back out of the palace door along with a man William presumed was the hospital doctor. As the driver remounted his horse, the doctor walked around to the rear of the cart and began his examination of Thomas and the others.

"You think you've been poisoned, do you? I'm inclined to agree with you. But all I can give you is some charcoal tablets. Other than that, we'll just have to wait and see. There are no beds for you here, unless someone has died in the last hour. Driver, take these three men to the public hospital. You know what to do with this unfortunate lad," the doctor said as he closed the boy's eyes with his hand.

"The charcoal tablets?" William asked.

"Inside, come on in with me and you can take it over to them. That's all driver take them on."

Thomas fell back down into the cart as the driver started around the street that circled the Palace Green.
"What's your opinion Doctor?" William asked as the two turned to go inside.
"They're in God's hands," the doctor replied. "They could go either way. It all really depends on how much is in their system."

"What about the one sitting up? He's my brother."

"I would say he's better than the others. But you never know. Have the doctors over there bleed him. That will get some of the bad blood out. If he was my brother, I'd stay with him tonight. If he's strong enough in the morning, I'd get him out of that   hospital. We set up over here for a reason. Ninety percent of their patients are lunatics. Get him home if you can, but like I said, if he's weaker on the morrow, it will only be a matter of time. Wait here at the door and I'll have someone bring you that charcoal."

"Thank you, Sir," William said as the doctor disappeared into the open front door of the palace. Ninety percent lunatics and they may bleed him once he gets there, William thought. He stepped inside and found himself in a round paneled room filled with sick men. He could hear the doctor order someone to bring out the charcoal from a side door that had once led to the governor's secretary's office. William walked over and took three small wooden boxes from a slave and dropped them in his shot bag and bolted back out the door. The driver of the cart was already halfway down the green as William cleared the palace gates. Breaking into a hard run, still holding his rifle in his hand he called to the driver to stop as he passed George Wythe's home. The cart came to rest at the side gate to the Bruton Parish Church. Catching up to the cart, William reached into his shot bag and pulled out two of the boxes. He pitched them to the driver. He walked around and put his hand on Thomas' shoulder and said, "That doctor said they are going to bleed you once you reach the other hospital. Do you want them to do that or not?"

"Hell no," Thomas answered.

"Why the hell not?" the driver asked, "They are doctors you know."

"It's my blood though," Thomas answered as William pulled him from the rear of the cart.

"All right then," the driver said as he drove off, "It's your neck not mine."

William helped Thomas to the ground and leaned him against the church wall.

"Stay here, I'll find us a place for the night, William said, putting Thomas' hat on his head. He stood up and walked into the churchyard. Making his way down the walkway on the back side of the church, walking among the many tombstones, he could hear the sound of an organ being played inside. Choir practice, he hoped, as he made his way around the corner to the sound of voices. William sat down his rifle, pulled open the large ten-foot door, removed his hat and stepped inside the church's tall foyer just under the bell tower, three stories above. A few more steps over the flagstone paved floor carried him into the grandest sanctuary he had ever seen. It was built in the shape of a cross, having the long main aisle crossed by a second, smaller aisle completing the shape of the cross that Christ died upon. On both sides of these beautiful aisles were rows of white paneled box pews with paneled doors. The white plastered walls were complemented by six fifteen-foot arched windows on each side and a round window at the three ends of the cross section. Ten pews down the main aisle and on the right side was a tall pulpit with a staircase leading up to it and covered by a large cherry soundboard overhead, at the end of the main aisle stood the congregational communion table draped with a white tablecloth. Overhead hung a balcony where the church organ was being played. As the choir broke into the first verse of Rock of Ages, the Reverend John Bracken spotted his guest and began to make his way to William who had stopped a few feet inside the sanctuary. At his approach, William hoped he had not made a mistake. Reverend Bracken was not a normal rector and this was certainly not your run of the mill southern church. Governor Dunmore had sat in his gallery directly across from Bracken's Pulpit before the war and his red canopy chair had been occupied by Governors Henry and Jefferson on Sunday mornings ever since. Reverend Bracken was a powerful and busy man. He was not only the leader of this magnificent church; he was also the president of William and Mary College. Would he allow two of the thousands of soldiers garrisoned in and around the town to stay the night in his church, having never even met them before? Praying for the best, William presented his hand and as the reverend took it into his own and began to shake it, inquired with a questioning look on his face, "Do you have news for me from the Marquise?"

"No Sir, I'm afraid not," William answered. "I am here of my own accord. Judge Wythe spoke very highly of you. I'm here to beg your indulgence for my brother. He is outside the church gates in need of your help. He has been poisoned by the British. The army surgeon told me that if he can live through the upcoming night, he would most likely survive. I have no other place to take him and can think of no better place for us to stay than here inside the Lord's house in our darkest hour. If he has recovered enough by sunup, we will be gone, and if not, I'll tend to his grave. I am humbly asking for your permission to use the church for the night."

Bracken paused for a moment raising his hand to his face and rubbing his cleft chin between his fingers, obviously in deep thought.

"May I have a word with you Reverend?" a feminine voice asked from the balcony above. "I could not prevent overhearing the young man's request. I may be able to be of some assistance to you both."

"By all means," replied Bracken, "I always have time to speak with the wife of our great leader, Mr. Peyton Randolph."

Mrs. Elizabeth Randolph, a woman well into her fifth decade who was known to all as Betsey, turned away from the balcony rail and descended the staircase. She was wearing a dark green dress and carried her favorite yellow fan in her hand. If William had not been so worried about Thomas he would have been awe struck to come face to face with the wife of the first President of the Continental Congress. He stepped forward on the stone floor and she smiled at him and motioned for Bracken to follow her to the end of the aisle.

"Reverend," she began, "everyone inside this parish knows you are one of the most daunting supporters of this war. However, there are whispers that the church itself may not want to break with the crown because it has so long been supported by the King's Taxes. This is a grand opportunity to show that is not the case. Giving refuge to a wounded patriot could end those absurd accusations."

"My thoughts exactly," Bracken answered, "and it is only one night."

"There, you have your answer," Bracken turned to face William. "Your brother will be in my prayers tonight. Bring him inside. He may have the use of the back pew."

"I am indebted to you Sir," William answered. "Judge Wythe was correct in his judgment of your character; you are truly a man of God."

Reverend Bracken inclined his head and walked back up the aisle, leaving William with Mrs. Randolph. "I'm not forgetting you either," William said sincerely. "I believe I am in your debt more so than his."

"Just win this war for my late husband and we will be even young man. I'll have some linen sent over from my home. Good luck to your brother and God speed." At that, she stepped out the door and disappeared.

Chapter 157
One Brother is Enough

William ended his prayer opened his tired eyes and raised his weary head to gaze on the cross that hung above the altar. He lingered there just another moment collecting his thoughts. He got up off his knees and made his way down the aisle. He slowed his pace as he passed the pew where Thomas lay. But he didn't stop, he continued on through the foyer and out into the new morning's sunlight. It was a little cool this morning, fall was finally arriving here in the tidewater, he thought as he stepped out into the churchyard. A coat would be needed if the campaign didn't end soon. He hoped he could find a wagoneer on the streets this morning. He had money to hire one, but wondered if any would be available. The army was using almost everything that had wheels, but he hoped he would be able to find one that was heading north empty. As he stepped into the streets William thought maybe he should head back to the camp where he might be able to find that whiskey peddler with his rickety wagon. But then he reconsidered and turned toward the Capital, not wanting to be put on any duty rosters today. Thomas needed to be attended to and he wasn't going to take the chance of being pulled aside by some officer wanting something. He had seen a few local farmers selling small amounts of vegetables and a few cuts of meat in the market square in the past. They always seemed to sell out within an hour, or less. They kept their wagons around behind the armory on Francis Street. Hopefully one could be talked into taking Thomas home with the help of James' coins. As he walked into the square, there were only ten or so people walking around one lone vendor. He only had a few baskets, one filled with squash, two with potatoes and one with green peppers. No meat at all and only one dozen eggs and a bag of feathers rounded out his wares.

"How are sales?" William asked as he looked into the baskets.

"Slow" the old farmer answered.

"Then lower your prices," a woman quipped while digging through the peppers.

"Believe me ma'am, I would if I could, but you know as well as I do that these paper dollars ain't worth the paper they're printed on. Pay me in coin and I'll adjust my rates. I'm lucky to have anything to sell at all with the British foraging everywhere. But this is the last of my crop I have to sell. The rest I'm keeping to get through the winter myself. I'll sell what I've got left by noon I'll wager."

"So, you're finished with your crops for the season?" William asked.

"That I am," the farmer answered as he lit his long cane stemmed corncob pipe.

"Then you're free to be hired?" William asked as the old farmer blew out a fragrant puff of smoke.

"Could be, I Suppose, depends on the task."

"I need you to take my brother to his home in Fairfax County with your wagon, a week's work I'd say.

"Why, what's wrong with him? If he has the pox I won't go near him. And if he's dead I sure ain't going to pull a corpse that far."

"He's neither," William assured the man. He's recovering from being poisoned. He's weak, but recovering. He'll get better care at home than here though. I have the means to pay you or someone else. In coin, mind you, not paper. If you're my man it will have to be done now, today."

"Where is he?" the farmer asked obviously considering the offer.

"Inside the church," William answered.

"Go and get him ready to travel. I'll be there with my rig inside the hour. You have your man," the old farmer grinned through tobacco stained teeth." But do you have your coin."

Thirty minutes later the doors of the church swung open and out stepped William, steadying Thomas. The two made their way down the street to one of the benches that sat next to the church wall. As they sat down, William looked down into the bag of walnuts that he had been carrying around with him for the past few days. He had gathered them while in camp and they would now supply him a cheap meal. Popping one in his mouth, he looked over to Thomas and said, "You sure had me worried last night. One brother was enough to lose in this war. I didn't want to have to go through that again."

"Well, I'm happy I could oblige you," Thomas replied weakly, smiling at his brother through charcoal stained teeth. "I hope I'm out of the woods, but damn it, I don't want to miss this. This siege is going to be something to see for sure."

"Maybe you'll get back before it plays out." William replied as he was reaching back into his bag as the wagon pulled up in front of the two."

"I hope you're not planning on paying me in walnuts," the driver said from atop his seat.

"No, I still have your coin." William assured him as he pulled Thomas to his feet.

He helped Thomas in the wagon and said, "I'll ride along with you for the day and come back tomorrow morning." He shut the wagon's tailgate and walked around to the driver and paid him. "Go on, get started. I'll retrieve my horse and catch up with you as soon as I can" As the wagon pulled away, William slapped its wooden side and said, "I'll be along soon."

As he watched the wagon with Thomas aboard roll out of Williamsburg, William was not completely convinced that Thomas was out of danger yet. But as the day wore on and into the night, he was able to ease his mind. Thomas was holding his own now, weakened yes, but not deteriorating any further. The two of them had begun to talk more now that Thomas was not in such pain. They even managed to talk about Joshua that night. They had not spoken of him much since their arrival in Lafayette's camp. The words had been hard to come by. William felt the stress of being so close to the British lines was enough to deal with. Being on the road home, away from the front, and seeing Thomas recovering had taken a great burden off his chest. He could tell Thomas was feeling the same, and by talking about their lost brother the two could keep him alive in a strange way.

William had begun this tour with revenge on his mind, but atonement had not come and most likely never would. Joshua's life had ended at the hands of Indians and none were here for him to take his revenge upon. Maybe it was for the best he thought, after all the good book did say, "Vengeance is mine, saith the Lord." Thomas' near-death experience had shown William that he could still lose a loved one or even his very own life in this war. Being hell bent on revenge could lead on to his own death, clouding his judgment he had come to realize. What good would it do Elizabeth and the children if he was killed? Joshua would never return from the Tennessee Mountains no matter how many Indians he killed. The best that he could do now was to fulfill his duties as best he could and try to make a better future for his growing family. Like so many times before William prayed for an end to this long drawn out war.

Chapter 158
The Devil's Own Play

Abandoned homes and plantations were quite common now, here along the peninsula. But something about this one seemed a little odd to William as he was returning back to his company of spies.

He had ridden by it just yesterday and had not paid it any mind. He supposed he was being extra observant and careful after what had happened to Thomas and his men. And maybe it had been too close to dark then for him to notice, but today his eye had been caught by the immaculate grounds. Everything was so neat and clean, flowers grew under the windows and a well-tended vegetable garden was just over the fence. Fall onions and turnips were growing alongside pumpkins and gourds, everything in good order. A potato hill had been dug just a few days before by the way they looked. If it were not for the open door and a few scattered items strew about the yard of this oxford brown home, William would have passed by without a second thought. But the sparkling white curtain floating in the breeze from a broken side window warned William that all was not right here. It was far too clean and white to have been exposed to the weather for any amount of time. Whatever had happened here had taken place either last night or early this morning. He pulled Sampson to a stop as the two reached the open front door. Against his better judgment, he dismounted and let Sampson have free rein of the front yard while he entered the house with his cocked rifle at the ready. It was completely ransacked. No, a single stick of furniture was undamaged in the parlor. An ax was still stuck in the top of the collapsed dining room table.

He pushed open the door that led to a small room off the hall, its floor was splattered with what looked to be buckets of blood, but there were no bodies inside. Turning away, he walked back through the parlor and followed the muddy tracks the intruders had left all over the bottom floor. Reaching the staircase, he took his time going up. He could see the second floor had not been spared either. The same vandalism as below was in evidence everywhere here too. His anger grew with every step he took. War is cruel when men are at each other's throats on the battlefield and horrible things happen, but this was not a battlefield. No ramparts or redoubts here. This was the home of a loving family that would fit in any neighborhood, here, Baltimore, or London for that matter. Whoever had done this was just using this war as an excuse to indulge evil cravings for wickedness he thought as he reached the top of the stairs. He looked in the first bedroom on his right and saw a large pool of blood under the bed. A woman's arm was hanging off the side already turning black. William quickly scanned the upper rooms but no one was there other than himself and the poor lady who had been killed in her bed. The sight was utterly unbelievable, far worse than anything he had seen on the frontier. This poor pregnant woman had been murdered in a most despicable manner, bayoneted through her ripe stomach. The bastards had even gone so far as cutting away her breast. He hoped it was done after she was dead, but probably not. Turning away in disgust, he could not believe that even the worst of soldiers could do something like this. Maybe a lunatic was loose, having escaped from the hospital in Williamsburg. Turning away to leave this place he saw a message written in this poor woman's blood over the doorway. It told the story all too well.

"Thou shalt not give birth to a rebel."

This had been the work of the British cavalry. God damn them, he thought. If there was ever a more devilish group than this, they had to be in hell. He quickly descended the stairs leaving the gruesome scene behind. As he reached the bottom floor, his thought went back to the laundry with all that blood. The woman upstairs was killed in her bed. Where had all of that blood come from in there? He once more opened its door and looked inside. He walked to the center of the room and saw a cupboard door cracked open ever so slightly. He took the knob in his hand and pulled open the door. There sat a row of severed heads on the shelf as if they were jars of fruit. He shut the door and quickly stepped out the back door where lay the bodies of the condemned beside the kitchen well. He had seen enough, he walked away, leaving them behind. Now he had another reason to hate the British. He had to go and report this to someone. He hoped he wouldn't have to come back for this had been the devil's own play and no one wanted to see that twice.

Chapter 159
Friendly Persuasion

"Come on James, play for us," Samuel pleaded inside their tent. "It's been a long time since I took a whirl with a pretty blue-eyed girl that's soft in all the right places."

"I don't have my fiddle with me Samuel, it's back home, you know that," James replied, lying on a straw filled bag he had been using as a bed. "Besides I don't know if they'd let me play one even if I did."

"She has one with her," Samuel answered with a grin on his face. "It's her daddy's she spirited it out of her house tonight. Besides it couldn't hurt to have a cheerful night around here. Hell, it just might keep some of the men from slipping off in the night. We're all about bored to death. It would be nice to dance away some of this idle time we've been having lately. I know you're a married man now, but I'm not. You still remember what it was like to be foot loose don't you? I really like this girl, come on, do it for me. Just a few tunes, that's all I'm asking. Besides, I already told her you would. You don't want me to look like a liar, do you?"

"Where did you meet this young lady?" James asked as he put his hands behind his head, clasping his fingers together, raising his elbows high in the air, giving Samuel a smug grin.

"Williamsburg. You know where I met her. She's right outside, don't make me beg."

"What if her father comes along looking for his fiddle with a squirrel riffle and I'm the one holding it? What then? Redcoats are enough to worry about without some crazed father shooting at me."

"Just run like the wind," Samuel replied laughing. "Besides I'd be the first one he would shoot at. She doesn't have his permission to be here anyway. Maybe we can get William to stand guard for us," Samuel said in jest.

"Well, I don't know, did she have enough good sense to bring a bow as well as the fiddle," James asked, rolling over on his side, resting his head on his bent elbow.
"Why sure she did, what do you think she is, a fool? Don't answer that. I know full well what you're about to say."

As James lay there laughing with Samuel, William stuck his head inside the tent flap and said, "You better get out here Samuel, you're about to lose her. One of those King and Queen County boys is about to steal here away with talk of blueberry jam and bread."

"See," Samuel pleaded, "if she pulls out on me it's going to be your fault."

"Very well," James replied "I won't have it said that I ever stood between you and one of your many love interests, but you better hope Lydia never gets wind of this back home. She will have your hide for sure. Come on, let's go get that fiddle."

William walked over and leaned his shoulder against a bitternut hickory and watched as Samuel introduced the local girl to James. They passed a few words between themselves before James took her fiddle and began to run the bow over its strings. James' music always seemed to have a calming effect on William. It was good to see some normal interaction among people again. It was a welcome sight after the unthinkable events he had seen at that roadside home with all its debauchery. William felt more relaxed now and as he watched this dark-haired girl move with all the ease in the world, he closed his eyes and imagined he was back home, dancing with Elizabeth and was looking forward to a time when it would not be a dream.

Chapter 160
His Excellency

William was sitting by his campfire on September 14, 1781, melting down a bar of lead in a small skillet. He was happy to receive the lead, newly arrived from France. He still had several rounds in his shot bag, enough to last a while, but this had given him something to occupy the rest of the day. His blood was up and this would help, even if it was just the simple task of pouring the hot lead into his bullet mold. The French were now supplying more than troops and money. Word was spreading fast of the French Fleet's victory over the British Navy at the battle of Virginia Capes. Even the rain this morning couldn't stop the spread of the good news. Cornwallis was ripe for the pickings and even the slowest minds knew it now. The Earl had put his fate in the hands of Admiral Graves and now he was sailing the remains of his battered fleet back to New York. Cornwallis was trapped, with nothing to do but wait for Clinton to come to his rescue.

It had rained for most of the day and the heavy downpour had kept him and most of the militia inside the tents talking over the good news until around two o'clock. The sun was finally popped out and everyone was outside, except for Samuel who was asleep inside the tent. After William and James had started the fire, James had taken to the woods to find more kindling. It would be wet and hard to burn, but with a few hours inside the tent it would soon dry out enough to start tomorrow night's fire. The lead had transformed into its liquid form and he was beginning to pour the silver mixture in the molds when James came back with some twigs and small limbs in his arms.

"Took you a while to find it this time didn't it?" William asked as he opened the mold, dropping the newly formed bullet onto an old piece of leather to cool.

"Having to walk further to find it," James replied, dropping the bundle just inside the tent's flap. "You know I have a craving for some fish tonight, but I don't see any need in going down to the creek. I'm sure the water's way too muddy to catch anything after all that rain."

"That would have gone down real nice." William replied as he filled up the mold again, "maybe tomorrow."

As James returned to the fire a loud cheer of "Huzzah" was heard coming from the other end of the militia camp capturing both men's attention. They're eyes locked together at the same time. "It's got to be him," William said, laying down the mold before trotting to the nearby road that ran through the center of camp. Men were lining both sides to get a look at the approaching riders. His Excellency, George Washington, the commander-in-chief was leading the way. He was followed by Billy Lee, his man servant. Washington sat upon his mount as though he was a part of the horse itself. A graceful and elegant rider, towering above the animal's back. William had always been told that Washington was a tall impressive man, and had often wondered if it was an exaggeration. Men of great reputations were sometime embellished, but not General Washington. He was everything William had heard and more, even with mud caked to his boots and trouser legs.

Ft. Pitts' old commanding officer, General Edward Hand was among Washington's aides. His eyes fixed on William as he rode by, but William was sure he would not remember a scout from his Squaw Campaign up the Mahoning River from almost four years ago. It was just a coincidence. William did not recognize any of the other American officers, but could see that General Rochambeau was wearing a pale blue coat trimmed in gold with a scarlet sash draped over his shoulder under his open coat to let everyone who saw him know that he was the highest-ranking officer among the French.

As another round of "Huzzahs," went up, William removed his hat and waved it high in the air as Washington's party rode away. After letting out a good yell himself, he put it back on his head and said to James. "Cornwallis's days are numbered for sure now, old friend. Washington's here." James just smiled and nodded his head as the two turned back toward the tent and with a few more strides were again beside the fire. As William picked up the mold, Samuel emerged from the tent rubbing the sleep from his eyes. "What was that entire ruckus out here a few minutes ago?" James acting as if he had no idea what Samuel was talking about shook his head with a confused expression on his face. "Nothing happened out of the ordinary. You must have been dreaming. We didn't see anything." Samuel yawned and scratched his head, then turned and stumbled back inside the tent proclaiming he must have slept awful hard to have a dream that wild wake him up. "I'm going back to sleep for a while, he announced as he dropped the tent flap. "I have picket duty tonight. Wake me up if Washington ever comes by. They say he's due any day now. I don't want to miss seeing him."

Chapter 161
Glowing Ships

As James was sitting on his horse, he reached down in his vest pocket and pulled out what was left of a cake of chewing tobacco. He bit it in two saving the other half for later on tonight. As he rolled it around inside his mouth trying to get it in just the right spot, he looked over Sampson's back to see if Samuel was anywhere near ready to go.

"Do you see him anywhere yet?" William asked as he tucked Sampson's ear under his bridle without looking up from his work. "We've got to be going soon."

"Yeah," replied James just after he spit the first of his juice from his new chew. "He'd coming along and that little gal is about ten paces behind him too."

"Well we don't have time for her this afternoon," William commented as he pulled himself up on Sampson's back. "Come on Samuel. Make haste" he called to his young counterpart. Samuel waved and nodded his head as he was approaching. Then he stopped and turned back to the girl and said a few words to her, but whatever it was, it didn't agree with the young lady for she quickly spun around and stormed off the way she had come, leaving Samuel standing there with his outstretched arms raised in midair.

"She didn't seem to take that too good, did she." James chuckled, turning his mount around. "This should be good. I don't know what you said to her Samuel, but you should try to store it away somewhere just in case you ever want to get rid of another woman sometime in the future."

Samuel shook his head as he pulled himself up on his horse. "I don't know why she got so mad. I told her right from the start that I wasn't looking for a wife. She'll just have to get over it. Come on, let's go and take a good look at those Frenchie's. I'm looking forward to seeing them."

"Well, one's going to be with us all afternoon from what I understand," William replied, as the three rode onto the sandy road that led to Williamsburg. "Let's go see what they look like. They say there are a thousand of them camping around the college." At that, the three of them raced down the road to greet the newly arriving French troops. General Washington's stopover at Mount Vernon on his trek south had not been enough time for the allied troops, made up of Washington's Continentals and General Rochambeau's Fusiliers to catch up with their commanders. Washington and his staff had been in Williamsburg for several days now waiting for the rest of their army to arrive. Washington had chosen to make his old friend George Wythe's home his headquarters, and not to be outdone, Rochambeau had accepted Mrs. Peyton Randolph's gracious invitation to occupy her large Spanish brown mansion which was located just off the Palace Green on Nicholson Street. The two generals could walk to the others headquarters within minutes if need be, and now that the army had caught up to the generals, spirits and expectations were running high.

William and the others rode onto the campus where they were to meet and escort a French courier around Yorktown and on up the river to where the French fleet was blocking the port. Dispatches needed to be sent to the fleet from Rochambeau and no one had become more familiar with the countryside than these three able bodied   militiamen. Their orders were to ride to the President's house where the French had been stationed, meet up with the courier, and show him the way.

On their arrival, William began to understand just how vital this siege would be to the war's outcome. The sheer scope of all the forces gathering here was mind boggling. Over eleven thousand French soldiers surrounded the college. Washington had fifty-seven hundred regulars under his command and three thousand militiamen, and word was that General Greene with his Southern Army, fresh from their victory at Eutaw Springs was on their way here too. A city of tents with their colorful regimental flags flying was spread as far as the eye could see.

The French were all dressed the same. The foot soldiers had the standard white uniforms, and the only difference that William could see what the color of the collars and cuffs. Most of them were trimmed in green but some of them wore sky blue. A few even had pink or red, much too feminine for William's way of thinking. All wore black cocked hats. The officers, however were a different matter altogether. They were clad in scarlet breeches, blue waistcoats with black lapels and brass buttons running down its length. William thought if they fought as well as they dressed, they would be a welcomed addition to the cause indeed.

William handed his orders to the French guard of the watch. A tall thin soldier with long heavy braids hanging on each side of his face read them over quickly and walked away into the Reverend Bracken's presidential house that the French had commandeered and was in the process of turning into their hospital. As he waited, William shifted his weight in the saddle and looked at Samuel and asked, "What do you think of them?"

"Let's just say I'm glad they are here and, on our side," Samuel answered. "They sure have a lot of guns. There is no way Cornwallis can get out of this now. And we haven't even seen General Washington's men yet. What firepower we'll have now, even without cannon. And you know there are tons of them around here somewhere."

"Why are they digging a ditch around the building?" James asked as he starred at a large work detail armed with picks and shovels. "Is it some sort of defense line? Surely they don't imagine for a second that the redcoats are going to attack Williamsburg now do they?"

"I don't know," William answered, "but I think this is our boy coming here."

A short thick officer strolled up to the still mounted men and said in a thick French accent, "Monsieur, lead on." he gave William no time to respond and walked off without another word, his crimson sash flapping in the wind.

"Well," James replied as he watched the officer walk away, "I hope they brought some horses along, for I can already see they have a few asses with them."

Two hours later the four had finally made their way around Yorktown and had reached the French fleet. Their ride had been surprisingly easy to William's way of thinking. No cannon had been fired at them, no dragoons were on the road to oppose them, and it seemed that the enemy was content to stay hunkered down behind their defenses this afternoon, saving their ordinances for the more formidable force that was sure to gather in the days to come. Still, William had taken his time moving through the countryside. He could tell the Frenchman was somewhat annoyed at the American's slow pace, but to his credit he had held his tongue. Now that he was sitting in the middle of a rowboat with his dispatches safely stowed in his brown courier case, the Frenchman felt it had been worth it, for he had made it safely through. All William and his friends had to do now was sit on the bank, watch the sun set and wait for his return. William walked down to the water's edge and watched as the waves lapped against the shore. He knelt down on one knee and reaching down into the water, cupped some in his hand and began to wash his face.

"Whatever came of that poor sentry that shot General Wayne in the leg a while back?" Samuel asked, as William stood up.

"Nothing as far as I know," William replied, drying his face on the sleeve of his shirt. "It was Wayne's fault in my eyes anyway. When a sentry yells for you to halt, you better do it, even if you are a general. I did hear some talk of a court-martial, but I believe that General Washington put a stop to all that nonsense when he was told the whole story."

"That's what I understand as well," James spoke up. "But they say Wayne was as mad as a bull when he was first put to bed. Cussing all sorts of profanities, swearing up and down that he would have that boy lined up in front of a firing squad before the day was out. I guess they call him Mad Anthony for a good reason," he chuckled.

"This would have been the time for you to catch those fish you were craving the other day James, said William, changing the conversation. "They seem to bite best right at sundown. If only we had a pole and a few feet of line we could fry some up tonight."

"Yeah, but for some reason, I'm not that hungry tonight" James answered. "I wonder how long that Frenchman will be gone. I hope we don't have to sleep out in the open waiting for him to come back."

"Me too", replied Samuel. "But I guess it's out of his hands. He'll have to do whatever he's told just like us, looks to be a long night with a chill in the air as well."

After waiting a few hours, the three came to the realization that they would be spending the night after all. They removed the saddles from the horses and fed them what little grain was on hand. Having attended to the horses as best as could be done the three men sat on the riverbank under a mulberry tree and covered themselves with their horse blankets. Talk had been the best way to pass the time, but now that midnight was approaching sleep seemed to be the best way to pass the remaining hours of the night. William volunteered to take the first watch while the other two fell asleep. It was a clear cool night with a stiff breeze blowing down from the coast. He had already seen two shooting stars overhead. He was looking for another, because Elizabeth always said it was good luck to see three in one night. The night was like so many others he had spent since the war began; it reminded him of all those nights on Captain Roger's unnamed boat on the Ohio with the sound of the waves hitting the shore. Wonder why we never named that flatboat? He thought.

Except for an owl behind him a few hundred feet, all was quiet and still. Needing to stretch his legs, he stood up and stepped out into the moonlight with his ever-present rifle, leaving the shade of the mulberry behind. He looked out into the river where the French fleet was anchored. A lone drummer aboard the nearest ship began to beat his drum, giving an alarm. William turned and looked upriver where he could see the glow of a fired ship silently floating downriver toward the French blockade only a couple   hundred feet away. It was a shocking but beautiful sight to behold. He looked back to the mulberry tree and saw the other two had been awakened by the sound of scrambling men aboard the French ships. Turning his attention back to the river, he watched as the burning English ship floated harmlessly by, missing all its targets. As James and Samuel walked down to join William a second fire appeared upriver, glowing in the dark, small at first, but growing as it drew closer. This one had a better line on its target. It was heading straight for the three French ships riding at anchor in a line. William could see the endangered ship's crew frantically trying to raise anchor to avoid the certain collision that was closing in on their ship. Having not enough time to raise it, someone had taken an ax and chopped the anchor's line, dropping it into the muddy river bottom below.

As the French ship began to drift aside, James said, "It's going to clear them again. I can't believe that Cornwallis is sacrificing what is left of his fleet for this. They're going mad up there; he laughed "I've never seen anything like it."

"Me either," William answered, "look, here comes three more. They could still do some damage yet. But I can't see this breaking up the blockade. They may hit one or two, but they can't destroy the whole fleet. We better get back under that mulberry and take some cover. They could have slipped some infantry or dragoons out of Yorktown with these ships."

The three of them ran back under the tree and watched as the last three burning ships sailed by. One of the French ships had to run herself aground to keep from being rammed, but otherwise the fleet was undamaged. As time passed it became evident that the attack, such as it was, was over
.

As James took his turn at watch, William lay down on his back and looked up at the sky and saw his third shooting star of the night. He rolled over on his side and his last though before sleep overtook him was that he wished Thomas and Joshua had gotten to see this night. But then he thought they both had in their own ways Thomas from his home in the arms of his wife and Joshua from above.

Chapter 162
Two Prisoners

Fifteen horses stepped out of the small wood that lay next to Wormley Creek and splashed into its waters. While still in midstream William glanced over to the spot where just yesterday a bridge had been standing. The smell of smoke still hung in the air. Poles that had once supported the bridge protruded from the water and puffs of white smoke rose here and there along the length of the burned-out bridge. Just another waste, he thought as he returned his attention to the matter at hand. Sampson's back leg slipped from under him as he climbed out of the water onto the steep bank on the opposite side of the creek, almost throwing William off. However, he quickly regained his footing, as did William in the saddle and they both made it onto the bank where the other riders awaited.

The British had been sending out more patrols the last few days and they had been doing a lot of damage on the roads while they were out. Beside burning most of the bridges, they had also fell several trees across the roadways wherever they could cause the most problems to the movement of cannon that they knew would soon be rolling down the road to begin the siege. Ever since they had seen General Washington riding around their outer defenses, showing no fear of their ability to harm him, they had known the siege was near. This made them more aggressive and desperate as the days wore on.

General Washington was now in Williamsburg tending to the last of his plans for the upcoming battle. This reconnoiter would most likely be their last before his army marched to Yorktown. William and his companions had already avoided two British patrols this morning and had come close enough to a redoubt that they could hear the Hessian mercenaries speaking German to one another. But now they had made it across what would soon be a vast battlefield and was coming up to the rear of the home belonging to Mr. Augustine Moore. This would be the end of their patrol today. The White framed two story house sat facing the York River only a short walk from its banks. There were two windows framed by black shutters on each side of the front door. The rear of the house had matching windows, and there were four more windows on each end, providing plenty of natural light inside the home. The second floor had five more windows protruding from the slanted roof line. Moore had not been back since he had met William and his friends on the road the day he had told them of the grain in his barn. It was a handsome home and William felt somewhat obliged to keep an eye on the place. Nothing had happened here before, but today was different. Two horses, wearing the green blanket of Tarleton' dragoons were tied inside the orchard on the south side of the lawn. They had their heads down, eating the apples that had fallen to the ground from the trees above. Both were still saddled.

"Prisoners," James whispered as he slid off Trace's back, holding his rifle. "I'll take the back door with half the men. You take the others and head around front. If there are only two inside, we'll have them between a rock and a hard place. Let's take six men apiece and leave one with the horses."

William agreed with a nod and slowly began to make his way to the front. Working his way along the wall of the house, as if he were in the woods of Kentucky, he stopped at the chimney. He peered inside the flanking windows, but saw no one inside. Continuing around the corner and past the front door, he once again looked through the windows of the other downstairs rooms and as before, he saw nothing. The first floor appeared empty. Turning back to the door, he saw that Samuel had pushed it open with the barrel point of his rifle. The lock had been chopped away by an ax and it swung silently open. Seeing nothing but the staircase, Samuel stepped inside, followed by the other men. They could hear the sound of voices coming from upstairs. William made his way through the hall and unlocked the back door to let James and his men inside. Placing his fingers to his lips he stepped back and pointed to the floor above with a smile on his face. Sitting on a table just inside the door in plain view, were two dragoon helmets and matching pairs of belts with two sabers still inside the sheaths, but no pistols were in sight.
The bottom board of the staircase popped as William placed his foot on it but the sounds of festivities from above prevented anyone hearing it. As he made his way up the stairs, William was relieved to hear the women were happily involved and had needed little persuasion to bed the two dragoons. Finding a rape in progress might have pushed him over the edge, with the visions of that poor woman dead in her bed still fresh in his mind. As he walked inside the right bedchamber, he lowered his rifle at the naked Englishman who rolled over and placed his hands atop his head as his partner jerked the sheet up as if to protect herself. The sound of a scuffle could be heard coming from across the hall, over the screams of a panic-stricken woman. "I'll part your head right down the middle," James announced, "if you go for that pistol again." As his prisoner was hurriedly putting on his trousers, William called across the hall, "Is all well over there?"

"Right as rain," James answered. "As long as you're not one of these Brits".

William crossed to the bed and pulled the woman out by her arm and said, "Samuel take her and the other one downstairs and let them get dressed while I have a talk with this fellow here."

"Gladly," Samuel replied, following her out of the room and meeting the other woman at the top of the staircase, without her sheet, but holding an armful of clothing below here breast.

"Thou shalt not sire loyal subjects to the King while in Virginia." William stated, remembering the message on the wall he had seen the week before. His captive kept his head down, looking at the floor, showing no reaction to William's statement, convincing William that these were not the men who had killed the pregnant woman and her child.

"Go ahead and finish dressing," he ordered. "I don't want to look at your naked ass all the way back to Williamsburg." Turning he left the prisoner with the other men and went downstairs to the room on the right of the front door where Samuel was standing guard just inside the threshold.

"Woman," William addressed the less modest of the two, "I know for a fact that you're not the owners of this house. What are you doing here?"

Her eyes narrowed as she looked at William. She raised her head in defiance but refused to answer. She looked him directly in the eye as she calmly pulled her blouse over head to finally cover herself.

"British troops have camp followers too," she said sharply. "What do you think we are doing here?"

"That one over there," Samuel broke in, pointing to the other woman, "Was in our camp the other night when James was playing the fiddle. She's a local girl, not a camp follower. You need to pick a side girl, you just can't flit back and forth from one side to the other," he advised.

"She needs to eat, don't she?" her partner shot back. "General Greene doesn't feed us like he does you."

"How did you get here?" William asked. "There are only two horses outside."
"We walked from Hampton."

"Then I suggest you walk back, the same way you came. You can't stay here and we're not going to take you with us. You walked coming in, so I guess you can walk going out."

After slipping on her shoes, she pushed Samuel aside and crossed the hall into the adjoining room and approached the fireplace. There on the mantle lay a tattered purse. She picked it up and tucking it into the top of her stocking; she walked out the side door followed by the other woman without a backward glance.

"Watch them close as they leave, Samuel. We don't want them marching down into Yorktown, at least not until we are long gone from here. I say that's where they'll end up tonight, now that we've put them out of business here." Samuel rolled his eyes and stepped outside as William looked back up the stairs. The two prisoners, now fully clothed were being led downstairs and out the back door, the butt of several jokes from their captors. James stood at the door and watched as William pulled the front door closed. As William crossed the hall to exit the back-door James said, "You know, in a way I kind of feel sorry for those two prisoners."

"I don't," said William. "The gaol in Williamsburg is a lot better than a prison ship."

"Not that," James chuckled, "can you imagine what they will say, when they are old and back home in England, and their grandchildren say 'Grandfather, they say you were captured in the war how did it happen'?"

Chapter 163
Cut to Pieces

William rode up beside one of the captured dragoons now that they were once again across Wormley Creek. He reached down to his saddle holster and pulled his pistol and pointed at the prisoner's head. "You see how fast I could end your days on this earth," he said, staring into the man's eyes. "You don't want to put me in a position where I'll be forced to do it because if you do, I'll drop the hammer on this pistol without any hesitation. We don't need you. Our plans are all set. You're just making it easier for us to take your horses back with us. If we run into any of your countrymen on the way back, don't make any trouble for us. Understand? If you'll give me your word and do as you're told, we'll treat you well. Otherwise there's always my pistol."

The dragoon nodded his head and said, "You have my word."

William turned in the saddle and looked over his shoulder to the back of the column and saw that James was giving his version of the same speech to the other prisoner. They had decided to follow Thomas's lead and split them up on the ride back. There was no need for them to be kept together. It was safer this way. Looking forward, William nodded for Samuel to ride to the front and to make sure nothing unpleasant was waiting for them up ahead. He and James had decided it would be safer to cross over Beaver Creek and return to Williamsburg that way. The course would be longer, but its swampy landscape could give them cover if needed. After riding for a while, William's curiosity got the better of him, so he spoke once more to his captive.

"Tell me, do you ride with Tarleton?"

"I am not at liberty to say," the dragoon responded after a brief moment.

"And I suppose there is no need to ask your name or where you're from?' William asked.

"That is correct."

"Then tell me, what do you think of America? No military secrets to give away in that response."

"I rather enjoyed the Northeast. New York was fine, but I loathe the South. July and August can be unbearable down here. I have never seen anything like it in England the heat reminds one of India."

"Do you miss your homeland?"

"Of course, I do, I have not seen England in two years, and I don't know when I'll set foot upon her soil again. I am looking forward to that day. I am betrothed to a lovely young woman back home. We will marry on my return."

"Why the military then, it seems to me you could make a living some other way where you could stay close by your loved ones."

"Let us just say that I was the last son born to a poor aristocrat. I have some family connections among the dragoons. With some hard work and ingenuity, I can move up in the ranks and make a name for myself someday. Now, may I ask you a question?"

"Sure," William replied.

"Why have you taken up arms against your King?"

"That's a bold question coming from a man in your situation," William replied, "but I'll answer it. How did you put it a while ago? You're not at liberty to say? Well, once we win this war, we'll be at liberty to say or do whatever we want."

The dragoon didn't reply, he just turned his head and stared straight ahead, plainly conveying that he wanted to end the conversation.

William obliged him, but gazing out over the landscape he felt as though he had won the debate. The creek was in view now. It had some type of brown grass growing out of its muddy water along the banks. It gave its course somehow, the look of a snake as it wound along. The trees along the banks were still green, even though October was only a few days away. This Englishman may not have liked the

South, but William sure did, he thought as he saw Samuel come riding back toward the column of riders.

"See something?" William asked.

Nodding his head with a smile, Samuel answered, "Do you remember that wheat field next to the creek? Well, there are about ten Lobsterbacks there, cleaning out the wheat. The dumb asses are all on the other side of the field and no one is tending the horses. They're ours for the taking if we want them."

"We don't need them," William answered, "and if things go bad, the British could reap more than wheat today."

"They say General Knox could use more horses to pull his artillery," one of the riders replied from behind.

"It will be a risk," William answered, "but that's why we're here I suppose. Let's go and get them, but we can't handle any more prisoners. If they can't be taken easily, we will just forget about it and pass them by."

"Agreed," Samuel replied, "But I still believe it will be easily done."

William looked back to his captive and said, "Remember the oath you just promised, because I will. If I'm forced to fire, you know where I'll shoot first. Don't say a word once we get down there, because if you do it will be your last."

After a short, intense ride of about a mile, William's party arrived at the wheat field and there, just as Samuel had said were the unattended horses, all saddled and ripe for the picking. They were all tied under a massive oak, just standing there swishing their tails at flies while the redcoats were down at the bottom of the sloping field, swinging sickles at the golden wheat waving in the wind. William held his piston on his captive dragoon while six of the men dismounted, untied the horses and led them back to the party.

James rode up beside William as the six were remounting, holding the reins of the stolen horses in their hands. "Hell William, they'll never know what happened until after we've gone," he whispered. "They haven't seen us yet." But then a shot rang out from their rear, as one of the younger patriots discharged his rifle at the working redcoats, stupidly alerting them to their presence.

William spun around in his saddle and yelled, "What damn fool fired that shot?"

Seeing the smoke still floating in the air around the young culprits' head was answer enough, without the youth owning up to his mistake. William looked back and saw that the redcoats were running toward the other end of the field, 'For their muskets,' he hoped, but that wish was soon dashed as he heard the distant cry of "to horse, to horse" as a mounted group emerged from the far side of the grove of trees.

"That will be the Seventeenth Light Horse approaching. You would be wise to let us go and make your own escape," William's prisoner smugly suggested.

"May be," William replied," but not just yet. Let's go, and remember our bargain."

"To the ford, Samuel" James yelled, knowing all to well that the bridge over the creek had most likely been burned. William and the rest of the men took to the road in a headlong race with Samuel leading the way. William took one last look back as he rode away, and saw that his prisoner had told him the truth. His patrol was literally in a race for their lives. The red coated Light Horse, with their black skull and crossbones helmets with red horsehair crest, far outnumbered his small patrol and their mounts were fresher.

Up ahead, William could see Samuel's horse Chance dive into the creek making a splash as it entered. The Charging British patrol had already cut into the patriot's lead. Two shots had been fired, knocking as many of the Virginians from their mounts. As Samuel rode up the far bank, he pulled his rifle and made a shot back across the water, hitting the lead pursuer and slowing the light horse for a moment. But now his rifle was empty and with no way to reload from full gallop, he had little choice but to continue his retreat. William heard the buzz of a bullet as it passed over his head and splashed into the water ahead while he was still midstream. More and more of his men were falling from the constant British fire all around them. He knew the only way to save his life now was to take to the brush and swamp as Samuel had. His captive had never bothered to enter the creek, having stopped at its bank. William had left him behind, not wanting to waste his shot on one unarmed man when so many behind were firing on his own men. As Sampson ran up the opposite bank, he was joined by several riderless mounts. Half of his number was already gone and he still had a good five hundred feet between him and the swamp. He reached over to one of the empty horses and pulled a rifle from under its saddle. Leveling it's sights on a saber welding light horseman, as he was overtaking James from the rear, William pulled the trigger, knocking the rider back over the rump of his mount with his saber still in hand. William dropped the rifle and pulled his pistol, putting a bullet hole through another charging horseman's skull and crossbones leather helmet as James raced out of the water and onto the bank. They were the only two left. Everyone else was either dead or wounded. His whole number had been cut to pieces except for himself and James, now that Samuel was safely inside the thicket. Their pursuers showed no sign of giving up the race.

The sod under Sampson's hooves flew high into the air as William turned him around, making the dash of his life for the thicket. More shots rang out as the two men bolted across the last clearing but none hit their mark, but as they reached the tree line, one last volley was fired and William heard the soft thud of a ball ripping into James' back. As James slumped forward, William reached over and grabbed his friend by his collar and with all his strength, pulled James off Trace's back and onto Sampson. With a few more strides they were out of sight and into the swampy woods along Beaver Creek.

Samuel had dismounted having little regard for his own safety. He, like William had gathered another gun from one of the stray mounts that had stopped in the thicket with Chance. Five of their pursuers were now in midfield, still in hot pursuit of the fleeing rebels at full charge. The leader was shot from his mount by Samuel's first shot. The other four made a sharp turn to get out Samuel's line of fire, but the last one did not have enough horse to make it to the trees before Samuel fired his last shot.

Samuel turned and while running for his mount, he pulled the wooden stopper form his powder horn and began to reload on the run. By the time he had gotten to his horse, he was reloaded and ready to fire again if need be. With one adrenalin filled leap he was on his horse and racing after his family, not knowing if James was alive or not. What he did know was that William had learned the lay of this swamp during their time here and if anyone could lose the remaining light horsemen, it would be him.

Chapter 164
Present our Guns

Sampson had been splashing through the swamp for about half and hour now, but it seemed like days to William. James was still hanging over Sampson's neck bleeding from the wound in the side of his lower back. William had put a rag over the bullet hole hoping to stop the trickle of blood coming from the wound by pushing down hard with his free hand. But he could still not see if James was bleeding on the other side of his body or not.

"William, we need to stop and give him a good looking over," Samuel said. "I believe we have lost them for now."

"James, are you awake down there?" William asked as he pulled Sampson to a stop, trying to see if there was any life left in James. He got no reply from his unconscious friend.

"Come and take him. I don't want him to fall as I get down," William told Samuel as he looked around the trees. Samuel pulled his friend from over the horses back and laid him on a fallen log to keep him off the wet ground. He pulled up Jamcs' shirt to see if the ball had passed through. "It came out more to his side than to the front of his stomach. Is that good or not?"

"I really don't know," William answered as he pulled some moss off a tree trunk. "I'm as dumb as a box of rocks when it comes to this stuff, but Mrs. Poague told me back in Kentucky when she was tending my arm that moss can stop the bleeding if you have nothing else to use. James, are you still with us?" He asked as he stuck the moss into the wound. Once again, he was not answered.

"We can't fool around out here too long, he needs a Doctor now. We need to get back on the road. We'll make better time that way. Let's get him back on Sampson, the road is just yonder. We need to get back before dark"

Within minutes the two horses were back on the road that ran around the swampy ground beside the creek. William put Sampson into a good steady pace, hoping the jarring from the horse's stride was not causing James more damage, but he felt he had little choice in the matter.

"Keep a sharp eye on our rear Samuel. They could still be out here among us," he called over his shoulder.

"I know," Samuel replied, looking back down the road. "They're here."

William looked back and saw three men of the Seventeenth charging from behind in full gallop with drawn swords. He and Samuel both turned at the same time and presented their rifles, but as they did so, the riders rode off the road, taking to the trees for whatever cover they could find, knowing all too well, that if these two pulled their triggers they would surely strike their marks.

"Don't fire," William told Samuel as he lowered his rifle. If we fire and they catch us with empty guns, we'll be done for sure. The prudent thing to do is not to fire unless we have a certain shot, but we need to get back off the road. We don't want to put ourselves in their line of fire either. If we can hold them at bay for three more miles or so, we'll be back at our own picket line." he said as he ducked off the road.

Samuel kept a watchful eye on their rear as they moved along the edge of the road, always keeping it in sight. After riding awhile, Samuel started to wonder if maybe he should suggest taking to the road again. They had slowed down considerably in the brush and they had not seen the redcoats since leaving the road. But before he could make the suggestion, he saw a flash of red in the trees.

"They are on us again, William, get ready to present your gun," Samuel said before yelling back into the woods, "Come on and show yourselves, you sons of bitches. What are you waiting for?" William turned Sampson around and like before, their pursuers disappeared from view after yelling a few choice words to Samuel.

"If they are in the brush Samuel, then we need to take back to the road,"

William said as he lowered his weapon for the second time without firing. Seeing William was already on the road, Samuel slapped Chance's back with his reins and bolted onto the road as well. After another run of about a mile, the light horsemen were once again in view, forcing William and Samuel back to the trees.

"Damn them to Hell, that's enough," William said through gritted teeth. Here, take him on in Samuel. I'm going back and kill those bastards, William said as he looked down at James with wild eyes.

"No William, there are too many of them for that," Samuel disagreed. "We can still make it out this way. It's worked this long. Don't let your temper get the best of you now. Come on, the picket's got to be close. Besides, you have the best horse to get him in on."

William nodded and started back down through the trees, but as soon as they had passed the bend that concealed them from those following, he took to the road for what he hoped would be the last time. As it turned out, it was, for the redcoats finally stopped the chase once they saw the two rebel horses pass the American picket line. All William could do now was to get his friend to the hospital back at the palace as soon as he could. Maybe Captain Babb could pull some strings and get one of the better surgeons to tend to James' wounds he thought as he passed the French encampment. Still in a full gallop he glanced over at Samuel and said, "Ride on down and find Captain Babb. He may be able to help." Samuel didn't take time to reply; he just took the eastern fork of the road at a hard gallop and disappeared into the American camp to find Captain Babb.

Chapter 165
Heaviest of Hearts

William put his quill back into it's inkwell on his makeshift desk made from an empty pork barrel that had been cut in two. With an ink stained hand he rubbed his reddened eyes in an attempt to make them feel better. The rubbing motion helped sooth them for a few seconds, but now for long. Picking up his letter, he began to blow on the still damp sentences trying to speed up the drying process. He wanted to reread it before folding and sealing it with the last of his wax. He had been guilty before of folding his letters while they were still wet, causing some of his words to smudge. Elizabeth always seemed to be able to make out the meaning, but this was too important a letter for William not to make his intentions perfectly clear. So, he sat down inside his newly pitched tent and started to read as a few drops of rain began to plop onto the canvas outside.

September 28 1781

Dearest Elizabeth

I take quill in hand today with the heaviest of hearts. Our dear friend and most trustworthy neighbor, James Tate has fallen to the hands of our enemy. Yet there is still hope, for the Good Lord has not yet see fit to bring him home. He lies, as I write this most disturbing of letters, within the walls of our hospital in Williamsburg. He may be at death's door, but as of this morning he was still upon this earth. The cause of this suffering can be traced back to a Light Horseman's ball through his lower back.

But Praise be to God it seemed to have missed his spine. Although he is unconscious to his surroundings, he was moving his legs about last night. In addition to mine and Samuel's prayers he is receiving the best of care from our surgeons. Good Captain Babb, with the help of Lieutenant Colonel Allison was able to persuade one of the better doctors; Dr. James Thatcher to oversee what we all hope will be his recovery. I have not taken the liberty to inform Prudence of her husband's bad circumstances. I am under the belief that this bad news should come from someone in person with the most loving and compassionate touch. So, this unpleasant task has fallen into your capable hands. I can think of no one better than yourself to relay this message to her. It is my most ardent belief that she should travel to his side as fast as she can make arrangements. I have no doubt her presence would greatly improve his recovery. As to my station, all is well. I do have some good news to depart. Today we the allied army has marched to Yorktown and invested the British works. This much talked about siege has finally begun which I pray will bring a fast conclusion to this great gathering of soldiers. I cannot say with any certainty what is destined to fall upon me in the coming weeks, however, I can tell you what is in my thoughts and heart. It is your face and those of our children.

Until I hold you in my arms again, you're loving husband,

William.

Chapter 166
Settling In

William and Samuel were now back within view of the Moore House, however this time a whole army was here to keep them company. Nothing like the day James was wounded when they were so few. The Militia was placed right behind Wormley Pond that took its name from the creek William had crossed so many times while out spying. Looking from his tent's opening he could see General Lincoln's headquarters. How times had changed. It was just last year that Lincoln had been besieged in Charles Town. Now the shoe was on the other foot. The British and their German allies were the ones about to catch hell. But Lincoln was not alone here. General Lafayette's army was on Lincolns flank camped next to the Hampton Road. Von Steuben's headquarters was placed on the other side, putting his men and himself between the British works and General Knox's artillery park to their rear. Across the little stream that divided the battlefield where the French cannon, placed in front of General Rochambeau's quarters. His French troops completed the ring around Yorktown, with another battery on the riverbank at the ring's end. And of course, His Excellency, George General Washington's large white tent was placed in the center of the field. It had been late in arriving and had not been pitched until this morning. Washington had spent the night with his vanguard under a mulberry tree, but now that its erection was complete, it allowed him easy access to the whole siege line. Cornwallis's outward route by land was now a thing of the past, although he still clung to the hope that Clinton's arrival by sea was only a few days away.

But bottled up across the river at Gloucester Point with his thousand men, Tarleton felt defeat and disaster was all that was imminent for the Kings forces here at this seaport post.

While the allied engineers were riding around the British perimeter planning where to layout the first siege line, William and almost everyone else were deeply engaged in the construction of gabions and fascines for the upcoming battle. Up to this point the allies had out maneuvered the British, but now the back-breaking work of digging the trenches was about to begin and that was just fine with William. He needed something to keep his mind off how James was doing. The fascines were easy enough, just cut, gather, and bundle wooden limbs together. The gabions took more time, having to weave the stiff grape vines around the wooden slats that held the baskets together. Most of these were about four feet around and some were as long as twelve feet, but no matter what their size all that had to be done to them now was to move them wherever the engineers wanted and fill them with dirt. No musket ball could find its way through so much soil and sand once they had been filled.

Last night Cornwallis had ordered the outer works evacuated the very ones that the British deserters had fled when William and his friends were out with Lieutenant Allison. No more mortar fire was to come from there any time soon at least not in this direction. Heading for Yorktown, maybe, but not to the allied lines William was relieved to know. Yesterday those redoubts had rained several cannon balls on the besiegers, killing a few of the French. They had been the subject of every discussion on how to proceed. Lives were going to be lost when these fortifications were to be stormed, but not now. Why Cornwallis had left only two redoubts manned by the Hessians was a mystery. He had not marched out of Yorktown to meet Washington on the allied army's approach and now this redoubt was just handed over without a fight. Maybe he was planning an escape across the river. The upcoming days would soon tell. At any rate, valuable ground had been cheaply won.

As William was working on another gabion, the British fired four rounds of artillery from their main fortifications around the town. Samuel watched as the cannon ball tore into the ground, throwing dirt and sand high into the air, but their impact was way short of the siege line.

"I wonder why they keep doing that," Samuel asked. "Don't they see they're not hurting us with those shots?"

"I suppose they want us to know that if we get any closer they can still do some damage," William responded, looking back the other way, paying them little mind. "But I did hear that one of those York boys lost a foot earlier in the day when he got too close."

"Looking for Captain Babb again?" Samuel asks as he looked at William.
"Yeah, he said he would ride out or send word if James should turn for the worst."

"That's why I don't look for him too much myself," Samuel replied, turning back to his half-made gabion. "No news is good news. That's one messenger I'll have no time for, even if he is coming from Captain Babb, or General Washington either for that matter."

"I wish I could do that too, but I've got to see the bad news coming for some reason," William admitted as he looked up at the dark cloud that was blowing in from the West "Looks like another wet night is about on us my friend."

"You know why I can't look?" Samuel asked. "After my folks passed the only good thing in my life has been your and James' friendship. I sure don't want it to end this way. I just can't deal with it yet. It's not because I don't care."

"I know that," William answered. "It's hard to be settling in for this fight and not have James here with us. But you don't have to say anything about your feelings for James to me. You're hurting same as I am. I know how you feel; it's in your eyes." William paused a minute as he watched an approaching wagon rolling down the encampment. As it stopped, the men inside began tossing out picks and shovels that would be used to dig the trenches. They were working in haste, trying to beat the approaching storm. As William watched he said, "You would think that making it through Joshua's death would somehow make this easier, but I reckon some trials in life are always going to be hard no matter what a man has experienced before in his past. I suppose death is always hardest on those left behind."

"That's true," Samuel replied, "But don't lets us put him in the grave just yet. We may yet hear his fiddle again."

Chapter 167
A Twilight Run

Yesterday William had worked beside Samuel far back of the lines, cutting down trees in a nearby woods. Every now and then they stopped their work and listened to the sound of British cannon firing on the ever-closing allied line. More lumber was going to be needed for the earthworks, and the militia had been assigned the task even though it had rained off and on for the most part of the day. Samuel had thought it was a hard detail until he saw a group of Pennsylvanians' pulling several large field pieces without the benefit of a horse or oxen over the muddy field. They were using rope and their bare hands tugging them along, similar to how Major Linn had pulled his boat around the falls back in Kentucky. But he'd had the help of the two oxen that Captain Rogers had provided. Falling trees had been tiring, but nothing like what those men were doing, and the hours of the day did go by fast for William as he and Samuel worked.

On the other hand, today had drug by. The militia had been relieved for the day and was ordered to get some rest and sleep if all possible. William had requested permission to ride back to Williamsburg to see James, but had been denied. The reason being that at nightfall twelve hundred of William's fellow militiamen, including himself and Samuel, were to relieve the Continentals building the works. General Wayne's brigade was to act as the covering party of the night. This would put the fatigue detail well within the British artillery range. Everyone was on edge waiting for the sun to go down below the horizon. Added to this detail was William's frustration at not hearing any news about James. Why Captain Babb had not come with some kind of news one way or another was another worry. The captain, much like Dan Morgan was having difficulty fulfilling his duties in the field and had been reassigned to Williamsburg. William was hoping his old Captain was just too engaged in his new duties to ride out and tell them that James was improving. The war still had to be won and he had things to do, just like William had these unfinished works to be completed tonight. They were being built just across the filed from the last two remaining British redoubts still being manned by the Hessian troops. Musket fire had been exchanged during the daylight hours between the two. William and Samuel had watched for most of the day. The covering party had taken the brunt of the enemy fire while the work crew had been unmolested for the most part. Now that twilight had arrived, every man had carried a gabion to the creek bank behind the new works. William stared out across the open field from under cover of the trees that lined the bank. As he stood watching the Continentals laying down their tools, he judged it would be about a three-hundred-foot run.

"Damn." Samuel proclaimed as he looked at William. "I sure do wish I had my rifle instead of this big basket. I kind of feel naked out here without it."

"I was just saying the same thing to myself," William laughed nervously. "I just hope Wayne's men can shoot as well as we can."

"Yeah, me too, I guess we're about to find out, here comes those fellows back."

As the New Jersey line bolted away from the works, the Hessians began to fire from the redoubt, but their muskets were ineffective shooting at the fast-moving men at such long range. William had anticipated as much, but he had no idea how accurate the artillery would be.

William looked over to Samuel and said, "I'll wager my morning meal that I beat you across to the other side."

"A race" Samuel inquired.

"Why not, we've got to make the run anyway."

"It's fine with me but come tomorrow when I'm eating your breakfast don't come crying to me about it," Samuel boasted as the militia took to their heels.

Another volley came from the redoubt, but William saw no one falling around him as he sprinted across the void. He could see a ring of smoke floating away from the main British fortifications, but had no inkling as to where the nine and twelve-pound rounds were falling. As he fell up against the mound of dirt that the Continentals had left behind, he looked for Samuel to his right. All he saw was Samuel's gabion being flung to the ground as he bent over, putting his hands on his knees in an effort to catch his breath.

Looking over at William, he accused, "your basket was smaller than mine. That's the only reason you beat me here." William reached down and picked up one of the discarded pickaxes that one of the New Jersey soldiers had left behind and said, "I thought as much. Why else would I make a bet with a faster man than myself?"

Samuel was about to reply, but one of the engineers who had stayed behind to oversee the militia's work came walking by.

"Bend your backs boys. The quicker we build this wall up, the safer we'll all be. Keep your heads down while digging. The likelihood of you stopping a ball decreases drastically if you stay low. All I want to see is asses and elbows. Do that, and come sunup we'll have another battery ready to be mounted." William swung his tool down into the damp soil, burying it to the handle. With an upward jerk, he tore the soil from the ground. As he was taking his second swing, Samuel scooped the newly loosened dirt up and into his oversized gabion with his shovel. The first night of October was going to be a hard one with all the British artillery shells flying overhead illuminating the night sky.

Chapter 168
Amen to That

It was now October 6th and William and Samuel were finally granted permission to go into Williamsburg for the night. The American and French hospitals that had been set up outside of Yorktown needed supplies to be brought in from Williamsburg and the two were happy to be chosen as members of that party's vanguard. This assignment would not only give them the opportunity to see what had become of James, it would also get them out of the fatigue details. There was to be another large party of sappers and miners going out tonight to dig the first parallel trench line. If all should go well tonight, tomorrow the first allied shells could be fired within the wall of the British fortifications.

The mood and morale in the American encampment was growing by the hour. Everyone was feeling as if the decisive moment was near at hand. Tarleton's horse had been defeated across the river at Gloucester Point. A combined force of French Hussars under Duke Lauzun and militia under Brigadier General George Weedon had won a skirmish with Tarleton. During the height of the battle Tarleton was thrown from his mount and nearly captured. Had it not been for some of his men returning to his rescue, he would have most certainly been killed. His whole troop of dragoons was pushed back into the earthworks having lost around fifty men. It had been a fairly small affair compared to what was yet to come on this side of the river, but would have a great effect on the outcome of the siege. Tarleton had been able to forage the countryside relatively unmolested whenever needed up until this point. The British navy would fire a cannonade from the river to open a path for him to get past the American lines. Upon his return from his confiscating expeditions with whatever loot he had accumulated, it was rowed across the river and fed to Cornwallis's men and horse. This supply line was now a thing of the past, thanks to this small victory.

As William and Samuel were riding back toward Williamsburg they were astonished by the sheer size of this army. If a census could have been taken tonight, he felt sure that Yorktown would have the largest population of any city along the seaboard. But what had really gained their attention were all the cannon and mortars sitting in the rear of the encampment. Row after row was just waiting to be placed in the trenches. Samuel had declared that he would not want to trade places with any of those British buggers for all the gold in the royal treasury once they were in place. The road between Williamsburg and Yorktown had been well traveled during the last week, but was still in fairly good condition considering all the traffic that had marched and rolled down it during that time, but now that they were coming up on the college, their thoughts were no longer on the siege.

"Tell me William, what do think the chances are of James still being alive," Samuel asked solemnly as the French hospital came into view.

"Not good. Lower back wounds are hard to overcome," William answered as the sour smell of pestilence entered his nostrils. "Good heavens, what is that stink?"

The two pulled their horses to a stop as four of the eight wagons pulled up and stopped in front of the converted hospital that had once been the home of Reverend Bracken. Now William could see why the French had dug that trench besides the building. It was not a defense works, but a massive latrine.

"Why would they put that in front of a place where sick and dying men would be?" Samuel asked.

"I have no idea," William answered, "but I'm thankful that James is inside the Palace and not here."

As the last four wagons began to make their way toward the Palace Green, William and Samuel put their horses to a faster gait and rode on ahead to see if James was still alive. Leaving the horses tied to an iron gate in front they made their way to the open front door. The only other time William had been here was the day he had gotten Thomas the charcoal. That day he had been told there were no beds available and if it was the case then, it certainly was true now. Every inch of the round foyer just inside the door had patients on the floor. Seeing the slave, he had met that day, William inquired if the man knew who James was and if he still lived.

"I can't say for sure," he replied. "How long has he been here? And why is he here?

"Ten days," William answered. "He was shot in the lower back."

"If he still here and alive he be upstairs on the second floor. These men here all got fever." William nodded to the slave and made his way to the large staircase in the next room that led to the second floor. As he reached the turn halfway up the stairs a sick feeling came over him. If James was alive the slave would have surely remembered him. James was someone not easily forgotten even if he was wounded. Reaching the second floor he and Samuel looked about the hall but saw nothing of their friend among the wounded. Continuing the search, they entered what had once been a bedroom but once again, James was not among the men inside. They passed into yet another room with the same results.

"He's not, here is he?" Samuel asked brokenly.

Not willing to answer, William continued on through a series of connecting rooms, fearing Samuel was right, but not willing to acknowledge the fact. As he entered the next room, he saw a woman sitting on the floor with her back turned, talking softly to a patient stretched out on the floor. Reaching down, hoping she may know something or someone to help them; he tapped her on the shoulder. When she turned and looked up at him, William found himself looking into the dear familiar face of Prudence Tate. She sat looking back at him and holding James' hand in her own.

Shocked to see the two talking to one another, a smile split William's tanned face.

"Where have you two been?" James asked from his makeshift bed. "I was beginning to believe that some damned redcoat had killed you both. What's become of Trace? I can't remember what happened that day?"

"I can't say for sure," William answered, "You were falling out of your saddle and I grabbed you and pulled you over Sampson's neck. He turned and ran into the tree line. After that I lost track of him, but I'll keep an eye out for him for you. But praise be James that's not why we're here." William answered. "I thought for sure I would never speak to you again. At least not until the great beyond. How is he doing Prudence?"

"Better, growing stronger all the time," she replied. "If he keeps improving at this rate, we'll leave for home soon."

"Are you able to walk yet?" Samuel asked.

"On the days they don't bleed me," James answered, "but they say that's all behind me now. They seem to believe they have gotten all the bad blood out."

Prudence got up off the floor and took William's arm and said, "Your letter home to me saved him for sure. If Elizabeth had not told me I would never have learned of it until he had died. I truly believe if I was not here, he would have passed on. He's still weak, but I think the worst is over now. Elizabeth is watching our son at your place," she said as she reached into her apron pocket. She sent you this. All is well at your home and she even had good news from Thomas. Your brother is doing well too."

As Samuel began describing how the siege lines were progressing to James, William stepped over into the corner and looked down at Elizabeth's letter that Prudence had just handed him. It gave him the best feeling he'd had in weeks.

"Hey William," James called with a smile, "You know this here room was once Lord Dunmore's bedchamber? Is that something or what?"

"Well, I suppose this room was due someone with good breeding. I'd say you broke its run of bad tenants" William replied.

"Amen to that." Samuel agreed tapping his rifle butt on the floor.

Chapter 169
Into the Trenches

This morning William and Samuel had spent the early hours of the day on the wet roads between Williamsburg and the siege lines. It had rained all night and the two were happy to have stayed inside the comfortable walls of Christiana Campbell's tavern, located behind the capitol last night. It was the first good night's sleep William had enjoyed in weeks. It could have been due to the fact that he had spent it indoors, but he knew what had really allowed him to sleep was his knowledge that James had survived his dreadful back wound. William had been speaking optimistically to Samuel about James' chances, but deep down he was convinced that not only was he lying to Samuel, but to himself as well. He was never more surprised in his life than when he saw James, alive and breathing yesterday. And if that wasn't enough good fortune, he had received news from home. Elizabeth had once again confirmed her love for him and had also relayed the good news of Thomas' improving condition as well. The sun was truly shining through in more ways than one today, as it finally breached the week-long cloudy skies hanging over Yorktown.

Now that the hospital supplies had been delivered and their horses turned out to pasture, William and Samuel were ordered to walk down Hampton road and enter the trench that had been dug during the night. This new zigzagging line was only six to eight hundred yards from the nearest British defenses. William was overjoyed and proud to see that his fellow soldiers had dug a four-foot-deep trench that was at least two thousand yards long in one night. He could only imagine how devastated the enemy had to feel this morning when they arose to see this new works right under their noses. The sergeant of the night would surely catch hell for this. The new trench spanned from the end of York Creek, across the road and all the way to the river's edge. All the gabions that had been made last week had been put to good use. They had been lined in front of the trench and filled with the sandy soil from to trench. There was no way for the British to force the allies back now. As William stepped into the trench, the British fired off several rounds of cannon fire, forcing him and Samuel to take a knee. The impact had fallen in front of them, throwing small amounts of dirt into the trench, but that was all the damage it had done. William looked at Samuel with a grin and took off running down the line as if he were a child just let out of the church door and happy to go play. Running up on a cannon being pushed into place, he stopped and helped to put it in line. Everyone was excited, working with zeal. No one seemed to care that they had blisters on their hands and dirt on their faces. Finally reaching their spot in the line William placed his long rifle between two gabions alongside his fellow militiamen and peered across the way to the enemy fortifications.

"About time for you boys to get here," Captain Babb remarked leaning up against the dirt wall.

"I thought you gave all this up," remarked Samuel. "What are you doing here?"

"I wasn't about to mess this." the captain answered with a smile. "No desk duty could hold me for long with all this going on so close by. I got here yesterday."

"Well tell us what we missed last night," William said.

"Oh, General Washington was back up to his old tricks," Captain Babb explained.

"You would think the British would have caught on to them by now, but they haven't. A little after dark he had the French make a fake charge on the other side of town to get Cornwallis's attention. The French spread out fairly thin, making a lot of noise, firing their muskets. The redcoats fired of a volley into the dark but there was little out there for them to hit. When nothing else happened, they let out a big cheer as if they had turned back the line. Then a little after that, he had us militia go over by their abandoned redoubt to build some campfires. It was hell getting them to light with all that rain but we finally got them going. Then we walked around the fires until they fired off a few shots at us with their cannon. But they must have been having trouble with the rain as well, because that was all the only round they got off. By that time the sappers and miners over here had enough trench dug to stay out of sight until this morning, and like all the Generals diversions, this one worked perfectly. When the sun came up this morning, Alexander Hamilton ordered the colors to fly and the drum to beat. Then he marched the New York and Connecticut lines into the trench. They're on down towards the end," he said pointing toward the river.

"How many men were hurt opening the works?" William wanted to know as he ducked down to avoid the latest round of British cannon fire.

"Not a man, as far as I know," Babb answered, dusting off his coat sleeve.

"When are we going to lay down a cannonade of our own, Captain?" Samuel asked rubbing his hands together in anticipation.

"As soon as General Knox gets his battery in order, he's building platforms for them now as we speak maybe tomorrow or maybe the next day. I'll say one thing for that fat bookseller; He sure has become one hell of an artilleryman over the course of this war."

"Did you ever see General Washington out and about," William asked, still looking out at the trench across the way.

"No, he was over here with the sappers. They say he swung the first pick ax. He wants to be able to say that he was the first to turn the sod on these trenches. I can't think of anyone more deserving of that honor than him. So, today we're the covering party. Just lay low and make sure they don't try to overrun this trench until the artillery is ready. The Marquis's division is going to relieve us tonight but not before we have some fun I hope."

After walking over to William's station Captain Babb pointed out over the field to a wooden platform in the British works.

"William," the Captain explained as he placed his hand on his best marksman back "twice already today there has been a British flagman standing up there signaling those last two redoubts. We have fired at him on both occasions but came up short. I'm hopeful you can remedy that for us. I've made a small wager with a Lieutenant from the New Jersey Line that we would put an end to that flag waving today."

"If he shows himself again, I'll put a stop to it" William answered as he pulled back the hammer on his long rifle.

Captain Babb turned and looked to Samuel and asked "You boys saw James yesterday I suppose?"

"That we did" Samuel answered "that's why we're so perky and in such good spirits today."

Smoke rolled from William's rifle after he dropped his hammer and flint down. The Captain stood up from his seat and without looking to see if William hit the flagman announced that he was heading over to where the New Jersey Continentals where to retrieve his winnings.

Chapter 170
The First Cannonade

The British artillery had been firing on the trench for two days now. They had succeeded in killing a couple of Marylanders and wounding a few men working on the batteries. But they could not stop the continuous buildup of the allied artillery. General Knox had finally placed the bulk of the weaponry. Installed all along the long parallel were the large twenty-four and eighteen-pound field cannon, dozens of mortars and the countless eight-inch stub nosed howitzers along with numerous three-pound grasshoppers and many garrison cannons these being the most difficult to install with their useless small wooden wheels on the carriage cutting down in the wet sandy soil.

On the other side of York Creek were the French Batteries which could not only bombard Yorktown, but could strike Gloucester Point as well. Even the British vessels out on the river could not hide now. William had estimated there were at least three hundred artillery pieces pointing at the enemy, maybe upwards to four hundred. Word had already come down that the signal to fire would come in the form of a raised flag. It would be run up a flagpole located in the center of the line. William and Samuel had kept a keen eye on this staff from inside the trench, eager to see if the American artillery corpse could silence the British bombardment.

The wait ended at three in the afternoon as the French shot the first bombshells into Yorktown. William could see the round rings of smoke floating from the French cannon across the field, but from his position he could not see the results of their   impact, but the cheering rising from the French lines told the story of effective firing.

Two hours later a roar arose from the American side. The long-awaited signal flag was struck. William jumped to his feet and looked toward the nearest and biggest battery.

"Look Samuel," he cried out, unable to curb his enthusiasm, "There's none other than General Washington himself standing behind that twenty-four pounder. He's going to light the first one of the days."

"Let's hope that bugger Cornwallis catches it on the other side," Samuel replied as he watched Washington step forward with the portfire staff in his hand. Its burning mixture of sulfur, gun powder and saltpeter set off the charge. The ground shook under William's feet as the large cannon discharged. It was percussion like no other he had ever felt before. He could feel the air being sucked from around that side of his body. Rising up, he looked out over the gabion that was in front of him just in time to see the brick and timber fly from one of the best's homes in Yorktown. Before he could look back at Samuel, another cannon was fired on his opposite side, with just as furious a report as the first. Turning to Samuel, he said, "Those poor dumb bastards will catch hell for another three hours before sunset. I can't imagine what it's like down inside that town right now. That one shot could have killed twenty men."

"Yeah, that's right," Samuel nodded with a grin.

But now that is was past dark and William realized that Washington was not going to call off the hounds of war, just because the sun had set. In the time between Washington's first shot and now, the British had been taking a sound beating.

Very little enemy fire had been returned as of late, but the American guns were pounding away, as was the French who had sunk the forty-four-gun ship *Charon* in the river.

Having been relieved from the trenches, William and Samuel joined Captain Babb on the banks of Wormley Creek and watched quite happily as bomb after bomb shot across the night sky, with red glowing tails streaming behind to slam into the dark seaport below. Closing the face on his pocket watch the captain announced, "It's ten o'clock. How many did you count William?"

"Seventy-two rounds, more than one a minute."

"How many nights do you think we'll have to watch this before Cornwallis strikes his colors Captain," Samuel asked. "I'm kind of enjoying this."

"If it was me, I would strike 'em at sunup, if not before. But Cornwallis is a proud man, and has his reputation to consider. But it's just a matter of time my lad. Unless he knows something, we don't."

"He doesn't." William replied. "This is going to be General Washington's finest hour. Who knows, this just might end this God-awful war for good and we can all get back to our own lives."

Turning his back on the besieged port and looking at William, Samuel said. "And just what might that be? This war is all I've ever known."

Looking up from his stool with a look of surprise, Captain Babb asked, "Samuel, just how old are you lad?"

"Eighteen, "Samuel told him, "see I got the whiskers to prove it."

Chapter 171
Your Glory is Now In Hand

The situation around Yorktown was changing daily and all those changes favored the American cause. The bombardment had been going on for three days now. The British batteries had taken a beating; half their cannon was out of commission; however, they were still able to fire back with a small number of their artillery, ineffective but still firing away. The Royal Artillery Regiment had been losing men hourly. Sailors with gunner experience had been brought in from the scuttled ships that now lined the harbor, to help fill the void. If Cornwallis was going to lose, he had determined that Washington was not going to be able to claim what was left of his fleet as a spoil of war.

The allies had been digging at night again. A second parallel had been dug only three hundred fifty yards from Yorktown. The artillery fire from the first parallel had kept the British far too occupied to notice the second trench being dug in the darkness. The last two remaining British redoubts were now the objective of this new line. To this point most of the allied fire had passed over the redoubts, landing inside the main fortification, but that had changed this afternoon. Each redoubt had been hit several times, weakening its defenses.

General Knox was again in the process of arming the new trench with sixteen-pound field cannon. Tomorrow even more cannon fire would tear into the streets of Yorktown, thanks to his hard work. Now, as darkness approached William and Samuel peered out of the first parallels in relative safety, standing on a couple of muddied   fascines. Since the closer, newest trench was receiving most of the British's fire, the men in the first line felt more at ease. Everyone knew that the redoubts were going to be stormed tonight, and William wanted to have a good view of the action. Just maybe he could get off a shot himself, so he and Samuel had stationed themselves directly across from the bigger of the two redoubts. According to the word going around the lines, two forces of four hundred men each were to charge at the same time. The first French, the other American. Alexander Hamilton had asked Washington for the honor of leading the American assault and had been granted his wish. He had handpicked his best men from Lafayette's light infantry along with a few sappers to carry the fascines, ladders and axes needed to reach the top of the redoubt. The French were to attack from the second trench while Hamilton was to crawl out of the first at dark, and lay in the field until the cannonade signaling the attack was fired. Waiting like everyone else, William looked down the trench and saw Hamilton leading his men through the five-foot-deep trench, armed only with a spontoon and his short saber on the way to attack the smaller of the two redoubts. As the long column filed by, William whispered to Samuel, "They're going to charge the one closest to the river. Let's follow them down after they pass."

Bringing up the rear were the sappers, with their fascines slung over their shoulders. As the last one passed him, William grinned and handed his long rifle to a surprised Samuel and bent down and picked up the fascine he had been standing on and fell in line. After a march of two hundred feet, the column came to a halt. Hamilton gave the order to fix bayonets. This order was usually given after the one to load. This could mean only one thing. No shots were to be fired tonight. The redoubts would be taken with only the cold steel of bayonets.

William turned, facing the dirt wall that was in front of him. As he stood there he reached down, checking his belt to make sure that the tomahawk Andrew had given him that night on the Ohio River was still in place. Behind him he could hear a few words of encouragement being whispered by an officer.

"Be brave my boys, your glory is now in hand. Up you go."

Without knowing why, William crawled out with the four hundred. As he cleared the gabions, the same officer who had just encouraged the attacking column reached up and grabbed Samuel by his belt and pulled him back down into the trench, "Not you my lad just the Continentals and sappers tonight. You'll have to wait for another day." Hearing this, William knew that Samuel had not made it out of the ditch, but he continued on with the others hoping no one had noticed his presence. After crawling half the distance across the field, William stopped along with everyone else. There, in the dark, he tucked his fascines under his elbow and pulled his pistol and blew some air down the breach, clearing the touch hole. Praying that it was in good order, he primed the pan and said a prayer. Jumping to his feet as the signal cannonade sailed overhead, he left his fascines on the ground. As he was running toward the redoubt his eyes fell on the wooden abatis around its bottom. It had been hit in only one spot today by the artillery as far as he could see. A few of the swifter Continentals had beaten him to the breach. They were going through as fast as they could, not waiting for the ax men to chop them a way through. As of yet, no British fire had rained down on the attackers. As William reached the abatis, he could hear a British sentry call from above for the pass word of the watch. Knowing that no reply would come, he jumped to the ground under the abatis, thinking that's what an Indian would have done under these circumstances, as the British fired a volley down onto the Americans below. He regained his footing and upon hearing the cry "Huzzah" coming from his fellow attackers, he jumped over the first ring of sharpened post and landed on a few fascines that the sappers had thrown over. He pulled his tomahawk free from his belt and using one of his powerful legs he pushed with all his strength, clearing the second ring of sharpened sticks in one leap, not waiting for the ladder bearers. A few more steps and he reached the top the redoubt. Using his tomahawk, he deflected the bayonet thrust being welded toward him and discharged his pistol in the redcoat's chest. He tucked his now useless pistol into his breeches and surged forward burying the blade of his tomahawk in the shoulder of his next victim, taking the dying man's Brown Bess in one fleeting motion. The British had reloaded, firing another volley into the dark. The glow from the powder revealed the fact that a British officer was charging toward William with a drawn swore. William used his newly obtained bayonet and stopped the man cold in this track. As he pulled the bayonet from the officer's body, he saw the remaining redcoats pouring over the other side of the redoubt in full retreat. After only about ten minutes, the redoubt was now in American hands.

William stood looking over at the other redoubt and could see the Hessians muskets firing in the night air in a vain attempt to turn back the French. As he stood there with the other survivors of the attack and their newly taken prisoners, he was joined by Hamilton holding his blood covered spontoon, who proudly announced, "The French may consider themselves professional soldiers but by the Almighty, they're no better than we are tonight." Thus said, he raised his spontoon high into the air, leading his men in a triumphant "Huzzah".

Chapter 172
With the beat of a Drum

To William's surprise, Cornwallis had held on for another six days. Maybe he was hoping that the fearsome rain storm of two nights ago would drown Washington's men inside the trenches. William and Samuel were thankful to be relieved from the trench before the storm arrived. It was a rough night inside the tent, several times he was sure the wind was going to rip the tent from over their heads, but it held. Neither had gotten much sleep, but at least they were dry.

Samuel was finally getting over the fact that he had not been able to join the charge to the redoubt with William. He had fussed about 'that captain' pulling him back into the trench almost hourly, and now that William had stopped teasing him about 'not being fast enough to out climb a fat fifty-year-old man' the issued seemed to be at rest.

A lot had happened in the time between that night and today. With another parallel firing into the port, Cornwallis had ordered a small night attack of his own. His redcoats ran into the trenches that were still being connected to the captured redoubts, spiking several of the allied cannons by breaking bayonets in the touchholes. The effort was of little consequence however, as within six hours of their having done the deed, General Knox had them repaired and back in firing order. British troops were deserting by the dozens every day at great risk of being shot in the back by their own men, as well as from the allies. Yet, despite still being completely trapped inside the port, for some strange reason, a few Americans were still fleeing across into the British lines.

Samuel had rightly put these American deserters in the 'crazier than hell' category
.

Two days ago, Captain Babb had joined William and Samuel for a ride behind the allied lines trying to get a fuller understanding of the siege, knowing they would never see anything like this again. As they were leaving the American side of the field, they stopped at a barn that was serving as a makeshift magazine. Lying next to the barn door was a sixteen-pound cannon with a split barrel. "That cannon has been fired once too often in the trenches," the captain explained. "They should be fired only once an hour. They need time to cool down. This one was fired too rapidly and that crack is the results." None of the three could speak any French so they never bothered to stop inside the French encampment. They did ride over to watch the French battery at work where they stayed long enough to see five consecutive rounds rain down on the British fortifications. On the fourth shot all three agreed that what they saw flying up into the air were the severed limbs of a Royal Artillery crew. Having seen enough they rode on downriver to get a view of Gloucester Point across the way. Once at the river they were met by the foulest odor any of them had even encountered before.

"What is that god awful stench" Samuel asked as he pulled his shirt over his nose?

"Death, my lad," Captain Babb replied as William rode Sampson on down to the water's edge.

"Down here," William called from the beach. "There are hundreds of dead horses lying here maybe a thousand or more. What a sin and shame. They must have tied them down at low tide and left them to drown when the tide came back in. This is no way for a noble animal to die, especially when they have carried men into battle as these have."

"I suppose they couldn't feed them all," Samuel said, shaking his head. "My goodness, I would have just turned them out before I would have done this."

"That's war for you." Captain Babb said. "They would rather have them dead than have them fall into our hands. Keep what you can, and kill what you can't. What a disgusting philosophy."

Turning away from the sad scene, William hoped Trace was not among the dead, but he had no way of knowing. If he were it would break James' heart.

Yesterday, William and Samuel found themselves back inside the trenches with cotton stuck in their ears. William had watched as the artillerymen working at a nearby battery pulled the corkscrew shaped wormer staff from a sixteen pounder, then using a ladle, he poured the black powder down the barrel. Finally, he had rammed the ball down and packed it tightly. Turning away, William pushed the cotton a little tighter into his ear and braced himself for the percussion of the discharge. But nothing happened. Looking back at the cannon, he saw the crew had stepped on to the gabions and was looking across the field. Pulling the cotton form his ears, he too looked out over the top of the trench. There, atop the British parapet, beating a parlay roll was a young drummer boy. The lad was displaying his mettle, as round after round kept flying in from the allied artillery.

"This is it," William predicted as he slapped Samuel on the shoulder.

"What?" Samuel asked.

"The Surrender," William answered as the cannon, one by one began to grow quiet.

"Hot damn, you really think so?"

The drummer was joined by an officer with a white handkerchief raised over his head. He was met at midfield by an American counterpart and led away into the American works, out of sight
.

"What now," asked Samuel as he slid back down into the ditch?"

"I really don't know," William answered, "we'll just have to wait and see."

Everyone in the lines was celebrating what they all hoped would be the end of the siege, but as the time passed, they began to wonder if they could be wrong. Twenty minutes became thirty, and thirty became an hour. Suddenly, a Pennsylvanian sitting on one of the gabions, yelled out, "Here they come back."

William had climbed back to the top of the trench and watched as the red coated officer disappeared in the British fortifications. Once out of sight, the allied cannon reopened fire with a roar from the far end of the trench. He rolled back down to the safety of the trench and put his cotton back in his ears and sat cussing Cornwallis for an idiot.

At three o'clock in the afternoon another cease fire was called. This meeting had lasted a couple of hours during which runners could be seen going into and out of Yorktown. Surely this meant the end was near. Finally, sometime after five o'clock the last British officer stepped into his works and no bombardment followed.

Last night a clear star filled sky looked down on the first peaceful evening since the siege had begun. A few of the men, like William managed to get some sleep, but others who were too anxious for news stayed awake playing cards or rolling dice as they waited. Once again rumors were sweeping through the ranks, but hard facts were hard to come by.

When William awoke this morning, Captain Babb confirmed the rumor that the negotiations had indeed taken place in Augustine Moore's house and around midnight the surrender was struck. Washington and the allied forces had captured eight thousand enemy combatants, one third of all the King's forces in North America. Other than Charles Town, the South was completely free.

As word spread through the ranks it was hard for the men to hold their composure and it was no different for William and Samuel.

"If only James could be here with his fiddle, we would have a dance," Samuel shouted.

"Hell, don't let that stop you," William replied as he locked arms with Samuel and began to twirl around in a circle, not stopping until they had gone around twice. As they broke loose, William clapped his hands together and said, "Eight thousand troops including Cornwallis and Banister Tarleton. Two of the best they can muster. What day is it? Does anybody know?"

"October 19th 1781," Captain Babb laughed, walking back to his horse.

"Don't you two get so carried away that you miss the surrender. You'll want to see Cornwallis' face when he hands over that sword to our Commander in chief."

"No Sir, Captain," William replied, "we wouldn't miss that for the world."

As Babb rode away, William glanced over to the roof of the Moore house, through the tree line that stood between him and the property. As he stood there looking at it, he thought it was odd that the negotiations had taken place where he had once run out a couple of women of ill repute. That would never be remembered, but the negotiations certainly would. The lord did indeed move in mysterious ways. Then his eyes fell on Wormley Creek. It was time to wash off some of the dirt from his face and neck.

Around two o'clock, Captain Babb rode back to William's tent. The sound of bag pipes playing could be heard in the distance.

"Come on," he called, "they're parading out."

William and Samuel quickly mounted up and as the three rode out of the militia encampment and past Lafayette's headquarters they could hardly believe their eyes.

Marching up from the port and past the first parallel was a long red column of soldiers marching to the tune, 'The World Turned Upside Down'. The line was already half a mile long and the Hessians and Tories were yet to show themselves.

The French, dressed in their finest uniforms stood on the north side of Hampton Road. The southern side was lined with the American Continentals. They stood taller today than they had in the past. They were still wearing the same dirty, ragged uniforms they had stormed the redoubts and manned the trenches in. As they had been during the war, the Continentals were solemn and disciplined, but the militia was having their fun. Most had taken a place along the road like the regulars, but many were moving around behind their fellow soldiers standing at attention. Yankee Doodle was the weapon of choice now that the surrender was in full flow. Jokes, cheers and insults chimed in between the beginning and end of the song.

Word of the surrender had swept across the countryside like a wild fire. Hundreds of the local citizenry were coming in to see this glorious sight. They were standing at the point where the British turned off the road to enter the predetermined surrender field, but from atop Sampson's tall back, William had a clear view over the tops of their heads as he rode along.

Despite the fact that the surrendering soldiers were clad in their best uniforms William could see through their facade. They wore the look of men who were tired and worn in both body and soul. When the column came to a stop, William rode Sampson as close to the American officers as he could get, but he could not hear what was being said above the noise of the crowd. Then, as the lead British officer came to a halt, a hush came over the spectators and he could hear almost every word spoken.

"Our Complements, where is General Rochambeau?" the British general asked.

One of the French officers nodded in Rochambeau's direction. Still on his horse, Cornwallis held out his sword, but Rochambeau declined, shaking his head and pointing to General Washington on the opposite side of the field.

"We are subordinate to the American General Washington," The French general replied. Cornwallis spun his black mount around and trotted to General Washington, who likewise declined. Then William heard the surrendering general address General Washington, "Sir, I regret to say that Lord Cornwallis is unavailable to make an appearance today. I am afraid malaria has raised its ugly head on his Lordship. Please accept his apology for not appearing here today."

As Washington nodded his head, Captain Babb leaned over and whispered, "Malaria, my ass, he's to red-faced to stand before his conqueror. That must be O'Hara, his second in command."

A deeply satisfying smile spread across William's face as he felt a swelling jolt of pride. Oh, how the might have fallen, he thought as O'Hara presented Cornwallis' sword to General Lincoln, Washington's second in command.

Then, one by one the proud British foot soldiers, the most feared army in the entire world lay down their arms before a rag tag group of former British subjects in a most unmilitary fashion. Mad, embarrassed, and ashamed they marched back into the streets of Yorktown, a defeated army.

Later that night as the militia sat around the campfires drinking rum, telling and retelling their thoughts of the day and what this victory would mean to the war, William slipped out of camp. He made his way along behind the first parallel, not stopping until he reached the bluff above the river. Standing there and looking up into the heavens, he had a feeling come over him like never before. As the waves slapped against the shore, he fell to his knees and thanked God for all the blessing that had fallen on him and his countrymen here today.

Chapter 173
Trace's Reins

Now that the siege and surrender were over, General Washington had a new burden to deal with. The French were only going to keep the eight hundred British sailors and marines, leaving a little over seven thousand prisoners inside Yorktown. Since the majority of Rochambeau's troops were going into winter quarters here at the port, the entire prisoner population had to be evacuated. This meant all the rank and file soldiers and non-commissioned officers who had been among those who laid down their arms. All of the high-ranking commissioned officers were to be released on parole. They could no longer take up arms in North America, unless exchanged, and were free to sail back to Great Britain.

This was not only a burden for Washington, but for William as well. General` Lawson of the Virginia militia had been put in charge of the prisoners. Since Dan Morgan had returned home, William and Samuel had fallen under his command. As fate would have it, half of the prisoners were to be stationed in Winchester, just miles from William's home. He had hoped to ride out today and with the help of Sampson's fast gate; he would have been home in a few days. Sadly, now he could go no faster than the British could march. But, at least they were heading in the right direction.

Yesterday, he and Samuel had toured what was left of Yorktown. The once beautiful village they had seen the day Cornwallis' forces had landed was now a thing of the past. Every house had some kind of damage, most were beyond repair. Shops had been looted; the roof of Swan's Tavern was all but completely gone. Streets and yards were littered with holes that had been blown from the allied bombardment, but miraculously, Grace Episcopal Church the town's largest house of worship had escaped unscathed. Anything of military value that had not been blown apart by the allies the British had destroyed. Little or no food was to be found anywhere. Residents like Charles Cox would have to muster up a lot of money and fortitude in the months to come in order to rebuild their lives and homes, but William knew they would manage. So now that all the prisoners were assembling on the road to Williamsburg, William and Samuel were mounted under one of the few trees that had made it through the battle.

"I wish we could get this thing moving." Samuel said, sitting on his horse. "I'm looking forward to getting home."

"No more than I am," William replied, looking at the long line of red. Putting Sampson into a walk, he said, "Look, there's the dragoon we captured at the Moore house."

"Are you sure?" Samuel asked.

"Oh yeah," replied William. "I spoke with him quite a bit that day. Let's go see what he has to say."

As they rode down the line of prisoners, they could not help but notice the different moods among the men they passed. Some were angry, some embarrassed, some wounded and many seemed resigned to the situation, obviously glad the fighting had come to an end.

"So, we meet again," William said, looking down at his former prisoner, who was now once again in William's custody.

"Yes, so it would seem." replied the Englishman, remembering his recent capture. "I see you made it out of that swamp alive and well."

"Yes, and I see you pulled through our bombardment," William laughed continuing the debate from their previous encounter.

"It appears I am destined to be under your yoke. But if not for that storm the night of the 18th, we would have escaped across the river and awayed to Gloucester."

"I heard as much," William replied, "Why do you think Cornwallis waited so long to try and get away?"

"It is all entirely on Clinton's head, the man replied. "We were receiving dispatches from him almost every other day. He kept assuring us that he was on the way to our rescue, but you see the results."

"Well, maybe now you'll have time to write home to your sweetheart." William remarked as Captain Babb joined them.

"Good news, my boys," the captain said, pulling his horse to a stop. "General Lawson needs someone to ride ahead home and tell the people of Winchester about all these redcoats coming in. Guess who got that honor?"

"Did you really?" Samuel asked.

"That I did, and I believe two good men like you two, should be my escort. We are leaving now. I hope this doesn't put a damper on things for you,"

"No Sir," William replied.

"Well then lead the way," Captain Babb ordered as he turned his mount around. "I have a pretty wife waiting for me at home you know."

Wasting no time, William and Samuel fell in beside the captain, leaving

Yorktown behind. William did not know if he would ever be back here or not, but he knew he would never forget what had passed here; Thomas' poisoning, James' wound, the nights in the trenches with Samuel, and of course storming that redoubt. Nor would he ever forget Hannah's rescue, Gibson's rotting teeth or any of those days in Kentucky with Joshua. Some memories were good like the night he smoked the pipe with the Delaware up the Allegheny. Others were bad, like the night on the Salt River. The war had been trying, but worth the effort.

Soon the three of them were in Williamsburg where the captain had to make one last stop on Duke of Gloucester Street, and as it happened, it would provide William with one last memory. As he stood outside of John Greenhow's store, a group of French officers approached riding down the street from the capitol. There, riding among them was none other than Banastre Tarleton, trotting along at a slow pace, engaged in conversation with his former enemies. He did not see the tall dark-complexioned militiaman step into the street, but once he had grabbed hold of Traces reins, William had Tarleton's full attention.

"Looking directly into Tarleton's eyes, Williams spoke very forcefully, "Sir, you need to dismount from this horse. He belongs to a friend of mine and I intend to see that Trace here is returned to his rightful owner."

Tarleton bit down on his lower lip as he looked at William. Without uttering a word, he dismounted, walked around to an unmanned horse that one of the French soldiers was leading and remounted himself on a horse of poor breeding and of little value. Riding away, he continued his conversation as if the encounter had never happened, but Tarleton's reaction was of no consequence to William, for he knew he had just gotten back James' most prized possession. As he and Samuel exchanged grins, they were rejoined by Captain Babb and William realized that the day they had all dreamed of was at hand. Each step forward left the dark days of war behind and soon he would be back home in his loved one's arms. He would ride down into his bottom, open the front door to his home and say, "Hello, my love," and all would end well.

The End

Author's Note's
&
Acknowledgments

The adventures of William Tipton that you have just read are not entirely a figment of my imagination. This account is based upon William's own words. An act of congress in June of 1832 was passed to provide a pension for American Revolutionary War Soldiers. The requirement for the benefits grated to the officers and enlisted men of the Continental Line, State Troops, Sailors and Volunteer Militia was simple. The applying veteran had to serve at least one tour no less than six months to be eligible. Later amendments to the law extended the benefits to widows as well. Sadly, a great many of the men who won our country's independence had passed away in the fifty years since the conclusion of the Revolution. There were others that simply refused the idea of a pension, not wanting to put a strain on the American Treasury. Unfortunately, many of the names of these noble men have been lost in time. Thankfully, William and his brother Thomas were not among them.

William appeared in open court on the first day of October 1832 before Justice Robert Trimble in Montgomery County, Kentucky. The declaration he made that day contained about 1300 words covering three pages. This does not seem like very much information, but his statement was much larger than most of his fellow patriots. It seems that a great many of the Revolutionary Veterans were not very long winded when it came to their war time experiences. Some were granted their pensions having only stated a single page in their declaration. I am thankful that William gave such a detailed account of his experiences. He told of being at Fort Pitt and going down the Ohio River to meet Captain Lynn at the Falls of the Ohio where Louisville, Kentucky stands today; of his stay at the lead mines in Maryland; of his trek south, arriving at Camden just a few days after the battle: and finally of his account of the siege of Yorktown. On only two occasions in my novel have I deviated from his statements, the first being thc Squaw Campaign. He actually was stationed at Fort Pitt during that time and he very well may have been involved in its outcome, but the pension does not speak of it. The second was Colonel Brodhead's Campaign up the Allegheny. For the purpose of the flow of the story, I felt compelled on this occasion to use the poetic license granted to writers. I used Andrew House, my 5th great grandfather's pension documents as a source of authenticity. Andrew was a member of that campaign and referred to it in his declaration.

Thomas Tipton was at the Battle of Saratoga and was indeed poisoned while at the Siege of Yorktown. This was all recorded in his pension documents in which he told of William having taken him home to recover.

Joshua Tipton sadly did die in Tennessee at the hands of the Cherokee, but it was much later in real life. The event took place in 1793 after he had fathered at least four children with his wife Jeanette Shields. William's reference to Joshua's son John Shields Tipton becoming a United States Senator from Indiana was true.

William's father was Mordacai Tipton; however, his mother was named Sarah instead of Sue. I made the change because William's daughter was also named Sarah and I thought two Sarah's could become confusing to the reader. Having a wonderful mother of my own I used her middle name instead.

Sylvester Tipton was also in the war. He was a school teacher afterwards, but his war time experiences in my novel were figments of my own imagination used to help move my story along. William's two friends, James Tate and Samuel Farra are fictional. There was a Samuel Farra that made his Revolutionary declaration in Shelby County Kentucky, but his is not the story or character used in my tale. I took James' surname from Tate's Creek in Fayette County, Kentucky. This watercourse got its name from a small battle between long hunters and native Indians with the only white survivor being a man named Tate.

Two of my villains, Aquilla Price and Ross Gibson are also fictional. They were based on the accounts of several actual men whose stories I combined to create authentic characterizations.

Captain Babb is recorded in William's declaration, but William never stated his given name, and being unable to discover his real name in my research, I bestowed him with Buxton with the help of my father who just liked the name.

The majority of everyone else in my novel where real men and women. Adam and Andrew House, Captain David Rogers, Major William Lynn, Gen. Dan Morgan, Blackhoof and Ann Pogue all lived during the time and in the location indicated. Did William Tipton really meet Simon Girty, James Harrod, Simon Kenton and James Ray while at Fort Pitt and on the Kentucky frontier? I can't say for sure but at that time there were only a few people on the frontier.

While I have no written proof of those meeting, it is my belief that he had to have cross paths with some if not all of them. While he was in Yorktown, he definitely saw our first President George Washington and General Lafayette. William's meeting with George Wythe is a long shot at best as is his encounter with Banister Tarleton. However, William's Yorktown experiences are as I related other than the fact that he did not take part in the attack on the redoubts under the leadership of Alexander Hamilton.

William and Elizabeth both died after living long lives on their Kentucky homestead. Elizabeth in 1833 with William following four years later in 1837. I have been on their farm and stood at their graves, which stand upon a hillside overlooking the farm. Having been addicted to genealogy for most of my adult life, I felt compelled to bring William and his family back to life in some way. I am very proud of my fifth great grandfather's history. I only hope that he would be happy with my efforts.

I want to thank my loving wife Samantha, an elementary school teacher, for all the times I yelled from my office door. I was always asking her to spell certain words for me that my dyslexia would not allow me to do. My two sons Harrison and Wyatt for keeping secret that I was writing this book in its early stages, and the encouragement I received from my father Hillis. I would also like to thank Robert Albrecht for his exceptional cover artwork which so completely captures my story. I would also like to thank my good friend Mary Jump for her great photography on such a poor subject as myself for the book's authors photo.

But the person I am indebted to the most for all her long hours of helping transcribe my manuscript is my much beloved mother Sue whose first name I will not reveal here due to the fact that I would prefer to live long enough to write a second novel.

Made in the USA
Lexington, KY
17 September 2019